The Diary of
ANNA GORGON

The Seventh Fortune

David Ryder

WESTBOW
PRESS®
A DIVISION OF THOMAS NELSON
& ZONDERVAN

WestBow Press books may be ordered through booksellers or by contacting:

WestBow Press
A Division of Thomas Nelson & Zondervan
1663 Liberty Drive
Bloomington, IN 47403
www.westbowpress.com
1 (866) 928-1240

ISBN: 978-1-5127-7682-9 (sc)
ISBN: 978-1-5127-7683-6 (hc)
ISBN: 978-1-5127-7681-2 (e)

Library of Congress Control Number: 2017902957

Print information available on the last page.

WestBow Press rev. date: 03/27/2017

This book is dedicated to the varmint. It was Anna's diary entry on October sixth that intrigued me enough to seek out the rest of her story, and you too will discover why as you read through Anna's diary. You may well even cheer the varmint on as the story unfolds. Don't expect that critter to stay around to get its head patted, tummy rubbed, or back scratched. No, it is not a tame varmint. Its teeth are sharp, it moves by stealth, and nothing escapes its notice. It is too wise and crafty to be caught or trapped, and free spirited beyond any hope of domestication. As Anna discovered on that day in October 1887, an encounter with the varmint is often only realized after the fact, evidenced by its teeth marks and paw prints leading away from the scene of the bite.

Contents

Preface

MY FRIENDS HAVE asked me to tell more of what I knew about my great-grandmother Hannah S. (Higgins) Ryder. When she married in Deadwood, Dakota Territory, she took her husband's last name as her own, but also took the opportunity to adjust her first and middle names to what she preferred, Anna Marie Gorgon. The source documents for this reconstruction of her legend were family oral history, Anna's incomplete diary, a letter found in Bibb's dossier, and Anna's short memoir. I am still uncovering new clues as my genealogical research continues. This book also provides more detail of the thirty transformational days in the life of the surviving Toivo twin as told in the book <u>The Hound of Tooty River</u>. Besides the historical significance to me, I hope the reader will enjoy the riches to rags story illustrating the inestimable value of a life changed for the better.

I wish I could say the mystery of the varmint is solved. Some pre-readers said yes, others no. Regardless, my hope is that you will thoroughly enjoy this under-current that reveals the power of kindness, security found in lasting commitments, and the excitement of an unfolding life purpose as Bibb and Anna suffer through their flaws and discover their strengths.

And one last thing… The varmint never fights fair.

Prolog

THE DAKOTA'S DEADWOOD Gulch of 1887 was at the zenith of its gold rush days. The Black Hill's city of Deadwood was the epitome of the untamed west and had two firmly established reputations. Deadwood was a place where the rich could get richer. Second, this jewel in the hills was known for its lively entertainment districts where madams provided dancing, drinks, dining, and the lucrative other 'd.' It was the 'dames that brought in the revenue.

The uncommonly beautiful Anna Gorgon and her husband, a sharply dressed gentleman gambler and savvy investor, came to Deadwood after a whirlwind romance in Saint Louis. They gained six fortunes together in Deadwood. They also lost five of them at poker tables, living beyond their means, and risky investments. And they fell out of love as easily as they dived into it.

Readers prefer stories where Cinderella is reunited with her glass slipper and where hard work and perseverance pays off in a rags to riches story. Those are stories of hope and longing, and rise above man's common fate of mingled comedies, tragedies, and too few happy endings. But as the elderly will attest, the destination of life is nothing compared to the significance of the many magic moments in the journey. Such is this slice of my great-grandmother's story taken from her 1887 diary.

Forgive her please. Anna's lofty opinion of herself in her earlier days, confirmed in daily entries that start each day's drama, was selective in detail and sometimes more opinion than fact. Following her daily entry is the more grounded family narrative provided by great aunts, uncles, and other relatives. Their recollection of Anna, that "bundle of trouble wrapped tightly in a skin of beauty" tells a more believable story of how she was separated from her sixth fortune and gained a seventh – a secure and lasting treasure hidden within the warmth of a green rag.

Friday, September 23, 1887

"Your man dead!" I don't know how Xue made it up the mountain to deliver the shocking news so long after nightfall. Thousands of thoughts immediately ran through my half-asleep mind. Xue said she learned the news from Bes's friend, and "She no lie!" I asked her how he died. She did not know, replying, "You safe now. You no hide no more."

I trusted that man with my love and he betrayed me. I still loved him anyway, but what a strange attachment. He provided for my welfare, but not my heart… Never again will a man be trusted with that treasure or my touch. They are an unworthy gender, and I will not be hurt by one of them again. Their words are smooth when they want something. Those silky-mouthed sweet talkers can keep on wanting, wanting, and wanting some more. Never again! Never again!

I soaked my pillow with tears tonight.

==0==

THE SMALL CABIN tucked away in the fold of the hill had been Anna Gorgon's home for several months. She had a hired man, a mute, to stay and work the small adjacent mine that overlooked Peedee Gulch just below her hiding place. His primary purpose was to scare all strangers away, and he had a perfect disposition for the job. Anna's cook, maid, lifeline to provisions, and all Deadwood news was a loyal Chinese woman who spelled her name Xue; and pronounced her name like the English word *shoe*. Citizens of Deadwood assumed that Xue was the mute's helper, or as the rumors described, his indentured servant. The arrangement kept Anna's concealment protected.

Their morning started with a thick frost, a down payment for the promise of frigid weather as the days grew shorter. This location had been a convenient hideaway for Anna during the warmer months, but winter on that windswept and treeless high ground called Lexington Hill would be too harsh for her liking. She also knew she could not keep her concealment forever, nor wanted to. What she wanted was sweet revenge, restored wealth, and her once high social status in Deadwood reinstated with due pomp. She did not want her husband dead. She wanted him to suffer in every way imaginable and live the rest of his life drowning in impoverished shame.

Over the last months Anna Gorgon had much time to ponder why her love for her husband had turned into hate. They had amassed six fortunes in Deadwood, and he with her help had squandered five of them. She and her husband were now major shareholders in several large mines, but more importantly they owned several businesses in town. Everybody knew the mines would eventually play out, but never the need for citizens to eat and stay warm.

The lure of the poker table gave way with time to newer carnal desires within her husband. Anna, on the other hand, started to think long term about her financial wellbeing. Their latest investments focused on both city and rural land, and jointly the Gorgons purchased property that would skyrocket in value if the railroad ever extended into Deadwood.

What hurt Anna the most was that her youth and vitality, which first attracted her husband to her, was no longer competing well with the newer youth and vitality found at the local saloons. In response, Anna became much more demanding of her husband, and her husband did not like it. He preferred brainless beauties who shared a common disregard for morals.

These later days were emotionally painful, and Anna was tired of it. Yes, there were moments of hope and suspension of hostilities between them, but the seething anger never went away. With the blossoming of her opinion came the blossoming of his, and the playful quarrels turned ugly. When he could not compete verbally, he competed physically and shut Anna up for weeks at a time.

Anna harbored even a worse memory of her husband's dark side. He had become loose in sharing his negative descriptions of his loveless wife within the social circles of Deadwood. He also applied his social charms (and up-front cash) to impress the bar honeys into showing a deprived man sufficient loving. He then made a habit of coming home late to brag to Anna how other refined women seemed to enjoy his company, – something she could enjoy if she just begged for it.

But it wasn't that simple. She blamed herself for not keeping her husband close. His wandering eyes could have been cured. She certainly had the beauty for it, but no longer the disposition. Anna's emerging desire for security along with her new demands to put away their childish rowdiness they both had enjoyed turned her husband against her. He protested; he wasn't done having his fun. The only words he wanted to hear from her then, and especially now, were those of adoration. He poked her back on this issue too. She was no model of maturity either. She longed for and would respond brainlessly more often than not to strokes playing to her vanity, and he knew it.

She often relived that fateful night when her husband came home late and woke the following morning with a painful social ailment. Her amorous Mr. Gorgon was suffering greatly from contracting a venereal disease, or maybe a herd of them. Without any sympathy or mercy for the man, Anna decided from that moment that their marriage was over. With this final betrayal, he forever forfeited all his rights and privileges as her husband. Forget the vows. Gone. Void. Null. The man she once loved would never touch her again.

With his demands came her denials, and vice versa. He could not stand her attitude and often told Anna he was no longer interested in hearing her opinions. She did not quit mouthing her strings of venomous words, and to shut her up he began to bruise her in retaliation. He never hit her in the face, but often the rest of her skin was left horribly discolored from the pummeling. She hid her battered body under fully sleeved and ankle-length dresses for the days following his rages. She also hid her loathing of the man, strangely often feeling guilty for getting him so angry. She felt trapped. There was nobody to turn to for help. All those bridges were burned.

One night in early spring, Anna and her husband provoked each other into uncontrollable rage. He threatened to kill her and this time she believed him. That night she escaped, vanishing completely from Deadwood. During the following months of hiding she learned more from Xue of her violent and unfaithful husband's dalliances. Initially, she had blamed herself for his bad behavior, but her summer spent in solitude on the hillside above the mine reversed that thinking.

But tonight was different. Her hundreds of plans for revenge on the man melted at the shock of hearing of his death. The news was totally unexpected. Gorgon had owned the town by using his money to corrupt officials and employing his darker criminal connections to bully the weak. He flaunted his ability to exercise his will in the face of the impotent law of the town. As far as he was concerned, he was the law, and his willingness to use his money to buy justice made Gorgon untouchable. He proved he could destroy anybody who challenged him, and that included his wife.

After a quiet dinner together Anna asked Xue once again, "Are you sure my husband is dead?"

"I no lie. My friend no lie. You cry now. You no cry now, you twice cry later. Cry must come."

"Is he really dead?" Anna asked again after wrapping herself in a shawl. The three candles lighting the room flickered in response to the drafts from the wind coming over the mountain and through the cracks in the cabin walls.

"Meese Gorgon, you must no make rash answer in Deadwood. You must cry now, you think tomorrow, Meese Gorgon. Okay to cry. I cry week after my husband die. You no like husband but you cry must. Make better think okay tomorrow."

"What do you think I should do, Xue?"

Xue knew Anna too well to answer that question. Anna was probing about options tomorrow, the day after, and the days after that. Anna was always plotting ways to inflict her will on people; if not that, revenge. Her employer was not one to take advice from anybody, especially a Chinese laundry lady. Xue wisely responded, "I tell you but you no hear. I understand. I tell you again, okay? You cry. Okay to cry. I wash dish, food put away. You sit chair. You wash heart with cry."

3

Anna got up and walked over to a padded chair where Xue normally slept. Xue's response had initially angered her, but she rethought her words before she replied. "Xue, I will try to cry but I have no tears left for that man."

"Tears are for you, not him. You no think now about tomorrow or day after."

Anna smiled. Xue's answers demonstrated a crafty refusal to give the advice Anna sought by diverting from her pointed questions. Calmly Anna said, "Xue, you are as clever as you are faithful."

Silently the normal rituals of getting ready for sleep were accomplished. Xue, as usual, combed Anna's hair, then each went to their place and the candles snuffed. There were some sniffles, but no more words spoken that night as they rested inside that cold, windswept mountain cabin.

Saturday, September 24, 1887

Xue delivered my letter to Mr. Franklin that asked him to kindly undo all the mischief he enabled my husband to cause. I think he will comply, and I plan to discuss this with him tomorrow. He has little choice: comply and be awarded his fees, or be embarrassed and disbarred. He knows and fears my temperament. Besides, he no longer has pricy loyalties remaining to my husband.

I still do not know for certain if he is dead; I shall visit the coroner tomorrow. I spent the rest of my day cataloging my property deeds and accounts. Mr. Franklin must be convinced I have the original documents.

I wonder how he died. Syphilis is a slow killer, and he was much too young for a heart attack. Was he murdered? Who could have done this, and what will be the law's response? Do I need to fear? What shall I wear into town?

==0==

ANNA GORGON HAD spent most of her sleepless night plotting her next moves. Getting up prior to dawn, Anna woke Xue and gave her a list of tasks for the day. Xue would deliver a message, find out the location of her husband's body, and then stay in Deadwood overnight. The next morning, Xue and Anna's butler were to bring a carriage and pick her up at a familiar spot. Her instructions to Xue contained much detail about a specific dress from her closet and which accessories to bring with it.

While Xue was preparing breakfast, Anna used the dawn's light to draft her letter to Mr. Franklin, the lawyer that both she and her husband relied on. Mr. Franklin was more honest than Anna and her husband put together, but that was hardly a high endorsement of his virtues. Over the last few months, Anna had learned that Mr. Franklin had drawn up her death certificate and successfully presented it to the judge. With that document, Mr. Franklin dutifully executed her Last Will and Testament and transferred all their joint property into only her husband's name. Anna was not surprised. This legal stunt only confirmed what she already knew about the man. Mr. Franklin, by necessity, and to be retained as their lawyer, had to be quite legally clever. Anna's leaving town six months prior with the original deeds and the keys to their bank lockbox merely slowed him down in accomplishing the required legal contortions.

Legal or not, Mr. Franklin's dirty work was personally hurtful to her. Both he and his wife had taken more than a professional interest in her – especially his annoying wife. Mrs. Franklin felt it a personal calling from God to be an outspoken replacement conscience for the one Anna seemed to have misplaced somewhere in St. Louis. At least Mrs. Franklin was kind enough to voice her concerns only when Anna and she were alone. Anna never took her concerns to heart, but merely considered the toleration of Mrs. Franklin's sweetly delivered pleas as an unavoidable component of the price to acquire Mr. Franklin's superior legal skills.

Anna began to laugh to herself. Mrs. Franklin's lectures on the recurring topic of "Anna's Lost Art of Moral Living" were tepid compared to the frank, honest, and ignored lectures that Mr. Franklin had delivered to her deceased husband. When Anna and her husband were both alive and still in love they enjoyed comparing notes and laughing themselves silly over the Franklin lectures. The Franklins really did care, and the Gorgons just as passionately did not.

After breakfast Anna returned to her business at hand. Anna did her final edits to the draft letter and then meticulously scribed a neater copy of the note to be delivered to her lawyer later that day. Anna, who never had misplaced a piece of paper in her life, reorganized her documents and filed away the draft along with the rest of her documents. She was happy with her latest composition and became anxious to set her plans into motion.

> *September 24ᵗʰ, 1887*
> *My dear friend Mr. Franklin,*
>
> *With the advent of my widowhood I am in need of your legal services to consolidate my wealth and properly transfer ownership of all the Gorgon assets into my name alone. I understand you are quite good at preparing death certificates and the execution of last testaments, yet I fear there has been some recent confusion. I am confident you will be able to correct this small error, for you see the court recorded it backwards. The death certificate you prepared and convinced the judge to sign seems to have had my name on it, and not that of my deceased husband. As proof of the error, I offer my signature below that will match my documents you have on file in your office.*
>
> *I cannot envision a more important appointment tomorrow than you entertaining me and my friend, the judge's wife, at my home at nine in the morning. You may invite your sweet wife to attend tomorrow also. Until then, your friend,*
>
> *Anna Gorgon*

==0==

Once she was satisfied nothing had been overlooked, Anna sent Xue from their cabin into town just as she had done several times a week all summer. Anna was jealous of Xue, but only in passing. Xue was a woman Anna had learned to trust, and that trust was fully earned. Xue was dependable, honest, and very loyal. What Anna envied was that Xue had no hint of vanity, a trait Anna was drenched in and wished to be drained of. Xue also had a habit of confidently sharing her opinions. This morning and without apology Xue gracefully but firmly told Anna that she needed to arrange for her husband's funeral before she spent time writing a letter to her lawyer.

Anna now had a hint of the pain Xue had long-suffered as a widow. A cloud of confusion surrounded how exactly Xue's husband had been killed at one of the mines, but few cared about a Chinaman getting justice. After his death Xue continued to work in Gorgon's cleaners and over time she became the only person that Anna trusted with her expensive clothes.

Xue, unable to afford an apartment on one income, took up residence in the back of Mrs. Gorgon's laundry business. She worked tirelessly with the goal of saving enough money to find a new husband and to return to California. She did not care which event happened first. Xue also had disappeared the same night Anna did. Out of loyalty to Anna, Xue never denied the conclusions of the local gossips who had assumed she regularly visited a man she loved on the backside of Lexington Hill. They assumed it was the mute miner of Peedee Gulch, but they were wrong. The man Xue visited, her deceased loving husband, had been buried on that hillside two years earlier.

==0==

The two employees at the Gorgon mansion were already distressed when the chimes rang at the grand portal. The butler who was also the grounds man, and the maid who was also the cook, were very concerned where their next paychecks were coming from. Neither wanted to answer to door chimes because they were expecting job termination and eviction notices. After spying out the visitor waiting at the door, they opened it and welcomed inside the very petite Xue.

Xue's English was good, but still heavily accented. "Meese Gorgon come home tomorrow. She say me sleep here tonight. Must get her closet ready."

"Mrs. Gorgon has been dead several months, and now also her husband. Pardon our skepticism, but why should we believe you?"

"This read. Meese Gorgon understand, expect you doubt. Here is envelope."

The butler took the envelope and opened it. Inside was Anna's signed note with instructions for them on how to prepare for her arrival, permission to let Xue sleep in her room, two weeks of pay for both of them, instructions to quickly deliver a smaller sealed envelope to Mr. Franklin, and to extend one other invitation.

"Xue, you must be hungry. When was the last time you ate? Let us go into the kitchen and fix ourselves something. You can tell us more about the lady of the house."

"I tell but you no talk others! Meese Gorgon arrival big surprise. Where Meester Gorgon sleeping cold?"

"He's at the undertaker's awaiting instructions. I'm sure that opportunist is expecting a large funeral rather than the city's standard five bucks for a box and a hole to put it in." The butler offered Xue a chair while the cook put together some sandwiches.

"How did he die? Does Meese Gorgon need to fear?"

"Mrs. Gorgon will need to fear the man who killed her husband, but not for a while. Our master called him out for a showdown. Mr. Gorgon fired the only shot wounding the man in the face. Mr. Gorgon never saw his demise coming, and lay dying in the street without a soul to console him."

"Is Meester Gorgon really dead?"

"He died heartless," said the maid, the only time she spoke.

"What?" replied Xue.

The butler continued. "A notorious outlaw came into town yesterday. I believe our master took matters into his own hands to rid the town of such vermin. You know he believed our sheriff to be quite the coward. Well, this outlaw is known for his quick draw, but worse, his lightning ax throw. Mr. Gorgon, may he rest in peace, died when Bibb's skill and speed rudely interrupted any evening plans our master had to later gloat over winning another duel."

"Bibb? The ghost called Bibb is in Deadwood? He never die, only kill." Xue, with revived superstitions, was visibly worried for Mrs. Gorgon. "Bibb very bad, will kill Meese Gorgon."

"Before you jump to that conclusion you need to read the papers. Bibb is near death himself."

"I no read. You read, yes, please? But first, I need carriage in morning. You take me, yes? We get Meese Gorgon near hiding place. Yes?"

It was now very obvious to the butler that Xue had nothing to do with the envelope except its delivery. Those instructions were also detailed in the note. "Xue, have you been hiding with her?"

"I no tell. Meese Gorgon will tell all what she wants known. She big plan all. You read paper now, yes?"

==0==

Mr. Franklin could vouch for the origin of the letter by the veiled threat before he considered the validity of the signature. It was Anna, no doubt, and no doubt there was a wagon full of trouble heading his way. He quizzed the butler who had delivered this letter to the mansion. Faithful to his instructions the butler gave no name, but did mention that he and the Gorgon's housekeeper were both very surprised. Although Mr. Franklin pressed harder for an answer the butler only gave a repeated reply, stating that if Mrs. Gorgon was alive, which was yet to be confirmed, his resurrected employer would answer those questions for herself in the morning. The butler did confirm that the judge's wife had already accepted the invitation. Knowing nothing good could happen if he stayed longer, the butler excused himself by saying he had to attend to his employer's other dictates.

Mr. Franklin told himself he was wrong about the wagon. This development was a whole freight train load of trouble. He was tempted to notify the sheriff, but that would require getting dressed and interrupting the only hours that man ever had some peace. And what could he do about it? Stake out the mansion? No. This smelled of being a hoax. Yes, the sheriff might find it curious, but this curiosity posed no harm to anybody but himself and his license to practice law.

When his wife asked who was at the door he glibly replied, "It was only a ghost."

"A ghost?"

"Honey, it was an invitation to breakfast for the two of us. An old client has returned to town. A messenger was the one who knocked at the door. We are to arrive tomorrow at nine in the morning followed by attending church together. Sounds delicious, and quite the surprise."

"Who invited us?" Mrs. Franklin mentioned, already in bed after washing her face.

"I left the note on the table. Honey, do you want me to go fetch it?"

"No, it will keep. I'm going to sleep. Blow out the candle, dear."

Mr. Franklin exhaled a deep breath of relief. At least one of them would sleep well tonight. Mrs. Franklin was always polite to their rich client, but she detested just about everything about the rancid behavior of the woman named Anna Gorgon, and with ample justification. When tempted to say something ugly about that beauty she would retreat to the reality that Anna's lack of virtue kept her husband busy, put wood in the stove, and coffee in the cupboard. Yes, their mortgage was paid in full due to that Gorgon woman's propensity to attract trouble and her husband's legal abilities to get her out of it. The lawyer's wife always wondered why God blessed the likes of Mrs. Gorgon, and not just a little blessing here or there, but everything she touched. It was inexplicably unfair.

To her shame, Mrs. Franklin had mixed feelings when it was reported that Anna was missing due to an untimely receipt of a merciless dose of coyote inflicted justice. Oh, no doubt Mr. Gorgon wasn't clean as the driven snow, but Anna gave the high society women of the town a bad name. In turn, Mrs. Franklin felt guilty that she lacked loyalty to Deadwood's sisterhood of leading women. She never could consider Anna an innocent victim of her husband's abusive behavior. It takes two to fight, and Anna was only armed with her wits; wits that proved to be no match for fists. Anna suffered greatly from that disadvantage. The only two in Deadwood who thought this truth was a concealed secret were Anna and her husband. In arrogance, Anna wrongly assumed that people were both blind and stupid. Conflicted within, Mrs. Franklin still cared deeply for Anna's soul.

And there was no pity or compassion left in anybody else's heart for Anna. It was unproductive and unwise to give any Gorgon any unsolicited advice. Unless the words said to them were akin to worship or praise, bad things happened to the family of the one who dared speak against them.

Sunday, September 25, 1887

Today I left my hiding place and returned to Deadwood. Mr. Franklin was very amenable to my suggestions, for he had no choice. Shortly thereafter the judge and his wife escorted me to services at the same church where my funeral was performed, sitting front row center at my request. My black widow dress was a delicious choice, and I believe the preacher was slightly and rightly unnerved. I only said one word to his wife after services, "Boo!" She did not think that funny, and I frankly don't care what she thinks. The preacher tried also to engage in a conversation upon our exit, and I said even less to him. I will not, would not, and did not entertain a single syllable from that man before, during, or after his fleecing of the flock. All he received from me was a deathly cold stare as if a corpse. We visited my grave in the cemetery adjacent to the church. My husband will have to settle for the same cheap tombstone and gravesite he purchased for me. When he looks up from six feet under, all that rotten fink will see will be my name written in stone resting heavily on his chest, lest he forget what he did.

The coroner showed me my husband's remains. I gagged and then I cried. His death was bloody. I imagined him lying helpless in the horse soiled dark street, recalling a lifetime of regrets as his exposed heart beat its last time; alone and without a lover. I had fantasized many deaths for that man, but none as horrific. I did love him once. His decaying body gave me the shivers. His abuses are gone forever; never again will I open myself to that suffering.

A modest funeral was all the undertaker got out of me. The sheriff found me there and I asked him if I was in danger from my husband's murderer. He looked in disbelief, and asked me to visit his office in the morning. He confirmed Xue's report that the man's name was Bibb. I am worried about Xue. Her belief that death does not end life causes her a fear of spirits.

I did not have to look for the newspaper reporter. He found me also. We quickly came to an agreement: Once I review all that has been reported about me and my husband since the night I disappeared I will grant him an interview at the mansion. I was not prepared for what I read today. This Bibb fellow, alias Tommy Toivo, and my husband both hailed from Fort Rice. That strange coincidence gave me a second dose of the shivers. I cried myself to sleep tonight.

==0==

Xue was not comfortable staying at Anna's mansion, and particularly sleeping in her bedroom. For one thing, the bed was too high, and her feet dangled off the side more than two feet from the floor. Next were all the mirrors in the home, especially in the Anna's closets. Xue never got used to seeing reflected movements all around her as she moved through the home. She had always wondered how the rich lived, and now she had ample reasons not to envy them. She did chuckle at the excesses as she spoke to herself, "When I put on my shoes, I have an easy choice. I must decide which shoe I put on which foot." Xue had but one pair to her name while Anna could spend all day in her closet deciding which pair of shoes would best match the chosen garb for the day.

Xue contrasted the Anna of the Mansion to the Anna of the Mine that she had lived close to all summer. Money was not Anna's problem; the detachment from her social status and the loss of daily control of her businesses bothered her deeply. Bitterness and revenge had reigned in most of their mountainside conversations, and Xue knew to just listen and avoid commenting… unless Anna threatened to do something harmful to herself. There was no doubt about it: Anna had a very high opinion of herself. Xue wisely chose to stay silent rather than feed her employer's vanity.

==0==

Xue and the butler were waiting at the trailhead rendezvous when Anna and her mute host appeared. The walk over the low pass and down Lexington Hill to Spruce Gulch gave Anna time to explain to her escort what had happened and why she and Xue were returning to Deadwood. He gave little response, but he seemed happy at the prospect of being left alone again and getting his cabin back. Sleeping in the mine was tolerable in the summer, but without the warmth of a fire he knew he could freeze to death during the winter. If the Gorgons hadn't owned the mine he would have run them off too. He considered Xue a joy to have as a neighbor, but Mrs. Gorgon was too accustomed to a soft life to be of any use.

Anna drank in the beauty of the moment as she and Xue shared the inside of the closed carriage. Better, Anna's heart skipped a beat as she once again put on her favorite shoes after exchanging her mountain clothes for her city ones. It had been months since she had applied cosmetics to her skin. It pained her deeply to see what the windswept and sun-flooded Spartan accommodations had done to her once youthful complexion.

Xue saw Anna's mood and countered with a compliment by saying "You wash up nice for mountain woman," and then asked Anna if she liked the dress. Anna responded with a half embrace, completely taking Xue by surprise. Anna gave out very few smiles, but now things were different. Her countenance had changed. She was going home as a free woman.

The maid was waiting at the back door when the carriage arrived. There was no fanfare upon her early arrival at the mansion. Breakfast was ready for all, and the maid informed Anna that all invited guests had accepted her call for morning tea. The maid was teary eyed, so glad to see that Anna was truly alive. She never could emotionally accept the stories that Anna had been murdered. While grateful for the continued employment from Mr. Gorgon, she took great offense in serving dinners to a painted parade of grown kittens that her master had entertained since Anna's disappearance.

Xue asked for a moment alone with Anna, and was quite direct in her question. "Meese Gorgon, now you home do you have need yes more for me? I know you plan many things, and I want to know if me included in them yes any. If no any, I go return to laundry as work lady under old rules. Yes, Meese Gorgon?" Anna whispered something into her ear and then Xue turned to go.

==0==

Julia, the judge's wife, could not contain her excitement over the news of Anna's return. Although habitually late for everything else, she arrived a full hour earlier than the nine o'clock invitation. There was no time to waste. She went out to the patio with Anna to catch her up on all the social events of Deadwood since Anna's departure earlier that spring. There was barely time enough to talk of anything except themselves. Who was new in town, and who had left since spring did make it into the conversation once or twice, but soon the competing pair of monologs returned to exaggerating their own social sufferings.

Anna did ask once or twice about which women in town caught her late husband's attention, but Julia diverted the conversation elsewhere without answering. Julia maintained her secret that she had been more than once the target of Mr. Gorgon's attentions; or rather the target for blackmail. The charming and sinister Mr. Gorgon would have used such a dalliance against Julia's husband if such a faux romance had ever been consummated.

Promptly at the appointed hour Mr. and Mrs. Franklin arrived in their Sunday best clothes. Anna had always been annoyed by Mrs. Franklin's unrequested mothering. They were brought into the parlor where Anna and Julia joined them. Mrs. Franklin, normally reserved, pinched Anna hard on the arm when they embraced as a greeting. Anna, hurt, recoiled and asked what that was about.

"Oh, nothing, dear. You know what people say about ghosts, and you certainly are a candidate. I'm glad you felt that, Anna. Thank you for your kind invitation into your late husband's home."

Anna concluded Mrs. Franklin just wanted to pinch her from spite. The demanding Gorgons had ruined many of Mrs. Franklin's evening plans to have her husband home alone for supper. Anna could not blame her or her husband for resenting the chronic but profitable habit. Nevertheless, Anna justified her behavior by considering herself to be an underappreciated great benefactress. Mr. Franklin had built his wife a nice home with all the proceeds of such petty inconveniences.

Mr. Franklin knew he would have to endure many unhelpful catty comments if he did not take immediate control of the conversations once they sat down. He was well aware of Anna's temperament and knew exactly why he and the others were there.

"Mrs. Gorgon, I want you to know that nothing that your husband did over the last six months was illegal. All the buying, selling, and managing of property was entirely above board."

"So you have maintained good records of all the transactions then, Mr. Franklin?"

"We both know that you kept track of the finances prior to your disappearance, and once you were gone I recommended to your late husband the services of a skilled accountant. Accept my sincere compliment concerning your business acumen, Mrs. Gorgon. There was very little difficulty during the transition period, except for the fact that many of the deeds and ownership documents had to be reconstructed from court records. The originals seem to have been misplaced."

"Mr. Franklin, they were not misplaced. I have them all, except for one. I am missing the death certificate that enabled my husband to remove my name from our property. Maybe before that was presented to the judge I might have been consulted. What was certified by the court may have been legal, but I am more concerned if was it honest and true. Please consult your wife if you too think I am something other than a living, breathing, warm-blooded woman. You be careful. She pinches."

"Mrs. Gorgon, it did not take you long to get to the heart of the matter. With your permission I will correct the difficulties that the errant document caused, but please be advised that assets sold this summer cannot be recovered. Be comforted that in those transactions the estate lost no wealth. Mr. Gorgon was quite savvy in his property acquisitions and divestments. What I can promise you is that if you retain my services that by two Sundays hence all property currently in the Gorgon portfolio will be solely in your name. I also pledge to you that your husband's last will and testament drawn up prior to your disappearance will be properly executed. I am quite sure the court will nullify the current will as fraudulent. I safely assume that you retained a copy of the prior one, yes? There will be standard fees, but Mrs. Gorgon, you have my word all will be made right."

"And the accountant, Mr. Franklin? What about those fees?"

"Mrs. Gorgon, your accountant has earned his fee. During the last six months the Gorgon estate net worth has increased thirty percent. You know that is better than any risky mine venture or financial instrument."

"That is a surprise. How did he pull that off?"

"Let me suffice to say that your husband invested well, and the main drain on resources was stymied. Forgive me, Mrs. Gorgon, while I state the obvious. No offense intended ma'am, but Mr. Gorgon suffered from a very expensive wife, and with her disappearance came stark financial advances. You may have noticed that Mr.

Gorgon reinvested much of the inventory found in your closets and parlors back into the businesses."

"That man sold my clothes?" protested Anna.

Mr. Franklin refused to get sidetracked. "Now, let us move on to my request, Mrs. Gorgon. You have grounds for complaint against my management of your legal affairs, but I ask you to overlook them in light of my commitment to make all things right. Please consider that we have much to gain by working together and much to lose by bringing in a third party to dispute the legality or accuracy of what has already transpired. Mrs. Gorgon, let us be reasonable and let me put aright the estate. Much has changed given recent events, may your Mr. Gorgon rest in peace. May I have your peace too? You have trusted me in the past, and you can trust me again."

"As to your assertion, I am not wishing that man any peace, Mr. Franklin. And as to your request," Anna Gorgon paused, put down her tea cup, stood up, and walked over to Mr. Franklin. He stood up in response to her gesture, thinking she might offer to shake hands. She did not shake his hand, but with all the strength she reached out and pinched Mr. Franklin on the arm. "Do not be surprised, Mr. Franklin. I wanted to know, using your wife's special test, if you were real too. I am putting you on notice. I plan to review your and my accountant's work at my convenience. I give you my peace, but cautiously. Your trust will have to be rebuilt by results. I am quite set back at the extent you enabled my husband to remove my existence from history. Though tempted, I shall not hold you liable for my late husband's acts of hatred towards me. None of us is without fault, Mr. Franklin. For the sake of mutual gain I agree we should put this horrid past behind us and move forward. Please notify the accountant to expect my visit in the morning. On Tuesday you shall have access to the original documents." Anna felt good after delivering her well-rehearsed tirade.

"There is one other liability that needs your immediate attention, Mrs. Gorgon."

"What is that, Mr. Franklin? Would you like more tea?"

"No thank you, Mrs. Gorgon. To the issue, your husband gravely injured a man two days ago, and the man is incurring debt during his recovery. There is little doubt that he has legal standing to demand to be made whole. I suggest you move quickly, in the name of justice, to limit your risks by absorbing his expenses without question. In fact, as your lawyer, I suggest you overwhelm him with kindness to deflect any future liability against the estate. The man's reputation is well established, and you need to endear yourself to him before he has a chance to think otherwise. I cannot say this anymore plainly. Not only is your estate at risk, but your very life."

"Can you handle this for me, Mr. Franklin?"

"Mrs. Gorgon, for your sake, I will not. You need to do this personally with each of the man's creditors, and may I suggest, without show or negotiation. You have but one chance at a first impression with the man called Bibb. You have this opportunity to resurrect your sullied reputation with the people of Deadwood too. My advice is not to squander it."

"I have my plans and I will do what I plan to do, Mr. Franklin. Thank you for the advice."

==0==

"Anna, please don't mention the funeral to anybody at church. There is nothing to be gained by it." Julia was unhappy with Anna's decision to go to church (alive) for the first time in her adult life.

"But they owe me! I want them to see how wrong and gullible they are."

"And what exactly do they owe you, Anna? What harm have they done you?"

"They participated in the fraud, Julia. They need to know and be sorry about it."

"Anna, the only 'they' you are hurting is me, and I'm already sorry. You flatter yourself. In your vanity you might have imagined a crowd, but not even one pew of the church was filled at your funeral. Not one of your employees came to wish you farewell. Your husband saw to that by refusing to give them time off to attend. Anna, as your friend, I spoke your eulogy, and the preacher commended you to God. Nobody injured or slandered you. Don't do this. The only fraud committed was that of your husband, and even that is in question."

"What do you mean?"

"Anna, he talked big, but he had no idea where you were. You deeply injured his pride when he looked for you in vain. I don't know who started the rumor you were eaten by coyotes or buried under the tailings of the mine, but I don't think it was him. When the papers published all that gossip he didn't deny the stories because he had no grounds for rebuttal. Eventually it became convenient to claim you dead. That was when he jumped on the opportunity. He hinted the rumors were true but never said enough to get him in trouble with the law. Anna, he cried at your funeral, and they were real tears. Certainly you had earned his wrath by goading him. Neither his love nor his hate could put you out of his mind. Anna, why do you want to do this?"

"Julia, this must be done, but I promise not to mention the funeral. Did he really cry?"

"Did you cry when you found out he was dead?"

"Julia, let's go. Don't call it vanity. I must go. I must see the scene and fix the memory in my mind. I will behave."

==0==

At the appointed time the butler was waiting to escort Anna away from church services. Before departing she took a silent trip through the cemetery and specifically to her grave. Once again she had thought more of herself thinking she warranted a larger tombstone, but that was not her life's reward. It was of the same size as many others there, common, and without frills. She pondered what a strange privilege to see one's own planted tombstone and wondered if there was any deeper meaning to it. No, it was all a fraud. It was a big lie by an unfaithful husband who had abused her and claimed to have killed her.

Uncontrollably, maybe by some deep emotion, something threw her to her knees and then to sit on her own grave. She stayed there for several minutes, holding back her tears. She was all alone, a widow with no kin for comfort. She vowed to herself that justice demanded that this is where her husband was going to be buried, nameless, and under her unaltered tombstone.

On the way home from the cemetery, Anna asked the butler to stop by the laundry to find Xue. She was there, and Anna asked her if she would please escort her back to the mine in the morning to bring home the rest of their belongings. Anna gave her money to buy provisions for their mute tenant and additional dollars to hire two men to drive the wagon and carry the burdens.

The next stop was the coroner's office. The butler stayed with the carriage while Anna went in. Up to this point everything today was theory and business. No longer; death had entered her matrix of realities. She noted the extent of the wounds and the grotesque expression on her deceased husband's face. He died eyes wide open, now dried out in their sockets. The body was there but he was gone.

She wondered what kind of man could do this act of slaughter to another. This mutilation was beyond any anger she could ever possess – even in her agonizing days of wounded body and soul. The act of malice that killed her husband was nothing less than the rotten fruit of evil.

Anna returned to the carriage after a few minutes. She bore the blush of an awakened soul. In silence they returned to the mansion where Anna immediately retreated to the gardens. She could not bear the thought of an empty bedroom.

==0==

It didn't take much time for the sheriff to be told by several citizens that Mrs. Gorgon had reappeared in church. The preacher and his wife also confirmed that indeed the infamous Angry Anna had returned to Deadwood and adorned with her spiteful attitude still in full bloom. The sheriff, half out of curiosity and half out of concern for the public's safety, visited the judge and his wife Julia. He got what he was mining for by only mentioning Mrs. Gorgon's name in passing. Julia not only confirmed that Anna was back, but just happened to mention that a Chinese woman named Xue was also at the Gorgon mansion that morning. The more he thought about it the more the sheriff was sure that Xue was the life-link between Anna and

Deadwood during her time of hiding. Xue may also know if Mrs. Gorgon had been plotting some sort of revenge against anybody in particular or many somebodies in general. On his way back into the business district, the sheriff stopped by a bar that served Chinese and asked about her. The patrons were very suspicious, but one man broke ranks by letting the sheriff know that Xue lived in the back of the laundry across the street from the drug store.

==0==

Later that afternoon the butler escorted Anna to the funeral home. Anna refused to grant her husband a church service and insisted that there would be no viewing. The ghastly look on her late husband's corpse could not be repaired through any cosmetic magic. If somebody had to remember him it should be in his charmed outfits and winning smile. Well-wishers would be welcome to visit and sign a ledger, but his body would be buried at night without ceremony in her cemetery plot planted six feet under the unaltered tombstone bearing her name.

The undertaker protested. He was prepared to make this his biggest event of the year, and he knew she had the money to pay for it. Many would come just to make sure Gorgon was dead. All the undertaker's appeals to protocol were in vain, but after negotiating a handsome price for almost no additional costs or inconveniences to himself he withdrew his complaints. All would be done as she insisted, and that would be the end of it.

The sheriff was waiting in the shadows of the funeral parlor until the business transaction was complete. When he saw Mrs. Gorgon start to leave he walked up to her prior to her exit. He asked by a silent gesture if he could have a discussion with her in a side room. She complied.

"Mrs. Gorgon, I am sorry for your loss. My wife also sends her condolences."

"What brings you here, Sheriff?" said with her arms folded across her chest as if inconvenienced.

"You do. This is as good of a place as any other to talk. You don't need nosy neighbors seeing me knocking on your mansion door."

"Other than your wife's well wishes, what concerns you enough to track me down here?"

"Mrs. Gorgon, Anna if I may, I do not plan to charge Bibb with your husband's death. I wanted to talk to you about this before I went official with it. Frankly, ma'am, I thought you were dead. The preacher came over to my home and mentioned that you were in church today. You made quite an unexpected ghoulish appearance this morning. I also came to warn you about another thing, but I probably don't need to tell you about the newspaper reporter. You know what he is capable of, and it certainly won't be long before he makes it his business to butt into your business."

"So you don't think my husband was murdered? You have concluded that no crime was committed in his death? Are you saying that because my husband often pushed his weight around this town and took great sport in mocking you? The dead man resting in the far parlor had a wife with a similar reputation too, so are you licking your lips with a little taste of sweet pay-back?"

"Mrs. Gorgon, I have no bone to pick with you. I am consulting you as a courtesy that I give to any new widow in this town. You have abused that courtesy because you are a Gorgon filtering things through Gorgon eyes. You are what you are, which is so sad. My responsibilities are now satisfied. You keep pretending all you want, but some day your vanity will get the best of you."

"Sheriff," she said in a more pleasant tone, "I was warned today that I need to turn over a new leaf. I was granted three chances to improve today and I have failed three times. This is difficult for me, Sheriff. Please thank your wife for her condolences."

"You have more problems than just your vanity, Mrs. Gorgon. The man who killed your husband has a nasty habit of filling cemeteries with those who offend him. Just today I received a dispatch from Miles City that two more men were found dead outside that town. Bibb is the prime suspect in the killing of at least five there, and had cause to up the ante when he left. We are not dealing with a passive individual here, Mrs. Gorgon, but a hot handed killer."

"Am I in danger, Sheriff?"

"Did your husband call him out and fail to kill him?"

"You seem to think so. So what is your point?"

"Come by my office tomorrow, Mrs. Gorgon, and we'll talk about this. Our other topics of discussion would not be appropriate at a funeral parlor either. You figure it out, ma'am. This is the third place he has visited since leaving Bismarck. Seven are dead in the first city, seven are dead in the second city, and he hadn't been here three hours and his first one is dead here. Death follows this man, and if history is any clue to the future, his next stop might be your mansion. Now I am not one for superstition, but his alias 'The Ghost of Fort Rice' didn't come easy. He rises from close brushes with death. As we speak, rising is something he may do again."

"Where is he now? And did you say Fort Rice?"

"Bibb is recovering at the Red Buffalo. The doctor thinks he might live and even hired three nurses to watch after the man. I find the doctor's behavior quite peculiar. I have never known him to go to this extent to arrange and finance care for his patients, especially a complete stranger so close to death. Somebody got to him with a secret to cause this reaction. Watch your step, lady. If this man rises up from the bed you better be headed back to the hills. And yes, I did say Fort Rice."

"My husband was from Fort Rice."

"I know, and he and Bibb knew each other. Your husband called him out over an incident that happened there, and now your husband is dead. I don't understand it. Your husband was never ignorant of reality. He knew what Bibb was capable of. What lunacy ever enticed your man to call him out I do not know. Your husband wasn't entirely stupid. Gorgon didn't intend to duel Bibb by the law of the west but decided to ambush the man. Stupid or not, the result was the same."

"Are you calling my husband an idiot?"

"Accept the truth, Anna, and you will be rewarded for it. If I said he was suicidal or insane, you wouldn't get his life insurance money. Be pragmatic. What do you want the doc' to put on the death certificate, Widow Gorgon? Is there any shame in saying he was slower than the man using a baby rag for a name?"

"He wasn't stupid, Sheriff. What really happened?"

"Anna, it really doesn't matter. You're a widow now. And a second thing because you brought up the subject, I have no need for sweet revenge. Maybe you should take that advice to start your life over tomorrow without that chip on your shoulder and a fresh wind of reality in your face. See me in the morning, Mrs. Gorgon, and leave your sour attitude at home in your fancy parlor."

"And what if I don't?"

"Be there, Mrs. Gorgon. Regardless of all the reasons to the contrary you may dream up, I'm still sworn to protect you. I do it because that is my job. There are some emotional twits in this town just as brilliant as your husband was that say I should arrest you for masterminding his murder. And here is another cold reality you can put in your bonnet. You sure are hard on men. Anna, face facts. You would not get an impartial jury in this town. You have earned every ounce of their heavy opinions."

"Do you think that way too, Sheriff? Do you consider me to be wicked also?"

"Come by in the morning. This isn't the place to discuss it. I will tell you plain: I'm the least of your problems. And some more friendly advice Widow Gorgon: Watch your back, young lady."

"I am capable to taking care of myself, Sheriff."

"There used to be a man in this town named Gorgon who arrogantly said the same thing to me. Whoever told you to turn over a new leaf gave you some sage advice. It would be even better if you actually followed it. Good day, Mrs. Gorgon." The sheriff left more uncomfortable then when he first approached her. Anna's soul was showing: dark and dangerous.

==0==

"Keep his diaper clean and keep giving him some of this filtered water when he wakes. Keep his hands away from the bandages and more importantly fill the air with your feminine voice. Find something positive to read to him, or better yet, sing to him if you can rise to the task. He must not feel alone. Give him words of hope if you got any, but regardless, fill the air with your soothing voices as best you can. When you speak words of encouragement touch him regularly on the arms, legs and chest, and keep his brow cool from fever. That is more important than my medicines. I will be back late this evening to give him more pain medication to take him through the night."

The three sisters had a very good patient, each instructed by the doctor to take an eight hour shift. All the wounded man could do was lay there and occasionally moan. They followed the doctor's orders and kept the man as comfortable as possible. They had little to read except the newspapers, and between their interest and his empty ears, these three nurses filled the time by sweetly rereading aloud all the newspaper articles. For fun these sisters applied simple nursery jingles to sing the printed advertisements to the severely wounded man.

==0==

As predicted, the reporter was waiting for Anna Gorgon to emerge from the funeral parlor. Anna, curious about what she could glean from him about Bibb, Fort Rice, and her husband, she immediately took the offensive in the conversation. Instead of dismissing the man, she achieved her goal of making a bargain with him. He reasoned she was going to find out anyway, so he conceded to her demands in exchange for an exclusive interview. She spent the rest of her day at the newspaper office reading all the articles over the last several months mentioning her, her businesses, her husband, or his mistresses. It was an emotionally painful exercise. Exhausted, she informed her willing and helpful guide to the archives that she was done for the day and prepared to leave.

When the reporter insisted that she had agreed to an interview she could only reply, "Later. I know I promised, but not now." He could see that she was exhausted. He bid her a friendly farewell happy in the thought that he had already gained a cache of comments from her as she perused the many articles. The articles she had most reacted to he turned sideways in the filing cabinet for future quick reference. He wasn't helping her; he was helping himself. She was a publisher's goldmine.

He could not go home. The story hound within the reporter cost him three candles that night. He was still at his desk taking notes, writing outlines for articles, and preparing for his exclusive interview when his editor walked into the office the following morning. Both knew the value of his diligence, and the editor encouraged him on. The editor decided on what day they would publish the articles and reassigned two others in the office with the happy task of selling extra advertisements.

==0==

Xue's superstitions and personality demanded an immediate answer. As Bes was ready to close up the diner for the evening Xue appeared at her kitchen door. "I come to help, okay, yes?"

"Help with what?" responded Bes, the owner, cook, waitress, and floor sweeper of the small diner across the street from the Red Buffalo Hotel. "The dishes are done and I'm ready to lock up."

"I come to help feed the ghost. You send food, okay, yes?"

"You're too late, Xue. His broth went over there two hours ago. What do you really want?"

"I fetch dirty dishes, bring back to you. Okay, yes?"

"Too late, Xue. They're back and washed already. Do you want to see the man? If so, just say it. There's nothing wrong with asking that. But think twice about it, Xue. You might not like what you see over there."

"I scared for Meese Gorgon. I must see if Bibb man is ghost or assassin to kill meese-stress. Can we go before rise of moon, yes, okay?"

"You sound scared for yourself too, Xue. Let your heart be still. The man is not going to kill or haunt the either of you. I was there before and after the ambush, and our good doctor is taking special interest in this patient. He's using his stock of pain medicines to keep the man calm. Tommy is drugged asleep most of the time."

"Tommy? Assassin name is Bibb. Did Bibb die, yes?"

"Bibb or Tommy, it's the same man, and no, he's still alive. He may die yet, but the doctor is betting his whole medicine chest that he will pull through."

"We alone when we visit, no? I no like go alone. You come with, yes? Is there a guard to keep assassin from escape, yes?"

"There's no need for a guard. The man has a better chance of placing a foot in a grave than one beside his own bed. He's hurt bad; a gunshot wound to the face. I warn you, Xue, the man is a repulsive mess."

"I must see, you take me, okay, yes?"

"The doctor insisted that I clean up prior to delivering his food, so I'm sure he will demand the same of you. I need a few minutes to finish up here, so you wash up over there. There's a nurse in Tommy's room that will even check your fingernails for dirt before you can go in. Don't you dare cough or sniffle."

==0==

The sun had set two hours prior to when Bes and Xue turned the lock on the diner and headed across the street to the hotel. Xue was visibly nervous and had half a mind to call off the visit. Bes announced her intentions to the innkeeper, proceeded upstairs, knocked on the door, and waited for a response.

The door opened a crack to reveal a woman dressed in white, obviously a nurse. She slipped out of the room and into the hall and addressed the visitors. "What do you want, Bes?"

"This is Xue, my friend, and she has asked to see Bibb."

The nurse looked at the short Chinese woman and replied, "I need a better reason than that. What is her interest in my patient?"

Xue replied, "Meese Gorgon my boss woman. Meese Gorgon want to know if Bibb live, yes? She bury husband tomorrow and so sad. I comfort her, yes? May I see patient, okay, yes? I no touch, just look, okay, yes?"

The nurse could not say no to such a sincere request, but she did demand an inspection for cleanliness. She also demanded that Xue hold a kerchief over her mouth and put a large hat on her head to put up and keep up her long braided hair.

They entered into the room, lit only by a single candle near the window where the nurse's chair was. The candle flickered with the new draft of air coming from the door. The shadows danced wildly around the room. Xue drew closer with Bes as they approached and beheld Bibb's face. Although Bes was acquainted with the sight, Xue was not. The wounds were more repulsive than promised, and what was left of Bibb's face was very pale, almost bloodless. Xue responded to the sight by grabbing Bes's arm tightly with both her hands in fear as they approached for a better look.

Standing over the patient, Xue took a complete visual inventory of the man lying there. Bibb was a smaller man than she expected. He was hardly the giant ogre that her imagination had formed from an assumed mold from which all gun fighters are cast. He was wiry thin, and the dried blood and forming scabs gave her comfort that he was not a ghost... maybe. Candlelight can be deceiving.

At that moment, Bibb turned his face towards Xue, looking directly at her through the one watered eye that wasn't bandaged. Xue froze as their gazes met. Bibb struggled to whisper out one word: "Anna?"

Bes commented later to the nurse that greased lightning was slower than Xue's exit from the room. She had completely come out of her shoes in her fright and flight. Never had Bes or the nurse seen somebody vanish that quickly.

By the time the door shut and the nurse and Bes returned their attention to Bibb he was once again asleep. Bes wished the nurse well, picking up Xue's shoes to take back with her to the diner. Bes commented that she had to see to her Asian patient now.

"Well, now I know how she got the name Shoe." They both chuckled as Bes left the room.

==0==

Xue entered the Gorgon mansion via the kitchen door not bothering to knock. The maid slowed her down, but only slightly, as Xue asked where Mrs. Gorgon was. As directed, Xue went into her bedroom and found Anna there.

"Meese Gorgon! Bibb man is a ghost, and he spoke your name! We must go! We must go!"

"Xue, settle down. What happened?"

"He looked me in eye! So scary, so white! He say your name! He know who you are! We must go! We must hide!"

"Xue, you cannot hide from a ghost. We are not going anywhere, but you may stay here with us if you are scared. Bibb is no ghost; no more than I am."

"You no comfort me with that word."

"Xue, all will be fine. Let us go downstairs to the kitchen to enjoy a bowl of hot sticky rice. There you can tell me what happened."

Monday, September 26, 1887

I sent the reporter away for another day. I am not ready to talk to him yet. My hair needs attention. There is a delicious irony that many in town think that I am a ghost. Let them think that; they deserve a little scare in their lives.

This morning we rode back to the cabin. Xue and I recovered our belongings and I took the mute some supplies. I later showed Mr. Franklin the stack of original estate documents. I did not allow him to take them. They will remain available to him at the mansion. I still do not trust the man. I also had a long talk with the sheriff, and this time I held my temper. My behavior has been quite bad lately, even by my abominable standards.

PS: They buried my husband tonight in my grave under my tombstone. No funeral, no service, no glory, just six feet of dirt over a body corrupted by a marriage destroying living death contracted from unclean lovers. May he stay put, never to bother anybody again. I almost cried. Call me cold, but I will save my tears for something more worthy.

==0==

THE SHERIFF KNEW it was time to make a decision. It was imperative for safety's sake to get Bibb out of Deadwood. The citizenry and the city fathers were unhappy with the doctor's efforts to keep the man alive. Shoot him, hang him, or let him die in the hotel room; they didn't care. Yet they had to acknowledge the sticky problem that Tommy Toivo, a.k.a. Bibb, was a trusted employee of the Governor himself. To harm him through neglect or injustice would cause twice the political harm to their city if such a story was made known east of the Missouri River. These local weasel politicians instructed the sheriff "Handle it, handle it now!" without suggesting specific remedies.

The sheriff found freedom in their approach. Since he was going to be criticized for anything he did, it really didn't matter what they thought. The sheriff was free to do what was right instead of what was expedient. The prior evening the sheriff talked it over with his wife and they settled on a strategy. Once the decision was made the sheriff contacted the doctor asking for a visit with the outlaw in the morning.

The doctor took serious pause at the inquiry. "Will this be a social visit, Sheriff, out of your sworn concern for our citizens' safety?" He took serious the sheriff's campaign rhetoric that boasted he would bring in criminals "Dead or alive, but I personally prefer bleeding bad." The doctor may have been the only one in town who did not praise that promise.

The sheriff easily discerned the doctor's anxiety given the inherent conflict in responsibilities between him and the doctor. "Social visit? If you expand the scope to those within my jurisdiction, yes. But no, Bibb is not a citizen of this town or even this country. Nevertheless Doc', I will make the visit look social. I plan to bring by wife."

"What is your intention, Sheriff? Do you plan to arrest him and haul him down to your filthy jail? I will not stand for that."

"The jail isn't that filthy, Doctor, and no, I do not plan to arrest him. I am seeking answers."

"Your jail is filthy, and you too! Much too filthy to see my patient in the morning! Maybe if you and your wife cleanup to Sunday meeting standards I might let you in. You must arrive spotless with no perfume or makeup, otherwise you can just turn right around and go back home. He hasn't much of a mouth or nose left to breathe through, and we are not going to shut down his respiration with some smelly eau de toilette. Do you understand? I'm serious."

"Doctor, pardon my curiosity, but what is your expanded concern with this stranger?"

"My expanded concern with the man is none of your concern, Sheriff. Suffice your curiosity with this: That man will not perish on my watch."

"Why?"

"You don't listen well, Sheriff. Or maybe you do but cannot stand not knowing everybody's business. Clean up, son, and no colognes. Bring your missus and meet me at the hotel around ten in the morning for coffee. If you want to make yourself useful, get the jail cleaned up too."

==0==

The mute had just enjoyed finishing his first good night of sleep in months when a cacophony of unwelcome female cackling approached his cabin. He quickly got decently dressed, and then tried to conceal his disappointment as they arrived. Back so soon, and just when the air on the mountain was being restored after months of endless chatter. So sweet was his sleep, and now a new nightmare was to begin. Xue was tolerable, but Xue did not come alone.

Anna acknowledged his gesture to come in, and then said, "We brought you some supplies to hold you over a bit. We are also here to collect the last of our things and then return to Deadwood." The mute had learned over the last six months that when Anna said "we" it often meant "he" and neither "she" in that "we" of women standing in front of him carried anything up the mountain.

The man's countenance changed as he saw the burdens that were being brought up the hill. He pulled out of his buttoned pocket some copper and silver nuggets and offered to pay for the supplies, but Anna would not entertain it. It was part of her secret vow to change her behavior, and she was determined to make it all the way to noon before she reverted back to her normal self.

The mute noticed that this was the first time she actually looked at him when she talked, which was rather scary. All the other times she seemed to talk around him or over his head or look down at him like a scab employee. Something was very wrong, as if she thought him to be fellow human equal in the eyes of God. He rethought. No, just different. Something was finally right with this woman, and for the first time he noticed that she had attractive eyes. He quickly shook off that thought as a bewitchment. She had been his overbearing ever-present landlord for too many months to become gullible now. Yet he decided to enjoy the respite while it lasted. It was quite refreshing, and Mrs. Gorgon's vacation from her normal self came with needed supplies.

==0==

Before going over to hotel the sheriff and his wife brought a dress and a shirt that needed cleaning to the laundry across the street from the apothecary. He asked the clerk where the pleasant Chinese lady was, the one that normally worked behind the counter. He was told Xue had not come back to her room last night, but she could be expected to return soon. Xue had told her fellow employees that she went to the mountain to meditate and talk to her late husband at his grave. She sometimes took fruit to offer to the memory of her man who had lost his life in an incident at a local mine. The sheriff was told not to worry, "So sorry; so sorry. She live here; always come back! You come back too. Tomorrow shirt and dress lick-it-ty clean."

==0==

Arriving on time, the sheriff and his wife passed the promised inspection prior to entering the hotel room where Bibb lay. The doctor had warned both the sheriff and his wife of what to expect so both might avoid a reflexive repulsiveness at the sight. The doctor seemed pleased with the progress of the healing and hoped to soon wean his patient from the heaviest of his pain medicines. The nurse gave her report about Bibb's conditions and changes through the night.

The morning light shone into the window and caught Bibb in the face. He was somewhat awake but remained slightly under the influence of the narcotic. Bibb responded to the opening of the drape thinking the light might be from heaven. That glorious thought was polluted when he noticed the man coming into focus was also wearing a seven pointed star. "No, this can't be heaven," Bibb thought to himself, "it is too hot in here and everywhere I look there seems to be a man wearing a badge." Bibb chose not to speak, nor could if he wanted to. Moving his jaw hurt too much.

"Tommy, I am the sheriff of Deadwood, and I want to ask you some questions. The doctor said it would be cruel to ask you to talk, so he suggested you to raise your right hand if the answer to my question is yes. Do you understand me?"

The nurse saw that Tommy was squinting, hoping to clear his one un-bandaged eye of an overflow of tears. After a quick dab from the nurse's cloth, Tommy looked at the man and then at a woman he did not recognize standing next to him. He did recognize the doctor by his stovepipe hat and the kind nurse by her soothing voice. He refocused on the star and considered it legitimate. Bibb then raised his right hand about three inches from the bed.

This was a good sign to all. Tommy had seldom been lucid since the shooting. The sheriff pulled out of his satchel a hatchet, to which the women of the room gasped in surprise. They thought the sheriff was only going to ask questions.

"Tommy, is this your hatchet?"

Bibb did not respond because his eye was blurry with tears again. Again the nurse dabbed his eye and the sheriff approached the bed with the ax. He rotated it around slowly so Tommy could see all the markings, to include the Toivo inscription on the handle. "There are twenty three notches on the handle of this ax. Does this ax belong to you?" asked the sheriff again.

Tommy did not reply by raising his hand but clinched his fist and then extended it with two fingers, clinched again, and extended it with four fingers. Then he raised his right hand again. The sheriff immediately knew what that meant. He just confessed without remorse to Gorgon's death.

"Good, now a second question. Do you swear what you told the reporter about Gorgon – the murders, robberies, and arson – all to be true? Bibb paused and moved his hand to the right and then left as if to say no or maybe.

"Did you make up the story? Then those tales aren't true?"

Much to the amazement of those in the room Bibb moved his hand left and right again. Had he slipped back into a stupor? The nurse got up and whispered something into the sheriff's ear, and the sheriff acknowledged.

"Are you sure that Gorgon committed those crimes?"

Bibb raised his hand to affirm the sheriff's question with the positive hand gesture.

"Is there evidence other than your testimony that would convict Gorgon of those crimes?"

Bibb raised his hand again.

The sheriff looked up and smiled at the young nurse, amazed by her insights. "You were right about what we have laying here. I'm satisfied."

The doctor was savvy enough to know the nurse's secret without being told, but the sheriff's wife would have to wait to be informed. The sheriff put away the hatchet and spoke as he prepared to leave. "Bibb, the city is not going to file a complaint against you for the death of Mr. Gorgon. Several witnesses have come forward and testified on your behalf, and I believe them. That does not clear you of other charges that have been forwarded to me from other jurisdictions, but those matters can wait until you are healthy enough to speak for yourself."

It was a nice speech by the sheriff but Bibb did not hear any of it. He had already drifted away into a merciful sleep. The chore of staying awake hurt too badly.

==0==

It was a beautiful morning in Deadwood. The sheriff helped his wife into the carriage and they proceeded back towards their home.

"So dear, what was the secret the nurse whispered into your ear?" asked the sheriff's wife.

"Some might think this trivial, but not is this case. The man refused to swear, yet he freely affirmed what he knew to be true."

"What is so significant about that?" she responded.

"I now know why the doctor is investing his fortune in the man. His secret is deeper."

"What he does with his money is his business. And as for his secret; are you hinting you know that too? And it is…?"

"This is not our good doctor's first rodeo, darling. The man can recognize a miracle when he sees one. There is more to that man than meets the eye."

"Which man?"

"Yes, I agree, dear."

==0==

The accountant feared for his career. He knew well the disposition of the wealthy Mrs. Anna Marie Higgins Gorgon. He also feared that every misplaced penny would be paid back ten times before he would be formally brought up on malfeasance charges. She was ruthless when it came to money and was never satisfied with the profits they had made. She was known to fly into public rants when she found out what her husband had spent money on, but gave herself a complete pass when it came to her own spendthrift ways. The young accountant, of all men in the gulch, most dreaded the consequences of Mrs. Gorgon coming back to life.

Mr. Franklin opened the door for Mrs. Gorgon as they entered the accounting firm. The accountant stood up and looked at what he thought for sure would be his doom. At one time he thought she was quite an attractive specimen out of the whole universe of women. That inflated opinion was before he was put in charge of the Gorgon estate. The accountant's wife once told him that men are handsome too until one looks closely. He was now convinced the reverse was true also. Women, like sunsets are beautiful too, but if a man is close enough to touch the daystar, he is close enough to get burned.

"Good morning, Mrs. Gorgon. It is my pleasure to finally meet you in person." The accountant did well to avoid looking nervous.

"You make too many assumptions, young man. Obviously you are sharp enough to correctly state the obvious. I hope you don't think you are to be congratulated for that. Yes, you have finally met me in person, but that is neither why I am here nor what I am paying you to do. Where are the ledgers for my estate?"

"I have the Gorgon ledgers on several tables in the back if you care to peruse them. Please note that we are not at month ending yet, so the standard accounting reports are not ready for review, nor have they undergone audit. Our last audit was at the midyear. We received an unqualified opinion, which, as you know is very good."

"Show me the books, young man. Lead the way."

Both Mr. Franklin and the accountant took her to the back room where the ledgers were arranged in order. "I have paper and ink for you, Mrs. Gorgon. Would you care for me to get them, and is there anything else you might need?"

She looked right past the accountant and addressed her lawyer. "Mr. Franklin, you may return to your practice to repair the damage my death certificate did to my estate. Young man, you can shut the door behind you as you return to your desk out front. I will look at these without your help. If I call for you, well, I don't want to think about that. On second thought, you don't want to think about that either. Good day, Mr. Franklin. I will visit your office after I conduct my first review."

Mr. Franklin commented to the accountant (after she had been left alone in the back and the door was shut) that he was justified to have complete confidence in his work. "I chose your firm because I knew your reputation. Don't become unnerved by her, well not just yet at least. Son, your problems are nothing compared to mine. We will get through this. That is my promise."

The accountant fetched the paper and quill for the lovely and gracious beast-ette in his back room. She concealed well the horns growing out of her head. He immediately shamed himself for having such thoughts concerning one of his wealthiest customers as he returned to his desk. He told himself that she was just being diligent in business and simply needed re-acquaintance with her finances. Right... and Stonewall Jackson only wanted to go trout fishing in Bull Run. He picked up the Deadwood paper and checked the obituaries for his name.

==0==

Anna was disappointed with herself that she did not make it to noon before she revived her pre-disappearance attitudes. She quickly forgave herself and doubled her heart's promise to behave when visiting the sheriff. His invitation was for the morning, but she missed that. "Brawn needs to yield to beauty," she thought to herself. "The man can wait. Should I buy a new hat before I visit?"

At half past two o'clock, Anna filed her notes in a folder and emerged from the firm's back office. The accountant stood up but dared not say anything. There was nothing to be gained in conversation. He carefully tried to discern her mood in other ways.

"Young man, have you had lunch yet?"

"No, ma'am. I seemed to have lost my appetite three days ago. And you, ma'am, you must be hungry. May I get you anything?"

"That is considerate of you, young man. No, I am leaving now and may be back tomorrow. I have some questions for you, but overall I am pleased with your work. Thank you for accommodating my curiosity." With that statement she walked out of his office and down the street, but not in the direction of Mr. Franklin's office.

The accountant sat down in his chair dumbfounded. He had no witness, but he was almost sure that Mrs. Gorgon had slipped out a compliment; or at least a close cousin to one. He immediately suspected something other, and told himself not to let down his guard. He pulled his lunch out of his drawer and went into the back room to discern what the Widow Gorgon had been looking at. His future may depend on that discovery.

==O==

Widow Gorgon decided not to get a new hat, but traveled in the direction of the sheriff's office. She was in a good mood springing from the state of the accounting records. There would not be a better time to visit the lawman. As she walked, because of her promise to behave, she decided to go to the sheriff's home instead of his office. She knew she behaved better with women present. Her real motive was to talk with his wife to discover any hidden agendas prior to facing the man. Better yet, after tea his wife might escort her over to his office. Either way, that would be better than just showing up fashionably late at the man's jail.

Of course, she would have to bring a present if she called on the sheriff's wife, and that would require shopping. Anna stopped by one of the Gorgon owned mercantile stores and picked up a clove of garlic and a pound of salt. Ghosts can't tolerate either, so in a small way her gift would be a poetic denial of the rumors. Even if they didn't get the joke, the gift would have some value for them rather than a useless trinket.

Widow Gorgon's arrival was a complete surprise to the sheriff's wife. She quickly dispatched one of her sons to fetch his father while they exchanged pleasantries in their small front room. The house was much too small for a family with four children, and she had to move folded laundry to make room for her visitor.

Anna marveled at the grace by which she garnered help from her children and accomplished the task of rearranging chairs and making tea. The woman had confidence and poise, but had no apologies for the smallness and fullness of their home. She seemed happy, and Anna knew happiness cannot be easily faked.

Twenty minutes later the sheriff arrived at his home where Anna greeted him upon his entrance. "Sheriff, you invited me over this morning, and I apologize for being late. What did you want to talk to me about?"

"Darling, please have the kids go out and play with the neighbor children. Some of the following conversation may get dicey." The kids did not need their mother's encouragement. Within seconds they were out the door.

"I forgot," said Anna. "Sheriff, I brought a gift for your family. My biggest fault is buying impractical gifts, so I changed my focus and brought you something useful. Please accept these items." Anna presented the garlic and salt to the sheriff's wife. She responded to the strange gifts with a simple thank you. There had to be some hidden meaning, but that was for a later discovery.

"Mrs. Gorgon, may I call you Anna?" started the sheriff. "Where have you been for the last six months? Certainly your abode has been one of Deadwood's best kept secrets."

"Some sillies say the cemetery, but Sheriff, pray tell me why that location is that important to know. I may have to return to my secret tomb if this Tommy fellow decides to seek revenge for the insults he received from my late husband. The man is rather notorious, wouldn't you agree?"

"Yes he is, Anna. My question to you is why I should care if he wants to go gunning for you."

"You obviously refer to my insults I had towards you yesterday. Forgive me, for then my fear was talking."

"Really? You have developed fears in the last six months? This is a recent character change."

Anna wanted to strike out at the man. He was baiting her. He wanted her to explode with penned up passions. He hoped she would reveal the hate within her to gain information about what really happened between her, her husband, and the man called Bibb. She would not accommodate his tactic.

"Good Sheriff, since you discern character for a living, I will agree with you that you are right to note that changes are rare. Well, regardless if I like it or not, change has come my way. I am a widow now. You might have noticed, in fact I am sure you have noticed, that while my husband was alive my bad behavior was protected by his money. People feared what my husband would do to anybody who challenged him about our behavior. Accidents happen, and accidents happened to them more."

"Anna, you are admitting to that? I might even believe you are maturing, maybe, if I thought you to be sincere. My first inclination is to assume you are conniving to position yourself for some great self-promotion. Tell me true, Anna, why the reappearance?"

"To reclaim what is mine. It is that simple."

"Not revenge?"

"Against who?"

"There are several that come to mind. On top of the list is Mr. Franklin. There are others."

"Mr. Franklin and I struck an agreement the other day. As long as he keeps his part of the bargain he will be rewarded handsomely."

"What about avenging the man who killed your husband? What do you know about him?"

"Only what I read about in the papers."

"Which papers? Just the local ones?"

"Sheriff, I have only been back in town for three days. I haven't had time to read other papers. Besides, you hinted to me yesterday that although this Bibb person killed my husband, he did not murder him. My husband called him out to his own peril."

"Did you hire Bibb to accomplish your revenge?"

"Sheriff, that is an accusatory question, and I will not entertain it."

"Why not? You wanted your husband dead for what he had done to you."

"What do you mean by that, Sheriff? My husband loved me, and he even cried at my funeral."

"Anna, did you invite Bibb to Deadwood?"

"Sheriff, I have heard of the legend, but I never assumed he was available to do dirty work. Is that your accusation? Shame on you! No, I have never seen the man or talked to the man. It wasn't until yesterday that I discovered he and my husband were both from Fort Rice. I certainly did not know there was any bad blood between the two. And for your next question, Sheriff, if I had known my husband to be a murdering, bank robbing arsonist I would have never married him. I married him because he told me I was beautiful, and I told him he was handsome, and we committed to make ourselves a fortune together. That arrangement worked until he found out I came equipped with both a brain and an opinion. Sheriff, you are wise to all the rumors and what happened between me and my deceased husband. Don't expect me to rehearse any of that in front your wife."

"Did you want your husband dead?"

"No. Absolutely not! I wanted him to admit he was wrong and come begging back to me. I would then shame him, take all the money, and leave him to die of the incurable and painful fruit of his unfaithfulness with his rent-a-honey heathens. No, he didn't deserve to die. He deserved to live and suffer a tortured life of ruin, pain and shame."

"You're lying, Anna."

"On what basis do you say that, Sheriff? What cards are you holding that would tempt you to call a bluff?"

"Anna, you live in an altered truth. You tell yourself how important you are and then you start believing it. Okay, so let's retreat. Let's pretend I do believe you. What are you going to do now?"

"That's none of your business, Sheriff."

"The Anna we know has returned, darling. That certainly did not take long." The sheriff's wife poured some more tea for all of them but said nothing more.

The sheriff returned his attention back to Anna from his wife. "It is my business, Anna. You are a woman armed with wealth and wild ideas, and I dare say none of them edifying to the community. Anna, you have one idol, and that idol is you. You need help, Anna. You have been separated from your moorings too long, like a kite detached from its string. Worse, as you flop around in the wind there is a man in town that on a whim could get out of bed and permanently return you to the cemetery. His only remorse would be he still had five people yet to kill before he left this city. Anna, I want you to go into hiding again, but this time with somebody that can help you. You are a danger to yourself and to others."

"That is mighty bold, Sheriff. Who is this lucky person you are thinking of to bring me back from the brink of insanity? If his name starts with Mister, he is already disqualified. I'm not taking any advice or lip from any man. While I was thought to be dead did some lucky quack build a nest in Deadwood in hopes of detaching this poor widow from her pittance fortune in counseling fees?"

"You are the lucky person if you admit you need help and commit to changing. Until you agree, the helper will remain nameless."

"I will think about it. But I don't believe any threat that my husband's killer is ready to get out of bed and murder me. Didn't you read the papers, Sheriff? It editorialized that I'm dead already."

"Seriously Anna, you need help, and now is the time to get it," interrupted the sheriff's wife in a compassionate tone.

"I think I have a better idea," Anna replied as she got up from the table. "Sheriff, enjoy your salt and garlic."

Tuesday, September 27, 1887

I spent the beginning of my day with the rude Mr. Franklin and that accountant. He told me that I had a choice: billing his time to the task of entertaining me or I allow him to get the legal tasks done. I suppose I must make an allowance for him. Men can only do one thing at a time.

I am still quite upset with the sheriff and the words he had for me yesterday. The arrogance of the man telling a successful woman like me that I need to change! He pretended to be kind because he wants something, and I am determined to find out his real agenda.

I took my lawyer's advice concerning Mr. Toivo's expenses. Outlaws are treacherous but sometimes can be good investments. Contrary to the sheriff's accusation, this is not a payoff for a prearranged accident. These payments must be made to avoid future losses.

I do not know why people are so unkind to me, and some are downright mean. I have never harmed them. I provide jobs to miners. I provide needed merchandise to the peasants and rich alike for a reasonable profit. I set a much needed social standard for women in this town they all can wish to achieve. Their ingratitude makes me want to leave this sick town and find a real place I can call home.

PS. The strangest thing happened to me tonight. I still think I am dreaming. It cannot be true. I am dreaming. These people are so mean.

==0==

ANNA GORGON WAS waiting at the accountant's office when he arrived for work Tuesday morning. Both he and Mrs. Gorgon had their heads full of tasks to be accomplished that day, and their lists were not the same.

"Did you have a good breakfast, Mrs. Gorgon? There is a fine diner on the other side of town that I could recommend to you." The accountant could tell she got the hint. She of all people in town knew where all the restaurants were, one of which was across the street.

"First things first," replied Mrs. Gorgon. "I need to withdraw some cash from my estate, but my errant husband saw to it that my name was taken off our account. I need to have a two hundred dollar draft drawn on the estate's account that I can present to the bank."

"I can give you up to twenty dollars in petty cash, Mrs. Gorgon, and that would be much easier. Will that suffice?"

"Kind sir, that is why they call it petty! I want two hundred dollars."

"Ma'am, where can you spend money like that in this town? Please, be reasonable. Will twenty dollars cover your immediate needs? You can draw twenty more dollars tomorrow if you need it."

"Write me a draft for fifty dollars then and I will overlook your unkindness to me."

The young accountant took a deep breath. If he didn't draw the line now he knew he would suffer more of her bully tactics later. "Mrs. Gorgon, as your accountant I want your trust, and part of that trust begins with calling things as they are, not as they are pretended to be. I have not been unkind to you. Twenty dollars is more than anybody, except maybe you before you disappeared, could spend in this town in a day. If you have an expense upwards of two hundred dollars, that transaction needs to be noted in the ledgers. I am not telling you no, Mrs. Gorgon. What I am telling you is that if I am to be retained as your accountant, I must demand certain financial disciplines to be followed. Nevertheless, have it your way for you are the client, but please note we can do this the easy way or the hard way. If you do not want my services, fine. You can be much more trouble than what my fee covers. I have a wheelbarrow out back that you can load your ledgers into and tote them back to your mansion to dump on your parlor floor if you like. I suggest an easier way, and that is for you to start showing more respect for my person and more reasoned justification for your requests. What I do is a professional trade and I will not be treated as anything less. You have enough money to hire all the sycophants you want, but I will not be one of them." The accountant could not believe what he just said, but he was glad he said it.

Unmoved, Anna replied. "You will not escape your responsibilities that easily. Prepare a draft for me immediately and I will return after I complete my business to discuss your offensive 'easy way' and your 'hard way.' Why are you still standing there? Prepare the withdrawal!"

==0==

As expected, the sheriff came by for his laundry around nine in the morning. Xue had been told that the sun had set in the east by the other Chinese worker when she arrived back at the business; either that or the sheriff and his wife really did need their clothes cleaned. Since the sun behaved on schedule, Xue concluded it was the local lawman that was acting outside of nature's laws. Xue was ready for him, and likewise his clothes.

The sheriff presented his receipt and received his wife's cleaned dress along with a shirt that wasn't his. It wasn't just any shirt, but one that their laundry service had ruined for another customer; in fact it was one of Mr. Gorgon's shirts that had burnt iron marks on the front of it. Xue, in her anger had also added some new bleach spills and removed buttons to make sure the subtle point she was making was not missed.

"Thank you for cleaning the dress, but I'm sorry, this shirt is not mine," said the sheriff.

"No mistake, receipt match. You pay now. Twenty cents please," said Xue.

"No really, this is not my shirt, and to be honest, this shirt is ruined."

"Good to have honest sheriff. Much better than ruined sheriff," she replied.

"The topic is the shirt, not the sheriff, and what is your name please?"

"I talking about the sheriff; and my name is Xue. You wait here one second; I go ask my husband about your shirt." She asked the next two persons in line for their receipts and she went to the back of the store to get their laundry. He wondered if he had heard her correctly; sometimes things are lost in transmission and reception. He was quite sure she said she was going to ask her husband, which meant that the widow Xue had remarried, was saying an untruth on purpose, or she was not Mrs. Gorgon's Xue. Xue did return with the other customer's clothes, they paid her, and left the store leaving only Xue and the sheriff in the storefront.

"So sorry; your shirt died. You take this one. You pay now."

"Is that what your husband said? May I talk to him?"

"So sorry; my husband dead. You pay now."

"I want my shirt back. Please bring it to me."

"I want my husband back. Please bring him to me."

"Neither this shirt or your husband are coming back from the dead. Xue, what is your point, and why are you making it? Please bring me my shirt."

Xue had planned for this moment. She put away her disciplined soft-spoken self and delivered a disciplined 'both-barrels of the shotgun' reply. "I no care about your shirt like you no care about my husband. You pay now. You take dead shirt. Show me the money." Another customer walked into the store. Xue continued in the same tone, "You must pay. I can no give you free just because you are sheriff. I must pay for your bill if you no pay me. Who arrest you if you steal from me?"

"Xue, I am not stealing from you. I am asking for my laundry, not somebody else's. But I am a reasonable man. Here is the money for this laundry, but please look for my shirt and bring it to my office this afternoon around three. I need to talk to you about something else too. You can bring a friend if you like. More than anything I need to understand what you are saying. I obviously failed at hearing you correctly this morning."

==0==

"I am sorry ma'am, but I cannot honor this draft. According to our records there is in longer an Anna Gorgon on any accounts in this bank. I will get fired if I honored this draft right now. I know you are Mrs. Gorgon. The whole town knows that, but I don't have fifty dollars to have taken out of my pay if I willfully break the bank's rules and give you cash for this draft. I am sure that your lawyer will have this all corrected soon, but until then this draft will have to remain with you. Would you like to talk to my boss? He will tell you the same thing, but you will have the satisfaction of getting your complaint more fully aired." Thirty minutes later Mrs. Gorgon left the bank; the manager with burning ears and she without her money.

==0==

The sheriff's wife started to laugh out loud when he brought into their home her clean dress along with the murdered shirt. "You do know this isn't your shirt dear, yes?"

"Xue said the receipt matched and I had to pay for it. The alternative was to look like I was taking advantage of her in front of other customers. She was making a point although I am not completely sure what her point was. I invited her down to the jail this afternoon to deliver my shirt first, hear out her complaint, and thirdly to discuss Mrs. Gorgon's reappearance."

"What do you think her complaint is?"

"I'm not sure but I think she wants to talk about her husband's disappearance. She obliquely accused me of not caring about her husband's death. Frankly, I don't remember it. There are many accidents in the mines and no shortage of workers willing to step and take the place of a fallen employee. I doubt if I will find anything about her husband in the files at the office. I don't even know his name or which mine her husband worked at. I have a feeling that I will be told everything I need to know before I am allowed to see the cotton hostage alive ever again."

"Can I join you? I'm sorry, but she will eat you alive if this is her complaint and you are left alone with her. It is deep in their culture. I can help by being there. She will be much kinder if she is worried about showing her face to somebody other than the one who unjustly treated her."

"When did I treat her unjustly? A Chinaman dies at the mine, okay, so where is my act of injustice in that? Dear, I don't see your point."

"You just made my point. We agree then. Let's hear her out together. True, there is probably nothing we can actually do to help, but that is not the issue. I will bring a snack. Food is a great peacemaker."

==0==

Anna arrived at Mr. Franklin's office in a snit. She had worked herself up into a lather walking the six blocks from the bank to his office. She found his office door locked, and she commenced to bang on the door. He arrived, opened the door, and invited her in to his waiting area.

"The bank would not give me any of my money, Mr. Franklin!" Anna declared.

"That is because technically it is not your money yet, Mrs. Gorgon. We agreed to a couple weeks and you have only given me a couple hours. Did we agree, or not agree?"

"We agreed. But can you hurry?"

"Undoing months of meticulous legal work in just days is already expecting a miracle, Mrs. Gorgon. Have you completed the more pressing task of taking care of Mr. Toivo's expenses? You have had two days."

"No, I haven't, Mr. Franklin. Do you expect miracles too?"

"Mrs. Gorgon, the only miracle I hope for, well never mind, you already know it."

"Spit it out, Mr. Franklin. What insult were you going to throw at me?"

"Anna, and I purposely call you Anna; the heart of the matter is your heart in this matter. It is a waste of precious time if you remain standing here expecting me to entertain you. I already cancelled all my other appointments to handle this work. Good day, Anna, and close the door behind you on your way out. We both have things to do that require our immediate attention."

Anna was furious. "I am not going to stand for your rudeness, Mr. Franklin."

"Stand? I will take note of that, Widow. If Bibb comes to kill you I will instruct the undertaker to lay you out with all the care you afforded your late husband! Widow, let me make this clear. Everything I do can be redone if I err, but you Widow Gorgon, if you make a mistake with Bibb you will end up dead again and this time dead for keeps. Do yourself a favor and do your duty and do it now! You are wasting daylight."

"You will pay for your insolence, Mr. Franklin."

"That is why I want you to stay alive, Widow. I expect to get paid for my services. Now scoot!"

"What about my fifty dollars?"

Instead of answering, Mr. Franklin stood upright and with a face that could terrorize any defendant, and pointed Anna to the door. He gave her the last word, but he took the last communication. To add insult to her injury the door locked with prejudice immediately upon her passing through the jamb.

Anna dared not go shopping. She now was certain that her credit was no good until Mr. Franklin completed his tasks. "Why was that man so slow?" she mumbled to herself as she walked back towards her mansion. She had more than two hundred dollars lying around in several safes in the house. She just wanted the satisfaction of gaining results from her demands, and resented severely being told what she had to do. Anna entered her home angry and empty, resolving Mr. Franklin's humiliating instructions would be purposely postponed until she decided the time and place.

==0==

Xue arrived at the jail at three in the afternoon with a package. She had been warned by her friends that nothing good ever happens to a Chinaman or woman at the jail. She told them that she was not afraid. She was not going to receive justice but to give justice. The sheriff's wife greeted her at the door with a smile and asked her to come to the back room so they could have a more private conversation. The sheriff had poured some tea when he heard Xue arrive and stood up to greet her as she entered the back room.

"Thank you for coming, Xue. Were you able to find my shirt?"

"Your shirt never lost. I gave you Mr. Gorgon's shirt. That shirt dead like Mr. Gorgon."

The sheriff tried to move the conversation towards his agenda. "Xue, I am glad you brought that up. I want to ask you about the Gorgons."

"He is dead, just like my husband," responded Xue.

"But Mrs. Gorgon isn't. Mrs. Gorgon owns the laundry where you work, and also provides to you a place to sleep in the back of the store. Is that correct?"

"After my husband died I no afford apartment. Meese Gorgon have mercy for price. She allow me to work many laundry hours. She also trust me with her clothes. Good for business, good for Meese Gorgon, good for me except very tired."

"I want you to tell me what you know about Mrs. Gorgon. You knew she disappeared about seven months ago. Did you know she was alive during that time?"

"I was very happy Mr. Franklin had bookkeeper. He nice man, and very on time with pay. Meese Gorgon not always on time with pay. Before she disappear Meese Gorgon always give me sewing job and bring clothes to Gorgon house. That extra money go away; so sad. Meese Gorgon no pay us anymore, we get money from accountant. I was told Meese Gorgon dead, like my husband. So sad."

"I think you know more than that, Xue. I think you knew that Mrs. Gorgon was alive."

"I think you know more about my husband die. I am very glad Meese Gorgon is now alive. I wish my husband alive too. I think you know more about my husband die, yes?"

"Xue, I need your cooperation. I am worried about Mrs. Gorgon."

"Why you worry? You care about Mr. Gorgon die bad?" responded Xue. "You worry about my husband die bad too?"

"I cannot do anything about either Mr. Gorgon or your husband. Xue, I want to know about Mrs. Gorgon. Tell me where she was living for the last seven months."

"You no care about Meester Gorgon or my husband problem, I no care about you problem."

The sheriff's wife interceded in the conversation that was going nowhere. "Xue, what was your husband's name? Maybe there is something we can do. Dear, when did he die, and at which mine?"

"My husband name was He Zhang, but at Seim Mine he a number; no name. He die when boss think he take gold, die, hire next Chinaman. I ask many times. Many time boss man many time say he no know He. Told me go away or get sheriff. He no get sheriff when I ask again, but get gun. Me no go back."

"Darling," said the sheriff's wife to her husband, "with this information why don't you start to look into this. Xue and I will stay here for a while longer." She could tell that Xue wasn't going to tell her husband anything. Xue was not angry, or controlling it very well, but she was resolved. Nothing he could say would bend her will. Yes, he could threaten her with some made up charge of withholding information, but in reality there was no murder to be solved. But that is not why she was asked to come down. The sheriff was worried about preventing one, two, or tally up even more funerals. Bibb and untimely deaths kept close company.

"Here is shirt, Sheriff. You find out soon."

The sheriff took the package and left the office. He was never very good at intimidating people, a fact that was proven once again. He left hoping that his wife would get answers to his questions. He headed over to Bes's and then to the hotel. He had a hunch, an ugly hunch, about something.

The sheriff's wife asked Xue, once they were alone, why she was evasive in answering her husband's questions. She assured Xue that her husband had a good heart and he wanted justice for all people in Deadwood. "Xue, my husband is a good man with a big job. Please don't be so hard on him. Give him a chance."

Xue replied, "Good heart hard to keep. If a good man does nothing when a bad man is bad, then the good man becomes bad man too. A good man must never stop doing good else he becomes bad. He no care about Chinaman because he too busy with too many bad men his skin?"

There was no good answer to her complaint so the sheriff's wife didn't try to answer it. "Xue, let us make an agreement to help each other. I promise you that my husband will look into what happened to your husband if you help us answer some questions. Can we do that?"

"Depend on question. I must be loyal to Meese Gorgon or I get fired and sleep in street."

"Did you help Mrs. Gorgon during the time she was away from Deadwood?"

Xue responded, "Yes, but no tell where. We hide again if Bibb man die and come alive again. We hide from outlaw. He know Meese Gorgon by first name. Meese Gorgon in big danger."

"But you did help Mrs. Gorgon, yes?"

"What is next question?" answered Xue.

"Is Mrs. Gorgon scared of Bibb?" asked the sheriff's wife.

"Bibb man kill Meester Gorgon. Bibb man will kill Meese Gorgon before Meese Gorgon kill Bibb man. Meese Gorgon run away from danger if danger too big. She no afraid of small danger. She quick to end small danger. She no punch a stand up man. She punch a lay down man. Poor Meester Gorgon. When he sleep, big punch by Meese Gorgon. She mean to sleeping bad man."

"Would Mrs. Gorgon ever kill anybody?"

"Meester Gorgon dead many time if Meese Gorgon want to kill bad man. Meese Gorgon say quick dead to nice for Meester Gorgon. He need to be blind and slow die by clap-clap."

"But what about a different bad man?"

"Me r'loyal. What next question? No, I go home now."

"Does Mrs. Gorgon have a gun?"

"Last answer then good bye. When Meese Gorgon want to come home I bring dress, hat, shoes, face paint, and gun. I no ask why. Good bye." With that Xue took one last sip of tea, stood up and headed for the door.

"Xue, before you go I want to say thank you. I will keep all your answers secret, and you were never disloyal to Mrs. Gorgon." The sheriff's wife approached Xue and although it seemed like hugging an adolescent girl she embraced Xue. It was somewhat awkward. It was the first time she had held close somebody from another race.

About thirty minutes after Xue left both the sheriff and his wife met at their home. He gave the package to his wife while he entertained questions from his children concerning their studies. From the kitchen he heard his wife laughing and all came into the kitchen to investigate. She showed her husband what had been wrapped up. It was a Chinaman's work shirt with a number stenciled on the front and back. And yes, the sheriff's shirt was still being held hostage at the Chinese laundry. Aghast, she quickly told the kids to return to what they were doing. What she did not want the kids to see was the evidence of foul play – a hole in the front and back of the shirt along with some very old dark stains. Alone in the kitchen, she told her husband everything Xue had confided with her.

The sheriff had hoped his hunch was wrong and what he had secretly arranged in town was a waste of time. After talking with his wife, both became afraid that something bad may happen, and soon. It would not be long before Bibb would be "stand up" as Xue described. It was a reasonable risk that Bibb might suffer a "lay down" lethal punch before he had a chance to "stand up." He asked his wife to arrange for child care during their date a Bes's tonight. He would return in an hour.

==0==

That afternoon Anna tried on many of her outfits that were stored in her closets. She enjoyed looking at them again as if for the first time. Some had the prices still attached to them. She took a shower followed by her maid fixing her hair perfectly. "What is the occasion, Mrs. Gorgon?"

"I am going out to eat at Bes's Diner and then go see the doctor about something."

"Ma'am, you don't look twice sick. You never ate at Bes's and you certainly don't look like you need a doctor's care. Tell me true, where are you planning to go?"

"I told you true. Don't assume I am the patient."

"I think I know where you're planning to go. You shouldn't go alone. Do you want the butler to escort you? He can at least wait outside in the carriage."

"I will think about that. Do you think I lost weight while away? I think walking those hills caused my figure to improve. What do you think?"

"I think I know better than to answer that question."

==0==

The newspaper reporter was outside the Gorgon mansion waiting for the lady to appear. He was very surprised that she chose to walk into town instead of taking her carriage. He shadowed her in his buckboard until she finally noticed him following. At eye contact he asked her first if she needed a ride and second if she was ready to keep her promise.

"You may offer me a ride, and you may join me for dinner, but where I am going after, there you may not go. I will give you information on that business if you promise not to publish it until after I give you my specific permission."

The ride into town was quite the sight for those who observed it. Never before had the reporter escorted such an elegantly dressed and behaved woman in his dilapidated buckboard. Unfortunately for the reporter, Anna was very aggressive and peppered him with questions before he got to ask his first one. He was not upset. The dam of silence had been broken. Besides, his hands were already full trying to guide the old mare down the lane. She had a personality of her own too.

Maybe by luck (but not really) the sheriff and his wife were enjoying a meal at Bes's when the reporter and Anna made their entrance. (Anna never merely entered a place; she made entrances.) It was such an odd couple that the sheriff's wife started to giggle. Anna, dressed in black, caught her response and diverted her path to their table. Anna asked his wife if the reason she was smiling was because her widow's mourning dress looked too baggy.

The sheriff answered, but not Anna's question. He looked directly at the reporter. "The last man who had dinner with a Gorgon in here caught a bullet with his teeth, and his tablemate was buried in an ill-marked grave last night. You might want to watch what you say. I will be. You two sit right here next to us and pretend I'm not listening."

Mrs. Gorgon snapped back. "That is a cruel and unfair statement, Sheriff, and you should not be eavesdropping."

"Lady Gorgon, eavesdropping is my job, especially when people end up dead, may your husband rest in peace. You still haven't answered all my questions yet. Moreover, when has fairness ever been included in your decisions and behavior?"

"You have misjudged me, Sheriff."

"I hope I have Anna, and I am anxious for you to prove my prejudices incorrect. Does that mean you will take me up on yesterday's offer for help?"

Anna did not appreciate that comment in front of the curious reporter. She quickly changed her countenance and responded, "We are sitting over there, Sheriff. My conversation with you is now over. May you and your lovely wife have a pleasant meal."

==0==

The reporter pulled the chair out for his beautiful date just as Bes came out of the kitchen to greet them. "Mrs. Gorgon, my name is Bes, and I want to welcome you to my diner. I believe this is the first time you have graced us with a visit."

"Bes, that is my loss. I have heard from several, even this week, that your dinner plate is the best tasting and most generous portion in the city. What do you suggest we have tonight? It is my treat."

"Mrs. Gorgon, tell me your preference; are you here to enjoy some hardy eating, or might there be another reason? No offense, but I'm being host to some uncommon guests tonight that is strangely too reminiscent of last Friday."

"You are very perceptive, and yes, if I may I would like to talk to you later in your kitchen about another matter. But for now, bring two of your Tuesday night specials out for us."

"Mrs. Gorgon," Bes approached closer, "Nobody is going to die tonight, are they?"

"I guess that depends on how nosey my dinner partner becomes, Bes." The reporter looked up not liking the question or the answer. "Don't worry. I only plan on getting him locked up in jail."

Bes returned to the kitchen and the reporter addressed Anna. "Mrs. Gorgon, your last statement, well, I only report the news, not make the news. What exactly are your intentions?"

"Kind sir, your fate is in your hands, not mine. Let us resolve to be very kind to each other. Do I have your word on that?"

"What do you mean by 'kind'?"

"We will make a peace pact. I propose that we agree not to hurt each other. Such an unkind action might prompt the offended to destroy the initial offender."

"Mrs. Gorgon, you have a strange sense of kindness. That sounds atroce[1], pardon my French."

"Trust me. I know how to be kind and I know how to destroy. I also have the means to do unto others before they do it unto me. As the golden rule says, She who has the gold, rules."

"Mrs. Gorgon, I think you're quoting from a source other than the Good Book. But even with that erroneous reference, you have delicately made your point. I caught your gentle nuance."

"That was neither delicate or a nuance. That was a promise, and I want to make sure you completely understand it."

"So what is your point in practical terms?"

"I will give you stories and you will let me approve them prior to publishing. If they are inaccurate, I want you to block them. Your boss can editorialize all he wants, but the news reports must be measured by how I define accuracy."

"And if I don't keep this promise?"

"Then I tell Bibb some lies I heard you say about him and where his ax can find you."

"That sounds more like vengeance than kindness, yes?"

"My husband died within seconds. Isn't that a preferred way to die rather than by a pickled liver, consumption, or syphilis? Now let us be reasonable here. Neither of us is going to hurt each other, are we?"

"No, ma'am, not when you make your position so politely and precisely clear."

==0==

After the fine dinner, Anna picked up the dirty dishes at her table and brought them back to the kitchen as if she was kitchen help. Her disappearance caught the sheriff's notice, and he immediately went out the front door, pulling one of his revolvers out of its holster. Simultaneously the sheriff's wife got up from her seat and went directly to the reporter's table. She was instructed, using her art of persuasion, to glean from the reporter what Anna had revealed.

The reporter noted the curious timing and inquired of the sheriff's wife, "Does the pleasure of your company have anything to do with a promise you may have overheard Anna say to me?"

She replied, bluffing, "That depends. What is she up to?" She purposely sat in Anna's chair.

"What if Mrs. Gorgon returns from the kitchen? This situation could become awkward."

---

[1]   French, Diabolical

"That's your problem, not mine. Is she packing?"

"I don't know! How am I supposed to know?" pleaded the reporter.

"Tell me what you know, and do it quickly. What you say next will be used to determine if you are an accomplice to murder. Speak fast and speak soft."

==0==

Bes gave Anna the covered bowl of a fragrant liquid dinner she had prepared for Bibb. When Anna asked, Bes told her that Bibb was in room number two in the hotel across the street. Once Anna was out the door Bes returned to the dining room and told the sheriff's wife that Anna was on her way to the hotel. The sheriff's wife, in turn, told the reporter not to leave his chair until she, the sheriff, or Bes said he was safe.

"She wasn't kidding about having me thrown in jail, was she?"

"I think her plan was to pin a murder on you. You will sit tight, yes? You are in need of witnesses vouching you never even left your chair, not even to sneeze."

"Glued."

==0==

Anna checked in with the desk clerk at the hotel to confirm the room number Bibb was staying in. He told Anna that Bibb was in room number two, and that the nurse had just stepped out. He volunteered another comment saying that the room door was unlocked and she could go up there.

"Well, it wouldn't be right to delay his dinner any longer. I imagine Bibb is pretty hungry by now. I will stay up there until the nurse or doctor returns. Thank you."

"Only a dead man could endure waiting for some of Bes's cooking to arrive." She replied with an odd smile to that comment. With a head nod she thanked the man.

Anna immediately went upstairs with the covered bowl of soup. Instead of knocking, Anna opened the door a crack and peeked in. The window shades were pulled down leaving the only light in the room a flickering lamp by the nurse's chair. There was the form of a man lying in the bed with his back towards her.

Looking left and right to see if anybody was in the hall, Anna quietly entered the hotel room and shut the door behind her. She laid the soup on a nightstand and started to pull up her dress. Strapped to her right leg was a holster holding a derringer pistol. As she started to reach for it, the sheriff came out the shadow stopping the woman by wrapping her up in his arms and throwing her onto the floor. Despite pounding him with her fists and her ferocious kicks, he immobilized her right leg and seized the gun before she had a chance to use it.

Upon hearing the commotion from across the hall the doctor came into the room along with the nurse. Between the three of them they handcuffed the violently thrashing woman's arms to the radiator pipe. Anna screamed rape, but it did not help. The sheriff grabbed a towel and gagged her. She kicked and fussed and wasted much energy flopping around on the floor as the three of them let her exhaust herself in her lashing out and muffled wailing. They were exhausted themselves.

Moments later the clerk brought the sheriff's wife up to room number two. The doctor dismissed the nurse to return to attend to Bibb's needs. He sternly warned her to keep what she saw secret from her patient who was in room number four. The bellman also returned to his duties at the front desk with a similar admonition.

"Will you do the honors, darling?" the sheriff said to his wife. "We are looking for a small vial that Mrs. Gorgon may have kept poison in to sprinkle into Mr. Toivo's dinner. Doctor, please supervise my wife's complete inventory of Mrs. Gorgon's clothes and person while I go and talk to our reporter friend across the street."

The sheriff dusted his clothes of all the cobwebs they stirred up in the confrontation. He continued instructing them, "Do not touch the soup. Mrs. Gorgon may get hungry later."

The sheriff then turned his attention to the widow. Looking at his disheveled captive he spoke sternly to her, "Mrs. Gorgon, do yourself a favor and cooperate with my wife and doctor. If you don't I will have the reporter assist me by holding down your legs while she inspects you from the hair on your toes to the hairs on your head. The complete search will happen. It is your choice if we do it the hard way or the easy way."

Turning to his wife again, "Darling, come and get me from the lobby if you need more cuffs to obtain the assassin's cooperation, or when you have Mrs. Gorgon dressed again whichever comes first. I'm taking her gun."

==0==

The sheriff was very careful in retracing his steps back to the diner looking for a vial. There was nothing on the stairs, nor did the desk clerk see her with one. The sheriff thanked the clerk for his cooperation in the sting and then searched the path from the hotel lobby back to Bes's kitchen door. He found nothing. Bes's eyes were wide with curiosity when the sheriff entered her kitchen. He told Bes that he stopped Anna before she could pull the trigger, and thanked her for her help in the ruse.

"I really wanted to think better of that woman, Sheriff, but to poison my soup is unforgivable."

"We don't know if she poisoned the soup. She had a gun, and you only have to kill a man once."

"Not that man, Sheriff. Once ain't near enough. You know that."

The sheriff smiled, and told Bes he had to get moving before the trail turned cold.

==0==

True to his word, the reporter was still sitting in the chair at the diner. Bes had made the wait worthwhile with three desserts. Regardless, the man remained very nervous.

The sheriff sat down at his table and laid the derringer between them. "Do you know where I got this gun? Be very careful how you answer."

"Honest, Sheriff, I had no idea Anna was packing."

"Why do you assume I got this from her? You did give it to her! Are you now going to deny it?"

"I'm telling you the truth. I never even suspected it, much less give it to her."

"Well, isn't that interesting... a reporter that both tells the truth and is completely free from suspicions. Son, I don't believe any of your assertions. By the way, she is currently across the street telling all sorts of stories. Why should I think she is lying and you are telling me the truth? If you immediately come clean I won't arrest you and throw you into jail."

"I don't know how to say this anymore sincerely, Sheriff. I had no idea where she got it. I never even suspected she would want to kill Bibb."

"I'm glad to see you are 'suspecting' again. Now let's work on your problem of 'honestly telling the truth.' How did you know that she wanted to kill Bibb? Did she say that to you? Is that why you gave her the gun so you could have some news? Come clean, boy! Come clean now!"

"Honest, Sheriff, I'm telling the truth. She told me nothing. Honest!" the reporter pled.

"So you choose not to talk. That is your prerogative. I suppose you didn't talk on your happenstance carriage ride here to the diner either. That is quite unique; both a deaf and blind reporter. Son, I have had enough of your dribble. Let's go, we are going down to the jail. You can hear her for yourself. Do you want me to call your editor? He could have an exclusive on you two conspirators."

"Sheriff, I don't know where she got the gun. It wasn't from me. I don't know how many ways I can tell you I had nothing to do with it."

"The problem with ineffectual denials is that they get so boring so soon. Boy, once more, are you telling me the truth? Weigh your answer carefully."

"Yes, I swear it."

"That was weak, really weak. How am I supposed to believe you with a simple 'I swear it'? Boy, I have other matters that I must attend to immediately. Fetch your editor, and both of you meet me at the jail in one hour. If you are not there, I will assume you have chosen to take flight. Son, I am taking your hat for scent for the hounds. Don't make me call them out. If you flee, despair that you have just eaten your last dessert." The sheriff reached over and took the man's notepad and then his hat. When he was naturally outraged, the sheriff pointed him to the door and demanded, "Now!"

==0==

The sheriff returned to the hotel. At the desk there was a note waiting for him that stated an exquisitely attired Mrs. Gorgon was waiting for him to call upon her in room number two along with his wife and the doctor. The sheriff was glad that Anna had chosen the easier alternative.

The beautiful and well-dressed Mrs. Gorgon was indeed upstairs, but she was in a rather foul mood. For good reason the sheriff's wife and doctor chose to leave her gag in place. Although she had agreed to the inspection in body, in spirit she displayed a much different temperament – amply expressed even with the muffler in place. She was laid on her back still with her hands over her head handcuffed to the radiator pipe. She was given a pillow for her head, but that was the only comfort.

"Mrs. Gorgon, when you are ready to explain what you are doing here, I am ready to listen. Are you ready to discuss this rationally?"

Her eyes told the sheriff her answer, beaming lightning bolts of hate in his direction.

"Darling," said the sheriff's wife, "I have some good news for her. I found no vial on her body, purse, clothes, or elsewhere in the room."

"I have some good news for her too," interrupted the doctor in turn. "Although her husband was stricken badly with social diseases, my opinion is that Mrs. Gorgon is completely healthy in that respect. I'm happy for her. It pains me every time I see a spouse of a wayward man suffer." The doctor turned and looked at Anna laying there on the floor. "No extra charge for that professional opinion, ma'am."

"Anna," the sheriff continued, "I am going to cuff your left leg to the bed post and then un-cuff your hands. That is so you can sit down on the bed. I have some questions to ask you. If you give me ladylike answers, I will treat you as if you are one. If you act like a criminal, we will reattach you to the radiator. You can show me your consent by nodding your head yes or no."

Anna consented, and the sheriff kept his promise. That did not remove the hate communicated through her eyes. He then proceeded to take off her gag. Fortunately, Anna did remain calm and ladylike, although the sheriff did stay clear of her un-cuffed leg in case she changed her mind.

"Anna, are you ready to talk to me?"

"I would like to have Mr. Franklin present with me."

"Mr. Franklin is not a criminal lawyer, nor have you been charged with a crime. You can call him tomorrow if you like. Anna, if you give me truthful explanations to my questions, this matter can be cleared up. It is my hope not to arrest you. My desire is to help you."

"Liar!" spit Anna towards him.

"Anna, that was not helpful. Did the reporter give you the derringer?"

"No, that is my gun that I keep with me for my personal protection."

"Did the newspaper man talk you into killing Bibb?"

"You are a snake, Sheriff! Your question is evil in intent and assumption. I never intended to kill Bibb, and that newspaper reporter didn't convince me into or out of anything. I have my own mind, Sheriff. My meeting with the reporter was to make a deal with him. I would give him my story if he told it my way."

"I heard the terms you gave him. They were not terms; they were demands. Why?"

"I do not need any bad publicity, Sheriff, at least until I rescue my fortune from legal purgatory. Don't blame me for my attitude towards the reporter. This was the same man that slandered me for seven months while I was hiding."

"So you wanted to extract revenge on him too? Yes?"

"I wanted fairness from him, Sheriff. Remember, you told me to be kind. I was, but firm."

"So, why did you pull the gun out when you entered this room?"

"Sheriff," she shouted, "the man killed my husband and thirty others. I would be stupid not to! He would want me dead too if he had the chance. I did not act irrationally nor did I have murderous intent. I wanted to see the man and negotiate a deal with him."

"So you asked Bes if you could deliver his soup to him? Was that so you could approach him while sleeping and all alone? Why should I believe your stated intent?"

"It is a maternal instinct to feed the injured and sick, Sheriff."

The doctor interrupted. "Pardon my candor, Mrs. Gorgon, but you have the identical maternal instinct I saw in General Sherman when we marched across Georgia."

"That is insulting, Doctor. Why do you say such hurtful things?"

"You're right, Mrs. Gorgon. Upon your insistence, I will apologize to the general for the unfair comparison the next time I see him. Mrs. Gorgon, you are not helping your credibility referring to character traits that you do not possess. Why did you want to deliver Bibb his supper?"

"I told you the truth. I wanted to negotiate a deal with him."

"What possible deal could you make with your husband's killer?" demanded the doctor in reply.

"I want him to take me home. I want him to take me to Fort Rice so I can be with my in-laws. I have no family, Doctor. I have no friends. I have no reason to stay in Deadwood any longer. I want to go home to a room full of lived-in chairs, home to a new place, a place I have never been to. I want to live with a family that I have never met and never met me, but family nevertheless. I want to live in peace; a life without the baggage of my past. I want to leave my current reputation and start over. I want to go home and be loved by a real mother, even if the only mother I will ever hold will be my husband's. This man can take me there and introduce me into their society. I swear it to you, and to you too Sheriff!" Anna broke into sobs. "That is what I want. You must believe me."

There was no mercy from the sheriff. "Wipe your face, Anna. Your tears count for nothing today. So you would leave your money and your mansion for something you have never had or seen? That is a wild wish, Anna."

"It's the truth, Sheriff. I have soiled everything I have touched here. I want to leave this place, and this man can take me and my wealth out of here."

"Why would he want to strike a deal with you?"

"I can furnish his room, his board, his doctor fees, his nurse, and whatever he needs to bring us home. Alone he is but an outlaw, wounded and ripe for a challenge. With me along he will be seen as an escort and assumed to be an honest man."

The doctor replied, "I would like to believe you, but what you brought into this room was a gun, possibly a poisoned meal, and certainly a motive ripe to commit murder. Show me the money, and tell me how you planned to accomplish this."

"You don't believe me, do you? Even if I showed you the money you still will not believe me! Well you are wrong, all of you. I have discussed this with Mr. Franklin, whom I am sure you will interview later. You are wrong, I tell you. Doctor, I am prepared to pay your fees even from before this man was shot. I am aware that Bibb asked for you to make a house call the first night he arrived in town. I also know that you have generously emptied your medicine chest to care for this man. You have also arranged for the Dowry twins and their older sister to watch him day and night. I know you are picking up the tab for meals and all of this, to include his room, which I honestly thought was this one. I have calculated that bill to be around $120 and I would need another $80 for his care until he was ready to take me home."

"That was the amount of the draft you asked for today, wasn't it, Anna?" inquired the sheriff.

"Yes, but you still won't believe me. You would rather relish the thought of putting me in jail for trying to pass a bad draft, wouldn't you? You don't believe anything I'm saying. And then the humiliation of what those two did to me! You are cruel, evil people."

"Anna, since you accuse me of it, I will meet your expectation of me. Here is my offer to prove you either honest or a conniving liar. I will believe every word you said if you do one thing."

"What is that?" she responded sarcastically in unbelief.

"Eat the soup. Eat all of it. If you eat the soup I will accept by faith all your other statements and promise to make good on your offer of charity. I don't care if it is from a heart of compassion or manipulation. Make good and I will accept it as goodwill from a sincere heart. I will go farther. Eat the soup and I will help you and Bibb get out of town free of the risk of arrest."

"All I have to do is finish Bes's soup? That is the sweetest deal ever I have ever been offered. You're tricking me. You must be tricking me. Bring me the soup."

"All of it, Anna."

You have no idea what you are missing out on, Sheriff."

"All of it, Anna."

==0==

The sheriff's wife first thought was that her husband was acting recklessly. There was no reason for such a gracious offer to be given to a woman like her, but the more she thought about it the wiser he became. If by chance Bibb would take that female fiend out of this town forever, the quicker peace could come to the valley. The wildcard was Bibb. He may not want anything to do with her. He also might agree, get a day's journey out of town and then grow weary of her. The deadly combination of an ability to kill without remorse and easy riches might become an irresistible opportunity for him to permanently end her continual complaining.

The doctor silently thanked God for answering his prayers. He had always been private about his faith. If he had been otherwise, it would have caused problems with those that expected too much of his skills. If she proved faithful to her promise he would have a completely restocked chest with current prescription drugs, not to mention being reimbursed for expenses he had incurred to date that he previously considered unrecoverable. The proof was still in the tasting of the pudding. She may have made all those statements as manipulations to get her out of this current predicament. Time would tell.

Anna had no hesitation to eat the soup. She still could not believe the sheriff's offer. Once completed, the sheriff asked her for two signs of good faith. First, she would immediately go downstairs and make arrangements for payment for all of Bibb's lodging with the hotel manager. The second was to commit to promptly arrive at his office at eight in the morning to discuss approaching Bibb with her offer. Anna agreed to both, but was still ruffled from what she had experienced just an hour earlier.

The doctor added one more condition. He said he would not stand for his patient to be moved from this hotel to one of Anna's properties. "If you are sincere, you will keep the man here. Your hotels are not as quiet as this one, and this one rents out rooms by the day rather than by the hour. Anna, don't you dare try to turn a profit on your promise! The deal is on the sheriff's terms, not yours! I insist!"

Anna was still flabbergasted. What caused this strange turn of events? In the time it took to eat some soup she went from presumed guilty of premeditated murder to completely free to fulfill her deepest longing. She still could not grasp the reasoning behind the sheriff's gracious offer. It had to be an evil trick, or a very good dream.

Upon her last spoonful of soup, the sheriff un-cuffed her ankle from the bed. She was free to go. She looked around the room. Those in the room were not smiling; all were in a very dour mood. Anna went immediately downstairs and made the appropriate arrangements with the management, promising to return in the morrow with specifics. She then walked home as if she was still dreaming, pinching herself along the way. The missing feeling of security that came with carrying her gun reminded her of the gravity of the incident.

$$==0==$$

The editor was just as distressed over his reporter's predicament as his own. He always had to walk the tightrope between being supportive of the town officials yet remain critical enough to sell newspapers. This event could be catastrophic. They were both waiting for the sheriff at the jail when he arrived.

"Good evening, Sheriff. I trust you have had a pleasant day."

"Obviously your reporter has not filled you in on what he did."

"Actually he has sir. Where can we assist you, Sheriff?" These words were simultaneously bitter to the editor as they were sweet to the sheriff.

"Sir, your employee worries me. There are times your man gets too close to a story. I often have cause to wonder if your man becomes a participant in making news rather than just a spectator. There was such an incident tonight. I have evidence to conclude that your employee was involved... (The sheriff took a breath. He so wanted to jail the reporter if only on the grounds that he was a daily thorn in his side) ...involved peripherally, not materially. I was prepared to arrest him tonight, but his story held true. I apologize for the fright I gave him. I do suggest you tell him to be more careful with the company he keeps in the future."

"What was the incident?"

"It concerned Bibb, and if it concerned Bibb, it concerned death. The gun was out, but the trigger was never pulled. When the story fully develops I will make sure your man gets the details. For now it must wait. This drama is not over; it can still go bad. Please, no reports on this yet. Are you satisfied?"

"Sheriff, I'll hold you to your promise, but you have my word. Peace. I assume he is free to go?"

"No, he is not," replied the sheriff gruffly.

"No?"

"No, but you may. This boy is about to learn my opinions on sensible limits to freedoms given to the press. Then he may go."

The editor responded, "Son, when you are done here, you immediately come back to the office. I'll be waiting there."

"But it's late, Boss. Maybe tomorrow?"

"I didn't stutter. Back to the office, boy. It's late, but I will be waiting."

Wednesday, September 28, 1887

I thought I was still dreaming until I visited the sheriff's office this morning. He was concerned I was going to renege on my offer. I wasn't exactly sure what yesterday's offer was so I wrote down this morning my desires prior to the visit. Later I spoke with Mr. Franklin and he set up an account at the bank for Bibb's expenses. And yes, this afternoon I visited Bibb's creditors and gave them instructions. The doctor and I ordered a new stocked medicine chest for his practice as well as replenishing his current one. That unpleasant man is my greatest critic and continual doubter of my sincerity. I purposely doubled down on his demands just to make him show some gratefulness. It worked; I am now back in control of this relationship.

I visited my husband's assassin for the first time this evening. The sheriff frisked me for my gun, an insult I fully earned. The doctor gave me no quarter either – no perfumes or dirty nails. I was told what I would see but I still was not fully prepared. The man isn't a man. Maybe the rumors are true, a ghost. There is no way he could have outgunned my husband. Yet, my husband is dead and this Bibb Being was breathing. Extreme cramping. Strange.

==0==

"I AM PERFECTLY fine, Doctor! There is no reason for you to invade my home and interrupt my breakfast!"

Prior to Anna's descent from her bedroom into the dining room the doctor had quizzed the maid and the butler harshly about when Anna arrived home and her activities overnight. Their stories were consistent. The visitor had already checked with the other doctor in town inquiring if Anna had visited him. Between his and his colleague's medical bag were the only two stomach pumps in town, something they used regularly to treat drug overdoses common to the painted ladies of the brothels.

"Anna, if you are fine then you will not deny me a listen to your heart and check your other vitals. You know why I am here, so let us not argue the point."

"You still don't believe me," retorted Anna.

"Not a drop of it, but I will if you let me confirm your claimed state of fineness. Don't worry, Anna. I will not charge you for this house call or another professional opinion."

"You, you…!" Anna calmed herself. Before she accused him of arrogance and mischief, she decided it would only hurt her own prospects if she refused. The butler had seen her anger before and he was worried she might pick something up off the table to throw at him, or worse, a knife to go after the man. Anna finished her statement in a calmer voice. "You, sir, may join me in the parlor along with my maid to satisfy your curiosity."

The doctor completed the cursory examination in just a few minutes. Anna was compliant but hardly amused; feeling like she was being handled like a ripe tomato at a farmers' market. She volunteered no information about her headache. Indeed, if Anna was suffering anything, she wasn't going to tell this man. She did complain that he was enjoying this touchy-time too much.

"That is because you are a Gorgon. No extra charge for that professional observation."

"What were you expecting to observe, Doctor?" came her snippy reply.

"The words of your maid were more important to me than anything you might say. She confirmed you came directly home last night. This morning your eyes are not dilated, and your tummy makes the happy sounds it is supposed to make after enjoying some of Bes's cooking. Anna, your problem is not in your ears, but what isn't being used between them."

"I will overlook your insult, Doctor, since you're not getting paid a fee for this visit. So do you believe me now?"

"No. I don't, Anna. Your body signs I can believe, but I remain unconvinced by your words. Keeping your promise will go a long way to convince me. That is yet to be seen."

Anna was still snippy with him. "And you keeping your hands off of me will go a long way in preventing you from being slapped silly. And yes, I will keep my promise, sir. Mr. Franklin will assure you that my intentions preceded last night's incident and this morning's insults. Maybe you will believe him. And you can believe this too: Never touch me again, Doctor. Good day."

"Be careful what you ask for or demand, dear lady. People hate both doctors and lawyers until they need one. The only thing I got out of your threat was that I no longer need to bother with the courtesy of asking your permission if I may touch you. And about Mr. Franklin, maybe I will believe him, even if he is a lawyer. Professional courtesy, you know. Since he can be trusted, I will also send him my fees and reimbursement request for Bibb's care. And oh, by the way Anna, nice tattoo."

"Get out of here!" demanded Anna.

"Good day to you too, Widow Gorgon, and you might consider taking a bath. Use some lye soap and a stout brush on those feet of yours. No extra charge."

It was all Anna could do to restrain herself from slapping the snot out of that man. Between her ears she reasoned that if she did strike him it would only prove him right. In a huff she instructed the butler to make sure he left the property. Upon their departure, she went back upstairs to sulk.

==0==

The butler delivered Anna Gorgon to the sheriff's office promptly at eight o'clock. The sheriff and his wife were prepared and waiting for her arrival. As planned, his wife started the conversation. "I am glad to see you in fine health this morning, Mrs. Gorgon."

"And why was I asked to come down here, Sheriff?" Anna purposely avoided greeting his wife.

"I want to reestablish what you agreed to yesterday. You surprised me. I fully expected you to bring Mr. Franklin with you this morning."

"I will inform him of his tasks, Sheriff. By the way, I have already seen the doctor this morning. He arrived an hour before breakfast."

"I know," the sheriff replied. "Mrs. Gorgon, there are two subjects we must discuss. The first involves reminding you of your commitments. The second is informing you of your risks."

"I am well aware of my commitments, Sheriff, and thank you for bringing up the issue. I have jotted down a list of them. Sheriff, you are well aware that I am thorough in business matters." She gave the list to his wife, her first acknowledgment of her presence. His wife studied the list and affirmed the list was complete.

"Mrs. Gorgon," the sheriff continued, "You are aware that Mr. Toivo is injured, yes?"

"I have been told that he has a face laceration and some problem with his chest."

"That's the greatest understatement of his condition I have heard yet, Mrs. Gorgon. I have asked the doctor if Bibb was well enough to visit with you. His answer was not medical. He said 'Show me the money.' He often says things like 'Words are cheap' but today he added that yours are especially worthless. Anna, I think you understand his desire to see more than lies and deceit from you."

"I am aware of his unprofessional opinions. What are his professional ones?"

"Bibb is getting stronger by the hour, and the doctor said at seven o'clock tonight you shall have your interview. Do not expect more than five minutes with him, and come clean, unarmed, and completely unscented."

"Sheriff, you divert. What are my risks?"

"Anna, I do not divert. You must agree to those conditions."

"Although I am not accustomed to agreeing with any man who humiliates me, I will agree to his terms for my sake, not the doctor's. What do I need to know about this outlaw?"

"My first suggestion is you not irritate the man. Even if Bibb currently lacks the reflexes and motor control of a murderer, he certainly has the mind of one. Your reporter friend told me you read all the Deadwood stories about him. That isn't even ten percent of the legends attached to that man. He goes by several names. He was born in Fort Rice with the given name of Terry Toivo."

"You said his name was Tommy."

"Tommy was hung for Terry's crimes. When the judge, now our governor, discovered a gross injustice he legally changed Terry's name to Tommy for a number of good reasons and a few ghostly ones. There is also a rumor that the judge ordered his brother's widow, like it or not, to become Terry's wife. From what I read, there is nothing to like about it. Her name is Anna, and she shares a similar reputation as Tommy in meanness and ability to handle a gun. I don't believe any marriage can be that bad, but I was told that one paper editorialized that his current punishment was worse than the hanging he was spared from."

"It is my opinion that men get what they deserve out of marriage. My friend Xue said that Bibb mentioned the name Anna. Do you think he was calling out to her?"

"I seriously doubt that, and nobody can know the genesis of what comes out of a drugged mind. Nevertheless, she is the least of your worries. Your worry is twofold: him killing you, and somebody killing him. Earlier this week I heard from the Miles City sheriff. He notified me that two more of Westum's ranch hands were found dead from bullet holes two inches above their noses."

"And…"

"Bibb had reason to kill them, and the means, and the ability, and the time. Bibb has a well-documented reputation of quickly hitting what he aims at. You have seen the recent evidence."

"And…"

"That makes seven of Westum's men that Bibb is accused of murdering in Miles City. The other five were murdered with an ax. The day before Bibb left town he had a showdown with Westum himself. It went badly for the man. Bibb threatened to kill him, take his wife, abuse her, and then trade her to the Indians for some buffalo burger. Bibb left the man alive, but rightly scared for his life. Take serious note of his low opinion of women, Anna."

Anna acknowledged and told him to continue.

"Anna, is this the type of man you want to hitch your fate to? You will be alone with him with all your wealth. You must admit you are incapable of defending yourself outside the safe confinements of a beauty parlor. You can call this off if you want."

"Sheriff, I want to leave Deadwood and go home; to the home of my kin. I am determined."

"And what if Bibb gets ambushed on the way home? Are you prepared to accept the same fate as promised to Westum's wife? That is more than a passing thought. Westum has many ranch hands that want Bibb dead if only so they can sleep at night. They are not seeking revenge; they honestly fear for their lives. There is bad blood between Westum's hired hands and Bibb."

"You exaggerate, Sheriff. Nobody would want that man dead."

"Your answer only confirms to me that you are determined to go east. There is still hope you will make it, if only on a wing of a prayer."

"Providence, Sheriff? You are now getting silly after all that seriousness."

"Providence, and a real good friend, Anna. Tommy works special assignments indirectly for the governor. His commissions come out of the army garrison in Bismarck. Nobody dares touch him for several reasons."

"What are those reasons, Sheriff?"

"First, the missions he completes for the governor are very important to the establishment of law and order in the west. He is a friend of the rule of law, and an enemy to the open range rancher and others who oppose statehood. Second, all those who have challenged him never lived past their next wink. Bibb not only has the most outstanding warrants for arrest in this territory, but he also is identified as the prime suspect for the most unsolved murders. He is not shy about his record either. Two days ago he intentionally identified your husband as the twenty-fourth notch to be carved onto his hatchet handle. Mrs. Gorgon, the man has ice water for blood."

"I am unmoved. Are there other reasons?"

"You told me you didn't want to hear it, Mrs. Gorgon."

"Are you going to spout off more myths of providence?"

"Mrs. Gorgon, regardless if you believe it or not, you have to consider the man's history. Bibb doesn't die, and his reputation as the man too mean to hang isn't because it hasn't been attempted. Although accused of being a ghost in this country and Canada, he is not. His fate is worse. He has the mark of Cain on him. Mrs. Gorgon, just because you don't believe in God doesn't mean there isn't one. Woman, face the facts. The man has beat death too many times to be unprotected by either dark places below or heaven above. I don't care which. I just want him out of town, and if the Ghost of Deadwood Gulch goes with him, that's a bonus for me."

"I am not amused by your sarcasm, Sheriff."

"I didn't give you that name. You earned the ghoulish title all by yourself, with a special thank you to some creative reporting. Personally, I think 'The Ghost of Deadwood Gulch' is a pretty fair assessment of what and who you are. You were creepy even before you reappeared."

"Yet I am neither humored by your insults nor deterred in my purposes. Thank you for his history, and I will see you in the Red Buffalo lobby at seven o'clock this evening. I am off to see Mr. Franklin, and then all of Bibb's creditors. I am sure you will be hearing from Mr. Franklin also. Until then, farewell. Don't ever call me that name again." She left after her evil stare transmitted an implied price tag associated with trespassing her will.

==0==

Anna arrived on time at the hotel lobby. Earlier that evening she ate supper at Bes's diner with her butler. The only passing words, referencing her new agreement with Bes, were questions asking if Bibb ate well today. There was nothing mentioned of the prior night's incident. Anna had already figured out who had played roles in last night's sting, and wondered if there were more involved.

The unusual event of Anna condescending to dine with her butler did not escape the reporter's attention. She was news, and he went where the news was being made. He withdrew after she gently rebuffed him when he came over to ask questions. He was still smarting from a pointed one-way conversation with his editor the previous night. Any complaint from anybody would get him fired.

In the lobby of the hotel the doctor, now satisfied with Anna's commitment to Bibb's recovery, greeted her more warmly than expected. He hugged her upon arrival and then asked to see her hands. There was nothing meaningful about the socially acceptable embrace. Anna was sure the hug was used as a graceful way to determine if she was scented and in a creepy way, to purposely touch her without her permission. Shortly thereafter the sheriff arrived.

After final instructions from the doctor, they all entered the room. The sheriff noticed that the bandages that once wrapped Bibb's face were now removed. The scabbing process was well on the way and there was no more need for warm towels. Likewise, there was no longer a need to guess how hideous the man looked. Bibb's color had returned and the doctor was pleased that when he tested Bibb's eyes both were tracking movements in the room. Bibb was propped up by pillows, and there was paper and a quill on his nightstand to respond to questions. He looked very much improved, but not for the uninitiated. Anna winced at the initial sight, even after being warned.

The sheriff walked towards the bedridden man and addressed him, "Bibb, I want to introduce somebody to you. She wants you to take her to Fort Rice."

Bibb looked up, blinking, and surveyed the room. He knew the doctor, nurse, and sheriff, but now there was a new person in the room, a woman dressed in black with an expensive veil over her face. Bibb, not wanting to talk, took to writing a note: *"On my horse? And now? And wearing that?"* which drew a chuckle from the men, the nurse, and eventually Mrs. Gorgon.

"My name is Anna Marie Gorgon. You may call me Anna. You killed my husband last week. As reported in the newspapers, one of the last words my husband said was that you were to take all his assets to his mother. I am one of those assets, and I am here to assist you in fulfilling your responsibilities."

Bibb returned to his writing pad, jotting down, *"Your name is Anna?"*

"Yes, it is Anna! Anna Marie Gorgon. I already told you that!" She turned to the doctor and asked if his patient was deaf, daft, or both.

The doctor held his tongue but so wanted to say that "daft" described her late husband's last, rather, very last decision. Bibb may be currently slowed by pain medicine, but regardless, the man was credentialed as the governor's envoy. Certainly governors and savvy politicians do not get where they are by hiring bumbling dummies. As the doctor was about to say something less caustic, the nurse responded first. "No ma'am, his hearing is just fine in the ear facing you. With due respect to your person ma'am, the problem isn't 'Marie' or 'Gorgon.' The problem part is the name 'Anna.' For some reason many of the women in his life come with that label, more than he can keep track of. Don't worry, they're all mostly alive, Miss Gorgon. Talk to him now, he's awake."

"Now that you made me into a widow, I no longer have a reason to stay in this town. I am ready for you to take me to my in-laws in Fort Rice. East of the Missouri we can get you some better medical attention. As for me, I plan to start my life over near my husband's family. You can take me and my luggage by wagon to Miles City. From there, we can take the train to Bismarck. I say we should plan to leave Deadwood about a week from now, or as soon as you are ready to travel."

Bibb again wrote, *"I can't afford a train ticket."*

The doctor whispered something in Bibb's good ear, and then a longer phrase. Anna was not happy with the doctor as a mediator, wanting to talk with the man directly. Bibb eventually lifted up his right hand, which to everybody else in the room indicated something.

"Anna," said the doctor, "Bibb has agreed to take you to Fort Rice. You can sign the documents that Mr. Franklin has prepared for you. Let him worry about the legal work and divesting. You can start packing. Let us go; the man requires sleep to regain his strength. He will certainly need it."

The doctor and sheriff escorted Anna out of the room. "I didn't hear him say yes, Doctor. I only heard you say that he agreed. Did he agree? I don't want to sell all I own without knowing for sure."

The sheriff answered, "Anna, he agreed. This man keeps his word. He raised his right hand; I saw it myself. You can start planning for your departure."

"You want me gone too, Sheriff, don't you? I haven't forgotten those insults you threw at me this morning."

"Anna," spoke the doctor, "you may visit him again tomorrow to confirm he didn't change his mind. I only warn you, don't insult the man with asking him the same question over and over. Do you mind if I come over for breakfast tomorrow? Your cook makes the best flapjacks."

"Doctor, you are free to make a house call at any address other than mine tomorrow."

"And Anna," continued the doctor purposely ignoring her insult, "You need to be thinking of more than just yourself. You not only own property, but you have many employees working at those businesses. Think of ways to be kind to them upon your departure."

"Good night, Doctor, Sheriff. I must go home immediately."

==0==

"This really hurts," Anna said to herself as she was trying to keep her face from expressing her pain in front of her butler. It was all she could do from doubling over from what she described to herself as death cramps. The stabbing misery during the ride home from the hotel was exacerbated with each bump that caught a wheel of the carriage. The last time she had been so afflicted was the night she met the dashing Mr. Gorgon for the first time. Thinking back she remembered how she had imagined that debilitating ailment as some sort of sign that Mr. Gorgon was to be hers until death do they part. Maybe it was, and by death he did depart. These cramps were timely; the severity untimely. She had so much to do.

Anna's maid greeted her at the kitchen door while the butler attended to the horses and parked the carriage. A couple of words were exchanged as she entered which prompted the maid to drop what she was doing to assist her up the stairs. Later as Anna prepared for sleep she looked in her mirror and contemplated her pains. "Sign? Ha! There is no such orchestrator in this universe, and if there is, he has a lot of evil to explain! All this needless suffering must be why those church mice call him a He. No woman would tolerate this."

Thursday, September 29, 1887

The dream is real. I will be leaving Deadwood. I cannot believe it. There is so much to do, but I cannot leave my bedroom. I don't even know this outlaw... I seriously doubt my sanity. What spell came over me to trust him with my safety?

Mr. Franklin came over at my request. He was pleased with the agreement. Tomorrow he will finish the appropriate legal arrangements reinstating my ownership of the estate. He asked me if I was happy with my accounting firm, knowing unpleasant words were previously exchanged. Instead of specifics, I only responded by giving Mr. Franklin five dollars and instructed him to tell the accountant to take his wife out to a dinner and a show.

I want to go home but I do not know why. This once playful daydream of a genuine home is now blooming into a frightful reality. What if… What if… What if...

==0==

"I NEED YOUR help, Doctor," said the reporter.

"You don't look sick. What do you really want from me?"

"I hope you will take this list of questions upstairs for Bibb to answer. I know he doesn't talk but I heard from Bes that he writes well. Help me out, please."

"Help yourself. Come up with me. I'm about to go there and quiz the nurse on how the patient fared the night. Let me see what you got there, and let me see your hands."

A couple minutes later Bes arrived with Bibb's breakfast which the doctor took with him upstairs. Much to the doctor's surprise, Bibb was sitting in the nurse's chair, and the nurse was sound asleep on Bibb's bed. When the doctor asked with his eyes what was going on, Bibb brought his finger up to his mouth and tried to say "shhh" to ask for quiet. Instead of "shhh" a wet whistle sound came out from his rearranged mouth. Despite the feeble attempt to give the woman a respite, the nurse woke anyway, and rather embarrassed.

"Doctor, Bibb said he was tired of sleeping, sir, and he saw me nodding off just after dawn. Forgive me, sir." She was off the bed before she got to her fifth word.

"Young man, I want no report in the paper that Bibb's nurse was sleeping in his bed. Do you understand? You boys can twist anything to sell a paper."

"Yes, sir, I mean no, I won't sir. This was an act of kindness, sir, and to imply otherwise would not be telling the story true. There is a man in this room that has personally warned me about committing that error, and totes an established reputation of reprisal on those who trespass. I trust he considered my work so far in the papers accurate. I had nothing to do with the editorializing though."

Bibb nodded to the man. There was no ire in Bibb's eyes to the relief of the reporter. By now the nurse had finished straightening out the sheets and was standing behind Bibb.

"Sir, we have had several breakthroughs last night. Bibb has taken several important walks down the hall and back. More important, he spoke several words to me last night. He asked me about his horse, although I misunderstood him as asking for a nurse. His lips are not working real well yet."

"Well then Bibb shall see his horse soon, maybe as soon as tomorrow." The doctor was pleased. "Bibb, you already know this man. He is asking if you would answer some of the questions he has written down while you are here recovering. Are you willing to write down some responses?"

Bibb motioned for the questions, his paper, and pen. After an initial review he wrote, *"If I find it to my advantage, Doctor. I will not answer questions that put me in jeopardy with the law."*

The doctor read it and gave the note to the reporter, who was grateful for the answer. Bibb's handwriting was superb. This was going to be too easy, thought the reporter to himself; yet it will be difficult to purposely misquote a man who writes out his answers so legibly.

"You may go now," said the doctor.

"Can you tell me what you think about the Widow Gorgon?" replied the reporter, speaking past the doctor.

"You may go now, son. The nurse and I need to tend to the wounds of a man that kills nosy people who ask poorly timed questions."

==0==

Anna could not move; she was suffering. So many heavy thoughts were going through her head. Nevertheless, when she heard that Mr. Franklin was in the house she picked out a housecoat to wear and then came downstairs. The maid saw her distress and came to help. Mr. Franklin joined Anna in the parlor once she was more comfortable.

The conversation was long and comprehensive covering all of her concerns. During the two hours they spoke Mr. Franklin reported his progress on his efforts. Although her agreement with Bibb altered his plans, there was no need for concern. Estate documents could be corrected at the record of sale now that the plan was to divest property upon receipt of worthy offers.

"Are you ill, Anna?" asked Mr. Franklin who obviously could see the answer to his question.

"Yes, and don't you dare tell that doctor. My ailment has nothing to do with poisons or perfumes, and I am not going to subject myself to the humiliation of another one of his house calls. My maid and butler are able to take care of me. That sheriff believes in providence. Maybe the next few days is no less than debilitating divine mischief at work so you and your accountant can do your tasks without me looking over your shoulder. I am so frustrated!" The room fell silent after the rant. It was the first time any voice was raised above a whisper that day.

"Frustrated over what?" replied Mr. Franklin quietly.

"I don't know. It is the changes, it is the trip, it is the divesture of what gives me social status, it is trusting this outlaw, it is… oh, it is… it is so much uncertainty… it is the hope of going home. I don't know, but I feel this change is good for me, but also I fear it will kill me. What am I supposed to pack? What do they wear in Bismarck? Do you think I have made a good decision?"

"Mrs. Gorgon, you certainly are not averse to taking risks. You have made many decisions in the past. Yes, some went bust, but more of them have paid out very handsomely. You have made other such decisions based on less information than you have about this man. My opinion is that there is more than a reasonable hope this will bring you financial gain while greatly adding to your personal happiness. You have no such hopes here. This town is approaching its zenith and now is the perfect time to sell. Since you are not in financial distress you have the luxury of waiting for your price."

"This outlaw is dangerous, isn't he?"

"And you're not, Mrs. Gorgon? Frankly Anna, you will be more trouble for him than he is for you. You need to lock your load of vanity in an empty trunk and not open it again until you are established in an eastern city. It would be even better to lock the trunk and bury it under your tombstone. Anna, I do not say this to be cruel, but sometimes you are your own worst enemy. Be not fooled by Bibb's silence. The man would just as soon deliver you to Bismarck as to swap you for supplies, or worse, well, Anna, you already read about the worse. The difference in outcomes may be as simple as whether or not you ingratiate yourself to him, or make him sorry he brought you along." He looked at her. She was in distress – body, soul, and spirit.

"You may go, Mr. Franklin. Thank you for handling all these details for me. I may want to rethink this."

"It is too late for that, Anna. You are all-in. Remember; the terms of the agreement are the sheriff's, not yours. He holds the aces, Anna. If you renege, he will press the attempted murder charge against you. Accept it, Anna. There may be more providence floating around this decision than just myself and the accountant finding time to get our work done. If you are burdened with worries, try thinking about what you can do for others before you leave. That will help clear your mind of worries… and your vanity."

==0==

The sheriff knew that a direct approach to finding justice for Xue would not work. He did the only thing he could do at the moment and that was to find somebody who had been working at the mine at the time of the man's death. One of the town drunks could be trusted with such work. He was a quiet drunk that was a volunteer enlistee in the payday platoon of undisciplined men found face down in an inebriated stupor somewhere the following morning. When he was sober he could ask around and fill the sheriff in on what he found out on his next trip into the pokey. He could hardly be suspected of being an informant in exchange for some bail and hangover relief.

What the drunk found out was that the enforcer at the mine when Xue's husband died had met his own demise earlier that year. He was a brutal man who was particularly mean to the Chinese working there. If the workers had plotted this revenge for his abuses nobody would ever know. The man met his death beneath fallen rock that had also killed another worker and injured a third, a common epitaph for those who worked and died underground. There was nothing that linked the man to the death of Xue's husband other than his now permanently retired heavy hand. The sheriff had hoped for something else to tell Xue, probably something she already knew.

The sheriff's wife commented to her husband that even without the help of lawmen, juries, and judges, justice is not mocked and time eventually evens out the score. "As the preacher would say, 'What you sow is what you will reap' isn't a negotiable contract. The offender might get a suspended sentence, but justice will eventually come calling."

"So, do you think Anna will get her just desserts traveling east with that outlaw?" he asked.

His wife answered, "She will certainly get her due if she stays here! The woman is ripe for another downfall and there are many in this town that would help nudge her over the cliff. She might change, but she won't be changing here. That is for sure. The death of her husband didn't do it. If not that, what worse life altering event could come her way to wise her up? I don't care if he is an outlaw, may God help that poor man. Bibb will be often tempted to oblige Mr. Gorgon's desire to have his widow join him at their fiery final destination."

"That was harsh, dear."

"So do you disagree?" replied his wife.

"I didn't say that. I only said that your words were harsh. I am a bit ashamed of myself for having similar thoughts. I'm not above treating a Gorgon unfairly. If I have to choose between fairness and justice, well, I might treat her fair after she arrives at the bottom of the rocky precipice." He took a deep breath to change is tenor. "I'm sorry, but those Gorgons bring out the worst in me."

"That too was harsh, dear. It is difficult to trust those with a habit of putting concealing sugar in their sentences. You're different, dear. You prefer salt, and one of the many reasons I love you so."

==0==

That evening Bibb took the list from the reporter and lined out the questions he saw no advantage in answering. Curiosity became so overwhelming to the on-duty Dowry girl that she begged Tommy to let her read his responses back to him out loud as a way to detect anything that could be mistaken by the editors at the paper. She could easily guess why some of the questions were lined out, but one question in particular raised her interest. When she saw that Bibb was getting tired she told him it was time to start the exasperating bedtime rituals. After that thirty minutes of essential walks and the changing of his clothes, Bibb was commanded to lay flat on his back in bed to await what he disliked the most about bedtime; her cleaning of his facial wounds.

"Tommy, you lie still. I will be as kind as possible. Both you and I know this will sting, but I can see that the doctor's medicine is working. Tommy, if it hurts too much raise your hand just like before. I will try my best to lessen your pain. Raise your hand if you are ready."

Tommy's response was both a wince and a raised hand. It was hard to refuse the young woman who was so faithful in following the doctor's orders. Even more disabling in raising a complaint was her double portion of the heavenly gift of compassion. Tommy was not ready for her next question.

"Tommy, you crossed out a question I want to know the answer too. I won't tell anybody your thoughts, but I desire to know, and as well my sisters." Tommy winced as one of the bandages that was too close to a scab was removed. "Tommy, the reporter's question asked if you had any regrets over what he cited as dying in Miles City. You lined it out. I won't ask why or what, but did you?"

Tommy responded with a moving his hand left and right as to signal no. She continued, "A lady who was at Bes's last Friday night visited this morning with the preacher while you were sleeping. My sister answered some of their general questions about your healing. They also had some questions about the healing of your wounded heart. Tommy, what's wrong with your heart?"

Tommy waved his hand left and right, but this time indicating the question was scratched out with her too. She responded with a second plea, and this one more emphatic than her first asking. Tommy replied, "Lll-ater. Miii 'ear(d)t is rr-righ(d)t, nnn-ot www-ong."

"Your heart is right, not wrong?" the Dowry girl asked. Tommy responded by raising his hand. That answer didn't make sense to her, but it was an attentive reply. She thanked Tommy for his answer and told him that she wasn't quite through applying the fixin's to his face. The last thing Tommy saw before closing his eyes for the night was an angelic smile of a very kindhearted nurse. If grace had a face, he had just seen it.

Tommy's answer frustrated the Dowry girl during the remainder of her shift, but his answer would have to suffice for now and she suffer the suspense. She hoped he would provide a better answer later. One thing she knew as true: Tommy trusted her and her sisters, and they trusted him.

Friday, September 30, 1887

None is this was my choice, I was tricked into this! That's my wish on how to rewrite history, but I admit to my diary that I was the one that brokered the deal with real tears. It was me that cried out that I wanted to go home. Why can't my soul accept an unwarranted gift? Do I not have sufficient cause to distrust and hate all men? A sheriff is commissioned to put criminals in jail, not to set them free. This is all backwards, and I hate being chained to my decision – Bibb is free and I am not. I am confused and scared. Is it because I cannot accept a gift, man or woman's, without suspicion? Am I that jaded with cynicism? Yet, I have been brought back from hiding, even from the dead according to the papers. That was not of my devising. Did just a selfish mere mortal of a man do that for me? If I say no, I must default to a worse conclusion: a controlling providence arranged it. This is all so unsettling; so wrong!

I am suffering less but still in bed; this month's is a bad one. I promise myself I will be more active tomorrow. I desperately need a diversion from lying around imagining all the things that may cause me pain and loss. I refuse to think this forced rest is a similar sign as the as last time – the silliness of that thought. Look at the trouble that misinterpretation caused.

==0==

AS PROMISED, BIBB'S nurse took him outside for the first time since he had been placed in that hotel a week prior. Around the corner and north a block was the livery where Bibb had sheltered his horse. To his joy, his faithful animal had horse-sense enough to recognize Bibb, even with the rearranged face. Bibb rewarded his steed with several treats. The stall was clean, even at this early hour, and the feed was ample. His horse had been well cared for. Although his mute companion did not need it, Bibb brushed it down and patted it once again in accordance to the ritual both he and the horse were accustomed. When finished, Bibb let out a deep-lunged sigh; the first in a week. He felt whole as if all was right again in the world. Bibb felt unworthy of such a champion. Only since Miles City had he come to recognize the true Benefactor who graced him with the spirited creature. Creatures require a Creator, and this horse as if by prescription was born to be his mount; such was the bond. He chuckled to himself when he thought that God cared so much for that animal that He went to the extra trouble to find Gorgon and had that scoundrel put a bullet hole through him. How else would that horse ever gotten such preferential treatment at the livery? Bibb only budgeted standard fare for his horse but now it was being treated as if it was the king of beasts!

Bibb was well pleased and went to visit the livery owner. He wrote down on a piece of paper a word of thanks for the good care of his horse. The owner commented, "That is a special horse. It is of superior stock and deserves the extra attention. That noble animal is not easily scared. There's an Indian that comes in here at random times that brushes it down. Nothing is said, but it is obvious the horse knows the Redman."

Bibb replied, even if it was in whistle words, "Anck oo." The nurse and Bibb left the livery and returned to the hotel. There was no doubt; Toak, his former trail partner and ax toting betrayer was on his trail again. Maybe his around-the-clock nursing care had kept him from receiving a murderous visitor in the night. Maybe not. Toak always had reasons for what he did, and it was no slip on his part to be noticed at the livery.

Bibb felt safe in Deadwood. If Toak's ax killed him in town he may also get blamed for Gorgon's death, and that followed by quick justice. The danger for them both would be out on the plains. One thing was for sure, Toak was patient. The question nagging Bibb was Toak's intentions. Toak's predicament was worse. Bibb wasn't supposed to survive Westum's lynch mob that Toak had arranged for him in Miles City, but did. Toak would also have to assume Bibb would have strong opinions about Toak's betrayal that led to his brutal beating. Bibb would also have equally strong opinions about a satisfactory final remedy.

==0==

That afternoon Anna was visited at the mansion by her accountant. He actually cared if she was feeling well and now especially curious after she failed to visit him. Besides having several business questions answered he wanted to thank her for her thoughtful gesture towards his wife and him.

Anna entered the parlor with uncurled hair and loose clothes that did not fit her to perfection. At first the accountant wasn't sure if it was her. He had never seen her without being adorned in the royal vestments of Deadwood high society. He called them royal because of the king's ransom that was forfeited to buy them. Obviously, unadorned, she was still not well.

"Have you spoken to Mr. Franklin about my immediate plans for the estate?" asked Anna.

"Yes, ma'am. That is one of the business reasons I came over. The other personal reason was to thank you."

Anna continued, "I need you to do me a favor. I want to know two things and you can tell me the next time we meet. First, I want your professional opinion estimating my net worth three months hence given my plans to liquefy the estate. Second, what will be my cash position one week from now? I may want to be generous to those who have worked faithfully for my husband and me since we arrived in Deadwood. Lastly, you are most welcome. You earned the bonus. Please wish your wife good health for me. Forgive me, but I'm not well and desire to return upstairs. Good day."

The accountant left without answers to his many questions, but happy nonetheless; he knew where to go next. Mr. Franklin's authoritative answers would lack the added drama that Anna could supply. That suited his accountant's mindset just fine.

==0==

The noon knock on the door brought Bes, a friend, and lunches for all of them. Bibb did not immediately recognize the other woman. Bibb's recollection returned when she had explained she had prayed for him a week prior when he walked out the door of Bes's Diner to face Gorgon.

After lunch Bibb wrote down on a piece of paper a request of her. *"Be kind and tell me your account of what happened starting that night. During my stay here everybody assumes I know what happened, but I didn't wake up until three days later. I'm sure I missed something. Begin when Gorgon walked into the diner. I'm also curious where this Anna Gorgon came from. She just popped into my life and I don't know what to think about that."*

"Bibb, it was a week ago today you came into town. My first meeting with you was during supper last Friday night. My husband and I were eating at Bes's diner across the street from this hotel. She must have been expecting you because not only did she have a table ready, but she had prepared a special soup for you that wasn't on the menu. Obviously others had heard you arrived in Deadwood because the newspaper reporter was also at Bes's that night. That man lives and dies by rumors, and he was not eating. He was only sipping a beer and taking up space. The reporter, noting you fit your description and a rumored list of injuries, came over to your table and introduced himself. You may recall that it wasn't long into that conversation that he and his notepad went scurrying back to his own table."

"You were done with your first bowl of soup and well into your second when Mr. Gorgon made his entrance. He was always well dressed, and that night he also wore his silver plated gun belt and pistols. Mr. Gorgon was one of the more successful gamblers and speculators in this town. If he cheats at cards, he is good at it. He certainly cheated on his wife and there was no love lost between the two of them once the unfaithfulness begun. Their fall from love was well publicized in the society gossip sheets and pulpits throughout this town. The man had eyes that could not be trusted. For years he greased with dirty money his agenda into reality in this town."

"Last spring Mrs. Gorgon suddenly disappeared. The rumor was that Mr. Gorgon drugged her and he left her exposed to the care of hungry coyotes. The man thrived on scandal, especially when another was weakened by it. His money had Mrs. Gorgon legally declared dead, and he mocked her fate with a solemn funeral all while feigning his loss. Nobody dared asked if her body was in the casket. He then proceeded to remove her name from everything, as if she had fallen off the planet."

"Last Friday night Gorgon wasted no time. He immediately recognized you, went directly to your table, and challenged your reason for living. You did not seem to take the bait. Not deterred, he sat down at the table and continued to throw insults towards you. He has shown hatred for many people, but this demonstration outranked all the others; quite an accomplishment. He called you a liar and challenged you loudly enough for all to hear. Bes came out of the kitchen and tried to defuse the confrontation, but Gorgon would have none of it." Both Bibb and the nurse looked towards Bes, and she confirmed with a nod the men's misbehavior.

"Later Gorgon took something you said as a threat and claimed loudly that you had called him out. You started to laugh at him for this ridiculous accusation. That enraged the man more, and I could see the veins pulsating in his neck from where we were sitting. You, pardon my candor, you seemed to enjoy having fun with the man, asking him mundane things like if he wanted a yeast roll. He responded by calling you a coward." Bibb nodded confirming her narrative.

"Your conversation turned personal towards him when you mentioned you had recently talked to his mother. You offered to deliver a message back to Fort Rice if he desired, saying that you planned to depart for there in the morning. That was the moment Gorgon burst. He threw his chair back and said you were not leaving Deadwood alive. You confronted the threat by accusing him of murders and bank robberies back in Fort Rice. He willingly confessed to them, as if above the law, and renewed his death threat towards you. You taunted him once more, warning him that a duel might not turn out as well as he was planning. That is when he boasted that if it didn't, it would be your job to deliver all his assets to Gorgon's mother in Fort Rice."

Bibb started to write. *"Really? That seems faintly familiar. If so, I did not take him serious. My nurse read to me the paper. The reporter certainly did, as well as his widow. Did I ever say I would? I do not remember."*

"I don't remember either. Bibb, that was when Gorgon left Bes's in a huff, with you at a table alone with his untouched steak. Bes came out of the kitchen and the two of you spoke. She was quite upset with you about discounting his threats. You seemed more interested in eating than dying. Likewise, both my husband and I were amazed by your unconcern about Gorgon's ultimatum, thinking you very naïve. Nobody is that fearless. You even invited the reporter over to your table to eat Gorgon's steak and to ask any questions he wanted of you. The unnatural silence in the diner prompted you to invite everybody to listen and ask questions if they wanted to, which we all did. Your peace was not natural, which added to our curiosity about you possessing an unwarranted pride in your own ability to defend yourself against the likes of Gorgon.

Pardon my candor, but it was like you were speaking your own eulogy – and not a sanitized one that a good uncle might embellish to say at your funeral."

Bibb stopped her, displaying a facial expression of dismissing an overstatement. He wrote again, *"Did you see where I was hiding my ax?"*

"No, Bibb, but who would be looking for an ax when you had pistols on your hips? Who in their right mind would bring a blade to a gunfight?" She thought about that and apologized, "I am not saying you are nuts, Bibb. It's just that a hatchet is not usually a weapon an outlaw takes to a shootout. Well… who could logically expect that? Certainly nobody at the diner did. And I am not calling you an outlaw either."

Bibb acknowledged her backtracking and whistled out the word, "Unck-kaaay."

"Bibb, you talked for almost an hour. You told us much about your and Gorgon's childhood in Fort Rice, and the details concerning the crimes we had just heard Gorgon confess to. You also spoke of your trial and the judge's response to your conviction that set you free but also punished you by saddling you with your brother's name and your brother's wife. You were asked questions how you got the name Bibb. You answered that and continued to tell us how you became hired as a courier. Another question the reporter asked (which you would not entertain) was how many men you have killed. As an aside, I'm quite sure that when that boy was an imp his mother fed him question marks for breakfast. The man never stopped asking or writing down what he heard."

It hurt Bibb to laugh, and that prompted the others to stop laughing too. Even if the joke was funny, Bibb's pain wasn't.

"To be honest, Bibb, I wasn't the only one wondering how a man as bad as you could be allowed to escape death so many times. Your resume has the devil's endorsement on every entry. At that low ebb you surprised me when you talked about meeting death again in Miles City. My ears perked up as if they were grabbed from underneath my bonnet. There you confided with us a confrontation with a tracker. It was a woman named Anna that finally cornered you, extracted your confession, and then drove a two edged saber into your soul. Without pity she watched you die."

Up to this point Miss Dowry, the nurse, was comfortable with the story. Bes, who witnessed the event, said nothing to contradict the retelling of it, nor did Bibb deny it. She had taken care of this man for a week and thought him to be just as alive as she was. She never considered the possibility that a man could be dead one day and alive the next, and have a reliable record of repeating the feat like some ghostly eternal phoenix. She broke the silence by asking the next question. "Excuse me, but what kind of demon have I been changing the bandages on for the last seven days? Nobody mentioned this to my sisters or me when they hired us on. Neither cats nor men get nine lives. What is going on here?" She had a chill come over her as she looked deep into Bibb's emotionless face.

"More than meets the eye, honey," responded the storyteller. She returned to speaking to Bibb, "It was at this moment I understood and shouted out 'Hallelujah!' I remember that you didn't deny my accusation that some religion found you, did you Bibb?"

Bibb waved his hand. This response was as bewildering to the young nurse as the phoenix.

"You see, Miss Dowry, Bibb, as I understand the man, has been chased by trackers all his life. The one tracker he did not suspect to corner him was the great hound. Bibb, you said it yourself that night. You confessed that you were tired of running and looking over your shoulder waiting for somebody to gun you down. It was in Miles City where you finally made peace with that hound of heaven, and from that point you no longer had a fate but a part. You surrendered your will to God in Miles City, didn't you Bibb?"

Bibb again wrote. "*I had no choice. Westum was going to kill me and I was too broken to defend myself. When I was offered God's protection I agreed to the deal as a preacher man explained it: life for life, will for will. The peace was indescribable and the release of my burdens unmeasurable, but I had no warning of the troubles that transaction would bring me. Now look at me! I'm five times more broken than I was in Miles City. Yes, I've lost many fears, but at a price. Worse than the wounds I've collected, worse than dealing with the dangers surrounding me, is a ruthless silent sleepless varmint. Miles City Anna didn't tell me about that companion critter that came with the deal.*" He handed the note, almost in disgust, to the hallelujah lady. She took the note seriously, and did not read it aloud, although asked by the others in the room.

"I know exactly what you are writing about, Bibb. It afflicts me greatly too. At another time I would like to discuss your comment, please, before you leave Deadwood."

Bibb was surprised by her answer, expecting a lecture from the storyteller. The answer revealed a mysterious bond she had with him. Her response countered his notion that he had some unexplainable inner distress unique to him that confused him so. He wrote another note, trusting she was not going to compromise his newfound trust in her. "*That varmint plagues me constantly! Not just every waking moment, but in my dreams too. I need it to stop before I go crazy.*"

She took that note too, read it to herself, folded it up with the other and put the writings into her purse. She looked over to the man. "Now I am certain of it, Bibb. We will save this for later."

None of this dialog was comforting to the nurse, and by now even Bes was curious what was going on. Miss Dowry asked her again if she was going to let them in on the messages from Bibb.

"Where was I? Oh, yes, I remember that you then threatened the reporter. He clearly understood that no mention of a woman named Anna of Miles City would find its way into print. I recall you said you would haunt him not only in this life but in the next one too. The man took you serious. For that fact, I bet nobody in that room has uttered her unmentionable name until now."

"There were so many questions that swirled around that diner. Of particular interest was a woman you called Humbird. I still don't know exactly who she is or supposed to be. Without warning after an hour of questions, you put your hands on your knees, stood, and declared it was time to face Gorgon. You warned the reporter to tell it right or face dire consequences."

The storyteller paused as if she needed to gain some composure, which added to the tenseness in the hotel room. "I will never forget the moment, Bibb. You stared right at me and paused as the diner went hush. I stood and became frozen in fright. You said to me that if I was the praying type, now was the time, and then you thanked me for it. My knees shook in fear as if my immediate appeal to heaven meant life or death, or worse, eternal death for two deadly antagonists."

"You floated across the room and went right to the door. It was surreal. You opened the door into the blackness and shut it behind you as if the darkness of a double death was swallowing you up." She paused, "And a breath later the gunshot was heard. I thought to myself. One shot made, only one dead. My husband sat me down. I thought to myself that one was still one too many."

The nurse was fully engaged in the story. She had previously only heard snippets of it. This was told as a firsthand account directly from the woman in front of her.

Bes spoke, noticing the nurse's condition. "Miss Dowry, I agree, it was surreal. There was no concern in this man's face. Even I started to wonder if this man was a ghost. Obviously not, ghosts don't eat my fixin's, but the moment certainly lent itself to the thought. When the gunshot went off, I ran into the kitchen to place clean rags in my pot of boiling water. Somebody *may* need to be cleaned up. Then I *hoped* somebody was going to need cleaning up. Then I *hoped both* were going to need cleaning up. Death bothers me and the thought of it turns my stomach. I was born to bring sustenance to people and murder is so against that. Women have more sense than challenging each other to duels. I do not know why men feel so compelled to."

The lady friend continued. "After the gunshot, several men to include my husband ran out into the street. They found you there, Bibb, on your back twitching in the dirt. You were bleeding badly. Four men, crouched in the darkness, carried you back into the diner. Several others in the diner, both men and women I suppose, sprung up from the seats and cleared off and put together some tables so the four could lay you down. That's when Bes arrived with hot towels, and some of the women started working on your wound. I didn't see the damage, but I thought death had come."

She paused as if doubting her own sanity. "I don't know what prompted me, but I steeled myself and walked out the door, through the blood in the street, and into the hotel to fetch the doctor. He had heard the gunshot, already had grabbed his medicine kit, and was coming down the stairs. He asked what happened and I told him Bibb had been shot but I did not know where. I told him you were laid out in the diner and the killer may still be roaming the street."

Bes then continued. "Bibb, your face was all mangled. When the doctor arrived he cut free some of your jaw, teeth, and pieces of shredded cheek to investigate what vitals had been hit. He had two of the ladies press down hard with the hot towels where your face was bleeding. Another lady was holding some sort of rubber something the doctor had forced down your throat to make sure the other two didn't suffocate you in their zeal to stop the bleeding. I must say I thought you were moments from termination, thinking you had passed at least three times. There is little doubt what our storyteller was occupying herself with at that critical time. She compelled her husband to get on his knees too. We went through three sets of boiled rags before the bleeding was stopped. Bibb, you were white as a ghost, I mean, as a sheet. We need no more of that speculation. Bibb, the doctor insisted your one eye remain open to discern if life remained in you, and that became my job. Your other eye the doctor had to close. It was flooded bright red with burst vessels within it, and so close to where the bullet exited your face."

"The sheriff arrived about that time. He asked the reporter what had happened. The man replied, 'It is apparent that Gorgon shot Bibb as he walked out the door about twenty minutes ago. Bibb wasn't even clear of the horse's rump before a gunshot was heard. His body laid just two steps out from the walkway, Sheriff, not even in the street yet.' The sheriff asked him if he thought Bibb had been ambushed. The reporter said he didn't witness the shooting, but the timing and placement of Bibb's body offer no other plausible explanation."

"A man in the room asked the sheriff if he needed help finding Gorgon. Another man agreed to help too. That was when the sheriff replied he had no interest in searching for the man. He said the priority was to keep this man in the diner, you Bibb, alive. I still recall seeing the doctor's half smile, looking at the sheriff, glad to hear the kindred spirit speak. The doctor and the sheriff are not always on the best of terms with each other."

"Ten minutes later boards were found long enough to place your body on, Bibb, and six men carefully carried you over to this room. I remember what the sheriff said as they were leaving. 'Don't trip on Gorgon's carcass lying in the street.' Nobody there, not a single one of us, had considered that possibility. Only one shot had been heard."

"Bibb, I know you have been told what was written in the papers so I will not tell you the gruesome details of the fate suffered by Mr. Gorgon. It was well lodged, and with a messy maneuver our sheriff took custody of your ax. A man stayed with

Gorgon's body until the undertaker arrived. Dogs came and lapped up his blood where he was lying, and by morning there was no sign left of the man's demise."

The nurse was totally engrossed in the story. She spoke up. "Bibb, I guess this is the time when I have to tell you what I know. The doctor often uses my two sisters and me to do nursing for him. We ain't real nurses, but we know his rules and that is why he trusts us. We are grateful for the work although it can get nasty." She paused for a second to think about what she said. "I'm sorry. You already know that. I apologize for mentioning that in front of the others. You know that each of us spends eight hours of our day to care for you. I'm so glad that this work is getting easier on both you and us. My sister stayed up all night with the doctor last Friday and into Saturday. You didn't really awake until Tuesday because of all the drugs. You sure did scare Xue last Sunday night."

Bibb looked at her in disbelief and replied, "Oouu?"

Bes answered, "Bibb, Xue is Mrs. Gorgon's seamstress and laundry lady. She is a pleasant Chinese woman that is very loyal to her employer. She came to the diner Sunday night curious of your condition. You were still heavily sedated, and the room rules were that she must cover her hair and mouth like we did when she came in here. Bibb, you were all bandaged up too, like an Egyptian mummy. All went well until you woke, looked right at her with your one good eye, and asked the one word, 'Anna?' Poor Xue bolted from the room having never been so scared in her life. By the time she vanished you were back asleep."

Bibb looked at her in disbelief.

"Yes, you did that, Bibb, but I know you meant no harm. But Xue will never be the same again."

He started to write. *"Should I apologize to her?"*

"Bibb, if you surprise her again like that you can put another notch on your ax without even throwing it." Nobody laughed. The nurse apologized for the thoughtless comment.

The hallelujah lady responded to the silence. "Bibb, there are some wrongs that don't need an apology. You meant no offense and Xue meant you no harm. Let this incident be forgotten."

The nurse continued, now more carefully, "Bibb, during those three days you had very few visitors. I did speak to the preacher once in the hall outside this room, and I didn't speak to the reporter on his nine attempts. Do you know about the incident involving a somewhat noisy attempt to deliver you your dinner?"

Bibb shook his head no.

Bes interrupted. "And if that woman wants that personal story be told she can tell it herself. She and Bibb will have several days together to share their stories."

Bibb wrote again. *"Do you mean Mrs. Gorgon? That was sweet of her to think of me, given her recent loss. I will be sure to ask her and thank her."*

Bes replied, "Bibb, I suggest you forget it. The whole incident was embarrassing for that woman. You will have challenges enough maintaining harmony with that beauty."

"Isss swse preeett-ee?" Bibb asked for paper again, he had used his last sheet by him. *"Is she pretty? She wore a widow's veil the only time I remember her visiting."*

"Bibb, she is known as a local beauty. No one dares to tell her different. You can draw your own conclusions, but I will warn you that some beauty is only skin deep."

"X-pwainnn," said Bibb.

"No I won't. You will have to discover that for yourself, and God help you if she confuses your mind in this matter." The hallelujah lady sat down, frustrated, resting her case. Bibb had seen that same facial expression in too many courtrooms.

Bibb wrote again addressing the nurse. *"Who else visited me?"*

"The doctor kept very tight control on that door, Bibb," replied the nurse. "Bes came over several times a day, and a hotel maid provided you clean sheets a couple times. Of course, my sisters, but you might think we are all the same person. The doctor did not want you to have visitors for medical reasons and the sheriff didn't want you to have any other visitors for his reasons. He said you attract trouble. Do you remember the couple times the sheriff visited, yes?"

Bibb nodded his head yes.

"Of course there was the doctor too. He has taken a profound interest in keeping you alive. You scared him several times. Last Saturday the doctor filled you with some heavy drugs. Twice we thought your heart slowed down too much. That is when the doctor found out how busted up your chest was too. No offense, but Bibb, you are a mess. You scared us half to death when you would stop whistling in the night. Seemingly switching your life on and off is not conducive to comforting me or either of my sisters. We seem to argue over everything, but having only one lit candle in this room at night gains unanimous agreement: one candle is ten too few."

Bibb wrote another note and pointed to the hallelujah lady to receive it. *"What do you know of providence? You make it sound like I am alive today because of it."*

"You can bet your last coin on it, Mr. Toivo!" responded the lady from her self-imposed silence. "I am no preacher but I been around enough years to know it when I see it."

That answer obviously did not satisfy Bibb by the look on his face. She responded again to him.

"Bibb, the way I see it is that providence comes in two flavors. The first one is general. That has to do with the changes of the seasons, the sunrise and sunset, birthing and dying. It is the natural order of things from thunder to ladybugs. I am not saying this power is humdrum. It takes a lot of wisdom and energy to keep this universe working like clockwork, but it isn't special or specific."

Bibb was receptive. She continued, "The second flavor of providence is God suspending the natural order to intervene in some matter. Some call such things miracles, large and small. Why would He intervene? I guess the big reason is so that He will be recognized for it. Another reason is because He delights being asked to intervene, and then to show those who asked He can answer specific prayers if it furthers His purposes. I prayed specifically that you would be spared that night. He chose to answer that prayer, not just because I asked, but because He had a greater reason other than to increase my faith."

He responded in writing, *"What reason could be imagined that would make this reasonable? He chose to keep me alive in this pain and with this disfigurement? That makes no sense."*

"Don't be so quick to judge the driver of the wagon. You are just a piece of the wheel."

"X-pwainnn," mouthed Bibb.

"Providence is much like a buckboard and we are like a section of a wheel attached by spokes to an axle. We go round and round, up and down. Every time we are on the bottom we seemed to be rolled through the mud, but then, up we go around to the top, to be on top of the world, then down we go again. Our lives are like that in cycles from suffering the mud to being raised to the top, just to descend and eventually splashed through the mud again. Now by spokes we are all connected to the axle, and for us that axle never seems to move. That is like God's love. It never changes, and if the pieces of the wheel focus on it only, it really doesn't matter how deep the mud is. But none of that is providence, I am sorry. The axle and the wheel and the buckboard serve one purpose, and that is to carry a burden. That burden is our purpose for existing. But providence is where that burden is being taken, and that depends on the driver. The driver keeps the wagon rolling and pointed towards the goal. From the perspective of the wheel we see nothing vast, and can easily doubt the wisdom of the driver. Neither does the wheel have any power in itself – that is the job of the horses out front. Our problem is we don't see that the driver is keeping us out the slime bogs, rock slides, and deep water. He carefully gets us safely home."

"Omme?" replied Bibb.

"Heaven, Bibb. The purpose is to get us there with all the treasures that can be loaded up in the wagon along the way. I'm not talking silver or gold, Bibb. I am talking friends, family, and precious memories. Some of those memories will recall how deep the mud was and how quickly you were pulled out of it. This miracle that you are still alive has been thrown in the back of that wagon for you Bibb, and it can never be taken away from you. Same with how well the doctor and nurses have treated you. Those blessing are secured in there too. Let me tell you a secret."

"Seere?"

"God has more than one wagon on its way to glory, and it takes four wheels to make any one wagon work. It would be nice if we were given more choices. You don't always get to pick who are the adjacent members placed next to your spot on that wagon wheel, no more than you get to pick your own siblings. You asked about that widow you are thinking of taking to Fort Rice, and now I will tell you my opinion. That Anna girl needs some wheel time. God Himself has decided to hitch that woman to the same wheel as you. I know He is going to take that wagon all the way home for you two, but trust me on this, there will be a lot of mud and humiliation between here and there for you both. And there will also be the highest moments of your lives. I just know it. I don't know what is in store for both of you, but you won't be the same people when you arrive at your destination. But you will be cleaner."

Bibb wrote another note. *"What if I don't feel like cooperating?"*

She laughed. "What does a wainwright do with a broken piece of wheel? Does he get a new wheel? No. He repairs the one he has. He gets out a bigger nail and drives that wayward piece of wheel back into place to carry its rightful share of the load. Kind of like a bullet through the chops, if you don't mind the metaphor. Does he nail the repaired piece upside down? No, he nails the wayward piece locking it in place where it can't but help but look only at the axle."

She continued, "Bibb, do not focus on Anna. She will get just as muddy as you, and in her pride she will throw some of that mud in your direction. If you are resolved with a mindset that you have been fitted to share the same axle with her, then there won't be anything she does or says that will tick you off. And this too shall pass. Be confident. When God is satisfied with the results He will release you. Be assured that in wisdom God governs this. It just may be possible that God decided the best way for Him to reveal His care for the Widow Gorgon was using the ways and personality of a notorious outlaw – and lookie there, you just happened to arrive in town and were available."

Bibb bristled at that concept. His notion of God didn't extend to anybody beyond himself. For God to be smart enough to work his will through two antagonists was something Bibb confessed he wasn't smart enough to think of by himself. He understood what the lady had said but wasn't willing to swallow any of that bitter medicine. Bibb was convinced God could not show His love through their mutual hate; that was so upside down. The lady had to be wrong but Bibb could not say why.

"Your trip will be hard enough and you don't need any extra friction between the two of you. Focus on the axle, Bibb, and ask the driver for some extra axle grease if the task starts to chaff you. Cowards look at the adjacent wheels and complain the others are not bearing their fair share of the load. That is an excuse of those who shirk their own tasks. Real men remind themselves of the destination and trust the driver. Bibb, keep your eye on the axle and keep your wheels a-moving."

==0==

"You had two visitors this afternoon, Mrs. Gorgon," said the maid as she brought her dinner up to her bedroom.

"Who were they, and why didn't you tell me?" replied Anna.

"They were two of your husband's lovers, and they were not worthy of your time."

"Did they say what they wanted? Had they left some undergarments here or had my husband promised them some treasure? Were they seeking blackmail?"

"I cannot tell, Mrs. Gorgon, but they asked to see you alone. I would not stand for that and I sent them on their way. They did ask me to tell you something."

"What could they say that would possibly interest me? And I am curious; do I know these women?"

"Yes you do, and no, I will not tell you their names. Some things are better left unknown. They told me that they honestly thought you were dead and now glad to know you are well. That was a lie. Anna, fear was written deep in their faces. They both trembled in voice stating…, no, emphatically pleading that they would have never shown your husband any interest if they knew you were alive."

"You're right. I don't want to know."

"When they left they added that they were truly sorry and wished you the best."

"Then I forgive them."

"They didn't ask for that. They asked that you would not destroy them."

"They asked that? Is my reputation that bad?"

"You have been good to me, Missy." She didn't answer the inquiry, but her deflection did. The maid had learned much about the Gorgons over the years. There was a heavy price attached to directly answering those types of questions to the mistress of the mansion.

Saturday, October 1, 1887

I am realizing the wonderful opportunity lying in front of me. I must stop complaining to others and myself. There is nothing in Deadwood for me. The future is bright, but I fear the trip... Who is this man? I married without really knowing the other one either – oh banish the thought! Flee from that hurtful fantasy! I will never again trust my heart to a man.

Bibb came over to see my wagons. I met him in the stable behind the house. I offered, but he would not come inside my mansion. He tries to whistle a few words; some I can understand. I told him my requirements on how the trip would be managed. He had other ideas. The Dowry girl spoke privately with me about his health while Bibb picked my best horse and went for a drive, as he wrote on the slate, "to judge her obedience." I will sell the other horses, the two carriages, and the unpicked wagon.

Mr. Franklin came over this evening with his wife to celebrate, and we did it right! I am now in full control of the Gorgon Estate, and by the way, he took the opportunity to give me a healthy invoice for his services. He will oversee the sale of the remaining properties as buyers bring in acceptable offers. I showed them the note from Bibb and without hesitation said, "Take it! Don't quibble." His wife said the usual malarkey. Later I pressed him for a second advisement (that is why I pay him!) and he went worthlessly into thought, as if ciphering debits and credits.

That half-man had opportunities to humiliate me in front of the nurse, but Bibb did not. Once his cards were turned face up he let me come to my own conclusions to what degree my demands were unbalanced. Why do I always want to control everybody and everything?

==0==

WHEN ANNA CAME downstairs for breakfast she had a smile on her face, the first one seen in a week. "Those days of darkness and gloom are over, and I'm ready to start packing. I'm going to miss this house. I will not miss some of the memories made in it. Oh well, time to move on! Giddy Up!"

The maid saw this as an opening for her question. "I wanted to ask you about that, Missy. What are your plans concerning your employees?"

"All of my employees can take care of themselves. I would not have hired them if they were lazy slackers. No, those who buy my businesses will not need my advice in keeping my good employees."

"What about the mansion? This isn't a business."

"Whoever buys this place will not be able to care for it themselves. Mr. Franklin will take care of that. He will lease it to one of many fish in the stream of fancy fellers coming in from the east with pockets full of gold and a wish to turn their investments into a million dollars. I also told him to sell the house if a worthy buyer presents an offer. As long as there is a tenant, you should remain gainfully employed. Once I leave town, you both are no longer bound by your contract and are free to look elsewhere for employers, or work here until your contract is up."

==0==

It was the butler who noticed movement in the backyard seeing a man and a woman snooping around the carriage house. He immediately went out to investigate. From the ugly wounds on the intruder's face the butler easily assumed the man to be Bibb. It could not be any other.

The nurse met the butler outside the barn door while Bibb continued his assessment. She told the butler that they did not intend to interrupt the lady of the house. "Sir, Bibb insisted on coming over this morning. He wanted to know what he had to work with in fear that he had to buy a different wagon for the trip. The doctor surprised me this morning when he said it would be okay for Bibb to leave the confines of the hotel and get some fresh air."

The butler replied, "I will tell the Widow Gorgon that you both are here. She has some things she wants to talk to Mr. Toivo about and this is a very welcome opportunity."

"Sir, please tell her to bring chalk and a slate if she expects responses from Mr. Toivo. Mr. Toivo's voice fatigues quickly."

==0==

Bibb had already decided what could and what could not be used on their trip when the lovely Mrs. Anna Marie Higgins Gorgon formally presented herself to the nurse at the barn door. Coming from the back of the building he quietly walked towards the conversation not wishing to interrupt the two of them talking. Anna's first visual impression on Bibb (truth be known her impact was not only on, but in, out, up, down, through, and around him) was that she was stunningly pretty, even if only one of his eyes was working well. Bibb had never seen such a fine young woman in a fine dress and in a horse barn before. So many odd things had happened, so why not another! He couldn't help but recall his mother's saying, "Too many odds make an omen." Another voice inside him brought to his mind what his daddy used to say, "Before you get too excited about a young lady, go visit her grandma and count the wrinkles." Bibb stabilized. This was the first time Bibb had seen her facial features. She was now out in the daylight instead of being something akin to a veiled lump of coal hiding in the shadows of a sick room. If there were such things as angels, her beauty certainly fit the definition of them he had imagined. But Anna of Miles City certainly didn't think angels were something delightful to look upon. The angels she read of in that paymaster's book could scare the feathers off of chickens when they showed up. That Anna never talked about girl angels.

Although her face was unfamiliar, he certainly recognized the voice. It was the same voice that produced all sorts of ungodly dialog across the hall the night before their first meeting. "Yes, that is the same woman..." Bibb quoted and then demanded of himself, "Don't be deceived by all the lace and grace, and don't you dare muddy your own thinking by looking at anything other than her eyes." Anna from Miles City had told him that more than once. At the time that seemed a strange proverb, and that Anna, well both of them for that matter, had eyes worth investigating.

Earlier that week while healing, Bibb had laid awake with a nagging curiosity about what sort of woman would voluntarily marry a gargoyle like Gorgon. Now he knew. There was no question in Bibb's mind why Mr. Gorgon would be attracted to her. Some things are as obvious as sunlight on a clear day. Her attraction to him on the other hand would remain a mystery, but obviously something must have been there, like distant thunder warning of future lightning strikes.

"Would you two like to come into my house? My cook made the best pastries this morning."

Bibb asked for the slate Anna was carrying with his eyes, and Anna complied with the request. He wrote in chalk, *"I came to look at your horse, not your house. TYA."*

Anna read the note and replied, "You have now seen the horses so let us retire to a place where we can sit down and discuss things comfortably. What does TYA mean?"

The nurse replied enthusiastically before Bibb could respond by stepping next to her and touching the bared skin of her forearm. "Mrs. Gorgon, it means *Thank you.* We have made up many codes over the last week. I think TY is Mr. Toivo's favorite phrase to write. TYA means *No, thank you* or *Thank you, anyway.* Either that or he holds up three fingers like a salute. It means the same. I imagine you will learn shortcuts too if you are going to communicate on the trip. When are you leaving? Did you know Bibb knows Indian sign language too? He has taught me some."

While they continued their conversation, Bibb pulled over two bite-sized bales of hay and placed them at their feet. He then went and got one more for himself, and then he sat on it. Bibb gestured with his hand for them to sit down and become comfortable. The nurse thought that as normal as rain, but the widow, conscience of her fine clothes, opted to remain standing. She looked at Bibb's face and thought it repulsive. She was going to have a difficult time speaking at him with such a distraction.

Anna was hoping to impress Bibb with her station in life as a precursor to her laying the law down on him. She had many demands formulated in her mind as to how their trip to Fort Rice would be conducted. She asked once again if they would like to go in the house. Bibb responded in chalk, *"I am comfortable here; I would not be comfortable in your house."* Obviously, the opportunity to impress him was postponed. And then Anna experienced an unexpected complication. Bibb didn't take his eyes off of hers, and his continued stare added to her anxiety.

Anna launched anyway. "Mr. Toivo, I want to establish some rules on how we are going to conduct ourselves on this trip." He didn't flinch. "I want you to know that I am going to expect the highest standard of conduct from you. I demand that you treat me with respect and honorable behavior. I expect you to provide me with all the social privileges and liberties I stipulate and no different from what I would expect from any man that was granted the honor and privilege of escorting me to the opera here in town."

Bibb started writing down some words as she kept up her lecture. He handed her the board and she read it. Her reply was, "No, Mr. Toivo, I am not done! I haven't even got into the specifics yet!"

Bibb responded with a hand with three fingers up. The nurse wondered if Anna had interpreted that correctly as a TY or as TYA. Obviously not, because Anna kept going.

Anna laid down another twenty minutes of expectations and additional rules. It only served to further convince Bibb of her naïveté of the ways of the plains. He actually started enjoying hearing her voice even if he wasn't actively listening. The nurse was wondering if she had practiced this oratory while living on the hillside all summer. It was quite thorough as if it was a recitation of a memorized East Coast charm school etiquette lesson recalled from Anna's childhood memories.

Bibb got up and retrieved the slate from the want-a-be schoolmarm, half wondering if she was holding class just to keep the conversation one directional. He added a word to the previous writ, *"yet?"* and handed it back to her.

"Mr. Toivo, have you listened to anything I have said?"

"Swall of ett," nodding his head yes.

"Well, do you agree with it?"

"Unnn of ett," he replied.

"Why, Mr. Toivo, do you disagree?"

He signaled for the slate, writing, *"Because it won't work. I don't follow rules; never have."*

"Well you will, and starting now!"

The nurse did a good job holding in her amusement at the contemplation of these two in the same wagon for more than ten minutes. The nurse had the advantage of getting to know the man longer than Mrs. Gorgon, and that added to the humor of her preposterous demands. Both women were wondering what was going on inside the man's mind while Bibb kept up his stare at Anna.

Eventually the gaze stopped Mrs. Gorgon's continuing rant. In the following silence she remembered how many notches were on Bibb's ax handle, and the additional one earned last week. Her husband was the last person that demanded something of Bibb. She was comfortable while she lectured at him, but very unsettled in the silence now present in the barn. Eventually Mrs. Gorgon asked, "Bibb, what do you have to say for yourself?"

Bibb kept staring at her for about ten seconds. Then he erased the slate and wrote *"I have a better idea."* He got up from his hay bale and handed the slate to Mrs. Gorgon without allowing the nurse to see it.

Mrs. Gorgon responded, "Well, it better be good!" Her tone had become even more condescending from what Bibb experienced at the beginning of her lecture. "So, what is it?"

Bibb took a sheet of paper from his pocket. It had about two paragraphs of words written on it, not readable because the paper was still folded up. He gave it to Mrs. Gorgon.

The nurse stood up too, partially in curiosity of the transaction. "What is it, Bibb? Do you need my help? What does the paper say?"

"Eeez go noaoww," Bibb said to the nurse, offering her his hand. He turned to Mrs. Gorgon, and in a half formal bow, he tipped his hat to her in farewell.

"Don't you want my reply? Let me read this aloud so we can all hear it and discuss it."

"No, ahmn. No, leeezz no. Laterr weeezz alkk." Bibb squeezed the Dowry girl's hand and politely escorted her out of the barn door. Intentional or not, it gave the nurse a hefty dose of the shivers as they curtly left Mrs. Gorgon alone in the barn. When Bibb looked back after about ten steps he saw the widow still reading the note. He decided not to look back again. Bibb let go of his nurse's hand once they were safely away.

==0==

That evening the mansion was bright with excitement and life. Several of Anna's friends accepted her invitation to join her for a formal banquette. Mr. Franklin and the butler, (the only two men there) quickly retreated to the billiard room once the feast was over.

The ladies talked for hours filling the home with cheerful discussions. Anna had privately shared Bibb's note with Mr. and Mrs. Franklin prior to dinner asking them for their candid opinion. Mr. Franklin's response was that it was odd that an outlaw would also be a bard. He consciously chose to leave the ladies to form their own opinions about such things, and they certainly accomplished that task over the next few hours.

==0==

The topic of the note Bibb had given to Mrs. Gorgon was brought up as her twin arrived at the sick room to work the next shift. "Bibb, my mind is simply wild with thoughts how you got such a reaction from Mrs. Gorgon. What did you write her?"

The other sister then questioned the incident, and soon she had a thousand questions too. The former took that opportunity to tell the arriving latter sister an embellished version of the story. While they were talking, Bibb disengaged from the particulars of the conversation. He started to write, and when they eventually noticed, it caused the young twins to pause and watch. When he was finished he gave the arriving twin the note, and she read it aloud.

> *Mrs. Gorgon and I have the same goal — to get home. I was glad to see Mrs. Gorgon was also prepared for today's meeting. It scares me that we think about the same things at the same time, but we think about them so differently. Frankly, we will die doing things her way. We may get home if we do things my way. Today she offered me a contract. I offered her a covenant. We may be kindred spirits.*

"Bibb..." came a response in stereo, amplified by the last phrase.
"Nod now, ladieezz. Aank ou."

==0==

The sheriff thanked his wife for paying the ransom to release his kidnapped shirt from Xue's laundry. The price of redemption was not monetary, but investing the time to sit with her in her back room and tell Xue what she and her husband had found out.

When he unwrapped the bundle and started to put on his clean shirt the sheriff's wife started to laugh out loud. Above the left pocket was embroidered the same number that was on the miner's bullet riddled and blood stained shirt. "Don't miss the point dear," she said with a smirk. "Her husband's number is now the closest thing to your heart. Xue didn't do that by accident."

Sunday, October 2, 1887

I was not expecting to, but Bibb and I had lunch along with the Deadwood parson and wife, Mr. Franklin, and the eldest of the three Dowry girls. I am quite sure that event will be in the newspaper. Bibb and I came to an agreement in general about the trip, but not in specifics. That outlaw fears specifics. He also fears me. He will be easy to control — all with a simple touch.

At lunch Bibb asked the preacher about providence, and got a heavenly answer that was no earthly good. Bibb showed cheek, pun intended (for he has only one left), to even ask a minister such a question. The preacher showed courage by serving up some bad tasting medicine for answers. He told Bibb to have perseverance, which was certainly an oblique insult aimed at me. I can take care of myself without any inconvenience to a man, any man.

That outlaw is recovering well. His wounds are revolting, but in time, I will get used to them. He certainly wasn't much of a man to start with, and now half shot up. His speech is getting better daily and none too soon. I just hate it when he dryly writes out his answers. I want to know how somebody feels. His statements are all substance. People can always change their mind about objects and actions, but seldom do they change their feelings. I certainly do not.

I'm going to bed satisfied in spirit and restless in heart. I cannot explain it. I feel I was made whole while at the same time missing something big. Is it possible to be peacefully anxious? I confess… I am lying to my own diary. I want to deny what happened today; fearing if I spoke the truth about the event it would actually become true. I can't believe I actually bit him, and so hard! I can't believe what my heart is telling me about what that rash act really means. Is there power in the blood? I am haunted by the phrase "Life for Life." I fear I do not know the full import of what it means yet. Yet… I fear there is a lot of "yet" yet to happen.

A late PS: When I tell myself that Bibb is an idiot, what does that say about me? I am allowing him to hitch his horse to my rig, so who is the bigger fool? Bibb is much smarter than he looks. I guess that really ain't saying much. I fell asleep angry tonight; now awake again. I'm still mad at Bibb for looking at my horses without permission and then having the audacity to tell me which one we would take. I again slept just to awake again later. I dreamt about little black pigs running up and down the staircases of the mansion. I also dreamed that the momma sow was in the kitchen and when I sat down at the table it touched my feet with its wet nose. I seldom dream but this one was so vivid. I need to go back to sleep, and stay sleeping this time. I must ask Xue if my dream means anything. She has lots of superstitions. No, I better not.

==0==

TO ANNA GORGON Sunday was another day of the week to make money. Mr. Franklin only protested momentarily when Anna made her request that he accompany her to visit Mr. Toivo at the hotel. The new dawn was coming. Mrs. Gorgon and her daily demands would soon be gone, only to be heard from again through the mail. He once caught himself praying for Bibb's speedy recovery.

At nine o'clock the butler delivered Mr. Franklin and Anna Gorgon to the Red Buffalo hotel. They proceeded to Bibb's room and upon arrival found Bibb fully dressed along with his nurse, the eldest Miss Dowry.

"You look all dressed up and nowhere to go, Mr. Toivo. What is the occasion?" asked Anna.

The nurse answered, "Bibb didn't figure you to be a church lady; but the business temperament in your blood caused him to expect to see you this morning. Bibb said he wanted to wear something presentable to meet you, an honor due a gracious-hearted lady like yourself. He also said he had plans, but conceded no hints one way or the other. Maybe you already know, Mrs. Gorgon. Based on how insistent he was to look nice this morning I think he was hoping to treat you to lunch."

The nurse received no hints from Mr. Franklin or the widow until she spoke, "Mr. Toivo might concede that a skunk in a shirt is still a skunk. Where did you get the oversized shirt for him?"

The nurse replied, "Bibb doesn't concede much, Mrs. Gorgon. I'm beginning to think he spends much of his time privately within his own thoughts, skunks or otherwise, even before he received his new speech impediment. I concede his humility is unpracticed, but I dare say he knows his predicament and acts accordingly. But to answer your question, I borrowed the clothes he is wearing from my neighbor for the occasion." Bibb was glad his nurse answered before he did. Anna was not a kind woman by nature, and he could have said something ugly just as easily, by nature.

"I am afraid I don't have any idea about Mr. Toivo's plans or humility, false or not, Miss Dowry. You have already proved you have more insights into Mr. Toivo's wounded thinking than I do. Mr. Toivo, this is Mr. Franklin and he is my representative. He has some items to discuss with you."

Bibb had difficulty in speaking and had developed a habit of retrieving drool with a slurping sound as he talked. This conversation was quickly surpassing his ability to respond without discomfort. He chose to stay silent. At a pause in the conversation, Bibb, by pointing asked his nurse to give up her chair and sit next to him on the bed. With another hand gesture he asked for his visitors to put the two chairs in the room near to the bed and then said, "Pleazzze sit (srpt)."

Both Anna and Mr. Franklin responded cordially. Mr. Franklin introduced himself as Mrs. Gorgon's lawyer and estate representative. Anna was hoping Bibb would be intimidated.

Bibb acknowledged his introduction. He pulled out several pieces of papers from his pocket, looked at them, selected one, and gave it to Mr. Franklin. Bibb then said, "Reeee dis (srpt) pleazzze."

Mr. Franklin took the letter and then read it aloud:

> *Mr. Franklin, please pardon my weariness of lawyers. My experiences with them often involve murder, gallows, and injustice. In one week Mrs. Gorgon will no longer be able to ask for, nor rely on, your wisdom; therefore I suggest she speaks for herself. My experience is that she, much unlike me, is a quick wit and well able to look out for her business interests and matters of the heart. You may give her all the advice she requests of you, but my conversation will be with her. Please take no offense. None is meant.*

Undeterred Mr. Franklin continued, "Mr. Toivo, Mrs. Gorgon wishes to discuss the rules of engagement for your trip to Fort Rice. She laid out many of the specifics to you yesterday when you visited."

"N-gage-ment??"

"Mrs. Gorgon wants concessions from you concerning how you are to conduct yourself while you are her employee."

Bibb looked at the lawyer with a glare that indicated he was done talking to him. Sorting his papers once again, he selected one, and asked his nurse to give it to Mrs. Gorgon. "Reeee dis pleazzze (srpt)."

Anna took the paper from the nurse and gave it to Mr. Franklin immediately. When he started to open it, Bibb stood up from sitting on his bed, walked over to Mr. Franklin, took the paper from him, and gave it back to Anna. "I musss be more clearrr (srpt). Reeee dis pleazzze, Mizz Orgon (srpt). No offfezze, Mr. (srpt) Franklinnn."

Mr. Franklin could not help but notice Bibb's recently cleaned revolvers and gun belt hanging from his waist. "No offense taken, Mr. Toivo. You have made yourself perfectly clear. I retain the right to advise Mrs. Gorgon if she requests it." Bibb's speech was slurred, but his body movements were nimble enough to throw an ax if he wanted to. Bibb did not return to sitting on the bed but moved towards Anna.

Anna unfolded the paper and looked at her lawyer before she started to read it aloud. She focused and began:

Mrs. Anna Gorgon, my resolution concerning your rules proffered yesterday has not changed. I will not submit to be your servant or employee on our journey together. Although your fears and concerns are valid, I reject entirely your approach to any such agreement. My reasons are many, but most importantly, your way guarantees failure and most likely death. I don't like death, and your experience with it is probably just as unpleasant as mine. I have suggested a reasonable alternative. Have you considered it?

Mr. Franklin interrupted, "Mrs. Gorgon did receive and read your alternative proposal."

Bibb looked at him, and then returned his attention to Mrs. Gorgon. "I askeddd youuu, Mrs. 'Orgon (srpt). Havvv you conssssiderratt itt (srpt)?" Bibb then focused on Mr. Franklin, saying, "Sheee godt morrr toungge ahd hhh'heart d'thann (srpt) I do. Letdt herr speaaa forrr herrselfff (srpt)."

"Mr. Toivo, I am very capable of speaking for myself. I asked Mr. Franklin to come with me to offer me his advice in this important conversation. Mr. Toivo, you must become more reasonable. I am giving you fair terms."

"Death may bee fairrr forrr meee, but (srpt) youuu hardlleee dessservvve ittt," answered Bibb. "Diddd youuu r-r-reeead-zz (srpt) my writtennn offfferrr?"

"I have seen it," responded Mr. Franklin.

Bibb noted the lawyer sidestepped the question. He looked at him directly and said, "Annd-zz?"

"We have it with us, Mr. Toivo," answered the lawyer.

"Whattt adviccce diddd (srpt) yooo givvv herrr?" asked Bibb.

"That was a privileged discussion, Mr. Toivo."

Bibb smiled, and thought about unlatching one of his revolvers, but opted to sit down instead. Mr. Franklin had irritated, but not offended. Bibb gestured to Anna to say something and waited for a response.

"Mr. Toivo, I am a woman of means and I am prepared to make you an offer of a handsome wage if you agree to my terms. Why will you not agree to them?"

Bibb wrote a short note on a piece of paper and walked over to Anna. At first Bibb did not let her take the paper. Bibb raised his finger to his mouth and whistled a soft, "Shhhh. Readdd dtdt'thisss, Anna (srpt)."

She did. The message said: *"There is nothing that you have that I want, and I am sure you feel likewise. We do have common hates and desires. We both want to be free and both hate to be beholden to somebody else."*

Bibb withdrew the paper, folded it up, and put it in his pocket with the others. "Mrs. 'Orgon, whattt (srpt) of my offerrrr (srpt)?"

"I have considered it, Mr. Toivo."

"Andddd…"

"I am not sure about it. I may need more time."

Bibb pulled out another piece of paper from his pocket, "Readdd disss, pleazzz. Shhhhh."

At first Anna was only annoyed, but now peeved by such a worthy opponent. Unread, she immediately handed the note to Mr. Franklin. She stared at Bibb with a look that both showed a wounded heart within her as well as one surrounded by pride. She wondered to herself why she felt that way. She came prepared to ambush this man this morning. Had she not learned anything from her husband's folly? Oh, how she hated the thought of somebody anticipating her next questions. Then she thought, "Why is that so bad?" She turned her gaze towards Mr. Franklin and when he had finished reading the note his eyes connected with his client's.

"Come with me, Mrs. Gorgon. Please excuse us for a few minutes, Mr. Toivo. You have given us much to discuss."

==0==

Mr. Franklin ordered coffee for two at the hotel saloon downstairs. The management had already cleared out the partygoers of the previous evening and transformed the room into something respectable again. They were the only two seated customers in the otherwise vacant room.

"Mrs. Gorgon, before you start to huff and puff, you need to settle down and relax. You did not display your best behavior in that room. If my wife were here she might advise you to loosen your corset a notch. You are not that far above his station in life as you might suppose."

"Are you saying I am a murdering, thieving, immoral outlaw, Mr. Franklin?" retorted Anna.

A long pause came before Mr. Franklin responded. He carefully aimed his words at her spirit. "At least you are not immoral, but only if I employ your loose definition of morality."

"That was harsh. What specifically are you trying to say, Mr. Franklin?"

"Mrs. Gorgon, neither of us wants to get into a discussion on the Gorgon history in this community. Your shrewdness has never been interpreted as business acumen by citizens of this town. You and your husband purchased a large share of unjust justice in Deadwood Gulch, and the bill for that behavior will come due very soon. That is why Mr. Toivo's offer is so intriguing. To tell you the truth, Mrs. Gorgon, that man upstairs is your late husband's better by half. As a lawyer, I am impressed by his preparation and thoughtful responses. Not once did he dishonor you or me. These notes were not composed by a depraved criminal mind. He admitted to lacking heart, but he credited you for having one, and he made a reasonable appeal to it."

"Let me read the note," demanded Anna.

"Anna, you made a rash mistake by handing this note to me instead of reading it for yourself. But that is history now. Tell me Anna, can you think for yourself, or are you dependent on me to make up your mind for you? I can help you with legal issues, business decisions, and estate planning, but I have no business meddling in these matters."

"Let me read the message," demanded Anna again.

"It will only make you cry. I know how much you hate tears, especially in a public place. Instead, let's first pull out yesterday's offer and discuss it."

"You are making me very angry, Mr. Franklin."

"Good."

"Good?"

"Yes, Good. Very Good! Inform me when you decide to shed your condescending attitude, and then we can restart this conversation. Anna, for you own good, think clearly. For one hour, please let your feelings play spectator to the rational woman that I know hides inside of you somewhere."

"You're talking to me like you're my father. What gives you that right?"

"Are you saying that because your father loved you?"

"What has that to do with anything?"

"You brought it up. I'm quite sure your father wanted the absolute best for his daughter, but he had to take that high spirited girl down a notch or two every once in a while. If that is the case, I accept your compliment, even if it was intended as an insult."

"You are out of line, Mr. Franklin."

"Really? This might be a good time for you to find a boudoir to freshen up a bit. Do yourself a favor and look into that mirror real deep. While you are there, you need to take time to read this. Before we return upstairs, please rid yourself of some of those anger wrinkles in your face. You have nothing to be angry about. I will be waiting for you here. On second thought, you may not be worthy of this note. Fix your anger first, and then come back."

"That is my letter, Mr. Franklin. Give it to me."

"I warned you, Mrs. Gorgon." He gave it to her. "If you decide to huff and puff, then don't waste my time by coming back out here. Shed your pride out here, and make yourself beautiful again in there. I have seen the beautiful Anna before. I know she exists. She is just hiding right now. My wife was right about you."

"You are wrong, Mr. Franklin. Very wrong. The beautiful Anna never left."

"Tell it to the mirror, Mrs. Gorgon. I have already made up my mind."

"You are so wrong."

Mr. Franklin, nodded, not speaking. She was not going to concede to him the last word. Somehow he expected to hear a mirror crack momentarily. He hoped he would hear a mirror crack.

==0==

Bibb moved to the chair over to the window where the nurse usually sat. He looked out and saw the normally rowdy town of Deadwood at its slowest. This town was no place to live. It might be a great place to get rich, but nobody could make a habit of enjoying a ditch in the middle of pits. For him the desires for luxury had long left him. It didn't hurt to have some money already stored away, but that really did not matter anymore. He had a very hard time putting his fingers on his desires. He wanted to go home. He wanted to go home to somebody. He wanted to be respected at home. He wanted to be more than a chicken farmer. He wanted to never have to look over his shoulder again. He wanted simplicity. He wanted that stinking hound that was driving him crazy on the outside and the varmint that was gnawing at him from the inside to cease their torment of him. He wanted to see the young Anna of Miles City and her parents again. He wanted to have peace with Toak.

After a few minutes of staring out the window Tommy took stock of the reality of the situation. He was a broken man in a broken town. Yet there was hope. He somehow knew that if he listened to the varmint there would be a reasonable expectation for having his desires addressed, or if not that, his desires changed. Then he thought of Humbird, his brother's widow and her claims on him. "Oh, what a messed up life I have!" he said to himself.

Tommy got up, picked up paper and quill, and returned to the nightstand and started writing again. The nurse returned to her window seat, observing everything in silence. "Was this man really a killer?" she thought to herself. "What tangled thoughts go on inside his head? Obviously they were coherent enough for Mr. Franklin to pull Mrs. Gorgon from the room. Or was that for her safety? Am I safe? Are my sisters safe?" The nurse decided not to listen to her fears. All would be well.

==0==

Anna sat down in privacy and read the note. In her pride she wanted to remain unmoved by anything a man could say, or in this case, write. It was written in perfect penmanship, another thing that bothered her about Bibb.

Anna's first response to the letter was a series of snappy comebacks for each phrase. She then asked herself why she was angry. "Other than being a lying murderer, why not trust him? Why am I even entertaining the thought? The man will kill me half way there and take all my wealth!"

Anna's second response was to make the men wait. She took his advice to beautify, and took her time, and even more time to touch up her hair and pay more attention to her dress. She did look in the mirror. Sadly, Mr. Franklin wasn't kidding about her anger wrinkles.

She sat down in a chair and reread the note once again, and reread the original proposal Bibb gave her in her carriage house. She knew that Mr. Franklin would want a thoughtful answer, not more of her drama. She read the newer note again and this time with an eye towards business.

> *Anna, I do not believe you need more time. You are an intelligent woman who knows her own mind. You have already made up your mind, but feel afraid to agree to a covenant. Do you think me not afraid of such an agreement? You must accept my proposal freely or not at all. Because you have already made up your mind, I will not plead logic with you. As dealing with your feelings, I am unarmed and inexperienced to enter that arena. I have no hope to convince you either way. Regardless, we must be free to be willfully kind to each other in spirit, and that is the foundation of my proposal. We must not be at each other's throats because of some perceived violation of some obscure section of some contract Mr. Franklin has drawn up. We have no judge on the plains to settle disputes. We must either trust each other or die. The cry of your mind and soul is to start your life over. Now is the time. You have my proposal. I appeal to your spirit. What is your answer?*

Anna had no answer, just more questions, and all beginning with the word *why*. She thought to herself many new questions. "Whatever came over that man to write down answers to my objections even before I had voiced them? This man is spooky. I guess if a man was locked in a room all day and night he would have time to think. How did he know what I would say? Did Mr. Franklin tell him? But why would Mr. Franklin do that? Mr. Franklin doesn't want me to leave Deadwood. He makes too much money off of the Gorgon estate to see it liquidated, not to mention my never ending legal troubles."

Sighing, she looked in the mirror once more to get herself ready to return. From close behind her came a female voice saying, "Does it hurt to kick the cactus, selfish blind girl?" Anna quickly turned around and saw nobody. She checked the rest of the boudoir and discovered she was the only one there. She peeked out of the door, and saw nobody other than Mr. Franklin. He stood up as the waitress came walking out the kitchen with more hot coffee.

Anna returned inside and checked around again; nobody. Her mind raced in thought. "It didn't happen. Nobody said anything. I am under stress and my imagination is getting the best of me. Liar. It was said clear as day. Ghosts don't haunt in the day. Liar. There was no voice. What an odd thing to say. Was it said to me? Who else?" She took a deep breath and returned to the waiting lawyer.

Immediately the attentive waitress warmed her cooling coffee too. Mrs. Gorgon made a special attempt to speak with her. "Are you also the cook this morning?"

"No ma'am, I don't cook. She left an hour ago to work at a real restaurant. I leave her biscuits warming inside the oven and keep enough hot coffee on top. Anything else, ma'am?"

Anna eliminated her. Her low raspy voice was nothing like the angelic one she previously encountered. What a strange message. Worse, it rang true. The voice knew her deepest secrets.

==0==

The sheriff was on his way to church when a non-standard post from Miles City was delivered to him. The letter had been entrusted to a miner traveling to Deadwood. The sheriff knew the grizzled courier because this wasn't the man's first trip to Deadwood to try his luck at finding "gold in them there hills." The sheriff offered him payment for his trouble, and the man responded that he would rather know that he had a friend at the lockup rather than an employer. The Sheriff offered him money again, a silver dollar, and the man took it that time, under protest. He had made his point.

To: Sheriff, Deadwood
From: Sheriff, Miles City

> *I received an urgent official telegram from the Bismarck garrison via the marshal there. For obvious reasons I could not have Bibb deliver this message, nor an Indian courier named Toak. Upon Bibb's departure from our jurisdictions, both you and I are instructed to collect up all records, notes, newspaper clippings, and any artifacts concerning Mr. Tommy Toivo, a.k.a. Mr. Terry Toivo, a.k.a. Bibb, and have them sent by a reliable party to the Intelligence Officer, a Major Ryder, at the Bismarck Garrison. If you package up your artifacts and send them to me, I'll wire the good major to let him know when he can expect our consolidated package by rail mail.*
>
> *Sheriff, another instruction in the telegraph bothered me. This collection is to be done as unnoticed as possible. A hint was given there may be national or international interest in this man. To evidence their seriousness and urgency (they want it all by November) the states' Department of State promised us both a fifty dollars reimbursement for our efforts. That goes well beyond dollars offered to snoop on a local rowdy vagrant.*
>
> *And yes, I still have five missing ranch hands and two more ranch hands with signature mortal wounds. The unanimous consensus is that Mr. Toivo knows more than passing details about the fates of these men. I want to question this "also known as" outlaw concerning these deadly mysteries when he gets back here. I am not looking forward to that. The man scares me and everybody else in this town. I don't care how busted up he is, the man is armed and therefore extremely dangerous. People have a tendency to underestimate his killing ability given the*

extent of his injuries. Tell that to the newly minted widows here. You probably already have a few new widows there too.

Be very careful. Death follows him. I don't know why Bismarck is so interested in him. I am to wire a certain Major Ryder with a code as soon as he arrives and when he departs Miles City. The telegram also demanded I actively assist in Bibb's return to Bismarck. Such a demand is noteworthy knowing they have no authority over Montana jurisdictions. But the point was well taken; whatever the deep unstated reasons are, we are by any means strongly obliged to push him safely on his way. I will have no pause in assisting Bismarck to get their man back alive. The faster Bibb is out of my town, the better. But I don't have to tell you that. If he has been in Deadwood for over a week, you already know firsthand. Peace.

==0==

Mr. Franklin dared not restart their conversation. He knew Anna too well to risk that. He studied her in attempt to discern her mood, but failed. She was never known to let quiet reign so long. Once she started he would bend the conversation to where it needed to go.

Anna broke the silence after both sipped their coffee several times. "Can you show me the contract you drafted for Bibb to sign?"

"I didn't bring it. It is a worthless piece of paper. Three hundred paces outside of Deadwood it will mean nothing. Yes, it would have been legal, but things can be both legal and wrong. I think you mentioned something like that to me about a death certificate."

"I thought we discussed something being both legal and not true. How could something be wrong if it advances my agenda? That is a whole different category."

"Someday you will answer your own question, Anna. Wrong is not as subjective as you might like it to be. I remain prosperous because of it. People wrong each other all the time, but who ever heard of righting somebody?"

"You digress and that bores me. Answer me, Mr. Franklin. What would it cost me if I agreed to Bibb's offer?"

"You only showed it to me once. May I see it again?"

Anna pulled it out of her purse and gave it to Mr. Franklin. "Please read it to me. I want to make sure I didn't miss anything."

He unfolded the paper. It showed signs of much folding and unfolding since he saw it last. He was careful not to see too much into that. In a subdued voice, he began to read:

Mrs. Anna Gorgon, surmising from your first words to me I gathered that you are a business woman and you think in business type thoughts. That dialect is a foreign language to me. May I propose a creative alternative to the shalls, musts, requirements, penalties and payments spelled out in a contract? Perhaps with a different yet still binding approach we may both get what we want on top of what we both need.

1. Life for life. My life for yours; your life for mine. You trust me to deliver you safely to Mr. and Mrs. Gorgon in Fort Rice. In trade, I trust you to superintend my medical needs. This goes beyond casual agreements. You must trust me in all aspects of the trip, from horses to hot lead, and never doubt my leadership. You will obey me without question in all matters concerning travel and provisioning. In turn, I will be unquestionably obedient to your management of my medical care, from showers to surgeries, to return me to be an able courier for the territory.

2. The only rule I will agree to is that we owe nothing to each other but kindness. We will use kindness in keeping our word to each other. You can talk all you want and I will listen all I want, but both will do it with respect. You do not have to answer all my questions, and I do not have to answer all of yours. In kindness we will tell each other what questions we are not prepared to answer. In kindness I will perform the chores that I can, and likewise you will do the same. In kindness we will cooperate with each other to achieve successful termination of this agreement.

3. I will not be released from this commitment until you say I am. You will not be released from this commitment until I say you are.

Please consider this a sincere and reasonable offer for us to achieve mutual goals and a basis for us to reside in peace until then.

Anna looked at him seriously. "Well, how big of a draft will I have to write against my account?"

"Anna, wake up! You are already legally liable for his bills because of your late husband's miscalculations. This agreement adds nothing to your costs, nor would you owe Bibb a wage."

"Answer my question. I know that already."

"Anna, why are you worried about money? Yes, you must agree to pay for his recovery. What? That was just two hundred dollars here. So you might need to have him see a surgeon in Bismarck. What would that cost, say maybe upwards of a thousand dollars? You make that in a month on your properties, and with liquidation that isn't even a pimple on your ledgers. But that is not your real question."

"That is what I figured it would cost, but you sound like I have a million dollars."

"Pretty close, dear-ee. But what this trip will cost you isn't in a currency you are willing to forfeit. You will lose your privacy. You will lose the comforts that your money now buys you. You will lose your access to power that your money brings you, at least until you reestablish yourself. You will lose friends, yes, but that's not much of a loss as shallow as many of them are. You will have to submit to the authority of a man as you travel. You will lose your fame, and replace it with an unwanted infamy. Be not deceived, your reputation will be tarnished by association with an outlaw for the rest of your life. You might learn to understand both respect and self-sacrifice for the first time in your life, and that might scare you to death."

"Dear me, Mr. Franklin! You said all of that right off the top of your head? You impress me. You may be totally wrong, but I remained impressed."

"I didn't say what I wanted to."

"Well, what is that, Mr. Franklin?"

"I will say it later after I am sure you are leaving."

"What makes you think I am even entertaining the thought, Mr. Franklin?"

"Because you are a brilliant woman, as well as a risk taker."

"You try to flatter me, sir. Are you really saying I would be an idiot to decline? Come now; that is cruel."

"From my mind through your lips, Mrs. Gorgon. And it is not cruel. Tell me true, have you made up your mind, or are you still waffling?"

"I can't stand the feeling I am being forced into a decision. I hate that. Everything seems to be boxing me in to give me no choice in the matter. The sheriff has an attempted murder warrant that he says he will use on me if I don't leave. You said it yourself that there are bills that were coming due soon, and reprisals are seldom paid with cash. My social status, like it or not, was buoyed by female sympathy while I was the abused wife of an unfaithful husband. That certainly will not last. And who would find me attractive here? The whole town knew my rat husband was clammed up from his rendezvous with naughty night-crawlers. I have friends because I am wealthy, not because I am friendly. Look what I did to the preacher and his wife! That snub certainly was not a brilliant maneuver on my part. The only hope for redemption in this town I irreverently squandered on bad prideful stunts. Everybody laughed at me behind my back when I wore that widow's gown. And Mr. Franklin, while I am at it, there seems to be too many coincidences about how you're pushing me out of town. Why do you feel this way? Why do I feel this way? Am I paranoid, or do people really want me harmed or forced to leave?"

"Mrs. Gorgon, Anna, as far as my loyalty to your person and estate I believe my actions will vouchsafe my plea of fidelity. As far as a conspiracy to remove you from your perch in society, I have seen none of it. The sheriff has other motives. More than anything he wants Mr. Toivo out of town. People die with him around. Take this as a compliment: He considers you too irresistible of an enticement for a man of Bibb's character to pass up. What young man would not want to be your escort and body guard for a thousand miles alone to anywhere?"

"You make me sound like some immoral widow anxious to snare another man with my enticements and endowments."

"Mrs. Gorgon, you said that. I didn't. But when a shoe fits, I have never known you not to wear it. But I was uncharitable. Mrs. Gorgon, down deep inside that dark little heart of yours resides a nugget of gold."

"Little? Are you commenting on my heart size or my capacity to care?"

"That is precisely what this next week will prove, won't it? I am wondering myself."

"I will remind you, Mr. Franklin, that I am a leading lady in this town, an inspiration of envy for many aspiring socialites. I will not entertain any more of the uncharitable thoughts you are voicing. This topic is now closed. Mr. Franklin, do you believe in ghosts?"

"Mrs. Gorgon, lower your voice, we have company coming."

"Mr. Franklin, I have never known you to shy away from questions. Do you believe in ghosts?"

"I'd doooo," came a voice from behind Anna. There was no doubt that voice belonged to Bibb. "Maaaay I joinnn (srpt) youuu?"

Mr. Franklin stood up and answered before Anna had a chance to. "Please! You and Miss Dowry join us at our table. I will fetch some additional coffee."

Once served, the nurse addressed Anna and her question. "Mrs. Gorgon, I find it such a strange coincidence that Bibb and I had just asked each other the same question. Don't you agree this is so astonishing? Did you know that Bibb has a well-established and unwanted reputation of being a ghost? We laughed ourselves silly this morning when he started to wonder if you were one too. We visited your grave the other day, and there is only one way for you to be both there and here. I know, I know, neither you nor Bibb are ghosts, but isn't it so uncanny that both of you have such like histories? It's just bizarre that you talk about the same things at the same time too. Isn't that just crazy? Just before we came down stairs he jokingly said he was once cornered by a ghost in Miles City. He wrote that it deserved him right after what he did to others. He complained that same ghost seems to have followed him here to this building. I told him that his jokes reminded me of Wild West legends you might hear from half drunken miners on a Saturday night."

"I wazzzn'nnt jokinnng (srpt)," said Bibb. All the party chuckled, except Bibb, at what was considered another tall tale to perpetuate his legend.

"Did that ghost talk?" seriously asked Anna. Her question sobered the conversation.

Bibb and the others looked at the asker with an interest in what prompted the question. He replied, "No'ma'ammm (srpt), not directly. D'that ghost spoke-kkk (srpt) throuuuugh a womannnn (srpt). Scarrrreddd meeee (srpt) toooo death-hhth."

The nurse wanted to change the subject. "Well, that is enough of that talk. No self-respecting ghost would show himself or herself on Sunday. Even they know the rules." The seriousness of the conversation was unnerving her since she and her twin sisters took turns working there alone at night. She wanted to hear no more talk of ghosts haunting the building.

Bibb discretely wrote something on a piece of paper and handed it to his nurse. *"The ghost that haunts me especially delights to work on Sundays."*

Mrs. Gorgon, thinking the note was a schoolboy prank took the paper from out of the nurse's hand and read it for herself. Once read, she apologized for her rashness and gave the note back. "This script was intended for you, Miss Dowry. I'm sorry."

Miss Dowry, catty at the insult, replied, "Mrs. Gorgon, I didn't know you knew that word."

"Script?"

"No, the last word you said." The returned insult registered on Anna's face. The nurse quickly responded, "I should have remembered my place here, and I quickly must apologize. You have been very generous to employ me and my sisters. I was unkind, and I did not think before I spoke."

Bibb raised his hand as if wanting to speak. He sputtered a few words but his scabs started to crack causing him to become abruptly silent. Then his eyes lit up as if he had remembered something. He left the table and went back up to his room.

The conversation continued around the table until stopped by Mr. Franklin. The chatter and topic at hand was a waste of an opportunity and they needed to put away all the silly thoughts about ghosts. Bibb deserved an answer concerning the trip, and urged Mrs. Gorgon again to give him one.

Bibb, who was beginning to move at his normal speed, returned from upstairs with a sealed envelope and gave it to Mrs. Gorgon. On the envelope was freshly written the text *"To be opened later while alone."*

Anna looked at him and the envelope with suspicion. Every time he had given her something to read it had an uncanny way of nicely painting her into a corner. It was the "nicely" that bothered her the most. By presenting his thoughts in writing she could not use her sharpened wit to retaliate without looking malicious. Maybe the reason so many were dead was because he disarmed his opponents before he killed them. She certainly felt declawed.

"Mr. Toivo, why are you pushing me into accepting your terms? What are your reasons, and how do I know your motives are pure?" asked Anna.

Bibb wrote on a piece of paper the numbers one, two, and three. Following three he wrote, *"I don't think my motives are pure. I don't think I ever had a pure motive. I never even thought about having a pure motive before. But that was before… a conversation for another day."*

Anna was reading his writing, even if upside down from her perspective, and was becoming irritated. She saw that Bibb was responding directly to her questions rather than reacting in anger. She knew Bibb could not match her wits emotionally and therefore easy prey to win concessions. She wanted to accuse him of improper thoughts, and he took away her leverage by admitting them.

Bibb then wrote behind the number two, *"See my answer in the sealed envelope later while alone."* Then behind number one he fumbled. He started to write and then scratched it out. Not only did he line through it, he made his false start unreadable. Oh how Anna wished she could have insight into that fallible mind of his. When Bibb was finished blotting out his words, he turned to her and said, "I ammmm (srpt) nottt pushinnng youuuu. I (srpt) havvv nottt pussshheddd youuuu. I will nottt pussshh youuuu (srpt) innnn daaah futurrrr."

Anna responded in a calculated level of passion, "You certainly want me to agree to your terms, and you have twice utterly rejected my terms. That sounds like pushing to me! You have not once hinted at compromise! You have not asked me once about my feelings! Don't you care how I feel?"

"Whyyy izzz rejjjectinnnggg yourrr termmmzzz (srpt) rejjjectinnnggg youuuu (srpt)? I dooo nodtt und,ddd,ddd,urrr,standdd (srpt). Helllppp meee (srpt) und,ddd…" then Bibb went silent. All could see it hurt the man to speak.

Anna answered in frustrated anger, "Because! Just because!"

Bibb looked at her with a puzzled face. He tilted his head to the side like a scolded puppy and looked into Anna's eyes.

Anna explained, slower, but very forceful, "Yes, Bibb, rejecting my wishes is rejecting me! That is so obvious! Can't you figure that out? Everybody sees it! You anticipate obscure thoughts with your stupid notes, but why can't you understand the obvious ones?"

"Excuse me," said Mr. Franklin, "but I need to redirect the conversation back to the issue. Anna, Mr. Toivo has made public his offer to you. His offer contains no penalties; neither does it specify performance requirements. It does establish kindness as a motivation in every interaction, but does not mandate it. Both parties are free to enter, but neither is free to leave without the permission of the other. The purpose of the agreement is life. Mrs. Gorgon, you want to leave this city and reestablish yourself in a community where you have family. Bibb has the ability, and has offered to do that. In return, Bibb wants his health restored and needs care in the healing process. You, Mrs. Gorgon have demonstrated your willingness and ability to do that. He has placed no new duty on you. He only asks you to finish what you have already started. Bibb, have I summarized this to your satisfaction?"

"Yesss (srpt)."

"Mrs. Gorgon, has my characterization of the agreement matched your understanding?"

"Yes."

"Mrs. Gorgon, what are your objections to the agreement?"

"What about my proposal? What about my rules for conduct?"

At that moment the hotel clerk approached Mr. Franklin with an urgent message. He was summoned to meet somebody in Bibb's room immediately. When asked for a specific, the clerk invited Mr. Franklin to join him after walking away from the table. Bibb took that opportunity to write a response to Anna's question.

The nurse volunteered some information to Anna. "Mrs. Gorgon, because of your kindness, my sisters and I have been Mr. Toivo's constant companion and nursemaids for over a week. During this week we have seen many strange things, but none of them indecent or immoral. Granted, he hasn't had a chance to be bad, but I will say that for an outlaw he certainly is a gentleman. Your grounds for hesitation are based on second-person accounts of his reputation, and granted, those stories may be accurate. Yet my sisters and I know of no such malice in this man, and that is from firsthand knowledge of the most intimate details of his life, wounds, and character."

Bibb looked up and with his eyes pleaded with Miss Dowry. Having no success, he said, "Pleazzz stopppp (srpt). Youuu arrrr morrr graciousss (srpt) thannn accurrattt. I ammm da mannn of da second-hand storriezzz (srpt). Annnnahhh hatezzzz phussshh (srpt). Pleazzz?"

"Bibb, I don't care," responded the nurse. "She needs to know. If she is too scared to go alone with you, can I travel east with you? I can help her keep her commitment to you just like I am now."

"Being scared or not is not the issue, Miss Dowry," replied Anna. "I can tell from your tone that your offer is genuine. Since I have yet to decide to go or not, it is premature to entertain your suggestion."

During that exchange Bibb continued to write on a new piece of paper. Both the women were soon more interested in what he was writing to continue their conversation. As Bibb was finishing, Anna's lawyer returned.

Mr. Franklin took immediate charge. "Bibb, I want to return to the conversation where we left off. Mrs. Gorgon presented you an honest objection. She asked you why you twice rejected her offer, and as she intimated, constituted a rejection of her. What do you have to say in response?"

Bibb folded the paper and handed it to Mr. Franklin which he started to read silently. Bibb indicated through a gesture he could read it aloud, and Mr. Franklin started over.

> *Mr. Franklin, I do not reject Mrs. Gorgon's rules. I reject having rules. Not one of her rules was tiresome to me. Truthfully, I intended for my conduct to go beyond the standards she proposed. Nevertheless, the presence of rules sets the expectation for failure. I want life. I want healing. I want to see the joy in Anna's face when she meets two of the most loving parents a daughter-in-law could ever want. I reject rules because I fail at keeping them. I do not want our relationship be one focused on keeping a contract with each other. I want the goal to be life and life abundantly, and the freedom to be kind beyond the expectations of the other. I do not reject Anna. I find in her a kindred spirit and a person I can learn to trust with my life. I hope she sees in me a man she can trust with hers. Mr. Franklin, Mrs. Gorgon isn't the only person who wants to start life over. Sir, I know what doesn't work: Rules. That is why I have proposed this agreement.*

"How do I know your proposal is sincere, Mr. Toivo?" responded Anna. Are you scheming to take advantage of me?"

"Becauzzz dazzze arrrr your termzzz! Youuu (srpt) propozzzed dhem dah firssstt timmme (srpt) weezzz meet. Remm,m,mem,m,m,ber? Youuu (srpt) prommisssed meee care forrr protectionnn (srpt) to takkke youuu hommme."

"Mrs. Gorgon, I remember that. You did say that. You demanded that Bibb keep the last wishes of a dead man, may your husband rest in peace."

"You have no need to remind me of that, Miss Dowry."

This was new information for Mr. Franklin. "Anna, I have a serious question for you. Were you the first to propose care for this man if he took you to Fort Rice? Yes or no. Don't weasel out of a straight answer. Yes or no?"

"Yes."

"Did Bibb accept your proposal?"

"Yes, he did, Mr. Franklin," said the nurse. "Both the doctor and the sheriff were there too. Mrs. Gorgon even asked a second time, and they both assured her Bibb had accepted it." The nurse's response did not please Anna.

"I dizzz (srpt) accepppt, s-ss-sir."

"So the question is not if you two are going or not, the question is under what terms, yes?"

Bibb nodded his head yes while Anna looked purposely unresponsive.

"Anna," continued Mr. Franklin, "It seems then there are two options for you. I do not find your approaches exclusive. Anna, if you agree to Bibb's terms, then you get your terms also. All your demands are satisfied. And you do not disagree with Bibb's proposed principles. Let me warn you about something. If you reject the principles and insist on your thirty rules, then Bibb has the right to insist on thirty rules for you too. Mrs. Gorgon, I know for a fact the only rules you like are the ones that you make and manipulate to your own advantage. Would you like me to recite some rules that your late husband imposed on you and led to your supposed death? So what is to be, Mrs. Gorgon? Principles or rules? Life or death?"

"S-ss-s-toppp!" Everybody looked at Bibb. "Dooooozzz nottt (srpt) puttt Annnn-ah innn (srpt) a corrrrnerrrr!" It was the first time that they heard the man raise his voice or show such passion. He immediately started to write something down.

> *Mrs. Gorgon must accept my offer in freedom and not by coercion! I do not care if she first proposed and I accepted. She is free to walk away without penalty. If she wants a different escort to Fort Rice or New York or Paris, I do not care. I offer myself freely to her if she will accept me. I will accept this arrangement only if she says she is entering into this agreement freely. Mr. F., please ask Anna the following questions: First, Anna, do you really want to go to Fort Rice? Second, Anna, do you want Bibb to take you? Third, do you understand you are under no obligation to agree to Bibb's proposal? Fourth, do you agree to all the provisions of Bibb's proposal? Lastly, would you commit to make your agreement with Bibb public? Mr. F., if Mrs. Gorgon says yes to the first four questions, and no to the last one, then I am convinced that she was pressured into the agreement. If she cannot sincerely say yes to all five questions, then she is unbound from the commitment she gave me the first time we met. I will go my way, and she is free to go hers. I will hold no animosity against her. I pray she will not hold any against me.*

Mr. Franklin stood up and took the note from Bibb, already read upside down, and with great intention took Mrs. Gorgon's hand. "Mr. Toivo, Anna and I are going outside to discuss this and one other thing. We will return shortly."

Anna did not expect this, but was glad for it. There was much to be discussed. She also had the sealed envelope that she was itching to open. They left the building leaving Bibb and the nurse at the table. Bibb proposed they should get ready to go for lunch. The nurse left first, asking for a five minute head start, while Bibb stayed and took care of the tab.

==0==

"Anna, I have two very important items to discuss with you. The visitor I had moments ago was the judge. Bibb is a person of interest in the murders of seven men in Miles City. Bibb will be questioned when you, if you, arrive there. Our own sheriff received word of this fact this morning. If it is any consolation, the Miles City authorities did not say they were going to arrest him. Does this change your mind about going?"

"Didn't the judge and everybody else already know that? Am I supposed to act surprised to learn that the man is a widow maker?"

"That is not all, Anna. The interest in Bibb has been elevated. The judge told me that everything concerning Bibb, all his writings, related newspaper articles, and statements from those he contacted is to be collected and sent east."

"So? He's just a courier indirectly working for the governor. Is there some sort of investigation going on? What isn't known about the man? He is infamous, and for all the wrong reasons."

"It isn't the Dakota Territory paying for the investigation, but asked for and funded out of Washington. Bibb must be involved in something well over our heads. I am telling you this for three reasons. First, Bibb is unaware of the investigation and must remain so. Second, I need your help in collecting everything he ever wrote to you. I will need to gain the cooperation of your employees too and gain their confidence. Last, I cannot advise you for or against this trip. It takes very little imagination to dream up all sorts of trouble coming into Bibb's immediate future, and to harm you by association. On the bright side, your chance of arriving safely with all your possessions is quite high. Even the most notorious of outlaws put considerable distance between themselves and Bibb. Your safety will depend more on you and your behavior.

"What do you mean by that comment, Mr. Franklin?"

"Anna, outside risks will happen, and Bibb is well able to protect you from them. It's those problems that arise within the buckboard that Bibb can't handle. Keeping your life will depend on you maintaining a cordial relationship with him. Bibb does not entertain nagging or challenges twice."

"What do you mean? I don't nag. I am merely compelled to repeat myself when certain others fail to see and respond to my wisdom."

"Call it what you want, Anna. Bibb is not known to wait for a repeated verse of the same song. He carves out his position on issues very quickly, and usually with his ax. Sober up, woman. If you die on this trip, it will be by his hand and your words. And unless you are willing to help, and I mean physical help instead of mouthing belittling advice, you will have troubles with this man. The man is wounded. If he needs you to quiet the horse while he changes its shoe, that means you actually have to get out of the wagon and touch the horse."

"Of course I would help. I am not a complete ninny! You are accusing me of acting like some sort of princess and expect him to be my servant."

"Do you really mean that, Anna? That's exactly what you advised me to put in that employment contract you wanted me to demand he sign. I can now assume you are no longer standing firm like a royal ninny about your demands? This is a welcome development. It allows me to go to my second issue. Here is Mr. Toivo's protest." Mr. Franklin gave her that latest note from Bibb and she read it.

"Yes to the first three questions, Mr. Franklin. I want to read the proposal again before I agree to the fourth. As for the fifth, I don't know, this is a new question. Let's go somewhere to discuss this."

"No, we owe that man an immediate answer. If you say no, then you can walk away free and clear while I go deliver the news to him. You're scaring me, Mrs. Gorgon. I have always known you as a woman who knew her mind."

"I still know my mind. I just want to read the agreement again. Are you sure there aren't any loopholes in there? Why is he giving me an escape clause without a hefty penalty?"

"Anna, it's a covenant, not a contract! Stop assuming everything is a contract!"

"Give me some time alone, Mr. Franklin."

"Five minutes, Anna."

"I need ten. I want to read what is in this sealed envelope. Bibb said he explained his thoughts in that letter and I intend to read it before I make my decision."

"I am not letting you out of my sight, Mrs. Gorgon. I intend to stand right over there. When you get up, I will return expecting your answers."

"Mr. Franklin, if I need more time, I will take more time. You be patient. Patience is a virtue."

Mr. Franklin held his tongue. Being lectured by Anna on virtues was always a humorous highlight of their relationship. Doubling the absurdity was that she was often serious.

==0==

The previous day Bibb had asked the nurse's sister to borrow some nicer clothes for him for a special occasion. They looked fine hanging in the closet, but now came the moment of truth. It took large efforts from both, but with her help they got Bibb into what he called "special event" clothes.

"Dewww I lookkk (srpt) preee-sent-able, Misszzz Dowrry?"

"Pardon my brutality, but your ugly wounds really distract from the fineness of the clothes. But of course, the clothes look good on you. They seem to fit well. You still haven't mentioned the occasion."

"Weee go to Sunday (srpt) luncech!" replied Bibb with a best smile he could offer. "D'there mighttt beee a (srpt) stoppp before we get d'there. D'that dependzzz (srpt) onnn Annnna-ah."

"Why?"

"I don't knowww Anna'zzz miiinddd. I'mmm (srpt) nodt surrre Anna-ah knowzzz Anna'zzz miiinddd (srpt). I hope sheee willzz anzzzwer (srpt) my fivvve qq-questionzz. Any-zz answerrr izz betterrr d'than (srpt) noo answerrr."

"Only one way to find out, Tommy." Bibb and his nurse walked from the room down to the table, but Anna and Mr. Franklin were not there. She felt bad for the reporter. By his absence he missed another opportunity to come to the wrong conclusion. Tommy looked presentable, but Miss Dowry outshined him badly in her mother's Sunday meeting dress. They looked much more than just friends if somebody didn't know better. His holding her hand going down the stairs could have been wrongly reported too. In reality she was helping him down the staircase, not the other way around. Bibb still suffered spells of the wobbly negotiating steps.

==0==

Anna carefully opened the envelope. Until somebody else claimed an interest in Bibb's notes she could care less what dust bin they ended up in. With outside interest in them she now considered them more of a personal treasure than state's evidence. She opened the letter and started to read:

The reason why...

> *Mrs. Gorgon, I was surprised to wake up earlier this week. I honestly thought I would not live through the ambush your husband had set for me. But I did. I started to think how lucky I was to be alive, and in truth, also wondered how your husband was not. I asked myself over and over and over again the question why I was spared. I do not know how certain things creep into my head, for some thoughts are certainly foreign to my selfish personality. As I laid there in my pain I was also strangely drowning in a foggy half-conscience peace. I felt I was spared for a purpose, or who knows, many purposes. Those details or dreams never crystallized in my mind but just floated out there.*
>
> *The night before I met you I was approached with a more specific thought. Up to that point most of my conscience thoughts were about my life, my pain, my recovery, my job, my future, my, my, my, and more my. Then an upside down thought came to me. How should I say it? Actually it was a right side up thought; it was then when all my thinking was inverted. I then realized my blindness. All my prior thoughts were base, disgusting, self-serving, and woefully in need of discarding. That is when the foreign mist came over me like a flood. "Take your eyes off of yourself! Your time is no longer your own. The mortgage on your life has come due." I thought about that foggy notion all night long.*
>
> *The following day when you entered my room I felt helpless and wondered if you were seeking revenge. You certainly could be packing, and you certainly had the right to kill me for your husband's death. Your intentions couldn't be discerned since your face was veiled. Despite your condescension I listened to your offer, and*

108

I agreed. My concurrence was not because you made such a good offer, nor was I desperate for your contribution. Neither was it about what I could give to you. It was because of the message in the mist.

I later asked my nurse if you hated me. I am still not sure if you hate me or not. Regardless, your feelings no longer matter. And even if a contrary mist whispers in my ear, that doesn't matter either. I agreed that evening, and I am bound by my word. Never again will I cheat a widow.

About the other... Anna, if you don't give me rules I won't break them. Show me your respect, and I am good for another twenty miles.

Regardless of your decision, I remain grateful for your current investment in my care. You did not have to do that, but you did. Your current kindness gives me great hope that we will be successful in achieving our goals. Your spunk guarantees an interesting trip.

–Tommy Toivo

Anna put down the note and started to think. She noticed Mr. Franklin walking towards her, and she waved him off. Her initial impression was that Mr. Toivo was trying to trick her into something with his sugar words. Not caring for her feelings certainly wasn't sweet, nor did his words contain veiled condescension. She read the letter again. The first time through she was looking for insults. This time through she looked for substance, and the semi-substance that bothered her most was the mist. She had heard a similar eerie message about a selfish upside-down life in the boudoir.

Mr. Franklin had waited enough. He approached and asked, "What did the letter say, Anna?"

"It was insulting and quite personal."

"Can I read it?"

"Not now, Mr. Franklin. Not now."

"That leaves one piece of business then, Anna. I need five answers from you, and I want to know what you are going to reply before we go back in there. You said yes to the first three questions. What about the last two questions?"

"I have decided to agree to the fourth question. You may have thought that was the more difficult one, but the fifth one puzzles me why he would ask. You will have to wait, Mr. Franklin. I am ready to return. Please escort me back inside."

==0==

Bibb and Miss Dowry stood up when Anna and Mr. Franklin entered the room. The waitress arrived with more coffee, but Mr. Franklin said that the meeting was just about over. "Mr. Toivo, Mrs. Gorgon is prepared to answer your questions." All sat down.

There was some silence, with the expectation Bibb would lead. He did. "Pwweeazzzz, Annn-ah."

"Mr. Toivo, I find your offer attractive. I agree to the first four questions."

"Thwee. Whatzz aboudttt Thwree (srpt)? Dooo yoooou agreeee freeeeleee?"

"Yes, Mr. Toivo. I will enter this agreement with you. I enter it freely without compulsion or force. I am agreeing because I want to do it. I hope you are doing it because you want to. Are you also entering this agreement freely, Mr. Toivo, or are you running from the law? Are you a coward wanting to hide behind my skirts?"

Bibb did not take the bait. He wrote a quick note down for her. *"You are well aware that I run towards the law, not from it, and besides, a gopher couldn't find room enough to hide behind your skirt. You should eat more."* Bibb slipped her the note.

"I will pretend not to be insulted, Mr. Toivo. You certainly are one not to talk about needing some extra beef on you." The others could only imagine what was written.

"Fourrr? Youuu agreeee (srpt)? Travelll myyy wayyy? Healll yourrr wayyy (srpt)?"

"Yes, Mr. Toivo, as well as the preceding provisions in that agreement. I will hold you true to your boast that you will exceed my expectations."

"Anddd youuu (srpt), mine?"

Anna did not expect that rebuttal. She thought for a while and replied. "Yes, you will be the trail boss. But I warn you, you will not like my standards on keeping clean or how I may decide how you are to be healed up."

"Fivvvve (srpt). Whatzzz yourrr answerrr?"

"Why do you want it public?" asked Anna.

"You knowzzz."

"What do 'I knowzzzz,' Mr. Toivo?" spit back Anna in a mocking contemptuous tone.

Bibb didn't reply. He sat waiting, purposely putting down his quill and sitting back in his chair.

"What do I know, Mr. Toivo?"

"Youuu arrre a smarzttz womannn (srpt). You knowzzz."

Anna was irritated. "I know why! You think I'm a floozy! Oh, you knew my husband well! You are thinking that unless I agree in public, I won't care about the shame of walking out on you if I have the whim to run. Well, Mr. Toivo, the same can be said about you! When have you ever kept your promises? Your record is to kill the people you have spats with! And where is your shame? Notched on your hatchet? You seem to confuse shame with pride, don't you Mr. Toivo!"

He wrote down an answer. *"You proved me right. You are a smart woman. Now answer my fifth question."* He slipped her the paper, she read it, and with extreme malice tore it into small pieces, throwing the remains into the cuspidor.

"Wellllll (srpt)?" asked Tommy, being entertained long enough watching the woman boil in her own juices. He started to write again. *"Anna, I am not good at keeping my promises, but when my word becomes part of the public record I remain true to it. This is for me... This is for you... This is for this town... This is for us... This may be for more than all of that combined. I do know one thing. I am not the only one around here that needs healing."* He handed her the paper.

Anna studied the note. She was much calmer now. She read it twice, and tripped on the word *us* both times. She longed to be part of an *us*. That was the deepest reason why she wanted to leave. She looked at Mr. Franklin, the nurse, and then Bibb. "Yes is my answer, Mr. Toivo. I am not ashamed of my decision. Is that public enough?"

"Yeszz is my anssswerr (srpt) too for d'the five questionszz (srpt)." Bibb had carefully avoided answering her question, but responded by purposely stating his common commitment.

Miss Dowry, relieved from the tension, was glad to make the announcement. "The reason Bibb dressed up is because he wants to take you all out to dinner. He said he wanted to try some food with some substance in it today! Please agree! I so want to go. This is so exciting!"

All agreed and Bibb was the first out the door. Mr. Franklin hadn't noticed it until now, but once Bibb stood up he noticed that in their absence he had gone upstairs and put on his gun belt. Maybe Anna had noticed that too. That question was for later. Anna was probably packing too. He wouldn't fault her if she was. That is what widow women named Anna do.

Bibb dismissed the butler who was still waiting to take Mrs. Gorgon and the lawyer home. There was room for only four and Bibb motioned that he would drive. He said he knew exactly where he wanted to go to celebrate. The four of them loaded into the carriage and they were on their way.

==0==

"Mr. Toivo, which restaurant are you thinking of going to?"

"D'the Sssilverrr Nail (srpt)."

"We passed it, Bibb," replied the nurse.

"I-zzz know-zzz (srpt) d'that..." as he kept driving.

"Bibb, where are we going?" asked Anna.

"I-zz d'the trail boss (srpt). Trussttt me-zz." It got quiet and nobody dared question him again. Anna wondered if he had just been toying with her and her emotions all morning. He sounded so trustworthy, and now he was acting strange, like a lying, thieving, murdering outlaw. Had he won, and now she wondered if he was taking advantage of her for some sick enjoyment. "Men!!" she thought, "They are disease infested rats! No! They're worse than that!"

As they went further down the street they saw many people walking down the avenue in the opposite direction they were heading. Bibb snapped the reins and the horses picked up their pace, and that made the passengers even more nervous. Bibb was almost reckless, and nobody could guess why he was in a hurry. And the Silver Nail was blocks behind them. Eventually Bibb pulled the carriage within five feet of the main door of one of the town's churches. Services had just let out and the parson was greeting the remaining parishioners.

"What is this about, Bibb?" demanded Anna. "This is where my husband was buried. This isn't funny. I insulted the preacher and his wife and I want to leave now instead of facing them."

"Number Five. Public-zzz! If (srpt) you say-zz yes in here, I know you-zz (srpt) meant-dt yes-zz."

She looked at him with piercing eyes and Bibb returned the stare. The spectacle was not missed by anybody, and Anna started to feel the eyes of everybody on her. Bibb reached to help her out of the carriage. She refused.

Bibb looked at her again. "Us. For-zz us."

For many reasons her countenance changed, but later she told herself it was the simple power of a two letter word earnestly said. She reached out her hand and Bibb held hers to help her balance. The strangest response came over him. The man was literally shaking in his boots. "What is with him?" she said to herself.

Once out of the carriage Bibb quickly let go, pointing her kindly to start a conversation with the preacher. Anna hesitated, so Bibb went on ahead, gave an envelope to the preacher, and returned to Anna. Mr. Franklin and Miss Dowry were now out of the wagon too, along with a small crowd from the last to leave the church that now didn't want to leave.

The preacher read the first paragraph and scanned the rest of the note. He motioned for the party to come inside, along with his wife and anybody else that wanted to. Anna was very confused but she was now part of the school of fish swimming into the sanctuary forcing her to float in with the tide. The preacher motioned for Mr. Franklin to come up to the front with Bibb. Mr. Franklin asked to see the letter, quickly scanned it, and gave it back to the preacher.

The preacher turned his attention to the others. "Miss Dowry, please perform the honor of escorting the Widow Gorgon up the aisle to stand before me here at the altar."

The pieces were coming together for Anna, and she was stuck. It was Mr. Franklin that spoke out, prophetically, "Anna, if you don't get up here, there is a good chance two people here won't live to the end of the day. Miss Dowry, bring her up here, and don't take no for an answer. Mrs. Gorgon made a promise earlier, and she now has a chance to keep it."

Anna, noticing all the eyes on her, had to respond. She had few choices for many reasons, and decided to turn the table on Bibb. He said she was smart, and she decided she was going to throw that man for a loop.

Anna dug her fingernails deep into the wrist of the nurse and proceeded to drag her up the aisle. The nurse responded in a high squeaky scared sound, "Let go, Mrs. Gorgon! Mr. Franklin, Mr. Franklin, This hurts! Let go… Let go…"

"You're coming up there with me, so enjoy it while it lasts, dear-ee," replied Anna doubling the grip on her wrist with both hands. They proceeded to the front by the altar where Bibb, Mr. Franklin, and the preacher were waiting, eyes wide open. "Now what did you want? I'm here now."

"I would like you to take this serious, Mrs. Gorgon," replied the preacher.

Anna looked at him and replied, "I am serious, sir, more serious than you have ever seen me." Anna turned around to the handful of people that were watching the spectacle. "Folks, you know who I am, and certainly by now you know the man with the hole in his head is Bibb. Before you all jump to conclusions and start all sorts of rumors, I want you to know I am doing this on my own free will. I am doing it because I want to do it. I asked Bibb to take me to Fort Rice, and he said he would. I said I would take care of him and get him to a doctor in Bismarck, and he said he would trust me. Bibb brought me here because he wanted to make this agreement public. He is the trail boss, and if that means walking over my husband's grave, well so be it." She turned to the preacher and continued, "Do your best magic, Priest. You ain't going to see me in here again."

"I would start by saying 'Dearly beloved' but neither of you fit that description. What is written on this paper will suffice; in fact it is quite good. Friends, you are here today to witness a unique event. The Widow Gorgon and Tommy Toivo have decided to enter into a covenant with each other, and chose this place to seal their commitment. They honor us by their choice, and we need to honor them in their willingness to submit to the authority of the church." A holy hush came over all attending; a complete stillness.

"Tommy Toivo, are you entering this covenant freely, without guile, and with a genuine concern for Anna Gorgon?"

"Yes-zzz."

"Anna Gorgon, are you entering this covenant freely, without guile, and with a genuine concern for Tommy Toivo?"

"I am."

"Tommy, will you trust Anna with your life in all matters of health until you are fully recovered and you release her from her fulfilled promise?"

"I will-zz (srpt)."

"Anna, will you trust Tommy with your life in all matters of travel until you arrive at your destination and you release him from his fulfilled promise?"

"I will."

"Tommy, will you in all your actions and conversations with Anna strive to make every word be filled with kindness and hold her in even higher esteem than you have for yourself?"

"I willlll (srpt)."

"Anna, will you in all your actions and conversations with Tommy strive to make every word be filled with kindness and hold him in even higher esteem than you have for yourself?"

Anna did not answer.

"Anna, will you?" asked the preacher again.

Anna reached over and took Tommy's hand, which he was not expecting. As she anticipated, Tommy started to shake all over. "Look at me, Tommy!" Tommy did and she waited until their eyes locked. "The man asked me if I would respect you and make all my words towards you kind. I don't know if I can all the time, but I'm sure going to try. With every ounce of my being I am going to outdo you in kindness if it kills me first or kills you second. Did you hear me, Bibb? And another thing: Touch me wrong, boy, and I will kill you in your sleep with your own ax. Treat me right, and your life will make heaven look like second place. Do you understand? Do you feel the same way?"

The preacher interrupted. "Anna, a simple 'I do' will work. Do you?"

"Yes, I do, and so does he."

"Tommy can speak for himself, Anna. Be kind."

"I s-sswear by the G-GGoddd of Anna'zzz motherrr (srpt) that I will be tr-r-rue (srpt), kind-d-d (srpt), rez-spectful, and committed-dd (srpt). I cannn't call on-zz (srpt) no higherrr authorit-t-ty."

"Who?" asked Anna.

"What-dt? Anna (srpt), can-zz you let-zz go (srpt) of my hann-ddd?"

"Whose mother? Tell me! Tell me now!"

Over the continuing bickering the preacher pronounced, "Friends, we have heard their public promise to each other, and in the sight of God they have committed themselves to kindness. As God's church we invite the All Loving to prove himself as the Almighty to help these two souls to honor and keep their confession! Tommy, do you have a sign as your pledge and seal of your covenant with Anna Gorgon?"

Tommy was stuck. He hadn't thought about that and now he was standing exposed in front of everybody. He looked at Mr. Franklin and found no help; maybe by some miracle he might have some spare jewelry. With his free hand Tommy pulled out a sizable knife from out of nowhere. He nicked his arm and spoke to Anna. "I h-have nothin' (srpt) but my-yy ownnn b-blood-d (srpt) to-to-too pp-p-ledge. It-t is-zzz my lif-fffe (srpt). May it-t commm-fort-tt you-you-yourrr mind-dd (srpt) an'-an' yourrr heart-dtt (srpt)." Bibb put away his knife, dabbed his blood onto his thumb from the wound, and marked in deep red the skin on Anna's forehead and then well below her neck. She couldn't breathe; frozen in awe, and in shock over his audacity to touch her. Did he dare to touch her wrong so soon after her threat?

"Anna, do you have a sign?" asked the preacher.

Anna's quick wit thawed her from her icy state of countenance. "Oh, yes I do, and one he will long remember!" she replied. She turned to Tommy and went close as to whisper something in his good ear. "Tommy, this is how close I will stay by you. I am who I am, and by this sign you will remember my pledge. Be comforted with this." Before he could respond, Anna bit him hard on the ear. Bibb's reaction was reflexive, quick, but immediately put back under control. Anna continued, "You said earlier that you were not your own man anymore. Tommy, I am laying claim to my piece of the pie. That one good ear of yours is yours no more. It is now mine and only mine until we get to Fort Rice. If I want to chew on it, it's mine to chew. Buck up, big boy. We're going for a ride."

The preacher thought these pledges unique, but so was this whole ceremony. At first he was unsure if he should participate, but now he was glad to be honored in being used. It was just a week prior this woman had been cold and bitter with an eye for revenge. He felt he witnessed a miracle anytime somebody in Deadwood had a soul movement towards a virtuous life. He was encouraged in his own calling, even if he had nothing to do the apparent change in the widow's heart.

Caught up in the personal excitement to witness these two – the black widow and the outlaw –standing before him pledging mutual kindness overwhelmed him. They couldn't pledge their love… neither of them had any. Kindness would have to do. He had no further script, and did what came naturally to him. "Having witnessed your pledges to each other at the altar of Almighty God, and by the authority vested in me by the territory, I ratify this covenant you have freely made. I declare you wed to each other in God's love and your kindness. You may kiss your bride."

Bibb's eyes never had opened so wide! This is not what he had planned. All he could exclaim was "W-Wh-Wha-Whatttt?"

"Kiss her while you can!" came unsolicited advice from a man somewhere on the right.

"Letz go of my hann-ddd, pleazzzze (srpt)?"

"No, No, No!" exclaimed the preacher. "I'm so sorry. She is not your bride. That slipped out by accident."

"There're no accidents at the altar, kiss her quick!" came a new unsolicited remark from the left.

A woman spoke loudly, "She really needs one, that frozen-hearted embarrassment to women!"

"Stop it!" The preacher lifted up his hands to regained control over the event. "My misstatement started this confusion, yes, but we must not stay in disorder. This is a solemn event that deserves reverence. I want to clarify that this is not a formal nuptial. It is still a covenant and most precious in the sight of God. Honor it. I command all of you in the name of the Lord to honor it!"

The preacher took more time to restore the dignity and quiet, and then continued. "And that command applies especially for you two, Anna and Tommy. God will not let you escape your responsibilities now. By invoking His help in His house at His altar, His reputation is now on the line. He will sic all of heaven's hounds on you quicker than lightning if you either of you even think of cheating. You three are bound, like it or not. You can't hide from a Ghost. Now go in kindness, respect, and peace."

Anna had no intention of letting go of Tommy's hand, but increased her grip. They turned to go and the several that witnessed the event started to applaud. Bibb's face flushed with embarrassment rendering him speechless. Anna thanked those that witnessed the ceremony and then took the frozen man attached to her hand towards, and then out the door.

After the newly-bounds left for the carriage, Miss Dowry asked the preacher if his wife and he could join them for lunch. "That is the least we can do for officiating this event."

The preacher acknowledged the comment and then turned to Anna's lawyer. "Mr. Franklin, I am curious. What did you mean that two of us might live through this?"

"Do not fret, sir. If those two didn't have an external constraint placed on them, they would kill or be killed. I am astounded Bibb not only thought of this ceremony but carried it out."

"This wasn't your idea?"

"No, it was entirely Tommy's. It is a mystery from which crevice of his tangled mind these thoughts came from. There's already a controversy whether Bibb is married or not. The paper reported it both ways. Something in his past may have triggered it."

"I don't think so," replied the preacher. "If he had thought of marriage he would have had a ring or something. Excuse my bias grounded in my profession, but I think providence is heavily involved here. When God has something personally important to Him to be accomplished He delights in taking the most unlikely among us and crushes them. He then takes the broken pieces and boxes them up to do His will. Bibb is about as crushed as a man can be, and Anna is boxed tightly. The freedoms that her wealth brought her are going to be dearly missed. For the first time in her life she is going to taste dependence. Humiliation or humility will be her near term fate. The result will be the same. That woman is bound for bruises in both body and spirit. Worse than death, Bibb might discover life; a new life after new birth. I read the papers. The darker the heart, the brighter the light appears. That boy opened the latch of heaven, and God is about to blow his doors off their hinges."

"You seem to be pretty sure of yourself, Preacher."

"I am speaking my prayer, Mr. Franklin. Faith often needs to be spoken to become real. God is certainly able to do whatever He wants with those two. I voiced my hope, and He heard my desire for them. Anything less will be tragic, but if they fail, it won't hurt God in the least. I pray He will use those two to maximize His glory and show His existence to doubters, like you, Mr. Franklin."

"What makes you think I am a doubter, Parson?"

"Your actions betray you, sir, but there is no shame in doubting. You are in good company. I shall visit you after these two have cleared town. For now, let us enjoy the moment. And you, Miss Dowry, did you expect the events of today?"

"I have never been so close to being a real Maid of Honor in my whole life. I realized that when we came forward. That was awesome."

"Nor I so close to becoming the Father of the Bride," replied Mr. Franklin. I feel obligated to pay for the almost-wedding reception. Let's join those two bumblebees for lunch together. My wife will never believe me. I can't wait to embellish this story to her. I can tell her the truth later."

"That's what doubters do! Let's go, friend."

Monday, October 3, 1887

I visited Mr. Toivo this morning to restate my concerns about the trip. My lawyer voiced my desires (Mr. Franklin warned me not call them rules) concerning how he will conduct himself as we travel. Bibb had the audacity to state similar concerns about me maintaining my behavior on the trek! Toivo irritated me to no end when he slurped "No matter what you do, Anna, I am keeping my vow." The prideful idiot is too naïve to know he makes me feel dirty when he uses his little religious words so innocently. There is nothing innocent about that scoundrel! It is all a lie! When I complained he replied in his spittled words, "Then I will show you, not tell you." After that insult that lawless creature had the nerve to give me a packing list with a weight limit! Mr. Franklin kept me from daring that dinky punk of a boy to put me and my luggage on a scale!

Mr. Franklin later presented to me a very generous parting gratuities plan for my employees. After I signed the legacy package he gave a final suggestion which I outright rejected. He had the nerve to recommend I should pay the preacher for his services! "You may kiss your bride!" That preacher man almost got kicked in his own kisser. My heart hurts from overwork today.

==0==

WHEN BIBB WENT to Bes's diner for breakfast a woman joined him at his table within seconds of his arrival. "Ma'am-zz, I don't believe (srpt) we have been introduced. My-zz name is Bibb (srpt), and I enjoy-zz eatin' alone (srpt). What did you-zz say your name (srpt) is-zz, and why are you-zz (srpt) at my table?"

"My boss said it has never been proved that you have killed a woman. That doesn't mean you haven't, it just hasn't been reported. I decided I would risk having this conversation as long as you don't invite me out into the street later. That wouldn't be healthy, so said my editor. I work for the newspaper as the social reporter."

"When you sat-zz down (srpt) I was-zz merely irritated. You-zz have exceeded d'that-zz now (srpt). State your-zz business."

"Yesterday you and Mrs. Gorgon came to an agreement of a peculiar kind. I would like to ask you some questions about that. I also would like to know your future plans."

"About-zz me killing women (srpt) or-zz you leaving my table? Have you-zz asked Anna (srpt)? She's-zz a good talker."

She leaned into the table towards Bibb with eyes flushed with excitement. "But you're a good writer, and you answered some of my colleague's questions. We have a list of thirty-eight more questions we would like you to answer. Pick which ones you like. I would be grateful if you just answered one. I would be overjoyed if you answered more. I know how you feel about reporters and I will not be pushy." She took from her purse an envelope with Bibb's name written on the outside and placed it on top of his silverware. "I know it hurts you to talk, and talking with pushy women hurts even more. I will frustrate you no longer, but will hope to see you here at this same time tomorrow. If not then, maybe the day after." Her smile could not be contained; this conversation had migrated past business into pure pleasure. She was fully alive responding to her life's calling.

Bibb took the envelope but did not open it, but placed it inside his hat. "Ma'am, you-zz might be-zz (srpt) a woman I-zz could oblige. I am-zz (srpt) not promising to-zz respond."

She reached her hand out across the table touching his forearm. "Thank you. I hope you do."

"You-zz did not say your name (srpt)."

"You're right. I didn't. Call me Bee. That is both ironic and poetic. You once called my colleague a fly buzzing around your soup. Bugs of a feather stick together!"

"D'that's birds."

"Bugs too, Mr. Bibb." She smiled as she saw something twinkle in his eyes. Gazing for just a second longer she felt that she was involuntarily reciprocating his compliment in her eyes. She left the table a happy bug.

==0==

The happiest man in town was the Gorgon estate's accountant. He successfully closed out the books for the month and quarter. He knew Mrs. Gorgon would certainly be pleased with the performance of her investments. She can leave Deadwood with great financial security.

The bookkeeper's future was just as bright. It would take over a year to liquidate the estate, and with it, handsome commissions. He was dreaming of a house he could buy if all went well. Better yet was the prospect that a fair man, Mr. Franklin, would be her proxy. Anna had a more demanding disposition, to understate the obvious. In a week she would be gone. The delicious rumor circulating through town was that the Black Widow was planning her second honeymoon. The unspoken subtext was that those spiders don't keep mates, they slay them.

==0==

A note was waiting at the lobby desk when Bibb returned from breakfast. The sheriff wrote him asking to stop by the office. Bibb's default answer was to stay away from any building with a jail in it.

Bibb had to tell himself to relax. He decided to ask the desk clerk to arrange a time they could visit over coffee at the Red Buffalo. Probably the sheriff only had documents to take to Miles City or Bismarck. If he was to be arrested, that would have been done already. He knew he was a marked man. It wasn't like he could hide in this town.

Bibb felt the pain of getting up from his sickbed too soon after the injury. He hurt all over; much more than in previous days. This would be a good time to write. It would be even a better time to sleep and would tell his doctor so when he visited his room later that morning.

==0==

The doctor came to examine Bibb once again just before lunch. With him were the Widow Gorgon and Mr. Franklin. Mr. Franklin, and not Anna spoke (because she had been previously asked not to add her commentary to anything), saying they were interested in seeing how his recovery was progressing. The doctor said there had been significant progress above the neck, but below the neck was a mess.

Mr. Franklin surprised them all by asking if he could have some of Bibb's attention concerning a legal matter. Anna was the most attentive to the new news. "Bibb, I have taken the liberty of drafting a Last Will and Testament for you. It is the least I could do for you considering the risky trip you are about to take. It is not complicated. It simply states that in case of your demise, everything you own at the time of your death will be given to a Mrs. Anna Toivo of Fort Rice. I recall that is what you said Humbird's legal name is."

"What's in it for you, sir (srpt)? I have learned to-zz be weary of lawyers bearing free services. D'that's how my brother got hung (srpt), and me convicted in-zz Fort Rice."

"That is a fair question. I will be the executor of your estate. My primary advice for you is to stay alive, but if you don't I will handle settling your property properly. I am allowed a small fee paid out of the estate for these services. It is limited to five percent of your net worth at death. Once you go to Fort Rice you can write a different will which will supersede this one. I need you to sign and since the doctor and Anna are here, they can be witnesses of your signature."

"Let me read it first (srpt)." It was as simple as Mr. Franklin claimed it was. There was no legal language that Bibb did not understand and the simple declaration that Humbird would get everything suited Bibb just fine. Bibb signed it first, followed by the doctor, but Anna took the one page document and read it for herself before she signed as a witness.

"Bibb," said Mr. Franklin, "I will register this document at the court today for safe keeping. There is no reason to take it with you on your trip to Fort Rice."

Bibb later asked the doctor if he could have something for the itch. The doctor asked him if he was in pain too, and Bibb replied yes. In response, the doctor told Bibb what he needed was some sleep. He instructed the nurse to stuff the man with egg sandwiches for lunch. "That will induce an afternoon nap better than anything else I know." What the doctor did not want to do was to give Bibb any additional medications. The boy needed weaning from the previous week's chemical cocktails.

==0==

Anna spent lunch and most of the afternoon with her lawyer. He discussed at length a plan to liquidate her assets, suggested a bank draft amount to take east with her, cash, and then gratuities for those who served her and her late husband faithfully. She initially thought the recommendations were too generous. Mr. Franklin held firm, saying that her growth in net worth that month along with a new find of ore in one of her mines more than covered the cost. She eventually agreed and instructed him to get with her accountant and set the plan in motion.

"There is another issue, Anna."

"What is that? Are you asking for something for yourself too?"

"Anna, that would be very unprofessional, but since you brought it up, no."

"Then what is it? Do you want me to make a will in case Bibb kills me on the way to Bismarck?"

"That was already on my list of things to do before you leave in light of yesterday's ceremony. You read and witnessed the will my wife and I prepared for Tommy. Anna, seriously, I do more work for you than just legal stuff. I gladly do these courtesies for you because you're still grieving the loss of your husband."

"Does it show?"

"No. But I need you and you need me. My fees for liquidating your estate will be adequate to cover my costs. But no, that is not the issue. What I want to convey is that I'm still grateful, and will remain to be so. You chose not press the errant death certificate issue with the court and I thank you. You could have ruined me, but you chose to trust me instead. I need no gratuity on top of my fee. I am more thankful I still have your confidence. That means more to me than any bonus."

"You are welcome, and I acknowledge the same. I have few friends in this town, a fact that I am becoming more aware of each day. Your suggestion of gifts may clear a worsening reputation."

"Technically you are providing this legacy to honor your best employees. Yes, it will help your reputation, but I know you didn't mean to say that. You were obviously thinking of others first and you doubtlessly assumed I sensed your unstated primary intent."

"You certainly are a sly one, Mr. Franklin."

"And you too, Mrs. Gorgon, as well as being a quick learner." He paused to gain her full attention. "I sadly have another bitter pill for you. Anna, it will not be easy to swallow."

"And what is that, Mr. Franklin. Have I made a second class fashion faux pas that you need to point out? Don't buttons go well with bows?"

"No, that is not it." He stood up. "What did you think of yesterday's ceremony at the altar?"

"I made the best of it, Mr. Franklin. Where are you taking this conversation? Are you reading more into that drama than what was there? I am quite sure you enjoyed it."

"Who wouldn't, Anna? That was a beautiful ceremony." His words had a tremble in them.

"Yeah... and I bet you were holding back your tears, Daddy. Hah! I was ambushed."

"And so was I, so don't you dare counter with any suggestion that I was party to a conspiracy. It was pretty obvious that Miss Dowry was surprised too. I really have to hand it to Bibb. He has one-upped you at every turn. Don't let his looks deceive you. What he lacks in looks he has in savvy."

"And are you implying anything like that, or a dark opposite of that trait in me Mr. Franklin?"

"Anna, let me tell you plain. You possess the most dangerous of all combinations. You have the looks, money, brains, and every once in a while, a mean streak. Not only that, you have a mystery wrapped around you – you have your own used tombstone and reputation as a ghost. Most women only get dealt one of those traits, and you got them all. Adding to that you now the kernel of a notorious legend. Mark my words; you will become famous or infamous. You have no other options, but you do have the choice between the two. I hope for famous."

"So, what is your point, Mr. Franklin? You are beating around the bush. Do you think I was ambushed?"

"Anna, that would certainly be poetic given Bibb's history with those named Gorgon, but Bibb did warn you more than once and you still didn't see it coming. No, the person that was ambushed was the preacher, and you need to compensate him. It is appropriate that presiding officials be paid well for their services."

"Competent ones, maybe!" burst out Anna, now standing engulfed in anger. "That man pronounced me and Tommy man and wife." The suggestion lit her eyes on fire with disgust.

Mr. Franklin purposely slowed down his diction. "That is because it just might be true."

"WHAT?" She was becoming panicked at the revelation; her chin fell as if to the floor.

Mr. Franklin pulled out an official looking envelope that had a seal from the courthouse on it. "I have a certificate here I want to show you, Anna. The preacher brought it by this morning. Your vows have been ratified and entered into the court record. It's official, and not easily undone."

"I don't want to hear it! I don't want to see it! I don't want to feel, taste, smell, or sense it! Fix it, Mr. Franklin! You said it yourself! Dead people can't marry! Undo this now!" she shrieked.

"You're right, almost. This may be a first. Yes, dead people can't marry living people, but there is no law against two dead people, the Ghost of Deadwood Gulch and the Ghost of Fort Rice, from matrimony. Anna Marie Gorgon, what went around has come around. You have been ambushed. If this wasn't so serious it might be poetically humorous. I know many in Deadwood would think so."

"This nor you are funny, Mr. Franklin! Fix it today! Fix it, or I will take my business elsewhere!"

"This is a strange time to threaten me, Anna. I am someone you said you trusted, and especially when none of this was my doing. Please calm down for a second and think this through."

"What is to think about? This has to be nullified!"

"On what grounds? Infidelity? Adultery? Unfaithfulness? Has he beaten you, or worse, have you beaten him? He will want severance, and that would be half your estate according to territory law. No, I am wrong about that. He would get it all. Anna, tell me true. What is your complaint about this court document?"

"I was tricked! I haven't been widowed two weeks yet. I haven't had time to properly grieve."

"You mean like spitting on his grave? I saw you do that. Anna, think clearly now. Many relationships start without partners loving each other. Look at all the arranged marriages, like Xue's. Was she happy? She certainly was."

"What part of 'fix it' do you not understand, Mr. Franklin?"

"Anna, sit down. Breathe deep." Mr. Franklin sat down first. "Are you going to let Tommy stay alone in the hotel every night between now and when you depart together? You have that big house, and why not bring him home? The man has done you no wrong, well, other than murder your husband. Remember, you did agree to the covenant."

"Mr. Franklin, why are you torturing me?"

"Because you desperately need it, and you are too old for a dad to take you over his knee and paddle your back side for your selfish outlook on life. Learn to see people as people, not pawns!"

"You have no right to talk to me like that! I bet you would enjoy turning me over. You are a sick man, Mr. Franklin!"

"You called me Daddy just five minutes ago. It must be quite a burden for you to bear – being the daughter of a sick deranged father. But you tried to divert the conversation, and you failed. Back to reality, Anna. What is your difficulty with this certified document?"

"That huckster tricked me!"

"Anna, you were the aggressor yesterday, and you boasted publically you did it under your own free will without coercion or threat. That man almost fell apart when you grabbed his hand. He shed his blood for you. Actually twice… the second time was when you bit him! Doesn't that count for anything, Anna? Where is your heart?"

"Where it needs to be, Mr. Franklin. I keep it safe, and I will keep it safe, where no man can ever trample on it again!"

"I am glad to hear that, Anna."

"What?" snipped Anna, now completely enveloped in anger.

"Your road with Bibb will be thorny enough without romance complicating things. I am glad to hear of your commitment to chastity."

"You are so out of line, Mr. Franklin! This is none of your business."

He stood, pointing his finger at her. "No, I am not out of line. You have made most of your life my business, Anna. One thing is for sure – I am one of the only people alive that will tell you what you need to hear!" Mr. Franklin seldom raised his voice, but it slipped out this time. "Anna, you must avoid the mistakes of your foolish, foolish past. You must divest yourself of your vanity and pride if you have any hope of starting your life afresh. I want you to succeed. In my most fervent prayers I ask that you will have the wisdom to succeed, and it is well within your grasp! Do not let go of this opportunity! Do not revert to your horrid past. Rise above it! Do it for God's sake if you can't do it for yourself. Recognize that there is more to this bizarre set of events than bad luck, good luck, or any luck at all. Life is more than just you and you scratching your own itches. There is more at stake than your happiness! Anna Marie Gorgon, don't you dare disappointment me!"

"Yes, Father, Dearest!" she said with a deeply mean and sarcastic tone. She got up, walked out, slamming the door behind her.

Mr. Franklin still smarted from being called a doubter by the preacher the day prior. "That will never happen again," he said to himself after she left. "I will return to my first love. If I am wrong, may He forgive me for what this daddy dearest is about to do."

==0==

Late that afternoon the sheriff came to visit Tommy in his hotel room. After dismissing the nurse, the sheriff notified Bibb that he just received a letter from Miles City about a rash of murders the day after he had left for Deadwood.

"I didn't do-zz it, Sheriff. Why did you-zz come (srpt) over here-zz?"

"Bibb, I know somebody heading to Miles City tomorrow. I am suggesting that you write the sheriff a note to be delivered to him. Tell him what you did and didn't do, and explain why it took you so long to get to Deadwood."

"I was-zz hurt (srpt)! D'that ain't-zz hard to-zz ex-x-s'plain!"

"Don't tell me, tell the sheriff. He is prone to believe you if you come clean with him."

"Come-zz clean? I hadn't heard-zz d'that phrase for-zz (srpt) awhile." Bibb had a peace come over him concerning the request. "Sheriff, I-zz will have-zz something (srpt) ready in d'the morning-zz."

==0==

"Ruined by a man again! I hate them! I HATE them! I HATE THEM!" Anna was beside herself as she thrashed in misery upon her bed.

Anna could not get over the turn of events, and cried with no hope of sleep this night. Riches to rags, and now married to the ugliest man in the Americas. She had a house, but now she was homeless. She had wealth, but not anymore. How was she to recover her losses? How did that ugly man dupe her so shamelessly? Why didn't Mr. Franklin stop it? "Ruined! Ruined! I hate men! If that Bibb mysteriously died I would get it all back! Oh... this can't be! I would be hung for sure by that dumb ox they call a sheriff. If he didn't get me, God would. Oh... this is so maddening! Bibb put me in a box! He's controlling me! This is so wrong!"

When the eyes became dry from having no more tears left in her to be shed, depression came over Anna like a heavy blanket. More than anything tonight she wanted her mother, but despaired that she had passed years ago. Anna longed to find a mother's love in Fort Rice. If that woman could understand her son, she could understand her daughter-in-law too. There was hope in this darkest of nights. "I will have to ride this agreement out to the end with my dear Mr. Double-ugly."

Tuesday, October 4, 1887

Some friends I have! Many are trying to tell me to stay put. They say I'm loved (more than my money) and how I set fashion trends in Deadwood. They like me most, I suspect, because "At least my husband isn't as bad as Anna's husband was!" Why do people like to compare themselves to others of lesser character? I guess for the same reason I do.

Mr. Franklin is a hateful man and last evening he set me up for abject humiliation. I talked to the preacher about annulling my marriage first thing this morning. He was confused, saying marriage is until death, and that my departed husband definitely qualified. After explaining, he better understood my request. He said he did not marry Bibb and I, but only certified a sacred covenant. He sternly warned me not to entertain breaking the promise. He said the territory can only jail me and society can but shun me, but God can take His hand of protection away and let the devil have his due for any unfaithfulness. He turned cruel towards me by arrogantly saying that if I didn't believe him that I should ask my husband if that was true or not.

I have yet to devise a worthy response to Mr. Franklin's deceitfulness. Did he deceive me or did I jump to a hasty conclusion? I accused that lawyer of being sly, and I fear my intuition is only half right. He warned me to keep my suspicions to myself lest he grow weary of them. He told me a story of an innocent husband that was so often accused by his wife of a trespass that the man decided to commit the crime since he had already endured the punishment for it. That man didn't change my mind but I did get the hint. Some days he irritates me so.

More rumors about Tommy arrive daily, and none of them good. One rumor about him inviting widows out for dinner is especially annoying. I correct myself... there are six gruesome newspaper accounts of his abominable misbehavior, yet his popularity gains as fast as mine decreases. Well, that just goes to show that if you are saddled with legend it is best to have a big one! People don't believe pie sized lies, but willingly swallow a whale of a tale. I can't believe that normally rational acting parents would allow that man to teach their kids how to shoot guns! Don't they know what kind of a man he is?

==0==

ANNA, CLOTHED IN one of her finest dresses, made an early visit to the parsonage. She did her best to conceal her anger and the ugly wrinkles her lawyer warned her about. The pastor's wife greeted her at the front door, presentable, but not yet dressed for outside the home.

"Is your man at home?" Anna asked.

"Where is yours, Anna?"

"That is the issue. I have come to speak to your husband about that man."

"Anna, please come into my kitchen. I have some coffee on. Would you like some? I was about to have a cup myself."

"Yes, but what I have to discuss with your husband does not qualify as a social visit. What he did to me was abominable and I am here to get it fixed."

"Anna, please come in, sit down, and relax. My husband has never done an abominable thing in his life. There must be a misunderstanding that can be explained. I was there Anna. It was a beautiful betrothal."

==0==

Sir, I was asked yesterday by Deadwood's sheriff to explain the shootings of two of Westum's ranch hands. Sheriff, I have no proof that I did not do it, nor do I have an alibi. I was not aware of the shootings until after I arrived in Deadwood. All I offer is my word (for what that's worth) that I had nothing to do with the shootings. Mr. Westum and I had already settled our differences before I left Miles City. We both walked away from the confrontation in peace. I harbor no bitterness or resentment towards the man or those employed on his ranch. I am no fool. If Mr. Westum wants to start something afresh, that is his prerogative. Whatever he starts, I will finish and gladly take the spoils of his foolishness home with me. Otherwise, peace.

My arrival in Deadwood was delayed by two situations. First, my pace was greatly deteriorated due to my rib injuries. Second, I was given shelter and food by a Lakota Indian band in route to Deadwood. I was cautiously shown favor and allowed to recover there for several days. I offer no proof of either claim. If you are still curious, my Deadwood doctor can give you his opinion as to my condition before I inherited my current set of afflictions. All I can offer to you is my word.

Your unspoken question most likely involves Toak. He arrived three or four days before I did in Deadwood and delivered our documents. I am told that he left for Bismarck with Deadwood documents days prior to my arrival. I have not seen Toak since my initial and unforgettable welcome in Miles City. Toak may have been in Deadwood several days ago but not seen since. He may still be here, or he may be in Miles City or Bismarck. Nobody sees a tracker, especially me.

I plan to return to Miles City shortly; maybe as soon as mid-month. I will be traveling in a buckboard with a lady passenger, the Widow Gorgon. She has asked me to escort her back to Fort Rice. In exchange, she will superintend my recovery from wounds. You know about my ribs, but I also inherited a bullet through the face during a disagreement with the widow's late husband. You are free to make your own assumptions and conclusions. I am sure the good sheriff has already informed you where he found my hatchet.

You are aware that persons of my caliber bring out the worst behavior in people. People have taken advantage of my poor reputation, done their dirty deeds, and let others assume that I pulled the trigger. That is not an alibi; only a recurring history lesson. There are over thirty unsolved murders in the Dakotas with my name mentioned with them. I am not admitting to anything, just restating the obvious. I bring out the worst in some and the best in others.

I am looking forward to seeing you and your charming wife again. I remain grateful that you protected me from a lynch mob, took care of me when critically injured, and found a place for me to heal secretly. I so hope to spend some time with them also. The Widow Gorgon and I will be heading east from Miles City when it becomes convenient, but we cannot tarry too long. There are not that many traveling days before winter visits the plains.

Again, please give my regards to your kind wife, and please also say hello to the widow I met right after I last talked with Mr. Westum. To answer another question: Yes, it has stuck, it is sticking, and will remain stuck. Reassure the preacher and his family about that. Peace.

//signed// Tommy Toivo, a.k.a. Bibb, a.k.a. Terry Toivo

==0==

"Preacher, I am here to talk to you about terminating my marriage. I am not happy about all the ambushing going on!"

"Anna," the preacher replied in a loving tone upon his arrival in the kitchen, "Marriage is a holy bond between a man and wife that God Himself endorses as good. If God calls it good, why are you describing it as an ambush?" The preacher sat down adjacent his wife, but Anna did not.

"You need to fix it, and you must fix it today!" demanded Anna.

"Anna, marriage is until death, and I don't do death. I do life. You need to align your point of view to match God's. God designed marriage for a purpose, several actually, and to violate His purposes, well, I will call it plain – that's evil. I don't do evil, nor should you. That is the message I preach every Sunday. What is your problem with that? Your husband is dead. I don't see your issue."

"Not according to my lawyer, Preacher. My husband is alive, and you filed papers with the court yesterday to register the event." Anna stayed standing even after prompted to sit a second time.

The preacher now understood her complaint, and wondered if he should have some fun with the situation. He could not resist the deliciousness of the opportunity. "Anna, it was my joy and responsibility to file the certificate. I normally would, but because you didn't specifically ask me to I delayed filing any paperwork to change your last name. And I will repeat myself: marriage is sacred. What are you asking me to do? If you are going to change your last name, you need to do it before you leave Deadwood together."

"I am not interested in changing my last name, Preacher!" Anna had to restrain herself from adding expletives because she still needed him to rescind the filing. Her angry delivery of what words she did say sufficed in getting the point across.

"Then what is the issue, Anna? We are so happy for you two. You received the blessing from the church. What more could you want?"

"I want you to nullify my marriage."

"Death nullified your marriage. There is nothing remaining to be nullified. What you are now is what you are. You will get used to it."

"Preacher, you are not listening!"

"And neither are you, Anna. But God didn't bring you here to talk about nullification. You have a bigger problem than that, and God has an answer for you."

"Who are you to speak for God? That's mighty arrogant!"

"Anna, coming from somebody who has no belief in God makes your accusation as laughable as it is meaningless. If there is no god, then you are accusing me of wasting air, and nothing more. Your problem, Anna, is not wasting air but being unequally yoked to a man you hardly know."

"And I am here to get that fixed, Preacher!" Anna's anger wrinkles were in full bloom now.

"Actually, I feel bad for Tommy. It's Tommy who is unequally yoked. You are the problem, not him. The full burden will be on Bibb. At best, you will be nothing more than an unwilling spectator. The man is to be pitied. This recent spiritual wound landed right on top of his physical ones."

"Are you going to help me or not?"

"Only if you want it, Anna. I cannot force it on you."

"Did you file a wedding certificate with the court yesterday, or not?"

"Did Mr. Franklin show it to you? Did I spell a name wrong? What is your complaint, Anna? I am required to register the exchanging of vows with the courthouse. Covenants are easy to get in to, but impossible to escape until fulfillment. We may generate a piece of paper that says the covenant is null and void, but that counts for nothing in heaven. In fact, it will be used as evidence against you when you get to the great judgment hall. Anna, it would be far better for you to embrace your covenant than to try to weasel out of it. God heard every word you said Sunday, and you will keep your word. You can willingly keep it, or God will hound you into keeping it. The same goes for Tommy, but his road will be easier. He has decided to enlist the help of God to keep the covenant instead of resisting it."

"You never answered my question, Preacher."

"I thought I did. What is it again?"

"Am I married to Tommy Toivo? Yes or no?"

"Anna, I made that very clear at the ceremony. Your vows at the church did not marry you and Tommy in the eyes of the territory. But because of your words coming out of your mouth right now your fate will be much worse than marriage. You have taken a very large risk, but with large risks come large rewards. In the end, God will either get you or kill you. Tommy, to his credit, knew that, and put protections into the covenant when he wrote it. It was not small talk when he invoked the God of Anna's mother to remain true, kind, and respectful towards you."

"What has my mother to do with this?" Still angry, Anna finally sat down.

"You think too highly of yourself, Anna. You may be the only Anna in your world, but not in Tommy Toivo's. Did I answer your question?"

"So what did you file at the courthouse?"

"A copy of your covenant. It was easy to take what Tommy had prepared to get it registered. I thought you said you saw it? It is on the same form as a marriage certificate, but I fill in the form different. To vouch for my truthfulness, the territory requires both of your signatures for marriage. To register a covenant only required witnesses and many more women than we needed volunteered to put ink to paper. Your lawyer Mr. Franklin made out more than one copy so everybody who wanted to participate had a chance to sign, even women that I know for certain don't particularly like you. But I digress. Marriage or not, you are in a binding covenant with that man. The more you think of it like marriage instead of a contract, the better chance you have of living through it and being rewarded by it. You would do yourself a great favor if you submitted to its provisions."

"Why do you keep insisting on that, and why do you think Bibb got the worse end of the deal? All he has to do is deliver me to Fort Rice and this whole mess is over. What's so hard about that?"

"Getting you to Fort Rice only defines the end point of the journey. It is the journey that will be difficult. It will be more difficult for Tommy because he is just learning how to be nice. His background was immersed in evil until Miles City. What will make it hard on you is your carnal knowledge. Tommy has never been married and therefore lacks understanding of the mysterious bond that comes with a marriage. Your relationship will be all the work of marriage without the enjoyments of marriage. You must both be kind to each other, or perish."

"Why do you keep saying that? Why are you attempting to scare me needlessly?"

"Why does a widow dress up and put on makeup early in the morning, and why does Bibb sharpen his ax? The answer is deeper than 'Because we like to.' Anna, do you understand what has happened to Tommy?"

"He was injured badly last week and I have promised to help him. He is young. He will recover."

"Anna, have you noticed that his reputation is not matching his behavior? Has he acted like an outlaw? Is it not strange he was not arrested? Is it not strange the Dowry girls haven't quit given what they know? Isn't it strange the doctor is actually interested in healing the man? Isn't it strange that your own Mr. Franklin sides with him on occasion and advises you to agree with him? Isn't it strange, Mrs. Gorgon, that your husband's murderer has not said one unkind or threatening word to you? Isn't it strange that you finally know what the inside of a church looks like?"

"Coincidence."

"Yeah, right. It will truly be hard for you to cross the plains with that man. A blind woman and a crippled outlaw! Isn't that a pair ripe for tragedy! You know very well that more than coincidence is going on here. Tell me, Anna, your story. A month ago you were in hiding thought by all to have been murdered by an irate husband. Isn't it strange what has happened to you?"

"I will write it down some day for you, but today is not that day. You said I am not married and I am satisfied. I will go now."

"You better not, Anna, until you know Bibb's secret," said the preacher's wife. "Your life depends on it."

"What do you, somebody who only met the man once over lunch, know of any of Bibb's secrets? You are baiting me."

"I am always amazed by people's ability to jump to conclusions, Anna," she replied. "Just because you were not present does not mean a prior meeting didn't happen. A lady in our congregation insisted that my husband pay Tommy a call at the hotel, and he was glad he did."

"Anna," the preacher followed, "that wasn't the only visit my wife and I received. The sheriff came by after a certain incident with you and some soup. The man protected your privacy, but did give me the indication of a recent traumatic incident occurring to you, other than the death of your husband. Tell us about this, and we can help you make sense of what has happened."

"Parson, I am a private person and I will keep that council to myself. That is really none of your business."

"Have it your way, Anna. Tommy is a very private person too. He has been forced to be. Outlaws can't afford friends. Some would say a miracle happened to Tommy. Not here, but in Miles City. That is his secret."

"I'm listening."

"Really? Are you ready to hear his story? Or are you looking for nuggets of gossip that you can use against him later? Your history screams that is what you do," countered the preacher's wife.

"So do you think I am that vain and cruel?"

"There's a reason Tommy keeps it a secret. And I will let you answer your own question."

"So why would he want to keep it a secret? Would he be subject to ridicule if it got out?"

Now the preacher responded, "Yes, and the person most likely to abuse him is in this room. He cannot keep the secret long from you given your future close quarters. Did you ever wonder why he insisted that the only command in the covenant was to be kind?"

"Kind? Preacher, you amaze me with that really stupid question. It's because that man doesn't have an ounce of character in him, much less love, or a heart to recognize it if any came his way. You said it yourself; he never married and probably never had a relationship with anybody."

"You are wrong twice, Precious," answered the pastor's wife. "But the only friend that man ever had betrayed him. He has lost faith in friendships. You do know that Bibb and your husband were classmates, yes? But there is another reason he committed himself to befriend you."

"Precious?"

"My fault, Anna," she replied. "I often see what people will be, not what they are. That comes with the role of being a preacher's wife. Bibb told my husband that he thinks he knows you from times past. Both of you, as he put it, 'are singing the same song.' He confessed something else to my husband. He said you could be trusted not to betray him."

"He actually said 'you alone' could be trusted." The preacher continued after interrupting. "I asked him how he knew that, and he said the varmint told him."

"Was he calling me a varmint?"

"Did you promise him that of all people alive that you would not betray him? No, so that rules you out as the varmint! Trust me, Mrs. Gorgon, if he had called you such a thing it would have been the greatest compliment you would have ever received in your life. The varmint is the secret you cannot understand unless I explain other things to you."

"Are you going to tell me, or are you going to start preaching at me, parson preacher and covenant keeper? I will tell you right off, I am not interested in a sermon from you."

"Then I will explain it, Anna," said the preacher's wife. "A miracle happened in Miles City."

"Who did it happen to? Bibb?"

"It happened to the whole town. It happened to the sheriff, the sheriff's wife, Mr. Westum and those on his ranch. It happened to a widow lady, and it changed the attitudes of many in that town. The focus of the miracle happened to be Bibb."

"You make it sound as if a man gave birth!"

A momentary hush came over the room. "How did you know? Who told you that?"

"I'm kidding! Can't you see I was joking?"

"No. I don't see it. Did Bibb tell you?"

"You, and you – both of you are nuts!"

"Seriously, Anna, how did you know? Did Bibb tell you, or did somebody else?"

"Is Bibb a woman? Did I make a covenant with a woman dressed up as a man? What's the child's name? Baby Bibb? This is too bizarre. Tell me it isn't so."

"Anna," the preacher's wife said, "I need you to listen to something that may be very foreign to you. Let me tell it all to you before you interrupt. I'll answer all your questions later if you have any."

"What could be as foreign as what you just told me? Go ahead, I'm listening."

"God exists. We may not like it, but that doesn't change the fact. He designed us to look like we look, talk like we talk, sing like we sing, and think like we think. He gave us an independent spirit and the freedom to do right or to do wrong. He rejoices when we make good decisions and He grieves when we don't. He did that on purpose – everything God does is on purpose – in order to give us the ability to love. Love is a choice, not a feeling. He has given us a desire to love and be loved, and then satisfies that longing with the opportunities and honest choices to actually love each other, or not. He wrote in His holy book that He loves us and that He desires, by acting on our own free will, to decide to love Him back."

"So what has this to do with Bibb and his secret?"

"Bibb has been given a new heart. In Miles City he came to the end of his trail. He was tired of running, killing, hurting, and living an evil life. He was tired of thinking there was a sheriff behind every tree and a rope for him on every gallows. He was told that he could start over if he accepted a grand bargain with God and God's Son. He learned that if he renounced his evil ways and let God rule in his life, he would be pardoned and given a new birth. In Miles City, Bibb accepted God on God's terms and became a new man, as you say, Baby Bibb. If Bibb ever had a heart, he had it removed early in his life. If Bibb ever had a conscience, he killed that in ages past. He is now a new man, but lost in a new world. He is confused, but he is learning fast. He has a new heart. He has a new conscience. He also has a new problem: the varmint."

"Why should I believe you? You Sunday morning people are always saying stuff like this."

"Has Bibb ever told you 'Not to believe what he says, but believe what he does?' Has he ever said that 'Who he really is follows him, and does not go before him?' When he was in Miles City the town was changed. Bibb took the biggest bully in the city and shook him down. He made that man plead for his life and his wife. The man changed, and fear came over the city. Not the fear of evil, but the fear of good."

"So why didn't God fix him, and why did this good God of his let that outlaw come to Deadwood just to get shot?"

"You," responded the preacher with great confidence, as if he was speaking down from the pulpit God's words directly at her.

"Me?"

"You, and I am beginning to think you alone. There are too many signs pointing to that. God is on your trail, Anna. He's fixin' to pitch his tent with you, just like He has with Bibb. I don't know where, when, or how, but I know why. You want reasons? Okay. First is that He loves you and wants you to respond to Him. Second, I think the Almighty has big plans, and you and Bibb are His chosen vessels to make it happen. Third, I think God sees the cries of your heart, and Bibb is God's chosen means to lavish you with riches that never can be stolen. Bibb will get you to Fort Rice, and he will get you to the mother you long for. He will also give you the respect and protection that a widow needs. He will teach you other things too, and God will reward your cooperation with a seventh fortune that can never be lost at a gambling table."

"Where do you come up with all this? This sounds like a fairy tale." Her words were bitter.

"A fairy tale that you desperately want to come true? Anna, it is in your grasp. Grab it! Live life to the fullest! Have your deepest desires come true! Anna, it can happen!"

"Why would your God, if He exists, show any interest in me, much less show me his favor? I have never done anything for him."

"Precisely! Anna, you do not know how right you are!" The preacher's wife continued, "God picked you for that very reason, and the same reason He picked Bibb. Nobody is going to accuse you of becoming so holy that God was obligated to grant you sainthood. No! He does not work that way. He changes people for his glory, not the glory of those He chooses. The reason they call it a miracle in Miles City is because what happened could never have been engineered by Bibb. God's hand is all over that boy right now, and the biggest mistake you could make would be refusing to cling to him under the shower of God's blessings already soaking that man. But it is your choice, woman." The preacher's wife was quite frustrated because Anna's reaction to the good news was skeptical at best. It was almost as if she was dead.

"Tell me about the varmint. That is where the secret is, isn't it?" asked Anna of the preacher.

"The secret is that Bibb was given a new life in Miles City. Some of the more excitable preachers would describe what happened to Bibb was that he was born again. I say he was regenerated in God by God for God. Makes no difference – we are talking about the same thing. Bibb accepted the grand bargain of exchanging his life for the sacrifice that God's Son made on his behalf. But God's Son isn't the varmint. Through the ages God reveals Himself to us in three personalities, God the Father, God the Son, and God the Holy Ghost."

"Ghost?"

"The Holy Ghost comforts those who are afflicted, showing them the love of the Father and the Son to those who react to His goodness in faith. Bibb's secret is directly from one of the other missions of the divine third personality. It convicts men of their evil deeds, their failures, their immorality, greed, and pride. What Bibb did not realize was that when he accepted the grand bargain was that the Holy Ghost would set up His abode inside his soul. He does not move in as a pleasant guest, but upon arrival starts to clean up the place. He is merciless in hounding the man into making past wrongs into rights. He also expertly guides the man into right living by dropping inward hints along the way. He knows exactly how to reach each person. He is known as the master persuader."

"Hints like a message in a mist?" said Anna tenderly. Her tone had completely changed.

The question caught the preacher off guard, but it did confirm that Anna was listening. "I haven't heard it that way before, but that sounds right. God talks to his own creation in many creative ways. He knows exactly how to reach each person. For the prideful, he will humiliate. For the rich, he will ruin. For the poor, he will raise up and give them their needs. For the vain, it might be speaking to them through a mirror. For the immoral, it could be through a venereal disease. For the student, it may be through textbooks. His word will make it to its target. The only question is what the target will do about it when it happens. God is a perfect gentleman. He can accept 'No' or 'Not now' or 'I am busy' for an answer. He is also the governor of the universe. When a hammer doesn't work, he politely backs off and goes to find the wood maul he has stored in heaven's barn. There are many ways, but there are two certain tests to know if it is the Holy Ghost speaking."

"What's that?"

"Anna, when you deal with Bibb over the next months, be kind. There is a varmint inside him that is torturing him day and night. It is reminding him of all the wrongs he has stacked up in his life and He is demanding Bibb to come clean. Bibb is miserable. Nevertheless, he also feels loved for the first time in his life. The varmint does not only condemn, but He restores and confirms. He touches the heart, and prompts for good and only good. The first test is that the words of the Ghost are good, and only good. The second test is truth. The Ghost never lies. It points back to holy living according to God's laws. This Spirit points back to God's Son who lived a sinless life and encourages his host to be like the divine Son. If there was a third test it would be that the Ghost gives the power and desire for that person to do what God wants done. In church we call that grace. That same grace is available for you too, Anna."

"So this varmint is a ghost? Like a good ghost?"

"Anna, do not use this information to torture the man. He has only trusted God for a month or so, and he is very immature in the faith. Take the extra step to be kind at every opportunity. The man is hurt, vulnerable, and inexperienced with relationships. You are strong, opinionated, and socially superior. Please don't take advantage of him, please don't try to control him, and please don't mock him. There is one thing he can do for you that will save you a lot of pain and questions."

"What can he do for me other than guide my horses, carry bags, and help me onto the wagon?"

"Anna, think higher. This is not just about what work he can do for you. Stop being Anna of Deadwood. Become Precious of Fort Rice." The pastor waited through the pause for Anna to reply.

"Change my name?"

"Not to Precious, but to Toivo."

Anna bolted from her chair. "What? I can't believe this! Outrageous! You were serious about that earlier, weren't you?"

"For the length of the covenant, borrow his name when you need too. There is protection under his authority and reputation. It will eliminate questions from being asked. It will also give you an attitude of respect for the man. If you honor him, he will honor you. I do not think it is possible for you to out give that man. Anna, please sit down and look directly at me." The preacher waited to get her full attention.

"I am."

"And listening too?"

"I am." Anna sat down.

"Anna, the big issue in your covenant is authority. In defined areas he will submit to you and likewise you must submit to him. I am not asking you to act married – that wasn't part of the covenant. I am asking you to honor the man, and by the varmint's insistence, Tommy will honor you. Isn't that one of the things you desire more than anything else?"

Anna was getting nervous. "That would be a pleasant change. I must go now. Thank you for the coffee and the conversation. I came here demanding you to annul my marriage, and I leave here thinking you actually want me to marry the outlaw. I heard what you said, but pardon my directness. The skeptic in me says this is all fairy dust. I never questioned my ability to understand any man. My worry is that he will not understand me." Anna stood up intending to leave the parsonage.

"Before you go, can we bless you with prayer?"

"If you believe in God, I don't have to be here for those prayers. If it makes you happy, pray all day if you want. I have business to attend to. I don't have it in me to wish you a good day. If you preacher people want to pray at me, go ahead and waste your time. I'm not going to waste mine."

Anna's shortness and faithlessness left the preacher and his wife disappointed. They tried to tell her about their faith, but the gospel fell on deaf ears and blind eyes.

They did pray after she left. The greatest concern was that the revelations they shared about Tommy would not be used for evil but for good. That night they spent extra time commending both Anna and Tommy to God's grace and care, pleading their conviction that covenants were more important to God than any marriage vow.

==0==

A knock came on the door around two in the afternoon. The nurse answered and found a small child, no more than seven years old at the door. The boy had on his hips a gun belt with wooden toy pistols. "May I talk to Mr. Bibb? Can he come out and play?"

"What do you want to ask him? He is sleeping."

"I want him to teach me how to shoot."

"Does your father know where you are?"

"I don't have one, and my mom said I only had to be home before dark for dinner. Can Mr. Bibb come out after his nap time?"

"I'll tell you what. I will write your momma a note, and if she says yes, I will talk Mr. Bibb into it. Right now he isn't feeling too good."

==0==

The reporter was not expecting a visit from Mr. Franklin that afternoon. They went for a ride in the lawyer's buckboard out to a deserted location overlooking the mouth of the valley. After securing a promise of secrecy from the man, Mr. Franklin showed him a document certifying the rest of a story that had not been reported in the social section of yesterday's newspaper. To affirm their agreement to help each other they concluded their business with a handshake and rode back into town. In two days they would meet again at that location to edit the final drafts of their agreed to work.

==0==

An hour later there were nine kids aged from seven to fourteen years old in the lobby of the hotel gathered "for Mr. Bibb to come out and play." The only thing that the nurse had required was that a parent came along. One of the three mothers went to Bibb's room and knocked on the door anxious to hear what her child was so excited about.

"My boy said Mr. Bibb would teach him how to shoot," she said to the nurse. "Is that true?"

She replied rather sheepishly, "Actually, I promised that. Bibb doesn't know about this yet. Please come in. He is decent right now. We can talk to him together."

Ten minutes later Bibb was heading down to the lobby with the nurse, who had been drafted to do his interpreting. She had already apologized to Bibb for making unauthorized promises for her patient. Bibb took the gaggle of boys with him over to the livery to get his rifle, and then to the jail. At Bibb's urging, the nurse explained to the sheriff about her promise to the kids. She also explained that Bibb didn't want to teach the kids about revolvers, but didn't mind teaching them about rifles.

The sheriff escorted all of them over to a flooded quarry pit. After the sheriff told them why everybody needed to know how to shoot, they each took turns being coached by Bibb on how to fire his rifle. Each of the boys (and two mothers) learned firsthand what the kick of a rifle felt like as they each shot several holes in the water.

The nurse ended the event when she told the boys that Bibb needed to get back to his room to recover from his bullet wound. Bibb's ripped apart face was a stark object lesson to each of the kids of the damage and pain a piece of hot lead could inflict. One of the mothers told the kids that Bibb would look like that the rest of his life. That fact made his wounds appear much worse than the initial repulsiveness. Class was over and the mothers took charge.

Bibb's and the nurse's slow stroll back to the livery started quite silent. Her shoulder still hurt from taking Bibb's advice to hold the butt of the rifle about an inch away from her shoulder (not snug like he told the others) when she fired it. Bibb was ashamed of himself for that petty prank, telling her she would be able to hold the rifle out there to avoid the kick.

Miss Dowry eventually could not take the silence anymore. It was as if Bibb was purposely walking and thinking in slow motion. Maybe not. Regardless, she was no longer able to hold in her feelings.

"You're mad at me, aren't you, Mr. Toivo?" she asked.

"No (srpt)."

"You have the right to."

"Yes (srpt)."

"Did you know that none of those kids had dads?"

"No."

"Did you see how happy their moms were watching you teach their sons about guns?"

"No (srpt)."

"Did you see how happy I was when you showed me?"

"No."

"Did you notice how quickly the sheriff volunteered to help without question?"

"Yes."

"Do you know why?"

"Yes."

"Will you explain it to me?"

"No."

"Why are you mad at me?"

"You know (srpt)."

"So you are mad, aren't you?"

Bibb stopped and turned to her, and she stopped in her tracks as if now standing in no-man's land. Bibb took a moment and physically adjusted his painful jaw with his hand. She feared.

"Woman," Bibb said, "Woman… What-zz you are (srpt)… What-zz you are is kind, and I am ashamed. You have hands d'that heal (srpt) and a voice d'that (srpt) soothes. How can I be mad (srpt) at somebody (srpt) I owe such a debt to (srpt)? I fear I abused your kindness, and now, woman, I fear I must ask you (srpt) another favor."

"What is it, Bibb?" as she looked responsively into to his eyes. She had no idea what kind of favor he might ask – anything from something intimate to demanding she stop her questioning.

"Can you (srpt) return my rifle to d'the livery (srpt)? I can't-zz go no farther (srpt) and must sit-zz down now (srpt). Please-zz (srpt)?"

"You stay right here then, I will be back directly." She saw the pain in his face and knew Bibb would be planted where she put him while she was away.

"Yes-zz." Bibb sat down on the wooden sidewalk in front of one of the stores not knowing she had already left. He leaned his exhausted back against a post and shut his eyes. It could have been two minutes, or ten minutes later when Bibb became aware that something warm was sitting next to him blocking the breeze. He opened his eyes and saw a kid sitting next to him as content as he could be. He decided to let him be and return to his nap. He was beyond just tired. Never before had anybody ever ventured to sit up close to him. "Being ugly wasn't so bad after all," Bibb thought to himself. "At least kids aren't scared of him, only adults."

The sight was quite a novelty for many in the city. Nobody dared say anything as they walked by, but sure did later – the lamb sitting down by the lion. When Miss Dowry returned, she sat down on the other side of Bibb, shushing the boy to remain quiet. She still couldn't get over Bibb's last words to her. This was the first time any man had addressed her as "Woman," and three times no less. Was Bibb angry? No. Was he sincere? Yes. Was he lucid? Maybe. Was it a compliment? Absolutely.

When Bibb eventually woke, she told Bibb that she was ready to take him back to the hotel and bring him his supper.

"Yes," Bibb said agreeing to her suggestion.

"Are you okay, Bibb?"

"No."

"Do you hurt?"

"Yes."

"Do you want me to fetch the doc?"

"Yes… No… Just dinner (srpt)."

Bibb's breathing was heavy as he stood up. Miss Dowry helped him until he motioned with his hand that he was able to walk by himself. He rubbed his chest several times, twice wincing in pain.

"Bibb, please don't think me out of line, but I must say it. I am so proud of you."

He looked at her in bewilderment. He gestured her to keep walking. Bibb's face betrayed to his nurse that something was messed up inside the man's chest. She risked his wrath by whispering a request in the boy's ear to fetch the doctor and meet them at the hotel. She couldn't wait to get him back into the room to get his shirt off of him, all the while praying that this outing hadn't reinjured Bibb. He certainly didn't give her any clues; he didn't have the energy to even eat dinner. For that matter Bibb didn't have the energy or will to say another word that day. She feared for the man, shedding tears in the candlelight as his breathing seemed so shallow throughout the evening hours.

In the wee hours of the morning after Bibb had slept several hours, he quietly got up out of bed. Without any more noise than the sound of cream being applied to his remaining skin, Bibb shaved what he could of his face. He was very careful not to wake his nurse who remained asleep in the chair by the window. Once finished, he walked over behind her and started to rub the shoulder that would have been bruised by the rifle's kick. The twin woke up, but was immediately shushed by Bibb before she could raise an objection. She dared not refuse the massage, but thought the man's behavior was quite out of character – he hated anybody to touch him, much less him touching them. Fifteen minutes later, Bibb without comment or any indications he was ever fully awake quietly returned to bed. He fell back into a deep sleep still under the spell of the strong medicine the doctor had given him earlier.

The next day the twin told her sisters what Bibb had done in the middle of the night. They could only assume that Bibb did not know they had a shift change while he slept, and the massage was meant for the twin that actually had the bruised shoulder. When she was asked what had happened, she confessed to her sisters and revealed her bright purple shoulder injury. They all had a good laugh; the man was confused, but a good confused. Even in his sleep he must have felt some guilt over the spiteful advice he had given her at the quarry. They decided not to speak of it again, and then returned to teasing the man-handled sister. Obviously she was enjoying her job too much to tell Bibb to stop.

Her reply "It's a tough job, but somebody had to suffer through it!" restarting the giggling.

Wednesday, October 5, 1887

I spent most of the day with Mr. Franklin reviewing and signing attorney stuff. With the help of the accountant, we set minimum and target sale prices for each of the properties and businesses to include existing inventory. I swore them to secrecy concerning our discussions and offered significant commissions if they exceed target prices at liquidation.

I was feeling better about the trip until Bibb arrived on his horse at the mansion. He reiterated his demanding irrelevant opinions on what not and what little to take. What does that man know about what a woman needs to have with her for a trip like this? I showed him what clothes I was going to pack. Without my permission, he went into my closet and picked out plain house dresses instead! The nerve of that man! He said where we were going fashion doesn't matter. Such impudence! Well, if fashion doesn't matter, I don't want to go.

After swearing me to secrecy, Mr. Franklin shared in confidence a copy of Bibb's letter to the Deadwood sheriff. He was not supposed to show me, but he changed his mind after considering my personal safety. The last paragraph intrigued me. I suspect it has much to do with what the preacher's wife confided with me yesterday. Mr. Franklin is a good man, but he drives me crazy. I am sure the feelings are mutual. Mr. Franklin and I are together a lot and I detect more than a passing interest in me and my safety. No, I don't catch his eye, but otherwise. He is old enough to be my father, and I enjoy teasing him about that. I wager that his wife puts him up to it. I wish she stop trying to mother me. The accountant… ugh! He has the personality of a lamppost.

I stayed the night at Xue's laundry. Mrs. Franklin sure did make the evening interesting.

==0==

REGARDLESS OF HIS many pains, Bibb was as restless as a man could be. He appreciated the medical attention he was receiving but he was tired of doing nothing but nothing in his room. Early in the morning he and the other Miss Dowry, not the twin, walked down to the livery to see if his horse missed him. Bibb fed it a couple pears and brushed him down. The horse did not need it. The livery owner said he was getting top dollar to care for the horse, and had gladly given it special attention. He also told Bibb he took it for a ride every day up to White Rocks and back. "I don't suppose that horse is for sale, is it Tommy?"

"Sir, you-zz would have (srpt) to ask its-zz owner, but only a fool-zz would sell-zz it (srpt). I cannot depart-zz with him. Can you-zz (srpt) take me up-zz to White Rocks? I need-zz to get out (srpt) of d'the gulch."

"Meet me here at noon. Do you mind if I invite a friend along?"

"I don't-zz care (srpt). It's-zz not like we-zz are having a-zz picnic. We-zz (srpt) are-zz just getting out-zz of town."

"Can I come, Tommy?" asked the Dowry girl.

"Why-zz?" replied Tommy, very surprised.

"Because you might need me."

Tommy looked at her, and could not say no. Her eyes were so deep with thought and emotions; she honestly cared for him. The way she talked forced him to consider the reverse. She had invested heavily into his life, cared for his most private of needs, kept his confidences, and cried herself in empathy when his pain was heavy. Bibb could only conclude one thing: she said that because she meant it. She was void of any other motive. "Only if you-zz (srpt) can ride next to-zz me (srpt), Miss-zz Dowry. Do you-zz (srpt) have a horse?"

Bibb's positive response to her was received as tenderly as it was said, nothing like what might be expected from a silly young school girl. "I will use dad's, unless he wants to go instead."

==0==

The maid notified Anna that a man on a horse had just ridden up the lane and was currently tying his horse up at their shed. She couldn't tell, but thought it to be Bibb. Anna quickly finished getting herself ready for a visitor, descending the staircase in time to meet Tommy at the kitchen door.

"What brings you here this fine morning, Tommy?"

"I-zz come to see-zz you (srpt), and what-zz you are packing. I (srpt) have another-zz reason too."

"I am packing what any sensible woman would pack. I have clothes for each day and the necessities to make my life comfortable. I think we will need another wagon, or maybe three."

"We will fit-zz in the wagon I picked (srpt), and you-zz will fit-zz all your stuff in one trunk (srpt). You will-zz find-zz a way to pack-zz (srpt) only what-zz essential. Can I-zz see?"

"See what?"

"What-zz you are packing (srpt), Anna." He wondered if she was purposely not listening to him.

"I have some of it laid out in my room, Bibb."

"Okay." Bibb started walking towards the steps. Anna's face immediately went aghast in protest.

"You stop right now!" she yelled loudly at him. "Where do you think you are going?"

"To your room-zz (srpt). You-zz said your stuff was-zz d'there (srpt)." Tommy was undeterred.

"I didn't give you permission to go up there."

"I didn't ask-zz (srpt) for it. Are you-zz coming up (srpt) or do I-zz have to pack-zz for you-zz (srpt)?"

"Tommy Toivo, you get back down here right now! That room is private and I will not have you going in there!"

"Be kind. You promised-zz (srpt). I am-zz helping you."

"Get down here! I demand it!" Bibb was already up the stairs when the last of those syllables were flying out of her mouth. She quickly ran up the stairs to find Tommy looking for her bedroom. He found it, and entered the room just as Anna caught up to him.

"Too-zz much stuff (srpt). Too-zz much wrong stuff. Sell d'this stuff Anna (srpt)." Bibb walked into her closet, which was almost a cave in size. He went through the dresses on the hangers and picked out four house dresses. "Wear-zz d'this, and pack d'these-zz d'three, and no more (srpt)."

"You will leave this room right now, Mr. Toivo."

"What-zz other stuff (srpt) are you-zz packing, Anna, other d'than (srpt) clothes?"

"That is none of your business, boy."

"It is-zz very much my-zz business (srpt). You-zz can pack-zz all you-zz want-zz, but I decide what-zz we take (srpt)." He pointed to a trunk she had in her room. "We-zz take d'that trunk. Put-zz your (srpt) legal papers-zz in d'the bottom. Put-zz (srpt) your most precious heirlooms-zz on top-zz (srpt) of that. Take nothing-zz (srpt) d'that will break. On-zz top of d'that put d'three days-zz (srpt) of clothes. Also wrap-zz one more set (srpt) in-zz a dry sack for our arrival in Miles City."

"Why only three sets? We will be gone two weeks or more to get there."

Tommy pulled out a knife and started to neatly carve his initials into the trunk lid. As he worked on that he told Anna, "One set-zz to wear, one set-zz to wash (srpt), and one set-zz packed away-zz washed and dried. October is-zz cool at-zz night (srpt). You will need-zz a blanket and-zz (srpt) a tarp for a covering. Consider taking a-zz rain coat too (srpt) and a useful hat-zz – not-zz one of (srpt) d'these-zz fancy feathery d'things-zz."

She was beyond angry. "What about your stuff? How many trunks are you taking?"

"All-zz I brought to-zz Deadwood (srpt) rode in on my horse. All-zz I take from-zz Deadwood will ride out (srpt) on my horse. D'there are (srpt) four other d'things-zz I need-zz (srpt) to carry in d'the wagon."

"What are they, Bibb? And why are you asking me?"

"D'they are d'things you have (srpt), or we need-zz to buy. First are all-zz (srpt) your combs-zz and hair brushes-zz. I need-zz at least two-zz dozen. I need-zz d'that big magnifying glass downstairs too-zz (srpt), and your husband's-zz rifle (srpt) above d'the fireplace."

"I understand the rifle, Bibb, but why the other stuff?"

"I need-zz ammunition too (srpt); four cases-zz should do."

"You will have to buy that yourself, Bibb. But answer my question. What is the other stuff for?"

"It will-zz provide us-zz (srpt) an escort to-zz Miles City. We (srpt) will be-zz like two ripe plums-zz for any bandit along d'the way (srpt). Anna, you-zz might have noticed (srpt) I'm not quite my-zz gun-slinger self lately (srpt)."

Her anger was defused by his sincere admission. She laughed and said she could make room for his extra stuff. Was he well in the head? She could not image him admitting that to any other person.

"Anna, don't fret-zz (srpt); we-zz can d'throw it on top. We-zz (srpt) will only need it-zz for d'the first day." That earned an odd look from her. She would have balked if Bibb had told her why.

"You can leave my room now, Bibb. You were not invited in here." Bibb responded by sitting down on her vanity chair. "You can go now, I said."

"Anna, do you-zz really (srpt) want-zz to go? Fort Rice-zz is-zz (srpt) too small-zz for you-zz. Bismarck (srpt) may-zz be too-zz small for you (srpt). Where-zz and what-zz (srpt) will make you happy?"

"I will be happy if you leave this room! I will be happy if you keep your promise. I will be happy if you do not take advantage of this poor widow. I will be happy if you stop all your gawking and take the stutter out of your brain. You need to start acting sensibly! I will be happy if you keep your business to yourself and act mannerly by understanding that my business is none of your business!"

"Okay. But we-zz (srpt) already decided d'that. Where-zz and what-zz (srpt) will make you happy? I am-zz asking so-zz I can-zz (srpt) understand. I am-zz asking so-zz (srpt) I can-zz be kind. Anna, I-zz really don't understand-zz women (srpt). Anna, I-zz really don't (srpt) understand-zz what makes d'them (srpt) happy. I don't-zz understand (srpt) why I-zz make-zz d'them so mad. If you-zz don't tell me (srpt), I will-zz not know."

Anna did not want to answer any question aimed directly at the motives of her heart. She turned the question around to put him on defense. "Why are you going? What makes you happy?"

"Anna, d'that's-zz (srpt) a fair question. I don't-zz have (srpt) a prepared-zz answer."

"You mean you didn't already write that down? You should have seen it coming! What's the matter with you?"

"I told-zz you what's d'the matter with me (srpt), but more-zz d'than anything I-zz want (srpt) to-zz understand you-zz. I want-zz you (srpt) to wake up-zz every morning (srpt) happier-zz d'than you-zz were d'the day before."

She heard well what he said, but she wasn't going to give him an inch. She replied in a snotty way, "Do you really mean that, Bibb? Aren't you forgetting that you are a no good lying murdering outlaw that kills people for packing too much underwear? Why should I believe you?"

Bibb sighed and paused before he answered. "I have-zz asked too-zz much (srpt). I deserved-zz d'that answer (srpt). But Anna, it's-zz my heart (srpt). It's-zz in my heart. It-zz won't-zz let me-zz (srpt) behave otherwise-zz (srpt). Good day-zz, Mrs. 'Organ." A very dejected Bibb got up to leave, and Anna just stood there staring at him.

Bibb was already down the stairs, out the door, and halfway to the barn when the translation of his mushy diction registered with its full weight. She bolted out of her room, out the door, and purposely stood wide-legged in the lane leaving the mansion grounds. Bibb was surprised to see her there, and as if she had the wherewithal to block his exit. Bibb suffered her actions only because of his promise to play nice. Anna was no longer a mere frustration, but a full sized thorn in his flesh.

"Bibb, you must answer me a question before you leave," she demanded.

"What's-zz d'the question (srpt), Anna?" replied a crestfallen rider on the horse. He was so sorry he had opened up to her like that, and his evil side dared him to run her over. He wondered if her beauty had bewitched him. Still, he promised to be kind, and that promise was registered at the courthouse. He was bound by his pledge. All she did was look at him. He asked again, "What-zz?"

"Who is It?"

"It? D'that It was once outside-zz of me (srpt). It-zz d'then was-zz living in-zz me (srpt). Now it's so in-zz me it is-zz me (srpt). None of d'that matters-zz. My word is-zz my word (srpt), and d'the It is my-zz problem, not yours-zz (srpt). But It is-zz good (srpt), and only-zz good. Honestly Anna, help-zz me be kind. I-zz *do* instead of *d'think* when-zz people pick-zz fights with me-zz, and my *do* is often very rash (srpt) and reckless. I don't-zz d'think-zz as fast as you-zz (srpt), so please-zz don't expect me to debate with you-zz. D'this-zz (srpt) kindness to-zz a lady is-zz new and-zz hard for me-zz. Let's-zz talk later (srpt). I hurt-zz."

"You hate women, don't you, Bibb?"

"Generally, and-zz it ain't hate hate-zz (srpt). I dislike what-zz d'they do to me-zz. Maybe some-zz I do hate-zz; d'the controlling ones-zz, for sure-zz."

"Is that an accusation, Bibb?"

"No, ma'am-zz (srpt). Controllers are-zz easy to identify-zz. D'they always-zz take-zz d'the last word in any dialog-zz."

"Bibb, you have no right to make such judgments! That is so arrogant!"

Anna wouldn't move from her spot. Bibb, having let Anna prove his point, tipped his hat in a proper goodbye and gently nudged his horse to go around her. She remained there holding her ground until Bibb was out of sight riding slowly off the mansion grounds.

As she walked towards the house she mumbled several unpleasantries. "That man is a liar! He claims he is slow, but he lies around in bed all day and plots how he is going to sting me! He has no reason to hate me! Look what I have given him and I ain't got a dime back on my investment!"

The Widow Gorgon was so beet red when she entered the kitchen that the cook asked her if she was flushed due to fever. The cook, a caring soul, was sensitive to Anna's moods.

"No I am not!" she barked back to the cook. Looking at the shock in her maid's eyes, she immediately calmed down and stated to her, "No, it is just that Mr. Toivo has made me very angry, and I am not accustomed to such effronteries. I didn't mean to take my anger out on you."

"Did you catch him in a lie, Missy? The man is known for that."

"Yes I did. He called me a controlling tyrant."

"He really said that? That's terrible! The man needs to apologize regardless if it was a lie or not."

"So you agree with him?" Anna's voice became shrill again and her face started to blush anew.

"Missy, what you need is a piece of cake, and I just happened to have some. Enjoy some of the comforts of home before you start on your journey. It will do you good."

"Tell me true. Do you think I am a controlling tyrant?"

"Ma'am, you have been good to me, and I will always defend you no matter what. You have earned my loyalty because you have been fair with me. If you really want an answer to that question, ask your accountant or Mr. Franklin. They can give you a professional opinion from somebody not obligated to show you deference to keep her job."

"I don't have to ask. That cake is a good idea."

==0==

Anna started to feel dirty for cutting the preacher off the day before in their conversation. He may have been speaking the truth. And this Bibb boy, oh, how he infuriated her. He was certainly an enigma. She wanted more clues about this man to use as future leverage. She wanted him in a box. She wanted to put strings through his arms and legs and manipulate him like a puppet. The more she wanted the more she hated his words.

While in her bedroom freshening up her makeup she started to think about Bibb and how his actions were not matching his situation. She asked herself, "How could a man that hurts so bad get up on his own horse and ride all the way out here and back?

Why would he? If he was in pain, he certainly hid it well! And his words… they were not the words of a self-confident gunslinger. No, he pretended to be timid. What a LIAR! Oh how he gets my back up. The man is a fake! He was only acting like he was emotionally hurt! LIAR!"

She calmed herself as she finished her eye makeup. She had to reconsider who was the liar, her or Bibb. Bibb never called her a controlling tyrant. "My husband wouldn't be dead if the man was a fake. Oh, but that Bibb lies! He said he was a slow thinker, and I am wise to that deceit! How did he get away with that? …Yes, I know, he played into my vanity by calling me smarter and quicker than him! He suckered me in! Oh, how he infuriates me, even if it is true!"

It then occurred to Anna that Bibb truly was in pain, and that reason alone could explain his timidity. He had sincerely said he wanted her happier in the morning then when she went to bed the night before. Anna recalled that she slammed him by calling him insincere and reminding him that he "was a no good lying murdering outlaw that kills women for packing too much underwear." With growing remorse she painfully relived the scene. Her tongue was too sharp. She remembered vividly the moment when Bibb's spirit fell and he turned his back on her to leave the mansion.

She had to admit that it might just be true that the pain he was suffering was not just physical, and that her words had something to do with a fresh injury. That was not a happy thought. "Well," she said to herself, "I have other things to do today than to worry about an outlaw's hurt feelings. He will get over it soon enough. It is a special kind of kindness on my part that I clearly showed him his proper place before we leave. I don't want him to get any foreign ideas once we are alone!"

==0==

The eight other riders, beside the owner, were waiting for a surprised Bibb when he arrived back at the livery. In the group were four boys, barely teenagers, and ready to ride. There were no females in the band, and Bibb's question was answered when Mr. Dowry introduced himself.

"Sir, you know my girls. They said you have treated them well while working with you."

"It is-zz d'they (srpt) who have-zz treated me-zz well, sir (srpt). You're-zz Mr. Dowry, yes-zz?"

"Yes, and please thank Mrs. Gorgon for her generous wage for each of them. She is not an easy woman to approach. Please thank her for me."

Bibb acknowledged with an affirmative gesture. It was encouraging that at least one soul thought that Anna woman was virtuous. Bibb still smarted from the morning's rebuke. He rode over to the livery owner and gave him a query with his eyes, and then pointed to his office. They went in alone.

"Bibb, I only told one of my friends to come along. Honest Bibb, how did I know it would turn into a troop? Can you blame them for being curious? Do you blame those dads for wanting their kids to ride a trail with you? Let's just go. Enjoy the outing. For you it's just another hill. For them and their boys it's a life event. One young man is the sheriff's boy."

Bibb looked up at him. "Where's-zz (srpt) my other gear-zz?"

"Locked up, Bibb, right where the sheriff put it."

"Please-zz (srpt) take me to-zz it."

"The sheriff didn't tell me I could return it yet."

"He didn't say-zz (srpt) you couldn't-zz either." Bibb's changed tone convinced the owner that it would be a healthy idea to unlock Bibb's property.

Several minutes later Bibb returned to the troop with his rifle, hatchet, saddlebags, satchel, sleeping kit, whip, and knives. He was watched carefully as he placed his personal arsenal on to his horse in the manner he was accustomed to. He asked one kid to hold his rifle and hatchet while he secured the other items. There was no talking going on. Silence.

"Lead d'the way-zz (srpt)," he told the livery owner. "I'll follow-zz, second horse-zz."

The rest of them followed in single line up the trail towards the top of the hill that overlooked the city and Deadwood Gulch.

==0==

They had been discussing for over three hours the plans for liquidating the estate when Anna changed the subject surprisingly. "Did you purposely deceive me about that marriage certificate?"

"Where did that question come from Anna?" replied Mr. Franklin. "Did your husband abuse you so badly that you will never trust a man again?"

"And where did that question come from, Mr. Franklin?"

"Do you assume all men are liars? It is a sad commentary that you assumed the preacher lied when he specifically told you that you were not man and wife. Lawyers are noted for exaggerations and deceptions, but not preachers. You owe him an apology."

"Until proven otherwise, yes, I think all men are born liars, thieves, and immoral selfish beings. They are depraved from birth."

"And women aren't?"

"My experience with women is that they are prone to gossip, but not betrayal. Men, or scant few of them, are redeemable. Fewer than that can be trusted. You and our accountant are members of that rare breed. Men talk of love, and then they stick a knife in you. A marriage certificate is but a license to abuse, and I will have no part in that again."

"And why can't you trust the preacher?"

"He has not proven himself trustworthy, at least not to me."

"And how does one earn that trust?"

"By obedience, Mr. Franklin. By obedience."

"To whom?"

"Me. If they want my trust that is how they must earn it."

"Mrs. Gorgon, what is your real question? You asked me if I purposely deceived you. What is the deeper issue? Did you embarrass yourself by going to the preacher's house to raise some dust?"

"I didn't embarrass myself. He explained what he did and I accepted his clarification."

"But not his apology or theology, I trust?"

"He had nothing to apologize for, unlike you Mr. Franklin. I didn't hear any of his theology."

"I am sorry that I did not argue with you, Mrs. Gorgon, concerning the certificate. I should have yelled back at you in like tones you used to counter or confirm your headstrong assumptions. In our business we presuppose that the customer is always right. In your case, the customer is often very wrong. Is that a good enough apology, or do you want me to get on one knee, Oh Queen, purest Daughter of Eve, and the woman of all women who must be immediately and completely obliged?"

"You mock me, Mr. Franklin."

"Only when you deserve it, Mrs. Gorgon. Can you not tone back your anger and passions? Granted, your continual jumping to conclusions keeps me employed, but it has done nothing to help your reputation. You are now going to a different playground. You need to know your place. If you are worthy, you will win the hearts of the socialites in that eastern city. Your money will mean much less there than it does here, and your demanding nature will win you nothing but scorn. Trust me on this, Mrs. Gorgon. Now, by your diverting answer, I am curious. What all did the preacher tell you?"

"Again you are wrong, Mr. Franklin. As for the preacher, he said that he was only doing his job. His wife was much nicer and spoke to me with words of reason."

"Did they tell you anything about what happened to Bibb?"

"What would they know? I left after I rightly concluded that my lawyer had deceived me."

"Oh, well then, let's get back to work on the estate plan." Mr. Franklin knew very well what had taken place at the meeting at the parsonage, but he wasn't going call his client's hand on it. She was never going to admit her tandem of conceits and deceits. It would prove nothing if he forced that. She was emotionally handicapped and deceivingly self-righteous from the ruination of her marriage. She would never admit weakness to a man again. Soon she was to be Bibb's problem, not his. "Hallelujah!" he said under his breath to himself. The word tickled his lips, even if he didn't know exactly what it meant. He was very satisfied with himself over never addressing her accusation.

==0==

Three quarters up the trail Bibb stopped and got off his horse. He started poking around and started to look off the trail for something. He had seen something in the dust that had bothered him, and now that something had disappeared.

"What do you see, Bibb?"

"It's-zz (srpt) what I-zz don't see, sir."

"And what don't you see?"

Bibb pointed to the livery owner to follow him back down the trail. By one of the boys Bibb stopped once again and saw exactly what he was looking for. It was the imprint of a horseshoe that had a small backwards curve on the end of it. Bibb knew that print well. It was the left hind foot of Toak's horse, and the print wasn't that old.

"I am-zz looking for d'the horse with d'this print, sir. I was-zz following (srpt) it up d'the hill, and it-zz disappeared." Bibb took a small limber branch of an ash tree, trimmed it with his ax, and tied it in a knot. "If I see-zz no more tracks-zz (srpt), I know d'that this-zz is where I need-zz to look."

"Look for what?"

"Tracks-zz."

"Of what?"

"A horse."

"Which horse?"

"D'the horse (srpt) with-zz a crooked shoe. Help me (srpt) spot-zz the horse track."

==0==

Anna was quite angry when she returned home. She was going to pack what she wanted to pack, take what she wanted to take, and sell what she wanted to sell. That ragamuffin named Tommy Toivo was the last person on earth she would accept fashion advice from. She promised herself that she would opt to die before showing up in civilization wearing common clothes. She had the butler bring up more trunks. All that evening she emptied her closets into them.

That afternoon Xue came to visit Mrs. Gorgon. She was invited up into Anna's bedroom and they started to talk about the clothes. Xue asked if she could sell all the dresses that she did not take east with her. She promised to bring Mr. Franklin the proceeds less a small commission. Xue told Anna she needed the extra money to buy a mattress now that winter was coming. The floor was starting to get too cold for her sore back.

"Xue, tell me true. Is that all you need?"

"You have more need than Xue," she replied.

"I will take your answer as a deflection. I already know your ethic. You want every dollar you have in your purse to be a dollar you earned."

"I also need no-dollar thing too."

"What is that, Xue?"

"Sheriff man ask many questions. I stay lroyal, I think very so. I stay lroyal lroyal but you might not t'ink so. I tell you first before you find out. I lroyal. Very lroyal." Xue was very nervous.

"What are you specifically worried about, Xue?"

"Sheriff man t'ink I secret agent for you. I no tell, but he t'ink so. I worried you fire me, but I lroyal. I no tell."

"It doesn't matter anymore, Xue. And I never doubted your loyalty, not once. The sheriff would have never bothered you if he wasn't worried about me. The sheriff only did what sheriffs always do, and this time he did it to you. Think no more of it, and yes, you can sell my dresses on commission. Xue, if you weren't loyal, you would have never come over here. Think of it no more."

==0==

At the top of the hill the troop stopped to rest. The view was nice. Bibb now knew why Toak had visited this particular hill. Bibb deduced from crispness of the tracks Toak had been there since the last rain. Other than the imprints, Bibb saw no sign of him. Toak never left many.

While there, a question came from one of the boys about tracking. In response, Bibb got off his horse and sat down on a stump. The others found stumps too or stood around.

"Ask-zz your questions, boy-zz (srpt)," said Bibb. And they did.

==0==

The knock came on the door late in the evening. Bibb was writing answers to several of Bee's questions while a Dowry twin was sitting reading a book in her chair by the window. They both wondered who it could possibly be. The nurse got up and asked who it was from behind the locked door. She recognized the voice matching the whispered name and let her in. She wasn't a woman Bibb recognized, and he immediately became cautious.

"Mr. Toivo, I have questions and you must give me satisfactory answers," stated Mrs. Franklin in an aggressive tone. Bibb did not respond but studied the woman. He was more concerned about what she was packing and where she was concealing her gun. Her questions could wait.

"What-zz about, and why?" answered Bibb. She started to inhale, but Bibb seeing the emotional huff brewing in her face, decided that he had suffered her enough and spoke first. Bibb asked her who she was and why he should care. When she looked insulted, in truth or faked, Bibb pointed to the hallway and told her not to let the door injure her heels on her way out.

"I want to know your true intentions concerning our Anna." She looked at the nurse. "This is a private conversation and you are to leave this room immediately, Miss Dowry."

"Your Anna? Well, d'that claim would make you a Mrs. Franklin, yes? I was warned about you, and you are again welcome to leave while you can. Are you Mrs. Franklin, (srpt) or am I mistaken?"

Miss Dowry answered for her, "Yes, this is Mrs. Franklin. Her husband is Anna's lawyer."

"Thank you Miss Dowry, but I can speak for myself, and please excuse us for a couple minutes. I have some frank discussions I must have with Mr. Toivo."

"She stays-zz, Mrs. Franklin, and for two-zz reasons. First, I have-zz confidence d'that when she is-zz asked to keep something secret (srpt), it-zz will remain secret. Second, I'm-zz not going to be alone-zz in a hotel-zz room with (srpt) somebody else's w-w-w-i-ife."

"I insist, Mr. Toivo. She needs to go."

"I said no-zz, Mrs. Franklin. Are we done here, or would you like to go down to d'the saloon?"

"Absolutely not! That would be such a scandal. I say a hearty no thank you for that suggestion."

"D'then again I wish you a good evening, Mrs. Franklin (srpt), and good riddance."

"Miss Dowry, will you swear to keep this conversation secret from all others, to include your own sisters?" Mrs. Franklin was very insistent and had no intention to leave the room.

"Bibb, I could sit outside the door if that would be a good compromise."

"No. You-zz stay." There was no *maybe* hiding in Bibb's command.

"Then I will go sit in my chair. Mrs. Franklin, you have my word that I will not repeat anything of what is said, nor will I admit to ever being privy to the discussion. Are you satisfied?"

"Bibb, has she proven sincere?"

"Have you-zz ever heard any gossip d'that she's-zz ever repeated (srpt)?"

"No."

"D'then you-zz answered your own first question. Do-zz you have questions (srpt), or are you only here to-zz lecture me? Mrs. Franklin, to be honest (srpt), I am not liking your attitude, something I rarely tolerate. I am not-zz responsible if you say-zz stupid stuff and I do something justified."

"Then I will get right to the point, Mr. Toivo. I have given Mr. Franklin three sons but no daughters. All our sons have moved east and we are quite proud of them. Anna Gorgon, who started as a daily menace in our lives, has gained our affections to become the fourth grown child in our family and the daughter I wished for but never bore. I cannot stand for one minute the prospect of that dear child being alone with you given your reputation, and it breaks our hearts that you are taking her from us. Yes, she is a grown woman, but we are very attached to her. It wounds us deeply that you might harm her. We suffered so at her first disappearance, and now you may take her away again from us. Mr. Toivo, what are your intentions? I must know."

"What kind of intentions are-zz you talking about, Mrs. Franklin (srpt)?"

"Tommy, I can step outside. Can I please step outside?"

"No, you stay-zz, Miss Dowry. Mrs. Franklin, what evil (srpt) do you d'think I intend for Anna?"

"You just said it yourself about me. Mr. Toivo, you have NO business sharing a tent together, OR staying beneath the stars, OR in any hotel room with a woman who is not your wife. It is wrong. It is vile! It is nasty, morally reprehensible, and against the laws of God! I will not stand for it!"

"But-zz it was her idea, Mrs. Franklin. Are you-zz your sister's keeper?"

"Mr. Toivo, I wasn't born yesterday! I'm no fool! And I'm not naïve to what kind of outlaw you are! She has suffered enough already and then to have the added humiliation of scampering across the plains with the likes of you! This is an outrage that I cannot bear. You must, in the name of that varmint that the town is talking about, arrest this immoral fantasy of yours. It is wrong, and it must be stopped, and stopped immediately! I want you to recant your covenant and back out of this arrangement with our Anna. It is so wrong and she is so vulnerable. She hasn't been widowed two weeks and you are taking unholy advantage of her weaknesses. Shame on you! You must recant now! My husband and I are prepared to make it worth your while if you just silently leave town alone. What is your price?"

"Does your husband know you-zz are here, Mrs. Franklin? Or what about Anna? Did she send you here (srpt)? Is she re-d'thinking her promise? I know (srpt) you-zz are smarter d'than to come here alone given d'the reputation you-zz slander me with. D'then again, we d'think with our brain but get stupid with our hearts. Miss Dowry, please walk-zz over and bring me her purse. I'm going to keep any d'thing she was fool enough to be packing (srpt). Don't you dare flinch, Mrs. Franklin."

"I am not packing. Miss Dowry, respect your elder and stay put!"

During the moment where Miss Dowry sat there frozen, Bibb took his gun out from underneath his pillow, stood up, walked over to Mrs. Franklin and took her purse. She dared not flinch. He opened it and found within a small derringer in the main cavity of the handbag. "Well-zz d'that answers d'that question. Mrs. Franklin I-zz believe you have been speaking with-zz your heart (srpt). Why did you-zz just tell your last lie?" Bibb inspected her gun. It was fully loaded.

"My last one or my latest one, Bibb?"

"I stutter. You decide (srpt)." Bibb took the gun and handed the purse to his nurse. "Don't give d'this back-zz to her until I say so. Now Mrs. Franklin, how about you-zz answering my question? What intentions did you d'think me capable of doing? Woman, don't lie to me (srpt) again."

"Then you don't lie either!" Mrs. Franklin shouted back. She was clearly undone and scared.

"Mrs. Franklin, you have reminded me once again-zz why I don't care to deal with emotional mothers (srpt). Miss Dowry, please go fetch d'the doctor. Take d'the purse (srpt) and lock d'the door behind you on your way out."

"I'll think I'll stay if that is okay with you, Tommy. Mrs. Franklin is a decent woman and it would be scandalous for her to be left alone with you in a hotel room." That response was insincere. The real reason she said that was because she was very scared what might happen to Mrs. Franklin.

"Miss Dowry, do-zz you d'think me evil too?" asked Bibb.

"Please don't make me go away Bibb. It ain't right."

"Mrs. Franklin, I will only ask one more time. What intentions (srpt)?"

"You are a depraved man and our Anna is vulnerable. From your depravity can come all sorts of vileness and violations injuring our dear adopted Anna. I cannot stand the thought of you touching her or threatening her or repeating any of those hideous acts reported in the papers about you. I cannot bear it! I cannot bear it. Please, Mr. Toivo, take the money and go. Ruin us, but leave her alone! If you must, take me instead. I have had a full life, but not our Anna. I plead with you! Tommy, don't do it. Please! I beg you with all the love of a mother's heart not to take our Anna from us."

"Mrs. Franklin, I am unimpressed (srpt) with both your offer and-zz your passion (srpt). I am taking Anna with me (srpt). We are going to Fort Rice. Anna is a big girl and has made up her own big girl mind. You have worn out your welcome here. You have nothing left to say I intend-zz to listen to. You best leave now (srpt) before…"

"I cannot leave, Tommy. I must have my way."

"Mrs. Franklin, I (srpt) cannot make d'this any plainer: The answer is no. Now go home."

"I appeal to the God of Anna's mother for you to change your mind. I have no other plea left to make. You must, you must give in. I have nothing left. You discount a mother's love, you balk at all the money I can muster, and you ridicule the passionate tears of an elderly woman. What is there left that I can plea? Bibb, you must concede or I will go to my grave bereft of my only daughter. Bibb please! Do I have to get down on both knees and beg? Can't you spare me of such shame?"

Bibb got up, holstered his gun, threw his coat over his shoulder and left the room. Every reason why he disliked women was in full display and he couldn't stomach another ounce of it. Bibb slammed the door so hard behind him that it was still rattling when the two women remaining in the room finally looked at each other. "Where do you think he went?" asked Mrs. Franklin.

"I'm scared," squeaked Miss Dowry. "I'm scared! We got to do something! Bibb never leaves town without seven dead, and you fired up the hate in him so bad. You saw his eyes! I got to run as fast as I can to get the sheriff. Is there any way you can warn Anna? There has to be somebody in the bar downstairs with a fast horse. Mrs. Franklin, quick, quick, we have no time to spare!" Miss Dowry flew out of the door, not even taking the time to put on her coat.

==0==

As Bibb exited the hotel he happened to see down the street the exact person he was seeking. Recognized by his hat, Bibb followed after the doctor as he was entering the brothel known as Fanny's Attic just downhill a few businesses from the Red Buffalo.

Bibb's entrance at the entertainment establishment was greeted by a woman who in that line of business might be considered past her prime. She sat him down at a table and offered him a drink. She started the small talk by asking him what took him so long to finally make his way down to her place for a visit.

"I'm here to see my doctor (srpt). I saw-zz him walk in here a few moments before I-zz did."

"He is currently upstairs. We make it a policy to never interrupt any guests once somebody goes through that door. We have several nurses in the house that can help you with your problem." The woman made eye contact with one of the ladies at the bar and she started towards their table. "In fact here comes Annie. Talk to her."

"I'm here (srpt) to see d'the doctor, and if you don't call him down (srpt) I'll go up and get-zz him. Send your bouncer over here-zz so I can speak my peace with him first (srpt). I d'think we can-zz reach an understanding quickly."

"The doctor is on a house call, not a visit. One of my girls got roughed up and she overdid her pain pills in a big way. He is upstairs helping her un-swallow what she should have only taken one of. Talk to Annie anyway. You're being here is good for business even if you want none of my business… yet."

"And you are fetching d'the doctor (srpt)? D'this is when you say yes."

"After my girl is attended to I will send the doctor down. Let Annie help solve your patience problem." Annie replaced her at Bibb's table as Fanny got up to leave.

"I'd ask what happened to you, but I already know." She could not help but stare. "Does your face hurt bad? Ugly is hard enough to suffer, but that looks painful deep down to the bones."

After a pause, and seeing no bait on that hook, Bibb responded to her. He was very careful to only look at her eyes. "Annie? D'that is your name?"

"Yes. What can I help you with? I know all about helping a man forget his suffering."

"Why are you here?"

"Here at the table with you, here in this hotel, here in Deadwood, or here as in being alive?"

"You pick."

"I want to talk about you. Are you as fast as they say you are? Finish your drink quick and I'll get you another one. I'm getting a bit thirsty myself. How about you buy me a drink?"

"How about you-zz going away (srpt)? I am wasting your time (srpt) and you are wasting mine."

"Wasting time? I'm not, but you sure are! Why aren't you at home with that rich itch of yours, or is that why you're here? Well, I certainly don't blame you." She read his face and changed her tone. "Loosen up. Relax. I'm ready if you are. Whisper to your Annie one of your little secrets into my ear. I won't tell. Do you intend to make an honest woman out of her? Good luck with that!"

"I don't-zz have any Annies. What do you-zz know about Mrs. Gorgon?" replied Bibb.

"Buy me a drink and I will tell you more than you want to know about her. Buy me a second drink and I will tell you what I know about her late husband."

"Interesting… (srpt)"

"Who knows what might happen then, Big Boy. Loosen up your wallet a bit and your Annie might start to sweetly whisper into your ear the secrets I know about you! Are you game?"

"Interesting… (srpt)" Bibb felt like he was being pulled into a conversation he had no business being a part of. He thought of waiting outside, but some dark curiosity kept him at the table. All of his internal self-justifications were lame, but yet he stayed there wondering what she would say next.

==0==

She was on her second drink when the doctor came downstairs. He had been told that Bibb was waiting for him. The doctor was quite disappointed to see his patient in the brothel engaged in a conversation with one of the girls. He felt Bibb would be vulnerable to Fanny's females, and the doctor wanted Bibb out of there fast. Bibb stood up as he arrived at the table, and so did Annie.

"Esther, what do you think you are doing?" asked the doctor.

"Entertaining Tommy."

"I d'thought you said your name was Annie," stated Bibb, suddenly feeling very gullible.

"But you like the name Annie, so I'm your Annie tonight."

"Esther, go tell Fanny to pay up. It will be the usual fee for the pump plus two bits for the extra bandages. Bibb must have a good reason to follow me here, so Esther, your turn is over. Be a dear and scoot along." She did. There were not many house rules, but Fanny enforced the few she had without mercy. Near the top of the list writ in stone was, "Thou shalt not disrespect the doctor."

Once the doctor sat down Bibb said softly, "I'm hurting, Doc. My innards are on fire."

"Do you know why I am here, Bibb?"

"No."

"It's because of a very confused girl upstairs decided to mix pain pills with some booze and it almost killed her. I see you have already had a drink so you can just forget about getting anything from my pantry."

"Are we done in here d'then (srpt)? D'there is nothing at d'this place for me. D'the music is too loud, and d'the drinks are twice d'the cost with twice d'the water diluting d'them down (srpt)."

"What are you doing out of bed and away from your nurse?"

"My room was invaded by a crazy woman (srpt) with a gun. I took-zz it away from her. She-zz wouldn't leave when I asked, so I left instead."

"Bibb, you need to learn how to roll over in bed and start to snore, not run down the street to the nearest brothel. I thought you would be worried about your reputation now that you're a married man."

"What-zz (srpt)?" answered Bibb.

"I didn't stutter. Let's get you back to your room and take a look at what is eating you." On the way out the door Fanny gave the doctor some cash and a thank you. Bibb was still wondering what the doctor had meant by his previous statement. The doctor continued, "What was her complaint? My guess is that your irritating visitor was Mrs. Franklin."

Bibb waited until they were away from the lights of the hotel. "How-zz did you-zz know d'that?"

"I didn't know that, but I saw it coming. She has some pretty strong attitudes about what is right and what is wrong. I venture to guess she might of have shared some of her core beliefs with you, or should I say at you?"

"She seems to be quite attached to Anna (srpt) and opinionated about who sleeps with who and how and by what authority. She (srpt) d'thinks strongly d'that I have no business keeping my promise to Anna (srpt) short of being-zz married to her."

"Do you agree with her or not? I am interested in your answer given what I have seen of your chest."

"What has d'that got to do with-zz anything?" replied Bibb.

"Your ribs are the same ones you were born with, but I suspect there might be a new heart in there somewhere. I bet my medicine chest on it. Let's sit down and discuss this more on that bench over there. So what is your answer, Bibb?"

Bibb stopped and stared at the man. "I-zz can hardly be expected to-zz marry (srpt) a woman I hate. Not just hate (srpt), but I-zz despise d'the woman front to back, top to bottom (srpt), and inside to outside. Everything (srpt); everything I have ever disliked about d'them beasties she is d'the fullest of d'the fullest of everything wrong about d'them."

"I didn't ask that question Bibb. I asked you if you agreed with Mrs. Franklin or not."

"If-zz I agree with Mrs. Franklin (srpt), d'then I would have to marry d'that despicable wretch, and I don't even want to d'think about d'that d'thought (srpt)." Bibb was starting to feel disrespectful and ungrateful to the doctor who invested heavily in his health. The man, without being asked, applied his all to save his life.

"Bibb, I can see why she hates you too. Can't you answer a simple question? Do you agree with Mrs. Franklin or not? I'm your doctor. Let's do some surgery here. You are committed by a holy covenant to take that woman to Fort Rice. So do you reckon that what God calls holy is less holy to man, as if man could dilute any proclamation of God? Are you telling me that God's opinion only matters as long as you get your way? Do you think that being bound by a covenant to God and Anna is but a happy convenience to get her to play nice? Is your covenant subordinate to a mere piece of paper that a judge can sign to make playing house with Anna legal? If you say yes to these questions I will be highly disappointed in you. What God has joined together let no man put asunder. Does that ring a bell, Bibb? Think higher, Bibb. Step back for a second. Tell me son, what do you think God thinks about this? Is a covenant, something God has freely bound Himself to mortals with throughout history, take a back seat to a visit with the Justice of the Peace? Bibb, you're playing with eternal fire here. When compared to what you and Anna did last Sunday, marriage doesn't rise to the level of whistling Dixie in the desert. A holy covenant is vastly more important to God than jumping the broom with a girl you might be fond of, or in your case, abhor."

"But-zz if I agree with-zz her… ugh, d'that is a living death! God ain't d'that mean, even to an outlaw! I was told He-zz was a God of mercy (srpt), but I ain't-zz been seeing-zz none of d'that!"

"Or mercy to a widow? Wake up, Bibb! Do you think she likes you or thinks you worthy of marriage to her? The man who killed her husband? Have I been giving you too many pain killers to fog your mind? And now the ugliest man in the territory comes waltzing into her life – a man that wants to take up playing house together under the stars and hotel rooms from here to who knows where? Bibb, do you really think she is ecstatic about riding with you to Fort Rice? And you still haven't answered the question. Do you agree with Mrs. Franklin or not?"

"I can't agree with her. I-zz just can't. God won't allow it."

"So God has been talking to you lately? Besides taking Anna across the plains without the benefit of marriage what else did the Almighty tell you? Did He also tell you to paint yourself up in mustard, crawl on the roof of a barn and howl at the moon? I would really like to hear the answer to this claim. There are not a lot of gray areas with God's opinion on marriage. I'm not interested in any can do or can't do out of you. I want a straight answer. Do you agree with Mrs. Franklin or not?"

"I can't-zz because I know d'that God wants-zz me to marry somebody else."

"Well isn't that convenient! You might have thought about that before your last trip to the altar! Bibb, are you lying to me? Up to now I thought you were honestly telling me what you thought. So are you planning to keep yourself pure for this other woman?"

"Yes."

"Yes, what?" replied the doctor, almost angry with his wounded patient. "Yes you were lying or yes about keeping yourself pure? Have you mentioned your romantic intentions to your new dearest betrothed yet? That would be a good start in convincing me. Who is she, Bibb? I hope it isn't your latest Annie. And I still want you to answer my question about agreeing with Mrs. Franklin or not."

"It is no secret who she is doctor (srpt), and no (srpt), I haven't declared my intentions to Mrs. Gorgon yet. The woman is my late brother's widow (srpt), Anna Toivo. To all d'the newspapers her name is Humbird. She has claimed me as hers (srpt) but I have refused her. D'that was until my-zz change of heart, or as you said (srpt), a new heart I-zz got in Miles City. Ever since d'that time I have completely changed (srpt) my mind-zz about her, like Boaz was to Ruth. I not-zz only have a duty but now also a desire to wed her. And yes (srpt), and laugh if you want, but I have never-zz been able to convince (srpt) any woman to become impure with me. I am what I am (srpt), and with a better heart, a despicable mind, and an untouched body (srpt), I hope to woo her. If God can fix my heart, He can fix my mind too (srpt), even d'though I'm not too fond (srpt) of His ways of fixing."

"So do you agree with Mrs. Franklin? Tell me true." The doctor sounded more sympathetic.

"I know Mrs. Franklin is right but d'there got-zz to be another way. I know d'that I know d'that I know I am supposed to marry Humbird (srpt). God would not put d'that desire in me-zz just to hitch me up permanent-zz forever and ever and ever with d'that Gorgon woman."

"Like it or not or thinking it or not, Bibb, you made your decision last Sunday in church."

"D'this is like death to a hope d'that I d'thought was surely from God. Like Abraham and Sarah never having kids, or Joseph d'thinking he would rule over his brothers just to find himself sold away as a slave. Not only d'this ain't fair, it is wrong. I hate d'that woman and every-d'thing she is. How can God tell me one minute to marry d'that monster, take her to Fort Rice and also tell me to save myself for Humbird?"

"Anna is not a monster, and you better erase that notion from your head. She may have scores of imperfections, but so what? If you only knew how sick we all are in body and soul you would be surprised that any of us would live to see lunch tomorrow. If God's justice ever overtook his mercy we would all be dead. But sickness is not the issue in play here. As far as I'm concerned you are more wed than most married people. Whose idea was that covenant anyway? Mr. Franklin or you?"

"It was me. I d'thought I was doing what I was supposed to (srpt). I see I have ruined not just my hopes, but Anna's too, (srpt) and also any hope for a long life with my Humbird."

"My Humbird? Do you really mean that Bibb? Are you that certain that God has ordained you to marry her? I'm not talking feelings here Bibb. Convince me you are telling me the truth about this 'My Humbird' of yours."

"I've d'thought-zz lot about it (srpt) and even wrote down my ten reasons. One I already told you; d'the Ruth d'thing. One was really bad and I am ashamed of myself. Humbird controls all my money (srpt), my stuff, my homestead (srpt), and every other material possession I-zz have except my guns and bedroll. I don't even own my own horse, and I want-zz all-zz my stuff back. D'that reason really stinks in God's eyes (srpt) and I'm ashamed I even catch myself d'thinking like d'that (srpt), but I do."

"Did you think this way before you entered the covenant with Anna?"

"Yes. I-zz d'thought d'there would be no problem traveling to Fort Rice together (srpt). She has all her rules about-zz d'this and d'that, and I had-zz no-zz problems with none-zz of her rules (srpt). She wanted me to always keep d'three feet away from her all d'the time. I would rather keep d'three miles away (srpt), and d'that might be too close to her. I really botched d'this up (srpt), didn't I?"

"Swear to me that you are telling me the truth."

Bibb replied, "I don't-zz like to swear. I'm cured of d'that."

"I know; that's why I'm asking. Swear it Bibb, and I will commit to help you."

"I don't want to-zz swear d'that-zz I-zz hates anybody. It's d'the truth. I'-zz hate-zz her, but-zz I shouldn't be swearing to-zz it. How can you help me anyway?"

"Swear it Bibb. Swear it by the God of Anna's mother that you have told me the truth."

"You really will help me (srpt)?"

"Yes, I will. There may be a way out of this."

"And keep my covenant (srpt)? You aren't telling me to sneak-zz out of town and break my promises, are you (srpt). I can't do d'that."

"Yes, the covenant stays unbroken, Mrs. Franklin is satisfied, and you can remain pure for your sweet Humbird. But I have to know you are telling the truth. Swear it, Bibb."

"May God strike me dead (srpt) if I have lied to you."

"You're not going to get off that easy. Swear it, Bibb."

"I swear it to God as my witness (srpt). I have told you d'the truth. I want to keep all my promises. Please help me."

The doctor shook Bibb's hand, not just in peace, but to test the words Bibb had just spoken. Bibb wasn't lying; he could tell. "Let's go." They got up and started back towards the Red Buffalo.

==0==

Miss Dowry, Bibb's nurse, was the first to bolt down the stairs to the lobby of the Red Buffalo. She pleaded with clerk to take her to the sheriff, and when he said he couldn't, she ran into the center of the saloon area and yelled with her loudest voice, made squeaky by fear, that Bibb was on the loose and the sheriff had to be told. The bartender whistled loudly, the musicians stopped, and the place went into an eerie silence. Miss Dowry made the appeal again, even more emphatic than the first time. A gruff old half sober miner broke the moment of silence and asked, "You say Bibb?"

She ran to him, which shocked everyone in the room, and the miner twice that. "Do you know where the sheriff lives? Take me there! Bibb may be set on deadly revenge." At that moment a gunshot was heard outside from somewhere. That was common in Deadwood, but the timing was almost evil.

Another man who noted the miner's condition spoke up. "He ain't takin' you ma'am. If he does you both might fall into a pit. Come with me. Let's go." The sober man and the nurse immediately departed into a very dark night. Other men, those who had a sense of manliness to be home to protect their families, left one by one. Another drunk was heard to say that if Bibb ain't here, then the Red Buffalo Bar was the safest place to be... and the music and dancing and winking and drinking and dealing and betting all restarted as if nothing happened.

Mrs. Franklin witnessed the event from the front door and hoped to snag a helper as some of the men left the saloon. She recognized one of Anna's mercantile employees and latched on to him. Her demeanor gave the man no choice, and she dispatched the man to the Gorgon mansion equipped with a short note she had quickly written. Anna was to flee her home immediately and to meet her at her seamstress's back room. The man was emphatically told as he mounted his horse to get her out of her house immediately and take her to Xue's just as she was found, and not to entertain any backtalk. Such was the tear filled appeal that the man did not hesitate. He, and everybody else in the hotel, knew something was up, and Bibb was unaccounted for.

A dreadful fear came over Mrs. Franklin. She realized that she might be number one on his list if Bibb decided to paint the town red with blood before he left the gulch. She had no escort and the night was dark and cold. She reasoned that Bibb had no argument with her husband, but if she went home immediately to be by his side Bibb might find them both, kill her, and then convict her husband of guilt by association and murder him too. She wanted to know immediately if Bibb came back and decided the best place to hide in that city was by the dish basin in the kitchen. Nobody would suspect her in an apron helping in the kitchen of a saloon, and from there news would be known quickly.

A quarter hour later she realized how confused she was! She was in a small room in the back with no escape. Just like a caged animal, if Bibb ever returned to the Red Buffalo she would be an easy notch on his ax. For only the price of a drink any drunk would delight in telling that killer where she was hiding. Then she remembered she was supposed to meet Anna at Xue's backroom and made immediate plans for her departure. She retrieved her coat and purse from the room and quietly stepped out alone into the dark of the night. Xue's laundry was only three city blocks away, but a long way to walk tonight. Her loaded gun left the hotel in the hands of an angry murderer.

==0==

While in the shadows near the entrance to the Red Buffalo the doctor reinitiated the conversation with his patient. "Bibb, why were you so surprised when I inferred you were a married man? I heard on good authority that the preacher pronounced you two man and wife."

"D'the preacher took it back, Doc (srpt). We ain't married."

"I heard of good authority that the preacher pronounced you and Anna man and wife."

"Doc, you heard wrong (srpt). I was d'there."

"I heard of good authority that the preacher pronounced you and Anna man and wife."

"What is your point? We only made a covenant (srpt). To be married you-zz have to sign some silly form (srpt) and have it-zz registered at d'the courthouse."

"I was happily surprised that Mr. Franklin, as part of his legal responsibilities, provided you with a Last Will and Testament just in case you don't make it to Fort Rice with your wife. Knowing your fondness for Humbird he prepared it so you would leave all your wealth, even newly acquired businesses, mines, and bank accounts to the one person you hope to grow old with."

Bibb couldn't believe what his good ear was hearing, and how dull a wit he was. He responded, "Anna knows d'that too, and it-zz says nothing about her getting-zz any-d'thing if I die. D'that sounds more like life insurance d'than a will. So you are saying d'that if I get a marriage certificate signed (srpt) and registered at d'the courthouse we-zz would be legally married? Okay, but aren't you forgetting d'that Anna would-zz have to sign the wedding license too (srpt)?"

"Mr. Franklin has Anna Gorgon's Power of Attorney. It is for legal stuff like deeds and things."

"But not-zz for a wedding license (srpt), and d'that certainly would be fraud."

"Lest you forget, Mr. Franklin also has a Power of Malarkey too. Somebody signed all those deeds and contracts when Mrs. Gorgon was in hiding for six months. And that signature is remarkably identical to her signatures prior to her disappearance and now found on your will."

"D'that would certainly be fraud (srpt) and he would lose-zz his right to practice law."

"And you would have a legal footing to have the wedding annulled once you made it to Fort Rice. Of course, that is only if the marriage was never consummated between here and there."

"He would still lose his license, and this plot is unfair to Anna too."

"She doesn't need to know. God knows and that is all that matters. He heard your vows, He heard her vows, and He heard the preacher in His name pronounce you wed. Sounds cut and dried to me. Your covenant with Anna cancels upon mutual fulfillment. Sounds like an annulment on the other side of the Missouri would be just as reasonable to cancel the marriage once the covenant is fulfilled. Man has more rules than God, so you might want Mr. Franklin to explain what has to be done and undone to satisfy the legal requirements of man. By the way, how kind do you plan to be to Anna? God heard your vows too. And about your claim this would be unfair to Anna? I say not. She was and continues to be the aggressor. One must be careful what one vows at the altar of God. She even sealed it with blood from your ear. A blood covenant trumps man's pen and ink on paper just as soundly as a royal flush outranks a pair of deuces."

"Mr. Franklin would-zz never do it. D'that is so wrong."

"So you think Mrs. Franklin and he are in disagreement in deep seated convictions about you two traveling and living alone together without benefit of marriage? I most heartily insist that is impossible. Mr. Franklin would love to see you two married. Not for your sake but so God's name isn't slandered. Mr. Franklin can't make you marry, but with proper persuasion you can make him prepare documents and register them at the court house. A man would do just about anything an outlaw would demand to preserve his life. Given a credible death threat scenario he would be acquitted of fraud. Now, if Anna never finds out and you can pull this off, you will be free to marry Humbird once the covenant is fulfilled. If Anna finds out you two are legally married, she just might keep you as a slave to her every whim and make your life miserable. Trust me on this. She knows how to make a husband regret every waking hour of every waking day, and to fear for his life by merely going to sleep at night before she does."

"What are you-zz saying?"

"I'm saying you have some Bibb work to do. I'll be waiting at the Red Buffalo to hear if you pulled it off or not, and then to look at that chest of yours."

==0==

The hotel clerk saw the doctor walk into the Red Buffalo and immediately approached him. "Do you know where Bibb is, Doctor?"

"His nurse should be watching him sleep upstairs. Is that not the case?"

"He left the hotel with a very hostile attitude almost an hour ago. He had a visitor that may have brought out the evil in him, and soon after her arrival he left. So did your nurse and Mrs. Franklin."

"So who was it that got Bibb angry, the nurse or Mrs. Franklin? Never mind. My nurse doesn't have it in her. Where did they go? Where did Bibb go?"

"All I know is that the nurse got somebody to help fetch the sheriff. Nobody knows where Mrs. Franklin is, but she better be careful if she doesn't want to be found cooling off at the undertakers."

"Was Bibb armed?"

"Who knows? He left so unexpectedly. For being so busted up he certainly can be fast."

"I'll be upstairs in Bibb's room if you need me."

"I'm sorry to say this, but you might have a busy night."

"It has already been a long night. I know firsthand that the natives are restless."

==0==

"The livery is closed," said the boy cleaning the barn. "Come back in the morning."

"I'm-zz not here for my horse, son (srpt)."

The boy immediately recognized the voice. "What can I get for you, Bibb?"

"I need-zz my ax," said Bibb with a voice as cold as ice.

"What for?"

"You ask-zz too many questions, boy (srpt)."

"You know the sheriff told us to lock your stuff up."

"What-zz has d'that to do-zz with you retrieving my ax, son?"

The stable boy knew exactly Bibb's point. "I will have to let the sheriff know I let you get your hatchet. He's worried about you getting in a mean mood, kind of like you are in now, no offense."

"I'm depending on you-zz telling him (srpt). You are wasting time, son. Giddy-up (srpt)."

Bibb secured his hatchet and disappeared into the night. The stable boy finished locking up the office and was securing the back door when another late evening visitor showed up.

"Bibb, are you in there? It's the sheriff."

The stable boy yelled back that he was the only one in the barn and was coming up to meet him. When they got into the light the stable boy told the sheriff that he had just missed seeing Bibb. "Bibb ain't been gone but two minutes, sir. He came by here and got his ax."

"It's supposed to be locked up, son."

"Bibb didn't ask nice, sir. I was armed with only a broom and he had his six-shooter on his hip. Given his mood I decided not to argue with him."

"So his horse is still here?"

"Yes, sir."

"Did he say where he was going?"

"Sir, with the way he was looking at me I wasn't going to ask nothin' and say nothin' but 'Yes sir' or 'No sir'."

"Did he mention any people's names?"

"No, sir."

"Which way did he leave?"

"Towards Main Street, sir."

"What was he wearing? Was he fully dressed? Did he have a coat?"

"He had on a wool shirt and a coat but no hat. He did have his knife by his boot. Sir, he seemed pretty intense and pretty mad. Somebody really upset him. He looked like he was going to do something about it, you know, permanent like."

The sheriff's heart sank into his chest. It would have been far better if the outlaw had an intention of leaving town. "I'm going to send one of my deputies to stay the rest of the night here with you. I want you to get Bibb's horse ready to ride with all his stuff packed and strapped to go. If the man wants to leave town in a hurry, I'm going to help him on his way. Somebody else can bring him to justice if need be."

==0==

The news the sheriff heard at the Red Buffalo further lowered his expectations for a peaceful ending to this evening. When he asked the clerk if he knew where Bibb was the hotel employee replied that he was seen buying drinks for a lady down at Fanny's Attic. As far as the sheriff was concerned that was a dead end. His experience getting information at Fanny's was that nothing true was answered to any of his questions, and with just cause. He went down the street to see if that assumption was still true, and to his surprise it was not. After being ridiculed the sheriff asked where the door leading back into the street was. The bouncer answered with the truth that time. In fact, Fanny walked him over to it just in case he got lost negotiating the tables on his way out. The sheriff's gut feeling was that Bibb had fallen off the virtue wagon, and in a big way. Tonight may be the worst crisis in his tenure as sheriff. His worst nightmare would be finding a bad Bibb in a bad mood doing a bad thing and he having the responsibility of bringing him in.

The sheriff had to act quickly, but wasn't sure what to do or where to do it at. One of his six deputies lived above a store a block away and he went there first. He instructed the man to get himself and the other five deputies to the jail within an hour. When the sheriff briefly explained the urgency even the deputy's wife offered to help contact the other deputies.

The sheriff returned and posted himself outside of Fanny's Attic. When the first John stumbled out the establishment he approached him and shook him down for some information about Bibb. The John protested in vain at the sheriff's threats and eventually told the sheriff he knew nothing nor saw nothing of Bibb there. A second victim of the sheriff's tactics was more successful, if that John told the truth. He did confirm a double ugly man, most likely Bibb, did buy some drinks for a girl there but left when an unknown man came into Fanny's and pulled him out of there. There was no evidence that either or neither man told the truth. A third man had the same story as the first, nothing of substance, but this time the sheriff convinced the man to return inside and ask Fanny to meet him by the back door.

Fanny did show up but she had very little to say. The sheriff asked direct questions and Fanny countered by asking what future favors she could expect if she cooperated. An agreement was made and Fanny offered one piece of information. She told the sheriff that earlier that evening a doctor found his lost patient and took him home with him. The sheriff couldn't help but wonder if that was a partial truth or a whole truth. He quickly walked back to the jail to meet his deputies.

He had to rely on his deputies to help with his plan to protect the town that evening. One deputy was sent to the livery as promised and with a task to get four horses ready to ride in case they had to form a posse. Two deputies were told to stake out Fanny's Attic in case Bibb had been delayed upstairs at that establishment. They were told to return to the livery in an hour. Two were sent to the Gorgon mansion, question anybody there, warn them, and return to the livery if there wasn't a trail of clues to follow. One deputy accompanied the sheriff to the Red Buffalo via the doctor's residence. All would meet at the livery no later than two hours from then, and quicker if they heard the church bell ring.

==()==

Mrs. Franklin saw no light inside of Xue's laundry but kept knocking on the door and windows anyway. The prospect of what to do if nobody answered was starting to cause her to panic. She wondered if she needed to go to the Gorgon mansion, but no, that would be as unwise as washing dishes. Mrs. Franklin stood by the window just in case somebody inside would want to make sure it was her (and only her) standing outside. Eventually the door opened a crack and Mrs. Franklin was whisked into the Chinese laundry.

Followed by a "shhhh" from Xue, Mrs. Franklin was taken through a labyrinth of laundry bags and doorways in complete darkness to a back room. The only furniture at their destination was bags of unclaimed laundry that had been converted into chairs. In one of those makeshift chairs was Anna Gorgon.

In words just above a whisper Anna started the conversation. "What is this all about, Mrs. Franklin? The person you sent practically man-handled me extracting me from my home. We rode double on his horse to within a block of here, tied up his horse and escorted me to the front door. Just look at me in my housedress and unkempt hair."

"At least you are alive, Anna. Bibb has been unleashed into an evil rampage on this town. I know because I caused it. I thought I was doing the right thing, and it turned out very wrong."

"What did you say to set him off?" asked Anna.

"I said I wasn't packing. At gunpoint he proved me a liar and took away my derringer. That was when everything went from bad to evil."

"Why would you even go there, Mrs. Franklin? Didn't your husband warn you not to go?"

"He did, but I went anyway. I didn't think it would turn out so badly. I really erred, and now your life, my husband's life, and every citizen in this town are in danger. A crazed killer is on the loose and it is entirely my fault. Anna, seriously, can we trust the man who brought you here? He won't tell Bibb where to find us, will he?"

"We must trust him. Where else do we have to go? I swore him to secrecy. He works for me and will not want to risk losing his employment."

"But is he willing to lose his employer? That is an entirely different question. Can we find sanctuary in the church?"

"And walk past that cemetery? No thank you, and somebody might find us there. Bibb was to hang for arson once and if a fire breaks out in Deadwood, somebody would go there to clang the bell. No, we are best off here."

"What about your barn, Anna?"

"Maybe, but let's stay put for now. We will be warm here. More important, my friend Xue is here and she can let us know when it is safe to leave. In the barn we only have our intuition and wits. Neither of those two weapons are sharper than Bibb's ax."

"I'm scared."

"Me too; very scared."

"You no worry please," interjected Xue. All worry all mistake. You sleep behind laundry, I watch door. You no so fuzzy think in morning. You wake with sharp think."

==0==

Not finding the doctor at home, the sheriff and his deputy returned to the Red Buffalo. Asking the clerk if he had seen the doctor, the clerk replied that he and the nurse had been up in Bibb's room waiting for Tommy's return. The sheriff was incredulous. If he had only asked about the doctor the last time through he would not have gone on such a goose chase.

The sheriff and his deputy were surprised when they caught the doctor and the nurse knee deep in lye and soap suds sterilizing the room. The doctor offered them both a brush to help clean but they declined. They were there for information about Bibb. Miss Dowry offered to tell the story once again (she had already told the doctor) and to answer any other questions they may have.

Ten minutes into the narrative the sheriff said he had heard enough to know where to go next. Mr. Franklin would need to be warned or rescued. He told the doctor he was going over to the livery and four of them were going to ride out to Mr. Franklin's home. In the sheriff's haste he had forgotten to ask the doctor if he had knew anything about Bibb's demeanor or whereabouts.

Once the sheriff left the room the doctor told Miss Dowry to go home and have her sister start her shift two hours earlier than normal. He didn't want the same nurse there when Bibb returned. He wanted to believe Bibb would have his emotions in check tonight, but his history gave evidence of deadly serious lapses in self-control. No, it would be better to be safe than sorry. The doctor changed his mind and decided to have all three Dowry daughters come to the Red Buffalo. Bibb may know where they lived, and they were safer with him than at home.

==0==

The note on the dining room table at the Franklin home disturbed her husband exceedingly. His wife had written to her husband that his dinner should still be warm in their oven and that she was going down to the Red Buffalo to give Bibb a piece of her mind. It was understandable why she left before he got home from the office because he would have tried to talk her out of it. He recalled his favorite complaint, repeating that he had "More influence on the behavior of polar bears in Alaska than he had with the dear woman God gave me." He knew she certainly was a determined woman.

This development had all the makings of a really bad decision, and something they had talked about several times since last Sunday. He didn't disagree with her in principle, in complete accord there, but very much so in approach. She did not give Tommy any credit for having a brain or a heart, and felt very strongly about her God given mission to educate him on the non-optional principles of life. Mr. Franklin looked around the house, and yes, she had taken her derringer. He prayed that God would protect his wife from Bibb's wrath. Bibb had very little tolerance for women with strong opinions, and especially those with a misplaced nose in his personal business.

Instead of eating dinner, Mr. Franklin made a sandwich and returned to his office. He fully expected a visit from the outlaw, and he did not want that visit to occur at his home. Bibb may have specific legal requests that could only be fulfilled at his office. He left an open note addressed to his wife placed on the front door of his house explaining that he had returned to his office to accomplish more Gorgon business. He also wrote at the bottom of the note for her to have fun at the lady's club tonight. If Bibb did show up, the note might redirect him away from his home. There was no lady's club but it did give an impression she would not be home anytime soon.

==0==

Bibb's predicament was that he did not know where anybody other than Anna lived in this town. As he left the livery he decided that he didn't need to know because he knew where to find somebody who did know.

As Bibb suspected, there were candles burning late at the desks of at least two reporters in the building just a block off of the main street. Bibb, spying out the place, also noticed a typesetter in the back of the building working the press with tomorrow's morning newspaper. The noise of the operation covered Bibb's entrance into the back of the building; the door was open to allow cool air in. The press operator never knew that Bibb went past him.

"Good evening, Bee (srpt)."

Bibb's unexpected announcement scared them both out of their wits. Both turned around at the same time and saw Bibb there with his ax in his hand and a pistol on his hip. Their faces turned white. Bee's knees gave out on her and she slipped back into her chair.

"Don't speak, either of you. Mr. Fly," continued Bibb, "D'this ain't no social visit. You-zz are coming with me (srpt). If you fuss, you-zz will still come with me (srpt), but to a plot adjacent to d'the church. If you understand (srpt) nod your head yes." Both nodded. "Let's go, Fly." Bibb looked back and continued, "Bee, if Fly doesn't cooperate (srpt), I will-zz be returning to take hostage your cooperation (srpt). Nod yes if you-zz understand." She did. "Bee, don't-zz be leaving here until Fly comes back (srpt). I know-zz where I can find you if you flee."

Once Bibb had left with his hostage in his buckboard, Bee ran to the back room and told the inker what had happened. She told him to immediately run to tell the sheriff. He told her to go herself to which she explained why she could not. He complied. She returned to her desk and wrote down everything she could remember from the incident.

The inker never did find the sheriff and returned to his post within the quarter hour. The paper had to be ready for sale by dawn, regardless if there was a Fly in deep ink or not.

==0==

Their first stop was Mr. Franklin's office. It was no secret how much work he still had to do to set Anna's deeds aright. Bibb decided he would check there first for the man. Bibb would instruct Fly to take him to Mr. Franklin's home if the man wasn't there, but he was. Bibb was glad he had to go no further to find him; he had already had his fill of Mrs. Franklin's whining today.

Bibb ordered Fly to get out of the wagon first and step up to the lawyer's office and knock. During the minute it took for Mr. Franklin to come to the door Bibb warned Fly that if he speaks, the Fly dies. Mr. Franklin did open the door and asked what the purpose of the visit was. Tommy told Mr. Franklin to invite them in and he would tell them.

Tommy explained to Mr. Franklin exactly what he wanted and wanted immediately. Mr. Franklin protested on legal and moral grounds. Tommy explained to Mr. Franklin that he wasn't asking Mr. Franklin's opinion on legal or moral issues but to prepare the documents immediately. Mr. Franklin protested again to which Bibb asked him if he could write with his left hand. Wondering why he inquired with that strange question, Bibb responded that he collects fingers from uncooperative lawyers. The newspaper reporter could only stand there in shock at what he was witnessing.

"Bibb, I have an extra copy of the certificate from last Sunday. It already has the signatures of three witnesses, but not yours, Anna's, or the preacher's."

"D'the preacher doesn't have to sign it. You-zz are a Justice of d'the Peace (srpt). You sign it."

"Bibb, this is highly irregular."

"Start writing (srpt) while you-zz still can."

Mr. Franklin completed the form, signed his name as the JP, and checked the box marked Marriage Certificate. "Sign it here as Tommy Toivo." Tommy did.

"Mr. Franklin, by your art-zz of persuasion, your life depends (srpt) on securing Anna's signature on d'this. The next order of business (srpt) is annulment papers. Prepare d'them, undated, and with-zz d'the reason being coercion of the JP, fraud (srpt), and failure to consummate. You get to sign d'this one too (srpt), Mr. Franklin, and d'then it will be my turn."

"Tommy, why are you doing this? Do you understand how many laws you have broken doing this? Let's pretend this never happened. Let's all go home and say this was a bad dream."

"Mr. Franklin, I am not-zz interested in your dreams. Sign d'the paper (srpt)." When he was finished Mr. Franklin signed it and handed it to Bibb for his signature too. Once done Bibb handed it back to Mr. Franklin. "Okay (srpt), now what must be done to-zz make d'this paper binding?"

"It will have to be registered at the courthouse. They are not open until tomorrow."

"Mr. Franklin, I believe-zz you are mistaken (srpt). D'they will be open tonight and d'this marriage will be recorded in the courthouse (srpt). Mr. Franklin, who has d'the keys to-zz d'the courthouse and d'the register? D'this in not a trick question, d'this is bet-zz your fingers and toes time (srpt)."

"The clerk would have both, but the courthouse is closed."

Bibb unlatched his revolver. "Mr. Franklin, you didn't understand (srpt). D'the courthouse is having special hours tonight (srpt). D'that annulment paper, well, you need to send that east to my good friend Major Ryder (srpt) along with d'the soon to be registered marriage license (srpt). Do you understand?"

"I could keep them here, Bibb."

"Yes you could (srpt), and if-zz Major Ryder doesn't have d'them when I arrive in Bismarck (srpt) Mr. Ax will be coming back to Deadwood for-zz your fingers. But what-zz good is a lawyer without fingers (srpt)? I guess I will just have to mercy kill-zz you. Do you understand me (srpt), Mr. Franklin?"

"This is highly irregular. I could lose my license over this."

"You-zz can also lose your wife too (srpt). Mrs. Franklin has already irritated me to no end (srpt), and she may also taste my-zz tainted form of justice, and before you do. You see (srpt), I don't trust lawyers. D'this simple d'threat isn't just a promise (srpt), it is insurance d'that you will follow-zz my instructions exactly (srpt). Are we-zz finished here yet?"

"I'll meet you at the courthouse, Bibb."

"Agreed. We will arrive d'there together 'cause you will sit in d'the front seat of d'the buckboard next to Fly (srpt). And don't worry about-zz the cold. You-zz can stay warm with d'the d'thought of what I'm packing and pointing. I'll be directly behind you to insure (srpt) your compliance. Fly, take us to d'the clerk's home. From d'there we can all ride together to d'the courthouse. Load up, let's go."

The next leg of the trip was rather tense, if seen through the eyes of Fly. Mr. Franklin suggested an approach that when they got to the clerk's home that first he would be the only one to speak, and second, Bibb do nothing to intimidate or coerce the man. Bibb replied to Mr. Franklin that he had but one chance to make things happen peacefully. (Bibb thought this was the portion of his plan that had the most unknowns and most risky. It made his trigger fingers itchy.)

When they arrived at the clerk's home, Mr. Franklin immediately apologized to the man for the late hour but it was exceedingly important to get a document recorded with the court before the midnight hour. The relationship that had developed over the years between Mr. Franklin and the clerk was one of mutual assistance, and it was at this moment that Mr. Franklin was calling in a favor much like the clerk had asked of Mr. Franklin many times. The man recognized Bibb not by his mannerisms but as the only man in town with such scars. Nor did he need any introductions to the reporter whose daily routine included checking the court register for news. It seemed pretty obvious to the clerk that if the reporter was with them to witness the recording of the document prior to midnight it could hardly be something nefarious.

The process to record the marriage had but one hiccup, and that was that it lacked Anna's signature. The clerk mentioned that small detail to Mr. Franklin as if this oversight was as routine as Mr. Franklin's response that the document would be signed in the morning. What Bibb thought was a show-stopper was but a yawn to the clerk. The deed was done, the document stamped, signed and numbered, and the record of action booked into the county register. Bibb and Anna were now officially and legally married. All had happened so mechanically that once done there seemed to be nothing left to do but to go home, pet the dog, drink some tea, and read a good book.

Mr. Franklin thanked the clerk once again as the buckboard with the four of them arrived back at his home. The reporter was quickly running low on self-control. He had to muster more from an unknown reserve to keep from speaking and apply his trade of asking questions. The next stop was back to Mr. Franklin's office. A similar good night was given by Mr. Franklin. He told Bibb to stop by next afternoon to see for himself a fresh signature on the document. In response, Bibb gave Mr. Franklin his wife's gun. This was not the time for conversation. Once inside his office, the anxious lawyer quickly inspected the gun. Noting it was still fully loaded, the man breathed a sigh of relief.

The ride back to the newspaper office was cautiously chatty. The newspaper reporter could not help but conclude that Bibb never suspected tonight's adventure had been anticipated by Mr. Franklin. The gun wasn't in the lawyer's plan, additional proof that Tommy's words and actions were as if he, acting independently and out of self-interest, was forcing his agenda onto others. Bibb's next words three times confirmed that the outlaw had no idea that Mr. Franklin and he had discussed the possibility of making legal Bibb and Anna's marriage days before. It was obvious that the clerk knew nothing of it either. Fly had to chuckle to himself, because until he saw the drama play out for himself he thought himself only inches from death too. He had to admit to himself he may not have been able to control himself from asking questions if Mr. Franklin and he had not previously discussed the subject discretely.

When they arrived back at the newspaper office Bibb hopped off the wagon with more of a thud than grace, and the face he made showed that it obviously hurt. He was still able to squeak out a strong admonition that none of this would be published until after Anna and he had left the city limits. Fly remarked he understood, to which Bibb repeated himself but this time reminding the reporter that as a courier he will be making several trips to Deadwood next year. The subliminal message was that Fly was a dead man if he couldn't keep it under his hat until they were gone.

Bibb walked into the livery hoping to quietly place his hatchet back in its holster and then return to the hotel. Once inside, he was surprised to be greeted by the stable boy, four deputies, and the sheriff. Bibb looked around, saw his horse ready to go as well as four other horses saddled. Bibb initiated the conversation, "What's up with-zz d'this, Sheriff?"

"Where have you been, Tommy? Let me see your ax."

"Put it away when you're done with it, Sheriff. You-zz seem to want to keep-zz it locked up. As for me, I'm going to bed."

The sheriff took the ax. "Not before you tell me where you have been, Tommy."

"Sheriff, can we-zz talk in d'the morning? I'll answer any d'thing you ask walking back to d'the Red Buffalo, but I've-zz got an appointment with d'the doctor d'there d'that I need immediately."

The sheriff inspected the ax and saw it showed more signs of rusting than of busting. It obviously had not been used to plant anymore citizens face down in the street tonight. He gave the hatchet to the stable boy and signaled a deputy to join him for the short stroll to the hotel. The only thing that Bibb confirmed to the sheriff on that short walk was that he had been entertained by Esther Annie at Fanny's Attic that evening. Neither the sheriff nor the deputy believed that alibi. What they feared was waking up the next morning to find mayhem as if a death angel had stalked the streets of Deadwood overnight.

The first question out of the doctor's mouth told the sheriff everything he wanted to know for the moment. "Bibb, did she hurt you or help you?" Both he and the deputy left Bibb to the doctor's care glad that, for now, all seemed aright in the city. He was glad he could tell his deputies to all go home. Bibb was back on his leash.

==0==

There was no Mrs. Franklin in the house when he arrived home from the office. Mr. Franklin was not overly concerned. Nobody was in danger anymore; well no more dire perils now than any other night in this rowdy town. He looked forward to hearing her story and hoped sincerely that she never connected the dots that would make her suspect he had anything to do with the event. He chuckled at her fate of hiding out somewhere overnight. He could empathize. He knew what tossing and turning on a cold couch alone was like on those evenings when he was told to go find a place elsewhere to sleep. Tonight she had been naughty, and it was her turn to chew on the soggy sandwiches and the bitter fruit of unintended consequences. Yet, his heart did hurt for her, but he had no idea where to start looking for her so he might comfort her and try to ease the trauma of the drama. His quickest hope of seeing her again was to sleep on his own familiar couch of banishment immediately inside their home's front door. Yes, it did hurt, and the longing to know if she was safe would rob him of his sleep.

Thursday, October 6, 1887

The varmint found me.

==0==

IT RAINED HARD for hours prior to dawn, and the change of weather exacerbated Bibb's pains. His first movement from the bed this morning reminded him of the thud he experienced climbing out of Fly's wagon late last night. All thoughts of getting out of his room today were cancelled. The doctor had succumbed to Bibb's sincere plea for pain medicine during his visit at breakfast, and ordered an all-day sleep for the man. His emphatic instruction to the Dowry girls was to keep Bibb in bed. The doctor said it twice to make sure he was clearly understood.

Undeterred by the rain, curiosity brought the preacher and his wife that morning to the hotel armed with some bread, wine, and a small vial of anointing oil. Miss Dowry was very talkative and Bibb did a lot of head nodding – not in agreement but as sleep kept overwhelming him. The preacher took the opportunity to pray for the man even if he wasn't lucid.

"We will come back at another time, Miss Dowry," said the preacher's wife.

"You better not wait too long. I think they plan on leaving early in the morning the day after tomorrow. They're having a party tomorrow night. Are you going to come?"

"I am aware of the types of parties Mrs. Gorgon is accustomed too, and we would not want to scandalize both her and us by attending. We will try again tomorrow."

==0==

Anna could not have been more miserable. The strange place to sleep, the leaking roof, the wet floor, and now all the noise of the laundry business made her wonder why anybody would put up with such conditions. Dressed as old ragamuffins she and Mrs. Franklin walked to Mr. Franklin's law office with laundry sacks over their heads to protect from the rain and hide their identities. Upon arrival Mr. Franklin's reaction was one of happy surprise. He said he was quite relieved to see them in whatever condition they arrived in. He brought them to the back office. Without prompting they immediately took up residence by the warm stove. It was a pitiful sight. He told his wife that once she was warm and dried out that he needed to notify the sheriff to stop his search for her.

"Why not me?" Anna was only hot on the inside. "Remember me? I'm the one who pays the freight around here! I was missing too!"

Mr. Franklin replied with sympathy to her outburst. "I'm sorry. I was not aware of your state of lost-ness. Anna, pardon my focus, but I couldn't think of anything other than where my own dear missing bride might be." Mr. Franklin redirected his conversation back to his wife and asked her why she decided to stay out all night. He gave her a gentle chastisement for giving him such a scare.

"If you only knew what I went through you would have more sympathy for me and my frayed nerves! Don't you know what happened last night?" said Mrs. Franklin to her husband.

"The only things I know about last night is that I got a lot of work done and that I came home to an empty house. Darling, please don't do that again. I need sympathy for frayed nerves too."

"And why didn't you come rescue me?" asked his wife.

"Rescue you from what? I thought you said you were going to a lady's club or something like that. I was more surprised this morning when you were still not home. On my way to the office I notified the sheriff of your disappearance. He did mention that you stopped by the Red Buffalo for a social call with somebody before you headed out to wherever you ladies hold your meetings."

"Didn't he tell you that Bibb had escaped from his hotel room and was savaging the city?"

"No, he didn't mention it. Which city are we talking about dear? Deadwood seems a bit wet, but completely un-savaged. But that doesn't change the present situation. How can I make you ladies more comfortable? You look, well, a bit rough this morning as if you two just finished a night shift at the sawmill. I bet you are hungry too. My courier will be back in about twenty minutes. Anna, may I send him to your home to fetch your carriage? I have some crackers here to hold you over. You both can eat a real breakfast and change out of those wet work clothes into something you are more accustomed to at Anna's. Darling, I would sure like to hear your story once you are happier with your condition. Anna, I will have some more documents later for you to sign. Maybe we could do signing over a late lunch here in my office? What about one o'clock? In the meantime I must return to my tasks. I need to get these documents registered today at the courthouse."

Within the hour the pair of wet hens were crated up and shipped over to the Gorgon mansion via a closed carriage with the window shades pulled down. Mrs. Franklin's intuition told her to be upset with her husband but she didn't know why. He had been very gracious to her this morning – something was awry. Her husband should have been furious with his discovery she had been at the Red Buffalo. She was beside herself because he did not even show a cupful of curiosity about how she ended up with Anna overnight. And she could not bring up the subject without paying for it.

==0==

Anna and Mrs. Franklin did clean up, ate a small breakfast and set out on their more urgent agenda. Mrs. Franklin was shown a guest room and Anna went to her own bedroom where they went about the task of recovering all the lost sleep they suffered overnight.

Except for Anna. When she married the notorious Mr. Gorgon they had a favorite verse they often sang with each other, a private love poem set to music. She had not sung it in months. But all night long at the laundry and now in her own bed during the day she was plagued with the ditty that would not leave her head. And the more she tried, the more it stayed. She hated the tune because it reminded her of her folly in marrying that no good man. She hated the tune all the more now because this version of the rhyme had different words:

> *Good and only good,*
> *You will belong to me,*
> *Kind and only kind,*
> *Precious Hannah Marie*

==0==

The nurse's will proved to be no match for a determined Tommy Toivo. After a good long nap, well past lunch and approaching dinner time, Bibb got up and decided to visit Anna. The real reason was to inspect her packing. She was a strong willed woman and Bibb had a nagging suspicion that Anna would take liberties with his instructions.

The Dowry twin protested for two reasons. First the doctor told Bibb to stay put. The second reason was her very bruised and sore shoulder, but she decided not to mention that. She knew that the trip to the Gorgon mansion would take at least forty minutes. There and back would be much too far for her Bibb. She caught herself wanting to take ownership of him. Introspection while helping him dress caused her to conclude that her answering of his most humble needs, reciprocated by Bibb in kindness (except for the incident firing Bibb's rifle) confused her heart. "Oh my, what would my mother say?!?" she spoke to herself. This latest nursing job certainly was an education in heart, mind, and soul, and they were not singing in harmony. Her mother had warned her about that earlier in life, and she was finding out how right she was.

None of the Dowry daughters' appeals ever mattered to Bibb once he set his mind on something, but at least this time he did say that she could come along. He was going regardless of what she decided. Resigned, she protested to her patient that he gave her no choice. She made him promise to protect her from the wrath of the doctor when he found out.

The freshness of the air after the storms proved too inviting. Bibb wanted to walk because he hated tramping his horse through the mud. After the heavy rain the streets were now part sewer and part muddle puddle. Miss Dowry gave in, bundled him up, and followed along.

==0==

The tune was still there, even at Mr. Franklin's office. Twice he asked Anna to go home to pack. He only had today and tomorrow to finalize all the legal papers and she was getting on his nerves.

> *Good and only good,*
> *You will belong to me,*
> *Kind and only kind,*
> *Precious Hannah Marie*

Anna eventually went back home. She was very frustrated and knew why. Besides that endless tune, she realized that nobody was kissing up to her anymore. There was a reason: she had no leverage. The day after tomorrow she would evaporate from their memories. Their boldness in speaking their minds proved they no longer feared her petty vengeances.

==0==

Bibb and his nurse knocked on the kitchen door at the back of the mansion. Bibb could never bring himself to ring the chimes in the front. They were too gaudy for his liking. The foreign noise of those gongs made his skin crawl. Understandably, Bibb hated loud unexpected noises.

The cook came to the door and immediately recognized the two. "Come in, come in! I just took some cake out of the oven. I want you to tell me what you think of it. I am trying out a new recipe with rhubarb in it. I'll go get the Misses." She cut them each a slice and went to find Mrs. Gorgon.

Anna was upstairs sitting on her bed with her hands over her ears. The tune was driving her insane, woeful as all day hiccups. When the cook notified Anna that Bibb was downstairs she commenced to throw a fit. There she was sitting in her bedroom in the midst of twenty trunks full of stuff and nowhere to hide them. He was surely going to want to force his way upstairs like he did before! The man was impossible… Oh, she wished that song would go away!

Anna put on a house dress, knowing that Bibb approved of those. Besides, she did not have the time to squeeze into a more flattering dress. She quickly put on some cosmetics and proceeded downstairs. She entered the kitchen just as Bibb and Miss Dowry finished their dessert.

"You-zz look lovely-zz d'this afternoon, Anna (srpt)!" said Bibb with a very sincere voice. "I am glad I-zz come over now (srpt). And Miss-zz, d'the cake was-zz very good-zz too. D'thank-zz you."

"What do you want, Bibb? Did you ride your horse over here? It could have broken a leg in the muddy streets, and then where would we be? And how did she get here?"

"Mrs. Gorgon," replied the nurse, "Mr. Toivo and I walked over here today. The color of the changing leaves is so delicious after the rain. You should go for a walk with us!"

Anna took the comment as an opportunity. She wanted Bibb as far away from the packing as possible, and she might walk him back to the hotel if she was clever enough. "Miss Dowry, you stay here and have another piece of cake. Mr. Toivo and I have some personal matters to discuss."

Bibb looked at Miss Dowry with the same look of surprise as on the other's face. "Sounds-zz good to me (srpt), Anna," said Bibb.

"I will get my shawl. Have another piece of cake."

Bibb wasn't going to wait for anybody to change their minds. He handed his plate to the cook and she gave him another generous portion. Bibb was delighted; finally something with taste that didn't hurt his teeth when he chewed it!

==0==

Anna went upstairs and changed her clothes once again. After emptying three trunks she found the dress she was seeking. She picked one that was shorter than her others because of the mud. She dug into another trunk and got herself a fashionable hat that matched her shawl and dress.

The real challenge was digging through three more trunks to find the right shoes for the event. Bibb had commented negatively about her shoes once, much to her aggravation. He said they were all worthless on the plains, and that shoes needed to be functional to have any value. There was so much that man did not know and needed to learn quickly if he expected to enjoy his trip with her to Fort Rice.

Once dressed, Anna went into her boudoir to fix her hair in the mirror and added a proper amount of cosmetics. While looking in the mirror the rhyme returned, but this time not in her head. It had moved! It was like it was eating into her heart! It was terrible! It was a bad dream! It was torture! The terrible thoughts it brought back of her husband; then it brought back of thoughts of the miserable time at the preacher's. The thought of her being stuck with that ugly outlaw in a binding covenant was indigestible. Then the despised name... then it came again... relentless...

Good and only good,
You will belong to me,
Kind and only kind,
Precious Hannah Marie

==0==

Anna and Bibb went through the great room and out the front door. There was a cool breeze in the air, a perfect late afternoon for a walk. They left the mansion grounds and headed towards town. Anna, emotionally worn, tried her best to be pleasant but was failing at it. She opted not to speak.

Half way back to the hotel curiosity finally overcame Bibb. He couldn't help but think Anna wanted him out of the mansion more than she had something to ask. He spoke first. "Anna, did you say-zz (srpt) you had something personal to-zz talk about (srpt)?"

"Yes, but I want to enjoy the moment. I have been in this town for all of my married life. I do have some good memories. Not many, but some. I want to remember this walk as how I will remember Deadwood. The lawns are beautiful and the leaves are on fire with color."

"It's-zz pretty (srpt). Tell-zz me when you-zz want-zz to talk (srpt). I'm-zz happy being-zz quiet."

They walked past more homes. Bibb had not seen such wealth since his time in Nevada. He allowed her to lead since she seemed to know all the pretty streets; places he didn't dream existed.

It wasn't long before the cadence of their walking matched that of Anna's rhyme, and it came back to her with a vengeance. "Did you hear that, Bibb?"

"Hear what-zz (srpt)?"

"Do you hear a song in the air, or a poem of a sort? It is such a catchy melody. Are you sure you don't hear it? It's soft, like a noise one would imagine a momma squirrel would sing to her babies."

"Sorry, Anna. I do-zz not (srpt). Can you-zz tell me the words-zz (srpt)?"

"Oh Bibb, I must just be imagining things. This time of the day during Indian summer is so pleasant. Mother Nature must be singing a song just to me."

"Oh."

"Do you ever get songs in your head, Bibb? If not a song, maybe a thought that won't go away?"

"I-zz remember (srpt) my mother's-zz nursery rhymes. D'those-zz are the nice things d'that (srpt) play in-zz my head."

"You ever have any bad things play in your head?"

"Mrs. Gorgon-zz, you don't-zz (srpt) want-zz to know about-zz d'the bad-zz d'things (srpt) d'that goes-zz on in my-zz head."

"How do you get rid of them?" She then baited him, remembering his letter to her. "It's kind of like a voice in a mist."

"Anna, what-zz are you-zz asking (srpt)? You ain't-zz hearing no voice (srpt) in-zz no mist. What's going on-zz? Are you-zz teasing me-zz (srpt) about my-zz letter? You're mean, but not d'that mean."

She stopped and looked at him after that reply. He immediately responded to his error.

"I'm-zz sorry (srpt). I need-zz to be kind (srpt). Anna, please tell-zz me what-zz happening (srpt)."

Anna jumped onto his statement with both feet kicking. "Bibb, who, what, how come, and why did you say you were sorry? Outlaws do not say they are sorry. Something inside of you – that wasn't you – something prompted you to apologize. Tell me, what was it? I don't believe you are kind by nature. Something triggered that, just as fast as you can throw an ax. Come clean, Bibb!"

Shocked, Bibb replied, "Anna, what-zz do (srpt) you know-zz about me-zz?"

"I know you aren't acting like a gun slinging murdering horse thief. Where is your filthy language? Where is your swagger? Where are your guns? Where is your quick temper? Why don't you carouse in the brothels? Bibb, were you castrated in Miles City? Tell me! You're holding out on some great secret, and I will not be comfortable traveling with you until I know what it is."

"Well… You-zz warned me-zz (srpt) you had something-zz personal to-zz ask (srpt), but I-zz didn't expect-zz castration (srpt). No, Anna, I am-zz just as much (srpt) of-zz a man now-zz as d'then-zz (srpt). Where-zz did you-zz (srpt) get such an idea-zz?"

"You tell me why you were so quick to apologize, and I will tell you why I think what I'm thinking."

"I said-zz I'm sorry-zz (srpt) because I was-zz not as kind-zz (srpt) as I promised. D'that's-zz all."

"But why so fast? What prompted you? Something prompted you. There had to be some voice in you that told you that if you didn't keep your promise it would bite you. It bit you hard, and it bit you immediately. You obeyed it immediately. What was it?"

"Anna, what's-zz bothering you (srpt)? Are you-zz being hounded by-zz a feeling (srpt) or-zz a song (srpt)? D'that happened to me-zz once (srpt). D'the song-zz d'that drove me-zz crazy (srpt) was while I was-zz working d'the rails in-zz Canada (srpt). It-zz said to me over-zz and over-zz (srpt), 'Don't you-zz want to know, Terry. Don't you-zz want to know (srpt)?'"

"What did you do about it?"

"Nothing I-zz could do. Well until-zz I found-zz out what-zz I wanted to-zz know-zz (srpt). It drove me-zz back to Fort Rice. D'that was-zz where (srpt) your husband did-zz me dirty." Bibb paused. "Anna, d'that was-zz unkind too-zz (srpt). I'm sorry. I need-zz to d'think-zz (srpt) about your feelings-zz before I say-zz stupid stuff (srpt). D'this-zz trip is going to be-zz so hard (srpt). Riding with Toak I said-zz what-zz (srpt) was on my mind when-zz I d'thought it (srpt). D'that's why I guess (srpt) God put-zz a hole in my-zz head. I need-zz (srpt) to d'think-zz before I speak."

"Who told you to be concerned about my feelings? That certainly didn't come from the heart of Bibb. Big boy, tell me what is going on here. You are holding back on some secret. I need to know the secret before I will be at peace with you. I don't want to hear another story about Canada or Toak or Terry what's his name. It is high time you 'fess up. Withholding the truth is a form of lying that I will not tolerate from you. 'Fess up before you get me angry and ruin this walk."

"Anna, I really want-zz to treat you-zz right (srpt). You deserve-zz a worthy escort. I asked-zz God (srpt) to tell me when-zz I have-zz not been-zz charitable (srpt). I should have-zz never asked Him-zz (srpt). He stomps on-zz every one-zz of my-zz bad sentences (srpt). By d'the time-zz He washes d'them-zz down, d'they are no longer my-zz words. It's-zz terrible (srpt). I have not-zz been neutered, but I-zz have been cleaned up some (srpt). Don't laugh-zz at me, Anna. D'this is so humiliating (srpt). I like-zz being tough, but once-zz I asked Him-zz (srpt) to help me behave better, He won't-zz let me un-ask Him-zz. Stomp-Stomp-Stomp (srpt) all over-zz my d'thoughts. And if I let-zz something unkind fly-zz (srpt), He stomps-zz on my tongue. I hope what-zz has happened to-zz me never happens-zz to you (srpt). D'the hound is-zz relentless, and will-zz chase you until-zz (srpt) you-zz are caught. You-zz can't outrun (srpt) d'the hound; d'the hound always-zz catches up (srpt). In d'the end, d'the hound always wins-zz. Tell me d'the truth, Anna (srpt). Did-zz some preacher pray-zz at you (srpt)? D'that's-zz what happened to-zz me."

"I asked you how to get the song to stop, not tell me another story. How do I get the song to stop? Bibb, focus on what I asked. How did you get the song to stop?"

"By behaving (srpt) and doing what-zz it wanted me-zz to do. When (srpt) I was-zz traveling home from-zz Canada (srpt) d'the song stopped. What's-zz d'the song (srpt), Anna? I am-zz curious."

"I kidnap you and take you to Mexico bound in chains where I force you to manage my chicken farm. You fall hopelessly in love with me but I deny you my hand to marry. As a compromise I let you serve me and make you walk barefoot through the thorny desert into town to sell my eggs and buy me more shoes."

"I'm-zz glad (srpt) to-zz hear d'that, Anna." Bibb couldn't help but notice that Anna had picked irritants from his newspaper history to divert from the truth. A least it was a humorous fib.

Anna was shocked at his deadpan response to her fabrication. "Why? What do you secretly want more of? Me or Mexico?"

Bibb let out a groan. "Anna, if d'that's d'the song (srpt), your only problem is too-zz much rhubarb pie-zz (srpt). D'the hound don't-zz bay d'those ballads (srpt). He is-zz good and only good."

==0==

Miss Dowry's curiosity overcame her. After feasting on cake she asked the maid if she could tour the mansion. "This is such a magnificent house. Can you show me all the closets, fireplaces, books, and paintings? This is like a dream come true. Please show me!"

"I guess the misses wouldn't mind. She is actually proud of this place. Finish your tea and we will go."

The house was as grand as advertised. It even had a suit of armor imported from England, or manufactured by a bored local blacksmith. The tall ceilings made Miss Dowry feel so small. The house was twenty times bigger than her home; it had a coal room bigger than the room she shared with her sisters! Even the horse had a bigger stall than her family's whole kitchen.

All went very well until they happened on Anna's bedroom. When the maid had finished in there that morning the room was tidy, but now it looked like a laundry bomb had gone off in it. There were towels and blankets thrown everywhere, two trunks of shoes turned over, and dresses stacked on the bed. The maid quickly ushered her out of the room, apologizing for the unexpected mess.

==0==

Anna's plan to safely bring Bibb back to the hotel worked flawlessly. The remainder of the walk, a quite indirect route, had been very pleasant for both. Anna told Bibb of her favorite memories of Deadwood and the excitement in gaining six fortunes and the heartache of losing five. She convinced Bibb that Miss Dowry was a capable young lady, and she certainly could find her way back to the hotel. Anna reminded him that she only hires the smartest people around.

"Tommy," Anna asked, "You are coming to the party tomorrow night at the mansion, yes? I invited you but I wasn't sure of your answer."

183

"Of course-zz! I will-zz be d'there (srpt). And I-zz will behave-zz (srpt). You have not been-zz d'the only one to ask me-zz. I am-zz looking forward to it-zz (srpt). Seems many of your-zz friends want to look-zz at my snout."

"You are silly, Bibb. They want to say they talked to you before we depart. Until then, Bibb. Good night." She started to leave the lobby. "Oh, Bibb... I made up the story about Mexico."

"It wasn't d'the kidnap-zz (srpt) or Mexico part-zz of the song-zz d'that-zz worried me (srpt). Are you sure parts of your song-zz weren't made up-zz? D'those d'thoughts had-zz to come-zz from-zz somewhere (srpt). Honestly Anna, have you-zz ever considered remarriage, even-zz if just a tease?"

"I will never tell!" She couldn't resist turning the tables on him. "And I'm warning you up front that I'll be askin' you about your wild wedding dreams in the morning!" His face showed the intended 'stunned chicken' result. She continued, "Good night. Sleep tight... Real tight, Big Boy."

She laughed as she walked away. There were very few men she had ever met that she could tease like that. Maybe she shouldn't kid him. She really didn't know him that well, and planting such thoughts in his head might have been a mistake. "No," she said to herself. "Let the boy suffer."

==0==

"Tommy, I don't know what to do! You're going to get mad at me if I do and mad at me if I don't. Mrs. Gorgon is going to kill me if I tell you!" Miss Dowry looked very distraught over her predicament.

"Sit-zz back in your-zz chair (srpt) by d'the window, and let's-zz decide together (srpt) about do-zz and not do-zz. Why-zz would Mrs. 'Orgon (srpt) be-zz upset?"

"The maid gave me a tour of the mansion. We never asked Mrs. Gorgon's permission. She was walking back here with you. Bibb, the house is simply grand."

"I see-zz no problem-zz with d'that (srpt). You-zz were with-zz the maid, yes?"

"We went to Anna's room. She must have a hundred trunks ready to go."

"Hundred-zz?"

"Twenty or twenty-five at least. Bibb, she has everything she owns packed or scattered everywhere. I know what you told her, and she doesn't care. She will need a whole wagon train to move her stuff. I wanted you to know, but Mrs. Gorgon will roast me alive on a spit if she finds out I told you. You got to do something, but can you do it without getting me in trouble? She will fire me and my sisters. Help me Bibb! Curiosity has just killed this cat, and the cat's two sisters."

"I will-zz d'think about-zz it (srpt). If I go-zz over d'there now she-zz will certainly blame-zz you. D'this can wait until-zz tomorrow (srpt). Let's-zz go over to-zz Bes's for some dinner-zz. I-zz can't wait to watch-zz you eat-zz my steak again (srpt)."

"And you-zzzz to eat-zzzz my-zzzz soup, Mr. Toivo!" She laughed first (at the pucker on his face reacting from the mimicking of his slurs) followed eventually by a half a smile and then a real laugh. She was glad that Bibb was growing more comfortable around her and her sisters, not just as nurses but also as persons with feelings and personalities. Bibb had a hard time with relationships, and from the newspaper accounts, especially with women. She wondered why he didn't turn on her or her sisters; they had been rough with him the first week they cared for him. They had no choice; bandages and plaster packs don't change themselves, and walking him down the hall... oh... She was glad that was over. She laughed again to herself. Bibb could recognize which of her two sisters was their older one but helplessly confused her with her twin. He had started to call them Sama and their elder sister Vanhin; Finnish words that meant something to that sinful saint.

==0==

The topic had come up at the Dowry house almost daily concerning their daughters' safety. Mr. Dowry wanted to see the answer in his girls' eyes, not just in their voices. He celebrated inwardly the day Bibb's heath had turned better, personally relieved that the doctor had ended the touching and singing therapy. His girls certainly got a lesson on the raw facts of life, death, and suffering caring for that man. He knew society needed nurses; he just wished they would be somebody else's girls.

Mrs. Dowry brought up the subject this night. "Honey, did you know Bibb gave our girls a gift?"

Seriously concerned he replied, "What was it? Did you approve of it?"

"There is no gift more valuable than a good name. Girls, tell your daddy all about it." And they did, and the names stuck. From that day nobody outside their home could tell the twins apart.

Friday, October 7, 1887

I did my final packing to meet Mr. Toivo's standards. I did not like his comments or his commands. I fussed, but he wasn't going to change his mind. He doesn't listen to reason. Don't forget, Tommy; your day is coming! Wait until I start handing out comments and commands about your medical condition! On that point, Bibb is healing remarkably well from the gunshot wound, most likely because he is as young as me. Most can now understand his mumblings. His ribs hurt him more than his face. He said something is in there still stirring the pot from the beating he took at the Westum Ranch in Miles City.

The party was divine! All my friends came and I gave them parting gifts. Bibb wouldn't let me take that stuff anyway so I divested myself of it. I actually had fun deciding who would get what based on what I knew they liked and what clothes would fit them. The books went to the library along with a monetary gift. They named a corner of the fiction section after me. Mr. Franklin thought that poetic.

My lawyer got it all done! After the party I signed off on the last of the documents, to include a will just in case Bibb gets hungry between Deadwood and Miles City.

==0==

THE JUDGE AND his wife arrived at Mrs. Gorgon's home shortly after breakfast. He insisted on having a private conference with Anna. In the meantime the judge's wife asked the butler and the maid what their plans were. They mentioned to her that new tenants had been found and the couple would be moving into the mansion in one week. That would not give them much time to inventory and store all the property that would not be part of the furnished home. Mrs. Gorgon had authorized an auction to sell those items.

Once in the private study the judge spoke first. "Anna, I still haven't received from you the artifacts and evidence that you should have been collecting."

"Oh, they're here and there around the house. Don't worry about it, Judge."

"Anna, this time tomorrow you will no longer be in Deadwood. This is important. I want you to collect it all and have it to me by noon. You are not to let anybody else know, to include your staff and especially Bibb. The staff will be interviewed later after you depart."

"That wounded man is harmless and easily manipulated. What is all the concern about?"

"Let me try this again, Widow Gorgon. The Widow Gorgon wasn't a widow fifteen days ago, Widow Gorgon. But this request is of you, not about you. If you can't get me all the stuff by noon, I will have the sheriff come down with a warrant and some deputies to help you find it."

"Judge, what I don't have, Mr. Franklin does. You will have to ask Miss Dowry about what he wrote down on the chalk board. Those messages are gone."

"So what do you have, Widow?"

"Why don't you go have some coffee, and I will be back in ten minutes. I have been keeping the stuff like I was told. You know I wasn't going to risk getting myself sidewise with the sheriff before I left. He still has an ace in his sleeve dating back to an incident with some soup."

==0==

Bibb was surprised to see the other two sisters along with Mr. and Mrs. Dowry seated at Bes's when he and the twin on duty arrived for breakfast. Thanks to the newspaper, there were very few in Deadwood unaware that the infamous "Covenant Couple" would be leaving in the morning. The two waiting chairs at the table told Bibb that he and his escort were to partake in a family style breakfast. Vanhin said it was her mother's idea since Tommy was almost part of the family.

He had to look at them twice, three, and four times. Bibb couldn't get over how much the daughters looked identical to their mother. Jokingly he asked her husband how he was able to tell them apart. He commiserated with Bibb. It was not possible except for the one he married was the sweetest and the nicest looking. She called his bluff and explained he could only tell because she wore his wedding ring. He couldn't be happier. She was raising their girls to be mirror copies of her in body and spirit, and that being the case he wished he had a dozen daughters instead of just three.

Mrs. Dowry had a slightly different opinion. A dozen Dowry girls might be nice, but she wanted them to be her grandchildren. She said her husband needed to focus on finding worthy sons-in-law rather than re-feathering his own nest with more daughters.

Her husband replied, "Honey, you have to admit we would be doing the world a big favor if we had nine more just like these three." Not seeing his hoped for reaction he continued, "Just like you."

Mrs. Dowry changed the subject. "How about you, Bibb? Do you have any brothers or sisters?"

"I was-zz a twin also, but my parents had no problem telling us apart."

"Any other siblings?"

"No ma'am. Just me-zz and my brother Tommy, and we-zz grew up on a chicken farm about d'three miles north of town on d'the side of a hill. I had a different name back d'then. After Tommy died his name was given to me. I had ruined mine and his name was still-zz plenty good, well, until I ruined it too. I'm good-zz at gaining bad reputations. You probably don't know any about d'that."

"But I do understand," said the older sister. "It ain't hard to collect bad ones. I had a friend who learned the hard way. It took her a whole lifetime to gain a good name and only seconds to convert it into a bad one. Bibb, tell me true. Did you break your momma's heart when you were young?"

Tommy was just about to answer that question when the preacher and his wife walked into the diner. They recognized Tommy right away, walked over to their table, introduced themselves, and asked Tommy if he would like to join them later for lunch. Before Bibb could respond they accepted Mr. Dowry's invitation to join them there for breakfast. Bes pulled over another pair of chairs and squeezed them all together.

"So Parson, what bring-zz you to Bes's, other d'then d'the good eat'n' (srpt)?" asked Bibb.

"Well there are a lot of good reasons and a few bad ones. We could talk about the bad ones later if you would like."

"Tell me your concerns-zz now. Present company and I were discussing my-zz bad reputation when-zz you walked in (srpt). You don't intend to scare d'them, do you (srpt)?"

"I will tell you plain then. Bibb, my wife and I worry that you are going to hurt Mrs. Gorgon."

Bibb thought his word was good with the man, but obviously not. "What concern is it of yours what-zz I do with or to Mrs. Gorgon (srpt)?" The tenseness at the table could be felt as that question signaled the end of pleasantries. "She likes frontier justice, and I might just give-zz her some (srpt) of her own medicine. You promote justice and such stuff like d'that in your church, isn't d'that right?"

The preacher's wife answered the accusation. "We love justice, but we love mercy more. You of all people should know that. Do you want to finish this conversation elsewhere?"

"No," snapped Bibb. Nobody could tell if he had killed the topic or asked them to continue it.

"Later or now, Bibb?" responded the preacher. "We got to talk; this is about life or death."

"D'then preach it preacher, but don't include me in any of your 'we.' I said my peace."

"Bibb, earned or not, the legend that follows you is that there is a steep fare for anybody that disagrees with or angers you. The notches on your ax give testimony that you settle arguments quickly, sometimes before the other person gets a chance to blink."

"What's your point (srpt)?"

"Anna also has a history. You know that she does not know how to control her condescending tongue. Combining her history and your history reeks of disaster. Let me say it plain: She has rejected the faith and if she dies before changing her mind I feel personally responsible for failing God and her by not explaining grace well enough to her. If she passes now, she is doomed, like you were before Miles City."

"D'that's pretty harsh preacher. Why are you-zz so worried about her (srpt)? She's a big girl, and if her mouth oversteps-zz her ability to defend herself, d'that's her personal responsibility and her personal problem, not yours (srpt)." Bibb paused for a second. "Preacher, I learned early in life not to stick my nose-zz into a place it doesn't belong."

"I agree with that. I also have no doubt that my heart, soul, mind, and even my nose says this issue is most certainly my business. It's my divine calling, Bibb. I have to worry. I was born to care about people, and I care about her, and I care about you. You must, not just have to, but you MUST keep your blood sealed covenant. You are irreversibly obligated, Bibb. You must be kind no matter what irritation she brings you. You must keep sober in spirit no matter what joy she brings you. You must be kind, no matter what crisis happens. You must fulfill your solemn commitment not just to her, but to God, and to yourself."

"And if I don't (srpt)?"

"She's dead, you're ruined, and God's name is dragged through the mud. Everyone is waiting to see if your change in direction and attitude is only until things get hard for you. If it really has stuck, well then God did work a miracle. If not, how would any thinking person conclude something other than God and His promises are nothing but a big fraud?"

"Aren't you readin' too-zz much into d'this drama, Preacher?"

"No."

"No, what?" replied Bibb.

"No I am not, Bibb. If you do just one thing I will have a sure hope that you will succeed. That one thing, Bibb, is that you see beyond your own nose. Look at the big picture. Your actions affect not only you, but all those around you, whole communities, and maybe even the territory. Look up, Bibb. Your help comes from above! Look inward, Bibb. Your help comes from within. Look next to you Bibb. Your help comes from those sitting next to you… today, tomorrow, and for the rest of your life. You are no longer just you. You must see beyond yourself. Your fame and infamy is to be used for good and only good."

"Do you really believe what you-zz just said (srpt)? Sunday preach'n' is-zz still two days away."

"Focus Bibb. Not only me, but a whole cast of people who want to see you succeed, from the hallelujah lady who brought the doctor to you the night you got ambushed to the governor of this territory. What about these girls here, Bibb? Look at all they have invested in your success! And back to the real problem. Bibb, promise me that you will not hurt Anna in any way at any time no matter the provocation. Promise me, Bibb. I demand it."

"What's in it-zz for me, Preacher (srpt)?"

"Stop saying *ME*!! Bibb, wake up! You have to stop saying *ME*! This is not about you anymore. That is my whole point. You are no longer a *me*; you are an *us!* And yes, if you can do that, there is something in it for you. You will become fully alive. You will have joy unspeakable. You will have friends that can never be lost. You can have peace. You can have assurance in your fate. Mark my words, Bibb. If you can see beyond the *me* in you, you will gain all the priceless things of life that really matter. I am not saying you must stop being yourself and become something you are not. I am saying that you must change inside, and live moment by moment as the ideal that you can become."

"And if I don't, or I fail-zz no matter how hard I try?"

"Bibb, who are you accountable to?"

"Why do you ask (srpt)?"

"What will you say to your mother when you get to heaven? And here and now, who has invested in your life and who is it that you do not want not to disappoint? After you make that list, add Anna Gorgon's name to the bottom."

"I really detest d'that woman (srpt). Why her?"

"Tommy. Get rid of the *I* and replace it with *us*. The covenant is sealed. You are now an *us*. If you win, she wins. If you lose, she loses. You and Anna are writ in heaven and bound on earth. If you do everything in your ability to provide for her success, you succeed too. Tommy, let me tell you plain. If you pass the covenant test, God will be able to trust you with even greater riches."

"You really believe d'this, don't you (srpt)? Why?"

"Tommy, you know all about passion. Answer that question for yourself. Tommy, promise me that you won't hurt that woman physically or emotionally. Promise me, and then promise God."

"I already promised God. D'that's why I'm taking her. D'the varmint made me do-zz it. And if it makes you feel better, I promise you too-zz, although you don't bite."

"Promise me that you will write both me and the preacher in Miles City when you make it to Fort Rice. We want to know if you kept the covenant. Can you promise that?"

"You'll get your letter, Preacher. Now you promise me something too. Have d'that congregation of yours pray d'that I don't slip up (srpt). Enough of d'this. Let all of us *us*'ngs at d'this table eat."

The rest of the meal was tame in conversation; from horses to hiccups. Of the latter subject the twins told on Tommy and how he suffered from them sometimes, and laughed how his hiccups were not normal hiccups. Then came out everybody's heart-felt sure-fire opinion on how to cure them. They all went home full of food and full of stories. Over the next week neither family ran out of discussion items from this time at breakfast. The nurses could not comprehend why the man they had grown fond of freely admitted with such passion that he detested the Widow Gorgon. That seemed so out of character, but then again, his history gave cause to wonder otherwise.

==0==

Bibb walked to the Gorgon mansion that morning after breakfast. He poked his head into the kitchen and told the cook that he was taking Mrs. Gorgon's horse with him to team it up with his horse at the livery. He left a pre-written note reminding Anna what specifically to pack and what specifically not to pack. He told the cook he wasn't going to stay around the mansion to defend the note either; there was real work to do. He asked her to tell the Widow Gorgon that he would be back early that afternoon to pick up the one trunk he had carved his initials into.

At half past noon Bibb returned to the mansion. The cook insisted on feeding him some rhubarb and egg soup that she made especially for him. "Mrs. Gorgon insisted that you eat this awful stuff to heal quicker. I never heard of such a thing. She said that this was Mexican rhubarb, a known aphrodisiac that also cures warts. I know what warts are, but the other sounds deadly if you catch it, so you better down this."

"What did she say-zz about-zz my note (srpt)?"

"After reading it she told me she plans to have you stand on your head for an hour while whistling Dixie to help your chest to heal. She said she was an expert in creative medicine, and that you had wholeheartedly agreed to be a cooperative patient."

"Tell her-zz one trunk, and-zz one trunk only (srpt). Tell-zz her obedience to outlaws (srpt) cures-zz warts too (srpt). I will wait-zz here (srpt) while you go-zz tell her."

The cook put her hands on her hips. "I dare you to go tell her that yourself, Big Boy. I declare, Mr. Toivo, you two will have quite a time traveling together. I figure you and the misses will either fall in love together or fall in a grave together. Mrs. Gorgon doesn't idle well. Based on how well you followed the doctor's orders to stay in bed, I figure you don't either. You two are like peas in a pod!"

"I'm just hoping to get-zz to Fort Rice alive (srpt). With her creative cures, I-zz might-zz not make it to Bismarck (srpt). But-zz she promised to be-zz kind (srpt), and she will-zz."

"Or else...?"

"You-zz just tell-zz her what I said about-zz d'the trunks (srpt). And don't-zz you believe-zz those lies-zz about me killing-zz tiresome widows (srpt). None-zz of the stories you heard are completely true. I never-zz liked cabbage (srpt) on my-zz rye sandwiches."

==0==

Anna was late in getting her trunk packed. Bibb patiently waited an hour, but his restless nature could wait no more. He had already picked up the ammunition and stowed all his belongings on his horse. After packing the necessities like a shovel, rope, hammer, and a stout oak pole, Bibb found a convenient place to store on the wagon the combs and brushes the maid had quietly collected. He also found a safe place to keep the magnifying lens the butler provided.

There was no sign of Anna finishing her work upstairs. Bored, Bibb decided to take Mr. Gorgon's rifle down from the mantle, collect up all the rounds in the house, and go to the garbage dump at the spent quarry on the edge of town. The gate keeper at the refuge pit obliged Bibb's request to familiarize himself with the rifle. By the time the loose rounds were expended, Bibb had harvested eight raccoons, twelve rats, and a bear. Later that man told the sheriff that once Bibb had the sights on the rifle set right, everything died.

==0==

The evening was gorgeous; the best of Indian summer. The small band Mrs. Gorgon hired to play lively music arrived earlier than all the rest and filled the mansion with the mood of celebration. Guests started arriving at around five in the evening and a banquette was served at seven.

As the house was filling up, Bibb and the butler wrestled the trunk on to the wagon. While the butler had to return to welcome guests, Bibb took his time to load their provisions. He also made a hay mattress for Anna in the back of the wagon next to her trunk, put into separate stacks their daily ration of foodstuffs, and then figured a way to affix a tarpaulin over the back to keep things dry. Once the back was secure he fabricated a place to keep his rifle and ax within easy reach while he was driving the wagon. Once happy with the loading he sat down to take a nap.

It was Miss Dowry that found Bibb sound asleep in the barn. Dinner had already been served and the party was approaching its climax where Anna would hand out her gifts to her guests.

Anna was quite insistent that she could accept no gifts given Bibb's quarantine against her receiving anything nice. She did explain that Bibb had his reasons to pack light and that for the first time in her life, she decided to listen to a man. The women thought that a funny joke, but one man commented that the essence of humor was a large dose of truth. Between the music, food, and the socializing the party was a complete success.

Bibb didn't have any party attire to wear so he stayed in the kitchen. When it was discovered that Bibb was in the house much of the attention gravitated his way. Several guests eventually cornered Tommy in the kitchen and asked if he needed anything. Some said they had some better clothes that would fit him. They were well meaning but Bibb really didn't have much use for these beautiful rich people. They had perfect diction and he felt that if he said anything it would only engender laughter and ridicule. If not in his presence, they would certainly enjoy their opinions in the back rooms of the party. He did write out on a piece of paper a note in response to the question about what he wanted. *"I want God to protect me and the widow while traveling, and a deputy sheriff to ride out with us on the first day of our journey."* It wasn't meant to be funny, but as Bibb predicted, they found amusement in it anyway.

Eventually the widow was told that Bibb was in the kitchen asking for favors of the sheriff. It was quite the new party subject. She broke away from being the belle of the ball to talk to Bibb. Several guests, full of curiosity (and a chance at a front row view of some fireworks) followed her into the kitchen, to include the surprised sheriff.

"Bibb, what is this about you asking the sheriff for a deputy to go along with us?"

"Just d'the first day, Anna (srpt). It's-zz for our protection from bandits."

"Well what is it Bibb? You want it both ways? You seem to be a bit unsure about this trip at this late hour. You already asked for God's protection! Why would I need you or the deputy if you are invoking God to watch over me?" demanded Anna, very close to a spiteful tone. Many were surprised at her blunt familiarity as she spoke to Bibb. They, knowing Bibb's low tolerance for condescension feared for her once they were alone on the plains. She could get away with that now.

Bibb stared at her for a moment and spoke, "Anna," but did not finish his sentence. He decided not to speak his response to her. He got out his little notepad and wrote her a single sentence.

Anna laughed aloud when she read the note. Others there demanded that she share his response with them. "Well, Bibb asked for God's protection for us and a deputy just to make sure. His response tells me he has a lot of faith in the latter, to your credit, Sheriff. Bibb, can I tell them what you wrote?"

Bibb acknowledged. She was going to read it no matter what he said.

"Bibb wrote, *I want a deputy to come along because bandits don't believe in God.*"

The sheriff, smiling, graciously granted Bibb his request, saying that was a reasonable price to get a man of Bibb's credentials safely on his way. He reminded Bibb that he was just like the other sheriffs. He would sleep well once he was outside his jurisdiction. The sheriff continued, taking the opportunity to tweak his host, "Bibb, I have a friend that tells me trouble seems to find you. Even I now believe all the stories I have heard about you. I hope your Widow Gorgon treats you well. I have known her for a long time and have yet to hear anybody accuse her of being trouble-free! And like I said, Bibb, you don't have to look for trouble. Trouble finds you, and behold, there she is."

Many laughed, knowing Anna's temperament. It was a delicious thought imagining those two sitting next to each other for their journey. They would love to be a bird flying overhead just to watch the sparks fly. A few guests came by the kitchen later to talk to Bibb candidly during the party. Their comments had the common theme that Anna would be a handful for him. Bibb knew what lay ahead, and he also knew Anna was not ready for it. Bibb was not shy about asking for their prayers for Anna. For most visitors that petition was hilarious but they knew better than to laugh about his request in his presence.

==0==

After Bibb left to return to the hotel the mood of the party changed for some. After initially making fun of the outlaw looking for divine intervention some noted that the man was sincere. Some felt a tinge of guilt and commented that if an outlaw could pray, then God might hear their prayers too. Many laughed afresh. A few felt ashamed of their mockery of Bibb... and God.

Although not invited, Xue came to the party late and long after Bibb had left. Guests there assumed, partly because she was wearing her work clothes, that she was asked there this evening by Anna to help her pack for the journey. She was nothing to the guests and they thought little of it as she went from the kitchen through the party area and up the stairs. Anna didn't see her come in, but some of her guests mentioned it joking to her that even up to the last few hours before her departure that Anna wanted more upgrades to her wardrobe. In a typical Anna-like response she said to her guests that they were jealous, but they had shown good taste by envying her. As the wine and drink increased, so did all the giggles and exaggerated accolades.

Nobody knew how late it was when Xue descended the stairs down into the party. She was carrying a towel over her arm and a basin of water in her hands. Her long black hair, never seen unbraided before, made her very noticeable in the crowd. She walked over to the table and stood by the end chair still holding her basin of water in both hands. She spoke nothing when asked. Eventually Anna was informed that her servant was acting strange and standing in her dining room. Curious, Anna went in there, and just as curious, many of the guests followed.

"Xue, what are you doing here?"

"Meese Gorgon, you must sit down. Please sit down right there."

"I must? Why must I?" answered Anna. Xue gave no answer. Anna was at first tempted to order Xue to go home, but seven months of unquestioned loyalty could not be overlooked. She asked again why she must sit down, and again Xue did not reply. Given the gaiety of evening Anna decided to sit down at her chair at the head of the table adorned with a big smile, a lubricated disposition, and many encouraging cheers from her guests. "Well, if I must, I must!"

Once Anna was seated in her chair, Xue did a most unusual thing. She put her basin of water down on the floor and knelt at Anna's feet. Xue reached out and took Anna's right leg by the ankle and started to take off Anna's shoe. Anna protested, for this was very embarrassing and promised to even become worse.

"Xue, stop this. You have gone too far. You must not do this."

Xue looked up at Mrs. Gorgon and spoke a phrase in Chinese to her. Anna's scorn melted into wonder as she saw tears well up in Xue's eyes. Not one soul around the table could overlook the event; all the lubricated joy turned at once into a silent sober moment. Upon unlatching Anna's right shoe, Xue removed it and placed it to the side with two hands. Not caring that Anna would not be able understand, Xue said another heartfelt and reverent phrase in Chinese. She took Anna's bare foot and placed it in the basin of warm water. Kneeling down over the basin, unconcerned that her hair was getting wet, Xue used some expensive looking soap to wash Anna's foot. After drying off Anna's washed foot with the towel, Xue washed Anna's left foot also. Before putting Anna's shoes back on, Xue pushed the bowl of water under the table, pulled some perfume from her pocket and rubbed a few drops onto the top of each of Anna's feet. Xue spoke a third time in Chinese towards Mrs. Gorgon's soul, stood up, bowed, and exited through the kitchen and into the night.

Once Xue had left, the party raged again. The seamstress's strange actions was the new topic of fun and commentary. Many thought it outrageous that she would go upstairs into the private chambers of the house and commandeer Anna's best soaps and perfumes for such a public stunt. They also knew better not to comment on how ugly the bottoms of Anna's feet were. That would be a joke for another day. Dead Mr. Gorgon must have made her feel the heat of his wrath, but to get scars like that would require a walk through fire. After a few more drinks, the whole incident was forgotten... almost.

One outspoken woman remarked as she was leaving that Xue took great liberties and assumed airs well beyond her station in life. Her audacious actions were meant to embarrass the host of the party and should have earned her the immediate physical removal from the mansion. Such presumption, and to go upstairs to steal the soap and perfume from her employer's private chambers! "Unthinkable! Unsupportable! Such unimaginable behavior!" the guest ranted.

Anna had nowhere as much drink as her guests and with good reason. She did not want a hangover in the morning knowing the early appointment with a wagon heading north. In response to the noisy guest, she asked her adjacent guests not to make quick assumptions. She told them that yes, Xue was acting well above her station, but the accusation of stealing the soap and perfume was totally false. Xue must have brought those things with her. Anna said she had never had such soaps or ornate urns like that in her home, nor did Xue leave them near the basin. They must have been Xue's. That didn't excuse her behavior, but malice had to be eliminated as a motive.

One couple as they were leaving, a foreman and his wife at one of her mines, was asked to stay until the all the others had left. The foreman was sure he knew why he was asked but his wife could not help but fear something bad was about to happen. She knew that Anna had earned very few, if any, of the nice things said about her that evening. She also knew that Anna had never been this nice for this long. The other shoe was about to drop.

Anna closed down the party in the wee hours of the night. She had given out all her presents and hugged the necks of scores of people. She was the Queen of Deadwood for the evening. All wished her luck and said they would miss her. Many instructed her to write when she reached the civilized east.

When the number of party guests was down to three Anna asked them all to sit down. Mrs. Gorgon sat across from Mr. Franklin and the other couple.

"Okay, tell me what she said," demanded Anna.

"She who?" responded the foreman. The foreman's wife was very nervous.

"My seamstress. I know you speak Chinese. What did she say?"

"Mrs. Gorgon, can we pretend I didn't hear a word of it. There is no reason to rain on your coronation. Let us call this a lovely evening and say good night."

"What did she say? Tell me anyway. I want to know."

"Mrs. Gorgon, the saying goes that at a feast of admiration and boasting, everyone leaves hungry. There was a large exception to that tonight. Yes, on your invitation you specifically stated that no one was to bring gifts. Obviously your servant girl did not adhere to your wishes."

"So she brought me a gift? I can't let you leave without an explanation of that statement."

"Mrs. Gorgon, do you really want me to translate the three things she said in Chinese?"

"How bad can they be? She didn't wish me dead or a pox upon me, did she?"

"The opposite, Mrs. Gorgon. She spoke three truths over you. She did not speak to you, and I assume she was speaking to either some great spirit, or her ancestors, or both. My Chinese is not that good. One thing is for sure, she wasn't speaking to you, but at you, through an unseen authority. Trust me; Chinese is hard to understand that way."

"So what did she say?"

"Mrs. Gorgon, I will tell you, but don't say I didn't warn you. The first thing she spoke was both at you and at herself. It was a short phrase quoting the proverb, 'If you bow at all, bow low.' The second thing she said was as she washed your feet. I think she said, 'The door to virtue is heavy and hard to open.' As she put perfume on your feet she kind of said, 'Humility has to be felt in your feet before seen in your heart.' I am not that sure on that last one. Instead of *seen* it might have been *experienced*. I think the gist of the quote was that you have to see humility in others before you can model it in your own life. Mrs. Gorgon, my Chinese is better barking in a mine than musing at a mansion. I'm not that good at translating it, especially something akin to spiritual sayings."

Anna dismissed his qualifier. "You're the best I got. So tell me your opinion. You understand them better than anybody else here. What do you think about what she said?"

"Mrs. Gorgon, it doesn't matter what I think. It matters what you think. If you think it was a big joke, well shame on you. If you think she tried to embarrass you, she could have easily done that by speaking in English rather than through her native tongue. I hope you take this event as I have. She spoke it as a gift in hope that your spirit, which speaks and understands a universal language beyond any human dialect, would accept her words and apply them in your life. Frankly, Mrs. Gorgon, since you gave me the freedom to comment, I will take this opportunity to tell you what I think. That little servant girl saw the biggest void in your life and she did her best in the only way she knew how to fill that vacuum. That display of love was truly extraordinary."

"Love? How do you conclude that?"

"Mrs. Gorgon, unlike shallow minds who think that hate is the opposite of love, that thought is so far from the truth. I've been married long enough to know the opposite of love is apathy. No, that girl could have let you leave town without her demonstration of appreciation, but no, she invested in your soul. Remember, as of tomorrow this town no longer has a Gorgon in it, but that servant girl, besides the expense of the soap and perfume, has to live with all the hee-haws and snippety comments from your high society friends. Some will get it; most will not, and continue their snippety ways and look down on people like that girl. Enough of that. I do have a question for you though. What happened to the bottom of your feet? Mr. Gorgon didn't do that to you, did he?"

"Thank you for your insights. I am embarrassed with what I first thought, but I am still far from agreeing with your conclusions. And no, Mr. Gorgon did not disfigure my feet. I did that all by myself when I was a young girl. Thank you for coming tonight and for staying late. I am richer for your consenting to translate Xue's words." Anna embraced the foreman's wife as they departed.

==0==

Just when Anna thought the day was over, Mr. Franklin interrupted her ascent up the stairs with one last stack of papers. "Can't we do this in the morning?" asked Anna.

"It is morning; sign these now." For the next half hour they wore out his pen putting her ink on all the bottom lines.

"Is this the last of them?"

"Maybe. I hope so. If not, I will have to send documents to you by courier. You will have to send me your address once you settle down."

"What don't you think of, Mr. Franklin?"

"You pay me to think of everything, Anna. But I will tell you one more thing."

"What's that?"

"Most of the women at the party were envious of you. You are getting to start your life over. You are confident. You are rich. You are business savvy. You are smart."

"And... Mr. Franklin. Your sweet statements always seem to have an ant hiding in the sugar bowl. Stick the spoon in a bit deeper and tell me what you find."

"But... Anna, don't break the covenant."

"That's it? That is the 'but'?"

"Anna, the covenant may end up being the best life decision you have ever made. High risk; high reward. Anna, I know you better than any person alive. I think, no Anna, I know that you can find happiness, joy, peace, relationships, and all those things your heart desires if you stay true to your word. Keep that covenant until both of you fulfill your responsibilities. Don't ever hint that you won't. Regardless of what Bibb does, you keep it. I also warn you. Don't even consider a serious relationship with the man. You have already had too many outlaws in your life. Commit yourself wholeheartedly. Above all, not just keep, but honor the covenant."

"Mr. Franklin, why would you think I would not keep it? I'm packed and ready to go."

"But is your heart packed and ready to go? I don't pray Anna, but I sure do wish a lot, and I also hope a lot. I have never wished for a person's success like I am wishing for you. You can do it!"

"Mr. Franklin, I'm astonished. Where did this sentimental outburst come from?"

"Anna, if you only knew my private thoughts... Well, I guess now you do... well many of them. Anna, I have been told by my parents all my life not to envy other peoples' fortunes, and so I am sure what I am doing now is wrong. I so wish I was Bibb, pain and all. It is so unfair that the life that I have longed for is thrust upon a man that has never pursued a moment of it. Life just happens to Bibb. He never asked for it. He never longs for it. It just happens. Some men are predestined for greatness and some of us end up being ho-hum lawyers."

"I will take your envy of Bibb as a compliment, Mr. Franklin. I never knew you could have thoughts like that."

"Anna, I plead that you make the most of this opportunity."

"Plead? That is a very strong word, Mr. Franklin."

"Threatening you doesn't work; never has. I feel so strongly about this that I am even willing to say beg."

"Are you that convinced, Mr. Franklin?"

"You will be the crown jewel in my life's work, Anna, if you pull this off. You may become the crown jewel in the whole territory... entertaining and dining with tycoons, statesmen, business leaders, and the famous from all around the country. You may be destined for even higher honors. Yes, I feel that strongly. Anna, do not disappoint me. If not for me, do it for your own daddy from wherever he may be watching over you."

She studied his face. He was a man whom she had trusted to manage her fortune, and he had done so brilliantly. Now he was asking that she would manage the next one for herself. "You have convinced me. I am committed. I am committed wholeheartedly. No matter what comes, mark my words, sir, I will stay true to the covenant."

"Thank you, Anna. Thank you. You have given me great joy. Good night." With that farewell Mr. Franklin left the mansion with a permanent and satisfying image of Anna's smile burned into his memory. He could not wait to get home and tell his wife of their parting words.

Anna was certain that fate would never let her see him in person again, but many times in her thoughts. He was to be the adopted daddy that would always be looking over her shoulder. She would long to hear those words from him in her subconscious: "Well done, Anna. Well done."

==0==

That night, when she lay in bed, she rehearsed all the compliments she had received. It was glorious! All those people that said they loved her and would miss her! Granted, many of the comments were platitudes, but that many people couldn't all be insincere! She was as high as a kite.

> *Good and only good,*
> *You will belong to me,*
> *Kind and only kind,*
> *Precious Hannah Marie*

Anna pulled the covers over her head. The song had come back. "No!" she yelled out loud from her bed, but the rhyme repeated. It was the antithesis of everything she wanted to repeat tonight in her mind to herself. She could not pretend it away or override it with quoting the suspect platitudes about her friendship and generosities she received from her guests tonight. Over and over again that rhyme repeated in a soft and gentle familiar musical cadence much like the sound of her horse's steps pulling her sleigh through fresh snow on a winter's night. But the cadence was not compassionate. It was as merciless as a hired murderer. It reminded her of her relationship failure with her dead husband. It reminded her of that nuisance preacher and his horrible wife. It reminded her of her covenant with the ugliest man on the continent. The worst word was the hideous utterance *precious*. That word was everything she wasn't. She longed for it, but not fool enough to hope to possess it – just to be mocked in her certain failure to achieve it. Even the handsome Mr. Gorgon never spoke so bold of a lie to call her *precious*.

"You will not rob me of my moment!" screamed Anna into the darkness of the room. Strangely the song went away. She thought to herself, "Can I resist this? How did the song just vanish?"

This was to be the last night in her house, her room, with her overstuffed closets, her shoes, her mirrors. She would miss all the things she liked, but she knew she had no future in Deadwood. "By this time tomorrow this city, this house, and my husband will be residents of my memory cemetery, buried forever and out of my reach." She took advantage of the silent room, a warm bed, a quieted heart, and from the energy expense of the day's overwhelming activity – Anna was soon asleep.

Saturday, October 8, 1887

This will be the most remembered day of my life. We left early in the morning escorted by the law, as if Bibb was being run out of town. Early afternoon the sheriff and his deputy turned around and Tommy and I were finally on our own. Bibb will eventually forgive me for over-dressing and over-packing. He has no choice because he has bound himself with a promise to be kind. I will have that boy so twisted in knots he won't know which way is up; but not today.

At evening we were intercepted by Indian scouts that recognized Bibb's horse – and then him. They brought us into their village. After some uncertain moments, we were welcomed by their chief. Bibb had this all planned, especially the expensive gifts, and chose not to tell me beforehand. I will eventually forgive him for this, maybe.

Bibb and I were assumed to be man and wife. He implied that to our hosts to avoid complications. Bibb was concerned that if I was not under his authority there was a good chance I would be auctioned into slavery. I don't know whether to believe him or not. We stayed in a teepee with two middle aged Indian widows. They were curious (I cannot understate this) about me and my clothes. Bibb translated for me at first, but eventually they could second guess me, and I them.

Bibb received the teepee treatment tonight. A bed could not have been more comfortable than what those widows provided us… or narrower. Us… I greatly long to be part of an us. Not an artificial us, but a real us with real feelings, real communication, real understanding, real sharing. Being bonded by only paper is a façade that degenerates into a farce. I might get something worthwhile out of this covenant arrangement. I am disingenuous. I am only trying to convince myself to make the best of my current situation. Right now I must. I have no choice.

I found the love note from Mrs. Franklin in the bottom of my trunk. Paper… Mrs. Franklin… Checkmate… The first time she pinched me was to see if I was the old Anna. The last time she pinched me was to see if I was the Anna that I can become.

==0==

THE BUTLER PICKED up Tommy and all three of the Dowry girls two hours before dawn. Upon arrival at the mansion the cook refused to entertain any notion of the whole troupe eating anywhere else but in her kitchen. Bibb wanted to eat at Bes's, but changed his mind when the food started coming out. She had put some thought into giving Bibb some tasty morsels that wouldn't loosen his teeth when chewing. The sheriff and the deputy joined shortly thereafter.

Bibb was anxious to get on the trail north. He had a destination in mind that caused him to insist on leaving before light. There were hugs enough to satisfy everybody that made Bibb even more anxious to leave. Anna mentioned that the

Dowry girls spent way too much time hanging on his neck. He didn't like it, but he didn't resist them. Anna concluded the reason that Bibb didn't fall apart was because they were but nurses to him, not the attractive young women that they were to everyone else. Anna laughed at the thought Bibb might hug her too. After all, they were a covenant couple. She could sense very well his true feelings about her, so there was no need to ask about the obvious. It was still funny anyway; just the thought of seeing that man shake himself apart caused inward glee. There wasn't any doubt in anybody's mind about how she felt about him either, that low-life widow-making half-a-man. Those attributes were the kinder things she thought about him.

The deputy teamed his horse with Anna's for the first leg of the trip. He also drove the wagon as they headed out of town. Both Bibb and the sheriff trailed behind them on their horses.

==0==

"Sheriff, you-zz aren't planning to-zz come with us (srpt) all d'the way to Miles City, are you-zz? We-zz are already past-zz an hour (srpt) from town. Don't worry Sheriff, I know-zz my way (srpt)."

"Can you blame me, Bibb?"

"Nope (srpt). But you have-zz no reason-zz to fret (srpt). D'the deputy will tell you (srpt) later we-zz didn't double back. I have no-zz cause (srpt) to return-zz to Deadwood."

"Stop here, Bibb. Let them get further down the trail."

"Why-zz?" asked Bibb.

"I have some questions for you."

"D'that you-zz ain't asked yet (srpt)? Is-zz d'this about-zz Gorgon (srpt)?"

"Who do you work for, Bibb?"

"I don't rightly know-zz, Sheriff. It keeps-zz changing (srpt)."

"Why were you in Canada?"

"I don't rightly know-zz, Sheriff. I'm starting to-zz d'think (srpt) it was to get-zz a Bible."

That answer was a diversion if the sheriff had ever heard one. "Why did you go to Miles City?"

"I was-zz taken there."

"Not how, Bibb, but why. Why?"

"I don't rightly know-zz, Sheriff (srpt). Maybe-zz it was-zz to deliver a-zz Bible (srpt). I just happened to get-zz in its way (srpt) and it-zz stabbed me."

"Bibb, are you purposely avoiding telling me the truth? Your answers aren't panning out to leave me any gold nuggets."

"Sheriff, try asking again-zz if you want-zz (srpt), but-zz I told you-zz d'the truth (srpt). I asked d'these questions to myself (srpt) long-zz before you-zz asked me. When-zz

I d'think about it, (srpt) d'these are d'the only answers (srpt) d'that make sense. Sheriff, I should not-zz be alive (srpt). I should not-zz have me a wid'r riding with-zz me either (srpt). I should be-zz in jail if justice had-zz her say. Why-zz didn't you-zz (srpt) put me in jail?"

"I couldn't."

"Or wouldn't-zz?"

"Bibb, there is much more to your story than I know. I think there is much more to your story than you know. I couldn't hang the governor's agent even if you killed Gorgon in cold blood."

"Enough-s of d'this talk-zz (srpt), sir. I'm smelling a noose (srpt) if I-zz don't shut-zz up. Is d'there anything-zz else (srpt), Sheriff?"

"Don't kill Anna. If you do, I will personally come after you."

"I will-zz try not-zz to (srpt)."

"Try? You tried not to kill her husband too, but oops, shucks, golly golly, an ax left your palm and a blink later Gorgon was face down in the street slop. Bibb, promise me you won't lay a hand on her. Promise me you will deliver her safely to Fort Rice."

"D'that's-zz the least burdensome promise I-zz ever been asked-zz to make (srpt). I can-zz promise you-zz that easy (srpt) because I have-zz already made d'that promise to God. I can-zz hide from you-zz (srpt). God's-zz much more sneaky d'than you (srpt), and He sees-zz in d'the dark. If I harm-zz Anna (srpt) you are my-zz least worry."

"Are you lying about God just to hide your evil ways?"

"Sheriff, we-zz just finished talking (srpt). You-zz answer d'that question later for-zz yourself. Trust your own eyes-zz, not-zz what-zz other folks seen. I ain't got-zz no secrets no-zz more."

"Bibb, take this letter to the Miles City sheriff for me. Don't open it. He is expecting it. There is another letter to Mrs. Gorgon in the bottom of her trunk from Mrs. Franklin. She said it was for Anna's eyes only so you need to keep what is left of your nose out of it."

"Don't worry-zz about d'that. I have-zz had my fill of d'that woman. She makes my skin crawl."

Bibb took the letter, tipped his hat, and galloped to catch up to the wagon. Bibb was done with that man. He thought his behavior in Deadwood was worthy of some trust from the sheriff, but obviously not.

By the time he caught up to the wagon Bibb had decided that dogs bark, toddlers spill their milk, and likewise sheriffs are obligated to suspect the dark side of people. Bibb was comforted by the axiom he had adopted: Who I am is known behind me, not before me. The sheriff will eventually answer his own question.

==0==

Around noon the deputy told Bibb and Anna that he was losing his landmarks and would have to turn back. Bibb acknowledged and thanked the man for going that far. They worked together to replace the deputy's horse from the team with Bibb's.

"Tell-zz your sheriff no hard-zz feelings (srpt). He asked-zz me some hard-zz questions (srpt) and he didn't get-zz d'the answers he wanted."

"I'll pass that on. Anything else?"

"Tell him I am not-zz evil (srpt). No harm beyond her due will fall-zz on Anna."

Anna looked up after hearing that comment. The sheriff must have let loose a whole Spanish Inquisition on her escort. Anna thought Bibb will have to fill in the details later. They would have time. Lots of time. She muttered silently, "If anybody was due their due, Bibb was overdue!"

Ten minutes later they were all alone. Bibb was driving the wagon harder than the horses would like to have gone. Anna's horse was suffering the most and Bibb made sure it got enough to drink. At the next water the "lots of time" had expired on Anna's internal clock and she could not hold back on her questions. "Why did you tell the deputy to inform the sheriff that you were not evil? Where did that come from?"

Bibb looked at her and asked, "Why-zz did you not listen (srpt) to my-zz instructions?"

"What instructions, Bibb?"

"What-zz to wear and what-zz to pack (srpt). D'the dress you-zz are wearing (srpt) is-zz too fancy."

"A woman has the right to wear what she wants when she wants, Mr. Toivo. I am not going to have you pick out my clothes like I am a little dolly. I am a full grown woman with a mind of my own, and you will not control me. You said one trunk, and all my stuff is in one trunk. What I wear is my business."

Bibb looked at her and opted not to respond to her emotional opinions, nor did he feel obligated to answer her original question. Maybe she would forget. Highly unlikely, but for now the original question was tabled. He finished watering the horses and pointed to Anna, and then pointed to the wagon. "Let's-zz ride."

For the next two hours Bibb pushed the horses hard. When they left the last watering spot Anna told Bibb she still wanted an answer, but did not get one. She sat there patiently knowing that she was not being ignored. No, Anna had learned that this man deliberates long to massage his real responses into kind answers. No answer from Bibb meant he didn't have a kind one to give her. That was admirable she reckoned, but she would rather know how he really felt about something.

Anna resigned to the fact Bibb had nothing good to say, so she occupied her time with enjoying the beauty surrounding her. The plains were gorgeous. They were gorgeous because they were not Deadwood. Deadwood's natural surroundings had been abused in every way by the hand of man to make a buck. Surrounding her now was an unmolested pallet of greens accented with dandelions and other wild fall blooms. She laughed to herself at her discovery. "Weeds aren't weeds out here."

An hour later they were still alone. The sun was approaching the slider spot – the point when it seemed to slip down faster than it moved all day towards the horizon. There was just over an hour of sunlight left and Bibb still had not said anything. He was driven by some unseen reason and Anna thought it best not to interrupt. She was not comfortable in the silence and fidgeted in her seat. Bibb's attention was focused straight ahead; thinking her squirming around was just a way to get noticed. Regardless of her growing list of discomforts, he knew where he was going and anxious to get there. All she knew, based on what was left of the sun, was that they were traveling northwest.

Later Bibb started to notice some sniffles coming from the seat next to her. With the sniffles came some moist eyes and more fidgets. "Do you-zz have to stop (srpt), Anna?"

"Where is the hotel we are staying at tonight, Bibb?"

"Mine is-zz strapped to my horse (srpt). Didn't you-zz bring a tent for yourself?"

"You mean there isn't a hotel? Why didn't you tell me? What have you done to me? Where are you going to sleep and what about my privacy?"

"Ma'am, until we-zz get to Miles City (srpt), you-zz will have to keep-zz yourself warm. After Canada (srpt), I am always-zz d'thinking I am living in-zz d'the desert (srpt). If you make-zz certain concessions, we-zz can keep each other warm (srpt), but I-zz would rather not."

"Are you serious? What man-brain concessions are you thinking of? After just one afternoon alone with me are you already thinking things like that? Shame on you!"

"If my plan works, we-zz will never be alone."

"This ain't no plan! This better not be your plan! My mother warned me about men like you!"

He looked at her in disbelief hoping that her misunderstanding of him was due to his mumbles instead of willful not listening. He thought more; it wasn't willful. She was just being an Anna. She, when upset, thought too fast. Anna was more concerned with what she was going to accuse him in reply to his first stutters. An Angry Anna never heard anything after his first five words. He sadly concluded that logic used after his first phrase was a total waste of his limited amount of precious syllables. Frustrated, Bibb decided his best hope was first not to get her angry, and second, speak deliberately measured to slow her brain down a bit. When all else failed, he should put his best points up front while she was still receptive. Of the three options, being kind to Anna was his best choice. She was much more reasonable un-angered. Bibb observed another thing about her over the last week. Men only had to be breathing near her to anger her. Bibb understood that sentiment all too well – he had similar feelings for females older than three days past birth. He felt sorry for Anna; he too once lived in that cave of constant complaining. There was now hope for his heart. Bibb now had eyes to recognize his invisible internal floating bitterness when it started to surface, and once discerned, it could be shed before it showed its dark self to others. This was not an easy lesson to learn. Although the analogy was flawed, he pictured himself as a piece of raw red meat readied for that varmint's bite while he harbored such rancor for another. She could use some of the same hope he had, but Bibb lamented that he was the last person on earth that Anna would accept advice from.

Back to the immediate situation Bibb concluded that she wouldn't believe his plan even if he told her. There was no utility in wasting that air. Concerning her outburst, he was trying to be kind while still telling her the truth about the realities on the trail ahead they would endure. Considering it unwise to answer the first question he decided to address the other. "About-zz your privacy, what are you-zz worried about? D'these last weeks-zz were d'the most embarrassing of my-zz whole life."

"I am asking about my privacy, not yours."

Bibb took that as a sign to go silent again and refocused on the trail ahead. Once again he was reminded that a person in emotional or physical pain seldom can think beyond themselves. That was newly obvious to him. Blind before, he now recognized that condition when suffered by others.

"Tommy, did you hear me?"

"Anna, if you-zz don't mind (srpt), please-zz do me a favor (srpt), and-zz don't whine about our conditions. D'they are what-zz d'they are (srpt), and d'they ain't bad. We could get-zz wind or a cold rain (srpt), or-zz worse, hail. Years from now (srpt) you-zz will have a whole arsenal of stories-zz to tell your grandkids (srpt) if you-zz get old. If you-zz want (srpt), and it-zz will be tight, you-zz can share (srpt) my bedroll with me-zz. Otherwise (srpt) you-zz sleep under d'the stars with d'the horse (srpt). You-zz don't snore-zz, do you? Horses don't like-zz snoring. It spooks d'them if you snort unexpectedly."

Anna had enough of that nonsense. "Is that my only choice, you or a horse's rump?" She laughed to defuse his passion. "Bibb, you are a bad man with a good heart. I have lived with the other and had my fill of it. But be warned, Bibb Boy, if you touch me wrong I will bust you in the mouth and loosen the rest of your teeth!"

"Is-zz d'that my only choice? Why not-zz poke me (srpt) in the d'the eye with a stick (srpt)? My chops-zz (srpt) are still tender."

They both laughed until it hurt, and it hurt Bibb a lot. That caused Anna to laugh even more. "Hey there, Bibb Boy, come and get it!" as she feigned being a boxer. Bibb sat there wondering what possibly she could be seriously thinking. Then he wondered if she ever did any serious thinking. She probably did, especially when it came to money and power. Bibb concluded that her primary source of entertainment was verbal sparring when she had the advantage. As for now, she was entertaining herself really well. He hoped she enjoyed it. He wasn't.

"Yes, you're right! My grandkids will never believe I shared a half a continent with the infamous murdering gunslinger Mr. Bibb." Her mind wandered more "...There we were crossing Montana all alone. ...Rain, wind, snow, hail, and sweltering heat – all in the same day. Bibb," as she spoke again directly to her escort, "I think you might be right. I can't believe it either. What would my momma say? She would be having a hissy fit for sure!"

"If you-zz don't tell my Humbird (srpt), I will not-zz tell your momma."

"Who is this Humbird? And tell her what? Sharing a ride in buckboard with you?"

Bibb got quiet again. Anna could see him thinking, and doing his best to conceal his emotions. "She's-zz my punishment for-zz murdering my brother (srpt). She's-zz mean and she's-zz ugly. She's bossy (srpt) and she's smart. She is-zz sneaky (srpt) and full-zz of knavery. Forget d'that d'thought (srpt). She has-zz a good heart. In every way-zz (srpt) she's-zz a better person d'than me-zz. I respect d'that. She can-zz make me-zz so mad (srpt) d'that all I-zz can do-zz is turn d'the other way-zz and spit (srpt). She always-zz knows what I am going to-zz say next (srpt), and ready to tie me in a knot with my-zz own words (srpt). With her, it's-zz just better to shut-zz up d'than to fall into one of her traps-zz (srpt). She always has-zz a list of promises she wants me-zz to keep (srpt), and d'then shames me when I-zz don't, even if I never agreed to d'them (srpt). She is-zz very aggressive (srpt) and keeps-zz me on my toes. Widow 'Orgon (srpt), I would advise-zz you against ever playing checkers-zz with her!"

"Whoa there, Big Boy! I think I just hit one of your nerves! That is the most you have spoken in a week. Bibb, I have a serious question, and you must answer me because it is directly linked to your health." She stopped speaking and waited for an indication that he was listening. "Do you love her?" Until now, the word *love* had been taboo to both of them.

"Love?" replied Bibb. "I-zz hate-zz love (srpt). Love is-zz a cruel demon."

Anna was not expecting that answer. All her life she had sought love. She thought that at one time she had it, but it only hurt her. "I thought love was good and only good. How can you describe it as evil?"

"I don't know-zz what love is-zz (srpt). But I-zz sure know what-zz it isn't. Love is-zz not a treasure (srpt). The person you-zz love is-zz d'the treasure. Loving love is-zz a lying love (srpt) and it will-zz betray you every time (srpt). Love is-zz not a feeling. I love-zz lots of d'things but I have-zz no feelings in me (srpt). Love is-zz a willful decision and never comes-zz without a cost or investment."

"Like a decision to be kind?"

Bibb was stymied and locked his lips. She had trapped him by his own words. A week ago he had insisted that she decide to be kind to him at the altar, and he swore the same decision to her.

It was minutes later that the silence was broken. "Maybe-zz," said Bibb.

"Maybe-zzzzzz what?" answered Anna, mocking his inability to spit out five words without having to zz-ify them and suck in his own spittle with a slurp "(srpt)."

Bibb didn't answer her response. He was serious and she was playful. Eventually she repeated herself, but more kindly. "Maybe what, Bibb? Are you admitting something? Confess it, Bibb!"

"Anna, I-zz have never been-zz here before (srpt). I know-zz what hate is, and I can-zz understand hate (srpt)."

"But not love? Me neither, Bibb." Anna went silent too, and then they both started laughing almost at the same time. "What are you laughing at Bibb?"

"You-zz never been silenced before (srpt)! It's-zz funny."

"And you have never said the word *love* before, well, and meant it. That's funny too! You're cute when you get frustrated." Without further comment they tacitly dropped the subject. It was that uncomfortable for each.

==0==

"I guess we should pitch a tent pretty soon," suggested Anna.

Bibb replied in a barely audible mumble scrambled with slurps, "I'm not-zz so sure I want-zz to share a tent with you (srpt)." She was not aware Bibb did not own or bring a tent.

"What do you mean by that smart remark? Are you afraid of something?"

"Not-zz in d'the least, Anna. I have-zz a better idea (srpt). You see-zz d'that smoke rising just beyond d'that ridge (srpt)? D'that means we will have-zz company soon (srpt). If-zz we have any luck, we-zz will have (srpt) better-zz accommodations tonight-zz d'than you could ever dream-zz (srpt). D'that, or a very bad haircut-zz (srpt). Anna, d'the next half hour will be-zz d'the most dangerous (srpt) part-zz of our trip. If you-zz don't mind, can I ask you-zz (srpt) not to say anything again until-zz (srpt) I command you to-zz (srpt)? Indians don't care for white women talk-zz."

"Indians? What Indians?" asked Anna.

With surprising anger Bibb replied, "I guess I-zz asked for too much (srpt)! I-zz will try again. Please, until I-zz give you-zz permission (srpt), please-zz purposely breathe only d'through-zz (srpt) your nose. People can't-zz talk if d'they breathe d'through d'their nose (srpt). Anna, I am-zz serious. Our lives-zz depend on it (srpt). D'those teepees tops on d'the horizon (srpt) tell me-zz d'that's a Lakota Sioux camp up-zz d'there (srpt). We-zz should be-zz intercepted by scouts any moment-zz now (srpt), most likely just-zz over d'the next rise (srpt). D'they are already watching us-zz."

"How do you know?"

Bibb quickly turned and gave her a glare that she would never forget until the day she died. She had just experienced what it felt like to be on the wrong side of a show down with one of the fastest guns on the plains. It tingled her down to her toes, an ugly fearful tingle, and she swallowed hard – on every word she had planned to say for the next two hours.

"Widow 'Orgon (srpt), d'there are some d'things you need to know-zz about Indian culture (srpt). You-zz ponder about d'this real good. If d'they d'think you are not-zz my woman (srpt) d'there is-zz a good chance one of d'the braves might want-zz you as a prize-zz (srpt). You are pretty and you-zz would be a novel beast of burden (srpt). If you act as if you-zz are my woman, you-zz will remain untouched (srpt). Second, d'their culture has-zz no quarter for women-zz (srpt) who rebel-zz against authority. Like it or not-zz (srpt), and for our safety, you must at least pretend-zz to be an obedient woman (srpt). When I ask-zz something of you, you-zz must respond immediately (srpt)."

She looked at Bibb as if he had been planning this for days. Fire was in her eyes. But she listened and obeyed.

"Widow 'Orgon, I have-zz no intention of taking advantage of you-zz in anyway (srpt). But-zz if I ask for something, I need-zz you (srpt), really need-zz you, to comply with my request immediately and-zz without question (srpt). I will-zz ask you to take-zz off my boots (srpt). D'that will demonstrate d'that you are bonded to me-zz (srpt) and not up for auction. But if you-zz insist (srpt) to have your independence, I can't be-zz held responsible (srpt) if things go-zz badly for you."

She looked at Bibb in disgust, not just because he told her what to do, but because she feared he was right.

"I can-zz promise you one thing, Anna (srpt). You-zz will never forget-zz d'this day (srpt) for d'the rest of-zz your life. I hope-zz it is-zz a long one."

==0==

As the shadows grew longer Anna disciplined herself to keep her wits and hold her peace. Not because there wasn't something to comment about, but she chose to save her words until after they ripened. Her trail boss had a muzzle on her. She didn't like it but Anna knew why. She had just been introduced to the foreign world of submission and obedience. If they survived this, she trusted Bibb's promise of kindness that her muzzle would come off as soon as she was safe.

When the two scouts finally intercepted Bibb they had already recognized his horse and what he was wearing. They found a place to block the way of the wagon. When Bibb saw their stand, he halted the wagon within fifty feet of them. He signed to them his name and his travel intentions.

Upon closer inspection the scouts confirmed it was Bibb, a more wounded Bibb than they had previously entertained. That did not stop the Indians from staring at the both of them. One scout stayed his ground while the other rode around the wagon. The Indians were carrying both an ax and arrows, and they wanted to see what weapons their visitors were carrying. Finally the one Indian blocking the way spoke to Bibb. He asked him both verbally and in sign who his passenger was.

Bibb did reply, but not to the question. He signed that he brought gifts for their chief, and asked permission to enter the camp. Before they responded he signed again to them that he was taking his woman to Miles City.

The lead Indian rode over to Anna's side of the wagon. He reached from his horse and touched Anna's hair almost in disbelief. Anna smiled, though not on the inside, as if the man was a friend. Bibb signed that there was no Indian word for her name, but the white man called her (and then Bibb spoke her name out loud) "Anna."

Anna was reassured that the conversation was about her name and not something else. Her hair, if not her beauty, had caught their eye. Through this she kept her word not to voice a single syllable.

The Indians spoke to each other and started laughing. Bibb had to smile at their comment too. Bibb then requested once again to enter their camp.

The lead scout indicated to Bibb that he may enter the camp, and that they were going to ride ahead and notify their chief of his arrival. They turned and galloped away.

Bibb told Anna not to be tempted to talk. There was still one scout that was observing them to their east. "To answer-zz your unspoken question, Anna (srpt), d'the Indians-zz made fun of my-zz face (srpt). D'they wondered how-zz somebody as ugly as me-zz (srpt) could have a woman as-zz pretty as you. D'this is not-zz a good sign (srpt). Anna, we-zz are not out-zz of danger yet (srpt). I am-zz going to ask you-zz to do something. If you-zz agree (srpt), please nod-zz your head."

Anna looked at Tommy without talking. She nodded her head as to say yes, wondering what he wanted her to do. There could be all sorts of unacceptable entailments that could go with the title of "my woman." Never had her beauty been considered a detriment. If Bibb could accept the insult of being called ugly with a smile, she could choke down this slight too.

"Anna, show no-zz fear (srpt). I am first going to give-zz your husband's rifle to d'the leader of-zz d'the tribe (srpt). After, when-zz I nod to you (srpt), get-zz out of d'the wagon, taking-zz d'the bag of combs (srpt). When I tell-zz you to, and not-zz before (srpt), come to-zz the leader, bow, and present d'the bag with-zz two hands (srpt). It's important, Anna; remember, two hands. D'that shows what-zz you have is a treasure. Look-zz at him in-zz d'the eye (srpt). Do not-zz expect him to return-zz eye contact. Stay still (srpt) until-zz I tell-zz you to return to-zz d'the wagon (srpt). Nod if you-zz understand."

Anna had listened keenly to the instructions. They would not be given a second chance at impressing the chief. It bothered her greatly about the scout touching her hair. It had been months since a man had touched her hair, something she once enjoyed. Now it could mean trouble. Anna nodded her head yes to Bibb. Her eyes also affirmed her commitment to cooperate.

"Don't-zz fear. For now-zz we are welcomed (srpt). Be-zz gracious in everything-zz d'that comes after (srpt)." Bibb reached under his seat and gave the bag to Anna.

Anna looked at Bibb with new question marks written in her eyes. She was already dealing with the fear of not controlling their situation. A new fear, the fear of the unknown, was overtaking her thinking. She was becoming scared.

"Anna, d'this will turn out really bad-zz (srpt) or really good. Be-zz flexible and smile. D'they understand-zz a smile (srpt). D'they understand-zz angry w'inkles too-zz (srpt). Don't-zz scowl. I'm praying-zz for good (srpt). You-zz do what you-zz want."

Anna thought to herself that was the craziest ultimatum she had ever heard; as if she was going to pray for a bad outcome! She thought to herself that God would never entertain her prayers anyway. Why should He, if He really existed? To the contrary, if He didn't exist, what would mumbling a few words to this unseen and mysterious "the Him" hurt. She wasn't doing anything else right then. Bibb had locked up her lips tighter than a cash box at store closing.

Her heart's attempt to contact "the Him" was overridden by her thoughts centered on how many of her rights were being violated. Contempt bubbled up inside her. Silently she said to herself, "I'll teach that man! He might be able to control what I say on the outside, but I won't let him control what I think on the inside!" She silently yelled a prayer heavenward. "Dear God! You seem mighty determined to take care of that man no matter what trick he gets himself into. While you are at it, take care of me too! That's all I am going to say to you. I already feel silly thinking this."

Just as her previous thoughts had been preempted, her thinking was overridden again. The words were strangely warm at first, almost comfortable; so difficult for her to describe to herself. This had never happened to her before. But a moment later those disdained words felt like a fire burning deep inside. She wanted to yell out, but she could not dare show her anger now – especially as they entered the camp. And then that ditty came again. She decided to resist it, and just like the last time, the tune went away. What she feared was that it went away not forever, but until next time.

> *Good and only good,*
> *You will belong to me,*
> *Kind and only kind,*
> *Precious Hannah Marie*

==0==

Bibb's arrival was now expected, and upon the wagon's appearance they were allowed guarded access inside the perimeter. Bibb recognized the teepee of the chief from a distance and would have gone there without help. That wasn't going to happen. An Indian guide had grabbed the rein of Bibb's horse, obviously the dominant beast, and was leading them to the center of camp. Many other male natives from the camp were coming along side too; all armed with hatchets and arrows. When Bibb and Anna arrived the braves were gathering in ranks in front of the chief's teepee. Anna thought to herself that Bibb could not shoot his way out of this situation. They were hopelessly surrounded and all she had to defend herself with was a bag of brushes and combs... and a smile.

Bibb was out of the wagon attending to his horses when the delayed chief appeared. One of the braves said a word Bibb did not know, much like a call to attention, as the chief approached. Bibb turned around to see the man standing directly in front of him. The chief was taller than Bibb (most men were) and looked intently down on him studying his face in the late twilight. Finally the chief was convinced it was Bibb and a large grin came upon him. The head Indian reached out his hand in friendship and Bibb returned the gesture.

Bibb spoke and signed at the same time. Anna now realized from familiar sounds of the syllables that this was a dialog that Bibb had been rehearsing at a whisper since the deputy left them hours ago. "I bring you a gift for your kindness on my last visit," Bibb said slowly in the Indian dialect. Bibb did not want to take a chance on being misunderstood. The chief was amazed that Bibb could talk giving the wound to his face. His words were confirmed by his hand gestures.

Bibb walked to the back of the wagon, turned back the tarpaulin, and slowly pulled out something wrapped in blankets. When he returned to the chief he asked one of the braves standing close to hold out his hands. He did, and placed the wrapped gift across them. Slowly and with great care, Bibb unwrapped the rifle from within the blankets. Soon the chief realized what the gift was and was visibly getting excited. Bibb took the unwrapped gift and with two hands presented it to the chief. He then told the chief that he also brought four cases of ammunition for him and his camp.

The chief was overwhelmed, hardly paying attention to anything else. He looked at the sights, the action, the stock, and the barrel. It was a prize rifle and the chief immediately recognized the quality. He could see himself in the polished wood. He looked down at Bibb and accepted the gift.

"My woman has also brought gifts to you, Chief." Bibb looked at Anna and she knew that was her cue. She dismounted gracefully from the wagon and proceeded to directly in front of the chief. She gave an appropriate curtsy followed by presenting the chief a large handbag, with both hands.

Given the quality of the bag, at first the chief thought that was the gift. When he opened it his eyes lit up like reflective diamonds in the glory of the setting sun. He shut the purse and in his tongue acknowledged her gift, all done without revealing the contents of the bag to anybody else.

"You must accept my hospitality. Will the accommodations you had on your last stay be acceptable to you and your woman?"

Bibb signed back that he was very happy with his offer. Bibb was happier that the chief established in front of all the others that Anna was his woman. This meant she was not up for auction, well, at least while he was alive. That was a risk Bibb knew he had to accept the day he had said yes to the blacked veiled widow.

The chief made some pronouncements and everything happened at once. One brave helped Bibb with the ammunition while the Indian women grabbed Anna leading her away from the wagon. Bibb barely had time to tell her all went well and that she was in safe hands, but warned her never to assume she was left alone by herself. Shortly the wagon and the horses were heading down to the river for care and grazing. Two other women had already unloaded Anna's trunk from the wagon and followed the other women that had circled around Anna.

The Indian women talked excessively, having been given permission by the chief to make the white woman welcome. They soon realized that Anna did not know their tongue, but that didn't matter. Between the gestures, smiles, and pointing Anna could tell where to sit, go, and stand. After a bed was made for her (she wondered where Bibb was going to sleep) she realized that they were all going to finish preparing a meal. There was no doubt that Anna was invited to help.

==0==

The stew was full of almost cooked buffalo chunks. Bibb knew that was exactly the way they liked it. The next meal from that buffalo would be much more roasted to help it keep longer. What was not eaten then would be turned into jerky. Bibb and the chief were at the center of the communal dinner with all the braves looking on. Bibb was able to share some funny stories that had universal appeal to the men. The women were off on their own side.

At the end of the meal the chief stood up and acknowledged his happiness with the fine gift of the rifle and the thoughtfulness of also providing the ammunition. It was truly a valuable gift. Then he said that the gift from Bibb's woman was equally pleasing. He called to the thirty-one oldest women to come to him, directing them to form a line from oldest to youngest. He made a couple of proclamations, which Bibb was not within earshot to understand, but saw the chief hand out a comb or brush to each woman in order of age until they were gone and all had one. The looks of gratitude on the women's faces as the chief presented to each their gift required no campfire to illuminate.

The women retired back to their own tents after the meal while the men stayed on by the central campfire. Bibb's reputation as a marksman needed no reintroduction. Plans for the next day started with Bibb teaching the chief how to use his new rifle. After that the chief ordered which braves would next be instructed on the use and care of the weapon. After repeating himself, Bibb made his point to the braves that they must also learn how to keep the weapon clean if the rifle was to last.

The fire was almost out when the chief dismissed Bibb to return to the widows' teepee. A woman close to the discussions was summoned to take him there. None of the braves were dismissed because the chief still had some instructions for them. This was not a surprise. Bibb was an outlaw and a white man. Trust was not something that could be bought with a gift.

The elders gave instructions to the tribe on how their guests would be treated and questions they wanted answers to. They gave specific assignments to individuals and detailed responsibilities to others. The chief spoke harshly to the matron of the tribe about his concerns with the white woman. Bibb was already known, but she was not. The medicine man was particularly distressed by a foreign scent she possessed. He also wanted to know how the outlaw could stand upright given his many injuries. The matron received specific instructions concerning that issue. The chief ended the council by telling his cadre to be aware that a great and higher gift may have visited upon their camp. Until proven otherwise all must consider the white couple friends of the Lakota. The medicine man, with a tone of solemn urgency used high ceremonial language to charge all to watch the warrior and the woman carefully. He identified one man in the inner circle as responsible to collect all the tribe's observations of all the visitors' words and deeds. The camp was on alert.

==0==

Upon arrival at the widows' teepee Bibb could see that Anna was in the thick of things – braiding and unbraiding hair, combing and having her hair combed. They loved touching Anna's hair. And the fun wasn't over.

"Can I talk to you, Tommy?" She whispered, purposely not saying Bibb.

"Yes-zz. Why?"

"There seems to be some rules here about women talking in front of men. You do qualify as a man, yes?"

"Of course I do-zz (srpt)."

"Then what are you doing in the women's teepee? You can leave now. I'll see you in the morning."

Bibb wasn't sure what she was hinting about at first. There was an awkward pause until one of the widows told Bibb that she had brought in his stuff from his horse. By the back of the teepee he was showed where she had stored it behind some blankets.

"What did she say, Bibb?"

"She was-zz telling me indirectly (srpt) d'that whenever I'm ready for sleep I-zz can bed down."

Bibb turned to one of the widows and asked her a question. Bibb pointed to Anna, which prompted the widow to get up and show him the bed she had prepared. Bibb spoke, gesturing in a nice way that the bed was narrow. The Indian widow grinned from ear to ear and pulled on Anna's arm for her to stand up and come close to Bibb. To add to the drama she measured the waist of each and then said something in reply to Bibb.

"What did she say?" Anna asked Bibb softly. She remembered to say it kindly even if kindly wasn't on her mind. This was not a time to show an anger wrinkle.

"Anna-zz, she said we-zz would fit (srpt). Honest, I did not plan d'this-zz. I'd rather sleep-zz with my horse (srpt)." Bibb realized too late how badly that had sounded and tried to recover. "Anna, we have-zz no choice (srpt). The chief announced to all d'that-zz you were my woman. We will get-zz d'through d'this. Pretend I'm not-zz here (srpt)."

"Well if the choice between you sleeping with a horse and me being auctioned off, I will have to make the best of this. My promise still stands, Bibb." Anna put the biggest grin on her face as she delivered her next comment. "Touch me wrong and I will slice you into coyote candy."

"Anna, trust me-zz. I will lay-zz down first (srpt) with my-zz back towards d'the fire. I-zz promise I won't even dream funny (srpt)."

Anna could not believe the situation she was in. She thought how every other man on the planet would be doing cartwheels over the prospect, but this man was honestly scared of her. Or this man was scared of Humbird, or whatever her name was, or both, or maybe something else too. His wicked side of life was well documented, but she hadn't seen it yet. Something was restraining the man. She almost pitied him, but chose not to.

"Well, keep your word then, Tommy. You have had a long day. Get ready for bed and go shut your eyes. Maybe you will sleep well enough and wise enough not to have cause or curiosity to open your eyes until morning."

Bibb took a moment to reply. "Anna," he said. "I wish... oh (srpt), I-zz can't say-zz d'things right."

"Bibb, what is it? Speak it out and don't fear about stumbling with your words. Nobody else here understands what you are saying."

"Anna." Bibb stopped for a moment. "Honestly (srpt), I did not plan-zz d'this. Wake me in-zz d'the (srpt) morning. The chief has busy plans-zz (srpt) for me tomorrow. And Anna, I almost forgot-zz to tell you (srpt). D'the sheriff said d'that Mrs. Franklin left you-zz a private note (srpt) in d'the bottom of your trunk. I am-zz going to sleep."

"Not so fast, Tommy." She said it kindly, but got his attention.

"I have been trying to communicate with these ladies for over three hours, and I want you to tell me what they really said. You sit right there. Until your lips are ready to fall off, you translate for us."

"My lips are already ready-zz (srpt) to fall off."

"I will be the judge of that, Tommy." She was perfecting the art of delivering kind sounding zings. "I will decide all your medical limitations and healing requirements. You need to exercise your throat some more. Be kind, my man."

Bibb complied. And complied. And complied some more. Eventually he fell asleep during one of the questions. Anna woke him and told him to go to bed pointing in that direction. Anna did not know that during the conversation one of the widows had asked him what white married men wear to sleep. Bibb's answer was much more modest than they expected.

To Anna's surprise, just as Bibb started towards his bed the widows jumped up and started to undress Bibb. To Bibb, the widows' response was helpful. This wasn't his first visit to this Indian village. They knew about his ribs and what trouble he had with clothes.

Anna initially looked on with protest, but quickly changed. Bibb saw her face's message, and told her that this was how they showed appreciation and kindness. He reassured her that there was nothing shameful going on. To the contrary, they were showing honor and respect in their cultural way. He was quickly tucked in for the night. Bibb said something soothing to the ladies in their own tongue, to which the ladies cooed back. It was so foreign to Anna.

Bibb knew what might happen next and prayed for death or a death-like sleep. The widow ladies would have some additional cultural expectations of Anna that she was not aware of.

==0==

While riding back into Deadwood the sheriff noted a lone Indian riding the trail northwest towards Miles City. Before meeting the man, the lone rider turned off the trail to avoid crossing paths. That night when his deputy arrived back in town he reported that he also had seen the Indian. The Indian had not avoided him, but approached him and asked him some questions.

"Sheriff, it was certainly strange to ride up to an Indian, and even stranger to be asked a question in English."

"What did he ask?"

"He asked me how long ago I said good-bye to Bibb and the Widow Gorgon. Sheriff, how did he know about those two? Why would he care, and what would he gain from knowing?"

"He could calculate how far up the trail they were. He probably saw you with them on the way out. Since you doubled back he could know with fairly good accuracy how far those two got tonight. That's if Bibb hadn't done her in by then. That Widow Gorgon can really irritate, and that outlaw has a short fuse. Did the man say what his name was?"

"No, but he had a horse with a government brand on its rump."

"It was Toak then."

"Who is Toak?"

"The Indian who betrayed Bibb in Miles City. When he meets up with Bibb, one, two, or three people are going to die."

"Do you think Bibb knows he is being tracked?"

"Did you notice if the government horse had a bent backwards shoe on its rear hoof?"

"How would I have known to notice that, Sheriff? Why do you ask?"

"My son told me that Bibb was curious about such a horse track found up on White Rocks. He also said that Bibb told those riding along about an Indian who had taught him how to track. He never said Toak when they stopped at the Rocks to rest, but whom else could it be? Toak was the tracker that got Bibb captured and beaten in Miles City."

"What can we do about it?"

"Nothing. Nobody takes better care of Bibb than Bibb. Forget about it. If providence wants to keep them alive, there is nothing we can do to change that."

"Did Bibb state a belief in providence?" asked the deputy.

"Bibb was silent on that, but his actions sure did indicate it. Why else would he have dragged our nightmare named Anna to the chapel? I also was privy to a letter he wrote to the sheriff in Miles City. Bibb wrote something in code that hints of belief. Regardless, the doctor surely thinks so. He bet a fortune on his hunch. Funny Bibb didn't mention anything like that to any of the Dowry girls."

"I can partly answer that, Sheriff. One of those girls told me something about Bibb."

"And..."

"There was an incident in the barn behind the Gorgon mansion. Miss Dowry said it gave her the shivers."

"And..."

"Bibb doesn't give any never-mind to Mrs. Gorgon. She laid out many demands and Bibb refused every last one of them. She was really mad, especially when he refused to go into her house. The nurse told me that Bibb eventually got fed up with her demands and walked away. Sir, she swore to me that she didn't tell Bibb about the soup. She said she thinks Bibb figured out the Widow Gorgon was the one who made all the noise in the hotel, and that she was out to kill him."

"How did he know about that?"

"She told me that Bibb recognized the voice from her visit the following day. And Bibb told the nurse that the Widow Gorgon's yelling in the barn confirmed it. They wrote some messages to each other in the barn that they did not show the nurse. Miss Dowry did say something funny that Bibb later told her about the incident."

"And..." The sheriff often had to lead his deputy on.

"She said Bibb told her a rule. 'The only thing lace was made for was to muddy a man's thinking.' Bibb told her that he wasn't sure if Anna was ninety percent lace and ten percent mud, or the other way around."

"What has that anything to do with providence?"

"I don't know, but it certainly wasn't love that brought them together. Bibb hates her, and not just a mild hate. He really detests rich, pushy women. And she hates him too. The nurse said I should have seen how she talked to Bibb. It's a miracle she is still alive."

"Why do you think he changed his mind about her?" asked the sheriff.

"I don't think he has, Sheriff. He just keeps it inside. The nurse asked Bibb about that. He said it didn't matter what kind of person Anna was. He made a promise to her and that settled it. He told her that he had learned the hard way that cheating a widow is worse than boxing with a ghost."

"What does that mean?"

"I don't know. That boy sure has had a colorful past."

==0==

The fire was going out in the widows' teepee. Once Anna was convinced, awake or not, that Bibb wasn't going to peek, poke, wiggle, or wince and locked permanently in position looking away from teepee activity, she decided to put away the nice dress she was wearing in exchange for comfortable sleeping clothes. That turned out to be a big mistake. Once the trunk was opened, the two widows sharing the same quarters revived. They acted as if that moment was bigger than any grand opening sale at a city department store!

The event was quickly out of control, and she couldn't yell at the widows and risk waking Bibb up. They loved all the dresses and undergarments. They each wanted to try them on, and after putting some of the innerwear on upside down and backwards Anna resigned herself to help them. It was almost comical, but in a lovely way. Then they wanted to try on the dresses too. Then shoes. Then they wanted to see how Anna fit into them. There was not one piece of clothes in her trunk safe from their curiosity. Anna had never seen two happier women in her life.

Their curiosity was not limited to Anna's clothes, but Anna's person too. They wanted to comb her hair, ask her about everything to include a late night stroll down to the river. When they returned one of the Indian widows offered Anna a pair of her pajamas to wear. The Indian ladies had already changed into their version of nightclothes down by the river. In the soft light coming from the fire within the teepee, Anna concluded that these pajamas were barely enough to be considered a respectable loin cloth. The women insisted that Anna comply. Anna couldn't find any of her nightclothes even if she wanted too. Everything was in such disarray and quite dark everywhere except near the dying embers of the campfire. She gave in at their insistence, and once again she could see their joy, even if was only in the white reflection of their eyes and grins full of teeth. There was no lack of help getting Anna into these pajamas. She was seriously worried that all the chatter would wake up Bibb and that would bring on a new set of problems.

One of the things that Anna did find at the bottom of the trunk was the letter from Mrs. Franklin. Since it was private this would be as good time as any to read the note. She opened the envelope as a pair of curious eyes watched on.

> *My dearest daughter Anna, you have no grounds to hate me now or in the future. I made my husband do this to protect you, protect Tommy, and protect God's reputation. I have no regrets for what I have done, and even if you don't agree with me yet, I would do it again because it was the right and proper thing to do. What you will find inside the inner envelope is properly registered at the courthouse. Also inside is a pre-release cutting from today's newspaper. Anna, there is no coming back to Deadwood; all your bridges have been burned.*
>
> *As your attorney, early today my husband started transferring the complete Gorgon estate into your new husband's name, and his alone lest you get any ideas to abandon the man in Miles City. Reading thus far, you have already realized that if Tommy finds out about your nuptials or tires of you (a well-documented possibility) he may dispose of you or sell you to the Indians and keep the entire estate for himself. Lest you forget, you witnessed Bibb's will and know full well who gets the entire estate if something deadly happens to him.*
>
> *There is an out. If you both fulfill your covenant and the marriage not consummated, my husband will process an annulment to un-marry you two and return the fortune to your name. He wants it in writing from Bibb's hand that you fulfilled your holy promises. Although I think it wise for you to endear yourself to the man to keep both of you happy and you alive, I think it best you not tell Tommy about the marriage. But you are a big girl and can make your own decisions, to include when and if to tell him.*
>
> *About the signatures? Surprisingly they perfectly match the signatures on Tommy's will. They are too good to be considered forgeries, and the witnesses to your vows would have to be proven liars. I am sure you will recognize their*

names. Gaining their future cooperation is highly unlikely given the years of fierce animosity between you and those three women.

Darling daughter, be not bitter, but be kind. You will thank me later. You may even thank God later. You had to lose your sixth fortune to gain a seventh.

We love you, Momma and Abba Franklin.

Anna was stunned, but not so the other two witnesses in the teepee. She put away the letter without opening the inner envelope. When she returned to the center of teepee more whispering began. They became more playful, and after she had endured all the sisterhood that she could modestly (and immodestly) handle, she quietly climbed into the bed prepared for her. Bibb had cooperated magnificently with her demands. Either that or he was so bone tired that not even a lightning bolt would jostle the man. This was so beyond anything she had imagined her wedding night would be like, banish the thought.

Unfortunately, the moment of her lying down sharing the narrow bed was when the chatter started afresh, and some of the sounds between the giggles indicated what was on their minds. Anna wished them good night and indicated by taking her fingers to show as if they were children that she was locking her eyes shut. She turned her back to them, pulled a small blanket over the top of her and Bibb, and snuggled up tighter than a tick next to "her man." She would not speak again this evening despite the universally understood commentary coming from the other side of the teepee.

As she lay there silently in horror that Bibb might awake, she thought of what really happened this evening and earlier this day. Bibb was right. These moments would never be forgotten. Her hosts were so happy. She thought to herself that she was happy too despite the note she had just finished reading. There she was, sleeping in an Indian teepee in a skimpy barely anything snuggled up next to an outlaw. No, this was beyond her wildest imaginations. It was beyond the wildest of her best dreams too. Then there was the risk. If Bibb awoke from his sleep her humiliation would be complete.

The Indian women had been so good to her, and so grateful for the gifts. How did Bibb know that such a little thing would get such a big response? And Bibb gave her all the credit for the women's gifts. She was being loved by so many without one ounce of merit to deserve any of it. Even bad girls have good days. She held Bibb so tight that even their breathing synchronized. She dreamed that their kindred hearts did too, or maybe that was already a reality. The last thing she remembered before falling to sleep was the sounds of coyotes howling at the moon.

Sunday, October 9, 1887

Utter poverty. I was blinded by juvenile adventurous notions that infected my mind last night. But the sun is now out... My new friends are not aware of their destitution, the hardships they suffer... the cuts that do not heal... the scars that mar all of their bodies... the broken legs that were never set straight... the plight of the pregnant squaw... the cough that never goes away. Their whole day is spent in finding food and gathering essentials, real essentials... not like stuff that rests safely as junk in my trunk. Yes, my heirlooms hold my memories, but little else. These people are too poor to afford memories. My blindness has fallen away and I am humbled.

Yet these Indians belong to each other. Their wealth is found in a good name; honor is their currency, their tribe is their identity. Obedience to authority is their dominant trait; they must obey to survive. Modesty is barely known to them. They cry real tears when their children suffer.

They think of me as a liability of the white race. I have no children and a wounded husband. They measure beauty in years of life and accumulated wisdom, not in the lack of blemishes or a natural attractiveness found in a body of balanced symmetry. They think me an unskilled wife because my husband lies broken and I do not cater to him.

At lunch the elder woman made a judgment about me which caused the squaws to laugh. I asked Bibb to translate and he would not. Later I whined until I got the truth out of him. She said "The spirit guides an ugly woman to a brave man. No other will have her. But a brave man is ill served until she gains a higher name. May he live that long." Those words are seared into my soul as well as every word of Bibb's comment about it. He said, "The good news is that you will not be up for auction nor do they have a good reason to kill me. Anna, ugly to them is similar to our term for a shy newlywed. They did not slight your beauty, but merely noticed your timidity towards me. Let them think that. She measured you by her cultural wisdom. I measure you by ours. Anna, I am so proud of you. I could not ask for a better partner. You are simply radiant."

I did not see those words coming. Bibb is so wrong. What have I done to deserve that praise? Whine? Hand out combs that I didn't want to bring — combs and brushes that my maid spirited out of the house without my permission or knowledge? My depth of selfishness overwhelms me. I am so ashamed. What have I contributed to our covenant to be his equal? Push him to his limits? Pack twice what he said I could bring and then dare him to say something? What have I done to be radiant? Feign true kindness and then mock his speech? The man is such a deceptive conniving liar, and as to his assertions — mark my words! I will prove that liar right!

My life has been filled with kicking and screaming, screaming and kicking. No more. I have kicked my last cactus. Not one cacti was ever hurt; only me. Not once did the widows complain.

==0==

BIBB AND ANNA'S teepee mates were up before dawn to get ready for the day. The fire was already regenerated when they woke Anna by wrestling loose the barnacle like grip that she had to Bibb's back. She woke in a daze, not to mention her fatigued arms and legs. The widow ladies also woke Bibb just to see if by chance he had been smothered to death overnight.

Anna did not like this development for the simple reason she was still in her Indian pajamas. She quickly grabbed some clothes and changed, concealed behind her trunk as to hide from Bibb's potential view. The Indian women, still in their pajamas, found the whole scene most humorous. Modesty was an inconvenient luxury they practiced sparingly.

All the bumps and bangs, the getting out and the getting in, plus the care for the horses the day before had worn Bibb out. He tried to get up, but his body said no. He tried again and soon resigned to the fact he was still severely busted up. His ribs ached, but that would have to be overcome. He felt like a calf that had been lassoed and freshly branded.

Bibb perceived what was going on inside the teepee from overhearing the chatter and kept his eyes shut. He decided the comments the widows were saying about Anna were, although humorous in an Indian context, best forgotten. Although sorely tempted otherwise, Bibb decided to keep facing the other way after hearing Anna's soft spoken protests. He took serious note of her useless pleas for privacy.

When the widows finished dressing they grabbed Anna by the hand and left the teepee. The quiet was refreshing and Bibb quickly, as if it was an unrequested gift from providence, dove back into a deep sleep – a welcome relief from the pain. The blessed respite did not last long.

==0==

Bibb did not notice when the women reentered the teepee. They kept quiet while they picked up after the clothing free-for-all they had enjoyed the night before. Anna silently showed them how to fold her garments and arrange them tightly into her trunk. There was no room to spare inside of it.

Nobody in the teepee but Anna seemed to notice that the fancy dress she wore the day before was missing. It certainly wasn't stashed away hidden in this teepee. Everything the widows possessed was in open view. Anna was confident that it would turn up, and probably adorned on the chief's wife. This was to be expected. Rights and privileges of ownership was a foreign concept to the women of the camp. Everything belonged to the male down to the moccasins on the women's feet, and the chief was the unquestioned local sovereign over everything.

All was going smoothly from Bibb's perspective. The women seemed to be getting along, and Anna was doing quite well for herself. The peace was refreshing as Bibb lay on their comfortable mattress meant only for one person. He still couldn't believe how last night's situations developed and happened so fast. He was even more astonished that Anna consented to the arrangements. It was now history, and if they lived, Anna and he would have plenty of time to discuss later. Bibb spent his time making mental notes to prepare responses to things Anna might complain about.

Bibb only had one immediate complaint, but sore ribs were certainly better than a bad haircut. Bibb laughed to himself, so glad the uncertainties of yesterday were over. "Scalping only hurts for a second. These Anna induced constrictions may hurt for days! Oh, I imagine I will get over it. I will tell her I will give her a week to stop snuggling so close to me, or else I will have to tell her to go sleep with the buffalo. That is certainly unkind. Maybe I will give Anna two weeks to stop it. Shame on me... Varmint, you don't have to say anything... I have already put that thought out of my mind. Go haunt somebody else. If you are really set on changing somebody's heart, go bother Toak. Go away, varmint! I have enough aches and troubles without having to deal with you too."

The little slice of Indian life that Anna witnessed in the last twelve hours showed her that possessing rights seemed unknown to the women of the camp. Even the combs belonged to the chief and could be recalled at any time. Anna saw that this custom enabled easy sharing of possessions among the women and limited any cause for envy. No woman owned anything to be coveted by another. Still, human nature, as it exists, exposed some selfishness, greed, and jealousies in the clan. If there arose any of that nonsense the matron of the tribe looked like she could nip it. She didn't get old by luck. There are no both old and dumb Indians. The silly ones don't survive.

==0==

The water was rudely cold. Bibb was perfectly happy laying there unmolested, but the women attacked him with water and rags to give him a bath. Once wet, the widows teamed up and chattered unceasingly to convince him to leave the widow's teepee. After chasing him out, the elder pleaded with Bibb to grasp a pole in front of him at slightly above eye level. Once he complied, they then mimed to Anna to start working on Bibb's face. Anna was much too slow for their liking as the widows grabbed more rags and started in on Bibb's arms and chest. Bibb did not like this at all, but none of his protests were registering. Anna seemed helpless. The widows were determined to remove all of the grime from all of the man, and if Anna wasn't up to the job, they were.

The energy Bibb didn't have earlier came upon him instantly with another jolt of the cold water. He couldn't suffer their kindness anymore and finally convinced the widows that Anna would finish the task. They started working on his legs and feet anyway. Once again Bibb insisted that Anna would finish the work. They complied, but visibly showing frustration with Anna's meager efforts.

Anna received countless suggestions from the widows on how the cleaning should be done. It was embarrassing for Anna and humiliating for Bibb. It was the first time that all of Bibb's injuries became exposed to Anna. The scars from the whip's lacerations on his back were bad enough, but his discolored chest was the most unsettling to her. There was obvious new bleeding going on inside of him. The back of his legs were also a ghastly shock to Anna. They looked almost inoperable to the point where Anna wondered how the man could walk. This morning was also the first time Anna actually touched Bibb's face, something that she really hoped to avoid. The bubble brigade at her side ardently insisted the man be thoroughly cleaned, and strangely scared, returned to helping.

Unexpectedly, the tribe's matron arrived at the melee. From her gruff talk Bibb found out that this cleansing treatment was not the widows' idea, but an edict. The widows were compelled to comply and were chastised for some of the scrubbing that should have been Anna's do to. After the matron left Bibb overheard that getting him clean wasn't the primary reason for the scrubbing.

"Anna, do not-zz be hesitant (srpt). Scrub-zz my legs as you-zz would scrub the dirt-zz off of your own. D'they are watching you (srpt). D'the tribe's opinion of white-zz women will be-zz set for generations based on-zz how and what you do now. D'they said (srpt) d'they were commanded to-zz have me cleaned. D'this inventory of wounds was not d'their idea (srpt) or d'the matron's. Please clean me good so-zz d'they don't get-zz in any more trouble. Kindly ask-zz d'them to help (srpt) and you-zz will win-zz d'them as sisters. Touch d'them when you-zz ask them (srpt), and hug-zz d'them when you-zz are done. The matron commanded that only you are to clean-zz my recent wounds (srpt) and let-zz them clean d'the rest. D'they are as curious about-zz white men (srpt) as much as-zz white women. You found-zz d'that out last night."

"Bibb, you really are hurt, aren't you? You weren't just saying that about your ribs, were you? You need to see a doctor and fast. You are bleeding in there; I can see it. And what did you do to your back and legs?"

"Anna, I'm-zz sorry I didn't tell you earlier (srpt). I made you-zz promise to care for me-zz (srpt) and you didn't know-zz how broken I-zz was."

"Tommy, enough of that talk. Shut your mouth and hold that post tight. I'm the trail boss here. They want you clean, and clean you will be. If I hurt you, speak my name softly, otherwise you do exactly what I tell you to do. In this jurisdiction men are commanded to be obedient and denied permission to speak unless their women allow them to talk… at least while they are being cleaned up." She said that with such a kind tone that the widows were satisfied Anna was accepting her responsibilities.

Bibb knew different. Anna was still smarting from Bibb telling her she couldn't talk when they entered the camp. She decided to have some devilish fun with the moment. She especially enjoyed applying several breath-taking applications of strategically placed ice water from the creek to her man. Bibb was immobilized by the embarrassment of the whole situation. There was nothing he could do about it except comply and hope Anna and the curious widows would hurry.

==0==

"Where are you going, Bibb? Are you leaving me?"

"Please-zz watch your tone, Anna (srpt). D'they cannot understand what-zz you say, but-zz d'they do understand-zz your feelings (srpt). My day is-zz not my own. The chief has-zz me riding with-zz his braves (srpt)."

"Must you, Tommy? I need you to translate for me."

"I must do what the chief has asked of me (srpt). I will teach-zz d'them how to shoot. I will (srpt) do what-zz d'they originally planned to do-zz before we came into-zz camp (srpt)."

"When will we be leaving here, Bibb?"

"I will ask-zz d'the chief for escorts (srpt) after we give-zz our second gift to d'the chief at d'the meal tonight (srpt). I hope you will be allowed to help deliver d'the gift. D'this morning observers told d'the matron d'that I did not act married to you. Anna, it is very important I change d'that perception. I want-zz to leave with you-zz tomorrow morning."

"Honestly, Bibb, you have nothing to worry about even if it takes a week for them to change their minds. I am in no hurry to leave. I will not complain if you want to stay longer to heal. I will not complain if we leave tomorrow either." She watched Bibb as she let her comments sink in.

"Anna, another d'thing I got-zz to ask. D'they d'think more of me d'than I'm worthy of, and if d'they see you get-zz me nervous and shake-zz, well-zz, d'they-zz will doubt our words-zz, and d'things will not-zz go well for us. Please don't surprise me. You know-zz how I-zz react to when-zz you bump me or touch me or, well Anna, d'this is not d'the time for d'that. Never is d'the time for d'that, especially now. I have to be-zz more man-zz d'than d'the man I-zz got left in me."

"Again you have nothing to worry about. Bibb, I know your weakness and I won't expose it to them. I am all in, Bibb. And that goes for you too. Don't you get any funny ideas either. I won't tolerate a single oops out of you. We can do this, Tommy." She was more sincere than he had ever noticed in her before. She continued. "Bibb, please tell these widows the same thing about what you have planned for today. If they wash clothes, I want to wash clothes with them. If they cook, I want to cook. If they sew, I want to sew. Please tell them. They have nothing Bibb, and I don't want to be a burden on you or them. Tell them I want to help them just as they helped me."

Bibb complied with Anna's request. The widows replied with puzzled looks. Bibb repeated her request to the widows, and this time Anna nodded and smiled. The widows smiled back and a deeper bond was formed. Within moments the teepee was empty and the full day had begun.

==0==

Bibb's morning was without rest. He first taught the chief how to fire his weapon, and then Bibb asked the chief for his permission to teach his braves how to use and clean the rifle. This request did not have to be voiced except for formality's sake.

Late that morning while Bibb was teaching them, one of the braves spotted a deer about 350 yards away. The brave asked Bibb if he could scare it. The rest of the party, about twelve braves, repeated the challenge to Bibb. The exhausted Bibb acknowledged the challenge and in return he challenged three of the braves to be ready to ride to finish the kill. At that distance the deer might not die immediately. Bibb reassembled the rifle, careful to adjust the sites to the settings he desired, and then asked the brave where the deer was. Eventually the mature buck would expose itself again.

Bibb would have preferred the prone position, but the grass was too tall. Bibb went to the largest tree and braced himself next to it to help steady his aim. Then the wait began for the deer to show himself again. During the pause a light breeze blew across and Bibb measured it by licking his finger to see how fast it dried. He changed his mind and found a smaller tree limb that could be used to steady his shot. Bibb knocked down the grass just in front of him that allowed him to see the deer if it popped up in sight again. Bibb assumed a sitting firing position stabilizing his rifle stock hand on the limb and patiently waited.

The moment came. Using the same techniques he was teaching the braves, Bibb gently squeezed off a round aiming up and to the right of the exposed antlers to adjust for distance and breeze. The round either scared the deer or hit it because the antlers immediately disappeared.

All the braves, not just three, jumped on their horses and galloped off on the chase leaving Bibb alone. Bibb tried twice to get on his horse but he could not. His chest hurt too badly. He decided to sit back down on the fallen tree and re-clean the rifle.

One brave came back to see about Bibb. He reported that his bullet had pierced through the lung and the heart of the deer. It had gone down immediately. There had been no need for a chase, and the other braves were already draining the deer and removing the entrails. There would be a feast in the camp tonight! The brave's excitement quickly ended when he saw that Bibb did not react to his joy.

"Why didn't you ride with us?" signed the brave.

"I tried. I couldn't get on my horse," admitted Bibb. Bibb showed him his wounded chest that was purple with internal bleeding.

"I will tell our medicine man. He will help."

"I am not worthy of his help. I am not Lakota."

"That is not your decision to make." The brave streaked away galloping towards the village.

When the other braves returned with the six point buck there was little doubt what they wanted to do. While one brave took the deer back to the camp, the others asked Bibb to teach them more aiming skills with the rifle. Just as Bibb thought he was done teaching and coaching, more braves arrived. Nobody had to be convinced of Bibb's marksmanship credentials.

By late morning every one of them knew how to adjust their individual rifle sight settings and could hit a small target at two hundred yards. Bibb would not take any of the praise. He (rightly) credited the skill of the braves and the quality of the rifle.

==0==

There was great concern in the camp when a brave arrived and asked their medicine man to leave the camp to care for an injured man. The elder left with the brave, adding to the anxiety among the women. It was very rare that the medicine man would leave the center of the village. To be traditionally accurate, the location of his moccasins defined the heart and hub of the camp.

Just short of an hour later a different brave arrived back in camp along with the medicine man. This brave was also carrying more meat. The medicine man provided details to the chief about an injured man. Little was told to the women other than the chief directed the tribe's healer to prepare something that was supposed to help.

The matron of the tribe summoned the widows and told them to inform Anna that Bibb was hurt. With a tear in her eye, the eldest of the widows approached Anna and drew a picture of a man in the dust, and then poked the stick into the chest of the drawing. Anna was confused, but when she drew a woman next the man, pointed to it, and then pointed to her, a pall of dread came over Anna. There was no doubt. The message they had for her was that Bibb was hurt.

Anna asked the widow to take her to Bibb. That conversation was obviously garbled because the widow ended up taking Anna to the medicine man. Through pointing, Anna was told to silently sit on the floor of his teepee along with and next to the elder widow.

Anna was sick with nervousness. This wasn't like life in Deadwood where she directed commerce with the flick of a finger. After the longest ten minutes of her life

Anna decided she could no longer wait. She started to get up to go search for Bibb. That was a grave mistake.

The medicine man sternly commanded something and motioned for Anna to sit. The widow next to her did not give Anna a chance to speak, but pulled her forcefully back to the mat. In an immediate response to Anna's look of outrage, the widow kissed Anna on the neck and held her hand tenderly. Anna obeyed, completely overwhelmed by the widow's unscripted response.

A second fear swept over Anna. Her living as a free woman depended on Bibb living too. Was the medicine man deciding which of his braves to have her for a slave? What of her riches? What of her freedoms? What of her desire to be her own authority?

Time went on in complete silence. A bitter smell was now filling the teepee. Anna continued to be very nervous as her mind filled with thousands of outcomes, and all of them bad. She couldn't cry; she was too busy planning her escape.

The young woman's sniffle gave it away; Anna saw a tear silently roll down the widow's cheek. Anna became ashamed of herself because she was only thinking of herself. Sitting next to her was an alien woman that showed more feelings for her man without trying – more than Anna could if she had a week to try. There they sat in the dark of the tent with a purposely silent painted man concocting something smelly. Was he preparing embalming chemicals? Anna started to sniffle, and that caught the attention of the old Indian.

After yelling a summons, a new woman came running into the teepee. The medicine man issued a very authoritative command to the woman and she immediately left. A minute later the other widow host appeared at the door, visibly shaken by the order to present herself at the medicine man's teepee. Another stern command was barked, and the younger widow came and sat down next to Anna. The command she was given was to comfort Anna as the first widow was dismissed.

The young Indian woman was frozen in fright, even more scared than Anna. The man's teepee was known as a tent of screams. Those that emerged were often healed. Those that did not were buried. Based on the medicine man's command, and not knowing what else to do, she sat hip to hip and embraced Anna. In doing so, the comb that was in her pocket poked into Anna's side.

Anna broke the embrace, and reached into the woman's pocket to retrieve the comb. Anna pointed for her to turn around, sit down, and face the chief. Anna sat behind her with the widow between her knees, took the comb and gently started to care for the widow's hair.

The medicine man saw what happened and stared at them as if in a trance himself and deep in interpreting revelation. Anna decided she did not care what that elder was thinking; she kept to her task entirely focused on gently removing tangles from her host's long beautiful hair. Later, breaking an almost sacred silence, the medicine man spoke again and this time directly to the widow in their tongue, "You are wise. We are most comforted when we comfort others. That lifts sorrows from hearts to hands." The young widow exhaled a deep breath of relief.

Anna spent the next thirty minutes combing and practicing a forgotten art of patiently being as quiet as the Indian widow was. She was in no position to demand anything. She especially wasn't going to ask about her favorite dress that was hanging from the highest point in his tent. At least now she knew where it was. She had worn that dress yesterday for one reason only: to frustrate Bibb. It now frustrated her. Bibb must have given that dress to the medicine man just to get even! "That man!" were the two words burning to come out of her for what he had dared to do! "He has no right to touch my clothes!" she seethed inside. Her inner anger was unwittingly transferred to the comb and she feared she hurt her widow friend when she squeaked. She forced herself to settle down realizing Bibb had no opportunity to do the dirty deed, yet a floating undefined hostility towards her escort remained. She almost felt guilty for thinking that way.

Several messages were delivered to the medicine man over the next hour. One message contained the word "Bibb" in it. Anna was still sick over the future that she might be facing. Her emotions had run the full gambit from the moment they had left Deadwood together.

The medicine man instructed the widow to take Anna to eat, or maybe just to take her out of his way. As they stood to leave, Bibb was brought into the tent by the chief. He did not look that hurt to Anna. She had seen him in much worse condition. One thing was for sure: neither her opinion, nor the opinion of any of the women in this camp seemed to matter much.

As she was pulled out of the tent Anna, against her inward desires, muttered an unspoken complaint to God. "You have given me the responsibility to take care of that man and you aren't letting me do it! Why are you preventing me when Bibb needs me the most?" Three steps later Anna hated the idea that she had repeated an admission there was a God, even if that God was dead or unresponsive; or worse, just dead to her. She complained to herself that this was the opportunity for her to be good and kind, and some old mystic was kicking her out of the healing chambers.

==0==

Anna ate with the other women after the men had been served their meal. There was much chatter surrounding Anna, yet she was still very much alone in her thoughts, in a sea of words and not a single drop of understanding. Her present situation reminded her of a saying her seafaring grandfather had passed down to the family.

"Water water everywhere and not a drop to drink"[2] was the song of thirsty sailors miles from port. She also remembered how he was involved in shipments of enormous wealth, but once he left the office he didn't have enough money in his pocket to buy his children shoes. Anna was verbally parched; nobody to talk to, and nowhere to spend her wealth. She was reduced to mute flesh and bones.

Anna pulled herself out of her self-induced pity party. The good news was that her worst fear that Bibb had died was abated. Why should she be surprised? The man cheats death as often as her butler takes out the trash. Second, her fear of enslavement also evaporated with the first dread.

Her third fear of powerlessness was not relieved. She saw true fear in the eyes of her widow tent-mate when she entered the medicine man's tent. Although she wanted to be with her man she now knew better. If there was anything to be learned from that recent episode it was to never invite herself into the elder's teepee. She feared she would now have to repeat what she so detested: wait.

==0==

Anna once told herself that no news is good news. That certainly wasn't a comfort to her now. Nevertheless, life in the camp didn't stop, and soon she was taken by the hand down to the creek with the rest of the women.

While in the midst of communal laundry, one of the little boys hanging on to his mother's arm was suffering greatly and saying so. Somehow he had gotten into some prickly vines with some of it now tangled in his hair. The child's situation was actually made much worse by the boy's own efforts to remedy the condition. As the mother tried to untangle the knots the child became more out of control in his misery.

While the attention was on the boy, Anna got up and went back to where she stayed the previous night. In the bottom of her trunk was an heirloom that she especially cherished. It was her mother's sewing scissors. She took them from her trunk and returned to where the women were washing clothes. She boldly approached the mother with the inconsolable child.

Anna showed the mother the scissors but nobody in that circle knew what they were. She mimicked using the scissors to cut her own hair, and then pointed to the child. The mother, at her wits end, consented to let Anna help. Before she approached the mother, Anna reached back and pulled some of her own hair in front of her face and cut six inches off of one lock. All the chatter immediately stopped, even that of the child's protest. Anna gave her hair to the woman next to mother with the child,

---

[2]   This common saying of sailors was coined by the English poet Samuel Coleridge in the late 18th century in his poem *The Rime of the Ancient Mariner.*

and by pantomime Anna instructed the mother that she should hold the child tightly. All eyes were on them. Once gaining the child's cooperation Anna proceeded on.

Within moments Anna had cut out the offending vines from the boy's hair and the crying stopped. Although the Indian women watched in silent curiosity, Anna thought no more of this incident any more than an ordinary five cent haircut witnessed fifty times a day in Deadwood. She motioned to the mother to continue to hold the child while she used a comb to make the boy's hair look like it grew out that way (instead of somebody taking a hatchet to him).

She wasn't quite finished trimming the boy's hair when one of the other women with especially long hair tapped Anna on the shoulder. She indicated that she would like about ten pounds of hair cut from her head. Anna, and wisely in hindsight, gave the scissors to another woman within the circle. Handing the scissors to the squaw, instructed her with gestures to cut off another lock of Anna's own hair as practice. It would not be missed. After that had been accomplished she mimed to the woman to cut the hair from the long haired-squaw. If that woman's husband got mad about his wife's haircut, Anna would not get blamed. The scissors were handed around to many of the women, and Anna sadly lost track of them. She stopped fretting when she thought that her precious heirloom would probably be soon hanging in the medicine man's teepee next to her dress.

As that excitement was still raging over the haircuts, Bibb came searching for Anna. Along with him was the elder matron of the tribe. When she approached the happy party, all activity stopped immediately. The matron was not happy. She walked up to Anna and indicated forcefully that she should kneel. Anna complied as the other women silently gathered around. The matron lifted in her hand the lock of Anna's hair for all the women to see and then quickly secured it in a fancy pouch. A terrifying silence continued. Anna was wide eyed and frightened. There was no doubt it was her hair that the matron had, but how she possessed it and for what reason the matron displayed the worthless lock confused her. The silence was ominous.

The sight tore Bibb at his heart. He knew what was coming and wished he could interfere. It was too late. Anything he did now would make matters worse. Anna was in the fix and there was no out of the fix except by going through the fix, if she lived. Anna had no idea of the size of her offense against the matron and the tribe. Bibb felt helpless and tried to extract himself but could not. It was no mistake he was asked (medicine men don't ask; they require politely) to witness the drama for Anna's benefit (and an implied necessity that he needed to become more manly). Bibb was not fooled. The matron had been told to keep an eye on Bibb too.

After speaking a sentence to all the women, the matron ordered Anna to stand again and began to talk sternly to Anna, nose to nose, as if she could understand. The speech was short but with so much passion that Anna was visibly trembling. At the end of the harangue the elder woman violently grabbed Anna's left wrist and slapped the top of Anna's hand with all the strength she could muster. Before Anna could react, the matron grabbed the other wrist and slapped the top of that hand too. It was a dreadful object lesson for the Indian women watching. (Likewise, if Anna by chance had insulted the tribe with her words, a hot rock would have been put in her mouth to blister her tongue).

Justice was swift in this tribe. Anna had been highly shamed in the traditions of her hosts. This public insult administered specifically to both her hands was the medicine man's ruling. The matron was to bring immediate punishment on to Anna for not taking care of her man, to be followed by a mandatory apology to each woman for her bad behavior. Little did Anna know that the hair incident was a separate issue altogether.

Anna, smarting physically, was frozen in fear with what might come next. The elder started waving her hand and was commanding her to do something. One of the widow women came to Anna's rescue to show her what she must do and say. Anna was to bow and say something to each of the women present in their tongue. Anna complied without understanding. What Anna did understand was that by her obedience the anger of the elder was abated.

The next act of the unexpected drama was that matron manhandled Anna to stand in her presence once again. Once Anna complied, for there was no option, the tone of the woman mellowed. She spoke words that suggested pity instead of anger. This sentencing was twice the length of the first, and eventually a tear came to the elder's eye. In sympathy, so did a tear arise in Anna's. None of this went unnoticed by the women there. Anna was surprised when the elderly woman embraced her. Anna could not let her arms flop around, so she embraced in return.

Then the matron's language turned rough again and started demanding Anna do something. Once again the widow came to her rescue. The widow got on her knees and touched her nose to the ground, then motioned for Anna to do the same. Once a very confused Anna complied, the widow backed away into the crowd of other women.

The elder made several pronouncements that must have called on ancestors or something from beyond. It was all very serious and Anna dared not look up or react badly. Once the matron was done speaking, she bent down and grabbed Anna's hair in one hand and chin in the other. In control of Anna's neck, and with Anna now into forced kneeling the elder blew heavily on Anna, once on each ear. Then she breathed once on each eye, then on Anna's nose. Releasing her hair, the matron took Anna's wrists and kissed the palms of Anna's hands. The elder woman then spoke again, and then bent over as if she was going to kiss Anna on the lips. Instead, the senior blew air towards Anna's mouth. Once done, with military like precision, the matron raised her hands and each of the women responded by saying a phrase in unison.

Anna did not know whether to get up off her knees or not. She was not to. The old woman took her hands and laid them on top of Anna's head, said what Anna supposed to be quite important, and then laid her hands heavily on the top of Anna's shoulders. Once finished, she motioned for Anna to stand up, turn around and bow again.

When Anna returned to look at the matron to see what was coming next, the matron had a folded dress in her hand. She indicated that it was a gift from the tribe to her. It was a sign, an exchanged gift, linked to the event that had just happened. The matron backed away from Anna and as quickly as the matron had appeared, she departed.

The whole group of women stood in awe at what they had just witnessed. There was no talking, but each of the women in an unorganized way approached Anna and wanted to see her hurt hands. They expected to see blood because of a sharp rock the matron would have in her hand when Anna was slapped. They were not disappointed. Bibb noticed that not one woman dared touch the dress.

Anna sought out Bibb's attention, and beckoned to Bibb with her eyes to come to her. As the women's curiosity was satisfied, Bibb was able to draw close. When they were closer Anna whispered, "What did she say, Bibb?" Anna dared not offend anybody.

"I won't tell you-zz, Anna (srpt). Don't ask-zz again. But for-zz your offense (srpt), you-zz have been lightly punished, forgiven-zz, and given power (srpt) from beyond to-zz never offend again."

"What did I do wrong?"

"It was-zz a capital offense to-zz d'these people (srpt), Anna. Don't ask-zz again. I-zz got-zz to go. I'm-zz being summoned-zz. D'the women (srpt) were told-zz to forgive you-zz too (srpt). You-zz can't help-zz being young and ugly." Bibb immediately regretted saying that unthinking post script.

==0==

Bibb spent the next hour with the medicine man and the chief. The medicine man gave Bibb some bitter medicine to swallow that was supposed to help his ribs. It did not cure the ribs, or take away the pain, but it sure made him not care much about it.

Bibb purposely steered the conversations to his travels. He wanted to generate an interest in the chief concerning unknown grazing lands, remaining herds of buffalo, and good water from lakes and streams. He offered, generally and not specifically, to show his scouts where some of these places were. This conversation lasted a good twenty minutes, verbal for the medicine man and the chief while Bibb used his hands (except for the words he did not know sign). Eventually the elders were both satisfied and guided the discussion towards their agenda.

The medicine man addressed the topic of the dress hanging overhead in his teepee. He said his widows were frightened by it. It contained a strange smell that persisted. The widows had asked the medicine man to cleanse it from the spirit that caused the strong odor. He had hung it up where all the smoke from his medicine making and warming fire would overwhelm the odor permeating the dress. If that or washing it several times didn't work, the dress would be burned outside the camp.

Bibb told the medicine man that he understood his concerns. In the white man's villages women put those smells on their body and clothes in hopes to enchant a man into marriage. It seldom works, but white women keep trying.

"And you? Where were you enchanted?" asked the chief. "Were you enchanted in the highest of the Black Hills? You had no woman on your journey south."

"Not by enchantment, honored Chief," Bibb replied. "We were both drawn in, but not by the cruel hand of enchantment. Honored sir, we freely committed ourselves to each other at the altar of the unseen guiding God."

"Where?" demanded the chief, as if this was suddenly very important.

"We were bound in the Black Hills in the white man's camp of Deadwood."

The medicine man continued the interrogation. "Then why does she still make herself stink if not for enchantment? Even more confusing, why would she make herself stink after being bound?"

"A man wiser than me will have to answer that question for you, Honored Elder. I have no answer that will pass a test of reason. I do have a question for you, sir."

"What is it, Bibb?"

"I am being followed by an Indian on a white man's horse. Are you aware of that?"

The chief answered, "Yes. Our scouts watch it. It dare not enter the village."

"Why?"

"It has no name. It betrayed the son of an elder of our nation to the white man for payment. A council of chiefs has removed its name from our race. It has no heritage. It has no home. It has no nation or tribe. It has no right to be in our presence. It has the right to die and become carrion. We will not even give it the dignity to die with one of our arrows. As its punishment it will roam in loneliness without a friend and without a spirit. It betrays blood." The chief then demanded a response from Bibb to his next statement. "You know of the living death of that punishment, yes?"

"Yes, I do. I know firsthand the burden and pain of that cruel judgment."

"What did you do about it?" asked the medicine man.

"Nothing."

"Nothing? I know that to be false." This challenge was purposely made to test for a lie.

"But I did nothing, sir."

Both the chief and the medicine man held there tongue. They wanted Bibb to recant or back away from his statement prompted by their intimidation of disbelief.

"I did nothing, sir. But I am not the same as I was."

"By nothing?"

"Honored and Wise Sir, I did nothing. The Great Spirit did everything."

"That is a bold statement, Bibb," interjected the chief. The chief was wondering about the strength of his will to counteract the effect of the mixture of bitter herbs.

"Kind Chief, I am grateful for your hospitality. But I tell you not what I think, but what I have experienced. I do not know the ways of the Spirit, but it knows my ways. But please do not believe my words, for I am still Bibb. But believe the Spirit that uses me and is known by the signs it provides that follow me."

"Why does death avoid you?" said the chief loudly in an accusatory and demanding tone. This was the heart of the matter.

Surprised at the chief's gesturing, but not alarmed, Bibb was realizing his thinking was strangely clouded, yet he felt fully awake. "Again, sir, I cannot speak with certainty. But I have learned that a good spirit has delighted by marking me. I have been marred physically, but strengthened in life. I have been delivered many times from the white man, from the red man, and from the forces of nature. You know of the betrayal of the unnamed tracker. You may know from your councils from other red brothers that they had their hand stayed when they wanted to strike me. Sir, I do not know the answer to your question. But there are two things that bother me. If I am not to die until an appointed hour by the yen of the spirit, there must be a powerful reason. This purpose I do not know. There is one thing I do know for certain. I am no longer my own man. My strength belongs not to me, but to those where I am sent. A Great Spirit took my will, and gave me continued life in exchange for it. I do not understand that mystery, but it stares me in the face every day. I no longer belong to myself."

"Who do you belong to?"

"I belong to your braves who went out with me shooting this morning. I belong to the woman I brought with me into your camp. I belong to the highest white leader of the east whom the white men call governor. I am here to serve my hosts and their leaders. I belong to a mere child in Miles City. I now belong to your widows. I also belong to a white widow in Fort Rice. Please do not think me great in character or noble in cause. I am still known as a killer of men and a notorious outlaw. My list of faults overwhelms me, and I am ashamed. My name is of dishonor to all the law men of the white settlements, yet their hand is kept from touching me. This is a mystery that I do not understand. I am not my own man. Please do not laugh when I tell you this. My experience now tells me to suspect that a certain Great Spirit delights to use me, the lowest of men, for his purposes if only to confound the wise and reprove the powerful. He has taken the most unlikely man in the west and has crushed him. And then that same Spirit raises that broken man up again to go where the man does not want to go and do the things the man does not want to do."

"What do you want to do, half a man?"

"I wish I could once again plow fields behind a mule. I want to plant wheat and bring in a harvest. I want to live in community with those of my heritage. I want to work hard, eat well, and laugh heartily. But sir, my body has been mutilated. Hard work is now too hard. My fate is set. I ride where my authorities tell me to ride to deliver messages from one authority to other authorities. I go where others send me. My superior sends me places where he cannot send others." Bibb sighed, and then continued. "Sir, I say too much. I need to do more. How can I help you and your people?"

"I still have many braves that wish to shoot well. Are you well enough to teach them?"

"Honorable sir, I was hoping you would ask. Please have them gather. I will meet them at the center of camp. With your permission, please allow me to speak to my woman first."

"You may go," said the chief.

"You may not ride," sternly added the medicine man. "The bitter herb that loosens your tongue and caused truth to spill will also spill you from your horse. You must stay close. You show our braves how to shoot on the other side of the river."

Bibb thought that he was strangely talkative. His hands were tired from all the signing. If the truth was easily spilled from his lips (and hands), he had better be extra careful with Anna. Her spirit was severely wounded by the matron after lunch.

==0==

As evening approached, Tommy took his and Anna's horse down to the river to drink. Anna found Bibb as he was walking on the way back to the corral.

"Tommy, I cannot wait to tell you all that has happened!" Anna's attitude was much more elevated than he had expected.

"We-zz will have lots of time-zz for d'that later (srpt), but-zz tell me d'the best."

"We absolutely had the grandest time washing clothes, Tommy! A dozen of us were down in the river and they were showing me how they scrub their clothes. After a while, somehow the splashing started. Oh Bibb, you would have laughed until it hurt. I haven't laughed like that in, in… years! Bibb, it felt so good. And your idea of the combs was genius! This is so much fun, and the kids are so cute! Bibb," and then she toned down her excitement, "Do we have to leave tomorrow?"

"D'that is-zz not our choice (srpt). D'the chief decides who comes-zz and goes (srpt), and when."

The answer reminded her how much authority the chief carries. She sobered more and said, "How hurt are you Bibb? Tell me plain."

"Anna, I hurt-zz bad, but not-zz too bad (srpt). I cannot get-zz on my horse. D'that (srpt) is-zz plum embarrassing. My ear still hurt-zz (srpt) from where you bit-zz me last Sunday."

"It does-zzzzz not-zzzz, Bibb."

"You-zz are right, d'that pain is-zz almost gone (srpt). But it's-zz more fun to d'think about my ear d'than my gut (srpt). I d'think you-zz marked me for life!"

"And life is what I will give you, Bibb." Anna turned to go, but then looked again to her man. "I will keep you alive, Terry Tommy Toivo, unless you touch me wrong. You and I are bound by a covenant, and don't you start assuming additional privileges as if we are married. You have no rights over me, and don't you forget it." Anna had smiled and put sugar on her words the whole time she spoke. There were many onlookers that only understood the tone of the conversation. Bibb's reaction confirmed that he didn't know what kind of response she was baiting him for, and Anna certainly was not going to tell him about Mrs. Franklin's love note.

Bibb returned to the center of camp to meet with the braves. He was elated that Anna's spirit was rejuvenated. Something had happened to her. The watery baptism by laundry administered in the river was only a symptom, not the cause.

==0==

The dinner that night was heavy in both buffalo and venison. Bibb worried about Anna. She had a continuous series of humiliating events since they rode into camp the previous evening. There are only so many smiles a person can wear in situations of constant kneeling below her accustomed station in life. Her bulging bank accounts and sycophant employees couldn't do anything to save her from the reality of these moments. Tonight wasn't going to be easier. She will be expected to cater to her man, care for his wounds, and take off his boots – all things that were once below her dignity.

"Honored Chief," Bibb asked after most of the knives were laid down, "my woman and I have one more gift for you. It is a strange gift and I do not know if you will want it. To the white man it has value. May we present it to you for your consideration?"

Permission was granted for Bibb to leave the gathering of men to bring Anna into their presence. She was glad to see him. Regardless, Bibb warned her of the non-optional protocols of Indian gatherings and the authorities involved. She told Bibb that she was anxious to present the gift. The other gifts had such impact.

Bibb and Anna came into the gathering place. Upon the sign from the chief they proceeded to a designated spot directly before him. Bibb signed again his desire to present another gift for the hospitality that they had received from his hand. He was again told to proceed.

"Sir, my woman will present you with a polished glass. It is a tool to allow man to improve their vision. In the daylight, it can focus the heat from the sun to start a fire."

"Let me see it," responded the chief. The command and nod from Bibb prompted Anna to present with two hands to the chief the magnifying glass wrapped in one of her finest kerchiefs.

It was a strange gift and the chief was not sure he wanted to hold it. "Medicine man, tell me your opinion."

The healer was given the glass and he played with it for a while. Not understanding it and how it worked he became troubled. "It contains a spirit!"

This was not a good development. The look on the chief's face questioned Bibb's intentions of bringing that gift into the camp. Bibb asked and retrieved the glass from the willing medicine man.

"Sir, this glass is a polished stone. It has no spirit in it. The glass is useful because it shows the truth about what it is placed over. The spirit resides in what is looked at, not in the glass. The glass reveals truth, but it does not contain truth. The glass is good and only good. I am sure of my words. Have your medicine man examine the ugliness of my face, and then the beauty of my woman's eyes with the stone. Look at my wounds and then look at her skin and teeth. Let him choose what to look at to see the contrast."

This was an acceptable test for the medicine man. If there was a spirit, Bibb would not subject himself for its use on any location of the medicine man's choosing, and especially his woman.

The contrasts were stark, and the medicine man took full advantage of the moment. After five minutes of examination, he asked the chief to use the glass to inspect his eyes. If there was a spirit, he would be able to detect it.

After that test, the medicine man became convinced that the stone was a valuable tool and not a medium. The medicine man asked the chief if he might possess the gift, and the request was granted.

As instructed, as soon as the gift was accepted Anna wasted no time speaking a phrase Bibb had taught her prior to their entrance. She was granted her spoken request to return to the other women.

As Anna walked back to her half eaten dinner she had to laugh at her own tired ways of thinking. At first it was her vanity that told her that Bibb missed her company tonight and wanted her to join him. Then she thought the worst of him to use her as a prop in contrasting extreme ugliness against the beauty of her frame just to prove a point to the medicine man. No. She must not automatically think it was all about her, and then to think it was all about him. It was entirely possible that Bibb wanted her to receive the credit for the gift, just as she did with the combs. The man was just trying to keep his promise to be kind. Granted, the situation got a bit out of control, but Bibb could not have anticipated that. For gain or ill, she was an inextricable part of the drama.

The longer she thought about Bibb asking for her, the more she thought the actual piece of glass had little to do with his motivation. What Bibb purposely did was to impress upon the tribal leadership that she and her man were inseparable. It quickly followed that Bibb had a higher purpose for her summons. That half-a-brain man, who thinks too much about everything for her liking, wanted to make sure that she was with him when he left the village. Their leaving together was not yet certain.

Back at the men's meal the chief offered a gift in return to Bibb. He asked Bibb what favor would please him. Bibb knew that he must be careful in his asking. If he asked too much, the chief would be dishonored, especially if it was outside of his ability to provide.

"Sir, I need your help. I am bound by a sacred promise to take my woman to the white man's cities of the sunrise. I am grievously injured and I am not able to protect her as I should. I humbly ask that you provide two scouts to ride close to us and provide us protection as we journey to Miles City. During the journey your scouts can discover winter quarters and new buffalo herds. They can discover good water and better knowledge of where not to bring your people. I am ashamed to ask, but I cannot adequately defend myself and my woman in my weakened condition."

"That is not a gift, Bibb. You know our ways and you knew that soon I would be sending out scouts to find winter quarters. What is your actual desire?"

"Sir, you are wise, but I fear my deepest request may be too high of a favor for a white man and white woman to ask."

"What is this high favor? And your woman too?" said the chief in an elevated voice. All the conversations stopped and the eating area went deathly silent.

"Sir, I am reluctant to ask. My greatest desire is that your medicine man bless us."

"You are given your first request. Tomorrow you and four of my scouts will depart for Miles City. In the morning you shall have my answer to your second request. Do you know what you are asking?"

"Because I know the value of the blessing, I risked hearing your refusal. I have no strength in myself. If the request is too high, your word no will satisfy me. I am already overwhelmed with your generosity to double our guard. I ask for the blessing in hope that someday I, just as you have doubled my protection, that I may double my blessings back to you and your people."

"Bibb, you have asked for nothing and you have asked for everything. Go in peace. Tomorrow you shall leave this camp."

==0==

Bibb was already in bed when the widows and Anna finally returned to the teepee. Bibb discerned from her excitement Anna was having the time of her life. It was a day of learning, laughing, working, and communicating side by side by pure wit. There was no agendas, no hidden meanings to speech. It was a most delightful day.

That evening's time around the fire with the other women was just as fun. The kids, several sporting recent haircuts, just couldn't get over the strangeness of Anna's hair and the color of her eyes. When the quartette of gigglers entered Bibb's teepee there was no whining or complaining to be had, except the moans coming from the only man in the room.

"Wake up, Bibb!" said Anna. I have been talking all day with these women and now I want to know what they really said. I want them to know what I said too. Bibb, you can sleep later! Get up!"

At her insistence, Bibb rolled out of his cocoon of comfort and came to join them at the fire. One other Indian lady was with them too. The subsequent conversation went too fast for Bibb, and he asked them to slow down and speak one at a time. The words exchanged were endearing. They were not words of daily chores and humdrum existence, but words of life and feelings.

Bibb had to stop the women several time to make sure he got the translation correct because of all the new words coming at him. The younger widow could not contain herself and burst with joy telling the story of the comb in the medicine man's teepee and being called wise by the tribal elder.

The thing that caught Bibb's eye, and he tried not to stare, was the dress that Anna now was wearing. It wasn't something any Indian women would normally wear; no, it was the gift Anna had received from the matron. The tribe must have come by it from a barter situation some time back – way back. It was barely, an overstatement, held together by frayed threads, and Anna taxed it greatly in the bust and hips. Bibb thought it amazing that Anna accepted the gift and even more extraordinary, she put it on. Never in her whole life had she had anything in her wardrobe like this.

Anna was entirely comfortable with her situation. The essentials of city life did not seem so essential anymore. She wouldn't like to live this way, but for the moment this time was grand. Anna dismissed Bibb to return to bed when all the yawns came out all at one time. It was already well past midnight and Bibb had mentioned that they were leaving in the morning... several times.

Anna extracted another promise out of Bibb before he was banished to the cocoon. He was to turn his back and close his eyes and not to move until morning. She got no argument out of him, but he did ask that she not crush his ribs like she did the prior night.

Bibb's whistle was a clear indication he was asleep. Anna, who had lost her sense of shyness with the women, carefully slipped out of her green dress and into her

Indian pajamas. With the freedom of movement from looser clothing she started to repack her trunk. The widows offered to help, but there really wasn't anything to do. During the day Anna had divested herself of everything that she couldn't buy new in Bismarck. It was the least she could do for a community of new friends that had so little. While Bibb slept, the women took Anna's trunk out to the wagon, went down to the river, and then three of them returned to a dying campfire in the widow's teepee.

To the sound of coyotes singing to a teepee lit by the glowing light of campfire embers, Anna took up her safe position behind Bibb in their cocoon. She whispered in his ear a few words, not really caring if he was awake enough to hear them. It did not matter. She had to say them more than he had to hear them.

Monday, October 10, 1887

I got very little sleep last night. The widows had us up before dawn and insisted we get ready. I thought it was to get an early start and I thought wrong. Bibb and I were painted by the medicine man at a dawn ceremony and afterwards the chief sent <u>us</u> on our way. The important word is <u>us</u>. There were more than words in his words. My soul is filled to bursting.

The tears I didn't shed for the man resting under my tombstone were poured out when I said goodbye to the widows. Never have I been so touched in heart. These women had nothing. I never want to return to this camp. Second memories would only pollute the blessed ones I have now grafted deep into my soul. How do I describe it? I feel light! I feel clean! I feel full!

Xue cleaned my feet several days ago. What is happening to me? I want to understand but I still seem dead to grasp if there is any "there" in all these recent events. I feel like I am trying to learn to dance to a different tune; clumsy, awkward, and humbled. Yes, humbled, and I will keep this humiliation to myself. If I confide in Bibb my thoughts he may try to take advantage of me. Why do I think like this? Broken Bibb can't even take advantage of himself, much less me. My memory of what Xue offered kneeling by my feet strangely comforts me, but I am not sure why.

All I can say is wow, and even that word is beggarly inadequate. I am crying now. I was a teenager the last time I shed good tears. Not tears of regret, pain, fear, or being denied my way. No… I don't know how to describe this. I can't control them. I can't generate them. She hugged me like she meant it; both of them. I certainly did not see this coming. We gently squeezed those wordless tears right out of each other. It has been years. Tears speak a universal language.

The top of my hands hurt terribly. I showed Bibb the ugly deep purple wounds. All he said was, "Yup," and kept driving. So much for receiving male sympathy; it doesn't exist.

==0==

BIBB HAD VERY little to do to get ready to travel, and quickly set out to do it. The urgency was not due to time, but because of the army of squaws that marched into their teepee well before the sun rose. They wanted to show their appreciation to Anna and respects to Bibb. Bibb was reaching his limit of the overwhelming female-ality of the moment. He dearly wanted to escape to make sure their horses were well hitched, fed, and shod, but Anna kept him close and part of the circle of chatter.

One of the mercies from his injury was that one of his ears could no longer hear higher pitched voices. He listened to all their lovely words, kind phrases, and sentiments gloriously filled with emotion. Initially all was tolerable and within his ability to translate. Five minutes later the excitement picked up as much as the pace. Bibb just could no longer handle the overwhelming amount of speech coming all at

242

once. That is when he decided to leave the women to their own intimacies. Anna no longer needed his help, nor was he able (willing) to provide it.

There was another reason Bibb retreated from the female festival, and he knew the varmint's bite was only seconds away for thinking it. What bothered Bibb was a soon painful payment for repeatedly entertaining the thought that it wasn't right that such an awful woman was given such honor and friendship. He reasoned that if they only knew what she was really like they would throw her to the mercy of the matron for proper punishment. No, Anna received just the opposite and he hated it. That woman, the Anna he knew, was receiving unmerited favor and lavished with love beyond understanding. It just was not fair. Bibb still harbored much hate for that wild widow and he felt confused and dirty about his feelings. His sentiments were emotionally sound but logically baseless. He certainly had received his bountiful share of unmerited honor too. He decided to do what he had to do: escape the scene of the crime. He gracefully excused himself to check on the horses.

It was a reverent dawn ceremony. The braves were decked with insignias and rankings, and the women ringed around the ceremony site made sure the children witnessed in silence. The only ones that felt underdressed were Bibb and Anna. Bibb advised Anna that once she was blessed that it would be wise not to speak until they were on their own and alone safely crossing the prairie. That seemed unfair, but once it happened she understood. Anything she muttered would have distracted from the solemn occasion.

==0==

As promised, the four scouts left with Bibb and Anna immediately after the blessing was pronounced on them by the medicine man. Ten minutes out of camp the scouts came to Bibb's wagon and told him of their chief's instructions for their journey together. They would travel as box corners a quarter mile separated from each other while Bibb and Anna would remain in the center of their moving perimeter. The scouts would stop when the wagon stopped. The lead scout told Bibb that at night one of them would come into camp to discuss the next day's travel strategy and get their evening and morning meals. Their wagon carried everyone's provisions for the trip. The eldest scout told Bibb that the last thing the chief commanded was for all of them to be wise in the ways of the plains and flexible in meeting the surprises of the Great Spirit.

From the lead scout's use of pronouns, Bibb, as if he had been adopted, was expected to heed the authority of the chief also. Not so for Anna. She was to remain only under Bibb's authority. Bibb opted not to translate to Anna this nuance of the scout's instructions. This was not in fear of her reaction but because of the revolting implications on him personally. Besides, it was the covenant that was the authority for

243

Anna's cooperation. The chief's word did not overwrite the power of their altar call, but confirmed it. Although distasteful, more than anything else those complementing thoughts gave Bibb reason to suspect the medicine man's blessing was in concert with God's will. Bibb knew that to be alive on this side of the teepees was a sure mark of providence. He thanked God for the scouts, the provisions, and the thought of going home. He grudgingly got around to thanking God that Anna was sitting next to him. Like it or not, she was his responsibility. Bibb wondered if it was just as distasteful to Anna as it was for him to be stuck in their awful *us-ness*.

Bibb's thoughts returned back the morning ceremony. It was hard to avoid the gravity of the words spoken. The origin of the utterances, whether of God, man, or evil, would be proven in time by the force of providence and not the hand of man. What the medicine man said should be only pondered in hindsight. Looking towards those words of destiny was a prescription for disaster and an unwise meddling in shaping the prerogatives of providence. That was God's work; not his.

==0==

Bibb was enjoying the quiet. After a short stop and the scouts went again to their points Anna asked Bibb, "Why do you hate me so?" She got no response. Later she tried again, "You really do hate me, don't you? I can tell about these things. I see it in your expression and in your eyes."

True. It was not only by intuition that Anna came to that conclusion. Bibb's disposition was soured as the reality of the morning's events and potential hazards in their immediate future crushed his thinking. Bibb had a head full of dislikes, but two were the most irksome. First, he was tired, sore, and miserable; second, the depressing thought he was responsible for the health and safety of the woman sitting next to him. That horrible thought came from reminding himself he was actually married to her. He wanted to think they were temporally married or almost married, but none of that thinking passed the logic test better than being temporally or almost pregnant. These thoughts composed of pure acid churned his innards worse than his busted ribs. He was too wise to be fooled by the kind sentiments the Lakota women had lavished Anna with before dawn; he knew the real Anna from Deadwood. He also knew he shouldn't be bitter towards her; yet it was eating him up.

Bibb had to consider that his wisdom was full of worms. Was he personally envious of the praise Anna had received? Did he secretly want those women to say something nice about him? Certainly the wake up crew had their chance to admire him but did not. By their silence Bibb had to deduce that there was nothing nice about him to say. Bibb was Bibb, and he was lucky to get out of there alive. It still ate him up, and Anna's dress wasn't helping the situation. Not at all.

Anna repeated her question. Bibb made a rude (and crude) gesture that indicated he didn't want any more noise out of her. Anna wondered why she got that reaction, and that was when a sudden fascinating intuitive leap of understanding came over her. It very much surprised her.

Her thoughts reverted back to the mirror incident at the Red Buffalo. Although she herself had experienced so many new things this month, all of a sudden she came to the eye-opening epiphany that these incidents were not just about a blind selfish girl named Anna. Her man, most likely for the first time in his life, had experienced many strange new things too. There was the solemn blessing, the washing, the drugged interrogation, and the high humiliation of not being able to get on his own horse. On the top of her list of his ordeals was the mystically emotional and physical bond of synchronized sleeping. Her heart told her she was right. His rude reaction was not out of hate. It was out of many unspoken fears. He suffered the fear of the unknown, the fear of touch, and the fear of kindled passions. The fear of emotional intimacy came immediately to her mind. She concluded he also feared the future. What happened to them since Deadwood was an irreversible blurring of the lines between a covenant and a marriage. She could tell from watching him in Deadwood that Bibb could tolerate shallow relationships, but his fear of fears was opening his soul to a deep relationship, and forbid the thought, intimacy. He was not going to risk suffering a betrayal again; that was his definition of death. Tommy had been burned indelibly by being both betrayer and betrayed. He hated the source of his deepest hurts and most painful memories. He knew how to prevent it too. The door to his inner being had been closed and nailed shut tighter than a horseshoe to a hoof.

She took her deductions to heart. Hate was a word that resides in the soul, and she had not been invited into that secret garden of his yet. She also knew she was the thorn bush growing in the center of his garden. His no trespassing gesture confirmed that. As she pondered her discoveries she laughed to herself under her breath. Her no trespassing sign was not only up but highlighted with a credible threat of dismemberment if she was ever touched wrong. She now knew why they were kindred spirits. Betrayal had happened to her too, but the only difference was that she deserved it.

Anna was at peace. The current mystery was now solved and she made a personal promise to tolerate his current and future coldness. She also wondered if she could make it until noon before she broke that promise. Her record of keeping personal promises was abysmal, but this was oddly different. The message at the mirror now made sense to her. She felt a new power enter into her life as the desire to be good and only good came over her like a flood. Then she hated what had just echoed through her mind. "Good and only good" was part of the silent rhyme she suffered going into her forced hush as they approached the Lakota camp. Yet the phrase "good and only good" was emboldening her with confidence to break the forced silence of her soul as they left the camp. She lied to herself when she dispatched that coincidence to a quirk of bad luck, and she knew it.

==0==

"May I talk now?" asked Anna.

"D'there would be nothing I could d'think of (srpt) d'that I would enjoy-zz more. I can't promise you-zz answers (srpt), but I will promise I-zz will listen."

Anna delighted in the response and his change of tone. "What did the medicine man say this morning?"

"You don't want-zz to know, Anna (srpt). He gave more-zz d'than a blessing."

"That was a short lived promise! Why wouldn't I want to know? Was it bad?"

"Would you-zz be upset if I-zz said he married us (srpt)?"

Her intuition was confirmed by his response. It was the cocoon experience in the teepee that was bothering him. She proceeded with her planned response, "Isn't it against the rules to be married twice in one week? Anyway Bibb, it wouldn't count." She paused to shift her topics. "I don't like it, but I'm getting used to your silly answers before you tell me what you really feel. And you can banish that thought about marriage, Big Billy Bibb Boy. You are not worthy to even have a dream that good, much less have your wild secret fantasy come true."

Bibb looked at Anna and then took some time to decide how to respond. "I reckon you-zz never promised (srpt) d'that you would answer my-zz questions either. D'that's fair (srpt)." Bibb paused a second time to get his mouth right. "All I have to say is (srpt) if marriage is like how you treated me d'there (srpt), it wouldn't be d'that distasteful."

"Put the thought out of your head, little boy. You have seen the last of those Indian pajamas."

"Did you wear pajamas (srpt)? Wow. My imagination (srpt) did play a joke on me."

"Bibb, are you lying again? Did you open your eyes when I told you to keep them shut?"

"Anna, can I tell-zz you d'the truth without you being offended?"

"Spit it out, Bibb. Offensive or not, say it."

"Never mind-zz d'then. Suffice it to say I behaved (srpt)." Bibb's tone turned serious. "Anna, I could not risk (srpt) looking."

"What do you mean by that, Tommy?"

"You know-zz. You were married once (srpt). Can we-zz talk about something else?"

"You mean like my first question about what the medicine man said? You were the first one to avoid answering questions directly. I hope you learned your lesson. Now answer my question."

"If I tell-zz you a lie, would you-zz be happy? D'the truth ain't so pleasant."

"Bibb, I demand a straight answer. What did he say?"

"You were destined to have seven-zz daughters…"

She interrupted immediately. "He didn't say that! Stop the silly talk."

"… and eight sons-zz. Anna, you-zz are going to be-zz one tired woman (srpt). You-zz might have fifty grandchildren! Now I know-zz (srpt) what you-zz will spend all your money on!"

"You're lying, Bibb! I can tell! You can't fool me! Lying is your native language."

"I told you I was-zz going to (srpt). D'there is no reason for you-zz to get all excited."

Anna knew how to get the truth out of Bibb. "I believe you told the truth about the marriage part. A woman can sense it when a man promises his heart to an irresistible and beautiful woman like me! Isn't it sweet! You are quite the romantic, Bibb, and now we are on our honeymoon! We can snuggle up tighter than bed bugs at night and start working on that Indian's prophecy! This is so grand! Should we start now?"

"D'that was-zz a-zz lie-zz, Anna-zz (srpt)! Don't tease-zz me-zz (srpt) like-zz d'that (srpt). I-zz am-zz a-zz (srpt) married man-zz (srpt). I-zz got-zz (srpt) to go-zz home (srpt) to-zz my-zz Humbird (srpt)." Bibb was very frustrated and stuttered terribly at such a thought. He didn't like his own fabrication turned on him.

"Well then don't say stupid stuff when you get all boxed in a corner. If you speak the truth the first time you don't have to backtrack on all your fibs-zzzz, Bibb-zzzzzzz."

==0==

Bibb was grateful for the early start that morning. While they were in the village their fates could have soured in seconds. Bibb also knew that his problems were not over; they were only different now. He was still frustrated from the last discussion he had with Anna. She could tell that she had gotten to him, and not exactly in a kind way. Bibb also noticed that she was very tired. He asked her if she would like to lie down in the back and let the wagon rock her to sleep. She tried to fight the notion, but eventually gave in to it.

While Bibb was riding alone up front he got a chance to rediscover his bearings. The plains seem endless, but there were enough landmarks along the way to guide his path. During the flatter stretches (which allowed Anna to sleep well) he could see five Indians on horses on his perimeter. There was no doubt in Bibb's mind who was riding the fifth horse. It was actually a comfort knowing where the man was as opposed to not knowing.

The fifth horseman did not show any signs of mischief. Once Toak discovered Bibb's escort and discerned the direction where they were heading he would ride ahead and wait. Toak was in more danger from them than they were from him.

==0==

Bibb asked Anna to wake up from her slumber. There was a river to be crossed and she would have to do her part again to navigate the obstacle. Bibb was surprised the wagon did not seem as heavy as expected, even with the added provisions. There was either a reduction in weight or he was feeling better. His ribs did not hurt as much as they did the prior morning. She had hurt him.

Anna became quite alert after the soaking in the chilly water of the river. She was still wearing the dress she had been given at the camp and Anna needed to be very careful with how she moved wearing it. After she climbed back into the wagon seat next to Bibb she offered to drive the horses while Bibb napped. Bibb kindly refused. He said he could not face the four Indians tonight if they noticed such a breach from protocol.

"Okay, Bibb, I'm ready to talk. It's time for you to come clean. Tell me about this morning."

"I appreciated d'that you-zz didn't hold me-zz (srpt) so tight last night. I felt good d'this morning. For (srpt) what-zz little we got, it-zz was great sleeping! You have hot breath. I guess we-zz all do."

"I could have used more sleep, but you were kind enough to let me nap just now. But you once again chose to deflect my question. What did the medicine man say?"

"He-zz blessed us good, Anna. The chief wished us-zz to be prosperous (srpt) and make it-zz home safe. D'that was d'the nice part."

"But what exactly did the medicine man say?" Anna was learning to be specific with him.

"He spoke over us-zz like he knew-zz our future (srpt). I couldn't tell-zz if he was-zz making it up, or if he-zz really knew something. Predictions-zz are cruel (srpt). Nobody ever benefits-zz from them. Only God know-zz d'the future (srpt), and He-zz keeps it mostly to Himself-zz. D'there have been times-zz (srpt) I guess He spoke to people. D'the guys d'that heard (srpt) d'the spirit tell d'them stuff wrote it down. I-zz guess (srpt) d'the spirit doesn't like-zz to be misquoted."

"Indians don't write."

"Yes, I guess so-zz. I just don't know-zz (srpt). It was-zz still interesting."

"So what did the medicine man say, Bibb? Have you noticed that I ask that question a lot?"

"Anna, I-zz still don't know what to d'think about it (srpt). What he-zz said about me was scary."

"So what did the medicine man say, Bibb?"

"He said several d'things-zz about me, most-zz of d'them unnerving (srpt)." Bibb looked at Anna and tried to defend himself. "Anna, honest, I-zz only asked for-zz a blessing (srpt). I didn't ask-zz for predictions. Honest, Anna-zz."

"I understand, Tommy. Do not get frustrated about this. I want to know, and there is no reason for you to withhold the truth from me. What did the medicine man say about your future? We are getting closer to you answering my question. I really want to know, Tommy, so don't make me keep asking you and don't be afraid of what the man said."

"Anna, he told me-zz three things (srpt). D'the best d'thing he said was (srpt) d'that I would die without my-zz name."

"That's good?"

"No-zz, Anna (srpt). D'that was just d'the best d'thing he said. D'the rest was-zz worser worse."

"What name did he say, Bibb? Your legal name Tommy? Didn't you say, or did I read it somewhere you were called the Ghost of Fort Rice? Didn't you already lose your given name of Terry?"

"I think he meant Bibb; he certainly implied it, Anna (srpt). D'these predictions are-zz so general; d'that d'they could mean anything. He said-zz it (srpt) like d'this was a blessing. I want-zz to d'think he meant (srpt) I would lose-zz my reputation."

"Your good one or your bad one?"

"Anna, I don't-zz have a good one (srpt). I d'think I made it worse now-zz too. I had an empty hand d'this morning (srpt) when d'they blessed us."

"You may have had an empty hand, but we didn't, Bibb. Don't you fret over that. Do you dare tell me the second thing?"

"Anna, d'the second thing d'the (srpt) medicine man said was d'that justice (srpt) will sit-zz on my shoulder d'the remainder of my-zz life."

"What's so bad about that?"

"He said wound-zz for wound, blow-zz for blow, blood-zz for blood (srpt), I will be required in my-zz body to pay (srpt) for d'the injuries I have inflected on others."

"That is bad."

"He said my-zz physical burden will be lighter-zz d'than d'the invisible one (srpt). I have-zz hurt people with more-zz d'than bullets. I scared people bad-zz (srpt), and d'threw out wounding words. Anna (srpt), if I-zz say something mean to you-zz, please correct me. I don't know-zz (srpt) when I hurt people some-zz time."

"That I promise. Have you really hurt that many people?"

Bibb purposely avoided a direct response. "D'the elder said d'that promise like it was a blessing too (srpt). He said I would bring-zz justice to the plains. I don't know what-zz d'that means (srpt). I have killed too-zz many, and not one of-zz d'them deserved dying (srpt). I-zz should have been bigger d'than-zz d'their insults (srpt). I've seen too-zz many judges and lawyers-zz in my life (srpt). D'that would be a very cruel fate to-zz become one of d'those. I didn't d'think (srpt) I was d'that evil to be punished d'that bad. Maybe-zz I have been."

"Does your list of not deserving to be killed include my husband, Bibb? And no, I'm not calling you out on this because I think you have been unkind. I simply want to know."

Bibb did not answer her question. He was more overwhelmed with the old Indian's words and the size of his burden. "D'that wasn't all of d'that blessing (srpt), Anna. D'the other d'thing d'the medicine man predicted (srpt) was that I would die in d'the grass of d'these plains (srpt). He said I would be taken to my-zz resting place (srpt) on a horse I did not own."

This meant something of immediate importance to Anna. She would not know what to do if Bibb wasn't at her side. These mystical words threatened her security and she began to fear. "Bibb, you should stay off of all horses. Maybe you should think about moving east too."

"I can-zz no longer stay off a horse (srpt) no more d'than a bird choose not-zz to fly. What-zz else can-zz I do Anna (srpt)? I am broken-zz. I have to-zz earn my keep (srpt). I need to keep-zz d'this job I got-zz. He made d'this prediction sound good too. He said (srpt) my-zz daddy will welcome me home."

"That is at good one, Bibb."

"You-zz don't know my daddy. He keeps pet varmints (srpt). I fear-zz d'this prediction (srpt) more d'than-zz all d'the others."

"When did you start fearing anything, Bibb? Is that the worst of it? Didn't you mention he said three things?"

"Another d'thing he said was-zz not about me-zz (srpt), but someone close to me-zz."

"I'm close to you. Was he talking about us?"

"Anna, he said I-zz would marry a woman-zz d'that was scarred badly (srpt). The scars will-zz become (srpt) beautiful in my eyes."

"Bibb, you said you were married to your brother's widow. The next time you see that medicine man you can tell him he got two out of three correct. That still isn't that bad at guessing."

"Anna, I'm not-zz married to Humbird. She says-zz I am, but I am not. I don't d'think I am (srpt). D'that woman hates-zz me. You are-zz d'the only woman (srpt) I have been to-zz d'the altar with, Anna (srpt), and d'that's-zz d'the truth."

"What are you saying, Bibb? So you lied to me about being married to Humbird? Why did you say that then? Marriage isn't something you are in the morning and aren't that night. Are you lying to me now? Did that medicine man really marry us?"

"No, Anna, d'the elder did not marry us (srpt). About Humbird, I really don't know-zz. I was at d'the trial (srpt) and d'the judge didn't say I was married d'then. Humbird said-zz d'the judge gave-zz me to her (srpt) to replace my brother after I-zz left."

"But you still say it Bibb. There has to be a reason. For a man who thinks a lot, why haven't you thought this through?"

"I have-zz d'thought it-zz d'through, Anna (srpt). I am ashamed of what-zz I concluded."

"Spit it out, Bibb."

"No. I won't."

Anna replied, "Then I know what it is."

"Good. D'then I won't have to-zz tell you."

"Spit it out, Bibb."

"No. I won't."

"It hurts that bad?" she fired back, her intuition ablaze in speculation.

"Would you like to know-zz (srpt) what the medicine man said about you?"

"Spit it out, Bibb. If you don't, the truth will eat you alive."

"No. I won't."

"Yes you will. It is unhealthy for you to hold it in."

"He said-zz d'three d'things about you."

"You can tell me later, Bibb."

"About-zz d'the d'three d'things?"

"No, about your stubborn reasoning! You can tell me about what the medicine man said now and the other later, or I will squeeze everything out of you." Bibb looked at her when she laid out that painfully credible threat.

Anna continued talking at the muted man, "Tell me the truth, Bibb, and not some story. Be kind, and tell me plain. It can't be as bad as what he told you, or your silly lie about bearing fifteen children."

Bibb went silent. It wasn't out of stubbornness this time. He really was collecting his thoughts. "Anna, d'the medicine man said-zz d'three d'things about you (srpt). D'the first d'thing really was about-zz your offspring."

"Not fifteen. He didn't say fifteen, did he?"

"No, Anna, he did not-zz give a number (srpt), but he-zz did talk about a specific one. He said a prince-zz of warriors (srpt) would give you-zz a boy in your old age."

"He said boy and not son? I am not planning to marry."

"D'there isn't much difference in-zz d'the Lakota language (srpt). I do not know. And old to-zz d'them (srpt) ain't old to us. He really-zz d'thought d'this was a superior blessing (srpt). D'the medicine man spoke (srpt) to-zz d'the women of d'the tribe of its-zz magnitude."

"That's better than dying on a borrowed horse. What is the second one, Bibb?"

"D'there was more to-zz d'the first one."

"More children?"

"D'that he did not say. He said-zz (srpt) d'that you would dine-zz with governors and kings (srpt), ambassadors and rulers. D'that's not-zz exactly right. D'their words for kings and rulers comes out more-zz like-zz champion of champions, power-spirits, and moccasins of authority. We're stuck with unpoetic and ugly sounding words for people of prominence."

"How will I do all that dining and dancing with people of prominence if I'm all scarred up?"

"Nobody said you-zz would be scarred (srpt). His second blessing-zz may be part of d'the first."

"What was that, Bibb? What was the second blessing?"

"He said you will-zz become beautiful (srpt)."

"That is it? I will become beautiful? Beautiful in the way they describe beauty?"

"You saw all-zz d'the women smile (srpt). D'they smiled when he pronounced-zz d'this (srpt) over you. D'this too is-zz a special blessing."

"Well, that is better than wound for wound. What is d'the third, Bibb?"

"I won't tell-zz you (srpt). I should-zz have told you he-zz only said two."

"Let me save you some pain, Bibb. Tell me now instead of later."

"No. I won't-zz (srpt). I will let you-zz know later, but not now."

"Is it bad?"

"Anna. Stop it-zz."

"Is it about us? His third blessing on you was about somebody close to you. Is this about somebody close to me?"

"Anna, if I tell-zz you, you will-zz d'thinks (srpt) I am just like-zz all-zz other men. Haven't-zz you been hurt enough (srpt)? I refuse to hurt-zz you. You will-zz d'think (srpt) I am-zz acting on dark motives. Just stop, please-zz."

"Do you have dark motives?"

"Anna, I am-zz what I am (srpt). Your opinions-zz about men contain (srpt) some logical conclusions-zz based on solid evidence."

"You think too much, Bibb. What makes you think women are not just as depraved?"

"I didn't say-zz d'that. I d'think women can hide it-zz better (srpt). I don't worry about-zz women. I have-zz (srpt) enough to worry about with men."

"So you think that I am depraved?"

"Anna, I have only known you-zz for two weeks (srpt). You have been kind to-zz me. I am trying my best-zz (srpt) to be kind-zz to you. I am bad, but you see-zz some good in me (srpt). I see-zz some good in you-zz too."

"Bibb," she said warmly as she turned to look at him, and waited for him to look at her. "That is a reasonable offer for peace. I accept it. When are you going to tell me the third blessing?"

"I'm-zz going to write down all d'that d'the medicine man said (srpt). I will send it to-zz a friend to keep it-zz safe for me (srpt). If it comes true in-zz my lifetime (srpt), I will show-zz you."

"Is it that scary, Bibb?"

"It is-zz for me! The medicine man said it was a blessing, and maybe it was, and one d'that had no ambiguity. D'the scary side of his d'third prediction was a sharp underside. D'that word from him came with a very mystical edge and I didn't like how it was said. Anna, please trust me on d'this. I must conceal it or else his blessing will become an irrevocable curse d'that would destroy our covenant. And Anna, don't let your mind go wondering what-zz it might-zz be, nor be asking me-zz about it. I want-zz you to hold-zz your momma in your arms."

"Bibb, allow me one question." She paused to get permission and did not. She asked anyway. "If the secret remains unknown to me, will the outcome be good and only good?"

"No Anna."

"No, as in you won't answer me?" She waited for his answer.

"No. It would not just be good and only good. For you it-zz would be best and only best."

"And for you? Good and only good?"

"You got your one answer to-zz your one question. Anna Gorgon, don't never ever ask again."

==0==

Anna was surprised by how comfortable her personal cocoon was this night. That was the only thing she knew for sure. Tonight was their first night together alone… No it wasn't. There were Indians out there watching them. Worse, all of them had the impression that she and Bibb were married. Yet Bibb, contrary to the sheriff's prediction, seemed to have no temperament to take advantage of the situation. He was perfectly happy sitting next to a tree or with his bedroll adjacent to his horse.

Because it was Anna's primary nature, she automatically felt insulted. Even with their close sleeping experiences over the last two nights Bibb still, as demonstrated by his actions, preferred sleeping next to a stinky sweaty animal over her. She logically concluded two things. She was just as attractive as she ever had been, and that man sitting under the tree was just not… just not right. There was nothing wrong with his eyesight; the venison harvest proved that. The second conclusion was that Bibb had more problems than just the physical. The bullet must have severed his brain from his mind, and his broken ribs must have separated any hint of humanity from his bruised heart. He was an emotional invalid. Or maybe not. He was certainly different. His heart and mind were far from her, resting in other thoughts. Or maybe not.

Anna spoke to herself as she looked up at the stars, "Tommy certainly is not a risk taker. Maybe that creature took me serious when I told him I would slice him up if he touched me wrong. It probably has never crossed his mind that women can exaggerate or lie."

Tuesday, October 11, 1887

Second day out from camp. My hands are ugly and hurt worse than yesterday. Our scouts surround us; Bibb showed me where to look. I thought the chief promised four braves; there are five. I recognized the one that came into camp tonight to take provisions to the others.

Bibb acknowledged me as a warm-blooded fully matured woman today. It is about time. Yes, he has always known that, he is not blind. For the first time he remarked that the obvious had entered into his thinking. Although he hinted I was beautiful, with the same man-mind that clueless outlaw found similar beauty in prairie dogs. He would be an easy man to hate, but I cannot. I cannot while I still need him. Hate? I don't even recognize myself as the sophisticated Anna of Deadwood anymore. Have I already used up my lifetime quota of hate? What am I becoming? It doesn't bother Bibb one bit if I hate him; hurts only me, much like kicking a cactus.

Bibb has an annoying habit of answering questions I do not ask. He claims to be a simple man, but frustrates me so when he bypasses my initial questions to answer the next one. I prefer small talk. I changed my mind; I was lying to myself. He is not clueless. He complains something is biting him but he will not explain. Ribs? Maybe, but more likely the preacher wasn't lying.

==0==

"ANNA, WHY-ZZ DO you keep looking at-zz me (srpt)? Of all-zz d'the d'things to look at (srpt), my face should be-zz d'the last on your list! Look at-zz d'these plains-zz (srpt); d'the blue sky. Truly d'there is an inspiring magnificent beauty in-zz all d'those-zz d'things (srpt). Even-zz d'the prairie dogs have sublimity in-zz d'their towns." Bibb looked at Anna and caught her rolling her eyes.

"Bibb, give me a direct answer for once. How many times have you almost been killed?"

Bibb wondered what prompted her question. "Maybe d'three times by-zz d'the law (srpt). No four… make d'that five, and at least a dozen by-zz d'the lawless (srpt). I don't know. I don't count. D'there's (srpt) no point in-zz counting." It was obvious to Bibb she wasn't interested in his topic.

"Why?" Anna replied.

"Why-zz what? Why not-zz keeping score (srpt), or why am I still alive against-zz d'the odds?"

Bibb surprised her with the second interpretation of her question. She replied, "I suppose both, but your second thought intrigues me. Does it still hurt to talk? You don't have to answer." Anna saw the pain in his face.

They rode for another mile and crossed a small river. Anna no longer had to be told what to do at the stream crossings. Her job was to wade out in front of the horses taking lead of the beasts eight times her size. Her horse was skittish in the water and she had to be savvy enough to guide their crossing on the shallower hard bottom. Bibb stayed behind to steady the load and use their long pole as a lever to lift an axle whenever a wheel needed to get past a submerged obstacle.

It was curious to Bibb that every time they emerged on a far bank, he could look around and see an Indian at each compass point – North, South, East, and West just outside of shouting range. He never saw much of this protection unless they were in a vulnerable spot. But no doubt they saw Anna and him continuously, and kept them encircled. Bibb would have considered himself in serious trouble if it wasn't for the chief's promise. He remembered such incidences on other plains where Toak and he, surrounded, had to make a dash for safety.

"Anna, you asked-zz me why I don't keep score (srpt), and I added the question 'Why am I still alive (srpt)?' I suppose-zz d'the answer is d'the same to both questions (srpt). What has-zz happened doesn't matter. It's-zz d'the *Who* (srpt) d-that scares me. D'that *Who* ropes me-zz (srpt) and drags me away from every demise-zz (srpt). It's scary to d'think who d'the *Who* is."

"Are you talking about providence?" replied Anna. "Save your breath."

Bibb saw her discomfort and waited ten minutes, partly due to his sore jaw and partly to think through how he was going to reply to her next five questions. Obviously Anna had no problem with saying something to voice her concerns; it was only a matter of time before her next comments bubbled up. Bibb had enough experience with her to know (if she wasn't angry) that Anna thought about her words before she said them. He also concluded that those moments of quiet contemplation was about the only thing that he appreciated about her. This wasn't his first trip down this trail; Bibb's experience was that all women named Anna were like that. It was in their nature, and God must have branded them with that name as a warning to other men. If it was a divine joke, Bibb failed to see the humor.

Like clockwork, the predisposition that Bibb predicted about Anna to say something eventually overcame her. "Bibb, how can a rascal like you talk of providence? That's pure nonsense. What credibility do you have in anything concerning religion?"

"None. But-zz I'm stuck for a different explanation. D'that is your real question-zz, isn't it?"

"I don't believe in providence. It is a very inconvenient concept."

"So I deduce you-zz prefer an impersonal God d'then (srpt)? So-zz do I."

"Bibb, have you ever been right about anything even once in your whole life? It is hard to tell if you are lying or just plain stupid." (Anna had already decided on liar. Bibb certainly wasn't stupid.)

"Stupid or not (srpt), I'm right about d'this," Bibb replied in an emotionless response. He realized his mistake; she was angry again. Bibb had learned he needed to avoid talking until she calmed.

She glared at Bibb, and then looked forward. Her mind had been fully engaged to anticipate and deflect the answer she thought Bibb was going to make, but he surprised her. She tried a different tactic. "You are being very inconsistent, Bibb. This proves my point about all this providence talk being nonsense. Either that, or you are baiting me with lies."

Bibb looked at her for just a glance and saw she was not looking for an argument. It never entered his mind that he had been laying out bait. He chose to remain silent, thinking to himself he better say something profound or not say anything at all. Nothing profound came so he took the opportunity to remain silent.

Anna did not allow a prolonged silence. She devised in her mind a set of questions to prove that she was right and then proceeded. "So why do you like an impersonal God? That is what you said."

"Anna, I said nothing-zz about liking God (srpt). I said an impersonal one would be-zz preferred. I certainly haven't been given a choice about it either (srpt). D'those-zz notions (srpt) have been-zz ripped from my head (srpt) like a rotten tooth. D'the extraction still hurts-zz (srpt), and you are making matters worse. I suppose-zz (srpt) you can't help it-zz."

Anna snapped back, "So it is my fault now?"

"Fault?" replied Bibb. "Hardly! You and God seem-zz to be working together (srpt) to gang up on me-zz! God has a rope around my leg and drags me-zz d'through places I don't want-zz to go."

"You are still talking nonsense." Anna voice was very much raised. "I have never been accused of assisting God in anything, so you have some big-X s'plaining to do!"

Bibb was visibly frustrated and clammed up. Anna saw that she had pushed him hard. She remembered what she knew from previous relationship failures; she had become overly demanding and demeaning. On top of that, her adherence to the drumbeat of the "nonsense" tune could be considered by some as nagging. Certainly her former husband would have thought so. Regardless of those thoughts, she reflected that her words lacked any hint of kindness. Strangely, she felt guilty about it. Soon, due to so much practice, she was easily able to dismiss those feelings of culpability.

She asked again, now much calmer, "Well Bibb, what is your answer? Are you admitting you are speaking nonsense? I thought more of you."

Bibb waited until he had guided the horses around a muddy spot in the trail. "Anna, you-zz are sadly wrong, my mouth hurts-zz (srpt), your back is up, a chilling breeze is blowing across our path, and (srpt) your dress is still wet. Can we talk about anything else (srpt)? You talk, and I will-zz look where we are going and gladly listen (srpt). We-zz get along best d'that way. Tell me about-zz (srpt) d'the dress store you owned in Deadwood. Start with-zz d'the reasons why you bought-zz it (srpt), and don't stop talking until you tell me why-zz you sold it."

Anna took the hint, not as an insult, but as a temporary cease fire. The man was wounded, and in a sad way, kind. She recognized that his last comments seemed to come out of nowhere. Yes, of course his jaw hurt and she was somewhat angry, but she sensed that beyond any doubt the real issue the man had was centered on the other two observations that slipped out of his mouth.

Anna, after wrapping up inside a blanket, decided to comply with his request starting with her motivation to make money retailing all the things she wished she could own. To her, the store was not a store; it was her giant personal closet, with rows of shoes, hats, and dresses. If somebody purchased something from her closet, she would buy something new to replace it. The whole scheme was quite grand until her husband turned ugly and she began to hide for her life. While on the mountain she so longed to peruse through her big closets but dare not. She resented her husband greatly for denying her of that joy.

Anna abruptly changed the subject. "So Bibb, you got your wish. It is now your turn to explain yourself. Go ahead, I am listening. You owe it to me if only to return the favor."

"Explain what? What I-zz d'thought (srpt) about your store?"

"Why you think I am in cahoots with God to make your life miserable."

"Anna..." Bibb responded with a disappointed voice.

"Okay, I will say it kinder," said Anna, "but it still means the same. Why do you think there is a providence and I'm cooperating with it? This theory of yours is vexing and needs dispatching."

"Anna..." Bibb looked at her and sighed.

"Well if that is too harsh, then start by explaining to me why you think God is not impersonal."

"Before I answer-zz d'that, I want to put-zz my own words-zz in my own mouth (srpt) without your help-zz. God is not making my-zz life miserable (srpt). He's-zz not like-zz d'that. Cahoots or not, He is using you-zz (srpt) to show me where I am ugly. D'there is so much to fix on me (srpt), I figure He-zz don't know-zz where to start."

"What does that stupid answer have anything to do with my question?"

"Anna..."

"Do you really think that? Be serious. Do you think I'm one of God's unknowing minions doing His dirty work?"

"Anna, if you-zz were mean, maybe (srpt). But-zz you're not mean. I see goodness (srpt) reflected in d'the deepest secrets of your eyes. I also see-zz loneliness (srpt) living in-zz d'there too. I recognize loneliness well (srpt). God is using you-zz because He can. You-zz have d'the right heart for it."

"Sweet-talk! That is all that is. Tell me the truth."

"Anna, have-zz you ever wondered why men cuss (srpt)? Women don't because-zz d'they are polite and gentle (srpt), but men smell up a room with d'their cursing (srpt). D'they delight in calling down God's wrath (srpt) on anything and-zz everything, as if God was obligated to destroy d'their enemies at d'their command. I was d'the king of d'them cussers. At least you-zz ladies are ladies."

"Don't underestimate women, Bibb."

"But don't you find it strange-zz d'that d'the same people-zz (srpt) d'that don't give a fig about abusing God's-zz title and reputation (srpt) delight in invoking his name for unneeded emphasis-zz in every sentence (srpt) out of-zz d'their mouths? If you want-zz to call something nonsense, d'there's your example. Before Miles City I said from one side-zz of my mouth-zz d'there was a God (srpt) in every sentence. With-zz d'the other side (srpt) I mocked him as if He-zz did not exist (srpt). I now realize how foolish I was-zz (srpt). I lived for years-zz with no fear-zz."

"What is so uncommon about men cussing, and why should any fear be attached to it? It isn't like someone divine is sitting around watching us and taking notes. In some ways it is quite humorous when you men cuss. I can remember many laughs over how mad people got and how they sputtered and said funny things when they cursed up a storm."

"Yes-zz… Yes-zz, it-zz was funny to everybody but-zz d'the one being mocked (srpt). Seriously, Anna, please d'think about-zz d'this (srpt). What if it-zz was your name being dragged-zz d'through-zz d'the outhouse (srpt)? Even if you'd didn't hear-zz it directly, if'ns you'd heard about it from others it would have crushed your spirit (srpt)."

Anna sobered. "It did crush my spirit."

Bibb saw he had emotionally slapped her accidentally. "Anna, I didn't-zz know (srpt)." He turned his head from the trail and looked at her. "Did Gorgon do-zz d'that to you?" Bibb noted the unsaid reply. "Don't answer (srpt). I am fitting-zz d'the pieces together. I so regret saying-zz d'that."

Anna responded quietly, looking the other direction. "Bibb, I baited you, and I accidently hooked myself."

"Anna, an impersonal God is all-zz well and good (srpt), and we-zz can pretend He-zz is gone away on a long journey (srpt) and He can't-zz hear what we-zz are saying about Him here (srpt). But my experience has-zz neutered d'that notion. I am so afraid-zz d'there is a God (srpt), and I-zz fear-zz d'that He hears-zz everything (srpt). Not only does He hear-zz everything, but is-zz actively doing-zz something about it (srpt). D'the insults He has-zz heard out of my mouth were taken personal (srpt), and His-zz response will be-zz personal too."

"If that was true, wouldn't you have collected a dozen tombstones over your head by now? Obviously you didn't, so that notion of yours is nonsense. Bibb, please, start talking some sense."

"His-zz response is-zz not revenge, Anna (srpt). No, it's-zz much more complicated. I'd once-zz d'thought even cruel (srpt). No, He doesn't sit-zz around waiting for-zz somebody to say a prayer (srpt) and-zz d'then decides if He-zz wants to answer it or not. D'that would be nice (srpt), but d'that's not His-zz style. No, He's-zz ruthless in His desire to reverse our directions-zz (srpt). Sad to say, but d'the Divine Dude is-zz very alive. He's-zz got my foot in his-zz noose and is pulling me-zz in (srpt). He's d'the hunter d'that peruses-zz his prey (srpt). He's-zz d'the father d'that puts a finger in-zz his son's chest and demands manly behavior (srpt). He's-zz d'the husband d'that leads his-zz silly bride into maturing situations against-zz her wishes (srpt). He's-zz d'the cowboy who lassos-zz d'the calf and runs-zz lightning fast (srpt) to wrap up its-zz feet for branding. He's-zz d'the king who tolerates naïve misbehavior (srpt), but never tolerates challenges-zz to his-zz sovereignty (srpt). And-zz d'there are-zz two other d'things d'that bother me more-zz d'than anything else."

"Bibb, are you okay? What brought this on?" Anna studied his face. She seldom saw such outbursts of resignation, and especially in a man. "What are those two things?"

"Can you-zz see why I'd rather have an impersonal God (srpt)? I want to run-zz my own life (srpt) and go-zz where I want-zz to go, but no (srpt). He's-zz chased me-zz close and drove-zz me into a box canyon (srpt). My desires are doomed, and my-zz will defeated (srpt). My-zz life is no longer my-zz own. I have surrendered, but He-zz still isn't satisfied."

"Who owns you?"

He held his breath and took a thoughtful pause. "Today it is-zz you. It's-zz also d'those-zz (srpt) Indians. It's-zz my boss paying me to deliver-zz d'the posts (srpt). It's-zz my Humbird. In Miles City it-zz will be-zz another sheriff (srpt). I am-zz called to walk like a man-zz, an honest man-zz (srpt), but everywhere I'm-zz being dragged (srpt). And to-zz be honest, d'the varmint is-zz killing me."

"I am not dragging you anywhere, and I am not a varmint!"

Bibb said too much and was sorry about it. He sobered, put his passion back into the recesses of his heart, and engaged his mind on how to get out of this predicament. After some quiet he thought he would get some peace. No, Anna was not going to let him off easy; her fidgeting told him so.

Bibb spoke again, "You-zz are right and I-zz was-zz wrong (srpt). You-zz are not dragging me-zz anywhere. Please-zz understand my-zz predicament (srpt). I see-zz more now-zz than I-zz have ever seen. I-zz see a pulling on-zz my life (srpt) d'that I never saw before. I-zz see beauty in-zz d'the simple d'things-zz of nature (srpt). I-zz see beauty in-zz people and relationships. I see-zz people loving people-zz d'that I-zz always overlooked before (srpt). D'this is quite overwhelming, and maybe God put-zz a bullet d'through my-zz tongue (srpt) so I would-zz d'think more and talk-zz less."

Anna accepted his wounded apology but then became curious. She was starting to understand him better, overlooking the sounds that happened every time he took a breath or prevent a drool. And most of his "*th*" sounds had a "*d*" in front of them because his tongue was forked. The man was really trying. "What was the second thing?"

"I-zz said it-zz already: Beauty (srpt). All-zz d'the beauty all around me-zz (srpt). It's-zz overwhelming and I-zz best shut-zz my mouth now (srpt). You-zz are a woman and I know-zz you know-zz what's-zz dancing around in my-zz mind (srpt). D'the varmint knows-zz too. Why couldn't I have been-zz left in-zz peace (srpt) as a no good always cussing rail hand (srpt) in Canada? But-zz no, cowards-zz don't get off-zz d'that easy (srpt). I am-zz done talking now."

==0==

Bibb was so sorry he had even attempted it. He had used the pole once again to lift the axle to pry a stuck wheel out of a mud hole's bondage. After freeing the wheel loose, he attempted to climb back into the driver's seat. A sharp pain in his chest betrayed the fact he had overestimated his healing, throwing Bibb back to his feet to stand beside the wagon. In reflex he simultaneously grabbed his chest and introduced some spicy words skyward.

Anna had long suspected those and other similar words to be trapped in the vile soul of that outlaw. She refused to react to Bibb's undisciplined response. This wasn't the first time she had seen him angry, but it was the first time she saw him slip up and be loose with his words. If that boy's god really did exist, fireworks would soon be coming. That same god Bibb just insulted, if that god was worth his salt, would deal directly with the curses and insults that were aimed in his direction just moments earlier. She had no business inserting herself into that fight.

Anna watched Bibb very carefully for the next hour. Unlike the miles before, he was holding the reins in his left hand and often subconsciously (or consciously) holding his ribs in the other. She could tell Bibb disliked it when she looked his way. Bibb's eyes betrayed his feelings. The man hated to look weak and if he caught her looking at him he quickly turned his eyes back towards the trail.

During that same hour Anna's thoughts evolved. She was so glad she had held her tongue when he had let loose with his tirade. Earlier she was ready to pounce on him for disrespecting her womanhood with such pollution of the air as if his words were a breach of his promise to be kind. She wisely decided that she was not the cause of the spillage. There was no reason to risk redirecting his foul mood towards her. Anna's second thoughts were those of shame. She could have been more helpful with the pole; there was enough pole left for her to put her hand to it to help lift. That thought was followed by anger that Bibb didn't take better care of himself, followed by remorse. Her first reaction should have been to keep her part of the covenant by actually applying some nursing skills, even if it didn't do anything to help. All the wishing in the world wouldn't convince anybody that her silence was therapeutic. Her inaction spoke louder than the possibly of her doing something hurtful like inspecting the source of his misery. Finally pity for the man rose in her heart. Pity gave way to a strange form of self-congratulations. She still pitied the untouched man, but felt good that she cared; a sweet care, a refreshing feeling last experienced too many years ago.

Like a surprise turn in a story, the sun broke free from the overcast conditions and seemed to light the trail in front of them. Anna noticed that Bibb looked up and around at the wonder of the moment and almost smiled. She jumped at the opportunity to ask, "Tommy, are you still in pain?"

"Pain hurts," Bibb replied in a death like rattle. "D'that is why d'they call it pain."

"How bad?"

"Why do you-zz even want-zz to know?"

That curt response answered Anna's question. After some silence she continued the conversation in almost a whisper. "Where does it hurt the worst?"

Bibb did not reply but pulled his right hand away from his chest. He look forward and snapped the reins if only to let the horses know he was still there. As Anna had predicted to herself, it wasn't long before Bibb had returned his hand to protecting his ribs.

Anna didn't like another dose of prolonged silence and attempted conversation again. "What can I do to help?"

"Shutting your mouth would be-zz a nice start."

"And then?"

"More quiet after d'that would be even better," replied Bibb, not intending to be cruel. It just came out that way.

"Do you want me to drive? I can control those horses."

"Control? No offense, Anna, but you-zz talk too much."

==O==

Anna dared not talk, and kept quiet until the point where she had to ask Bibb to stop at the next set of bushes. Bibb's response was strange, as if he had just woken from a deep sleep. In reality Bibb hadn't even considered anything else in the universe except his persistent affliction. Of course he would stop; besides not being unaware of Anna's needs, he was ashamed that he hadn't even thought about resting and watering the horses over such a long stretch of the trip. He had been consumed with his own inescapable circumstance.

Anna wasn't the only one that noticed. The scout that had been riding on the south point behind them caught up to the stopped wagon. Bibb and he exchanged some speech and sign, and Anna was savvy enough to know the subject of the scout's question; the Indian inquired about Bibb's physical condition. She didn't know the details, but was quite sure Bibb didn't tell him to "shut up."

Once pointed and traveling north again Anna kept her wits about her. Her intuition had told her to rein in her controlling ways and keep a keen eye open for any sign of change in her man. Once Bibb had let loose of his ribs, Anna decided to engage again. "Bibb, I am not a stranger to pain. I know you don't want to talk, but it would be for your own good if you vented your aggravation. Tell me about what you are suffering. You talk, and I will listen."

Tommy looked her way. As much as he wanted to he could not pretend she wasn't there.

Anna waited a bit longer. Eventually she spoke again, looking forward down the trail, "I'm not angry with you, Bibb. I'm concerned; honestly concerned. You asked me not to talk, and I won't until the next time you ask me a question. But Bibb, I want to know, not because I'm curious, but because I really ache with you. I've spoken enough. Our next shared words will be from your lips."

The pain had already pushed Bibb to the verge of tears. Her calm and kind words added to the pain and pushed him onto the knife edge of controllability. The undeniable forming moisture in Bibb's eye as he looked at his wagon mate gave Anna an answer, although she had no idea what that answer was. He unknowingly had acknowledged that he had heard her plea; that would have to suffice. His silent response could have meant a hundred things, but none of that mattered. From out of nowhere the word *precious* entered her mind. Over the last weeks she had loathed that word as part of the terrible recurring ditty that refused to dislodge from her subconscious. When bathed in a man's tear, *precious* became precious again. She turned the other way as that thought was soon bathed in a woman's tear too. Her heart could not lie to her. She did care; deeply honestly cared.

==0==

Anna thought the amount of perspiration on Bibb's brow was abnormal and had been getting worse over the last hour. Yes, she was warm too, but the dress was cool. He was possibly fevered which sorely tempted her to go contrary against Bibb's wish for silence. He saw her growing fidgets and responded to her with a question.

"Can I ask-zz you for a favor, woman?"

"Yes," she said softly, carefully avoiding any emotional baggage.

"Don't-zz let me stop. I may not start up again."

"Bibb, let me drive."

"I may."

"You say when, Tommy. I'm listening. I'll hear you even if you whisper it."

Bibb looked at her and then gently snapped the reigns once. He detested the nightmare he was living through. He detested the fact he may need somebody, that somebody named Anna in particular, to help him make it across the plains. He detested the possibility he was broke and possibly beyond repair. The medicine man may have been right; he might die on the plains.

Tommy could only wish for sleep, the pain was overwhelming. His hands were bloodless white and hurt from clinching the reins so tightly. He needed not do that, but his whole body demanded the hardening of his muscles and joints. The pain reminded him of vast loneliness of Utah's desert; pain as unbearable as the glare and heat from the sun reflecting on that salty white ground. He was miserable. His own sweat could not penetrate his clammy skin and his own breath was trapped in his own chest. It was as if tortured by hornets, and when the sting left him half dead the pain doubled, tripled; to unbearable of unbearable. He knew he would gladly swim through the floors of cattle cars if he could just get two minutes of relief. He was desperate. His heart was angry; aching from considering the possibility that God had lied to him. The Anna girl of Miles City had said that God would never leave him "no matter what," and it seemed that the current "no matter what" he was suffering had run the God-critter clear out of the territory. He could not take another blow.

"Anna," asked Bibb.

"What, Tommy? What is it?" Her response was soft and immediate.

"Talk to me. I don't care about what. Just talk to me. Take my mind off of me."

"I can drive, Bibb. You can lie down in the back."

"Anna, fill the air with your dreams and desires, and don't ask-zz me any questions. If something worries me, I'll let you know."

Anna first thought the request was a test, but then considered even if it was, it would be a most delightful examination; she had no risk at failing. Her man never once interrupted as the sun's shadows gradually crossed from the left side to the right side of their wagon. At times she imagined that it almost looked like he was listening. When they remounted the buckboard after resting and watering the horses Bibb didn't even ask her to exchange seats with her after switching the horses too. He just did it, and she was warmed by his answer why. He wanted his good ear facing her direction on the next leg of the trip. He would just have to risk the pain of getting his ear bit again. She laughed, but Bibb could not, barely having the energy to use a rag to wipe the sweat off of his head and arms.

They were many miles down the trail when Anna asked Bibb to speak his mind. She insisted that it would be good for him, and secretly she wanted to have a new subject to talk about. She had to admit to herself she had run out of monolog that wasn't monotonous.

"Anna, first, second, and my next d'thought is d'that I am about to die. D'the gnawing inside is relentless and is blackening my outlook on life. My remaining d'thoughts don't make sense."

"Let me help you make sense of them."

"You are d'the other d'thoughts. It's you d'that don't make sense."

"I make perfect sense, Bibb. What don't you understand or mistake as illogical?"

"Answer me one question d'then, Anna."

"What?" she replied. She thought to herself this might be about her dress, or her late husband, or her nagging. She wish she had responded, "I might" instead.

"Why did you go to d'the altar with me? You knew-zz what I was, and still am."

"I will let you know as soon as I sort that out myself, Bibb. But I will offer you a clue about how I became to be me. My daddy was harder on me than my brothers and sisters. He said I lacked the discipline that my siblings had and that he was going to do his best to instill some into me before I ran away from home. I hated when he kept telling me, in fact he even wrote it over the door of our room, to *'Obey first and understand later.'* Our preacher said that too, but I was bad about sneaking out of church when we were still living together as a family."

"Well at least you obeyed once in a while. I-zz never obeyed or understood."

"You obeyed ten days ago, or was our trip to the altar a defiant act of rebellion? And in that shot-up half of a man-brain of yours I know that you already have guessed what I'm going to ask in response to your next answer."

"Tell me more-zz about your daddy, and why-zz he named you Anna."

"I will, but you are warned. You are only on parole. I will also be asking you later a question you don't want to answer now."

"D'then, Anna, I will answer you now instead-zz of risk being called a coward. What I understand now d'that I didn't understand ten days ago is…" Bibb fumbled with his side for a moment, "…is d'that I desperately, actually more d'than d'that, I need you. Not your money, not your touch, but I need-zz you – not d'the you I can see, but d'the you d'that lives inside of you. Let's not bring up d'the subject again."

"I will talk about my daddy then. And I never called you a coward. I only thought it." Anna said and thought about a lot of things in the next hour. His declaration was totally unexpected. She convinced herself it was his pain talking, not the real Bibb. She also knew through her own experiences that pain is the great megaphone of life. It causes you to lie loud or tell the truth loud. Loud lies are easy to detect, and the sincerity of Bibb's declaration left her few options on how to interpret the admission. A breath of a thought went through her mind; she – the *she* that lived deep inside her – was lovable again.

==0==

It could not have been a better traveling day. Indian summer on the plains is one of the best times of the year to travel, but not for distances that consumed weeks. The lovely weather can give way to the first hints of winter overnight. Bibb always considered the first frost of the year a rude awakening to what was coming. Bibb could tell that first frost was now overdue as if it was crouched ready to pounce on the high plains.

During the half hour before setting up camp for the evening Anna and Tommy discussed how to eliminate the awkward time they had the previous evening getting ready for nightfall. Anna was specific in her questions about the boundary between trail bossing and hygiene bossing. Anna had the verbal advantage because Bibb had already expended the total amount of words he was allocated for this day. His mouth really hurt. The silence told her that his "everythings" hurt from toe to top.

Not talking didn't stop Bibb from thinking. He wondered if there was a connection between the medicine man's prediction and the fact that Anna would not change out of her dress. There was not a lot of dress left in her green dress, but he dared not mention anything lest he would get a lecture about changing his own clothes more often. Nevertheless, his experience could easily predict that a day or two more in the same clothes was going to win her a ridin' rash. Then the same thought came to him about him... he just best keep his thoughts to himself.

A different Indian came into camp this night to pick up provisions for him and the three others. Bibb and the scout had a short discussion about something; only a lot of pointing when seen from Anna's perspective, and then the Indian returned to his brethren with his and four other provisions.

Anna was not a complete city girl after all. She showed some skill in tending the fire, and offered ample commentary concerning the trip while she poked at the small blaze. Most of all, she talked about the women at the Indian village. It might have been just the healthy campfire, but Bibb couldn't help but notice that Anna had a glow about her as she talked on and on.

"Do you want to talk, Tommy?"

"No, ma'am."

"Ma'am? What's the matter, Tommy?"

"Nothing."

"What's wrong? Spit it out, and call me Anna."

"Nothin's wrong (srpt). It's almost like too much is-zz right."

"What's right, Tommy?"

"My-zz heart."

"Does it hurt? I thought your chest hurt you most of today. Where exactly does it hurt?"

"Anna, never mind-zz d'that. Yes, it does, and I mean it hurts, but it d'thinks (srpt) too. Something is wrong, Anna. Well not wrong, really (srpt), it's just not broken like it usually is."

"You have a broken heart, Bibb? You sugared my curiosity. I'm listening. Now explain."

Bibb couldn't put his thoughts into words. Everything he wanted to say would work him into a deeper conversational pit with that Anna woman. He opted to just stay quiet. He didn't know that his silence would prompt even more curiosity within Anna. He was wrong no matter what he did.

"I'm waiting, Tommy. What is on your mind?"

"I should be d'thinking about d'the horses (srpt). I'm going to check on d'them. Anna, you-zz do what you have to do to bunk down in d'the wagon (srpt). I'm giving-zz you ten minutes of privacy."

"Is that what's on your mind, Bibb?"

"No… I mean yes… d'the horses need my attention (srpt). I'm going now. I'll be back soon (srpt) with some more sticks to burn. Anna… Oh, never mind."

"That's okay, Bibb. I can read your mind better than you can read your mind. You go fetch some wood while there is still some twilight."

"D'then what-zz was I d'thinking?"

"Peace, Bibb. Am I right?"

Bibb was really confused. Was she toying with him? He thought more to himself, "No, she said it with kindness. That is my corrupt thinking, not hers and…"

"Bibb, have you ever experienced such a peaceful evening? I bet you have. You are no stranger to starry nights. I bet you were thinking the same thing I was. A reliable source in Deadwood said that we might be kindred spirits. Tell me true Bibb, were you thinking the same thing I was?"

"Maybe." Her eyes were dreamy and he was helplessly drawn in by the pure tone of her voice.

"Well if you weren't, you should start thinking about it. I am. Nights like this were made to drink it all in. Surrounded by such majestic wonders are… it is… well, don't get this wrong, but the word that naturally comes to mind is intimacy. Intimacy with the unknown… Oh Bibb, I prattle on too much. Get done what you need to get done, and I will do the same. Give me about fifteen minutes to get situated for sleeping."

Bibb almost blew the whole moment by verbally responding. He wanted to ask her "Who made the wonders?" and "The unknown isn't so unknown." He feared that would bring the providence topic up again. Bibb sorely wanted to avoid that. He would tell her his opinion if she asked, but he dared not hold his breath waiting. It could be years before he heard that topic come from her mouth again. Bibb did leave as asked. The real reason he walked away was to avoid her magnetic eyes.

"That woman can really confuse me about her intentions," he mumbled to himself while he walked towards the horses. "I think she throws in words like 'intimacy' just to see me squirm. Maybe not. I can't blame her; that is what women named Anna do. I wish I could be as relaxed in my conversations with her as she is with me. No, I don't either. She is just making it hard for me to hate her. The woman is baiting me. There is no 'naturally' in her nature. Yes, she is. No, she isn't. She is keeping her promise to be kind; something I should work harder at keeping too… Well, in a half hour she will be to sleep and I will get some peace… Oh, that woman really did know what I was thinking. The varmint must have whispered it in her ear." Bibb missed talking with men.

Wednesday, October 12, 1887

Our third day out from the Indian camp. Bibb is getting more talkative every day, which means he listens less. That is okay, there is little left of my shallow "dead-wood" history I care to talk about. Tommy's good attitude makes me feel dirty about my past. He is either faking the pain or faking the joy; those two don't mix. Maybe he is faking both.

Eventually that man answers my questions, but never on the first ask, or second, or third asking. He is so simple and so complex, or dare I say, deep (and sometimes dense – he can get me so angry). I have never met a man until now that finds me both as appealing as a gold strike and as uninteresting as last year's bird nest. As much as he complained about not wanting to be my employee, he treats me as if I was the Chairman of the Board. Respect is nice, but sterile is unbearable.

We happened upon a dead Indian today. Bibb would not pass it by. I helped him bury the man. He even insisted on a ceremony. I wanted to move on instead, but I am not the trail boss. Bibb has expressed no desire for an assistant trail boss either. Bibb showed his anger wrinkles.

Late tonight Bibb came to the back of the wagon where I was trying to sleep and took the moccasins off my feet. He tucked my covers tight around me and then vanished like a ghost. I spoke not – in fear of unfriendly others still around the camp. Miles City could still be a long dangerous week away.

I was but a little girl the last time somebody tucked me in. I really wonder what Bibb was thinking or not thinking. He gives such conflicting clues. Truthfully, I bet he doesn't know either, or how a woman might react to what he does. He is so clueless it makes him appear sincere – the tale-tell mark of a very good liar. I laugh; there was ample opportunity but no "oops" in all of that tucking in. Even in the dark that man carefully respected my threats. Shame on me for anticipating a small accidental oops as he, without asking, made sure I would stay warm and covered overnight. He is either trying to be faithful to the covenant; or he's varmint scared.

==0==

ANNA DID NOT sleep well. All the entrails placed on her from Mrs. Franklin's love-note were heavy on Anna's mind and soul throughout the night. She thought of a thousand ways to get even with the Franklins for what they did to her behind her back. Then the reality of her situation set in. Like it or not, she was all in and there was no going back. She was as married as married could be. She laughed to herself at how the word *us* had turned her thinking around earlier that week. And now she was truly an *us* legally, and according to the preacher, spiritually too. Yes, her fantasies wished for a more handsome man, a rich compliant man, but no, she went to the altar with Mr. Ugly and agreed to the promises. She was now part of an *us* and there was nothing, absolutely nothing she could do about it. She was truly torn up inside. All her life she craved *us*-ship. Now that she was part of an *us* she balked. Her first *us* was never an *us*. He beat her and abused her. This one would not dare. He would either be as kind as possible to her... then reality set in... or kill her. The man had no middle.

Her success depended entirely on her first being on her best behavior and secondly controlling the wants and desires of her male escort. Of the two problems, the first was the worst. Her second problem was made more difficult due to the pain of suffering an annoying man that noticed too many things, thought too much, didn't answer her questions, went mute when he hurt, constantly lied, never took her advice, and didn't speak his feelings; all things she thought she could fix over the next few weeks. She resolved that she would treat Bibb as if they were merely engaged. She loved her previous engagement period with the dashing Mr. Gorgon. During that glorious time in their lives she treated him well and he treated her even better. They teased each other often, had heart felt conversations, but never dared crossed the line of, as Mrs. Franklin would say, "right and proper." Funny... she was the enforcer of that standard although he lustfully wanted to take liberties.

No, Anna's sixth fortune was not lost; it was being held in escrow by a very clever lawyer that suspected correctly that she had planned to abandon Bibb in Miles City once she was through using him. Yes, she had hired Mr. Franklin in the first place because he was clever, but she never expected his cleverness to turn on her. Was all his loyalty to her feigned? Then she had to reexamine that assumption. If she double-crossed Bibb what would keep Mr. Franklin from double-crossing her? Was he really disloyal? What made him (or his wife) plot this out? Anna had to conclude that in his mind, his customer's ethic had to be forced to yield to a higher ethic. The only question Anna still had on her mind was how long he had been planning this. It seemed so curious that he had her sign Bibb's Last Will and Testament. In hindsight, that was no coincidence. Oh... that man! Oh... that woman! Mrs. Franklin pinched her good this time!

Except for the three witnesses who signed the marriage certificate Anna had to concede that nobody wanted her to fail – not a single soul. To win back her sixth fortune she had to win her seventh first. Then she got mad at the Franklins again. Then she resigned to her inner soul that right and proper might be right and proper because it really is right and proper based on a higher societal norm than her own flighty opinions. She didn't want to think about that anymore; the thoughts of a higher authority had a lot of extra baggage. It included the finger wagging of that detestable Deadwood preacher... who also wanted her to succeed.

Anna became confident that if she could conceal this inconvenient legality from Bibb she could pull this off. She was glad that she had buried the letter deep in the envelope with her other papers while still in the teepee. Bibb would never have the audacity to look through them. The man treated her one piece of luggage as if it was full of a feared feminine fungus, as if touching it somehow would instantly sissify him.

==0==

Anna and Bibb were three hours down the trail from camp when they came upon the body of a Blackfoot scout. He had a single feather in his headband. The body was lying face down with drying blood under it. There were no arrows stuck in him or any other signs of mischief. Regardless, it was a corpse, and it had been lifeless only for a few hours.

Bibb asked Anna if she would like to help bury the man or stay in the wagon. She did not commit, nor did she leave the wagon. Bibb jumped out of the wagon and turned the body over, seeing what he expected. "Look-zz d'the other way-zz, Anna." Bibb returned to the wagon and pulled the shovel out of the back.

"What did you discover, Bibb?"

"It was-zz a skilled hatchet job."

Anna looked the other way, composed herself, and then returned to looking at Tommy. "Did he die like my husband died?"

"No, ma'am. D'this hatchet was-zz not thrown (srpt). It was-zz done eye-zz to eye-zz, most likely d'this-zz dawn."

"I want to see anyway. Take my hand, Tommy, and help me out. I don't think this dress will hold together much longer." Tommy came back to the wagon to oblige her request.

Anna, by her response, really didn't want to look and stayed on the far side of the wagon. Tommy returned to the corpse and lifted the stiffened arm. When he rolled it over, the wound he had warned Anna about was in full view. Even from a distance Anna thought it was as bad as what had happened to Bibb's face and her husband's chest.

"How painful was his death, Bibb?"

"Ma-am-zz, I don't know. Bad, but-zz quick. Dead is dead, and death is-zz a door (srpt). Indians say so. I'm not-zz curious about what's behind-zz d'the door, either."

"You believe that too, don't you Bibb?"

Bibb stuck the shovel into the ground and it did not go anywhere. The ground was hard and his body was soft. Bibb looked around and found a patch of taller grass about a hundred yards from the wagon. He started to dig there finding the ground more moist and amenable to his task.

Anna watched the man struggle. He was as determined as he was hurt. She looked around and saw nobody, which was often the case, but knew that she was not unwatched. That was both their fate and fortune. She went around to the back of the wagon and found Bibb's bag of clothes. They were all smelly, but so was hers. She knew she could not work in what she was wearing and certainly was not going to help naked. Her practical side did not care about possible hurt feelings. Finding a shirt and pants, she changed into them. Other than long in the arms, short in the legs, and tight in two circumferences – they would do. Anna then walked over to where Bibb was digging a grave.

"I have come to help. Here is some water and hand me the shovel. I'm calling in your promise to listen to me about your health, and you have no business with a shovel in your hand. Give it up."

"You are-zz wearing my-zz clothes-zz!"

"And you-zzzz are digging your-zzzz grave if you don't stop! Go back to the wagon and rest. I demand it." Anna was as forceful as she was mocking.

Bibb looked at her and stepped out of the shallow hole he had completed already. Bibb sheepishly handing her the shovel; rather she grabbed it from him. It hurt too bad not to comply, and neither he nor she was in the mood for an argument.

Once out of the hole he just stared at her. Bibb offered her some advice on how to do it, and she half-listened. She did take his gloves when he offered them. Yet he was still ruffled by her brazen act of sifting through his stuff and commandeering what she wanted without asking.

The varmint bit hard. His memory keenly went back to the time when he took his brother's clothes without permission. He hated that varmint. Bibb could sometimes anticipate encounters with it and given time, prepare his justifications for his actions. That never worked; the varmint bit him anyway. He loathed how it continually proved him a liar to any claim of his own innocence.

The varmint was proof of what that Miles City mama had told Bibb to be true. She predicted as a gift from providence that Bibb would receive an improved recollection of everything he ever did. He didn't recall her telling him that most of what he would remember was his bad behavior, and a swift kick in the pants to make all wrongs right. Maybe that was because she didn't tell him... oops; must have slipped her mind.

That daydreaming did not help the current situation. Bibb was still infuriated over Anna appropriating his clothes. The following thought was even worse. He seriously wondered about the possibility that if he complained about her taking his clothes then he may be due the same fate his brother suffered. The medicine man said every evil he had committed would be specifically paid for.

No matter how he tried to get it out of his mind, it still twisted his sensibilities that a woman would put on his clothes. There was something very wrong about that, but he could not identify it. Was he angry because his manly pride was hurt? Was it his self-centered nature? Is there something immoral about a woman in men's clothes? Was it that he had to admit like a coward that he was injured and obviously in pain? Why didn't she have a problem with this gender violation?

He suffered with the thought that the situation might be only what she said it to be. His anger was totally unwarranted. She was being practical. In kindness she wanted to get the shovel out of his hand. Also, she did tacitly agree that the Indian needed to be buried instead of leaving the corpse to decay in dishonor.

Anna was also smart enough to know he was too stubborn to stop unless she forcefully took over. Bibb also had to admit the dress she wore would not have lasted a minute of labor. Bibb had no recourse but to shut up for now and to thank her later. It was easier to rationalize that she took over because of his health rather than the painful thought of losing his manly right to be leader. He had agreed to the idea to place his healing in her hands. He had no reason to legitimately open his mouth again on the subject, unless of course he was hungry enough to delight in a force fed portion of gravel flavored humble pie.

The problem with rationalizations is they never satisfy the cry of the heart. The effort to outsmart himself provided to be a short lived peace. He could not get out of his mind that she was wearing his clothes! It was a grace a bullet had been put through his face; otherwise he knew he was very capable of saying something stupid before he thought this all through. But… She had gone through his stuff and had taken what she wanted!

Bibb couldn't take watching anymore. He walked back to the wagon, unhitched his horse, got his rope, and lassoed the corpse by the feet. Before he dragged the body over to the hole, he gathered up the Indian's weapons and then removed the scout's moccasins and headband.

It started to sprinkle which soon gave way to an exceedingly hard rain. Once at the grave, both Anna and Bibb used the rope to lay the body to rest in the grave. Bibb would not tolerate Anna refilling the hole, saying it was his job. She was invited strongly to use some lye and the cloud provided shower to clean up and change back into her lady's clothes, which she did on the other side of her horse.

Bibb placed three rocks on the muddy grave and wrapped the scout's headband around them. He then took the scout's one feather and planted it vertically between the moccasins. He mumbled a few words and walked the horse back towards the wagon. He knew he was being watched, and not just by Anna. He would feel better once he was again close to his rifle. He hoped Anna had sense enough to cover it up from the rain.

Anna was already in her dress again and sitting in the wagon when Bibb returned. Bibb hitched the horses back to the wagon, washed off his shovel, secured the load, and returned to the driver's seat. "Where is-zz my rifle, Anna?"

"Covered, and under your seat."

"Thank you-zz."

"For what, Bibb?"

"I will tell-zz you-zz later. You are kind."

"How?"

"I will tell-zz you-zz later. Let's leave this-zz place before we-zz have company."

==0==

It did not take long for the news to spread around Miles City that Bibb was returning to town. The sheriff wished he could have controlled that rumor, but news was news and scary news travels fastest. The preacher's word that Bibb was a changed man did not square well with the funerals of two ranch hands with leaky foreheads and recent news of a duel in Deadwood. The legend that the ax was faster than the gun was discussed in every business in town. Nobody in Miles City doubted the outcome of the Deadwood event as the whole story was becoming known.

Some of the rumors included a strange twist. Bibb was returning with a woman, and not a tame one. Some said they married, some said no. Some said Bibb was already married, and some said he was a bigamist. There was also speculation inflamed by a Deadwood newspaper editorial that Bibb would arrive alone repeating the rumors that Bibb rid himself of female traveling companions if they became too irksome. Some wanted Bibb thrown in jail. Most wanted him to bypass the city.

The sheriff told the town council his intentions on how he would deal with Bibb. He tried to make the case that the city was safer with Bibb staying in it than Bibb wandering around the outside of it. That was not a complete fabrication, but close to one. The sheriff had enjoyed peace ever since the man left town several weeks before. The law of the gun had given away to the rule of law.

==0==

Towards evening Bibb found a suitable place to make camp. While still daylight he scrounged around for some kindling and wood for Anna to start the fire. He then took their horses down to the bank of a stream where they were tied with long ropes to a nearby tree.

When Bibb returned from brushing down the horses Anna had already heated some water for coffee and had beans cooking over the fire. She mentioned to Bibb that she was getting tired of hard tack, beans, and jerky. Bibb responded that the menu was on purpose to motivate them to keep going. Anna agreed with him that after a week of that fare any steak in Miles City will be like heaven.

Bibb set up the rest of camp and refilled the canteens they were carrying. He took special note of where every tree was around them; there were not many; the Blackfoot never died alone. It was a lovely place to stop, given the protection from the wind and the sound of the river. That pleasantry would have to do for their daily dose of optimism. The hard tack was still hard, and Bibb gave her all his jerky. His teeth couldn't do much with it. He had to tear it into morsels and swallow it whole.

The time around the fire was lovely for Anna. This was better than any adventure she had taken with her family as a child. Bibb was still ugly, but because it was dark enough outside that particular sin could be overlooked. She had to catch herself on judging him too quickly; she was starting to look a bit overripe herself.

Anna had very few complaints as she told Bibb more of her childhood. Bibb could not help but notice two things. First, Anna's childhood was a lot better than his, and second, that dress she had on contributed nothing towards keeping her warm. Anna did comment (not quite a complaint) that during their daily feast of HT, B & J that Bibb took better care of the horses than he did her.

"D'that's-zz not true. You're eating more d'than grass, you're not getting a whip put to your rump if you move too slow-zz-ly, and you've got a brush to lay down your hair nice in d'the evening. D'the only d'thing my horse suffered d'that you haven't (srpt) is a good breeding at d'the Indian village. Anna, right now-zz is a good time for you-zz to stop your whining. I saw-zz your mare winking mighty friendly at my-zz steed (srpt). What-zz are you trying to say, Anna?"

With a new found dose of ill attitude Anna stopped that topic dead in its tracks. "I'm not saying anything you are thinking about, Mr. Toivo. Good night!"

For Bibb, the newly found quiet was quite nice. She was every bit of the promised handful. His tactic had worked well until he opened his mouth again. "If you want to wear-zz (srpt) my longer pants and sleeved shirt (srpt), you are most welcome to-zz d'them. What-zz you are wearing is not too warm (srpt)." It was obvious to Anna that Bibb was choking out those words against his normal will.

"Yes, thank you, and please, may I? I was so cold last night. Will you pick out some clothes for me, Bibb?" She was testing the sincerity of his offer. He confirmed his offer by bringing his warmest pants and shirt, and then returned back to the fire purposely having his back to her as she changed.

After a minute she told Bibb she was done. She returned to the campfire to sit beside him. "Bibb, will you be kind and go down to the stream and wash this dress out for me? When you are done, hang in on the tree to dry. And can you help me turn the hay mattress over? I never worked so physically hard like today ever. I'm bone-deep tired."

Bibb thought to himself that kindness is a gift that won't stop taking. Once a man is kind to a woman, they will keep asking for more. Then he told the varmint to stay away from him before it bit him again. Anna deserved some kindness and no more of his smart mouth.

Bibb walked over to the wagon, helped her with the bed, and asked for her clothes. She made him reach for the dress, almost toying with him. When he reached into the wagon, she touched his arm, saying, "Thank you. You're a man of your word, Tommy Toivo."

"Where're-zz d'the rest of your clothes, Anna (srpt)? Do you want me-zz to wash d'the other stuff too?"

"Bibb," she said, still holding his arm, "that one piece of green cloth is all there is so please be very gentle with it. And thank you for your clothes to keep me warm. I promise I won't soil them if that is what you are so worried about. I never saw you with anger wrinkles until today."

Bibb almost said something but let her have the last word. It was hard enough just to loan her the clothes. He had to think that the same stream used to wash her clothes could wash his too. He left with his other dirty clothes too. He wondered if she told the truth about having nothing else.

Bibb decided two things at the river. She sure did know how to get under his skin... and into his mind, and secondly she was comfortable with his company. If she was scared she would be formal and standoffish. Wearing his clothes... that still bothered him, but he would just have to get over it. He never estimated the price of kindness to be so high.

==0==

Bibb had dozed off while leaning against a tree by the campfire when he heard familiar noises. First it was the horses that alerted him to company. He went down and brought them up to the fire. Over the next thirty minutes he heard what he had heard many times before. Bibb prepared for the visit.

The reflection of the camp fire light in the wolves' eyes let Bibb count how many there were. He saw four and suspected six in the pack. They were on the hunt, and they were interested in anything they could scavenge. Bibb let them get close enough to hear them breathe to increase his chances at ending their visit his way.

Anna was sound asleep in the back of the wagon when she was jolted awake by the sound of three rounds of gunfire fired in the blink of an eye. Her first thought was a fear that Bibb had been killed and evil men were coming to sell her into prostitution. When she peeked out the back of the wagon she saw nobody. She thought that better than seeing a dead escort by the tree.

"Anna," said Bibb in a subdued voice from behind her. "D'they won't be-zz coming back soon. I got-zz (srpt) d'three of d'them! Two-zz in d'the head, and one-zz in d'the other end (srpt). How do you-zz want your puppy chow?"

"Who did you shoot? Not our escorts, did you?"

"Anna-zz... No-zz... I shot d'the wolves (srpt). I don't kill friends! Are you-zz hungry?"

"In the morning, Bibb. I'm not getting out of this wagon until I can see where I'm walking. Bibb, are you okay? Tell the truth. Are you hurt?"

"No-zz, just cold. But skinning d'these wolves-zz will warm me up (srpt). You-zz go to sleep, little birdie. Keep d'these loaded revolvers (srpt) by your side to keep you safe and-zz warm."

That comment gave Anna two things to think about as she tried to fall asleep. She asked herself first if he was telling her the truth about being cold, or was he just hoping somebody warm would invite him into her cocoon for some teepee treatments. Second, she knew all too well that his "maybe his wife" was also named Anna, and he called her a bird, specifically a Humbird. What was that man thinking? Without trying he had teased her back for touching his arm. There was also the other repugnant possibility that they were gaining feelings for each other.

She returned to her slumber position fairly certain that this heartless man never had feelings for anybody. What she experienced was the unexpected familiarity that came with a mutual promise of kindness, and nothing more. As she fell back asleep she knew exactly how she was going to test her theory in the morning.

There was nothing warm about Bibb's revolvers.

==0==

Bibb suspected visitors would be coming into camp later tonight. The Blackfoot never traveled alone, and they certainly were going to have questions. At the burial site Bibb saw two of them on horses as he finished hitching up Anna's and his horse to leave at the gravesite. They would have seen both he and Anna bury their brother with dignity.

That afternoon Bibb took the opportunity to plan his discussion with the Blackfoot. Certainly they were not there by accident; they were too far away from their nation to be satisfying personal curiosity. Bibb assumed they would have inspected the grave soon after he and Anna had departed. They would also have a very good idea who killed their partner. Tonight's visit would be to gain answers to their questions, not to seek revenge. Then again, Bibb had to consider the possibility he could be killed without notice in the night as he exposed himself in the campfire light. Bibb had listened all afternoon to Anna's adventures in Saint Louis, but now his mind had to focus on what questions his visitors would have for him tonight.

Bibb purposely kept the fire hot and bright. He did not want to be mistaken for a scout killer. The bright light from the fire would expose his unmistakable mark of Cain. He slung his hatchet under his shoulder like he had done many times for his own protection and calling card. With his knife he skinned the wolves and roasted the meat as he began the waiting.

Around midnight Bibb noticed two approaching by stealth. Bibb made no sound until they were close, still tending to his roasting wolves. When his back was turned to them he spoke calmly in a voice loud enough to be heard in a tongue he hoped they recognized, but not in a yell: "Blackfoot two feather, you may enter my camp in peace. Blackfoot one feather may stay close and watch. I have your brother's weapons to return to you and a gift for your chief. You have nothing to fear from Bibb."

Anna woke from her sleep at the noise of Bibb speaking in a foreign tongue. She was again amazed that such a man like him would have that knowledge. She keyed on his word *Bibb* wondering why he would refer to himself at the end of his own sentence. Slowly she adjusted her position so she could watch through a crack between the slats of the wagon. She now knew why Tommy parked the wagon that way.

As Tommy tossed more wood on the fire Anna saw a shadow of a man approach from behind him. Without turning, Bibb addressed him in the Lakota tongue. "You are welcome here, Two Feathers. Join me for wolf."

"Peace?"

"Yes, you have my bond of peace."

From the dark side, Anna watched the approach of an Indian wearing a headband touting two feathers. Bibb motioned for him to sit. Bibb stood up, and from that point on he signed his conversation with the Indian, explaining that he had great pain in speaking.

Bibb sat down. In turn, the Indian chose to sit almost directly across the campfire from him. Anna was frozen in place as she continued to peek out from under her blankets through a crack in the slats. She saw both of them clearly. There was no noise but the fire. She dare not move and risk discovery.

Bibb signed. "I sit with my back towards One Feather. I have no reason to fear him because I have done him no evil."

"How did you see me?"

"I heard you first. My ears were awakened to your steps, and though dark I have been given great sight to count your feathers."

"Where did you get your great sight?"

"It is not mine. Do not call it mine. I am Bibb, but do not believe me because I say so. My name follows me. It does not go with me or go before me. What is your name?"

"Call me Two Feathers. That is more honorable than my given name. May I see your ax?"

"You have already seen it. You may hold it."

"Is it a magic ax? What spirit does it possess? I am sent to find out."

"There is no magic in the ax, but like me, it too is known by where it has been. There are no new notches on the handle today."

Bibb stood and handed him the ax, and in an act of clumsiness the ax was dropped in the exchange. The blade nicked Bibb's ankle which started to bleed slightly. The Indian was terrified and quickly picked it up.

Unaffected by the slip Bibb continued, "Two Feathers, share meat with me."

The Indian did not know how to respond. He just kept looking for his doom to occur. Bibb crouched to the fire, pulled his knife out of the log where he had previously stuck it, and heated it over the fire. Bibb's ankle was still bleeding but no mention of it was made. Bibb took out two plates, sliced and placed a piece of roasted meat on each.

"Two Feathers, choose which one you want. I will eat the other."

The Indian pointed to the one on the left and reached out for it. Bibb kept the other, stuck his knife in it and started to eat it. He signaled for the guest to do the same. With hesitation he did.

"Two Feathers, I know you visited the grave of your fallen brother today. I buried him with his head towards the dawn and his feet towards the mountains. He will not be hindered on his way to the Great Spirit. His feather marks his grave, and I have his weapons to return to your tribe. With the weapons also take these wolf pelts. There is one for your chief, one for you, and one for One Feather. You may tell One Feather to come eat."

"There is no One Feather."

"There is no hiding from a ghost, Two Feathers. Did he gain or lose a feather in the last hour? Do you want to call him or do you want me to go get him? There is no reason for you to test me, and I have no reason to test you. Call One Feather in to this fire to receive his gift."

"Where are the weapons?"

"I have them put away safely. They are the weapons of a One Feather and only to a One Feather they will be returned. If you choose not to call him in, I will take one feather from you so you will be worthy of them."

That statement was completely unexpected and a serious affront to the guest's honor. The Indian studied the man. Bibb continued to eat and remained extremely calm for having delivered a threat of such magnitude. Bibb signed to his guest, "Call him in with your whistle. He is watching and will know that it was your whistle and not mine. Call him now."

The signal went out and One Feather came into the camp. He did not have to be informed of the conversations; he had seen it in their hands. Bibb took his plate and used it to cut a fresh piece of meat for One Feather. Bibb handed it to him and motioned for him to eat. One Feather looked at his partner and received an affirming prompt.

"I will go get your weapons. I will soon return."

The two Indians sat by the fire while Bibb went to the wagon. They started to talk rapidly in an Indian dialect Bibb did not recognize. Bibb approached the wagon where the all but sleeping Anna lay. While there Bibb whispered to the motionless lump under the blanket not to fear, not to move, and keep the guns close to her side. He also told her to knock softly with one knuckle against the slat if she had heard him. Bibb returned with the Indian knife, bow, four arrows, and the knowledge that Anna was awake.

"These belong to your tribe," signed Bibb. I never had intentions of keeping them, but kept them to make sure you came to me tonight. This appointment was not of your choosing, nor mine. Two Feathers, you came here to ask me questions. Ask them." Bibb reached down to his ankle and unconsciously irritated the recent scrape, causing it to bleed afresh.

Aware of the new bleeding, Bibb continued. "You did not mean me harm, and I mean you no harm. I pledge my answers will be as truthful as I have knowledge of." Bibb took fresh blood on his thumb and dabbed his forehead one way and then the other in the shape of a tilted X. "I require no pledge of you. I will not require of you any answers."

"Are you dead?" signed Two Feathers.

That was a strange initial question Bibb thought, and certainly not his own idea. His medicine man must have instructed him to ask it.

"No, I am alive as you. I live, breathe, eat, sneeze, and cry the same tears as you. I suffer pain. I cherish joy."

"Then you are not a live spirit in a dead body?"

"No, but I have been thought to be. I have been told a ghost now lives within me. This ghost has no evil and reveals to me some truth. I cannot explain, but I know the ghost is there."

"Show me the ghost."

"I do not control the ghost, but like the wind it goes where and when it wants to. The ghost chooses when to hide from me, but no one can hide from the ghost. It is known by its fruit."

"What fruit?"

"The fruit of this spirit is found in its goodness."

"Show me this fruit."

"You see it now, but you will not recognize it until later. How much later I do not know. Tonight you are a witness of the ghost's signature."

"You are not this spirit?"

"No, I am not the spirit nor do I possess the spirit. My name is Bibb and I am a wanted man."

"Where are you going next?"

"I am on a sacred pledge that was not of my choosing. I have been bonded by the spirit to deliver a woman who does not belong to the west away from the west. I must take her back to the east beyond the large river called Missouri. She also has been bonded to deliver me from my suffering by bringing me to a powerful white medicine man.

"Where did you come from?"

"From a place of many chickens."

"What?"

"From nothing have I been raised up. To nothing I will return. My life is not my own and the plans the spirit has for me are hidden from me. My country has disowned me. I belong to no tribe or nation."

"How is that possible?"

"I had an evil past before the spirit chose me. That bad past caused the white man to take away my feathers. Many times white man authorities decided to kill me to satisfy their justice. Every time I was rescued. I am spared for a reason only known by the spirit. The spirit has not told me my fate."

"You killed a man in Deadwood. Why did the authorities let you go?"

Bibb wondered how they knew that. "They sent me away. I now go to Miles City where more men have died. The authority there will send me away too. I am bound by a sacred oath to deliver my passenger far to the east, and to the east I must go."

"Where is your partner Toak?"

"I was hoping you could tell me." If they knew his name, then they knew his history, and if they knew Toak's history, they would know their shared history as couriers. They would also highly suspect Toak killed their brother today.

"You do not know?" signed Two Feathers.

"Nor do I know his intentions. He is not bound by any oath to me. Just because we share the same pain of excommunication from our nations does not mean we are still partners."

"Did you fight with Yellow Hair at Greasy Grass?"

This change of subject was welcome to Bibb. He knew this question was a direct reference back to the Blackfoot medicine man's initial one. The concern about Bibb's history, outrageous or not, was based on the superstition that it is impossible to kill a man that is already dead. Bibb had heard the rumor shared among several Indian tribes of the plains that both Bibb and his valiant horse did not survive Custer's Last Stand[3]. Bibb now had a chance to correct that tall tale.

---

[3] 'Greasy Grass' is the Indian reference to the Battle of the Little Big Horn, and 'Yellow Hair' the white man's leader, General Custer. Although almost half of 7th Cavalry survived the battle, there were no survivors found from the five companies of soldiers surrounding General Custer.

"No. I have never put on the white man's uniform. I do ride the white man's horse."

"Why is that?"

"Trust."

"Who?"

"The white man's great leader trusts me. I bring his messages to his people."

"Why you?"

"My name."

The senior Indian spoke out loud, "Bibb?"

Bibb confirmed with a nod. Two Feathers was satisfied. The name Bibb needed no further explanation. Two Feathers continued, "Why do you speak and sign a red-man language?"

"I deliver messages. I deliver people. I deliver hope. I deliver gifts. I deliver peace. I deliver fear. I also deliver death. I do not decide what to deliver, I only deliver. The Spirit now demands I deliver truth. Today I delivered honor to your fallen partner, and now I deliver his weapons to you. What were you expecting from my camp tonight? Have I delivered to you what you seek? Do you dare seek other treasures from me? I say you dare not. But you are not bound to answer. I am."

"Who are you? Who is 'I am'?"

"I am Bibb of the forked tongue and the wounded body. I roam the land of no authority. I am a man with an evil past. Do not believe me for what I say, but what you have seen of the spirit called 'I am'."

"Do you have a message for my chief?"

"Yes, Two Feathers. Tell your chief that I hope to be honored to share meat with him and his medicine man when the day of appointment comes. Tell him no honest Blackfoot need to fear my campfire. And I also have a message for you, Two Feathers. Go and come in peace. You honored me with your trust under these stars. May the same stars remember tonight when difficult days arrive, for they will come. Have you found what you sought? If so, take meat for your journey, the weapons, and the skins."

One Feather took the weapons and Two Feathers took the gifts. They departed as quietly as they came into camp. Bibb waited about fifteen minutes and then took the horses back down to the trees by the river. Upon returning he found Anna either asleep or faking it very well. It did not matter. He took his guns back, removed her moccasins, tucked her in, and returned to his place warmed by the night's fire.

Bibb decided he liked Anna better at night. There was no light to illuminate her distracting features. Better yet, she did not talk when she slept. As Bibb watched the fire he eventually concluded that the undistracted peaceful life is not really life. That is called rest. Life begins again afresh at dawn.

With all of the day's distractions, what most stole his sleep was that he still could not get over her earlier taking and wearing his clothes without permission. He was also glad about the ax incident. If his words didn't convince the Blackfoot, maybe the fact that he bled might. Or more rumors will start. That thought was overshadowed once again by the brazen audacity of that woman taking and wearing his clothes! It really bothered him, and it bothered him more that there was nothing he could do about it. The Deadwood sheriff was right about her. She was one frustrating woman! Did it bother her? Not in the least, as evidenced by the dainty snore coming from inside of the wagon.

Thursday, October 13, 1887

Fourth day out from the Indian camp. At breakfast that man told me what happened in the wee hours last night. I should have been more scared than I was. Bibb said there were still five Indians surrounding us. The dead one and the two that visited last night were infiltrators and sworn enemies of Toak's tribe. Bibb said their chief had much wisdom in sending scouts that knew Lakota. Bibb does not speak Blackfoot. There are many things Bibb ain't, but he certainly is a protector.

Bibb will not let me wear my dress! What a strange turn in him. What am I saying! What a strange turn in me too! Who would have thought that a worn rag would be the catalyst in bonding us as a team? Not the spark of romance... not a loving touch... not the femininity found in perfumes and fine gowns... not even in heartfelt compliments – it was the clothes I wore to dig an Indian's grave that turned his mind. Remarkable? Yes! Dare I say miracle? I dare not. That would admit to something that contains more baggage than I am willing to carry. Regardless, this trip is now bearable, despite the HT,B & J, and the d'Entrée du jour, wolf steak.

PS: I must guard my heart. I have been widowed less than a month and need time to mourn properly. I was worried about his attraction for me. Never did I think I would have to check myself against the possibility I might gain feelings for him. No... the man is quite repulsive in every way. What I enjoy is not him, but the security I have with him around. I must not confuse my joy in seeing my deepest longings for home and family becoming reality with the means by which that hope is enabled.

==0==

ANNA WAS COMPLETELY unsatisfied with Bibb's first narrative of what happened overnight. He had shared much of the what, but none of the why. He had said enough to scare her, and now she wanted enough to comfort her. He answered questions she didn't ask and avoided the ones she did. Why the judge demanded all of Bibb's artifacts made more sense now, and the midnight visit gave evidence of much more mystery to Bibb than his outlaw reputation. She decided to probe more, not out of simple curiosity, but because her life may depend on knowing more than what she knew now.

"What really happened, Tommy? Why did you give me your revolvers? Didn't you need them?"

"D'they respect-zz d'the ax. D'they despise the guns (srpt). You could have been-zz hurt. Respect saved our lives-zz (srpt). You needed to have the guns, not me-zz."

"That doesn't make sense, Bibb. And how did you know they were Blackfeet, and that one had one feather and the other had two?"

"Blackfoots, Anna. Not Blackfeet. And my vision is-zz good, and sometimes gooder at night. But I cheated yesterday (srpt). I saw d'them before dark. Toak taught me-zz d'their ways (srpt). D'they knew my ways-zz too. D'they were chosen to meet us-zz (srpt). I knew d'that when d'they spoke my tongue and read-zz my sign. D'they risked-zz d'their lives to meet me (srpt). I risked ours in return."

"They didn't see me, Bibb. I remained hid."

"D'they saw you dig. D'that saved your life (srpt), and-zz mine too."

"And you think Toak killed the scout?" asked Anna.

"Toak? What-zz do you know about him d'that I didn't tell-zz you? Our guards would have told me if one of d'them did it. Yes, it was Toak, and it happened before we came in d'the area. D'the Blackfoot were waiting for us when-zz Toak must have stumbled onto one."

"So Toak was your partner? What happened between him and you?"

"Toak left me-zz for dead."

"And what happened?"

"I didn't-zz die (srpt). D'that happens-zz a lot."

"Where is he now?"

"He's close. He is Indian number five-zz. He doesn't ride-zz d'the compass points-zz (srpt). His birth nation is at war with-zz d'the Blackfoot."

"Don't you want to meet up with him?"

"D'that's-zz complicated, Anna. We need-zz to get going (srpt). I will fetch d'the laundry. Can you put-zz away breakfast?"

==0==

Mr. Franklin followed Anna's instructions with true delight. Together they had devised a plan, a legacy will, by which her most faithful employees were secretly rewarded. Mr. Franklin arranged for proxies to visit the two dozen of Anna's favorite former workers with conditional offers. Anna instructed that none of them would receive a windfall, but each to be presented with a lucrative opportunity if they accepted certain risks and invested some of their own resources. Mr. Franklin didn't mention the details to Anna on how he would distribute the propositions before she left. He thought it ironic that local deacons would help. No one would suspect Anna as the mortal source.

The mute miner was allowed to purchase the claim and mineral rights for fifty cents on the dollar if he was willing to sign a bank note. Xue was allowed the choice to become a partner with the manager at the cleaners or a loan for fare to California and a sum to help start a business there. Anna's faithful pharmacist was given a scholarship to cover half the cost to go to school in Saint Louis to get a real diploma (unlike the questionable one that was hung in the store).

==0==

285

Anna still had much on her mind that morning. So much had happened in the last three weeks that she wondered if she could keep this pace up. "Do you ever long for a normal life, Bibb?"

Bibb really didn't want to talk, but she eventually shamed him into it. She reminded him, in fact several times, that it wasn't kind to respond to her with a silent ugly face. He tried to smile but obviously failed. She said it wasn't working and to try harder. Bibb eventually mumbled that there was no quota of "normal" remaining for him on any ledger.

"Spit it out, Bibb. How is anybody supposed to understand your mumbling rumblings?"

"Normal simple living stopped for me-zz d'the day Judge Church hung my brother (srpt) for my despicable crimes. D'that ain't the worst of it (srpt). I really would-zz like to have a boring life too, but any hope-zz of boring stopped d'the day I-zz realized another man had died in my place (srpt) for all my other crimes. I used to call myself lucky (srpt). I'm not lucky. I'm not lucky at all (srpt). D'the d'things d'that happen to me-zz stopped being accidents."

"Was that the day Humbird came into your life?"

"She didn't come into my life (srpt). She ripped into it with a wood maul and hot smithy's pliers. No, Anna, come to d'think of it, d'that's not true (srpt). D'the first time I met d'that beauty I was in jail. D'that night she forgave me (srpt) for murdering her husband."

"Bibb, I thought you gave up lying."

"You're right, Anna. I only shot my brother while he slept (srpt). I also shot d'the horse I stole, and he was accused and tried for d'that crime. The hangman finished what I started (srpt). My brother Tommy was-zz convicted for horse thieving and my-zz other crimes (srpt), like bank robbing."

"Liar! How can you tell me such things? Just when I started to trust you, you start in with this foolishness! Now try to tell me the truth, if you can. The newspaper quoted you saying that this Humbird was mean and ugly. I think you actually said 'the meanest and the ugliest.' You just told me she was a beauty. Come clean, Bibb. Is she attractive or not? Did you lie to the newspaper reporters, or are you lying to me?"

"I guess I lied to both. Humbird is not a pretty woman (srpt). She bears d'the permanent blemishes of a dreadful childhood disease (srpt) d'that killed her father, and almost killed her. Personally, I hope-zz d'that my disfigurement doesn't make somebody like me ugly forever (srpt) like it did for her. What do you d'think, Anna?"

"I think you're trying to change the subject, Bibb."

"No, I'm trying to have a conversation with you instead of an inquisition (srpt). In a real conversation both participants get-zz to ask questions."

"Nice try, big boy, now tell me, is Humbird attractive?"

"If we make it to Fort Rice, you can judge d'that for yourself (srpt). If we don't make Fort Rice, d'the fact she is ugly or not really doesn't matter one grain of rice (srpt). Anna, let's not talk about my past (srpt), and let's not talk about Humbird. I prayed d'that never again I'd say one mean d'thing to or about d'that woman, and d'the best way to do d'that is to d'think about something else."

"So you do think she is attractive. I thought so."

"Stop it, Anna."

"Why would you pray for that, Bibb? I bet you caused all heaven to burst out laughing when such a liar like you would make such a request."

"How did you know?" asked Bibb, sounding very serious.

"You're lying again, Bibb. Stop it!"

"I'm not lying, Anna (srpt). I got two specific answers to d'that prayer. Neither was something I was expecting."

"God doesn't answer specific prayers, Bibb."

"I would call you-zz a fool, but d'that would be unkind (srpt). To boast d'that you know all what God does and doesn't do, and d'then which prayers He answers and which ones He doesn't (srpt), and how specific or general His answers are, you-zz would have to be (srpt) all knowing, all seeing, and everywhere all at once (srpt). Here you sit on a buckboard in d'the middle of Montana telling me God doesn't exist. At d'the same time you are telling me (srpt) you are greater in wisdom and knowledge and power d'than d'the very d'thing you are trying to deny. Nice try, big girl (srpt). From your boast, a really really really big girl."

"That was unkind, Bibb."

"I'm sorry, Anna (srpt). Now you see d'the tortured world I live in. I so want d'there not to be a God, but He doesn't give me-zz d'that choice anymore. I can't rationalize God away (srpt). I can't deny all d'the answered prayers or all d'the coincidences d'that have kept me alive (srpt). I can't deny d'the majesty of d'the starry hosts we see-zz above us at night no better d'than I can pretend away d'that gnawing newborn conscience He stuck-zz inside of me (srpt). I am without rest (srpt). I am d'the most miserable of souls. I so want to live life my way, but d'that is no longer possible (srpt). I will never have a day of peace again."

"Is that why you looked at me funny when I mentioned peace the other night? Never mind. So what did you have the audacity to ask this starry newborn conscience of yours?"

"I asked God why he made Humbird so ugly (srpt)."

"That is not a prayer. That is a question. God doesn't answer questions. And why...?"

He abruptly cut her off. "I forgot-zz you knew everything, big girl. Why are you asking me questions if you know-zz more d'than God knows?"

"Bibb, learn this and learn this quick. Given a choice, it is better to be kind than right, and right now you are being neither. You must cease being both mean and unkind. Stop it, Bibb."

"I'm sorry. I will start-zz over. God answered d'that question by showing me d'that Humbird is no longer d'the ugliest person I know."

"And who is that? Are you agreeing with that Indian matron? You are being mean, unkind, and rude, on top of being insulting!"

"Anna, stop it! You weren't d'the one shot in d'the face! God's answer to my prayer was (srpt) for me to understand what she has suffered all her life! It's not fun being marred (srpt). It's not fun to be the butt of jokes (srpt). It's not fun wondering if anybody could ever love you (srpt). Just stop it, will you! I'm not sure what hurts more (srpt). D'the physical pain of hot lead through my lips (srpt), or a verbal knife to d'the heart. At least d'the doc could drug me up with d'the head wound (srpt). I know how Humbird feels now, and I'm very ashamed for saying so many cruel d'things about her."

"Tommy…" She almost got out her next words.

"What, Anna?" Bibb rudely yelled back interrupting her next thought. "What could you add to improve on silence? Nothing! Just shut your mouth and be quiet." Tommy was really irked and tired of the accusations and questions that appeased her vanity.

"Okay," replied Anna ignoring his outburst and poised to retake the offensive, "Let's pretend I believe you and you take back all those mean things you just said. What was the second prayer?"

"I asked to stop being a mean, selfish, murdering liar. I asked God (srpt) to make me into something honorable."

"Well you certainly proved God wasn't up to that task just now! What circus trick were you expecting for him to perform for that to happen?"

"Anna, it is not a circus trick d'that He is going to do (srpt). It's a miracle He's already done."

"When? Where?"

"When-zz Bes made a hot bowl of soup in her kitchen two weeks ago Tuesday."

"That makes no sense, Bibb."

"You just proved my point. D'that was no circus trick, and you ain't no clown."

"Bibb, you are talking nonsense. Tell me your point plain."

"Anna, if you were God, and d'this no good reprobate honestly asked to have his life changed for-zz d'the better, what would you do to make sure it happened?"

"Are you saying he would have a woman deliver hot soup to the wrong room of a hotel?"

Mentioning without prompting the wrong room supported a notion that Bibb had long suspected. "And, if you were God, and some rich widow cried out d'that she wanted to go home and start her life over (srpt), what would you-zz do to make sure d'that happened?"

"Make sure Bes had the soup ready on time?" Anna said sarcastically. "Goodness gracious, Bibb, you are seeing too much much in this too much much."

"Anna, have you-zz seen a change in me?"

"Let's drop this topic for now, Tommy. You are still a no good, thieving, lying outlaw."

"I know."

"And me? What are you implying about me? You and your sanctimonious theory of yours?" She was sorry she asked. In her spite those questions came out too quickly, as if daring that man to say something ugly.

Bibb sighed before speaking. "Since you asked…Vain as a peacock, Anna. Vain as a peacock."

Anna remained silent over the next hour. Bibb had laid out the case, like it or not, that God gave them to each other. The very thought that God would dare bring a man into her life angered her. She wanted nothing to do with men – she had already been hurt too much. Bibb's hypothesis that God was answering two prayers at once was at first stupid to Anna. Then it was plausible. Then it was possible. Then it was probable. She reset that thinking by speaking to herself that Bibb was lying in order to gain control over her and her emotions. She never prayed to go home or have a family; she had kept that very much to herself. Bibb never prayed for a bullet to go through his mouth either… Her inner thoughts were boiling over. "Maybe God doesn't wait around for us to pray for what we need. No… this is all too silly. There is no grand orchestrator of lives and events… I dislike uncertainty as much as things outside of my control. I must control myself, and I must control that outlaw. I can do this. I will prevail!"

During that same hour while Anna was simmering in her own juices, Bibb was relishing the fresh air as well as enjoying the quiet. Nothing was bothering him. He had said his peace and was glad he did. He was sad that he had been somewhat unkind to Anna, but he got over it. That extraction of shame took nine seconds short of ten. It was a beautiful morning.

==0==

Around noon Anna and Bibb happened upon a clear stream and a good place to rest the horses once on the other side. The conversation from the morning had blown over and they appeared to be back to being kind once again. Anna knew that this was a good time to count Indians, and she was not disappointed. She saw four of the five.

"Bibb, have you ever thought about going out west? I have considered it. I have heard that California is full of opportunity."

Bibb looked at her for a moment and then returned to checking the shoes on the horses. She could see that he was thinking. Many of the questions she asked caused him irritation, especially today. Actually it might have been the tone of her questions that irritated him so. This softy spoken question did not seem to be like the others, yet he did not reply.

Anna actually thought that Bibb was preparing a well-rehearsed answer for her. What was actually on his mind had nothing to do with her question. He was glad his own clothes were clean and all of them in his sack again and, more important, she was wearing her dress. He hated the thought of her sweating inside of his clothes. He definitely wanted to avoid any ridicule that would certainly follow if he was ever caught in a shirt that had been pooched out.

"Bibb, why won't you answer me? I know you heard me. You gave me your ear at the altar. I guess when I had the chance I should have claimed your mouth for my own too. Is it because it hurts to talk, or does it hurt more to dream?"

Bibb laughed to himself. Why was she bringing up the altar? That seemed to be the farthest thing from her mind an hour ago. "Nothin'-zz to dream-zz. I was d'there."

"When were you in California? Where did you go? What did you see?"

"Greed and killing (srpt). You asked-zz me d'the easy question. D'the hard question is why I-zz came back."

"How about you answering the question I asked?"

"I did-zz. I answered d'the d'third one."

"Tommy, the visible, not the invisible! I want to know what you saw before you pass judgment on what you saw. I want to know where you went before you tell me about what you perceived was there. *When* has a date associated with it, not some character assessment. Tommy, I am not asking this to be mean, find fault, or fill the air with noise. Context before content, analysis, and opinion please. Remember that I committed to be kind too. I want to know to whom I'm being kind to."

"Fair enough-zz."

Anna waited for a few minutes, distracted by a bird that decided to perch on the back of Bibb's horse. It was a mocking bird and began to look surprisingly content. Bibb pulled his rifle out.

"Don't kill it! It's meaning you no harm!"

Bibb responded, "Sh-hhh" and motioned with his hand for her not to talk. Instinctively she started to look around. There was something other than the bird that spooked the spook.

"In the wagon, Anna. Look-zz forward. We need-zz to leave now."

Ten minutes went by as Bibb continued to guide the wagon up the scant evidence of a wagon trail. He was on alert, but very calm often checking to his left and right. He purposely guided the wagon to a higher point where he would have a complete view of his surroundings. He got out of the wagon and retightened their load, but also taking the opportunity for a complete scan of the horizons. "Stretch, Anna, please-zz."

She got out and walked away from the wagon to a respectable distance. She kept her eyes open to see what Bibb was trying to see. She again saw two separate Indians, one to the north and one to the west. She decided to let Tommy worry about them. A minute later came Tommy's "Press on!"

One other thing she did not have to worry about anymore was her new dress becoming dirty. What she wondered about now was if that patchwork of frayed threads would ever survive a real cleaning. The dress she was wearing was quite revealing even by Deadwood standards, well beyond by what was seen in the brothels. It came down to mid-neck and covered to mid-thigh. Depending on the one adorned in it, the dress allowed for displaying ample cleavage, a considerable problem for one as endowed as Anna. There were no holes worn through the dress, but acceptable portions of it were so thin as to become semitransparent. There was very little holding it together.

Along with the dress she wore the moccasins given to her. Everything else, except papers and heirlooms (less the scissors), was left at the Indian camp; no socks, no hats, nothing. She had never been more grateful for anything as much as the dirty old blanket that they also provided her. It came in handy to keep her warm and keep Bibb from becoming distracted.

The Deadwood mansion's overflowing closets had never given her the same satisfaction than the wardrobe she now possessed. The thought of providing those Lakota women something… anything… everything… warmed her heart to near bursting. She was thoroughly astonished at the feelings she was experiencing. She had always hoarded clothes in Deadwood and it bothered her greatly when another woman's fashions outshined hers. In Deadwood (and to the Anna of a month ago) this dress would have had no worth.

That last thought haunted her as they rode across the endless prairie. This was the first dress she had worn in her adult life that she did not buy. It was without price to her, and she laughed to herself when she deduced by reversing the syntax that this barely more than a green rag was her first priceless dress. The next thought was worse than the first. This was no Indian dress, and there was a strong possibility that the dress's previous owner lost her life when she lost her dress; a priceless price indeed. "No, no, no," she said to herself. "The dress belonged to a princess and a member of royalty." The next thought put a lie to that. No princess would ever subject herself to such a lowly estate by wearing such a rag. Finally she faced the fact that there was a princess in it now; the medicine man said so. Such a mystery!

Everything was so different; her heart said so. As proof she remembered that every woman in that village reverenced the matron's gift when she received it. As more proof her teepee widows made sure that it was worn at the dawn ceremony, and only to be put on after she was cleaned and received her ceremonial paint. The widows had insisted, and there must have been a reason.

The dress was truly special. Even if it was an old dress wrapped in a stinky blanket, for the first time in her life Anna felt full contentment with her attire. She was no longer an ugly woman in nice clothes. She was enjoying being a nice woman in ugly clothes. The words erupting from her heart once again overwhelmed her: "I feel clean! I feel free!"

The quiet she suffered earlier that morning gave her time to think as they rode silently across the plains. Her first thought was that she had lived this many years and never saw the needs of others. How much good she could have done for those without proper raiment in Deadwood if she would have just noticed them! She saw, but never took the time to really see them. To her the poor were only slow paying on-credit customers.

Anna's second thought was worse. All those slow payers definitely saw her and what she was wearing. She admitted to herself that they never wished to be like her (as she had previously assumed in her vanity) but they simply only wanted to be warm. How they must have resented her. She actually thought she was doing them a favor by setting the fashion standard. What they saw was the flaunting of her wealth in their faces. How those poor mothers with scantily dressed children must have loathed her for her callous spirit.

Anna reflected that she had no adopted sisters to share her soul with in Deadwood. Then she thought back to the Indian camp. What a change! How she loved those shortest hours of her life! In a way, they were the only hours of her life... real life. She lamented how much of life had passed by her since she moved from Saint Louis, strangely enough, to find life.

She soon got over those thoughts replacing them with something more pleasant. She turned her musing to laughing to herself at the freedom she had from not being encumbered with so many layers of fabric. She had learned much about unbound living from the Indian widows!

She laughed again to herself as she thought why civilized women wore so many layers of clothes. First in her mind, because it was her mind, was that the purpose of clothes was to be fully elegant and attractive, especially to men. She also concluded that reason was a dead issue with the scrambled-brain man-creature that rode next to her. That led her to her second thought, and that the clothes were a layer of protection from men with immoral intentions. Bibb, the deadly dean of depravity, (that thought tickled as she thought of the alliteration), did not even raise his one remaining eyelash over such concerns. In fact, the recent bruises on his chest betrayed the fact that Big Chief Bibb of the Broken Belly was more scared of her touch than she was of his.

At the next stop Anna's thoughts became more pragmatic. As Anna headed back towards the wagon she spoke to herself again, "Enough of this silliness. Clothes were not to keep men close; they were not to keep men away; but simply to modestly protect people from the environment. She sure wished she had a hat right now. Clothes were also worn to help keep their bodies clean, and that was a growing problem. Until they arrived in Miles City there would be no changing her situation, and that was still days away.

She concluded Bibb didn't care two figs about clothes and probably never thought more than ten seconds about it. Men miss out on a lot of important thinking, especially the one she was with. They must think about something. They must care about some things too. All these thoughts were interrupted when she saw Bibb return to his seat in the wagon. It was time to drive on. "Load up!"

"Load up, Press on," she muttered to herself. "Press on" is what that man cares about.

==0==

At mid-afternoon a sprinkle of rain began to fall. She quickly put away the blanket to keep it dry for later. Mile after mile they drove on. They both became soaked from riding for over an hour in an unseasonably warm rain. It wasn't a stinging rain; actually it was quite refreshing. But the moist wind blowing strongly from behind them was an omen of what was coming.

Of the many perils on the plains Bibb feared hail the most. The smell of such a storm was in the air and worse, felt in his knees. Bibb took comfort in the words he remembered that the young Anna from Miles City had told him while he was recovering. She said that fear was like giving the devil permission to have that demon bring your fear upon you. She read him a story in the book about a man named Job that had his fears come upon him, and his case turned more pitiful with each page she read. She seemed serious but he discounted her words deeply back then. But now was now, and right now Bibb was carefully watching a wall of blue bellied white topped storms building in the western sky moving in their direction. Bibb wanted no part of pitiful calamity that Job brought upon himself by worrying. With a flick of the reins Bibb urged his horses into a trot.

The fear still lingered. Actually it grew as the western horizon filled. Bibb eventually told the varmint that he was deeply concerned for his own, his escorts, and his Anna's safety. Those weasel words fooled nobody but himself, and that feeble attempt at masking his fear failed too. Bibb eventually told God that he hated hail and asked none of it would come their way.

Later that afternoon Bibb found the shelter he was looking for. Relieved, he rounded up some wood to start a fire in the stove while Anna brought the food inside the one room cabin. There was no sense in heading out again today even if the storm passed. Guessing that the rain was not going to stop before dark, Bibb searched for and found nearby the large flowing spring he had remembered. Actually Bibb's horse had the better memory. It walked right to it.

While Bibb was gone Anna found some dry clothes in Bibb's saddle bag and helped herself to them. When Bibb returned he found the dress hanging outside in the sprinkles and he found her inside cleaning and organizing their stuff. On the only flat surface in the shelter there was served a prepared supper: another dose of HT, B & J, with some aged wolf.

"D'thank you-zz, Anna. You read-zz my mind well."

"That you are hungry, or something else."

"Yes'um."

"Yes'um what? Which is it, Tommy?"

"First is d'the vittles. Second is-zz d'the something else (srpt). I don't want-zz you to wear d'that dress again until we-zz get near Miles City. Please don't."

"What's wrong with the dress, Bibb?"

"Nothin-nnn-nnn."

"Tommy..." she snapped as if it was an abbreviated command to confess.

Bibb stumbled around, desperately looking for something to occupy his hands. He grabbed a couple pieces of jerky and started towards the exit of the shelter.

"Bibb, I asked you a question."

He turned. Instead of locking onto her eyes, which had become his custom, he never raised his chin and looked at the floor in the general direction of her feet. "Anna, it's-zz what-zz in it... d'that's-zz... never mind-zz. I'm going to tends-zz to d'the horses. I can't fault you-zz for putting on something dry."

Before she could respond he was outside back in the rain. Both knew the only clothes that were dry were Bibb's. She had nothing else.

Anna decided that Bibb was washing up or something else important to him to explain his delayed return. She kindled a fire, something Bibb said he liked to do, and started to re-cook the remaining wolf meat. She decided an hour later that Bibb was not delayed by something, but by anything.

Anna put on her wet dress again (she didn't want to get his dry clothes wet), and went to look for Bibb. He was found down by the horses sharpening his ax.

"Bibb, come in and eat. Dinner is getting cold."

Bibb did not answer, but he did slightly turn his head to acknowledge her presence. He returned to his whetstone and blade. Anna came and sat down on a log next to the one he was sitting on. "Bibb, we have to talk."

"About what-zz?"

"Me, you, and the rabbits."

"Talk."

"Bibb, there is no such thing as two rabbits. You either have one or you have a hundred."

"I'm listening."

"Let's be kind to each other. But let's be kind beyond what the eye may see. Let's be kind to our heads and our hearts. I cannot help the body I am stuffed into, and you cannot help the body you are left with. Let us both look past that. You have acknowledged that I can catch your eye, and I now realize my vanity has been satisfied at your expense."

"You're admitting vanity?" responded Bibb, but in a nice way.

"Vanity is a wretched thing Bibb, and I am sorry I have put thoughts into your head that cannot be rightly satisfied. What I used as a weapon against my husband – teasing and then denial – lead to two ruined lives. The only adult relationship I ever had in my life I choked to death with pride and vanity. I want to run away from those appalling memories in hope to build new and real relationships based on trust, love, respect, and admiration."

"Anybody in mind? You Anna women never stop planning ahead. Who are you d'thinking of?"

"No Bibb, I am talking about me in particular and you are so wrong to lump me in with other women you can't deal with. And it is so wrong that when I finally confess a personal weakness to you that you assume every woman named Anna has a similar weakness. You listen good to me right now, Tommy. You know by our mutual pledge why I am traveling with you to Fort Rice. I long for a clean sheet of paper to rewrite my life on. I wanted life to start over from the moment we left and only to remember my horrid past as something never to repeat. I confess that today I degenerated back into my past, not learning from my own history. Do you understand what I am saying?"

Bibb looked up at her eyes, and then returned to sharpening his ax... again.

"Tommy, say something."

"Anna," and Bibb paused, "We-zz need-zz to be a pair of one rabbits. D'this one rabbit will keep his pledge to d'the other one rabbit-zz."

"Tommy, I too pledge to keep my one rabbit business to my one rabbit self. That I promise. And the commitment I made to you at the altar also remains intact. But I need your help, Tommy."

"With what-zz?"

"I need to wear your clothes until we get to Miles City. May I wear them?"

"I said 'Yes' before, and I say 'Yes' again. And yes, d'that will help me-zz with my two rabbits problem. But it won't fix it-zz. I can't fix me-zz."

"Bibb, you're not making sense. Just listen to your conscience and you will be okay."

"Nope. Won't work. My conscience is easily bullied by-zz my will (srpt). It's worse d'than dead. It's weak (srpt). I wish it was-zz dead so I-zz have an excuse. My will sometimes likes-zz being bad, and sometimes-zz I don't have-zz to even d'think about-zz being bad (srpt). I just does-zz it. I just can't fix-zz me (srpt). You said if I-zz touch you wrong you-zz would kill me with my ax. I want to make sure-zz d'the ax is sharp. A dull ax don't kill-zz, but maims (srpt). I'm tired of maimed-zz."

"Aren't you being over dramatic here, Bibb? Aren't you forgetting that down deep inside of you, you are good?"

"I used to-zz d'think d'that, but it was a lie. I am real good at lying (srpt), and d'thinking d'that I was good in my core was a whopper. It's worse now-zz d'than when we-zz were in Deadwood. You was-zz so easy to hate d'there. D'this kindness promise is-zz d'the problem."

"You hated me? Why?"

Bibb didn't answer immediately. He wanted to let her form her own answers. "D'that's all different now. I figure only Humbird is keeping me-zz alive now."

"Humbird? What does she have to do with the here and now?"

"Humbird has-zz d'the fear of being replaced (srpt). She gets jealous and mad over anybody who's weaseling away somebody's heart out from her hands-zz (srpt). She hates-zz me, but hate-zz me with somebody else worse. She would kill you dead if she saw you now (srpt). You-zz have changed. I have-zz such a hard time hating you now (srpt). If I stop hating you, d'then she-zz would know-zz it and kill you dead (srpt). I would rather die d'than have you hurt-zz over her jealous rage."

"Good, then it is agreed. If you just keep hating me we will do just fine. I will just keep hating you too. You will be so surprised how kind I can act while hating somebody. I have had a lot of practice at that." Anna got up and stood behind Bibb. "Let's get dry and eat."

"Anna, my conscience says-zz d'that's a good plan. D'the problem isn't my-zz conscience. It's-zz my will (srpt). I am done with-zz hating. Hating is like being lost in-zz a cave. I want-zz to be new."

"If you can't behave because you are weak, then behave out of your fear of Madame Humbird. A little fear isn't so bad. In this case, a lot of fear isn't so bad either. Bibb, sometimes I think you think too much."

"Ha! I d'think too little! Or maybe I d'think too-zz much about d'the wrong d'things."

"Like what? Or shouldn't I ask?" She watched the man's countenance sober into silence.

"I have a serious question for you-zz, Anna (srpt). I'm not sure about-zz d'this and-zz please don't be-zz offended by my-zz asking, but I gotta' know. Anna, I know-zz what touching you wrong is, but what would be touching you-zz right be?" Anna could tell by his softer speech the man was bent over backwards with frustration, and had just delivered an honest question.

Anna took the step towards him from behind and laid her wet hand on his shoulder. "It depends on the purpose, Bibb. There were no rabbits in our teepee.

From now on, if we see one, let's see who can kill it first. That doesn't mean we don't touch. I cannot keep my pledge for your healing without touching you. We need not be afraid of touching each other. If we commit to keep the bunnies out of our yard, I will have no fear of you, you will have no fear of me, and neither will have any fear of any bunny business. Agreed?"

"Anna, I-zz understand what you're saying (srpt), but-zz it just ain't helping my mind."

She got very quiet and then came even closer behind him. In a soft whisper barely audible to even herself she asked in his good ear, "Then what does the varmint say, Bibb?"

"Varmint?" Bibb was alarmed by her question, stood, and turned looking towards her, almost in shock. "What does-zz d'that have to do-zz with-zz anything?"

"Bibb, I know your deepest secret. I did not believe what I was told at first, but now I know it is true. It is the truest thing I know."

"What-zz?"

"Sit down, Bibb. Keep sharpening your ax if that comforts you. Your secret is safe with me."

Bibb complied, still visibly undone, and now determined not to speak again. Once he sat down with his back towards her, Anna drew close to his good ear again.

"The varmint is good and only good, isn't it?" She paused a second and then said, "I am this close, but the varmint is closer." She then bit his ear gently.

Bibb turned and looked at her again. For just a second there was more than just a twinkle in her eyes, leaving Bibb even more confused. She gave him no chance to respond.

"Tommy, you finish sharpening your ax and then come up for supper. I'm going to quick change out of this dress. I will have some hot soup and dry clothes ready for you when you get up to the shelter. Give me about ten minutes. Bring some more wood, okay?"

"Yes-zz'mmm, I will." They looked at each other like they never had before. They were both scared, both happy, and both feeling more married than married people.

==0==

All the plans that Anna had thought about walking back to the shelter were soon altered. Upon her arrival at the shelter she found a horse outside and an Indian inside. Two months ago she would have been terrified walking into that situation. She spoke at the man with the only words of greeting to a man she knew in his tongue and then asked a single question, "Bibb?"

The scout affirmed that was his desire and she motioned for him to come with her. He followed her down to where Bibb was collecting wood. As they walked, she longed to get out of that dress and into some dry clothes. The weather seemed to be getting worse as the day was slipping away. The wind rushing into the storm was now strong enough to make it hard to hear each other. Fortunately the lightning was still far to the west. It would not be long before a serious storm hit.

As Bibb and the scout were discussing something, she knew not what, she could not help to think that her plans for the evening were now scattered to the horizons. Thousands of possible situations were swirling in her mind about the implication of this visit. Worse, she started to feel guilty when she caught herself thinking so selfishly.

By intuition Anna deduced that the men were discussing the strong storm moving in their direction. Bibb and the scout seemed to make an agreement and the Indian took off in a full run.

"Did you invite him to join us in our shelter?" asked Anna.

"So you understand-zz d'their language now, Anna? I'm proud-zz of you (srpt). He just left to signal d'the other d'three. He was more concerned about-zz d'their horses (srpt). D'they will be acting spooky if d'that weather delivers-zz what it looks like it's promising."

"Aren't there five Indians without shelter?"

"D'the other one will be-zz asked, but he will-zz not come."

"How do you know?"

"Redbird." Bibb paused and realized that Anna did not know about Redbird. "Anna, d'the fifth Indian's wife is named Redbird (srpt). D'that man's child and its mother live on my farm in Fort Rice. He wants to see-zz d'them again in d'this life."

"Would you kill him? Or them? Bibb, what kind of monster are you?" She meant to say "man" rather than "monster." She so wanted to unlearn her habit of accusing first and thinking second.

Bibb looked at her eyes and decided to overlook the insult. "I don't kill-zz people on purpose. Anna, of all d'those d'that died I-zz only murdered two... Maybe three. I don't-zz count no more."

"So they just fall over dead when you show up? Bibb, come clean. Did you kill all the others by accident? Did you notch your ax each time by accident too? You scare me, Tommy."

"D'they meet me, d'they talk big, and-zz d'then d'they call-zz me out into d'the street, Anna. Same story, different details-zz, same outcome (srpt). D'the ones I-zz murdered happened different. D'they never saw-zz d'their death coming (srpt). I feel really bad about-zz d'them. Anna, you look wet and-zz cold. Go up to-zz d'the shelter (srpt) and put-zz on dry clothes. It will-zz be a long night."

==0==

Anna knew enough of their tongue to welcome the scouts as they arrived. Bibb had them unload their burdens inside the shelter and then led the scouts down to the spring to corral their mounts with the other horses. Anna cooked some remaining meat, along with snake soup. She also threw into the pot the roots that Bibb and the scouts had found.

Dinner was strangely lonely for Anna. Much was said spoken between the men. She was not even noticed as if she was a second class citizen. Ironically, she was the only citizen there.

To pass the time and to make herself useful while they talked, Anna boiled up some water to make sassafras tea. She brought it to Bibb who offered to share to communal cup. They only packed one pot and cup for the trip.

It felt so strange to Anna to remain quiet, but she knew better than to interrupt. She also felt strange wearing Bibb's dry clothes; certainly they were talking about that scandal. Or maybe not. Her vanity was showing up again in her thinking. She remembered how much attention the men showed the women back at the Indian village. It was the same amount she was receiving now: none.

She secretly hoped in their conversations that they would tell Bibb about Indian number five. Over time Anna changed her mind. "Why should I care?" she asked herself, as she was experiencing the strange new world of self-examination. Then an answer came to her mind she didn't want to accept: Bibb was becoming important to her. Why else would a threat to him be a threat to her?

All the conversations abruptly ended with a very bright snap and crackle of light immediately followed by a thunder clap so loud that could be felt. The storm had arrived. The men did not think it strange that Bibb got up and headed out into the weather, but Anna was caught unawares and was distressed. She got up too and came over to Bibb before he was able to leave.

"Don't leave me here with them, Bibb. I don't feel safe. I want to go where you are going."

"I'm going to stay-zz with d'the horses, Anna. You'll-zz be okay."

"Bibb, they won't care that you are my man if you are gone. There is no chief here to make sure they behave like they did in the village."

"What makes you-zz d'think I will behave better d'than d'them (srpt)? Anna, you stay here and stay dry. D'they won't even notice you."

"Bibb, I want to be with you. I don't want to be alone with them. And what about the other Indian? Tell them something why I have to go with you. Bibb, honestly… please. There is something in all this that makes me nervous. Please? Look at them. They are just filthy from several days of dust. Tell them I am volunteering to do their laundry or something."

"You would do-zz d'that?"

"To be near you, yes. Yes I would. Their women showed me how, and the outflow of the spring has plenty of clean water." Her softened words received no recognition from any other except Bibb.

"You would really do-zz d'that?"

"Bibb, these men have risked their lives to protect us. You made me promise to be kind. It is okay for me to be kind to somebody other than you, yes?"

"Anna…"

"Well, then, go tell them. I will change back into my wet dress. You gather up their clothes and let's be off."

==0==

For the next four hours Bibb stayed down by the half a dozen horses to keep them calm. He rubbed each one of them down purposely spending time calmly talking with them. Anna was perplexed that a murdering, lying, thieving outlaw could comfort animals – even during thunderstorms.

At one point Bibb left the corral and neared the place where Anna was washing their clothes along with the Indian's. She heard his steps and yelled at him telling him he should have announced his arrival. She quickly hid behind a bush and shooed him away.

Bibb forgot what he was going to tell Anna as he returned to the sanctuary of the corral. It didn't matter if he remembered why or not; he wasn't going back there for a second dose of that noisy treatment! He was quite embarrassed over the whole incident and wondered how he was ever going to explain himself to her. He thought he should have seen it coming… the varmint always did.

Bibb told the horses his frustrations. Bibb forgot that God had developed a very nasty habit of overhearing all his conversations, especially when he promised something (like what he had committed earlier to Anna.) It wouldn't be long after he personally committed to something that he would be tested… just the length of time it took to be distracted by something else, and then would come the slap in the face. Each of these varmint sponsored tests was to see if he really meant what he previously said. It was emotionally painful – and wearisome – as if the critter never slept.

Anna of Miles City, that sweet young girl with blonde hair, failed to tell him about the varmint. The grand bargain seemed too good to be true. Why didn't she ever complain about varmint biting her? Maybe it had. Anna never lied, nor was she a whiner. Nobody can tell all the details up front. But this small detail… all those slaps… all those tests. Even a non-whiner would say something.

Bibb felt ashamed. This thinking was wrongly finding fault in that decent Anna-girl of Miles City. She didn't do anything, no nothing wrong never ever. The varmint ain't one of her pets – heavens no – it ain't no tamed varmint of nobody no how never

ever. Bibb was further ashamed that he didn't see the recent test coming. He should have known that his Anna would not be decent while washing the clothes. The woman deserved some privacy after putting up with him all day.

About an hour later Anna returned to the corral with her arms full of laundry. "Bibb, the storm is over. Help me carry these back up to the shelter. We can hang this stuff up to dry over the fire."

Bibb waited for the hammer to fall, but it did not. He knew one thing for sure: he wasn't going to bring up the river incident. Bibb decided to quickly start the conversation on something practical. "We can use my-zz whip and d'the wagon reins to hang d'them on once we get d'this laundry inside the shack. It won't-zz take me long to fetch 'em. I'll meet you up d'there directly."

Anna chose to wait outside the shack for Bibb. When they entered the dark shelter together they discovered all the men soundly asleep. As quietly as possible Bibb strung up the leather and rope he brought with him. Likewise Anna threw the wrung out damp clothes over the top of them to dry. Bibb tended to the fire and made sure the flue was open properly to let it burn slow and hot.

Anna walked over to Bibb and whispered in his ear. "You take off those wet clothes and hand them to me. Then go dry off, climb into the sack, and shut your eyes."

Bibb thought this was in a small way her response to the earlier river incident. Too busy thinking instead of doing, Bibb hesitated. She repeated her instructions, still thinking him not moving fast enough. She approached him and started to unbutton his shirt and then handed him a rag to dry himself off with. "Now scoot! I will follow shortly."

There was no need to keep a guard. The storm was over with dawn not far away, and those scouts needed the rest. She issued her last instructions to her patient, "Those boys think we are married and I'm not going to give them any clues to make them think different. What don't you understand about my telling you to 'scoot'?"

Bibb followed her last instruction without hesitation, not because she commanded him but because he was too tired not too. He laughed to himself. She was in charge of keeping him alive, but her leash on him was short and tight. With her, there were no excuses or second chances allowed, and being in close proximity was no excuse for an accidental oops. If he faulted an iota in his sleep he would be prematurely showing up in a sliced and diced condition at God's Judgment Hall.

About five minutes later a warm body slipped in behind Bibb wrapping her arms around him. He was too scared to speak, but she wasn't. She whispered in his good ear, "Good night, my man. Don't you even think about even twitching your toe, or anything else." As a bonus she softly bit his ear but not enough for him to notice. The nibble was a reminder for her, not him. Even if her man couldn't enjoy some of the simple benefits of being fully married, she decided she wasn't going to be denied. What he did not know would not hurt him. They weren't one nor would they be, but they were an *us*, and being a part of an *us* is what she secretly craved more than anything else in life.

Strangely, as a kindred spirit, Bibb was thinking an identical thought. He prayed that the varmint would dispatch immediately and permanently any bunnies that might come within twenty miles of the camp. He didn't have to give it another thought, either the varmint answered the request or he was too tired to care. As if a gift of mercy from his suffering and any possible improper thoughts, Bibb was deep in sleep within seconds of his request. His pawed benefactor graciously granted him a blessed pain-free rest.

Anna lay happy, very happy. "Good and Proper" did have its benefits. There was a mystery and intrigue in this moment, but absolutely no shame. Yet the longer she thought about her innermost secret delights being satisfied the more remorse entered into her thoughts. She began to regret deeply her misplaced anger with the Franklins and the preacher. "I really don't have a reason to hate them," her heart spoke to her gently. "Momma and daddy Franklin really do love me. I didn't know it two days ago, but I know it now." She had to admit that "Good and Proper" was truly good and proper.

She squeezed her man and got an unexpected moan. She inadvertently may have hurt him again. Her mind wandered more as the dainty remaining rain was calling her further into sleep. She thought if there was ever a sign from heaven that moan would have been it. She needed to treat the man with kid gloves physically and not to tempt the man mentally. Her own spirit groaned inside of her, "Help me God to know how to love your man..." Her last thought was that she might have uttered a prayer but before a protest could be mounted she was gone... Her prayer, even if it was against her will, was rewarded with a glorious and peaceful sleep. She was gone... a deep sleep that took her down to the bottom of the ocean.

Friday, October 14, 1887

Fifth day from teepee town. My dress was fire-dried when I woke this morning. After breakfast I packed it away in my trunk. I was certainly surprised when I opened my luggage. The Indian women had put a small amount of a dried food I liked where my clothes were once packed. How sweet of them! There was also a feather. I am quite sure it was not meant for me. No Lakota style pajamas in there... That's a good thing given Bibb's weak heart. The dress is risqué enough. Those women... those sisters... those wonderful memories.

It is not strange to know stories, but it is strange that stories would cause somebody to act weird. It isn't like history repeats itself. I didn't ask Bibb where he had heard the stories about the lambs; I already knew them from my grandmother's knee. In these many hours of quiet I am delightfully recalling more of my childhood. My days are no longer cluttered with business matters, social events, and addicting gossip. I need to cherish this refreshment. Today was a most delightful day, except for that hard headed man being so stubborn. He calls it backbone.

==0==

"THANK YOU, TOMMY," came a feminine voice from inside the bedroll on the far side of the shelter.

"D'thank you-zz for what-zz, Anna?"

"Letting me remain in the bedroll until the scouts had left. That was very un-Indian of you."

"You weren't-zz presentable, and neither were they. D'they were thankful for-zz your gift of clean clothes. D'that was-zz a high compliment (srpt). Seldom do Indians d'thank their women for-zz d'their efforts. D'the women don't-zz d'thank d'their men (srpt) for d'their food and protection either. The gratefulness is-zz d'there, but not-zz said. It's deep in-zz d'their culture."

"White wives have a culture too, Bibb. When somebody says *Thank you* the other says *You're welcome*. I wanted you to know that I appreciated your kindness last night and this morning. Be a dear, and take down the leather and return it to the wagon. I need about ten minutes alone to get up and get ready."

Bibb did not like her word "wives" at all. He looked through the hanging clothes and saw only her mouth, nose, and two brilliant eyes peeking out from the top of the bedroll. He acknowledged her request with all the smile he had, took down the clotheslines, and started out the door.

"You forgot something, my man."

"What-zz? I got-zz it all."

"You can say *You're welcome* now. It is a cultural responsibility."

"Anna…" Bibb was very frustrated. "It's me-zz d'that needs to say-zz d'thank you. I didn't do anything d'that I wasn't supposed to do-zz (srpt). All I have done-zz is keep my promise."

"Say it anyway, Bibb. Say *You're welcome.*"

"You're welcome. Now let's get going." There was nothing in his voice that gave evidence of gratefulness or acknowledging a favor.

"Bibb, try again. Say *You're welcome* with meaning."

"You're welcome-zz with meaning." The pause in the dialog and the look on her face gave him two clues he had not scratched her itch. "Isn't d'that-zz good enough or do you demand gooder?"

She laughed. "Bibb, when I told you to say it 'with meaning,' that meant to say it from a sincere heart. Your rote 'You're welcome with meaning' means nothing. Try it again, Bibb."

"Can I try again later, Anna? We got-zz a long ways to go today. You get up now, okay? I am going outside now (srpt), and I will be back in ten minutes. Please don't wear-zz d'the dress. Promise me now (srpt), or I'll take it with me out to-zz d'the wagon."

"Bibb, you pick out what you want me to wear and lay it on the table. I'll decide between the dress and your clothes once I get up."

"Are you-zz going to change your mind in-zz d'the next ten minutes (srpt)? Why can't-zz you-zz decide now?"

"I can and have the right to change my mind a hundred times in ten minutes. Bibb, don't ask again. You said we needed to leave soon, so get hopping, Bunny Boy."

"I-zz not-zz no-zz b-b-b-bunny b-b-boy, Anna (srpt)!"

"You're burning daylight, Bibb! Now be a dear and go hitch the wagon and bring it up here."

Bibb looked at her one last time. Her face looked so different without her hair exposed. She was still pretty, but that didn't matter. There was no *You're welcome* left in him for her now, with or without feeling. He really disliked being teased. He proved there was no bunny in him and she knew it! He behaved all night long! It was a tease just to get him to sputter – and it worked.

"Bye, Anna," and he left. If there had been a bucket to kick, he would have kicked it.

Anna waited a minute to make sure he was gone. She wondered if that man was really that dumb or if he was just teasing her. "You-zzzz are welcome-zzzz (srpt) with feeling-zzzz," she mocked his deadpan tone to herself. Either way, it provided a good chuckle. She already knew how important the two words *Thank you* were to him. She also knew how *You're welcome* tied up his tongue, as if it put him under some obligation to return a favor, or worse.

Bibb did the only thing he knew to do. He talked to his horse the whole time about what to do about that irksome Gorgon woman. He was not angry, but he was plenty irritated. He could never yell at his horse – it was not in him. He calmly laid out his complaint and asked his horse several pointed questions about mares. He didn't get a response. He was happy just to talk to somebody that didn't tease him back.

The varmint overheard the whole conversation and reminded Bibb that he once had a brother like that. His twin never cared much for being outsmarted and teased, and preferred to be alone rather than to suffer ridicule. After Bibb stewed on that thought awhile the varmint also told him that Anna would have never risked teasing him if she didn't trust him wholly – she trusted him to retain flawless honor for her body. Bibb had other thoughts enter his thinking too. He was starting to place worth in her emotions, and he felt called to protect her from her deepest fears. Then came the bite: "Tommy, if you touch her wrong you have touched me wrong. Expect deadly results."

Bibb had to think long and hard about that thought. He wondered if it was the varmint speaking or if he was so used to having the varmint around he had started thinking like it. Certainly the varmint had saved his life too many times to count. If the varmint could choose to spare a life, it could certainly choose to end a life, especially if it meant keeping Anna whole. Bibb recommitted to do himself a big favor: maintain their covenant to be kind.

Lest Tommy start feeling good about himself, the varmint did what the varmint always did; it bit him again. It sternly warned Bibb to keep it that way. "She isn't the only one you made promises to, Bibb! If you sow wild seeds in your imagination you can expect to reap a crop of thistles in your thinking! But never fear, Bibb. I am in here watching everything, and I will help you. Trust me. Let me make it plain in a way you can understand: She belongs to me, not you. Don't be fool enough to touch wrong what is mine, and only mine."

Bibb so wished the varmint would stop sitting on his shoulder, or more accurately, eating at his innards. He especially disliked that it seemed so right. *Right* just wasn't the right word. Maybe *good*, or *pure*, or… It was easier to describe by what it was not, like dirty, or filthy, polluted, or corrupt. Bibb would have described the varmint as holy if he had any idea what holy meant, other than a swear word. Those thoughts hurt and he was ashamed of himself. "Why can't it think about my good too?" Bibb complained. It was always thinking about others' needs. He started to wonder if there really was a varmint or not. There was a good possibility it was just an overactive conscience, and he knew how to kill that.

Threatening to drown the varmint in booze didn't help. Bibb spoke to his horse as if it was a proxy for the varmint. "She doesn't even like me, so why do you go to such trouble to push me into treating her nice? Why not make her treat me nice?"

Bibb backed down with his complaint before another piece of flesh was lost to the varmint's response. The varmint had been good to him, and only good. Anna had been very good too, and she had made a promise to help him with his greatest fear, his broken body. Bibb felt ashamed at his short memory and tirade of ungratefulness. He sincerely apologized to the varmint once again.

Bibb loaded up the wagon with some wood and led the horses back to the shelter. On the way he told both of the horses that his good behavior for this many days in a row had flat worn him out. "It isn't hard to be bad, but you two wouldn't know." Bibb had suffered through two arguments that morning, and he had lost both. At least his horse still liked him.

==0==

Anna still wasn't ready when Bibb arrived back at the shelter. Bibb said nothing about it. He knew better. It was only half past dawn, whatever that time is, and he already had his fill of her commentary. He took the extra time to gather and stack wood on the east side of the shelter where there was some protection from the prevailing winds and weather.

"Why are you doing that, Bibb?" asked Anna from inside the cabin.

Against his better judgment he answered her. He did because he promised to be kind, and no other reason. "A widow once told me-zz to never show up with an empty hand (srpt). She told me she would get me if I ever left a place poorer-zz d'than when I arrived. Are you done in d'there yet?"

"Widows are drawn to you, aren't they? Bibb, speak louder so I can hear you, and no peeking!"

Bibb shook his head. Anna was being so Anna. "Like-zz bears to honey. I have done nothing to deserve-zz d'their notice (srpt). God just piles-zz d'them on me like tamarack wood[4] into a hot stove."

"Just like a man. Why do you keep blaming God for your troubles?"

"I'm not-zz complaining. Before today I never had cause enough to kill me a wid'r."

"You certainly say stupid stuff when you get put into a corner, Bibb. Tell me true. Why do you always blame God?"

"Sometimes God deserves-zz d'the blame. He certainly loaded me down with a wagon load of women named Anna, and go ahead and try to convince me d'that ain't

---

[4] Tamarack logs burn so hot that they can melt grates in stoves.

306

(srpt) his doing! I bet He d'thinks-zz d'that's funny too. D'the angels in heaven must be bust'n-zz d'their guts out laughing."

"That sounds like a complaint about both God and women. Clean it up, boy."

Bibb moved the wagon forward, noticing there was no *bunny* adjective before *boy* this time. Her question was legitimate. "Maybe God is a woman. He sure can confound me like a woman does (srpt). I guess not, all d'the preachers call Him a Him. Makes no never-mind anyway (srpt). He is God and I ain't. D'that kind of settles the matter for me. I ain't saying it settles it for you-zz. I suppose you just d'think I'm babbling. D'that's one reason I don't like to talk to others (srpt)."

"If you would talk sense maybe that would change, and people would start to listen to you."

Bibb was at his limit of female condescension when Anna exited the cabin. "Anna, I'm tired of you-zz saying d'things like d'that (srpt). In some ways you really are smarter d'than me, but likewise d'there are ways I'm smarter d'than you-zz. Like knowing when d'the man you are riding with (srpt) has just about exhausted his patience with-zz you. Now get in d'the wagon, woman."

"That was unkind, Bibb. Say it nice. Do you know the word *Please*? Just because I'm wearing men's clothes doesn't give you-zzzzzz d'the right-zzzzz d'to d'talk d'as d'iff-zz I-zz was-zz a d'man."

"I've been known to tell both men-zz and women to shut up when d'they have pushed me too hard. What you're wearing is-zz a completely different issue."

"Is that what is really bothering you, Bibb. What are you really asking for? Do you want me to put on my dress again? What would the scouts say? Well Bibb, I'm tired of your silliness too! Just back off with all your complaining and begin keeping your promise to be kind for once!"

Bibb couldn't take any more of her words, ways, and attitudes, and without thinking he decided to do something about it. "You want kind? I'll give you kind!" Bibb jumped out of the driver's seat and stomped around the back of the wagon. Bibb knew he was losing his grip on his anger. He hurt even more as the thud from jumping out of the wagon registered in his ribcage. As if a precision strike on his chest, in his rush racing to her side of the wagon Bibb nicked the corner of the buckboard dead on his deepest wound. The pain was sharp, but his anger remained sharper. He stumbled right up next to Anna and became angrier because he realized he had to look up to her in order to gain eye contact. He couldn't stand up straight from the sharp newly registering chest pain, but gritted what was left of his teeth, straining there until he had her eyes' full attention.

She could see him thinking, and feared he was turning evil. She unconsciously checked to see where his weapons were, and yes, his revolver was on his hip. She was very nervous, scared like when her late husband was angry enough to beat her. She voiced an urgent plea in her heart for the varmint to seize him; to seize him now before it was too late. No miracle happened.

Anna took the defensive opportunity to return the glare, looking deep into his eyes, as if this moment was to be a life ending showdown. She found none of the expected rage, but still she didn't know for sure. Not knowing why, other than she felt she must, she had pushed him hard again that morning. She now feared she had crossed the same line that had gotten her hurt in times past – terrible times past. She refused to speak again for risk of provoking a beating. Without warning, in just a blink, an inner ray of light sparked inside Bibb's better eye. She swore it was something but it was over in such a flash that the reason within her denied what she thought she saw. Fear gripped her once again as she could see his pain overtaking his ability to reason. She was scared for her life and had nowhere to flee.

"Anna," sputtered Bibb, obviously in great pain. He turned around wanting to walk away in a desperate act of kindness. Two steps later the word *coward* flashed like lightning into his mind and stopped him dead in his tracks. He turned again towards her and started to point his finger at her face, but couldn't as his chest pain arrested the gesture and produced a horrible burping cough. Bibb, swimming in frustration, pain, and emotion spoke directly into her eyes while holding tightly to the side of the wagon for balance. "Anna, listen good and live. I know you don't-zz believe in-zz d'things like providence, but I do-zz (srpt). I am-zz in such a knot, and wishing you-zz weren't so irksome, but I keep coming back to a truth d'that I wish were a lie. Anna, even with all your, your, your, oh… Anna, against all d'that is within me I have resigned to d'the truth d'that you are God's way He has chosen to show me His love; and worser d'than worse, d'the same me-zz to you-zz. I hate-zz d'those d'thoughts, but d'that's d'the d'thoughts I-zz cannot escape as if d'they-zz were branded on top-zz of my shooting hand. He knows I reject what I can't see, like Him, but He knows I can't reject what I can see. Call me dumb, but I can't get-zz it free from my mind d'that you are His confounding love gift given to me in-zz d'these hours of my greatest need. If I dishonor you, I dishonor God. Go ahead, call me-zz simple. Call me-zz silly (srpt). Call me-zz stupid. Call me anything you want. Even call me-zz an idiot and you won't change my mind (srpt). When-zz I treat you right as I ought, you shine. When you-zz shine, I see-zz what-zz I can become. My problem is d'that I lack d'the good I need in me to make you-zz shine. I just hate-zz it when He never lets my mind idle. He is always making me-zz d'think and wonder and remember and… Oh, Anna, help me."

She paused, dismissing his anger and emotion. "Love gifts? Bibb, where did those words come from? And what do you know of love?" She wasn't sure; his spittle may have had fresh blood in it.

"D'that's why you're here, Anna, to teach me (srpt). You-zz make me say-zz d'things I normally can't, like *You're welcome*. I hate-zz it! I really hate-zz it. I liked being what

I-zz was and d'the respect I was-zz given, but-zz d'those outlaw days are over. Back d'then I set-zz my own ways and I walked my-zz own paths. Nobody dared tell me what-zz to do. I liked d'that."

"Are you okay, Bibb?" He didn't answer but turned around and limped around the buckboard back to the driver's side. His retreat made her momentarily speechless, caught completely unprepared for this turn in the conversation. When the gravity of what Bibb confessed registered in her heart, she deliberately turned the other way for fear he would see what she was involuntarily broadcasting through her eyes. She had longed for a reciprocating love endorsed from above, and for years she had denied God her affections because such a love was unfairly denied her.

"Tommy, let's talk more after we pack up and get on our way. You pack the pot, spoon, cup, and bedroll, and I will check around to see if we are leaving anything. Once you get that packed, you can help me with the trunk. It's ready to go." Anna's inner thoughts were even more painful than his suffering. She could not look at Bibb. The risk of showing empathy (or weakness) was too high.

"Anna, are you-zz okay?"

"Yes, now let's get going." Her mind was elsewhere. Bibb's pet varmint saw her intense soul suffering. That critter had dared to rip open her deep ancient scars and was delighting in his deed.

"D'thank you for choosing to not wear-zz d'the dress." Bibb's words were said slowly. Bibb couldn't speak quicker if he wanted too. Anna knew Bibb's *thank you* wasn't from him. The varmint was never satisfied with one bite. Those words had the same effect as twisting a knife in her heart.

At that moment Anna's could not even whisper out a "You're welcome" to the man. Her only hope was silence and continually facing away from him. She had heard his words. The man was clueless, or he hurt too badly to notice her lacerated heart. She occupied her hands with busy work to tidy up the place, all while taking deep breaths to regain her composure and control of her eyes. "You're welcome, Tommy," still with her back towards him. "That was the best decision I have made so far today." She was very glad her trembling soul wasn't reflected in her speech.

Anna was doubly glad she chose not to wear the dress. She was even more relieved, though she was tempted, that she didn't throw herself into his arms like some brainless bar-baby. Either of those errors would have ruined this gigantic moment. Reason had returned. Her promise to herself remained intact. She would not fall for sentimental words again, even if they were well aimed and heartfelt. Men lie. That is what men do. She re-determined in her heart to overcome her greatest weakness and felt proud of herself that she did not succumb to a liar's open-heart confession.

They worked together to load the wagon and then Anna assumed her place as a passenger. Bibb took extra time to tighten the load and then to recheck the horses' bits.

Once on their way, in the silence Anna told herself she had witnessed a miracle. Her heart (but not her mind) was changing about that half-a-man, and she found herself speechless in awe of the confession and commission – she was to teach the man what he did not know. She then considered a second miracle: a man had actually listened. Not only listen, but her opinions counted. This was the moment of soul bonding she had dreamed of in the darkest scars of her heart. More than that, she actually longed for and even prayed for such a relationship. For years she had deeply resented God for not providing one.

It was even more of a miracle because the man with the reins, her man that was holding the reins, was clueless… He didn't know how deep her feelings were running. Finally she had become an intimate friend to a man, a real friend – not the fake stuff of social posturing or physical attraction. She knew it was real when she confronted him in anger and he chose not to retaliate with brute force. He had a history of lashing out violently at others. He certainly could have attacked her.

As they rode farther down the trail she soon concluded that this morning's words were not Bibb's. His well of wisdom only goes down six feet deep – deep enough to bury somebody. This was entirely the varmint's fault. His paw prints were all over it. Bibb had told her that the varmint didn't fight fair. It was true. She had prayed in that desperate moment for the varmint to seize her man, and she now smarted for it. Something else might be true also. The preacher had told her that this might be the first time in Bibb's life he had experienced love; her love; a love from a woman's heart. She felt ashamed that she intentionally made sure he stayed well outside of her charms and purposely making sure he would never experience any affections from her. She had served him nothing but cold, cruel, disrespectful gruel, heavily salted with condescension. That thought hurt. She parsed his words back to herself, and realized that was not what Tommy had said. She could kick herself for poor listening. He had said love was coming through her, not from her. Anna concluded that her man says smart stuff more by accident than on purpose. "Yes," she thought to herself, "the varmint doesn't fight fair. She or He or It took a bite out of me too." Once that critter was summoned from the shadows, nobody was safe. Bibb wasn't the only one who got bit.

==0==

The plains were wet from the previous evenings soaking. The creeks were tricky to cross because they were flowing to the limit of their banks. She would have had no clue what to do earlier in the trip but Anna was now comfortable in her role, and the horses were comfortable with her leading the way across the waters. She was really enjoying the trip now. It no longer mattered how physically ugly the man sitting next to her was … or how he talked… or didn't talk… or how he thought. She enjoyed

310

the friendship. The greatest change was that she started to enjoy being with herself. She liked the woman she was becoming. Even if nobody else noticed, she noticed.

Anna decided to bring up an issue to see if her man had any objections. "Bibb, did you know the preacher man in Deadwood gave me some advice about our covenant? I'm seriously thinking of taking it." She waited a moment hoping that he might be thinking of a response. He wasn't; not even close. He was in his own little world. Her statement didn't even merit a glance in her direction.

"The preacher said I should appropriate the name Anna Toivo until our covenant is fulfilled. What do you think of that suggestion?" Again, her statement and question did not earn a response from the man. After becoming frustrated with his silence she added, "Well, I'm perfectly content in bringing some honor to your name. It could use some."

Bibb did not share her feelings of contentment, or anything else for that matter. If there had been something strong to drink, he would have consumed it. He was tired of being pinched by her and bitten by the varmint. The question that kept coming back to him during his daydreaming was "Tell me there, son, how much has all this female frustration hurt you?" The answer was worse: "Buck up, big boy, you ain't seen the worst of it yet."

==0==

At lunch Anna asked Bibb where the eagle feather came from. He was caught unawares, not knowing that it, or the dried food, was hiding in Anna's trunk. This was no minor revelation. He acted quite distressed.

"What's the big deal over a feather, Bibb?" she asked.

"It's a symbol of identity, Anna. In d'the lower ranks it indicates trustworthiness and-zz maturity. It's also the only d'thing d'that a scout or brave really owns. Everything else belongs to-zz d'the tribe, and specifically d'the chief. To steal it is to steal a soul."

"So who decides who gets what and who hands them out?"

"The medicine man recommends and d'the chief bestows if he agrees. D'these eagle feathers are hard to come-zz by and very easy to lose. Trust is everything in d'the Lakota tribe, and once violated it-zz hard-zz to win back."

"So why are you so worried?"

"It might have been stolen. We-zz may have been set up for death because of it. If our scouts find out about it, d'they may conclude we stole it and immediately administer d'the tribe's justice."

"Over a feather? That sure is harsh!"

"Anna, d'this isn't a new story. Similar dramas of deceit and betrayal are-zz as old as the sea."

From that point in the conversation Bibb told Anna what he claimed to be a true story about ten of twelve brothers that traveled across a desert in search for food from an ancient African ruler. The ruler was shrewd. He accused them of being spies and jailed them all for three days before sending nine of them home, keeping one in jail as surety. To accomplish an undisclosed plot the ruler had secretly restored their payments in their grain sacks prior to sending them back home. Several times Bibb interjected his personal distaste for jails. "D'this feather is like d'their returned payments."

"I know the story, Bibb. It has a happy ending."

"Why didn't you-zz say something d'then? It hurts me to talk."

"It is exercise for your mouth, and I am in charge of your healing. Keep talking. I like it. The more you talk, the better I can understand you. You ain't slurping and 'd'ing and 'z'ing on me as much as you used to. I really think you are healing up. This is good for you."

"Later, I hurt." Bibb didn't speak again until they stopped to rest the horses after crossing the next creek, and his words were only to issue instructions on where Anna was to lead the horses.

Bibb later found and drove the wagon into a grove where nobody could see them easily. While there Bibb had Anna retrieve the feather, and then instructed her to go into the woods to stretch. Anna cheated, and looked back to see him hide the feather in one of the cracks in the wood underneath the wagon bed.

Once on their way again, Anna asked Bibb why he did that.

"Did what-zz?"

An hour later, Anna connected Bibb's fable with his strange behavior. "What about the feather, Bibb?"

"You never saw-zz a feather, heard of a feather, or would know what a feather was-zz even if you got tickled with one. D'the only treasure in our trunk was extra dried vittles."

"That's silly."

"Not to d'them. Indians and white men value different d'things. You-zz would not be spared if d'they d'thought you took it. I would have a chance to repair my reputation given I'm known as a liar and a thief. Women-zz don't rank high enough in d'their view of d'the world to receive mercy."

"They will just have to become civilized."

"Before or after d'they d'kill you? Anna, just accept it. D'there is a chance d'the feather was a gift of honor. I didn't hear d'that at d'the ceremony, so we need to be very cautious. If we are searched and d'the feather is found, Anna for your life's sake say you knew nothing of it."

"About what?"

"Exactly."

==0==

Late afternoon one of the Indians rode into their location and told Bibb and Anna to abruptly turn and head east. On their present path there was an Indian village that needed to be bypassed. They were not enemies. They would ask them to stay for many days, days that neither they nor the scouts could afford. Bibb expressed his gratitude for the information and told the scout that he would swing to the right for one hour and then turn north again.

Anna deduced that the change of direction had everything to do with the scout's visit. "Bibb, are we lost? When are we going to get to Miles City?"

"Anna, d'the scout told me d'that an hour detour may save us several days of travel. We are not in danger of losing anything but time."

"How about answering my question?"

"No-zz, we are not lost, Anna. When do we-zz get to Miles City is another matter altogether. Without difficulties, we could be-zz d'there in four days. Between weather and herds in our way, it will-zz probably take us five days. D'the dangers will increase when-zz we get into cow country and d'the white ranchers."

"Why?"

"Generally d'they hate trespassers and specifically d'they hate me. Other d'than d'that we-zz will be okay."

"Are you scared?"

"I would prefer we-zz be riding our horses rather d'than pulling a wagon with a trunk. Trunks attract d'thieves. D'the horse is much safer, and nobody can out-shoot me on my-zz horse."

"Are you scared? You don't answer questions well."

"No-zz."

"No, why? Answer the question."

"Anna, you-zz didn't ask why. Give me-zz some credit for listening to you-zz. You say I always answer questions-zz d'that you didn't ask, and now you say I don't answer d'the questions you didn't ask. Honestly, Anna, how am I to know what you want-zz?"

"Why not?"

"Why not-zz what?"

"Why aren't you scared?"

"Don't ask questions if you already know you won't like my-zz answer."

"I don't know your answer, Bibb."

"Providence."

"I knew that."

==0==

Bibb was not as familiar with the land they were now riding in. Being more cautious than usual, he was glad when the lead scout asked to stop to make camp well before the sun went down. Once making eye contact Bibb signed to the man, "Is there a problem?"

"No problem, Bibb. We want extra time to scout this area. Our chief is looking for a winter village location. The next stream is deep and will not freeze over. There are many edible plants in the valley. One of us will stay close tonight while the other three will go explore farther out."

"What about the fifth Indian?" asked Bibb.

"He was ahead of us when we turned. He will catch up tomorrow when he discovers us missing. He will then backtrack, find, and follow your wheel marks."

"Do you need some additional food? We have more than enough to share. Please help yourself."

Bibb took the scout over to the trunk and they opened it together. The Indian was very happy to discover their favorite dried foods inside. "Where did you get this?"

"We just discovered it. My woman had offered her clothes to the widows, and I suspect a woman from your tribe placed this food in here after we had loaded the trunk."

"May I take enough for me and my brothers' ride tomorrow? We want to have time to search thoroughly around this location."

"Do not consider it a gift from us, but from your own women. We only need food to get to Miles City. You take this food so you can quickly return to your village without a need to hunt."

The lead scout was pleased, in fact smiled, which hadn't happened often. Bibb was happier than the scout because there was no reaction to a missing feather. The scout was either a very good actor or he did not know to look for one. That was the best news Bibb had received all day. He was going to have enough trouble with the white man. He didn't need any trouble with the red man.

Camp was set up by the stream and soon Bibb had a good fire going. A north wind was blowing gently through their camp on the cloudless evening. The promise of frost rose with the moon.

==0==

"This jerky is exceptionally good tonight, Bibb."

"Jerky tastes best by-zz a fire on a cool night."

"You promised we would talk about something this morning, and you didn't bring it up all day."

"Anna, instead of having me-zz guess wrong, can you just tell me-zz what I forgot?"

"You really forgot?"

"Anna, how does a man know-zz what he forgot? If I-zz knew what I forgot it wouldn't be forgotten. Be kind. Tell me what-zz I forgot."

"Two things, Bibb."

"How about telling me one-zz d'thing first? We can talk about it, and when we-zz done maybe I will remember-zz d'the second-zz d'thing. Anna, d'this isn't hard. Tell me what you-zz want to talk about."

"Do you want some coffee?"

"Anna, yes, and you look-zz like you would like some too. I will get up and make some. Was it coffee-zz d'that I forgot-zz d'this morning?"

"Thank you."

"You're welcome." Bibb started to walk towards the provisions stored in the wagon.

"Bibb," she raised her voice as he walked away, "*Thank you* was what I wanted to talk about. I wasn't thanking you for getting up to get the coffee. Get back over here and talk to me."

"Anna, I-zz wants some coffee and I-zz am going to make some coffee. If you like what I'm making you can have some. To show my petty kindness, I will ask you if you want it-zz strong or weak. You're getting what-zz I make regardless."

"Weak, please. I want to sleep well tonight. I hate being cold."

"D'this ain't cold like Canada. D'that was cold. Cold down to-zz my bones."

She rolled her eyes marveling at Bibb's innocent ability to stray off of the topic. She decided to have some fun with his diversion. "Then if I ask you for your bedroll tonight you won't complain?"

Bibb wasn't ready to surrender that. He returned to the previous subject. "Anna, what's your question about-zz *d'thank you?*"

"What about the bedroll, Bibb? How are you going to stay warm by the fire?"

"We will-zz figure something out, Anna."

"Thank you."

"You're welcome."

"Bibb, I wanted to talk about *Thank you* and all you're thinking about sharing blankets with me. Let's keep on the issue here. You promised you wouldn't think about things like that."

"How about we change-zz d'the way we are talking? You-zz ask d'the question, and I will-zz answer. I am so confused about what-zz we are talking about."

"Thank you."

"You're welcome."

"Bibb!"

"What-zz?"

"Never mind. I'm going to walk over there into the dark. I will be ready to share a cup of coffee with you when I get back." She was enjoying tying the man in a knot.

"Anna, are you-zz sick?"

"Bibb!"

"Anna!"

"Bibb!"

"What-zz?"

"I asked first! You tell me."

"Thank you-zz."

"For what?"

"I will tell you-zz after d'the coffee is made."

==0==

The stars where extra bright this night due a dry sky and endless vistas. The Indian scout that was staying close had brought his horse into camp with Tommy and Anna's and commenced to make something like charcoal out of what was left of the fire. He then dug a small trench in the ground and placed some of the hot coals into it. He then covered it up with dirt he had pushed aside and then prepared for sleep.

"What are you planning to do now, Bibb?" asked Anna.

"Anna, we can either freeze separately (srpt) or stay warm together. We can sleep on d'the hay and share our blankets, but only if you say it's okay."

"Bibb, tell me true. Are you attracted to me?"

"Anna, can-zz you just stop all your teasing? I am really tired of it. I need you and you-zz need me. Attractive or not has nothin' to do with d'this or d'that."

"So you don't deny my attractiveness."

"One d'thing I can't deny is your vanity! You don't need-zz me to tell you d'that you're young and pretty. You-zz know d'that already. You just want-zz to hear me say it (srpt). Okay, you-zz are young and pretty. Is d'that good enough? I'll even say it again: You-zz are young and pretty with-zz feeling-zz-zz-zz-zz. Now d'that I have scratched your itch, can we-zz talk practical sense?"

She changed her tone. "Tommy, you gave me the best answer a woman could have desired."

"You're nuts-zz, Anna." Of all the ways a woman can talk, Bibb hated gooey the most.

"And you just undid any happy points you might have earned, boy! Oh! You can really snap my whip. Have you ever interpreted correctly a single word of true feelings? Don't answer that, Bibb, because it might make me change my mind. You convinced me by your past inactions that I can trust you in my sleep. That decided, regardless if one or both of us are nuts, I'm going over there anyway to prepare a place for us to sleep."

Bibb had no idea what feelings she was talking about. Her thinking was somewhere out by the stars. It must hurt for her to be so… so… He couldn't even think of a word to follow *so*.

Anna interrupted her floundering man. "Bibb, listen to me!"

"I'm listening." That was a lie. He was getting very weary of her, and avoided her eyes.

"Bibb, I have a fear of being cold, and my feet and hand freeze up fast when I'm not bundled up. I have a serious favor that I don't want you to take wrong."

"D'that would be a change, Anna. It seems like everything I-zz do you d'think is either wrong or dumb. You don't-zz hand out a lot-zz of compliments. You're short on pleasantries too, and when you say something nice I wonder about-zz your motives. Anna, not only I can't understand-zz you sometimes, but sometimes you-zz scare me (srpt). I'm not saying you're wrong or something is wrong with you-zz, it is just d'that I'm not hearing with understanding what-zz you are saying. Anna, I am a simple man. Whatever you-zz wants, please tell me exactly what-zz you want-zz. When you tell-zz me generally, I fail. I can't read-zz your mind. What in-zz simple words do-zz you want? Don't give me just hints. Tell me plain."

"Bibb, shame on you," she said all of a sudden sweetly. "That Indian might think you have started to hate me with all your whining."

"I already told-zz him d'the truth, Anna. He knows how I really feel about you. My horse also knows."

"What did you tell him, Bibb?"

"It was good, Anna."

"Specifically, Bibb. Don't give me just hints. Tell me plain." She really liked to poke him, and he wondered if it was just the Anna in her being Anna. Before he replied she stated, "I want the exact words, not another commentary, and not with feeling or your lack of feeling."

In response, Bibb spoke the exact words he had told the scout earlier, and the scout's ears immediately perked up, and so did Anna's ire.

"Bibb!" Both her hands went up straight up as if a plea to heaven for common sense to smite that man back into reality. "Bibb," she said slowly and more sweetly than what was boiling in her, "What did you say to him in English? Tell me, please."

"D'they were kind words, Anna. Now drop it, please. What's-zz d'the favor you want? Settle down, Anna. Are you settled down?"

She took a deep breath. "Okay Bibb, I will tell you plain." She had to check herself due to the frustration in her voice. In her kindest anger (and shelving her embarrassment) she told Bibb exactly what she wanted. "I want you to hold me tonight. All other times I have had to lay close to you I held your back, but even then I got cold. Can we switch? I will get cold if we don't, and I hate that."

"Anna, you figure out what you want-zz and I will have to hold my breath long enough (srpt) to do it. Tonight will be cold, so double up on my last set of clothes and d'then put my coat on over it. I can promise you I will fall asleep first. I'm tired and can barely move. First one-zz to sleep (srpt) wins. You-zz are starting a snoring habit too. Anna, I'm ready for d'the back of d'the buckboard."

"Let's go. Peace?"

"Peace."

"Do you think I am attractive?" asked Anna quietly.

"When I open my eyes up in d'the morning, maybe, but for now, I can't tell and don't want-zz to guess (srpt). I want to go to sleep. You are wasting time tickling your own vanity (srpt), so why don't you scoot over to d'the wagon and do what you got to do (srpt). I will be back in five minutes."

"Peace?" asked Anna again.

"Peace."

When Bibb returned, the next minutes were spent in arranging blankets and accidental elbowing each other. Eventually they were settled. Bibb was enjoying the peace and desperately wanted to fall asleep first. That was when the dialog started afresh.

"What did you tell the scout?"

"D'the obvious. Good night-zz, Anna."

"Was what you said to him about me good?"

Bibb did not answer, but he did squeeze her from behind for about five seconds. That was a good enough answer. The more she thought of his response the better it was than anything he was capable of saying. Anna wondered if it was because they were actually married that God gave Bibb self-control, or was it the Indian sleeping just ten feet away, or was Bibb just plain weird? No matter, she trusted him because he had behaved in the past and the *us* in them was right and proper, even if he didn't know it.

In time she was proved right. Because of Bibb's cooperation with her wish, Anna was warmly wedged and covered perfectly in a sleeping cocoon. What Bibb lacked in virtue would be forgiven because of his stillness and warmth. The quieter moments of Bibb's breathing reminded her of a purring cat. Anna never liked cats because they did not like her; cats preferring her siblings' laps. She wondered if cats could like the Anna she was becoming. Maybe yes, maybe no. She laughed. The thought of becoming kind and only kind would be a God-sized task. She deeply desired to be able to pass what she jokingly now named her tabby-test. If her heart was not right, no kitty would spend time in her lap, regardless of the enticements. Her job was to make the Tommy-cat keeping her warm feel loved enough to return. She quickly amended her thought to '*comfortable* enough to return.' Her attractiveness was of no use. Cats do not care if you are beautiful. They discern your quota of kindness. Gaining some of that would require her to radically change her attitudes. She decided she was wrong about that. She admitted to herself that she was not a kind woman and knew she could not give away something she did not have. Anna opened her eyes and looked out into the darkness. She would have to ask for kindness from another source to be spilt on her, have it pass through her, and then on to her Tommy-cat.

She pulled on his arm that was draped over her shoulder tight around her. He moaned. She smiled. He purred. She slept.

Saturday, October 15, 1887

Sixth day out from camp. The scouts searched for a winter site while we stayed put. Bibb was glad about that because my horse needed the rest. Our bones needed the rest too; I am weary from the endless miles. Bibb said we are about four days from Miles City. He also said that our wagon pullers won't move on the ninth day if we don't rest them by the eighth.

Bibb's mouth is healing and he speaks much better. The worst threat to his life is his poking ribs. After bathing Bibb showed me what weeds were edible. To the delight of our scouts we boiled them up for dinner tonight along with some fish.

I wrestled the truth out of Bibb about his presumptuous promises he has made with God, why he is so convinced there is one that hears promises, and why he kept it a secret from me. I should not have asked. His answer stung my soul badly. I am not sure if he has a low opinion of all women or just me. I wonder if he was jilted earlier in life. I wouldn't blame the woman.

==0==

BIBB HEARD A lot of moaning coming from the buckboard as the sun dawned. "Anna, do you ache all over?" He got up from the campfire to investigate, curious if Anna was ready to get up.

Earlier that morning Bibb had breakfast with the fourth scout before he left to check out the nearby areas. The other three had fanned out while it was still light the prior evening to cover the farther possibilities. The fourth Indian told Bibb that they all planned to return by sunset.

Bibb discovered his Needle in the Haystack was quite a sight to behold, much like a thistle stem. Even beauties have bad days. While he stood there thinking of what to do next Anna spoke in a foggy tone, "Bibb, let me sleep some more. I don't want to get up. My body refuses to move."

"I'll take d'that as a *not yet* from you. I will go check on d'the horses and see if I can find some wild onions (srpt) down by d'the creek to make some tea." Bibb laughed to himself. She was a wreck.

"When are we going to get there, Bibb?"

"Never, if we keep-zz sleeping our days away (srpt), but you never mind d'that. Today is a rest day for us and d'the horses. D'there is no need for you to get up now."

"No chance of it. It even hurts to talk." Anna was sore all over. The daily grind of the trip was wearing her down, and she was so used to having her employees do all of her manual labor. Her muscles were sore from the pulling, her joints were sore from the carrying, and her bottom was sore from all the sitting. Her hair was a collection of hay infested knots and the pores in her skin were clogged with dust blown in all the way from Oregon. She was sunburned on the arms and the face, and her tingly feet hurt the worst. Other than a new born migraine and a tummy ache from aging beans and jerky, all else was just fine.

While down by the creek Bibb cared for the horses and cleared an area to build another fire. Filled from the stream, Bibb started to heat up some water in their bucket. He also used the tarpaulin from the wagon to make a small lean-to around a flat rock next to the fire. In about a half an hour Bibb had the site turned into a functioning poor-man's sauna just like his parents used to assemble. He remembered from his youth that if it was Saturday, it was Sauna-day.

Bibb returned to the wagon and found Anna still asleep. He gently woke her up, not an easy thing to do given her perfect imitation of a boulder. As she rubbed her eyes he softly told her that her tea and crumpets were ready. Once awake and smiling in anticipation, he then mentioned her morning meal was waiting for her down by the creek. He tried to say it sweetly but could not counter her disappointed look. It meant little that he had taken the time to prepare her some breakfast if her breakfast was not to be served to her in her royal haystack.

"What did you make me?" asked Anna, hoping against hope he might redeem himself.

"Anna, you-zz can have anything you-zz want for breakfast menu as long as it is hard tack, beans, or jerky."

"Why did you wake me up, Bibb?" said the sleepy and considerably less than cheerful woman.

"Because your bath-zz is also ready, Madame."

"What?"

"D'there is a hot sauna waiting for you down by d'the creek. D'the water is almost to a boil and you-zz need to take advantage of it. May I help you-zz out of your carriage, My Lady?"

Slow at first, augmented with an abundance of unintentional moaning and groaning, Anna became almost upright, bent at the belly. As she slipped out of the wagon she felt the abrupt chill of the October morning and was tempted to immediately return to the hay basket.

"Bibb, what did you say there was down by the creek?"

"I put-zz together a washing shack for you Anna. Take a change of clothes (srpt) and you can use what you got-zz on for a towel. When you-zz are done, I will wash up."

"Show me where."

Anna followed (slowly) and couldn't get over how clever the whole setup was. She was going to enjoy this. She instructed Bibb that he needed to rest too, and told him to take advantage of the warm hay bed she had just vacated. Bibb brought over some more wood for the fire, now wonderful coals, and then told Anna he liked her suggestion of sleep.

"When I am done here, I will come wake you up."

"Take d'this gun, Anna. D'this morning I saw a snake by d'the creek. If I had my gun earlier we-zz could have had it for lunch. With all d'the ruckuses I made d'this morning I am quite sure it and all its brothers and sisters have cleared out also. Don't be afraid to shoot it if you-zz fear anything. I will come immediately if you do."

About two hours later, almost noon, Anna found her Little Boy Blue under their haystack fast asleep. She woke him up and told him it was his turn to take a bath.

"Anna, I'm sorry. I was-zz going to make you lunch. I fell asleep. It was a deep one! What-zz time is it?"

"You wash up, Bibb. When you come back up here we can share some beans. How did you think of that Bibb? That is about as good as bathing gets out here in the middle of nowhere."

"D'that was grand-daddy's idea from d'the old country. It was mom's idea d'that-zz we had to wash up once a week regardless if we-zz needed it or not. My twin brother and I used to make a party of it every week after our fish fry."

"Bibb, the bad news is that the creek water is as ice cold as it's clean. The good news is that it makes that shack all the warmer when you get back into it."

"Are you a Finn?" asked Bibb. "Only Finns do d'that."

"No, but the preacher suggested I should act like a Toivo; at least temporarily. Now go wash up, and when you come back up we will have some lunch."

"Keep d'the gun close, Anna. I'm taking d'the other one with me."

"Why?"

"Toak. He may visit. He may want to take you-zz."

"Take me where?"

"Kidnap you, Anna. He may take you in order to strike a better bargain with me (srpt). If he was to visit, it would be today, most likely d'this afternoon."

"What bargain?"

"Simple. His life for yours (srpt). He will return you to me if I choose to let him live."

"And what if he disagrees, gets the upper hand, chooses to live and take me with him?"

"I suggest you start whining. After a few hours of your company he-zz would pay me to take you back (srpt). He has no tolerance for a voice like yours, especially d'the squeaks you give off when you get huffy." Bibb said it as a reasonable statement that was part of a legitimate survival strategy for them. He never considered the possibility of an emotional response from Miss Needle.

"That is as unkind and as stupid a thing as you could have ever said. Take it back, Bibb. Take it all back right now!" she said in a higher pitched huff.

Now realizing his error Bibb responded, "I guess d'the truth can be said badly. But Anna, Toak would kill you if I didn't take you back immediately. No doubt about it; d'there wouldn't be any negotiation. He's a very serious man. He wants to live, and he wants-zz even more my word d'that I won't kill him."

"Why wouldn't he kill you instead?"

"He needs d'the work to feed his family. Without me, he would be hunted down and killed. D'the only question left if I die is who would kill Toak first, the white man or the red man."

"Why don't you kill him first?"

"I might have to, but I don't want-zz to. I need him too. He has saved my life several times. He's d'the closest friend I have, and it pains me what happened (srpt). We will see. If you see somebody you don't recognize, fire a shot into d'the air (srpt). I will come running back."

"Bibb, do you really think he will visit?"

"No, but he might, and we have to be ready. Don't let him take you. He won't kill you until he negotiates with me. You-zz are no value in trade if you are already dead."

==0==

The sheriff of Miles City received a package from Deadwood courtesy of a mercantile agent. After the sheriff spent time reading the items in the package he invited the preacher over for lunch, show him some excerpts, and to get his opinion on how to keep the town safe.

The preacher found Bibb's post script of his letter quite encouraging. The sheriff thought the same letter was quite threatening. The sheriff would make arrangements to talk to Westum and his wife after church. They could agree on what to do about Bibb's comments then.

The package came with a written promise for more to follow. It was re-bundled and given to the conductor of the Limited for immediate delivery to Major Ryder at the Bismarck garrison.

"When do you think he will get here, Sheriff?" asked the preacher as they walked back from the train station.

"Too early to think about that. Don't worry. The news that Bibb is close will travel much faster than the buckboard he is riding in. Our friend Mr. Westum will make sure of that."

==0==

"Stop d'that Anna! Why do you-zz always want to know about personalities, thoughts, feelings and gooey stuff like d'that? None of d'that matters nothing to nobody never."

Anna sincerely answered, "Bibb, stop being so purposely silly and admit those are the most important things. Horses and cows, tools and guns, well, that is all just stuff. Nobody cares how high a mountain was or how fierce the wind blew. They want to know how you felt about it."

"Anna, I don't-zz know how you could be any more wrong d'than you are right now. Can't we just enjoy our beans? Or do you need-zz to know how I feel-zz about my-zz beans too? I think-zz my beans are good. I think-zz my beans feel good d'that I am eating d'them. I d'think my tummy will feel-zz good after eating d'them too. Anna, did you know-zz d'that my gizzard is telling me-zz it doesn't care-zz beans about your beans? It must be a male gizzard. It ain't got no-zz feelings!"

"Have your fun, Tommy, but I know you don't mean that. I can prove it to you."

"How?"

"I just have to pick the right topic, and that gizzard of yours will be singing its heart out. I can prove it but I'm not going to now. You foolishly have decided to mock me instead."

"How do you feel about-zz my gizzard mocking you?"

"Stop it Bibb. You are only proving my point."

"Anna, now you done it! My gizzard is starting to cry. I can feel it leaking all over me inside. Bad gizzard! Bad gizzard! You buck up right now and act like a man's gizzard. There ain't no-zz reason for shedding girly tears over beans!"

Anna held her breath and refused to engage Bibb anymore with this childishness. Showing some irritation she changed the subject, "Bibb, can you show me what the Indians find to eat out here? I know they like certain roots, and some of the nuts are edible too. Why don't we go harvesting and cook something special for our scouts for when they return?"

"D'that is both a sensible and kind suggestion. I won't even have to consult my gizzard about d'that. We can do d'these dishes by d'the creek and d'then go speculating for some vegetables."

==0==

"Bibb, what is the one topic you won't talk to me about?"

"Anna, I came down here to pick these chokecherries and collect some roots. Can we save this conversation for later?"

"Yes, but I want you to think about it now so you can talk about it later."

"Why don't you see if d'there are any plums left on d'that tree over d'there on d'the other side of d'the creek? D'the plums may be old, but we can cover our hard tack with some of d'the natural jam. I'm going to pick some of d'the greens growing on d'the bank of d'the creek."

"Bibb, the water is cold!"

"Finally, Anna, we found something we can agree about! Just go do it. It's cold for me too-zz. We need-zz enough food to feed six tonight, maybe seven. You know-zz how to cook fish?"

"Yes, I tell them when I want my dinner, my butler buys it, and he brings it back to my maid to cook. Nothing could be easier; same with tonight. I tell you what I want and you make it happen."

"If I-zz catch 'em, will you-zz cook 'em?"

"Bibb, no I won't. I don't know how. I'm wearing man's clothes now so I don't cook. Are you trying to embarrass me into wearing that dress again?"

"Embarrassed in front-zz of who? Honestly, Anna, if you don't know-zz something just say so. D'there is no shame in d'that. I'll teach you-zz."

"If you catch some, I'll try, but don't expect me to cut them up."

"I got-zz to catch d'them first, Anna. No sense worrying about cleaning if d'there is no catching."

"Where's the plums and berries, Bibb? I can catch them."

==0==

Bibb preferred resting at the same location where they had slept the night before. It would be very hard for anybody to sneak up on them there, and at night if one of the scouts was late they could easily see the campfire.

That afternoon Bibb had disassembled the sauna and brought the wooden pieces up to the wagon along with the horses. He used the tarpaulin to set up a windbreak for them and their campfire. Anna thought it was nice plan to keep some of the warmth from the fire from blowing away. She told Bibb that once her feet were cold, they stayed cold.

Bibb showed Anna how Toak had shown him how to prepare some of their harvest. While she was doing that Bibb took out his hammer and made a mess separating the meat of the walnuts from their shell. Every once in a while a nut wouldn't be hit quite straight and it would end up shooting in a random direction. Both were quite amused, and Anna teased him about his poor aim.

There was no sign of Toak all day. Bibb concluded that Toak was thinking more about his escape than any confrontation. He knew that the scouts would have sworn their lives to protect Bibb and Anna. Toak's success infiltrating (and keeping his heartbeat) would be short lived if he did any harm to either of them. There was no mercy remaining for that man if he raised his fist.

Anna noticed that when Bibb was the teacher and she was the learner she could ask him anything and get an honest answer. She tested her theory several times and was astounded each time as Bibb opened up more and more. He thrived on her respect for what he knew and how well he could teach it. That afternoon she enjoyed learning some Lakota words and some handy sign language along with the cooking lesson. She actually caught herself having some fun too, a far cry from her earlier pitiful moans.

"Bibb, before we left Deadwood I had a long talk with the preacher who performed our covenanting. I honestly thought the man was wrong, but I am starting to change my mind."

"About what?"

"Why you changed."

"Why would you be-zz wanting to know about d'that?"

"I didn't ask him that, nor was I curious about it. He told me. He wasn't nice about it either."

"About why I changed?"

"No, he meddled me hard about why I didn't care. He was very blunt and painted me as shallow and apathetic. Both he and his wife said many hurtful things to me about me."

"Were d'they true?"

"Bibb! You're supposed to say 'How did they hurt?' or 'What hurt the most?'"

"D'the truth hurts d'the most (srpt). I know d'that better d'than anyone. What hurt you, and what can I do-zz to take away d'the pain? Was d'that said better enough gooder for you? Did I have enough gooey 'with feeling' in my response?"

"Bibb, you are… never mind. Bibb, I confess I went there with full intentions of getting our agreement annulled. He said he could not nor would not undo what God brought together. His wife and he talked me into cooperating with you, giving me several reasons to change my mind."

"Cooperating and changing-zz your mind… hmmm… Anna, pardon my skepticism, but my daddy told me d'that only what's down in d'the well comes up in d'the bucket." Before Anna could respond Bibb said, "And now Anna says, 'D'that was mean! Take it back.' And d'then I say-zz, 'What part of what-zz I said was mean? Was my daddy wrong?' And d'then Anna says, 'You're refusing to be kind and you know I-zz changed. Admit it!' And d'then I say-zz, "Anna, do you believe everything I tell-zz you?" And you say, 'No,' and I might mention no, with feeling. And d'then I say-zz, 'D'than why do you d'think it's strange I-zz don't believe everything you-zz say?' And d'then you get huffy again and before you start sprouting d'those wrinkles again I say-zz, 'What were we talking about? Cooperating and changing your mind?' Anna, it's your turn to talk now. I just saved us some time and wrinkles."

She was hot. "Yes, cooperating and changing my mind Bibb! Why do you look so surprised?" Anna wanted a confirmation of her efforts to improve, not another "daddy said" saying. She was fishing for a reciprocal revelation to come out of the living irritation sitting across from her.

Bibb saw he was heading for trouble and hoped to divert the conversation before it turned ugly for him. "What's d'this have to do with walnuts?"

"Did you hear what I said, Bibb? We are not discussing walnuts here. We were talking about the preacher's reasons for me not to annul the agreement. It was his thoughts but his wife's words."

"Oh. I d'thought walnuts. Can you tell me-zz what d'the wife's reasons were? I didn't ask because I d'thought d'they might be too private. I don't want-zz to tread where I'm not invited."

"They were humbling, Bibb. Actually they were humiliating, and at the time I resented both of them for it. Bibb, I don't think I am the same woman I was a month ago."

"I don't know-zz nothing (srpt) about women enough (srpt) to compare-zz one to-zz another (srpt) or whatever, and-zz I know nothing-zz of your mind (srpt) to know-zz if you-zz really changed your ways (srpt) or if you-zz are just toying with-zz me (srpt). You're asking d'the wrong man-zz (srpt) to comment (srpt) if you-zz are d'the same (srpt) as you-zz were more (srpt) d'than a month-zz ago (srpt)."

Anna noticed how Bibb reacted to this sensitive subject and pounced. "I didn't ask you for a comment! You're supposed to listen, not analyze. Listen to what I am saying, please, will you Bibb? The preacher said I was vain, cruel, and that the Anna Gorgon he knew would delight in destroying you bit by bit, snipe by snipe. He wasn't wrong then, but he's wrong now. Honestly Bibb, I now realize I need you just as much as you need me. I don't want you to think you have to do all the giving and I do all the taking. No. No. A thousand times no. I have changed. Do you see that?"

"No, I don't," replied Bibb in a matter of fact way. "You may be nicer to me, maybe just to get me to d'think d'the way you want me to d'think about giving and taking. I don't know your mind. Nicer d'than what? You had no nice in you d'three weeks ago so I guess even d'the smallest hint of nice would be an improvement. And your comment 'You need me?' Where did d'that come from? Honestly, I don't know. Maybe you need me until we get to Miles City. I hope not, but your history suggests you will drop-zz me like a hot rock once you hear d'that train whistle, pack up all your treasures, and ride d'that iron horse east never to be seen again. You made all your money by making and breaking contracts. D'that's been your secret to wealth, but never is d'that a way to true riches."

Anna's face went pale with disappointment. "Bibb, that is the cruelest thing you have ever said to me. I'm really hurt that you feel that way. You didn't see one ounce of sincerity in my confession, did you?"

"Was I supposed to? I wasn't supposed to comment, remember? And Anna, I didn't say it to be mean. I said it to express my fears about-zz your covenant with me. I so want you to have riches d'that can never be lost. I am scared for both me and you. We have a chance to be either rich or destitute, and if we-zz are not careful we-zz will both suffer beyond what words can express."

Anna was stung by his bluntness. She could not help but strike back at the man. "If you are so smart, poor boy, what is this great secret of yours to be rich forever, as if you have a clue?"

"Do you really want to know, or do you-zz want to mock me? It ain't what you-zz want to hear. It was painful for me to learn, and it-zz will be just as painful for you too."

"I will be the judge about pain around here."

"Have you ever decided d'that you cared for d'the long term welfare of a stubborn man?"

"Why should I? You would only insult me every chance you get."

"Have you ever decided d'that you cared for d'the long term welfare of an insensitive man?"

"You are as insensitive as they get, and yes I said I would try. What is your point?"

"Have you ever decided d'that you cared for d'the long term welfare of an unlovable man?"

"This ain't funny no more Bibb! I know where you are going with this!"

"Secrets aren't meant to be funny," responded Bibb.

Anna fired back, "Have you ever decided d'that you-zz cared for-zz d-d-d-d'the long term-zz welfare of an unlovable woman? No-zzzz, you-zzzz big liar!"

"I will concede d'that trying to love an unlovable woman has done nothin' to change her. I must admit d'that it has done everything to change me."

Anna was beet red and getting madder. "So you think I am the same woman I was a month ago! You have seen nothing positive in my behavior, have you? You think I am worse, and only being kind to manipulate you into doing what I want? Admit it! You think I am vain and cruel! Admit it! You make me sick. I hate you with every inch of my body!"

"It is good d'that you see yourself true, but to do nothing about who you really are, well, d'that is worser d'than unintentional ignorance. D'that is evil."

"Evil???" Anna could not stomach any more of this man. She picked up an unpeeled walnut and threw it at him as hard as she could. Proving her good aim, she nailed Bibb right in the forehead. Before the stunned Bibb could recover from the first surprise a second walnut hit him full force in the chest, and that one really hurt. Instinctively he picked up her artillery from the ground, having a half a mind to return the favor to her forehead. He sensed the varmint's presence. He was now more exposed to an inwardly painful injury than any well-placed walnut. He let them drop.

"Anna, I'm just a blind old buzzard," he coughed, "with holes in my wings. I don't see nothin' but d'that means nothin' (cough). No, d'that is wrong. Maybe you have changed. I don't know. All I know is d'that I have. You stated your opinions quite clearly. If it is any consolation (cough), I can't no longer hate you no more. I hated you fierce in Deadwood, but d'that varmint, no, it's you and d'that varmint (cough) d'that has changed my mind."

"Or your heart, Bibb? What of your heart? That is where your evil resides!"

"I don't know, woman! What heart anyway (cough)? Can we talk about anything else? D'this subject is making my guts churn."

"Yes, we got to talk about something else because you ain't got a clue about feelings, or a heart, or kindness, or sense, or women! I am so tired of your cowardly ways of always shifting the blame to me! Yes! We can change the subject, but you will not deny me my due! You owe me full explanation and a full apology afterwards! You have hurt me to my core! I hate you!"

"Anna," Bibb sputtered doing all he could do to control the rage within, "I got to get up and take a walk. Why do our conversations (cough) always have to turn into mush? Just stop it, woman! I feel like (srpt) I'm caught in a giant spider web and about to get eaten. To be as kind as I must, I'm not telling you no to your demands, but for now I have to get up and go (srpt). Spare me d'the pain, Anna. I hope d'this is what you meant at d'the creek by the one topic I wouldn't talk to you about. I cannot bear (srpt) another 'promise me d'this party' out of you." Bibb, thoroughly upset, got up and turned pointing his finger at her nose. "Anna, when I ask you to talk about anything else, you might seriously consider putting a cork in your bottle before I do (srpt)." Bibb walked away.

"Bibb, please? Do you have to go? Don't retreat from me."

"I'll be back, Anna. Stir d'the berries. Maybe I will get lucky and see d'the fifth Indian." Bibb walked away and didn't look back.

She had it on her lips, but she swallowed them; she gave Bibb the last word.

==0==

Anna sat by the fire ashamed of herself. She had wanted to be kind, but the fire in her always went after the man as if he was inferior and assumed to be withholding information from her. She had just been making progress, and then she did it again. She so wanted to control him. She likened him to a wild horse that needed to be corralled and broken. She felt ashamed about that thought too. Had she not learned anything from today? If she showed him more respect certainly he would openly reveal his heart. That was the problem. She had convinced herself there was not a man alive worthy of her respect after what her husband had done to her.

Anna stirred the berries and turned over some of the beans she had ground to a paste and was baking on the coals. Hopefully it would turn into something like bread. In her time alone by the fire, a new fear come over her like a flash. Terror entered her soul when two close gun shots rang just behind her. She grabbed the gun Bibb had given her and ran to settle her horse.

Bibb's horse was no stranger to the shots but hers was jumpy with the sudden sounds. She really ran to hide between them but found herself occupied with a handful of problems calming her horse. She looked to find where the shots came from and saw no one, not even Bibb. She wanted to cry out for him, but what if it was Toak, and Bibb had been killed? A new fear of being taken came over her. She looked all around – no sign of him.

"Anna! Look-zz what I got!"

Looking off to the side she saw Bibb walking up the rise with two pheasants, one in each hand. "Bibb where did you go?"

"I felt like killing something (srpt), and d'these poor birds showed themselves to me. We-zz will dine like royalty tonight."

"You didn't see Toak?" asked Anna. That was her first assumption after hearing the gun shots.

"Nope."

"Well I am glad you found something then. There ain't nothing else around here to kill but me and the horses."

"Don't worry, Widow Gorgon, d'the horses aren't in any danger. I like horses." Tommy saw the look on her face and then saw the enormity of his oversight. He could think of nothing to say that would undo his comment and not sound lame.

Anna grabbed her gun with both hands. She was shaking. She didn't know what to think. Was this the end for her? She had heard all the stories about Bibb never returning from the prairies with any widows he had taken out with him. He had walked away from camp in red hot anger because she was being her old self. She feared that inside of Bibb's dark soul that a hateful murderous fire was rekindled and burning uncontrollably hot. She could only assume that any nicety he might dream up and then sweetly spit out was nothing but a ploy to get her to let down her guard.

"Put d'that gun away before you hurt yourself, Anna. Toak ain't around here. Help me pluck d'these birds." Bibb knew she was shaking and pointing a loaded gun at him. As long as she stayed on the defense he felt no concern to disarm her, or worse.

Anna watched Bibb as he walked past her and sat down near the fire. "Anna since you're already standing next to the buckboard, can you at least bring over your pillow so I can-zz put-zz d'these feathers in it (srpt)? What's your problem, Mrs. Toivo?"

Anna felt that Bibb's address of her, new words to come through his lips, was a deadly lure. He had never called her Mrs. Toivo before and the timing was very strange. She spoke nothing as she watched Bibb manhandle the birds into fillets. How easily that man took apart something that had been alive just minutes before, nor did he have any problem slashing their throats and ripping their heads off. She looked to see where he was hiding his ax.

"Mrs. Toivo, d'this is d'the quietest you have been on d'the whole trip. If you ain't bringing d'the bag of feathers to me, I guess I will have to bring d'the feathers to d'the bag."

"Mr. Toivo, what are your intentions?"

"Mrs. Toivo, my intentions are to put d'the feathers-zz in your pillow so tonight when you-zz sleep you will be more comfortable. D'this ain't real complicated, Anna."

"Say it again, Tommy."

"D'this isn't real complicated."

"No, say my name again, and say it as if you cherish it-zz."

"Anna…" said as if she was being a silly goose. Bibb blew his chance and saw it in the fear renewed in her eyes.

"Anna, the first day out we-zz both had trouble with the 'L' word. I d'thought we had agreed to not discuss it. Both of us are proven failures at it-zz."

"Are you talking about love, Mr. Toivo?"

"Yes, and I only like horses. I have a different feeling-zz about widows. God has put many widows in-zz my life for good reasons."

"Are you saying that you are fond of widows?"

"I'm not saying d'that at all. Widows are to be appreciated, not to woo. Widows don't belong to me. D'they are more like a flock of human angels sent-zz to cure me."

"Cure you of what?"

"Cure me-zz of me."

Bibb got up from the camp fire with his hand full of feathers. He asked Anna to open up the feather sack so he could deposit them in there. When he walked up close to her she put down the gun and opened the sack, and the deed was done. He started to return to the camp fire when Anna stopped him with her touch.

"Say it again, Tommy."

"Say what-zz?"

"My name."

"My… Oh! How much I… never mind… I got to get d'those birds ready to cook up." Bibb started to walk away and mumbled as he went. "My, nothin'," Bibb muttered. "I can't say stuff like d'that. She's not mine. She belongs-zz to d'the varmint."

Anna overheard him and commented, "Is that a good thing?"

Bibb looked back at her. "No, it is not a good d'thing. It is d'the best d'thing. Anna, let's talk about something else. Help me with roasting d'these birds."

"You're not mad?"

"Angry, but not mad. D'the price of being unlovable causes me to choke, but I will get over it. Don't be asking for an apology anytime soon, and I will take care of all d'the walnuts from now on."

Anna had forgotten about throwing the walnuts at Bibb. She knew that in the past that during her rages she was capable of throwing anything and everything, and equally capable of not remembering it later. Her late husband never forgot about her aim, nor could she expect Bibb to either. Her hate for Bibb subsided, but her hate for her own behavior did not.

==0==

The day had actually warmed up nicely, and once the sun went down so did the wind. Bibb could now take down the windbreak and later burned the poles in the fire. One by one the scouts returned, and each was treated to what Bibb called a big-sky feast upon their arrival.

Later that evening they all enjoyed time by the campfire. Bibb brought out some bark he had peeled from a tree that he knew they enjoyed to smoke. One Indian brought his pipe, which became communal. The Indian claimed it was from the pipestone quarry now in the white man's land.

Bibb signed back, "Then it is from the graves of the ancient ones."

The Indians went silent in wonder how Bibb had obtained that knowledge, but Anna jumped on the opportunity of stillness to interrupt. She asked Bibb to tell their guests that he was going to translate everything to her as it was said. All the Indians thought that was rather strange. First because they assumed she already (by some mystery of the spirit) understood their language. The other reason was their Lakota customs assumed she would have no interest. Her request was very un-Indian. Bibb made a joke about it but failed to translate, but it was unmistakable to her that the English word *bird* was said. Their joking aside, she got her way so nothing else mattered to her.

"So you know of the ancient ones?"

"I know no more than to respect their name. I do not know their ways or actions, but because my hosts honor them, I gladly respect them also. Tell me about Unktehi."

"The rock from which this pipe is carved is stained red with the blood of our ancestors. It is most sacred. The stem of the pipe is from the backbones of our buried people, and the smoke from the pipes is the breath rising from our fathers long dead."

"Did they die with honor?" signed Bibb, and then again he translated the words to Anna.

"When the world was fresh and without blemish the enemy of all people, Unktehi the water monster, caused a great flood. Our peoples climbed the hills above the

332

pipestone quarry as the waters rose. The waters caused rocks to fall and crushed our ancestors. Their blood pooled and forever colored the rocks of that scared place."

"I thought your people believe the Badlands near Deadwood to be the bones of Unktehi. Her ribs are the strange rocks sticking up out of the ground there. How can that be?"

"You do know some of our legend, yes? The Great Spirit's name is Wakan Tanka. He let her out from her bondage to fulfill his great purpose of improving the human race. The lore is unclear. Maybe Wakan Tanka was angry with the human beings and longed for a new people; a new people filled with wise warriors and beautiful women."

"But what of the bones of Unktehi?" asked Bibb.

"Tunkshila, the Grandfather Spirit captured and punished her by turning her to stone. If you stand on her backbone at that sacred place she will shake you off."

Anna inserted herself with a practical question and Bibb translated it. "How did your people survive if all were killed?"

"All but one, Ugly One." (Bibb only translated 'All but one'.) A great eagle, full of spots, allowed a beautiful girl to grab its talons and she flew off to the eagle's home in the highest point of the Black Hills. The eagle's name was Wanblee Galeshka and by a mystery the eagle and the girl married. She bore the eagle twins, one boy and one girl. When the waters receded the twins were the only people of child bearing age. The Lakota Oyate nation was born from the offspring of the eagle and the beautiful maiden through those twins that married."

"So the eagle explains your heritage of being both warriors and wise," remarked Bibb.

Anna also remarked, "And your women beautiful."

When Bibb translated Anna's words the Indians were pleased with her unexpected and sincere compliments. The elder of the scouts asked Bibb if the white man had any ancient legends.

"The white men living in this land are not of one nation, but of many origins. Sadly, many of our memories are only one generation deep. But of those traveling from east to west there is a common ancient story."

Anna looked at Bibb and was just as intrigued as the scouts were. She was unaware that the white man had any origins story.

"Does this story make a lie of the Lakota legend?"

"Or does the Lakota make a lie out of the white legend? You decide. I am not one to pass judgment on our elders. I can only tell the story as best as I remember."

"Then tell us," remarked the eldest scout.

"Like your story, it goes back to when the earth was fresh. The legend starts with a man and a woman, and they had two sons, an older and a younger. In our history these ancients also knew of a senior Great Spirit called the Father and an equal Great

Spirit called the Son. There is also the great enemy of man who delighted in tricking man into believing that the Great Spirits were liars, cruel, mean, and unloving. In truth, the opposite was true. The great enemy was the father of all lies."

"Did the Great Spirit banish the evil one to the Badlands?"

"No, but this enemy's banishment is coming according to the white race's medicine men. Our ancients called them prophets. The trickster of man is still up to his mischief even today, and is one reason why some white men give up being good to become bad. Likewise, the Great Ones causes some bad to become good. There is a war between good and evil, but I must continue my story."

"This great evil enemy is a man, not a woman?"

"Yes, he is referred to as a male, but I do not know why. Let me tell you about these boys from the first man and woman."

"What did they do?"

"They were tricked and they both misbehaved. The Great Spirit had a rule from the foundation of time that all misbehavior must be paid for with blood. Either the misbehaving person must pay with his own blood or find another to shed blood in his place. The Great Spirit would accept the shed blood of a perfect animal, like a lamb, to satisfy the Great Spirit's requirement that all misbehavior must be punished. One of the boys believed the Great Spirit and when he was called to account for his misbehavior, he obeyed and killed his own lamb to satisfy the penalty for his faults. The other brother believed the enemy who told him not to offer blood, but to offer grain instead. The Great Spirit rejected that sacrifice because he mocked the law of the Spirit. That brother's name was Cain."

Anna's ears perked up. She had heard that name before, and it wasn't in a nice context. She asked, "What happened to Cain?"

"He was permanently disfigured, divinely protected from death, and banished from his society; but the story continues on. Like in your history there was a giant flood because the Great Spirit was angry from man's mocking of his wisdom. The Great Spirit found one honorable man and warned him about a coming flood. The Great Spirit told him to build a very large boat for him, his wife, their three sons and their wives, and many animals. When the flood came, only they and the animals on their boat were saved. All the others, the spiritual descendants of the marked brother, perished."

"Was this man saved by an eagle? Did the eagle guide his boat?"

"I do not know, but the Great Spirit saved both the man and at least two eagles. This man, his name was Noah, also saved some lambs, perfect lambs. When the waters receded this faithful man followed the Spirit's instructions exactly, but this time instead of one lamb for one man, the Spirit allowed one lamb for a family of men to satisfy the penalty of listening to the great enemy."

"Did this faithful man have more children?"

"No, but he had many grandchildren, and from them grew many nations. One of these nations was particularly bad but the Great Spirit loved them anyway. Over many generations this family grew into thousands of people, but they were captured and made into slaves. But the Great Spirit saw their tears and told their prophet about the law of the lamb. The nation's wise men listened to the prophet, and convinced each household in each tribe of this nation on one special night to sacrifice a perfect lamb. If they did, the Great One would destroy their oppressor and they would be freed from slavery. They obeyed, the Great Spirit destroyed their oppressor, and they were freed."

"The importance and power of a lamb is increasing. But what about the trickster?" asked the eldest Indian.

"You are right. And later this band of freed thousands became a nation many times bigger, and like all their ancestors, they were not wise to the ways of the trickster. Once again the Great Spirit called upon a wise elder to remind them of the law of the lamb. At the first full moon of the melted snow they were to take a perfect lamb and sacrifice it, but not for each, but now for the whole nation. They obeyed this rule of the lamb, and each year the Great Spirit overlooked their faults."

"Do they still do this?"

"No, because they don't have to. Many generations later the whole world was being tricked by the enemy to not believe the Great Spirit's words. The Great Spirit decided to end the mischief of the great enemy forever. The Father Spirit sent the Son Spirit to remind all men of the rule of the lamb. The men of the world didn't like being told they were both bad and deceived. These bad men decided to kill the messenger. To their surprise this messenger after three days being dead came back to life by the power of the Father Great Spirit. He did not only come back as a man, but also as a divine lamb. And this lamb not only paid the penalty for the misbehavior of one boy, or one family, or one household, or one tribe, or one nation, but this special lamb once and for all time, paid the penalty for all men's mischief for all time, and all nations."

"So why isn't everybody good then?"

"Because the trickster is still running around causing mischief, and man still likes to believe the enemy's lies or believe in only themselves rather than to trust the Great Spirit. In your tradition the trickster is already turned to stone. In our history the trickster's trial is over. He has been convicted and his executioner is waiting on the gallows."

"So in our tradition we have brave and wise men, and beautiful women. In your tradition you have good men who believe the law of the lamb and bad men who either deny it or fight it?"

Bibb continued, "And in your lore the fight between good and evil is over and your trickster already judged and punished. In the white man's tradition the fight between good and evil continues and the trickster is judged but not yet punished.

Our traditions are not the same but have some common themes, one of which is acknowledgement of a trickster and a war between good and evil."

"But many differences," responded the scout leader.

"And I do not have an explanation for those differences. I am grateful I have learned more of your history tonight. I hope you now understand the white man better by hearing some of his tradition."

"But what about you, Bibb? Is this Cain man still alive? Is he marked and banished from his peoples? In the war between good and evil where do you stand?"

"I stand miserable. I do not have an answer. My trail has been that of one who listened to the trickster. I am permanently marked as a descendent of the bad brother because of my many years of denial and warring against the Great Spirit. My trail has been of great mischief, death, meanness, and cruelty beyond measure. I am ashamed of that trail, and my burdens are heavy."

"But you are not walking on that trail now. Our medicine man said so. He spoke of justice following you through the grass."

"Any justice that follows me are not prints from my feet. If the Great Spirit has use for one such as me, He will order my steps. This I do know. I no longer deny the law of the lamb. If the Great Spirit decides to use my feet, I have no choice but to obey. I am not a wise man. I am not a prophet. I am a broken man. I am no longer my own man. I belong to no nation. I belong to no country. I have the mark of Cain upon me, but yet the Great Spirit has chosen to put his moccasin marks over my footprints where I have walked. I cannot explain this, nor can I understand why I have been branded for the tasks that are placed upon me. I am a confused man. I am a wounded man. I do not know my future. I may be killed tomorrow. I am ashamed of myself. If anything good happens when I am present or after I leave, it is not my doing, but of only the Great Spirit's favor. I want to go home, but I have no home. I want safety, but I will never have safety. I want a family, but I never will have my own family. I want citizenship, but I will never have my own citizenship. I want peace, but I will never have personal peace. I no longer own my future; I have traded all of those things away for something higher."

"And what is that?"

"I have been promised I will see the smile of the Father Great Spirit. There is no greater honor than to hear the Son Great Spirit say to me when I reach my end, 'Well done, good and faithful man. Enter into my peace.' For this I will live; for this I will die. May the Spirit's moccasins cover all of my tracks."

==0==

Each of the Indian scouts headed off in a different direction but not very far from the camp. Anna wished them well using a phrase in their tongue that Bibb had taught her. She then went about the business of protecting any food that could be eaten later.

Anna had one word for Bibb once camp broke for the night. Actually it was a gesture, a finger pointed toward the hay bed they had shared the night before. Bibb needed no further prompting, and Anna could tell her wounded man was in one of his thinking stupors. She was right. Bibb was stung by many points in the evening's conversation, but none more than the scout's reference to Anna as the Ugly One. Their phraseology was not simply ugly in the common Indian language, but in their conversation tonight references to her included ceremonial suffixes. What he thought a humorous and harmless name a week earlier had bloomed into a prophetic moniker. Anna would never need to know their low insult or her high epitaph – that Indian name would soon be legendary at council fires and would follow her to her grave. If the medicine man spoke the truth, Anna would grow out of the low meaning of ugly. Bibb connected the clues and soon realized that this wasn't just about Anna. The medicine man had ordered this precise test of Bibb's mettle. How he reacted, whether puffed up or humbled, or choosing to immediately translate to the Ugly One as if they were one, or if he reverenced her name and held it close, would be reported back to many Lakota camps.

Bibb kicked himself for being so dense. "Eagle feathers," he mumbled to himself. He felt that the scouts were sent to watch him more closely than they were sent to watch the trail for dangers. "D'that's okay," he whispered. He was strangely at peace. He remembered the words that Anna of Miles City had said to him: There is no safer place to be then in the center of God's attention. Bibb voiced a prayer heavenward thanking Him that they were safe, they were warm, and they weren't hungry. Bibb almost thanked Him for the varmint's watch over him, but Bibb never quite could get those words out of his mouth. Right or wrong, Bibb concluded that Providence was protecting his trail and the varmint was protecting his soul. The Ugly One? No idea… everything about that woman defied logic. It was never said, but implied by the scout's words that the kindred spirit riding in the wagon with him was suspected to be his twin, repeating and amplifying the ancient Lakota legend. "What a pair we are," chuckled Bibb to himself, "Ugly and Double Ugly." If those rumors were spread, their lives were in grave danger, and there was no humor in that at all.

Anna would have to remain a mystery; and Bibb was okay with that. He pondered the possibility that the eagle feather was Anna's and not his. It was put in her trunk, maybe as a sign of an ancient father. Bibb thought to himself that his credentials were already established with the Lakota. He didn't need any feathers; he was the warrior of Greasy Grass. That name wasn't going away, and if he denied it the title would only stick worse. Bibb fell asleep thinking he was thinking too much. He told himself that he didn't know nothin' about anything anyways, so why should he expect to know anything about the unknowable? Anna wasn't that ugly anyways; only the parts above her ankles.

When Anna arrived at the bed in the wagon Bibb was already asleep. She saw that he had not even taken off his boots. She removed them for him and then climbed in next to him.

She pinched him hard on his ear; hard enough that he woke up. "So am I one of those burdens you have to bear? What did you mean by that?"

It took Bibb a few seconds to collect some consciousness. "D'that's so backwards... Later we will..." and Bibb returned to sleep. Anna snuggled up in front of him, took his leg and threw it over the top of hers and then took his top arm and did the same. Then with some effort she got the blankets over the top of both of them. She was now happily warming inside of her cocoon. This ugly, small, wounded man next to her did have some deep passions. She had looked for them in all the wrong places. His words tonight were of a different language, almost an ancient language. They did not flow like the words he had spoken to her over the last month. They projected authority but there was no condemnation. He spoke almost in a medicine man's cadence. As she closed her eyes she could now understand how her man had internalized his wounds and had come to grips with his disfigurements. Her Cain was a poet and didn't even know it.

She lay perfectly still reliving their afternoon argument, not out of passion or topic, but in victory. Despite his rage she had won. He had addressed her as Mrs. Toivo. Through his own lips he had voiced willing ownership of his responsibilities. She concluded that if the feeling she was feeling right now was a manifestation of what that Deadwood preacher sketched as "decent, right, and proper" ownership, she was okay with that. Her Mr. Toivo was clueless. She was okay with that also.

As she lay there she thought that Bibb's leg and arm should be heavy. They were not. They were warm, and in more ways than she could express. Her last lucid thoughts were even better. There was no ownership involved here, it was co-submission. He was all in. She was all in. He had voiced his dream of seeing her in her mother's arms, and now by some miracle she was dreaming of seeing her Tommy in her mind's eye walking straight, smiling, and riding a horse like a teenager. Although her hair was in knots, her fingernails broken, and in desperate need of cosmetics, there was nowhere under the moon she would rather be tonight. Anna's longed-for communion of being *us*, ugly or not, carried in its unseen pockets wrappings of beautiful warmth. She was more than okay with this situation; strangely contented and... the word escaped her momentarily... but whole, wonderfully whole in newfound happiness. She could not put any magic words to her feelings, but tried. Voiced in her heart she sang a new song in a minor key, "A willing *us*, a kind *us*, a bruised *us*, but fully *us* nevertheless."

Poor Mr. Toivo. He had no idea about the deliciousness of his situation. For that matter, he didn't even know he had gone to sleep with his boots still on.

Sunday, October 16, 1887

Seventh day out from the blessing. The rest was good for both the horses and us. We traveled as many miles today as on our first day. We are seeing less buffalo and more cattle. The scouts told Bibb that they have accomplished their chief's mission of finding wintering grounds. They said they will return to their camp when we discover a wagon trail into the city.

Our best talking day yet. That might have something to do with me losing my sharp tongue. The one question that Bibb ~~hates~~ dislikes hearing is "When are we going to get there?" It just keeps bubbling up and spilling out. Bibb answered many questions today about Miles City, Bismarck, and Fort Rice. The other question he ~~hates~~ dislikes is "Are we lost?"

I am anxious about returning to the land of women. This man's world is harsh and smelly, and I can't help but feel like I am but a ~~burden~~ parcel to be delivered. I very much dislike the possibility that Bibb knew best about what to pack and what not to. That is not completely true. What bothers me greatly is the bitter medicine of knowing I was wrong. Worse; he was right. No, he was lucky. He had no way of knowing what was going to happen in a widow's teepee.

Oh, Bibb finally addressed the question my intuition demanded to be asked. He admitted he was a liar, and his answers allow me to believe what I want. What he doesn't suspect is that I know the truth; and the truth is tucked away in my trunk. The price of my demand was to sleep alone tonight. It was worth it. Out of this spat will come, I dare say, a healthy love.

==0==

ALL WERE UP before dawn. Good dinner, good conversation, and great weather caused all to have a great sleep. Bibb did not even remember going to bed. He just found himself there in the morning, woken by mocking bird perched on the side of the buckboard above his head announcing the soon dawn. He also found out why his arm was asleep. There was an Anna-bird perched on it. Bibb apologized to the Anna-on-it because he was unable to extract himself from the cocoon without waking her. The day had started for both.

"Good morning, Mr. Toivo."

"Good morning, Mrs. Toivo."

"Bibb, you knew that is what I wanted to hear, didn't you?"

"I have no idea what-zz you are talking about, Anna. But look at d'this dawn. It's going to be-zz our best day yet. Where did you hide d'the leftovers? I'm hungry."

"I'll get them, Bibb. I'm getting up too. Are our guests still here?"

"I don't know, but I-zz will find out."

"Did you stay warm last night?" asked Anna in a way to hide her suspicions.

"Perfect." His comment won him a strange smile from Anna. Bibb rethought his comment. He should become stingier with his warm words lest the bunnies overrun the camp.

"For me too, Tommy; let's get going. I can almost smell home from here."

==0==

Anna spent the first miles of the morning wagon ride bundled up. The wind was blowing into their face and Anna wanted nothing of it. Bibb enjoyed the quiet but not the chill. Their first stop was short, about an hour ride north from where they started. The horses enjoyed a patch of green grass and some water from a small creek. Within ten minutes they were on their way again.

"Bibb, I'm really surprised you didn't pick flowers for me this morning. You had a chance at that last stop."

"Why would I do d'that? What have d'those flowers ever done to make d'them worthy of death by pluck'n'? Even d'the weeds are God's favorite flowers growing where man d'thinks otherwise."

"It's our anniversary. Two weeks ago this noon we knelt at the altar together. Did you forget to get a gift for me too? You are supposed to remember such things. Now my feelings are hurt."

"Yeah, mine are hurt too, really bad. I'm about to cry me up a river (srpt) of (srpt) tears (srpt)."

"That would be a change. Up to now you surely haven't shown them. Do you even have any?"

"Someday I might. Liars don't need-zz feelings. Feelings are how lies are squeezed out-zz of honest people. Lies don't have to be squeezed out of liars (srpt), d'they just come out naturally."

"Bibb, honest people can have honest feelings. You need not be so quick to condemn them."

"D'the feelings or d'the people? And d'then you will respond by saying both, and d'then you will ask if anybody I know has ever had-zz honest feelings, and d'then I will say I will d'think about it. Can we drop d'the subject now?"

"So where is my gift, Bibb? I thought for sure you would have one ready to show your appreciation for my companionship."

"Hmmm… What would a woman who has everything, knows everything, is smarter d'than everybody else, and-zz needs no beauty enhancers? Hmmm… (srpt). D'that's a hard one. I know what she doesn't have. I will give her d'that."

"What is it, Bibb?" she said with heightened anticipation.

"Silence."

"That is not a gift!"

340

"Oh yes it is! Believe me. It's a wonderful gift. But I tell-zz you what; for our anniversary I will grant you d'three questions. You d'think of your d'three best questions (srpt), and I promise I will answer d'them, but only if you can keep quiet for ten minutes."

"Bibb, that is not appropriate in our relationship because that isn't being kind. That covenant works two ways, you know! You can prove your kindness by starting to answer my questions now. I will be gracious, and your answers better be too."

"Two ways? It works six ways, Anna, unless you fired and replaced God Almighty."

"That wasn't kind either. Take it back."

"Anna, when you-zz got a problem with me, instead of beating me up with your zings (srpt), why don't you complain to God about it? He has big shoulders, and He can tell you if your complaint is valid or not. If it is, He is big enough to apply corrective action (srpt) to d'the stubborn old goat you're riding with. D'there is no reason for us to argue."

"So you probably have complained to God about me, haven't you?"

"Several times. He is really good at changing you, or changing me, or both."

"Give me an example!"

"I still don't like you much, but I certainly don't hate you anymore. And you've changed too (srpt). Two weeks ago you wanted to sue because you thought you were branded Mrs. Toivo. Now you honor me by accepting my name (srpt). D'that's too big of a change for me to be guilty of rigging. No, God did d'that. I'm not so sure I like d'that or not (srpt), but I'm not going to tell God He made a mistake. God doesn't do d'things for our convenience. Your change in attitude is not just so I can feel good about it today. Your change in attitude is because God is preparing you-zz for something big in your and other's futures (srpt). D'that was how God answered my biggest complaint."

"And what was that, Outlaw?"

"Anna, my complaint was d'that you didn't respect me."

"So you and God are teaming up against me?"

"No, we are teaming up for you. My greatest joy will be (srpt) when your mother-in-law accepts you-zz as her own daughter. Maybe God d'thought it would be productive to polish up d'the gem hidden inside of you (srpt) before you arrived in Fort Rice."

"That is really arrogant. You act as if you are talking for God. A liar and a thief should be more reserved in making such statements."

"You're right. Can I give you d'that gift of silence now?"

"Maybe I should complain to God about you! The problem I would have is not knowing where to start!"

"Start with my arrogance (srpt), since you brought up the subject. He already has me turned around on d'the thieving. D'the lying problem may take considerable more time (srpt). It's so second nature to me-zz. Be careful though. He might take a swipe at your vanity (srpt) while you're listing all my faults."

"Arrogance again! Who are you to know what God is thinking? Who are you to complain about the grease spot on my clothes when you are awash in manure?!!"

"Anna, you-zz have voiced many complaints about me. I know-zz most of d'them if not all of d'them are valid. I knew d'that we would eventually have d'this discussion ever since d'the meeting we had in your barn. Women always find-zz d'thousands of complaints about me. Maybe d'that's why I try my best to avoid d'them beasties. D'the happiest women are d'those who never met me."

"You can't avoid them, Bibb, especially when you're sitting next to one of those 'burdens' you insult as a 'beastie' crossing the continent in a wagon with you."

"Anna, d'that is why I had you promise (srpt) in front of God to be kind to me. If you can direct your complaints to God about my-zz faults and still muster some kindness to me, we-zz both will be better off. Anna, give God a chance to fix me (srpt), and He just might surprise you. D'the important d'thing about God when-zz He answers d'the prayer is d'that we say d'thank you. He delights when we give Him d'the credit for His work. And Anna, I really do want to change, but I can't help-zz but bristle at your high-pitched nagging."

"I don't nag!"

"Honestly Anna, I d'think God has brought us to d'this point for a reason."

"Spit it out. You are going to say it anyway."

"I d'think God wants to get-zz you mad enough to where you finally will talk to Him. If you just believe d'that He exists and give-zz him a chance to show Himself strong to you, you-zz might just be surprised (srpt) how-zz able He is. And what does it cost you if d'there is no God? Even if you are just talking to the stars(srpt), you will discover it's healthier to d'think out your complaints before you launch your tirades into me (srpt) solely based on emotions (srpt) rather d'than logic (srpt)."

"Is that what I do? Is that why you never show any emotions? Well, you ain't that smart either, big boy, and your logic is awful rusty. Arrogance and rust! That is what you are made of!" Anna was really in a huff.

"Can you squeak d'that out for me with a little higher voice (srp.)? I prefer-zz nagging that scares the coyotes too, not just men. Have I got you mad enough yet? Anna, I dare you. I dare you. I triple dog dare you to complain to God with d'these offenses. Tell d'the Al-wimpy you don't d'think He is man enough to be able to fix a single one of your complaints. I just ask-zz you (srpt) to wait-zz until d'the sun comes out before-zz you start whining to God. I don't like-zz close lightning."

"Bibb, you are baiting me to do something you know I won't do."

Since Anna had accused, convicted, and ready to punish him for baiting her, he decided to go ahead and commit the crime. Bibb put the worm on the hook. "Anna, you're heart smart. Can you tell-zz me what is worse, vanity or lying?"

"Why can't you just fix yourself? Why can't you just stop your reprobate ways and change?"

"To become just like you? What's worse, Anna, vanity or lying?"

She hated it when Bibb thought ahead and prepared an answer for her following questions. She took a deep breath to calm herself. In a less shrill voice she spoke, "Bibb, I am tired of you poking that vanity accusation at me."

On purpose of not, Bibb's response was immediate and said loudly without any hint of kindness. "Well d'then why can't you just fix yourself, Anna? Why can't you just stop your reprobate ways and change? I'm sorry. D'that is just what you-zz told me to do (srpt). How careless of me to remind-zz you d'that we are both nothing better d'than rust and-zz rotten eggs."

"Stop the wagon! I want out!" Her shrill control was short lived. She had tried to be reasonable.

"Anna, I won't. If we-zz do d'that, our scouts will come running here as fast as d'they can. D'the wounds on top of your hands testify d'there is no quarter in d'their world given to women who disrespect authority (srpt). D'they are bound by an oath to deliver me to Miles City. If you make it d'there too it will be because I chose to let you ride with me and you chose to conduct yourself in regard to your right and proper station in life. D'they may punish you. As you know (srpt), Indian punishment is immediate, painful, purposeful, and harsh. I will not stop d'the wagon and risk your life. You need to swallow gracefully what you d'think are emotional insults d'that are not insults. Both of us need fixing and d'that is just an undisputable fact you illogically want to dispute."

"Liar! What do you know, Mr. Fork-Tongue, about the scout's behavior away from their chief? All men are bent morally!" Truth be known, Bibb's use of the clause 'Right and Proper' irritated her badly. This worried Anna. Bibb had to know something about the envelope hidden away in her trunk. Anna's mind raced with self-justifying reasons she could use to prove Bibb as the only illogical person in their conversation. Mr. Franklin? Mrs. Franklin? Somehow Bibb knew.

Bibb replied as calmly as he could to her accusation. "Have I been wrong so far about d'their ways? Maybe you-zz could catch a ride with Toak. He will be glad to offer you a ride (srpt), or at least tie you-zz up and drag your carcass behind his horse."

Anna changed her tone. "Bibb, let's be reasonable."

"What do you-zz suggest?"

"I suggest we start this conversation over."

"Just so we could do-zz it all over again later d'this afternoon? Anna (srpt), I have a sincere request to make of you d'that will resolve all of d'this."

"What is that, Bibb?"

"Will you pray with me d'that God will fix my logic, my arrogance (srpt), my thieving, my lying, and as well as your most recent complaint, being morally bent?"

"Are you serious?" She was surprised he had listened to her. She hadn't been listening to him.

"Do you-zz want to see lasting changes in me?"

"Absolutely! Starting right now!"

"Let's start right now d'then."

"What are you suggesting?"

"Hold my hand, Anna, and I will do d'the praying."

"That's it?" She reached over and took Bibb's closest hand into hers. "Okay Bibb, I will cooperate. This better work."

Bibb responded without closing his eyes or kneeling or even stopping the rig. He then voiced a simple prayer aloud and fast. "Father, you have heard all-zz of Anna's complaints. She wants you to fix me to where she-zz can respect me. I want to be fixed, and I want you to get all d'the credit for it. Amen." He let go of her hand as the *n* in *amen* was escaping from out of his mouth.

"That's it?"

"Wasn't d'that enough? We asked for more d'than most folks could request in a whole year. You held my hand, so it-zz was your prayer too (srpt)."

"Don't I have to ask for something?" replied Anna. She grabbed his hand again.

"Anna, the prayer is over. You can let go of my hand now."

"No, there are some other things I want."

"Well you tell Him d'then. I can't read-zz your mind."

"God, fix Bibb fast so he doesn't embarrass me when we get to Miles City. Amen."

"Anna, d'that was a good prayer, and you are hurting my knuckles. Please let go."

"Why?"

"I need-zz my hand back, Anna, and we-zz said enough to God."

Anna, exasperated with the man and thinking him condescending, spoke the word *dunce* under her breath. She dared to ask, hoping that he might redeem himself. "Why was that a good prayer?"

"Because you-zz were specific. You made it easy on God to prove to you He is worthy of your trust. You can let go of my hand now."

"Can we talk like normal couples now?"

"From what I know of married folk we-zz have been talking like normal couples for almost an hour! Can we give it a rest for a while (srpt)? My mouth hurts, and let go of my hand, please."

"Mine too. Bibb, let's promise each other that we will be especially kind to each other for the rest of the day. I don't want to fight no more." She noticed immediately that in Bibb's previous statement that 'normal couples' evolved into 'married folk' all in the same breath. She suspected now more than ever that Bibb knew the truth.

"Anna (srpt), I must confess to you a weakness."

"What is it Bibb?" She really wondered what else was on his mind.

"I can't fight with you if you-zz are holding my hand."

"Well then, you should hold my hand more often."

"Anna, I fall apart when we do d'that. I get d'the shakes and my mind goes mush and-zz splatters in a d'thousand directions. No, I can't do d'that. D'there has to be something really bad happening for me to want to do d'that. Anna, can you keep my secret? It's so embarrassing."

"No."

"Why not-zz?"

"It's not your secret anymore. It is our secret now, and it is safe." Anna took his hand by the wrist and told him to stick out his little finger. He complained but she took control of his hand anyway. She took the pinky from her other hand and wrapped it around his and squeezed it.

"Bibb, our big promises we will take to the altar. Little promises, like this one, we will seal as a pinky-promise. With this little squeeze of our littlest members, we promise to be faithful to each other. Bibb, I promise to keep our secret secret."

"Isn't d'this childish, Anna?"

"It would be if it was trite, and if a woman's touch wasn't so traumatic for you. Tommy, this will be our simple way of showing that we have peace with each other and a renewal of our covenant of kindness. Do you agree?"

"Can't we-zz just say it?"

"No, Bibb. That ain't good enough. God hasn't fixed your lying problem yet."

"Anna, I have another confession."

"What is it, Bibb?"

"D'this is d'the very first moment I have been comfortable being next to you. D'the air is clear, and we-zz are now a d'threesome."

==0==

As the sun became full overhead it became comfortably cool, so Bibb took advantage of that to push the horses a little harder. Anna's horse was now up for the challenge. The streams cooperated too, being shallow and not requiring either to get soaked. What made it the most comfortable for the passengers was that they were not fighting anymore.

"Bibb, have you thought anymore about the words of the medicine man? Evidently our scouts have. One made reference to it the other night."

"You know-zz I didn't ask for any of d'that prediction stuff, Anna. I only asked to leave d'the camp in peace and-zz with a short 'God bless your journey' from d'the chief. All d'the medicine man's words were totally unexpected."

"Why are you so defensive? You act as if you didn't like it. Didn't it make you feel special?"

"Too special. Yes, too special. His d'three predictions for you were something to look-zz forward too. D'the d'three predictions for me were death and pain. You know-zz d'they won't keep d'those predictions secret, don't you? D'they will be-zz discussed at many councils and pow-wows. Expectations will be-zz set. D'those at war with d'the Lakota will delight in proving d'the Lakota medicine men to be false seers by-zz preventing d'the blessings to be fulfilled."

"How would they do that?"

"Do you d'think d'the chief sent four scouts instead of two because he was overjoyed d'that we gave him some practical gifts? D'there may be another reason. D'there is-zz another reason."

"You said it was to search for winter camp. Do you now think otherwise?" replied Anna.

"Anna, it would be harder for me to carry out justice on d'the plains if I was dead. It would be equally hard for you to give birth to a prophesized child if your reproductive organs are harvested from you alive and-zz offered to a foreign spirit."

"Bibb, that can't be."

"Okay, should we-zz agree d'that d'the chief did d'that because I'm as cute as you-zz are ugly? What two virtues did d'the scouts elevate in telling d'their origins legend?"

"Beauty in women, and the wise warrior traits found in their men."

"Anna, nothing has changed in d'these people. We entered d'their camp with unexpected gifts and high respect for d'their culture. D'they d'thought d'they saw something in us, or at least in you, or on you, d'that reminded d'them of d'their legend. Just like with d'the lambs, d'their legends repeat d'themselves over and-zz over with increasing scope. D'their legends increase with power too."

"Bibb, did you see those prophecies coming?"

"Never in a million years, Anna. I was glad to leave d'there alive and with you as a bonus. I did not piece d'the puzzle together until d'they told us d'the pipestone legend at-zz the campfire. D'that-zz was not a mistake. D'that story was told on purpose. D'they have hundreds of legends, but d'that was d'the one d'they chose, or was commanded to tell us. Scouts don't carry sacred pipes when searching out buffalo. D'their medicine man must have given d'them d'that special pipe, and with it, his instructions."

"Are we in danger?"

"Cherish every breath you breathe, Anna. Not-zz only here, but wherever we end up. D'the prophecies do not cease at d'the borders of d'the Indian nations. I actually hope for your sake d'that d'these prophecies were from God. If God gave d'these secrets to d'the medicine man (srpt), d'then you will have a boy. God's promises cannot be frustrated by man. You will have at least nine months more to live (srpt). But if d'the predictions were just wishful d'thinking, d'then we-zz both could be catching arrows at any time. We are much worse off for d'these predictions. Anna, we-zz are now marked for life, however long d'that may be. Like it or not, your story and my story will be forever linked in d'the red man's legends. Mrs. Cain, for d'this I am deeply sorry. You deserve better. I have to ask. Did you-zz really give a lock of your hair to one of d'the Lakota women?"

"Why are you asking me that now? Bibb, this is unnerving. You make it sound like I need to be looking for danger over my shoulder for the rest of my days."

"If I live, I will see-zz d'that lock of hair again. Anna, you were warned (srpt) about hitching your destiny to mine. Welcome to my fate. Not-zz only do I want to get you to Fort Rice (srpt), I want to hide you-zz in Fort Rice."

"Bibb, I can't take any more of your lies! What gain are you expecting from scaring me so? You need to come clean! What nauseous thoughts are you brewing up in your thinking?"

"Anna, I'm serious. Go ahead. You put together d'these pieces and tell me what your conclusion might be. Anna, consider d'this from d'the medicine man's point of view. D'the fairest of maidens arriving in a princess's dress bonded in an all-night death grip to-zz a spotted eagle. What-zz was he to d'think after getting d'the scented dress and d'the widow's report about our first night together – Lakota hug d'their women, not women wrapped so tightly as to injure d'their men. Anna, connect d'the clues. D'the woman and d'the warrior. D'the prince bearer and d'the justice bearer. Anna, you must see d'this with d'the red eyes of d'the medicine man. D'they look for signs of d'the spirit and d'then d'the physical marks of proof. Anna, consider you with your princess hair bearing gifts of combs; and d'then my fighting spirit bearing scars of a soldier. Anna, all d'these pieces are coming together for me and-zz I feel so slow in wit. I should have known. You must tell-zz me true. I-zz already know what you were d'thinking wearing d'that expensive dress on our first day; and guess what – you guessed wrong. I pray your decision d'that morning to wear d'that worthless fancy and lacy d'thing was an unwitting cooperation with providence. If it wasn't, d'then d'the medicine man's blessings may all be devilish and we-zz will end up tragic actors in an evil outcome. Anna, tell me true. What were you-zz d'thinking to give d'them your hair? I got-zz to know."

"How was I supposed to know about this deep under-story?"

"D'this will all happen fast. All d'the ingredients calling on strong medicine are in place. All but one. D'they need-zz to lure me into a convergence."

"Bibb, what's that, and what do you mean by strong medicine?" Anna suddenly wished she had changed the conversation rather than ask those questions. Bibb was deep in thought.

"Anna, you know not d'their ways yet. Tell me exactly how d'they got your hair."

"You answer me first. What convergence?"

Bibb thoughts were already putting a *where* in place of Anna's *what*. "D'the prediction is now running d'the plains. Some will want to prove the Lakota liars. Some will want to use d'the convergence to bring war. D'the holy men will want to bring peace. D'the suffering souls of d'the tribes will want icons of healing. Did d'they take your hair or did you give it?"

"Bibb! Answer me. This isn't funny. Focus. What convergence?"

"Anna, I really don't know. D'this ain't funny to-zz me either! I will be summoned, but I do not know how. I will be lured, called, or dragged. I do not know if I should cooperate, because it may be, or-zz will be my life. My guess is at a sacred site of d'the ancients; a ceremonial site. Under another pretext, valid or fabricated, I will find myself bled out in-zz d'the midst of something well beyond my understanding."

"What will happen? What do you think might happen?"

"Anna, I don't know, but for d'the convergence d'there must be a presence of Unktehi, and I have no idea what d'that would look like or be. Anna, I answered your question. Now you answer mine. Anna, yes or no. Was d'that a lock of your hair d'that d'the matron had? How many locks-zz does she have?" Bibb's tone was unmistakably urgent and sincerely serious.

"You scare me Bibb, and without cause. You make it sound like if I did not give it to them then they would have scalped me! They may want to scalp me now! Stop it!"

"Anna, d'think like d'they do. D'think calmly. D'they don't engineer history, d'they live history. Your hair would be worthless if d'they took it from you. Mrs. Cain, d'this is entirely different. You gave it to d'them, didn't you? You gave it freely without being asked?" Bibb paused to think as Anna kept her silence. "Yes, d'that was d'the sign. D'that was d'the sign d'that pulled d'the trigger. How did you cut your hair, Anna? Tell me true."

"With my grandmother's scissors."

"And where are d'they now? Where are d'the scissors?"

"They have them. I never got them back from the Indian women."

"I will see d'them again."

"Well then, bring them back for me."

"D'they ain't coming back. D'they were recognized and received as a gift to d'the Lakota."

"Bibb, why don't you and I run away together far away from all this drama? Why not California? Why not Boston? Why not Europe?"

"Anna, we did run away together, and look-zz at d'the mess we are in. Anna, we have nothing to fear from d'the Indians. D'the one I have to respect and fear crossing (srpt) is d'the varmint."

Anna didn't say it, but the logical underpinning of Bibb's theory was that Bibb's courage and reputation were no accident, nor was her beauty. She had liked to think that she was beautiful because she took extra time to care for herself and she made herself that way. She had to consider the possibility that there was a God, and He had fashioned her specifically for a role in this drama. Bibb had said that he didn't believe in luck anymore. Too many coincidences put a lie to that. The Deadwood preacher said to her that God had his hand all over that boy. Looming large in her soul was the possibility God had made her exactly the way she is for this exact place and moment in time.

Ten minutes down the trail her smile caught Bibb's eye. Little did he know that she had put all that legend talk in the imaginary fate bucket and threw it out the back of the buckboard. She turned to much more pleasant thoughts, like planning ways to control her spotted eagle… and he had a lot of spots to rub out of his character. The only certain thing she concluded in those minutes was that all her nagging of Bibb was ordained of God for his benefit. It was her job to make an honorable man out of him. No, she could never change him by nagging. Real change in that man would come from holding his hand… and yes, salted with some respect. She signed up for that man's physical healing, but she would count it all joy as she labored at the bonus task of fixing the man's heart. She knew that to accomplish that task her heart would have to be set aright too. She knew her dark heart could use some improving too, and now she had a noble reason, a calling, to rid herself of her stink'n' think'n'. She had never attempted anything noble in her life and it was about time she started to show something for all the blessings she had accumulated. Her mind wandered back to Deadwood. Mr. Franklin had said she, if she succeeded, would be the crown jewel in his life's work. What would be hers? She had many thoughts, and all of them purposefully delicious. "For this and more I may have been born," came a whisper from deep within her soul.

==0==

The conversations in the wagon got increasingly more pleasant for both as they journeyed northward. She asked once or twice, or thrice "When are we going to get there?" and all Bibb could say was that he was recognizing landmarks again. She creatively asked "Are we lost?" in at least a dozen different ways mixed in with all her other questions that afternoon.

"Anna, can you change the subject please."

"Now that you are not acting so spooky, you can finally answer my question. Tell me why Toak would want to take me alive? He believes you would trade any promise he would ask in exchange for my life, yes?" She smiled. He wanted a new subject and he certainly got it!

Bibb answered soberly. "You mean his life, and pray-zz he does not yet know d'the predictions. Toak is no rash fool. If I could win Toak as a friend again, your safety would improve greatly. Toak's home is in Fort Rice, and based on our past bonds, he would become your Indian protector. D'that is a very large if. He is your worst enemy until he and I settle d'the betrayal issue."

"What betrayal issue?"

"I was naïve. I did not see it coming. He taught me tracking. I taught him d'the rifle. He taught me d'the ax. I taught him d'the whip. He taught me how to fish with my hands and I taught him how to cook. Toak has saved my life many times, and I also saved his. He taught-zz me his language and I taught him ours. On horseback we shared our lives over d'thousands of miles. D'the bond could not-zz have been any deeper. For d'the first time in my life I d'thought I had a friend. But my ribs and legs tell-zz a much different story. And Toak's story did not start with me. He is a master betrayer of both red and white. But I do not want to slander him. I try my best not to speak ill and eat myself up with bitterness. D'that is so hard, d'the hurt is d'that deep, but I still-zz wonder-zz if d'this can be fixed. Ask my brother; Toak is no worser d'than me-zz. You read d'the papers. I have nothing to add to d'them. D'there may not be-zz a bottom to d'this deep well."

This lamentation was almost incoherent. Anna knew Bibb's brother was dead. She keyed her response to Bibb's last phrase. "So deep you will never want a friend again?"

"Yes."

Anna was very frustrated but dared not show it. She had hoped for a different response that might show a return on her emotional investment in the man. His not mentioning her as a friend or potential friend hurt. She redirected the conversation away from what she first perceived as an insult but quickly recognized as a bitter truth. "Bibb, please answer my first question. Are we in danger?"

"I'm d'thinking not so much now, but d'there is a lot of pieces still d'that haven't made sense yet. I don't d'think d'the feather was a gift anymore. Naw, Mrs. Toivo, I'm seeing way too much *much* in this too much *much*. We have more miles behind us d'than in front of us. It won't be long and we will-zz be on d'the train east and d'then shopping for real clothes in Bismarck. Come spring, my chest will be fixed and you-zz will have a real ma hugging on your neck."

"Are you admitting you are wrong about all those Indian tales?"

"I'm admitting I don't know hardly nothing 'bout anything, but you knew d'that."

"But you currently have strong misgivings about past and future friendships, yes?"

"I know I am naïve about people. I need to pick people d'that aren't as smart as me for friends, but-zz I ain't sure d'there are any such critters. And stop what-zz you are d'thinking. Yes, d'that was stupid. Anna, I ain't good at-zz friends. God will have-zz to pick me one; I pick-zz awful."

She let him have that last word on that subject. She silently gave the man a compliment about his candor and a scolding about calling himself stupid. She saw his need, and for the next couple hours their discussions were lively and colorful. Bibb was so much better at communicating now, and she was so much better at ignoring the slurps, dahs, and zz's. They talked much of Anna's childhood, how she happened to fall in love with Mr. Gorgon, and her desire not to become pregnant. She explained she did not want to be a dependent nor have a dependent. She also said that she used sex to control her husband. Not only did she consider such marital obligations messy and primitive, but over time she learned and perfected the tease and denial tactic to always get her way. Besides destroying their marriage, she mentioned that tactic got her beaten regularly and him becoming a willing victim of the clam. Anna was shocked how easy it was to tell Bibb these intimate secrets without shame or fear. She, in her heart, concluded it was their covenant of mutual kindness.

Anna also extracted many stories out of Tommy. Much time was spent telling about the real Tommy and his misbehaving twin brother Terry. Bibb also told the story of the haunting of Fort Rice. His joke on the town really boomeranged on him. On the bright side, he mentioned that his most favorite families were the Finnish sodbusters up on the prairies just west of the valley edge.

==0==

Despite Anna's urging otherwise, they made camp late this night. The scouts were fed and then went back to their posts on the perimeter. Anna offered Bibb a warm spot next to her on the hay mattress but Bibb told Anna that the horses were getting very jealous of her. Bibb went down the hill to take extra time to brush them down, gave some extra feed with some horse-apples found in a thicket by the spring. As a treat that only a horse could enjoy Bibb started to sing them to sleep. Anna heard his bad attempt at a yodel from a distance noting that man would never be allowed near or in a church choir. It was so bad it was good. The spirit was good. The sound was terrible. Because it was a sensitive spot Anna thought, "And that man complained about her high-pitched nagging!"

Anna decided it was now time and sweetly approached Bibb who was still brushing down the horses. "Bibb, there has been something that has really bothered me for several days, and I want you to come clean. Now that we are getting along better I feel safer in asking you a simple question."

Bibb's response to her tone was not what she desired, but in fact the opposite, putting him on guard. "Is it-zz d'that bad? I promised I wouldn't touch you wrong and I haven't."

"Safe emotionally, Bibb, not physically. I already trust you physically. But I can't help but think that varmint of yours is evil."

351

"Oh Anna, do not say d'that. You can say d'the varmint is mean, you can say d'the varmint is annoying, but never be so wrong to say d'that d'the varmint is evil. It is good and only good."

"But that varmint of yours is either lying about something or you are lying to me about something. I want you to come clean so I know which one of you is trying to deceive me."

"D'that's easy, Anna. Given d'that choice, it's me d'that has-zz been d'the bad boy. What did I do so wrong for you to decide d'this?"

"If I ask you something, will you swear to me that your answer is the truth?"

"Anna, I don't swear-zz no more. What's d'the question?"

"Will you swear that you have truly given up lying and murder? I want to be able to trust you."

"Anna, if I tell-zz you I'm telling d'the truth, what is stopping d'that from being a lie?"

"Because I know your horse would know if you're lying. If you lay your hand on your horse, and I ask you if you have given up lying, and if you say yes, and if your horse doesn't react, I'll know you really have given up lying. I am certain your horse can tell by your nervousness that if you said yes and it was a lie, your horse will react, and it probably will never trust you again. Bibb, for me, can you submit to that simple truth test? I just can't stand not knowing for sure about you."

"Anna, isn't d'this just a bit silly?"

"Don't you believe in horse sense? Is the price of your assumptions of silliness worth more than the peace of mind you can give me about my deepest question?"

"Okay Anna, I will put my hand on my horse, and you ask-zz your question. Sometimes I really don't understand you. If you d'think my horse can detect truth and for you to gain peace of mind, go for it. Ask your question, and d'the horse will tell you true. Really, Anna, has it come to d'this? I already told you I don't lie, cheat, and murder no more."

"Then you will have no problem putting your hand on your horse and give me a truthful answer. Bibb, there is your horse, put your hand on its neck. I will ask my question, and I will know for sure when you give me an answer whether you are still lying to me."

"I'm not 'still lying' to you, Anna. I have given up-zz on lying."

"Put your hand on your horse then, and let's see what your horse has to say."

"D'this is silly, but to be kind and to satisfy you not only will I put one hand on my horse, I will put both arms around its neck. It likes d'the lovin' anyway." Bibb started talking to his horse and it responded to his presence just as so many times before. "Okay Anna, ask your question if you must and I will answer it if I must."

Anna stood near Bibb with both hands on her hips. She changed her tone from all sweetness to more like a boardroom strategy session. "Bibb, are we married?"

Bibb balked and the horse sidestepped. Bibb, stunned, was pushed into a panic by her question.

Anna shouted at Bibb, "I thought so, you big liar!!! Sleep with your horse if it will have you!!! You are more despicable than the low life crud of barnyard scum! Every word out of your mouth for the last month has been a lie! You disgust me, Mr. Terry Tommy Toivo!!!"

"I didn't answer your question! How did I lie?"

"You didn't have to. Your horse answered the question for you!"

"Anna!"

"Don't call me Anna!" She stomped back up the hill to the buckboard leaving Bibb in a fog.

==0==

Bibb did not see that coming nor could he ignore it. He had to do something, but what? If he would go up the hill to the buckboard and try to reason with that wet cat, well, other than getting his eyes scratched out what would that accomplish? If he didn't go up the hill and try to reason with the wet cat, well, that would be the same as telling her that she concluded rightly. He felt bad that he had scared his horse badly when he recoiled at Anna's question. He comforted his beast, rubbed it down some more, and talked to it softly concerning how much he appreciated all the work he had done this last two weeks. The horse felt better, but Bibb was still tied in a knot.

Bibb decided he could not avoid the confrontation forever. He knew that she would not have been mentally idle since she stomped off in a huff. He considered taking the offensive in their next conversation. He did what he usually did when he was stumped about what to do; he sat down on a stump and sharpened his ax. His remembered what his dad had told him as a little boy, "That is why they call it stumped." He never remembered his mom and dad arguing, but did remember dad going back behind the shed when things weren't going well between them. He now smiled. Maybe he inherited this habit from his father to withdraw and sharpen his tools when frustrated by women.

About fifteen minutes later Bibb caught out of the corner of his eye a figure walking down the hill with a stick still burning from being taken from her campfire. It was not terribly bright, but it did the job to help her down the dark hill to where Bibb was sitting. She called out to him, "Bibb, I am coming down the hill to talk to you. Where are you?"

"I'm over here," replied Bibb. "You stay where you are and I will walk to you. We can walk back up d'the hill together." In just a few moments Bibb's face could be

353

seen by Anna. She also saw he had a whetstone in one hand and his ax in the other. She was already nervous, and this didn't help. "Anna, follow me. Let's sit down by-zz d'the campfire and talk d'this out." Anna did not speak, but followed him up the hill where they both found places to sit opposite each other with the fire between them.

"I made some coffee, Bibb. Would you like some?"

"It would be-zz awful hard to share the same cup on different sides of d'the fire, Anna, but yes, I-zz would like some." She got up, poured some for him, gave it to him, and returned to where she had been sitting. He seriously wondered what she was thinking.

"Anna, I did not expect your question, and I jumped. My response surprised my-zz horse and it gave me room to catch my step. I did not lie. What is d'the real issue here? What is wrong-zz?"

"Bibb," she said coldly, purposely trying to remove the emotion from her hurt, "I have woken up each morning when we have slept close with a nagging thought that must be resolved. That varmint of yours will not let you even look at me funny, will not let you lie, will not let you feel ill towards another, allows for no oops in the night, will not let you swear, nor will it let you say any evil towards Humbird. Yes, that is all good, but why does this same varmint let you sleep with me, you holding me or me holding you, without a peep out of that critter? No soul on this earth has to go to church to know how God feels about two unmarried people sleeping together, even if it is just an *us* and not as one. You said the varmint is good and only good, so why does that critter permit this? What am I to conclude except that we are somehow legally married? What have you done to me? What have I done to you? Why are you not bit up one side and down the other by that varmint over this gross trespass of the law? We must be married. There can be no other explanation if that pet varmint of yours really is some kind of agent from God. And what about your overactive conscience? Why isn't that newborn conscience of yours hoppin' upset? Tell me Bibb, are we married? Did you pull some rabbit out of your hat before we left from Deadwood?"

"D'there are no-zz rabbits, Anna, and d'this has bothered me more d'than you will ever know. I want to remain pure, and with a pure conscience to ask Humbird to marry me when we get to Fort Rice. I feel very, very strongly d'that Humbird and I are fated, d'the best fate a man could ever wish for, to be wed and grow old together. D'this isn't a new feeling. Many in Deadwood know d'this deep conviction of mine. Anna, marriage to you would be convenient for now as we travel across d'this continent together, but so ill-advised in so many other ways. I'm not wronged, but you certainly would be ruined and tortured to be married to me. Banish d'the d'thought. No, don't banish d'the d'thought, but consider our covenant to be stronger d'than words, witnesses, and court registers. Our covenant was blood bonded at d'the altar of God, and like marriage, what God has joined together let not any man trifle with. I am not worthy to even touch your hair, much less ask for your hand."

Anna kept staring. She disciplined herself not to speak and risk side-tracking him. He may not be lying, and even if so, Bibb's wounded heart was laid bare. She was not going to put words into Bibb's mouth. This moment may never come again. She kept silent, communicating with her eyes.

"Anna, I have d'thought much about d'this and you must consider other d'things. D'the first night we met, you in d'the black veil, I felt compelled as if it was a calling for me to agree with you. D'there was no desire in my heart, for I truly hated you with all d'the hate I could hate with, but d'the varmint said yes, and I obeyed. I feared for my very life as I lay severely wounded at d'the Red Buffalo, and for what? D'this I do know: God gave me my very life back, so who was I to say no? It was at d'that very moment I was joined to you, and what I feel very strongly about, actually more d'than a feeling but a divine appointment, is d'that varmint has surprisingly given me d'the gift of peace about us. To answer your question, I must rely on what a widow once told me explaining why I can remain close to you when our eyes are closed. It is a matter of child's play, and no more complicated d'than d'that."

"Child's play?" replied Anna, not knowing if that was an insult. "Explain."

"Anna, Fort Rice has a small school and very little room outside d'the building for children to run and play during recesses and lunchtime. Our teacher, d'the Widow Nelson, couldn't stand us children not running around and staying huddled around d'the doors during our free time. She solved d'that problem by getting d'the banker to put up a picket fence around d'the school grounds. From d'that very day d'the kids played right up to d'the fence edge instead of huddling close to d'the doors. Horses and cows are d'the same. Put d'them on d'the free range and d'they will stay close to d'the barn. Put up a fence around d'the barnyard and d'they will wear a path within inches of it all day long."

"What is your point, Bibb?"

"At d'the altar you added to our promises a new promise of your own. You drew d'the fence line for me. If I dared touch you-zz wrong, you would end my life. Period. End of Bibb. End of story. Because of d'that standard, your standard, (and I like to d'think also ordained by God and sanctioned by d'the preacher), I have had peace in d'the teepee, in d'the buckboard, in d'the dark, and at d'the campfire. I also want to make something very clear to you, Anna Gorgon. I have no feelings for you in any way d'that would ever hint of a desire for marriage, banish d'the d'thought. You are what you are, and a d'thousand percent full of everything d'that I consider irksome about any woman. You have brought out d'the best in me and d'the worst in me. If I had my choice you would still be in Deadwood. My feelings have softened, but I am still far from liking my lot in life. God didn't ask me if I liked my lot in life. He told me to obey first and I would understand later. Okay, I understand a lot more now, and my lot ain't as bad as it was, but to tell you d'the truth I ain't d'the happiest man on d'these plains. For example, you don't know how badly you have hogtied me by wearing my clothes. D'that is so wrong, but I had to swallow d'the notion d'that maybe I was d'the one d'that was wrong and realize how disgustingly selfish I am-zz. So why have I stayed close to you each of d'these nights? D'the practical answer is d'that I don't like to be cold either. D'the real answer is d'that your life depended on it. If d'those scouts ever suspected you were not my woman, you would be taken away from me and auctioned off for d'the highest price. Anna, my dislike for you doesn't matter a hill of beans compared to d'the value God puts on your life and d'that varmint makes me honor. Once we are away from d'those Indians, Anna, be not offended, but I have no intention whatsoever continuing d'that habit. Why do I carry on d'then and not leave you on d'the side of d'the trail? D'there's a spiritual reason, and no court paper or a register in some log book will change d'the clear truth I have about our covenant. D'the covenant is primary. If we are married, which was your chosen topic for d'this evening and definitely not mine, d'that would be secondary. I am-zz to honor you-zz with my whole life, and if need-zz be, my whole death. It doesn't matter one iota if you misbehave or not, my role in our relationship is set. I must fulfill d'the covenant or die trying. It is not an option, and if marriage is required, well, marriage is required. Some say yes like d'the very opinionated Mrs. Franklin. Some say no, like Fanny down d'the street from d'the Red Buffalo, but d'their opinions don't matter. It is d'the covenant, Anna; it's d'the covenant. And d'the covenant has its own reward in its wings upon fulfillment. I will be healed, but you, Anna, you will be fulfilled. D'this is as true of a truth d'that can come out of my mouth. My deepest desire in my heart is to see you in Fort Rice embraced and adopted by Mr. and Mrs. Gorgon as d'their very own and only living descendent. I can see d'that in my mind's eye right now better d'than I can see you at d'this campfire. D'that is my calling. D'that will be my life's reward. I am not going to muddle up anything d'that might interfere with d'that possibility, and marriage to you would kill me, kill you, and kill your in-laws. D'they hate-zz me Anna, and d'they will hate-zz me worser d'than worser when d'they find out about d'their son. But Anna, trust me on d'this: d'they will love you, love you, and love-zz you more. D'they will love you with everything in d'their heart, mind, and soul, and more d'than your heart could contain or ever dream of d'this side of heaven."

"Oh." That is all Anna could say. Her eyes were wide open.

"Anna, do you want-zz me to say we are married? Okay, we are married. If you want-zz me to say we are not-zz married. Okay, we are not-zz married. I am a liar and you get to pick d'the lie you like d'the best. But Anna, my heart is set; my will is resolute. I will-zz get you home. Not for me. Not for you. But because of d'the varmint. D'this is all his doing-zz, and if d'there is blame for it, he gets it. If d'there is credit for it, let him get all d'the glory. If I get healed up or if I die, d'that is for his credit too. Regardless, my job is to obey first and understand later. Good night, Anna. I am sleeping with my horse tonight. I scared him bad and I'm not-zz going to leave his side tonight." Bibb took the first sip of his coffee and left into the dark of the night.

Anna sat there awhile wishing her husband might return. Ever since she was a little girl she thought marriage was the ultimate level of a relationship between a man and a woman. Her Tommy certainly had different thoughts, and she had to grant him the possibility that he was right. Would the varmint be leaving Bibb alone if they were just married and not bound in a covenant? No, the covenant was superior to the marriage, and the law of marriage shrank into the shadows of the light from the beauty of the covenant. Their marriage license gave her and Tommy privileges and status; but the covenant gave them and made them *us*. It was the *us* that she wanted, and in her heart she believed Tommy did too. He said he wanted two things; he wanted to learn how to grow old together with another and second be a man who could be respected by a woman. How many hints had he already given to her about that? He was begging for help because he honestly did not know how to relate to a woman. From childhood she had learned that in a marriage the bride and groom are gifts to each other. She started to count the ways that Bibb had told her that she was a gift from God to help him. "Oh," she spoke to the campfire, almost involuntarily.

Anna turned the table on her own thinking and sighed. That is the difference. Bibb would never give himself to me. That boy fears the critter, and its bite makes him absolutely obedient to the varmint's demands. She considered what were those demands and how burdensome could they really be? She remembered their fight where she feared she had gone too far. Bibb had been quite clear when he said that he was to be the means by which God loved *His Precious Hannah Marie*. She immediately balked. That varmint had snuck those despised words from the poem into her thinking.

As she watched the fire die she resigned from keeping any hope of Bibb returning tonight. She slowly found her way to the hay mattress, climbed in, and silently and alone looked up at the stars above. She wanted to fall asleep but had too much to think about. Obviously Bibb had thought much about her intuitive observation long before she had. The last word she said to herself as she drifted into sleep inside of Bibb's warm cocoon was "Oh."

Monday, October 17, 1887

Eighth day out from camp. We were delayed by somebody shooting at us. One of our scouts was nicked by a rifle shot. Bibb and a different scout went out tonight to eliminate the danger. Bibb never said what happened, but he brought back an extra horse. I don't want to know...

Bibb told me a story about my late husband from their school days. He knew about my husband's hidden leg scars. Bibb's explanation didn't match my late husband's heroic and glorious account of their origin. Are the problems we have later in life nothing more that unresolved problems from our childhood? Am I the only one who thinks that? No, it is much simpler than that: all men are born depraved, and then they get worse.

I must, and I must not write this. Despite his severe character flaws, I have never been so glad to see a man in my life as when Bibb rode into camp tonight. And look at me... One moment I hate men with every ounce in my being, and then my mind and heart happily go another direction. This I know: Sometimes when you wish upon a star, dreams do come true.

==0==

"WHEN WILL WE be there? You are lost, aren't you?" asked Anna.

"Would you like me to stop at-zz d'the next tree and ask for directions? I am sure d'there would be a wise old owl d'that could give a hoot."

"Now I am sure you are lost. You only say stupid stuff when you don't have a good answer. What is it Bibb? Am I right? Are you really lost?"

"Mrs. Gorgon, I travel by keeping landmarks on my left and on my right, and I dead reckon d'the rest. Our advantage is we got d'those Indians making sure we don't ride into trouble. Come to d'think of it, getting lost might be fun. I'm starting to enjoy your company."

"You are not, Bibb! I can tell about these things."

"Well d'then, Mrs. Gorgon, enlighten my ignorance. Beyond what I d'though I knew, treat me to everything you 'I can tell-zz about d'these d'things' to me, O Omniscient Anna."

She rolled her eyes. "You already know the obvious. I need not expound on your sullied reputation. As for your current condition, you remain very much like a man."

"I will enjoy d'that as a compliment, Anna."

"It wasn't."

"What was it, d'then?"

"A statement of fact. I will have to endure the burden of dealing with your shortcomings."

"Mrs. Gorgon, flaws aren't so bad. You might want-zz to collect a few shortcomings for yourself someday. You would have to give-zz up being perfect, but being flawless isn't as exciting as most would d'think it would be. Contrary to your presumptions, being a man-zz isn't so bad. I actually enjoy it. I only have to d'think about one d'thing at a time, I don't have to worry about how I look-zz, and I can burp anytime I feel like burping."

"It is now for certain. Another silly answer. We are lost. Bibb, when are we going to get there?"

"How about if I tell you d'that I don't know? D'that way I can see your femininity come into full bloom. Besides, I kind-zz of like being lost. You-zz are good company when you-zz are a damsel in distress. Come to d'think of it, I d'think damsels like being in distress. D'they like being flustered so d'they can justify d'their cattiness. At least d'that is my experience."

"Bibb! I know what you are thinking and your thinking is wrong. Your little joke at my expense has gone too far. Stop it. You promised to be kind."

"Anna, give me an honest answer. Do you really d'think you know me? Do you really know how I d'think?"

"Tommy, I am fairly confident that I can always guess your next words. Yes, you do surprise me once in a while, but most of the time I can anticipate your thoughts. Be warned! I also enjoy more than my fair share of female intuition. The next thing you are going to say is 'Really?'"

"Really?" Bibb said without thinking.

"See, I told you so. Now is your big opportunity to say, 'Anna, you look beautiful today!'"

"Anna, you-zz certainly look-zz pretty today."

"Am I not beautiful? Why can't you say it?"

"Because I d'think you're pretty. Anna, let's not talk about who is pretty and who is ugly. My face is hideous, and I'm not-zz happy with it. I wish I was restored, but d'that wish will never come true. I will never be normal again. D'that's a cold hard fact. I will have to be content with what I am. I don't like it, but it is-zz what it is. And Anna, you amaze me. You already know d'that God made you-zz pretty, so what's d'the point of asking me about it?"

"You are digging yourself into a very deep hole, Bibb."

"And you-zz tease me about-zz not answering your questions? Okay, you-zz don't got to. I imagine it is more depressing to-zz maintain 'pretty' over improving on 'almost pretty.' Being ugly isn't hard at all. D'there isn't anything I can do about my scars. You seem to worry a lot-zz about keeping your youthful attractiveness. Anna, I didn't say-zz I was enjoying your company because you are pretty. I'm enjoying your company because you-zz are kind to an ugly old guy. You really do have a sweet heart when-zz you want to, and lately you have shown you want-zz to. I really appreciate d'that. Let's not talk about d'this anymore."

"But you still won't say I am beautiful. You still agree with the Indian matron, don't you? She said I was ugly."

"Anna, you have only been a widow d'three weeks. How can you-zz expect to be beautiful yet?"

"Why do you have such a high opinion of widows?"

"Because d'they-zz are beautiful."

"That is circular reasoning, Bibb."

"Anna, you-zz make my head-zz hurt. Let's stop talking about d'this."

"Name one widow that you don't think is beautiful."

Bibb looked at Anna and almost said something he would have badly regretted. He paused in silence for a couple seconds. "Some widows enjoy men d'that dig deep holes."

She read his mind. "Other than me, Bibb. Name one!"

"I can't. And I never said you-zz weren't beautiful. I just never said you were."

"If you are smarter than you look, your next words will be an apology!"

Bibb decided to let her have the last word. He thought he had given her a compliment, but she wanted only to see a zing from it. That is what she does, and only God can un-rot them rotten apples. Nothing he could say or do right then would be helpful, and to apologize would only appease and encourage more bad behavior. On the bright side, he was so ugly that anything he said was smarter than he looked. He further thought it really must be tough to be an Anna. He looked at her and smiled. She certainly was a big bag of frustrations tightly wrapped up in a basket of beauty. He certainly wasn't going to feed her vanity by calling her beautiful.

==0==

"Bibb, tell me what you knew about my husband."

"Besides-zz d'that he hated me?" responded Bibb.

"Why did he hate you?"

"Haters don't need-zz a reason to hate. D'they hate because d'that's what d'they do. His boasts were always bigger d'than his britches, and he always said he had more bigger and more better everything d'than he really had. Only con men market d'things d'they don't own."

"You think my husband was a hater and a con man?"

"I know-zz all about haters. A preacher told me once d'that-zz d'the reason I hate-zz is because I don't have any love, well, except-zz a love for myself. I guess if you-zz don't have any love, you-zz have to steal love from someone else. As soon as I get some I quickly soil it. Anna, you-zz didn't ask me a fair question. You knew Gorgon better-zz d'than me. I only knew him from-zz our kid days. D'that's why I can-zz only talk about my hate. I like-zz to d'think everybody grows up someday, but I'm-zz wronger d'than righter most of d'the time. Like I said-zz, you know-zz better d'than me."

"Name one thing you remember about him."

"He has a puncture scar on his right d'thigh."

"How do you know that?" asked Anna.

"We got-zz into fights. Sometimes he would win, and sometimes I would win. We-zz always ended up bloodied."

"And…"

"Well, one time he whooped me good-zz. I had two black eyes to his one fat lip. When he wasn't expecting, I got-zz even."

"What did you do?"

"I hit-zz him with a piece of lumber."

"And…"

"I still remember him wailing. D'that was such a sweet sound. Revenge when done well certainly is delightful, don't you d'think so?"

She glared at him as if that was an indictment of her behavior. "Bibb, did you enjoy beating your mother?"

"I NEVER BEAT-zz MY MAMA!"

"And likewise I know nothing of getting sweet revenge! Bibb, be more careful with your questions. But if I thought revenge was delightful, I certainly would enjoy it. And remember… the lumber… continue…"

"Oh, yeah. He went crying to-zz d'the teacher because his left d'thigh was punctured."

"I thought you said the right thigh."

"I got-zz him again in d'the other leg to twice mark-zz him-zz as a coward. Just once would only be-zz gettin' even. Revenge needs two helpings to be done right."

"Was it from a splinter?"

"No, it was from an old rusty nail. It took me-zz d'the longest time pounding d'that-zz crooked d'thing through-zz d'the board before I got it to stick out about a half inch. Your husband was such a whiner. Did you learn d'that from…"

==0==

Anna wasn't ready for Bibb's instinctive reaction when they both heard rifle shot from north of where they were at. "Hold-zz on, Anna!" Bibb grabbed his whip from somewhere and snapped it over the horses' ears. Bibb's horse had no problem – it was used to galloping towards danger, but Anna's horse needed the encouragement the snapping sound provided. The wagon sped over the grassland much faster than Anna was comfortable. Bibb saw the Indian's horse, but no Indian. Anna was scared, but Bibb knew how the Indian fought… if there was a fight… if he was alive.

When Bibb got to the unmanned horse he could see the three other Indians riding hard in pursuit of a white man on a horse. They were more interested in identifying the man for now, and when satisfied they quickly returned to where Bibb was. Their mission was to protect Bibb and the ugly one with the princess's dress, not to chase assassins.

When the three returned they found Anna caring for their brother who had a significant but not critical flesh wound in the forearm. She had already ordered Bibb to surrender his shirt and knife. She cut off the sleeves and used one for a tourniquet and the other for a bandage. The bleeding stopped before the full pressure was needed. It nicked him good, but the rifle round did not do grave damage.

The others also assessed the injury. Their discussion convinced the wounded man that it would take a while to heal. More important, it looked like he would recover without much loss of ability.

The next topic was what to do concerning the sniper. Bibb told the men he would ride the wounded brother's horse on point. Since the Indian's horse knew nothing of being part of a team pulling a wagon, Bibb chose to ride it rather than his own horse. The wounded man would have to drive the wagon. The scout riding on the west point told the wounded Indian where to take the woman to set up camp, a creek he had crossed about a half mile southwest of where they were at.

Before Bibb told Anna the camp arrangements he warned her not to complain or make a face. Secondly he made her acknowledge that he was still the trail boss. The plan was actually anticlimactic to all the fears that ran though her mind. She took it as a compliment that the wounded Indian would trust a white woman to stay by his side to care for his arm.

"I will drive the wagon, Bibb. The man is hurt." Anna said this as a heartfelt offer of help.

"D'that's a kind d'thought, Anna, but it will-zz not work. Anna, let-zz d'the man drive. He needs to contribute to-zz save his dignity. He will tell his grandchildren-zz d'that he got to serve and to be served by a white princess. Take care of that man's arm more d'than you would look after me."

"Princess?"

"Don't forget, Anna, he heard-zz d'the medicine man too. D'that was not a private ceremony."

The scouts agreed to let Bibb ride point in their formation. He would set the pace, being injured himself and not used to bareback riding. His reputation for tracking preceded him, and they acknowledged that Bibb possessed a range advantage over the sniper with his rifle and eyesight.

The men conversed for several minutes more before they broke up to go their separate ways. Before mounting himself, Bibb quickly reminded Anna of several key

Indian words for yes, no, okay, water, pain, and the phrase *please eat some more*. Anna thought it clever how Bibb carried his whip, rope, and ax. Obviously he had gone on manhunts before.

As he was leaving Anna spoke again to Bibb. "What else do you want me to do while you are gone, other than to look pretty and act like a princess?"

"You can pray for-zz d'that idiot who took a shot at your escort. Justice will-zz be visiting him soon." Bibb sounded strangely evil.

"If I get the notion to pray, it will be for you."

"Be careful, Anna. God might turn you beautiful on me while I'm gone, and what-zz am I supposed to do if d'that happens?"

"Bibb, be careful. Please, be careful." Anna was scared not for herself, but for the repulsive half a man she was starting to admire.

==0==

Anna had a dinner ready for the four men but only two returned to camp. The mature campfire was welcomed by the arriving Indians due to the nip in the air. Anna had already surrendered her hay mattress and blanket to the wounded Indian sleeping comfortably in the back of the wagon. Anna shared the jerky, hard tack, and some beans with the men, but was careful to save some for Bibb and the other Indian.

The men paid very little attention to Anna, which added greatly to her personal comfort. When she left Deadwood she never dreamed that she would be sharing a campfire with three Indians while void of an escort. The Indians did not seem to have any anxiety about the earlier incident, nor about the two that were not in camp. They actually asked her about laundry but she pretended she didn't remember those phrases. She would talk to Bibb later about that, if Bibb returned. She was worried.

Anna was getting cold and her blanket was wrapped around the wounded Indian. She so wanted to take Bibb's bedroll off Bibb's horse, but did not want to give the men any ideas that she was ready for bed. She couldn't sleep anyway. She approached the most talkative of the Indians and asked in his tongue, "Bibb okay?"

A different Indian stood up and answered her with a message he had received from Bibb before they parted ways. He struggled with it, but did say three understandable syllables to Anna: "Found white man."

==0==

The sleeping assassin never had a chance. Bibb knew exactly what he wanted to do to fully immobilize the man and immediately pierce his soul with the fear of judgment. The snap of a whip scared the man's horse which rudely awakened him as a rope went tight around his legs. When his eyes opened the man found himself looking at a strange angle at the ugliest man alive. He instinctively reached for his gun and then lost it when another snap of Bibb's whip took the weapon out of his hand.

"Who are you?"

"If you are not truthful, I may be-zz your executioner. Some call me Bibb, and how-zz do you prefer justice administered? Ax, whip, knife, rope, revolver, or with your own rifle?"

"I didn't do it!"

"D'the man riding your horse shot-zz and hit-zz my point man in his right arm. If not you, d'then who? You-zz are d'there only person with d'the only horse in d'this camp."

"It was only an Indian!"

"And I am-zz only a ghost." With the crack of a whip the man received a laceration to his right forearm, strangely identical to the wound inflicted on Bibb's point man's arm.

The man, flushed and immobilized, shook involuntarily as he tried to reckon his current situation to reality. "I know who you are! Shoot me now, Bibb. Don't torture me."

"D'this ain't torture. I know torture. I don't do torture no more. But I will-zz let you-zz pick what-zz your rightful punishment should be. Tell me what's you-zz d'think is fair."

"Let me go on my word never to shoot at an Indian again."

"Sounds fair. How should I prove to my scout you will never shoot-zz at him again? A trigger finger; maybe two? D'that sounds like d'the reasonable d'thing to do. I don't know which hand. I will have to detach d'them both." Bibb took his ax from its holster and laid the blade in the hot coals of the man's campfire.

"Take me to the judge. He will be fair."

"D'the judge ain't here and my Indian scouts want d'this resolved. I'm letting you be d'the judge, or if-zz you prefer, you can-zz rely on my mercy. D'that would really be dumb, but you-zz already proved your lack of smart-zz to me."

The man watched Bibb. He turned his ax over on the coals. The blade had started to change colors as the metal reacted to the heat from the man's camp fire. Fear was written deep into his face. Blood from his wounded arm would not stop flowing and splattered all over him as he writhed in pain. Bibb methodically collected up the man's weapons: a gun still in a holster, his rifle, and the blood splattered gun he had previously attempted to use. He also found the man's knife. Bibb emptied the man's rifle, the other bullets on his belt, found all the other loose ammunition and secured it all in the man's saddlebag.

"Cat got-zz your tongue? Well I guess so. I gave you-zz a chance to come clean, but you-zz lied to me anyway stating you didn't shoot my friend. D'that was unwise given d'this predicament of your own making. So you-zz prefer not to answer my-zz questions. D'that's your choice, but I will give-zz you one more chance to-zz change your mind. I don't recommend it, but if death is what you desire, what name do you want-zz on your tombstone?"

The man reconsidered his silence. "If I tell you what do you plan to do?"

"Bring your stuff to-zz your next of kin. Come clean or die dirty – your choice. I-zz believe in proper burials; I've had several. You prefer buried dead or alive? No matter to me."

"Shoot me, Bibb! Shoot me! Have mercy and shoot me!" The ax was now a throbbing red hot.

"I asked-zz you your name, Sniper."

"Carson."

"Carson, you asked for mercy, and I may give-zz it to you." Bibb walked over to fire to check on the ax blade. "Who's your next of kin? Anybody in Miles City? I will deliver d'this horse to d'them."

"I have a brother there."

"His-zz first name?"

"Bobby."

"And your name?"

"Tommy."

"Ooooo. Bad answer."

When Bibb finished administering a strange display of grace the man was left asleep without the benefit of consciousness, a mercy from the pain he would wake to. From behind the thicket his Indian scout showed himself and then signed to him. Bibb answered likewise in sign, "He asked for mercy and he received it. He did not ask for justice, and he received that too. He will not be shooting at any Indians for a long time."

Bibb laid the man's canteen, rifle, empty gun belt, and two loaded revolvers at the man's feet. He took the man's bedroll and laid it on top of him. Everything else he packed on the man's horse and led it away from camp. Once back at their horses, Bibb chose to ride the sniper's horse and asked his Indian brother to lead the other horse back to their camp.

"I hurt," said Bibb to his companion.

"You chose not to kill him. Why?"

After gaining eye contact with the scout Bibb signed, "He will live scarred and with the wisdom that a white man brought him his due, not Lakota. Fairness may have required his death, but the law of the ancients' limited justice up to what I delivered."

"Why not seven times the wound he gave my brother?"

"Friend, he did not have seven arms. I could not take more than an eye for an eye, wound for a wound, or blood for blood. That blood I drew from his right arm. Justice also allows for inflicting a limited reminder to the offender not to repeat the deed. The book of the ancient's law allows no more than two parts of ten to the original injury, and he received the full measure of that. Beyond that is revenge and cruel torture. Less than that is unmerited mercy. Do not fear. The name of your brother's avenger, a white man, may stray from his lips and the blisters on his trigger fingers may heal, but the scars will stay to remind him forever. The Lakota will remain blameless."

"What about the horse?"

"I will deliver it to his brother in Miles City."

"You know this man? How do you know this man?"

"I do not know the man. He told me his brother's name before we left. I will tell his brother where to find him and what happened to him."

"His brother will kill you."

"No. His brother will not. He will not risk dying for his brother's folly. He will trust my word."

"Why?"

"Because someone must carry on the family name, nor would he be fool enough to attempt avenging his brother without truly knowing his brother's offense. Because of the horse and tack he will be unsure if his brother is alive. He will not rest until his brother is found. And other reason too."

"Because of what the medicine man said?"

Bibb smiled but did not reply. He didn't even think about that. Bibb thought that God had other plans for him. He felt ordained to deliver Anna to her mother-in-law. No, he didn't feel invincible, but he had the confidence that God would let him keep his promise, and to let Anna keep hers too.

On the ride back Bibb convinced himself that it was his pain that confused him. What else could explain a smiling varmint he imagined in his mind's eye? He had been viciously cruel tonight, but a good cruel if there is such a thing. This was the first time his wrath had stayed under control and inside limits. This surprised him. Before the varmint became his constant companion he would have enjoyed killing the sniper an inch at a time until he was bled out. Bibb bristled at the thought of how utterly evil he used to be when he was out of control.

==0==

Anna was still awake and sitting by the fire with the wounded Indian when the noise of coming horses was heard outside the camp. Her initial fear of being alone with three Indian scouts disappeared hours prior – along with the setting of the moon. She did not care anymore about that. She was cold, and fear or not, she wrapped herself in Bibb's bedroll when not tending the fire.

In response to a strange sound, the Indian next to her made a different call back. That was followed by another whistle that broke into the silence of the night. Within minutes the two missing men entered the camp with three horses. Anna knew immediately what that meant. The good news was that Bibb was alive. The bad news was that the owner of the horse Bibb was riding was left in no condition to voice a complaint. She saw the dried blood on his ax and asked no questions.

Anna was already out of the bedroll when Bibb rode closer to the fire. She noticed immediately that he was sore, if not hurt, and maybe hurt bad. Between the sleeves cut out of Bibb's shirt and the fresh blood splattered on it, what was left of that piece of cloth was due a demotion to a grease rag.

The scout arriving with Bibb walked his horses down to be with the others. Still mounted on the assassin's horse, Bibb translated Anna's statement to the scout that a dinner plate would be ready for him when he returned. He acknowledged and then fielded questions from the other two scouts.

Coming close, Bibb spoke to Anna softly, "Anna, I'm sorry to bother you, but I need-zz your help getting off d'the horse. Can-zz you hold d'the horse still while I slide onto d'the buckboard?"

After some effort Bibb was off the horse and back standing on the ground. He walked up to take control of the horse and unintentionally ended up standing face to face with Anna, whose maneuver to get there was very intentional. She could tell that he was favoring his left side. Anna forced herself into a muted reaction much contrary to the symphony of questions and fears that sang within her. "I am glad to see you, Tommy. Where do you hurt?"

Tommy pointed to his chest and almost had a chance to reply before Anna moved closer. She surprised Bibb by putting her hand to the skin where he had pointed. Bibb's immediate reaction was to back away a step.

"Bibb, did that hurt? I'm sorry. You must be hungry. What do you want to eat?"

"No, your touch didn't hurt; it-zz just surprised me. Anna, I'm sorry. You-zz were just trying to be kind, and I should have accepted d'that gesture. My brain is slower-zz d'than my body right now. If it's all the same to you, Anna, I'm-zz worn out. Where's my-zz bedroll?"

"By the campfire. The inside is warm already. Bibb, don't argue with me. You know what I want and what the Indians will expect. Let's start by me taking your boots off, followed by you jumping inside your bedroll."

"Can you take d'the horse down to be with d'the others? I can if you-zz are scared. Did anything happen here while I was gone?"

"Bibb, stop talking and march where I told you to march. It's time to get your boots off and you into d'the sack."

"And you-zz? How will you-zz keep warm?"

"That's a problem. I'm keeping my wounded Indian in the back of the wagon under his blanket and mine. I'm not going to take it from him to keep myself warm tonight."

"I see. I understand. Anna, I promised I-zz would never touch you wrong, and I-zz meant it."

"There are no bunnies in the camp tonight, Bibb." She paused to seriously assess the possibility the man had suffered a lower brain injury from cantering bareback on the Indian's horse. "Bibb, honestly, how can you think like a man at a time like this?" She realized that sounded a bit dumb after it was said. She recovered and asked, "How bad do you hurt?"

"Sore. I will feel-zz it more tomorrow. I'm not injured. D'the blood ain't mine."

"Bibb, I promise you two things tonight. You will stay warm and I won't hurt you anymore than you already are."

Bibb was fumbling for something to say. Her comment was so unexpected. He replied, "I'm glad-zz to see you too, Anna. I'm starting to-zz understand why-zz people long to come home."

"Bibb, what do you need? Anything?"

"Warmth sounds good; really good. Anna, let's not argue. I'm going to walk d'the horse down to d'the others. I am stiffened, and I need unstiffening. Can you fix a plate for my brother and me, and we will be back soon to nibble on something before going to sleep. Keep d'that wounded man comfortable. Anna," he shut his eyes for a second and almost losing his balanced he reflexively steadied himself by holding on to her forearm. "Anna, never mind; some d'things are best left unsaid." His eyes relayed his thoughts anyway. For a prolonged moment as they were locked in a stare something they both feared might happen: time stood still.

Bibb left into the darkness. Awaiting his return, Anna went and found a place clear of sticks and rocks to lay the bedroll down. All the time she was preparing the nest she relived his words about home. Never before had she received such a genuine compliment, and surprisingly indirect. Bibb voiced her same longing for home, not as a place, but a relationship. Her Tommy-cat voluntarily desired to be near her, and it was her heart that had won the moment. Her warmth was just a bonus.

The sharp cold of the air reminded her of the reality of the situation. She told herself that she must check her passions also. She looked up to the stars and gave thanks to whoever might be listening. She wished into the dark unknown asking that she not hurt the one entrusted into her care. It was a bonus that the man was also her husband. Her intuition told her that he knew that they were married too. He would not have been so careless expressing his desire to return to being *us* if he was ignorant of their bonds, legally and soulfully. The more she considered her recent verbal and visual exchange with her man, the more her heart told her she had never received a compliment as large as his tonight: where she lay her head was home, and he deeply longed for it. Not a lust, not a like, but a longing. She told herself that was the key between their legal and, dare say, spiritual bond. Longing… Yes, and the satisfaction of sensing an unseen hand guiding them to a glorious fulfillment. Not a fulfillment of riches, fame, or power, but the quiet satisfaction of knowing and being known completely and without reservation. And the cost of sharing their spirits did not have the entrails of marriage, but a much higher reward. It was a longing for a far off country. It was a sure hope of a great fulfillment. It was for a place where her past would be forgotten; a place where who she could become, she would become; a place she would find complete soul contentment. For sure, Bibb was neither marriage material for her, nor she for him. "Mrs. Franklin, did you know something beyond yourself to pull this off?" she spoke to herself. Anna fully intended on taking the escape provision promised in Mrs. Franklin's love note that an annulment could provide, but she also decided that was a decision for another day.

The realist in Anna began to doubt all the thoughts she was having while waiting for her man to return. They had only known each other a month, but what a month it had been. But tonight he was hurt and it was her solemn promise she would to attend to the healing of that man. He was living on the edge, and all these thoughts of a happily-forever-after needed to be tempered against the reality her trail boss was half dead. Maybe her thoughts were all fantasy, but if they were they certainly were blissful ones, and wholly without guilt. One thing she had learned… covenants promised at the altar bare no shame.

This was a new feeling for her. She was not in love with *love*. She was not even in love with *like*. There were no bunnies invading her thoughts. This was so different. Oddly and wonderfully she didn't want to show her affections as leverage to get something back in return. She now actually cared. Their relationship was no longer a contract to her. She didn't belong to him and he didn't belong to her. There are no ownership issues with being *us* and being *us* is what they were; if not by a courthouse document in Deadwood, then by the blood bonding at the altar. As for the company they kept, they were *us* by edict of the Lakota Chief. The scouts certainly thought so.

This was all so strange and she began to doubt her thinking. It seemed all too good to be true, and her experience agreed. Things too good to be true are usually untrue. What she did know without doubt: she knew within her deepest soul that she was not the same self-serving Anna that lived on a mountainside a month ago. She decided her next words would be said in the morning. Anything said now could ruin the joy.

When Bibb returned he remained, as always, clueless to Anna's innermost thoughts. He was hurt and his pain was dictating his inward conversations. He thanked her for the light dinner, her care, and help with his boots. Bibb wished her a good night, changed his shirt, and fell asleep.

Anna finished some last minute clean up, checked the covers on the wounded Indian, and put on another layer of Bibb's clothes. With all the noise of owl wings and the rowdiness of a robin's feather, Anna settled in for sleep next to her husband. She recalled the day's fears and fumbles. Xue's proverbs came to her, sticking deep in her mind as she tried to drift away into slumber. She now understood why her Tommy did not believe in luck.

For some unexplainable reason Anna recalled a fairy tale from when she was a little girl. When everything in the story was about to turn out happily-forever-after she remembered a proverb her grandmother told her. She said that the main reason for the story was to teach that good eventually triumphs, but to also teach little girls that when two people love each other, time flees to the trees.

Promises... Proverbs... Friends... Fears... Fumbles... Promises... Proverbs... Friends... Promises...Oh... Oh, oh, oh... Oh, oooh, oooohhhh... Anna was now asleep.

Tuesday, October 18, 1887

Ninth day out from camp; to my shame this is my first day of my purposely living within our covenant. We must be getting closer to Miles City. Early this afternoon Bibb and I approached a homestead ranch. We asked to stay in their shed but we were invited to share their humble home with them and their three children. Upon those arrangements Bibb returned to the scouts and released them from their oath. They immediately headed south with what we had left for food. Bibb showed me a knife I had never seen before. I knew intuitively that it came from the owner of the extra horse. I did not want to know so I did not ask. He gave it as a gift to the wounded scout. I asked Bibb about the fifth Indian and received no answer.

Tonight I was surprised at what Tommy did. Over dinner conversation he gently enticed our host to tell Westum's story as if Tommy did not know who this Bibb fellow was. I thought that Bibb was a grand embellisher; nothing compared to what we heard tonight. Actually, I am now prone to think Bibb understates his role when he shares his stories with me. Take it from an expert — that is a form of lying; or humility. I need to stop assuming malice out of the man.

The first snow of the year tonight! Our scouts must have gotten very cold and wet. They were good to us and to me in particular. They were the first men I ever deliberately washed clothes for, and the first time I actually wanted to. I certainly don't feel like an Indian princess being this dirty and my hair so full of knots. I hope by my actions that the scouts can honestly report to the matron that I am no longer ugly. Just as Bibb has his varmint, I have my matron.

==0==

THE EARLY MORNING ride started cold and was getting colder due to a north wind blowing in their faces. Anna wrapped up in her brown blanket and looked almost like a giant piece of chocolate sitting next to Bibb. She had delighted in a sleep filled all night with pleasant dreams. While inside her chocolate covering she was having fun letting her mind wander but had to silently chastise herself for seeing too much *their* in their situation. Anna reminded herself that the man next to her could easily return to being a monster. The rider-less horse trotting behind their wagon was a stark and continuing reminder that Bibb was capable of mayhem on a moment's notice. He was just as depraved as all other men. Bibb's depravity was just more obvious.

Still covered up in blankets Anna started a conversation. "Bibb, I would love to think I might become something special in the future, but princess like thoughts and all those other things only feed my vanity. Still the Anna in me would like to think they might come true. How do you know if what that medicine man said was truth?"

"I don't like-zz your question."

371

"Why?" replied Anna. She considered it a fair and reasonable conversation starter.

"My opinion of d'the man's wisdom grows, but so do my doubts. Not all d'that is wise is true. Anna, my innards give me-zz no clues and I am very perplexed. Time-zz will tell, I guess."

"Perplexed? Don't guess, Bibb; just answer my question. It perplexes me when you don't answer the questions I do ask and then answer the ones I don't ask. I bet you have never thought about how annoying that is. Now Bibb, please answer my question."

"Please?" Bibb didn't see that word coming. "I figure it is true if it comes true. But even so, you can't wait-zz for something to happen just because a medicine man said so. D'the only way to know it was true is only after it happens. I figure d'there are only d'three possibilities. Either d'that medicine man made it all up in his own mind, or a lying spirit told him, or a spirit of truth told him. D'the problem I guess about untrue spirits is d'that d'they are still mostly right. It is d'the slightly wrong part d'that is so bad. D'there are no partial truths comin' from d'the spirit of truth."

"So what should I think about it?"

"Don't d'think about it one bit. Anna, you can't plan your life around what-zz other people predict. If it happens, well, d'then it happens, and d'then you have to suffer d'those who like to say 'I told you so!' I didn't believe it when your husband said he-zz was going to kill me. I d'thought he would be smart and go home to his pretty wife after making all d'that bluster. Well, I was wrong and-zz he was wronger. Predictions are cruel because we live-zz in a cruel world."

He paused and looked at Anna. "I'm sorry, d'that was a poor example. I didn't mean to bring d'that up. I can be so un-d'thinkin' at times."

Anna was just as anxious to change the subject. "What did you think of the medicine man? Do you agree with me that he was a cruel tyrant? He certainly demanded obedience; he even had the audacity to demand my obedience."

Bibb's unresponsiveness prompted Anna to loosen the blanket wrapped tightly around her to better look at her riding mate. She had learned over the last week when her man was being thoughtful and when he was being stubbornly silent. This was the former; the answer was in his eyes. (She also could immediately detect when he was about to say stupid stuff.)

Bibb spoke after some thought. "He is a servant of his people and very meek. His kind of people will inherit d'the earth."

"Weak?!? He didn't look weak to me! If you want to know what weak is, try sizing up yourself for once!"

"Anna," Bibb replied sorrowfully. "Did I mumble? I will assume d'that, instead of d'thinking d'that all Annas are d'thinking d'three words in advance of me actually saying d'them. I d'thought I said meek, which is great power under greater self-control. Weak is little power under littler self-control."

"So you ddd'think ddd'that medicine men will ddd'take over ddd'the world? That would be a sorry day for women."

Bibb ignored her mocking. "No, Anna," he replied. "D'the meek will inherit d'the world, and providence don't care about d'their color or d'their culture. And d'they won't inherit the world by some sort of divine reward. D'they will have to take it because God said so, maybe even against d'their will. God ain't dumb. He can't afford to give it to anybody else. All d'the non-meeklings among us would ruin d'this place if we were ever put in charge."

"You mumbled, Bibb," (which was a lie), "but you are forgiven given your weaknesses. I resent your generalizations about women named Anna, and specifically your false accusation that they don't listen and hear only what they want to hear. You never denied he was a cruel man, so you confirmed my conclusions. What do you say about that!?!"

"Experience has made him hard; his burden has made-zz him demanding, but I saw no cruelty in d'the man."

"That man took my dress! That was certainly cruel!"

"You be d'the judge, Anna." Bibb became more subdued as he rehearsed many of his past thoughts hardened by the miles. "He said d'that dress belonged to a beautiful princess, a woman of all women, an heir to great power, and-zz a woman who will restore glory to d'the Lakota."

"At least one man in that camp thought I was beautiful. What else did he say about me?"

"He said you were strong, well not you, but your body. He said your odor was as strong as twenty buffalo. He asked me why you stunk like d'that, but I had no answer for him."

"You are lying again! Bibb, how do you ever think you will earn my trust when you say rude and dumb things like that? Admit it! You made that up, and you can apologize now before I get really angry with you!"

"Anna, I wasn't lying. You need to consider d'things like perfume from d'their perspective."

"So, Bibb, do you think I will get my dress back then? That was one of my favorites."

"Anna," saying his words apologetically in anticipation of her response, "You will have to be happy with d'the dress d'they gave you. D'the dress in his teepee belongs to a princess, but Anna, d'that princess hasn't been born yet. Anna, understand d'this. Indian legends do not fade away. D'they repeat over and over again with increasing intensity, just like d'the legend of d'the lambs."

"So you think my green dress is generations old and belonged to a princess once?"

"I don't know. Could be." Bibb sighed. "D'the medicine man said it belongs to one now."

"Well, that explains why it is holding together. It must be magic."

Bibb let her have the last word as he thought to himself. Magic? No. Providence? Good chance. That dress certainly had an effect on him.

"Aren't you going to say something, Tommy? You still owe me an apology too!"

Bibb shook his head to loosen the tense muscles in his neck. He had nothing to apologize for. He snapped the reins and the horses responded. One thing was for sure. She could not be told about her third blessing. If she gained that knowledge, the blessing would become a curse.

==0==

Bibb told Anna that the landmarks were becoming more familiar now and that their arrival in Miles City was but a day away. Anna was happy with the thought and voiced her desire (several times) that Bibb should hurry the horses. Bibb replied that he was glad he didn't hire an assistant trail boss, and that their current pace perfectly suited the real trail boss.

Anna countered with many teases culminating in her accusing Bibb that his only reason for delay was because he couldn't get enough of her companionship. Bibb had smiled many times on the trip, but this was the first time she had heard him fully laugh since he was wounded. It was a terrible combination of sounds. The cacophony of odd gurgles made Anna laugh all the more.

Cows. Hundreds of cows. Anna was tired of them blocking their progress. Bibb warned her that cows are not to be rushed, and worse, the ranchers don't like travelers interfering with their herds. Bibb said persistence and patience is the best and fastest way to navigate through these beasts.

Along the way they started to see ranch hands and an occasional sod-buster. Even once they saw a salesman. Bibb had hoped they would see the circuit rider, but that didn't happen.

"Why do you want to go slow, Tommy?"

"I don't want our arrival to be a surprise to d'the sheriff. I figure at least d'three of d'the dozen or so ranch hands we've met will let Westum know we are just a day's journey out. D'the second reason is d'that I want-zz to arrive in d'the evening tomorrow after a good night sleep tonight."

"Where do you have in mind?"

"With some of d'the friendliest folk in-zz d'the west."

"Anybody in mind?"

"Not yet, but d'the sooner we find a place, d'the sooner we can send our scouts home. We are out of Indian controlled lands now."

"Bibb, I'm starting to get to know how you think better. What is the third reason you don't want to push on and arrive late tonight? With you there seems to be a real reason behind the reasonable reasons you throw my way first."

"You don't want to be crossing d'the herds of cows at night. D'that is d'the venue of rustlers, and rustlers get shot. I suspect it was d'the cattle rustlers d'that killed Westum's men."

"Why would they do that?"

"To take d'the cows, and hand me d'the blame. D'that's a low risk high profit opportunity. I bet I won't be in Miles City a whole day before d'the sheriff will be asking me questions about it."

"Why not talk to him directly?"

"I want to find out d'the mood of d'the town first. Sheriffs' have a nasty habit (srpt) of jailing me first and asking questions later. Did you know d'the Deadwood sheriff asked me to write d'the Miles City sheriff a letter to explain-zz myself?"

"What did it say, Bibb?" She purposely avoided answering his question.

For the next ten minutes Bibb recited the letter to Anna almost verbatim. She never told Bibb that under Mr. Franklin's strictest confidence that she had been allowed to see the letter. She almost wished that Tommy would have embellished some of his narrative so she could have proof that he lies. She was ashamed of that thought. Her Tommy told the story true, and if he could tell that story true, then she could trust that the other stories he told were true too; maybe even understated.

"Tommy, what has stuck, is stuck, and will stay stuck?"

"If you don't know by now, I ain't telling you. Anna d'there is another reason I want to spend one last night on d'the road. You need a chance to-zz make yourself pretty. I want-zz you to find d'that green dress of yours and put it on for our last leg of d'the journey."

"What is your motivation to suggest such a thing, Bibb?"

"Acceptance."

"Acceptance of what?"

"Acceptance of you. I don't want you to be ridiculed by d'the society ladies in town. It would be better for you to arrive in woman's clothes, no matter how tattered, d'than to subject yourself to d'the ridicule of shallow minded women over d'the scandal of wearing men's clothes. D'the west already has more d'than its share of manly women-zz, and d'the girly women despise d'them. You will win d'the society women's help in getting you a new wardrobe if you wear d'that dress into town. If you wear my stinky rags d'they will d'think you no better d'than an outlaw's pet slave."

"Did you think of that all by yourself or did the varmint tell you?"

"I have been d'thinking about d'this since we were grave digging."

"And you would also like getting your clothes back too. Yes?"

375

"Absolutely," Bibb snapped, even scaring himself with the passion of his reflexive reply. He sobered before giving a more tempered reply. "Anna, you have no idea how much you wearing my clothes drives me beyond crazy. Tell me true. Doesn't it bother you any to wear my clothes?"

"Not in the least, and I would do it again if given a chance. I figure technically they ain't your clothes anymore; they are our clothes. Bibb, you listen and you listen good; I'm only saying this once. You have no idea how much your first unselfish kindness meant to me. Before putting on your clothes I considered all of your acts of being nice were made out of social obligation. Not so with sharing your clothes. That was different; a big huge different. But Bibb, I didn't answer your question. Yes, I will honor your request about wearing the matron's dress into Miles City. I will not fuss, but Tommy just be warned, this drama isn't over yet. Face it now, or face this truth later. Neither of us will leave Miles City wearing the clothes we arrived in."

"What are you planning to do with my clothes, Anna? D'they're mine, not yours, not ours. You should leave d'them alone."

"Didn't you understand me? I guess technically you are right if you once again conveniently leave your God out of our relationship. Did I quote you right, Bibb? If they are yours and not ours, I will just have to claim them as mine and only mine and watch you fail in trying to retain title to them. Yes Bibb, I'm now claiming title on them for me and only me if you unwisely decide to thumb your nose at God and not call them ours. Yes, they are now and forevermore my new nightgowns. And be not deceived, I'm not going to let you run around Miles City in my new pajamas – how scandalous! Well, not new new, just new to me. Now that they are bust'n out and fitting me good, I figure you wouldn't be caught dead wearing them anyway. It's all for your better health, you know."

"D'that's, d'that's, d'that's just wrong! You need nice feminine stuff, not my rags, and I'm not willing to surrender my stuff to you. Anna, why would you do d'that anyway? It's wrong wrong."

"Just to watch you squirm. Forgive me, but this Mrs. Toivo loves doing that to her altared Mr. Toivo. And I didn't stutter. I meant *altared*, not *altered*. And stop looking at me like that, Bunny Boy. You think I'm really something special wearing this shirt, don't you? Plant your eyes back into your head and put a stop to all those lustful thoughts you're thinking right now. That ain't healthy for a man who can't even get off his own horse without a woman's help."

Her taunts had gotten Bibb all wrapped up at first but her string of absurdities absent of malice let him see her words were all in jest. He could breathe again. They both started to laugh. Anna thought further to herself. "What happens if I actually tame this lion?"

Bibb had different thoughts. She could have been beaten for saying that to the wrong man, and most likely did. If she feared him, Anna would have only thought those thoughts, not said them. Bibb took her trust and tease as an oblique compliment. She was no longer the high and mighty chairman of the board or the queen bee of the hive. Although a bit peppery, she was the real Anna being Anna, and happy living free within her own skin. Yes, but the clothes issue was front and center again in his thinking. He could not deny that there was an unexpected and deep intimacy (he could not come up with the right word to describe it) in sharing his clothes. He bristled as the word entered his thinking. Bibb had long beforehand concluded that intimacy only destroys. Maybe not this time. He was still very far from accepting the wrongheadedness of her wearing his clothes. It was just wrong, and no matter how hard one might try to rationalize it, wrong was still wrong. As much as he disliked it, it would have been wronger of him to make her wear her green dress riding across the freezing plains. His mind wandered more as the horses' footfalls beat out a rhythm. He found himself thinking that at the altar she had promised to be 'this close.' What could be more of a visual reminder of their covenant? What could be closer than being in his clothes? As much as he resisted the thought, Bibb could not deny to his heart the warmth of that strange intimacy in light of their promises at the altar. "Ugh!" Bibb said to himself recoiling in these thoughts. He knew himself better now; he had to see to believe because his faith was still so babyish, and there was no denying the obvious sitting next to him. This whole thought stream was unbearable for Bibb. He forced himself to change the subject within his mind. The clothes issue was petty compared to her blooming freedom of personality. She was being her true self without reservation. He preferred the real Anna to a fake one. But the clothes! That was wrong wrong, and nothing but wrong!

==0==

At lunch Bibb had the scouts gather and he told him of his plans from this point on. They agreed that as soon as the wagon trail was established going towards Miles City that he and Anna would find lodging with an immigrant family. The scouts were made welcome to take the remainder of the victuals, save two rations, for their ride home. The scouts were pleased with the plan.

Further up the route north Anna could tell that her man was thinking again. His intense look on his face gave him away every time, and she had learned not to interrupt. Bibb eventually asked, "Anna, what names should we use to hide our identities from our hosts tonight? We will have to use something I can remember."

Anna looked at Bibb in total disgust. Bibb prompted her for an answer once again, and still got no satisfaction. Something had gotten her tongue. Then he wished it had.

Anna replied with a chip on her shoulder, "I guess you weren't lying when you said at my party that 'Outlaws don't believe in God'."

"Where did d'that come from, Anna?"

"Let me explain this plain for you Bibb: You're a liar, liar, and a liar again! You disgust me, Bibb! Have you been lying to me all along?"

Bibb thought about her outburst and came up short of ideas to rationally explain what caused her turn in countenance. He eventually replied, "Lied about what?"

"You lied to me, you lied to yourself, and you stinkin' rat even lied to God. You are pathetic!"

"About what, Anna? What-zz did I lie about? And you don't even believe in God! Explain yourself, will-zz you!"

"I believed you believed in God, and now I know it was all a lie. I thought you believed God was answering your prayers about our protection. You really suckered me into believing that untruth! You are really a hypocrite, Bibb. You disgust me! You lie just like every other man lies. Can I ever trust you again?"

Bibb tried his best to fit together the pieces. All he suggested was a name to conceal their identity. Or was it something else? Did it have anything to do with the dress? Bibb was really confused. "Anna, please tell me my lie. I really don't know."

"Bibb Boy, you sure don't have any problem being proud of your soiled reputation with the Indians or with me, but when we get within spittin' distance of the smoke rising from the houses of civilization all of a sudden you want to hide from your past! What is it Bibb? I thought you were trusting in God to protect us, and now you want to lie about who we are! You even want me to be a part of your big lie! I don't know about God, but if that varmint bites you for even thinking about something sideways, why do you even think he will put up with your intentional deceit of hiding our identity? Was all your talk about a varmint a big lie too? Are you saying God ain't capable of protecting us without you assisting him with your big lie? You are Tommy Toivo, and the preacher said I was Anna Toivo, and that is who we are – nothing more and nothing less. You ain't a Bibb anyway! That was your outlaw name, and you ain't no outlaw no more. You are more of a church mouse than a real man. Oh, you disgust me! What are you, anyway? I am glad I ain't got another dress to loan to you until you decide what you are! Just when I thought you were something resembling a real Montana Male! Oh! I'm so mad I could just spit. Bibb, tell me, what are you?"

Bibb responded slowly and measured. "Anna, I take it you're not too fond of my suggestion."

"Answer my question, Bibb!" she demanded in no uncertain terms.

"I see your point."

"You need more than fixing your sight, Tommy! You have to figure out if you believe in God or not. If you don't, well, act like it. If you do, well, then act like it. I can't stand this muddy mush in the middle with your thinking. What is it Tommy? What side of the fence do you stand on?"

"Anna, we are and will continue to be Mr. and Mrs. Toivo until our covenant is fulfilled. You are right, very right, and I was completely wrong. I was blind to my hypocrisy. I have never been a hypocrite before, and, well, it ain't-zz a good feeling. I am truly ashamed of myself for making d'that suggestion."

"Well, your contrition ain't done yet. I ain't the only one you lied to. You better make peace with that varmint before he eats us both up."

"Do you believe d'there is such a d'thing as d'the varmint?"

"I think you do, and that's what counts. You are supposed to be the protector around here, and you really scare me when you stopped believing in providence. Don't do that again, Bibb!"

"Anna, I still do believe-zz in providence. I believe-zz you are right d'this time. I see my error, and I'm back on d'the right path. You had every right to be mad, and I deserved your words."

"Do you really mean that, Bibb?"

"Watch what I do, Anna. I already know-zz your strong opinions about d'the truthfulness of d'the d'things I say."

"I wish you would stop it! You made me so mad, Bibb! I don't know why I get so angry. What dark cause is making me be so unkind to you in my words? What drives me to such disappointment in your behavior? Why do I even care what you think?"

"Do you know-zz what faith is, Anna?"

"I know what I think it is, but it probably ain't nothing like what you think it is. Why?"

"If faith was a rattler' you would have fang marks on your legs. As your protector, I guess I would have to come and cut you, and suck d'the venom out."

"You would probably like that."

"What? Choosing your venom instead of d'the snake's venom? No d'thank you. Oh, Anna, I don't know what I'm saying. I'm so bumfuzzled. You really proved me wrong and I am rightly embarrassed. I am so wrong. I didn't mean it. I wasn't d'thinking right. I'm so knotted up. I really am sorry."

"So what do you call faith?" replied Anna overlooking his awkward apology. She was far from being ready to give him a drink from the cup of condolences.

"I don't know. I just recognize it when-zz I see it. It's like seeing a situation from d'the varmint's perspective, and d'then volunteering to cooperate with it instead of whining about it. Faith is like agreeing with God, and d'then doing or saying something about it as if it was your own d'thoughts."

"Why did you bring this up, Bibb?"

"Because you saw my life from God's eye, and said something when you saw I was faithless."

"I didn't see the heavens open wide and hear God proclaim mysteries, and then order me to chew you out when you were so wrong. You were just wrong, and anybody could have seen that."

"I didn't."

"Now you do. What's your point?"

"You asked God to fix me quick before we got to Miles City. I guess he also picked you to apply d'the fixings. D'the problem with prayer is d'that God often fingers d'the asker to do d'the fixings."

"You were wrong, so I had to!"

"Who told you I was wrong, Anna?"

"What are you trying to say, Bibb?"

"Boldness comes from knowing you are toting d'the truth. You knew you were right, and said d'the truth at me regardless of d'the consequences. Faith made you bold."

"Faith in who, Bibb? Faith always needs a *who*. Without a *who* it's noth'n but a worthless wish."

"I can't answer d'that question for you, but you sure did seem certain d'that I wouldn't strike at you back. You had faith in somebody d'that something would restrain me. I'm so embarrassed."

"But that was because I was right, Bibb. Nothing more."

"D'that wasn't what I saw."

"What did you see, Bibb?"

"The old Bibb would have killed anybody else who talked to me like d'that. You I cannot. You I cannot. I cannot. To hurt you is to hurt me. It would stab-zz me like a knife if I ever laid a feather on you. I cannot, Anna. I cannot. I am so embarrassed. Maybe-zz I have become a church mouse."

"I don't think so. I was cruel to suggest that. You are Mr. Tommy Toivo, and I am Anna Toivo. No more, no less…" She became un-expectantly bold again. "No, I am wrong about that. I am your Anna, and you are my Tommy. Until you are well and I am in my mother's arms, you will just have to accept our inconvenient marriage."

"Anna, I am just sick about this. I disappointed you, I disappointed God, and now d'that d'the truth is dancing in front of my nose, I disappointed me too. Anna, humiliation tastes like gravel."

"Welcome to my life, Bibb. Welcome to my fate." Anna was becoming quite somber about this whole incident. She also noticed he didn't balk at her phrase "our inconvenient marriage."

Bibb remembered those were his words to her now spoken back at him. He hadn't even noticed or felt the extent of humiliation she had endured over the last weeks, but now those thoughts were overwhelming him like a flood. It hurt Bibb to his core that he didn't see her pain like he felt it now.

After about ten more minutes of muddy ruts and silence, Bibb did the only thing he could do to comfort himself and her. He slipped his hand over towards hers and offered her his pinky. She felt it and returned the gesture without looking in his direction. She could not. She dared not. They both experienced the short squeeze of peace. There was nothing else to be said. The covenantal commitment cooled their heated words into warm respect. Kindness had won the day, and in their hearts they both blamed God for it. The good varmint never fights fair, and he always wins.

==0==

About an hour north from their lunch location Bibb and Anna secured the favor of some sodbusters for shelter. It didn't hurt that Bibb also showed up with two rabbits to put in their stew.

Anna stayed with the family while Bibb rode on his horse back to the scouts and wished them farewell. Bibb told them how much his woman appreciated their protection and then sent them away with his blessing, which now meant something. Besides giving the guard the last of the rations, Bibb presented the elder of the scouts a recently obtained knife to pass on to the chief. Bibb knew that the chief may want to award the weapon to the wounded brother for his role in protecting their future history alone in a hostile environment. That embodied history had a name, the Ugly One, and she was entrusted and enriched by a princess's dress. As they departed all hoped that their trails would cross again.

==0==

The family that invited Mr. and Mrs. Toivo into their home was first generation Germans. They had two boys and a daughter all under the age of twelve. The girl had an extraordinary fascination with Tommy's facial injury and immediately wanted to play doctor on him. With Bibb's cooperation and Anna's supervision the young girl learned a lesson in cleaning messy wounds. If it wasn't skin little Heidi would call it by the scientific name: *innards*. This opened the way for other conversations. Good schooling helped. The children's English proved better than that of their parents.

Tommy naturally gravitated to help with chores. He and the father went out to the barn where he saw where he could help. Tommy pulled out his whetstone and started sharpening the man's tools without being asked. It took until dinner time, but Bibb re-shod the man's two work horses.

While Bibb was in the barn the young girl wanted to play doctor on Anna, but had to settle for combing out knotted hair and each getting wet washing each other's faces and arms. (Her brothers were very uncooperative with her medical passions, and her dollies were so operated on that they were beyond further repair.) Her mother was delighted having the rabbits Bibb harvested, and her two boys were busy digging up the last of the potatoes and getting them stored in the root cellar.

At dinner time the little girl's curiosity could not be bridled. Her first question after grace was pronounced was directed at Anna. "Don't you have any clothes?"

"I have only one dress, little Heidi, and I am saving it for tomorrow. Mr. Toivo and I will be going into Miles City tomorrow."

"Do you want to wear one of mine? My mom made me one with warm sleeves for fall."

"Do you sew too?" asked Anna.

"No, but my mom lets me put the thread into the needle's eye. Mom said her arms were too short to see 'goot' enough to do that. We try, but we don't say *good* good here, so we say *goot*. You should try it. It tickles when you say it."

Heidi's mother asked Anna, "Mrs. Toivo, do you need some sewing done? I have some darning to do tonight. We can do that too. Pardon my asking, but don't you gotts any socks? You need socks or your feet will freeze." The clues to this riddle were not adding up for the mother. This couple had three horses, a very nice buckboard, and a large trunk, yet she only had one dress and no socks.

"No, ma'am, and did I hear your husband say your name was Helga? That is a pretty name."

"So is Anna. Those Indian moccasins will not get you through the winter. Mr. Toivo, tell me true, can't you even afford shoes and socks for your wife?"

"Helga, you are kind to-zz notice our needs. One of our reasons we are traveling to-zz Miles City is to purchase essentials for Anna to wear. D'those moccasins are now one of Anna's greatest treasures. D'they were a gift from special widows of a Lakota tribe we stayed with ten days ago."

"Lakota?" The older boy Hans spoke up at that revelation. "You stayed with the Lakota?"

"Hans," replied Anna, "Mr. Toivo is a trusted friend of the tribe's chief. He has spent several days living with the Indians this summer learning their ways."

"What did you do to become friendly with Indians? Aren't they wild? Aren't they savages?"

"Hans," Bibb said, "I did nothing to earn d'their respect or friendship. D'they showed me-zz mercy when I didn't deserve it. Just because d'the red man does not trust d'the white man does not mean d'they are savages. I am a broken man, and d'they took me in not because I am white or red, but-zz because I'm human."

Heidi spoke up, "How come you don't have moccasins and why is your wife wearing your clothes? Don't you care about her?"

Helga spoke up, "She didn't mean it that way, Mr. Toivo. Heidi, of course Mr. Toivo cares for his wife. Isn't that true, Mr. Toivo."

"Heidi, Mrs. Toivo has a heart as big as Montana. D'there is a secret why she has an empty trunk and only moccasins to wear. Maybe she will tell you d'that secret tonight. It is not my secret to tell. And you are right, her feet do get cold. She told me d'that she is looking for a little girl to keep her warm tonight. She can tell you her secrets and what it is like to be a princess."

"A princess? Are you a princess, Mrs. Toivo?" asked Heidi.

"I will tell you about that later when we go to sleep tonight. Will that be okay with you, Helga?"

"Will it be okay with your husband?" she responded.

"I must confess," Anna responded, and reached over and placed her hand on Tommy's. "Mr. Toivo and I are not fully married yet. We have made deep promises to each other before God Almighty, but our formal wedding is still in the future. He would prefer that we sleep separately. We are traveling east where we will meet my parents. To tell you another secret, Mr. Toivo prefers to sleep with his horses. Isn't that true, Mr. Toivo?"

"Our horses seem to prefer d'that too, Anna."

"How did you get hurt, Mr. Toivo?" asked Hans.

"I was shot in d'the face, Hans. Heidi, one of Anna's secrets is d'that she was d'the one who made sure I got well. She knows a lot about doctoring. D'that is how we met."

"So you are not Mrs. Toivo yet? Isn't that a lie then?" asked Heidi.

"Our preacher said it was okay," Anna answered quickly. "He recommended I should call myself Mrs. Toivo while we are traveling out of respect for my partner. The preacher even filed a piece of paper at the court house to make sure our covenant was official."

Unlike Anna, Bibb was not enjoying this conversation at all. Several times he unobtrusively tried to get his hand unstuck from Anna's grip, but it was not going to happen. Bibb could think of nothing else. And her comment "not fully married yet" was tearing him up. He would have to save his questions and comments for her until later. He wasn't sure if Anna was making that preacher stuff up or not. It could have happened. He certainly wasn't going to question her about it now.

Anna later called it a desperation move when Bibb finally got a chance twenty minutes later to unlock his hand from the intentional 'fully married' until death-like grip Anna had locked on him. Bibb asked about Miles City. "I heard d'the big rancher in town is named Mr. Eastum, or a Mr. Westum? Anna and I found one of his horses out on d'the range and we want to return it to him."

The father, who was quiet until now, spoke up. "His name is Mr. Westum. He and his new wife run a ranch west of the city."

Helga spoke up, "Actually, Mrs. Westum is the one that has a new husband. Mr. Westum had an accident that changed him from being bad to becoming goot. It is quite the story."

"Accident?" asked Bibb.

"Yeah, he fell off his high horse," answered Hans.

The father continued. "About two months ago an outlaw came through town. You might have heard of him. His name was Bibb."

"His name was Bibb? Was he killed?"

"No, but mighty close. Westum's ranch hands decided to have some fun with the man. They beat him senseless not knowing who the man was."

"They don't know it now either," inserted Hans.

"Why not?" asked Tommy.

"They're all dead. Bibb got them. All of them."

"Son, we don't know that for sure, so stop speculating," inserted the boy's father.

"Bibb does know for sure, that's certain. All my buddies said Bibb took after them with his ax just to make it personal."

The other brother added, "Or shoots them in the forehead. Dead is dead, and Westum has had a hard time finding ranch hands to work for him ever since."

"What happened to Westum and what happened to Bibb?" asked Anna.

"The sheriff rescued the outlaw from Westum's ranch. He actually put him in jail for horse thieving. This Bibb guy was thought to be on the edge of death and then mysteriously disappeared. Many in town thought he had died and considered the whole matter buried."

"Until the papers came in from Canada," said Hans. His picture was on the front of their newspaper and it said the man was known as the Ghost of Fort Rice."

"Where is Fort Rice?" asked Bibb.

"Somewhere east of here. But that was when all the ranch hands started to disappear one by one. Everybody in town was wondering about a lot of things, starting with why the sheriff didn't return the horse Bibb rode into town on to its owner. All sorts of Wanted posters started popping up around town. It was rumored by some of the sillies in town that Miles City was being haunted."

"Son, don't overstate the case. Yes, but the sensible people in town didn't care."

"But Mr. Westum cared, Papa. He was losing ranch hands and he had to do his own work."

"What about Mr. Westum's accident? What kind of accident?" asked Bibb.

The father continued, "Mr. Westum made the accident of going to the same restaurant where this Fort Rice ghost was waylaid. That is when this Bibb fellow suddenly reappeared and was strangely whole – far from the shape he was in when he vanished. Bibb threatened to expose Westum's evil heart with his own signature style.

That credible and immediate threat convinced Mr. Westum to sing out his sins with gusto lest mercilessly his own brand of frontier justice would visit him immediately. Their discussion was heard by the sheriff and a whole room full of others. Confused by the outlaw's strange reappearance from the dead and the certain knowledge that the outlaw's just revenge upon him physically would be worse than death, Mr. Westum confessed to several crimes this strangely resurrected man mysteriously seemed to know much about."

"That knowledge really spooked a lot of people; I told you that, Dad."

"Hush, child," responded Helga. "Mr. Toivo, it was actually Bibb's credible threat concerning his wife that changed Mr. Westum. Bibb threatened to take his wife for his own immoral pleasures and then sell her as a slave to the Indians when he was finished using her."

"Why didn't Bibb just kill him and do that anyway?" asked Anna.

"Tell them what the preacher said, Schatz[5]," said Helga. "It was certainly strange."

"No, I will tell him what I think. The preacher can talk for himself, and often does talk on forever and ever. I think Bibb thought it would be a greater revenge to make the man change his ways. Bibb gave him a choice: Die, or no longer live for himself. Westum chose life and became a slave in the service of our city."

"And his wife," added Helga. "Westum changed from being a bully to becoming a real husband. That Bibb thumped Mr. Westum goot. Bibb threatened Mr. Westum and told him if he ever went back to his old ways he would personally and slowly take his life from him an inch at a time as a just reward for the beating he suffered."

"So what happened to Bibb?" asked Tommy.

"He just disappeared again. Vanished like a ghost," added Heidi. She had obviously heard her brothers say that often.

"That's strange. Why would an outlaw do that?" asked Anna.

For the next two hours Anna and Tommy were told the many legends of the notorious Bibb. No mention was made of Toak, as if he never existed or part of the story, nor did the preacher get mentioned again. Anna mentioned that nobody could be as bad as they made the outlaw Bibb seem to be. All the children disagreed strongly and their parents fell silent to let them speak their opinions.

Bibb asked a question as the yawns started to appear and the candle was going out. "Maybe we should pray for this Bibb guy. Do you think he is so bad that he could ever get changed like what happened to Westum?"

"Nope," said Heidi. "That man is going to burn for sure."

"Heidi! Don't say things like that! God can clean him up goot if He wanted to."

"Why would He want to?" the daughter asked her mother.

"Because God is goot and able to fix bad," said Helga.

---

5   German: term of endearment, i.e., sweetheart, pronounced 'shot-zee'

"What good would that do? Can God make rotten pears ripe again?" she asked. The little girl never ran out of questions.

Bibb announced he was tired and was going to the barn to stay with the horses. He asked if anybody needed anything, and if not, he would see them in the morning.

"I know what God would do with a cleaned up outlaw!" said Heidi in a new burst of excitement as Bibb was getting ready to go outside.

"What is that?" asked Anna.

"Well if Mr. Westum was given a new wife after he changed, well, maybe if the upside-down outlaw Mr. Bibb has truly turned right-side up, maybe he could be rewarded with a princess!"

Bibb was not amused as the others were. "Good night, you all. I'll be out in d'the barn. D'thank you for d'the wonderful meal and your hospitality. You have been most kind. Anna, do you need anything from out d'there?"

"Can you bring in my dress? It needs Helga's help."

They all stood up, said good night to Tommy, and started cleaning up after the feast of hase (rabbit) stew. Heidi was particularly excited. "Let's go! Let's go, Mrs. Toivo!"

"Where to, Heidi?"

"To my bed! You're going to tell me all your secrets!"

"Okay, but first I'm going out with Mr. Toivo to say goodnight and fetch my dress. I'll be back."

"Doesn't that just beat all," said Hans. "That little sister of ours never wants to go to bed. Mrs. Toivo, you just might be a princess."

==0==

Bibb helped Anna get her dress from the trunk. The candle they took out to the barn didn't survive the blowing wind or the snow that was now falling hard. By the soft glow of the wood stove they eventually found their prize. She thanked Bibb for his help. It was quite dark in the barn.

"Do you have anything else to say to me tonight, Mrs. Toivo?"

"I never felt more like royalty in my life. Maybe the medicine man was right." Her words were said so softly that it shivered Bibb. He did not like his current predicament and knew he had to turn the conversation elsewhere. Her eyes glistened as if they had just caught some of the new snow.

"Anna, d'thank you for not giving away our identity. D'that would have complicated d'things. I don't want to be kicked out tonight into d'the cold and wet."

"Bibb, did you almost propose to me tonight? You said something about us waiting until we got to Fort Rice to get married."

"Anna-zz, excuse-zz me-zz, but you-zz said d'that, not-zz me."

386

"But you said nothing to correct the thoughts I knew you were having."

"Anna, let's not-zz talk about-zz d'this. I know-zz you're just teasing me-zz. You're a whole lots smarter of a woman d'than d'that to-zz even be-zz considering such a d'thing. Haven't you-zz heard enough of my-zz legends tonight to know-zz what I am?"

"You're right about that, and I knew your answer before I asked."

"D'then why-zz did you-zz ask it-zz, Anna?" Bibb just despised being boxed up like this.

"To clear the air. I don't want you getting any funny ideas about desiring marriage while you're sleeping out here with the horses tonight."

"Anna, are you-zz telling me-zz d'the truth? I have-zz a hard time-zz figuring out what you-zz are d'thinking sometimes."

"Good. Can you walk me back to the house now? My feet are freezing. Please?"

Bibb saw a wheelbarrow by the door and told Anna to sit in it. "Your royal carriage awaits you, Your Highness!"

Anna laughed, assumed the somewhat rickety throne, and then commanded her lowly knave to roll her and her royal vestment back to the castle. Once back at the door to the home she asked Bibb again if he really preferred to sleep with the horses.

"I must. If I-zz was under d'the same roof with you tonight I wouldn't be-zz able to sleep. Good night, Anna. Sleep well. Tomorrow will-zz be a trying day."

"Bibb, I sure enjoyed this evening. You are a dear sometimes. Good night, Bibb."

Bibb tipped his hat to Anna, turned, and happily returned the wheelbarrow to the place he found it. The man said to himself as he put more wood in the stove, "A warm barn full of horses and an unloaded wheelbarrow. What more could a man want in life?" That question haunted him most of the night. Plagued with a pretty princess once in a while wasn't as bad as he once thought.

Wednesday, October 19, 1887

Bibb and I arrived in Miles City late in the day. We were not even inside the town limits before Bibb was confronted by the law of the town, the sheriff's wife, and two other people. Bibb made no effort to introduce me. He was cold and quarrelsome – and not the same man I had gotten to know over the last month. I got Tommy to tame the bad boy Bibb inside of him once the sun went down, and none too soon for my liking. I enjoyed peace tonight. Indescribable peace. My greatest fears are now behind me, and I can almost smell the aromas of the eastern cities. The sound of a train whistle is as glorious as the blast of angel's trumpets, confirming my certain call to find my way to my new home.

We rented room number three in the only hotel in town. (I have an aversion to rooms numbered two or four.) I immediately went shopping for necessities and later Bibb and I ate a real meal together. Along with clothes and essentials I also purchased a gun. Bibb fell asleep at my side tonight – on the park swing. Bless that man. He has no idea what that meant to me. It has been years since a man has been that comfortable and trusting around me in public. To the contrary, the single bed in the hotel was the cause of our biggest test of wills ever, and I won. I am the trail boss now.

To my shame, Mrs. Franklin was right about the old me. She may never know that the old me was washed away in the creek running through the Lakota Camp. I am not the new me yet; feeling much like a caterpillar climbing into a cocoon. What I know for certain is that my dreams are standing at my doorstep. A cocoon... who would have ever thought that? Many transforming moments come to mind... who would have ever thought... Bibb still scares me. I scare me. I am now in full control, and strangely that has a bitter price. I do not feel like we are the same us as I did on the plains. No, I feel, notice, and see a lot of the old controlling Anna fighting to have her way in every way. Mrs. Franklin was right, sorely right.

==0==

THE TOIVOS GOT an early start on the rutted trail to Miles City. Three inches of snow had fallen overnight and with the bright sunshine made the whole prairie dazzling white. Before departing they were served a modest breakfast of two slices of butterbrot and coffee, which was no more or less than their hosts enjoyed. Moist bread was a real treat after ten days of hard tack.

As soon as they were headed north Anna asked Bibb if he froze last night in the barn. Bibb responded that he was no colder than their horses. Before he could ask Anna the same question she volunteered that she had to give the teepee treatment to that little furnace her parents called Heidi.

"What's d'that? What do you mean by d'the teepee treatment?"

"I had to crush her ribs in my arms and wrap my legs tight around hers. The little girl kicks in her sleep and it was the only way I could avoid getting more bruises."

"Yeah, I know. D'that teepee treatment is pretty brutal stuff. Makes me glad I have a horse. But did you sleep well?"

"The girl reminds me of me. I was called Hannah of 10,000 Questions by my teachers when I was her age. That little girl could not stand me leaving any of her questions unanswered."

"D'that apple didn't fall far from d'the tree, did it? And you were worried you wouldn't find a kindred spirit in Miles City. I'll bet you a silver dollar d'that her middle name is Anna. Hannah?"

"Okay, Bibb, you have had your fun. Now it's my turn."

"I wouldn't recommend starting a snowball fight in what you're wearing. D'thank you for taking my advice and wearing your dress today. You need to stay-zz under d'those blankets for now. It should warm up nice today. I bet d'the snow is gone by noon."

"That's not the fun I was thinking about, Bibb."

"Anna, why don't you tell me what your idea of fun is?"

"Bibb, my hands are cold. Can you hold them and keep my fingers warm?"

"Anna, forget it. I ain't going d'there. When I stop I'll get you something else to wrap up in. You almost shook me into a d'thousand pieces last night at dinner. You know-zz how much d'that bothers me. Please don't do d'that to me again. It ain't right and generates in me d'thoughts and feelings I shouldn't be having. D'that's not playing fair, or fighting fair, or just not fair, period."

"Now this is my kind of fun!"

"You're a tease, Anna."

"And my next step is the denial. This is really fun."

"Now d'that you had you fun, can we talk about Miles City?"

"What about it?"

"It's a gamble for me to show up with one of Westum's horses. After what Hans said last night, I'm afraid d'the prevailing opinion of me is d'that I'm so bad to be unredeemable. D'that means d'the sheriff may use one of his two murder warrants to d'throw me in jail."

"Why can't we just sneak into town, Tommy?"

"D'that would be nice, but I know d'there is little chance of d'that. I hope I can avoid both Mr. and Mrs. Westum. He has reason to stay clear, but she might go after me. She is not exactly as pure as d'the snow surrounding us."

"Well then, if you are scared, I'll meet with her then."

"I recommend against it, but Anna you're free to do what you want. Once we hit Miles City I plan-zz to spend my time in jail or at Anna's house. Once I round up enough provisions to take d'the buckboard to Bismarck, we need-zz to be heading east before winter arrives."

"Excuse me, Bibb, just in case you haven't noticed, winter is already here. No, Bibb. That is not what is going to happen. Once we hit Miles City there will be a new trail boss on this trip of ours. You promised that I would be in charge of your healing, and you are not getting out of it. Suck it up, buttercup. You are about to lose your control. If you treat me nice and cooperate, you might even learn to enjoy your pain. I will."

"Now d'that is a pleasant d'thought. Anna, I'll do my best, but d'there are some d'things I will not be able to handle. You have to give me some freedom to be me."

"I'll give you all the freedoms and kindnesses you gave me on this trip. When I tell you not to talk, you are not to talk. When I tell you to bow, you bow, or go here or there, that is where you must go. I am going to enjoy this. How are you at doing laundry?"

For the next half hour it was quiet between the two of them. They found a lone tree and stopped in its shade. Bibb got out of the wagon and found more clothes to wrap around Anna. All this was done without benefit of conversation.

"When are we going to get there, Tommy?"

Tommy didn't answer.

"Okay Tommy, you made your point. You have my permission to talk now."

"I don't need your permission. You ain't d'the boss yet. I didn't talk because I enjoyed d'the quiet. I do have another request to make of you, Anna."

"What is that?"

"Pretend d'that you know nothing of Toak or Westum. I need you to do all d'the listening and none of d'the talking about d'them."

"Why?"

"If I get thrown in jail you won't be assumed to be a co-conspirator. If d'that happens, you need to get on d'the first cattle train out of town. With me pushed aside, only bad d'things can happen to you. I d'threatened my revenge against Westum's wife, and if d'they are vengeful you will be d'their target just to watch me suffer."

"So you do have feelings for me. I knew it."

"Will you stop it, Anna? I am really tired of you needling me about having or showing feeling about you, d'the moon, or hard tack. Just stop it. You know I do, otherwise I wouldn't have said what I said in d'the barn last night. I don't want to fight, but you are pushing me too hard in d'that direction. Please stop. You don't know how much you twist me in knots. And your teasing about not fully married yet, and preacher talk, and courthouses, oh! Please, Anna, stop it. I can't handle it. I need to d'think clearly today and you are muddling up my brain with feelings and... and... oh, never mind..."

"I just wanted to know your heart, Bibb."

"D'that is not a wise pursuit. Anna, my heart is desperately wicked. D'the varmint has bitten off more d'that he can chew. Do yourself a big favor and stop looking for light where d'there is only darkness."

"That is a lie, Bibb, and you know it."

"What's my lie d'this time? I ain't said no nothin'."

"There is light in the dinky little heart of yours. I've seen it. And Bibb, where there is light, darkness has to retreat. The darkness that used to own your soul is not surrendering peacefully, but it is putting up a fight that it cannot win."

"What do you know about d'that?"

"Bibb, I don't know, but I can feel. I have seen that light in what follows you. When I'm with you I can't stop arguing with you, but that is because of what I have seen following you. Based on what is behind us I know the path in front of us will be good. I don't trust you fully, but I do trust the varmint that you talk about. Bibb, let me tell you true as true can be about me. I so want to be kind to you but it is not in my nature. I always want to win. I always want to control. I always want to fix those I care about. After I get on your case, I feel just terrible. I promise myself to be nice the next time, but you say something stupid and I just launch on you again. But Bibb, accept this to be true about me."

"Which truth? I already have experienced several helpings of all of d'that winning, whining, controlling, launching, and fixing, not to mention all your talk of feelings."

"This truth, Bibb! I can't sit still if I see you misbehaving or saying something stupid. Bibb, I see who you really are. You are so different from your reputation, and you learn fast, and you honestly care. Best of all you honestly give me a fair hearing. You don't always like what I say, but you do listen. That has been your greatest kindness towards me. It has been the piece of my life that I have missed the most, and now that I have experienced it, I don't want to give it up. But then you say something stupid and I start to fuss again. Bibb, you can drive me crazy sometimes!"

Bibb almost said something stupid again about who drives who insane. That would have not been helpful or kind. "So Anna, what do you want me to say or do? You never say anything unless you want to make a point, and sorry, but I missed it d'this time."

"Start with saying nothing. You don't say stupid stuff when you breathe through your nose."

"I can do d'that." He was very glad that the woman gave evidence that she had also listened to him. Humility is a hard lesson, but the lesson she learned entering the Indian village would be kept for the rest of her life. Breathing through his nose was a happy compliance.

==0==

391

Anna and Tommy stopped for lunch on a rise in the land. The snow had already melted almost everywhere and the ground was sloppy and slippery everywhere they stepped. They celebrated their last meal of hard tack and jerky with a smile. They ceremoniously divided the last piece and washed it down by sharing a snowball Anna had made. Anna thought this was as big of a little moment she had experience in years. She saw it as bread of affliction and the cup of coldness that was no longer going to be part of her wandering in the wilderness. She stared a Bibb, wondering if he was attaching any meaning to this special event. Nothing. Absolutely nothing. Bibb was being Bibb; all man. He was eating the snow because the hardtack was dry and stale. No more. No less. Bibb once again was missing out on all the glory.

"Bibb, let's call this our fighting food! Whenever we feel like getting after each other about something we can break out this dry stuff and exchange some verbal jabs."

"You sound like you enjoy getting after me." Bibb was still was wishing for more of her silent treatment.

"I'll never tell. Then it is agreed then! I will have to stock up on this stuff."

"How about we agree d'that d'this is fighting food, and never buy any more of it? I prefer d'the kind Anna over d'the kindled Anna. She can get pretty hot and doesn't keep her fire in her belly."

"And I enjoy the kind Bibb over the stubborn one!"

"Anna, it sounds like you are asking me for another piece of jerky. Is d'that what you want?"

"Are you saying I'm looking for another fight?"

"If d'the shoe fits, wear it. By d'the way, are your feet still cold?"

"No, and thank you for asking. Bibb, when do you think we will get there?"

Bibb rolled his eyes. She couldn't help her own nature. She couldn't stop asking that question any more than she could stop breathing. "It depends on d'the cows. D'there's a good chance we will see many more before we arrive. D'the good news is d'that we crossed our last creek. We-zz will stay on d'this ridge and drop down into d'the Tongue River Road about five miles south of town." Just as he finished saying that the north wind blew past their ears the faint sound of a train whistle.

"Bibb, it's true! We are almost there. This is so wonderful!"

"It will be more wonderful once I get you to d'the mercantile. You are due for some new clothes. Anna, please let d'the ladies in town help you. Don't take on any airs. Don't act poor, but don't act snooty. If d'they suggest a red dress, buy d'the red one. D'this is not where you should display your superior knowledge of fashion and design."

"You're the trail boss for now. I will follow your advice. So how long from here?"

"Is d'that because you were planning to do d'that anyway?" accused Bibb.

"Yes. It is scary we are starting to think so much like each other. My good sense is starting to rub off on you."

Bibb was tempted to take the last word, but seeing Anna's mood, his next reply would have not been the last word. She was acting spirited and aggressive. Bibb assumed it was because they were getting close. He later concluded the train whistle had brought that on.

Once they were heading north again Anna asked Bibb if he saw anything of Toak at the last stop. He responded in the negative, and unless the tracks were recent they would be hidden by the snow and mud. Toak would know that too.

Because she could sense such things, Anna started to watch Tommy's every move as he drove the wagon. He had a most serious look and his face, and by her reckoning, very deep in thought. "Bibb, are you worried?"

"I'm worried about my anger, Anna. I'm just a bag of vengeful hate right now, and I can't seem to lick it. So many d'things could go very wrong, and I'm in no mood for another dragging and whipping courtesy of Westum's boys. I try to d'think of good d'things, but dreaming of revenge and hate just comes back."

"Maybe that pet varmint of yours is letting you whet on yourself here instead of when we get there. Bibb, here is my promise to you for what it is worth. I'm all in. I'm standing behind my man. You say it, and I will obey... as long as you don't touch me wrong."

"You would even pray for us?"

"I'll think about that. I ain't saying yes, but I ain't saying no." Once again he zinged her with the most secret of her magic words: *us*. She thought to herself that was not possible. *Us* isn't in that man's vocabulary. No, Bibb didn't zing her, but she knew what did. That varmint doesn't fight fair.

After a long pause Bibb asked, "If you can't pray for us, can you pray for me?"

That settled it; another zing. The varmint was showing Anna his varmintly grin as if laughing out loud. God's hand was all over that boy. She was glad to be sitting next to him and his protection.

==0==

The German family enjoyed their meals together. Work often caused them to skip meals, but last night's snow kept them inside to work on some home maintenance. They gathered as a family for an early lunch to eat, plan their afternoon chores, and discuss the company they had the previous night.

The conversation swirled around the table for several minutes. Heidi was used to not getting a chance to talk. Her mother would sometimes force a break in the conversation so Heidi could say something. The general consensus at the table was that both Toivos shined with the glow of being newlyweds. The father stated that it did society goot when goot people get married.

"Are you talking about the princess and the bad man?" asked Heidi.

"I'm talking about our company last night. I thought you said you enjoyed sleeping with Mrs. Toivo last night in your bed."

"I did, and she told me many secrets. She said a medicine man predicted that she was going to be a mother of a prince. That would either make her a queen or a princess. I don't know how that is all supposed to work."

"And what did she say about Mr. Toivo? He would have to be the king then!"

"He is no king, and his name isn't Mr. Toivo."

"Then what is it?"

"Last night when they went outside to get her dress he brought her back to the house to say goodnight to her. I watched from the window. I thought that was really sweet. Did you know he gave her a ride in our wheelbarrow so her feet wouldn't get wet in the snow? She called him by his real name twice. His name is Bibb."

"What?" replied the father. "Hans, run to the barn. I'm turning sick over this. Hans, see if that man robbed us blind. Quick, go, son."

"Yes, he is that bad man we talked about last night."

"Are you making that up, Heidi?" The big German father reached over and held his little girl's hand. "Heidi, tell me true," he said tenderly.

"That's his name, Papa. I guess I'm not very good at keeping the princess's secrets. I'm sorry."

"It's always appropriate to let your parents help you keep your secrets. You did good, Heidi," said the eldest son.

"Well, he certainly behaved and helped out here!" replied Helga. "Except if you were a rabbit; all were blessed to have them stop by."

"Are you sure, Heidi," her father asked again. "His name is Bibb?"

"Yes, Papa."

"Shouldn't we tell the Miles City sheriff he is coming?" asked Heidi's brother. "They have to be warned, especially Mr. Westum."

"Too late, son. They will be there before we could get there to make a difference."

Heidi interrupted them by saying, "I liked Mrs. Toivo. Shouldn't we pray for her?"

"Dad, come quickly," said Hans who had just returned from the barn. With a new sense of urgency, the man of the house and Hans quickly got dressed for the cold. Out of compulsion the father grabbed his gun and followed his son back to the barn. The three remaining in the house cleared the table and got ready to go outside too. Helga was scared because her husband was scared.

He entered the barn expecting the worst. That is not what he found. Bibb had worked most of the night cleaning out the stalls and sweeping out the place. All the father's tools were picked up off the benches and sills, and returned to their places hanging on the wall. There was new hay given to their horses and each showed signs that they had been recently brushed down. The inventory complete, the patriarch sputtered something in German giving his son an impression of disbelief.

The two in the barn were headed back into the house when something caught Hans' eye. Scratched by a fingernail in the frost on the window glass was the letters "dunker-surn" with the word "Bibb" under it. "What does it mean, Father?"

"That is how a Finn would spell *Thank you* in German. It also means that woman may really be an Indian princess. Go fetch your sister, will you? I'm going to stay out here and look around. That boy had to have been up half the night cleaning this place. Tell your mother too, and have them all come out here and see this. Don't tell them. Let's surprise them."

The big German father put some more wood in the stove to get the barn warmer. Soon his whole family joined him out there and gathered around the stove. Once warm they had Heidi try to read the name in the frost since she was just learning her letters. Her eyes lit up when she discovered it spelled Bibb. They brought her back and placed her in the center of the family circle. Her older brother asked, "What other secrets did she tell you, Heidi? We want to know!"

Heidi did not disappoint them. She was the special friend of the princess.

==0==

"We got a welcoming party, Anna, and it-zz might be trouble." Bibb looked around to see first if there was a bypass and second if there was the fifth Indian. The sheriff had placed his carriage on the road in a place between the valley wall and the Tongue River. There was no avoiding them. Subconsciously Bibb checked to feel his revolvers on his hips, the ax under the seat, and the rifle by his side. Anna was not comforted. This looked like a prelude to a gunfight to her.

Bibb pulled his wagon close to the sheriff's so that all parties were facing each other. Next to the sheriff was his wife, and behind him, Westum and a woman just as formally attired. Bibb assumed her to be Mrs. Westum.

"Mr. Toivo, welcome back to Miles City." The sheriff was hoping to get a similar greeting.

"Mr. Westum, d'this extra horse belongs to you. One of your men took a shot at us. It was-zz rather unfriendly of d'the man. Before I step into d'the jurisdiction of d'the sheriff I want to return it to you. D'the man's name was Tommy Carson, and he won't be taking shots at anybody anymore."

"I got your letter, Bibb, and Mr. Westum instructed his hands not to get crosswise with you."

Anna interjected herself when the tension in the air got too much for her. "Crosswise? Tommy, who is this Mr. Westum, and why are you picking a fight already?" She was ignored by all.

"Before I start any disagreement with Mr. Westum," said Bibb, "I want to know if Tommy Carson works for d'the man, or if was he a rustler d'that had stolen one-zz of Westum's horses. He was working alone when-zz I tracked him down."

Westum told the sheriff that Tommy Carson was one of his hands, but if he had taken at shot at Bibb it was against his specific orders.

"Do you believe him, Sheriff?" asked Bibb. "Words are cheap. Carson talked with his rifle. I talked to the man with my whip and d'the blade of my ax."

"I know for a fact that Mr. Westum told his men to give you a wide berth. I was there."

"D'then I believe it's d'the truth, Sheriff. It still doesn't answer d'the insult d'though. I asked Westum for peace, and right-zz or wrong, Carson answered d'the question for him."

"Being a renegade comes with a price," the sheriff responded. "Both you and Carson might be aware of that inconvenient truth. Tommy, I want you to cut Westum some slack. He did his part to promote peace."

"Maybe." Bibb paused to switch subjects. "Sheriff, I got something for you from Deadwood. It's a letter from d'the law d'there. He asked me to give it to you." Bibb got out of his seat, gave the sheriff the sealed envelope, untied Westum's horse from his buckboard, and retied it to the sheriff's.

While Bibb was taking care of the transfer, the sheriff opened the envelope. There was a short note inside, *"Just in case you have trouble, Sam."* The note was attached to two orders signed by the judge in Deadwood. They were warrants for the arrest of Bibb for the murder of Mr. Gorgon, and an arrest warrant on Mrs. Gorgon for the attempted murder of Mr. Toivo. The sheriff quickly put the envelope in his vest pocket.

"What did he have-zz to say, Sheriff?" asked Bibb.

"It was a personal note and some legal stuff. Nothing much; a routine transfer of jurisdiction in some cases we are working. Bibb, you look hurt and you're walking funny. You need to see a doctor. Why don't we put you two on a train for Bismarck?"

"If it all d'the same to you, Sheriff, I will go d'there when I decide to go d'there and how-zz I want-zz to go d'there. How did you know-zz when I was coming in today?"

"Several folks who saw you mentioned it to me. We are glad you made it."

"Was Toak one of d'them?"

"Who's Toak?" asked Anna. She was ignored again.

"Yes, Toak came into town this morning. He told Anna's mother when to expect you. She relayed the message to me. She said Toak was very cordial. She also said he left as secretly as he arrived."

Adding Toak into the conversation, and especially the fact he had talked to (young) Anna's mother, bothered Bibb much more than it should have. It immediately showed in his conversation. For the next ten minutes the old Bibb came back. Mrs. Toivo could do nothing to stop a vulgar rant; so unlike anything she had ever heard come out of the man's mouth before.

It was the sheriff's wife that had enough of that and ended the rant by forcefully overriding Bibb's topic, changing the subject to an appeal to meet Mrs. Gorgon's needs for clothes, shelter, and a good scrubbing. She promised that she would personally meet Mrs. Gorgon in the lobby of the hotel with the owner of the clothing store at four o'clock to go shopping.

Anna's eyes told Bibb everything he needed to know; her piercing stare finished changing his demeanor. Bibb's quick calming showed her that he tacitly agreed to cooperate with the plan. He was still angry, but Bibb dared not express it. He also saw that her pinky was extended as she cupped her other fingers inside her thumb, a sign all others would miss even if they knew to look for it.

Before they went their separate ways, the sheriff secured from Bibb certain promises about behavior in his city. He also suggested Bibb stay away from the preacher's home until tomorrow. The sheriff passed on to Bibb that he had been told that the parson was going to be late returning from his circuit. Bibb need not set that good family up for scandal by silly gossipers by staying there overnight without the man of the house at home. Bibb also agreed to stop by the jail in the morning for coffee. The subject of the meeting was clearly implied, but not specifically stated in front of the Westums. It was said as an invitation but Bibb sensed immediately that the invite wasn't optional.

Bibb and Anna's ride to the hotel was not cordial at all. Bibb was showing his dark side again and Anna was confused about it. Her theory about light and dark not coexisting together sounded good, but didn't look like it was holding any credibility given the vile attitudes she was witnessing. Through intuition and kindly proffered questions (ugly) Anna discovered the source of Bibb's anger. He was upset by Toak's unknown close whereabouts along with his ingratiating himself with (young) Anna and her mother. Bibb seemed quite possessive of that special friendship and he told (ugly) Anna that "Toak was up to no good," but with many more vulgar adjectives.

"A penny for your thoughts, Bibb? What's bothering you the most?" she asked softly. She knew this was not the time to react to his words. She needed to do her best magic to calm her man.

"I don't believe my own words, Anna. D'that is what bothers me d'the most."

"What words, Tommy?"

"I told you never to believe d'those predictions. D'they are bothering me, Anna. Toak can kill me with no trouble whatsoever in d'this town. He knows my safe place too. D'that bothers me."

"What words, Bibb?"

"D'that I would die on d'the grassy plains. I can't afford to believe d'them. Death is following me, Anna. I can smell it. I can't afford to let my guard down. Toak has d'the upper hand. I am d'the hunted, he is d'the hunter."

"He wouldn't dare, Tommy."

"Why?" asked Bibb. "He would know nothing of d'the medicine man's predictions."

"Predictions? Honestly Bibb, that is the least of his worries. He doesn't dare touch you. He ain't that stupid. If he does, he is doomed!"

"Doomed?"

"That cub molester will have to suffer the fate of dealing with mother grizzly. He will pray for death, but I won't give it to him until the full price for his trespass has been paid seven times."

Bibb smiled at Anna. The essence of humor was the tinge of truth laced between the syllables. Tommy could understand why just one seventh of that fate would be enough of a deterrent. Bibb tried his best to improve his attitude.

"Can you be kind and do me a favor, Tommy?"

"What?"

"I can't ask you to be friendly to the Westum's, but can you at least be pleasant? You scare me Bibb. You scare me bad when that dark side you have oozes out of your pores. Yes, I understand you have to be cautious not only with Westum's boys but Toak too. You accused me of having faith earlier, and I have not forgotten it, Bibb. Well, here's that faith thrown into your face, Mr. Toivo. I am trusting God that He will force you into delivering me to my mother's arms, so get over it. Bibb, you ain't getting out of this covenant that easy."

"You believe He will do d'that?"

"You believe it, and I believe you. And another thing Bibb… I made a promise at the altar that I would superintend your healing and you promised that you would cooperate. You're stuck, boy. No man ever born has out-foxed that varmint of yours and it's almost time for you to start taking your bitter medicine. Bibb, listen good and weep. That varmint is going to let me get my licks in on you."

"You-zz make it sound like death might be preferable."

"Bibb, you know my words are strong but my heart is kind. Trust my heart, Bibb. Trust my heart." Not getting through, she put her hand on his to get his attention. "Bibb, trust my heart."

Bibb removed her hand gently. "You know, Anna, I d'think I have been a bad influence on you. You are becoming better known by where you've been rather d'than where you are."

"Is that a compliment, Bibb?"

"About d'the best I can come up with. I'm still in a pretty foul mood. Anna, your heart is still a mystery to-zz me. I don't know-zz if I can trust it or not."

"That is a mean thing to say."

"I can trust your eyes."

Anna looked at him. She thought Bibb's words to be a devious verbal escape, but he might have been telling the truth. "You're forgiven then. To be honest, Bibb, I don't trust my own heart either. So, Bibb what exactly are you promising me? Are you promising that you will trust my eyes?"

"Yes Anna, I will."

"And what sign do you propose to seal this promise with?"

"Will you-zz trust me too, Anna?"

She thought his response clever when he pinned her into a commitment too. He had a quick wit and didn't even know it. She responded, "I will, Bibb. I am all in. You have no idea how in I am."

Anna reached her hand over towards her driver and Bibb was ready to receive it. They both hated arguing, both hated not having their way, both had an extra dose of pride to protect, and both wanted control. Both wished the other would learn the art of compromise and compliance. But all that was put out of the way once again. For now, kindness had won the moment with a short twist of a pinky.

Bibb responded once she withdrew her hand, "I am all in too, Anna."

"Bibb, you worry me. The sheriff is worried too. He thinks you might go dark again and start killing people. Why do you give off such terrible frights to people, especially the sheriff and Mr. Westum? I really don't understand. You are much smarter than that."

Bibb's answer was his silence.

She saw that subject was closed. "Do you really think somebody will help me find a place to get some clothes? This town ain't that big. Your clothes are really starting to stink too."

Bibb resisted the opportunity to remind her who had been wearing them. "And yours too, Mrs. Gorgon, and you should do something about it."

Bibb did not have to remind Anna of anything. She definitely did not take his comment as it was meant. Then he tried to encourage her to spend time with the ladies shopping. She took that comment as an insult too. Bibb tried to dig himself out of the hole, but it just got worse. Then he said a few more things he soon regretted. Then her prior husband's name came up as a topic. Then Toak's name entered the conversation. It was terrible for both of them. If it wasn't for arrival at the hotel neither would have given an inch moving off their strong opinions.

It wasn't more than ten minutes earlier they were at peace, and now this. Bibb finally resigned, got her registered into a room, and hurried off to spend some quality time with his horses down at the livery. He knew exactly what happened – it was that varmint testing him again. He had made a serious promise, being all in, and just like church bells on Sunday morning that varmint wanted to know if he was meaning his promises or saying it only to get his own way. Bibb could kick himself for not getting any wiser when it came to entertaining that sleepless creature. He should have seen it coming and been prepared for it. Better yet, he should have been more true to his promises. If he had done that, the varmint would have stayed well mannered.

Then the varmint did what it always did. It bit him again. Bibb knew what was coming. He would be gnawed upon until he apologized to that Gorgon woman again. Bibb complained to his horse that insufferable humiliation would not be necessary if he was a scout and she was a squaw. He banished that thought before another hole was chomped out of his back side. Bibb was running out of places to get bit, and that varmint never took a nap. Entertained? Never. Obeyed? Always.

==0==

Anna joined the party of happy shoppers right at four o'clock to acquire some clothes and other essentials. When asked about her ragged dress she offered no explanation other than it only had about ten minutes left before its official retirement.

"Well Mrs. Toivo, we shall certainly help you out of it! Your green dress is quite unique in a strange way," declared the preacher's wife. From then on she only listened.

"Its value to me is where it has been, not in where it is going. Do they sell shoes in this town?"

The sheriff's wife was at quite a disadvantage. Unlike the other ladies, she could not find herself warming up to the Widow Gorgon. Her husband had told her in confidence about her reputation in Deadwood, as well as the contents of the envelope Bibb had brought with him.

While Anna prattled on about life in Deadwood to the other ladies, the sheriff's wife could only think that this woman was still capable of treachery and murder. Her socialite airs were only skin deep. She purposely shied away and let the other ladies do all the talking. It was time for her to listen, not to talk. Besides, this was the moment that widow had been longing for since she first climbed into that buckboard. Let her have her day!

==0==

Bibb was glad Anna was not in the hotel room when he returned from the livery. He was not enjoying the prospect of having to talk to her. He had spent an hour with his horse rehearsing his answers to the questions that a certain noisy female would soon be throwing in his direction. An apology was not going to be good enough with her this time. She would want to know the reasons and the feelings behind everything he said too. Bibb washed up as best as he could, but his fatigued body still looked like it had been run over by a herd of buffalo.

Anna came back later that evening with several packages. She didn't overdo her shopping adventure, but she did buy herself a supply of under essentials and a pair of nice dresses. She also purchased under essentials for him, much to his embarrassment, as well as a new shirt. She knew Bibb would not easily depart with his comfortable pants. Shirt today, pants later. She had learned her man was only fixable in increments.

After Bibb changed his clothes, Anna and he went for dinner at their hotel. Anna never thought a steak could taste this good. The supper was later than usual but well worth it. Anna particularly enjoyed re-experiencing the luxury of using silverware and to eat on a real plate! Wow! What a treat!

Afterwards the Toivo's (as they checked into the hotel as) went for a walk across to the park. They ended up on the swing in the gazebo in the park center, and within minutes of rocking in the cool breeze Bibb was asleep.

==0==

"Stop it, d'this ain't right!" They hadn't been in the hotel room five minutes together before this new conversation with a new reason to disagree erupted. Bibb insisted that he was the one who would sleep on the floor so that she could have the bed.

"I got bad news for you, my dear retired Trail Boss. We reached the end of your jurisdiction about three hours ago. Get over it, Bibb. There is new management in place now."

"We ain't in Fort Rice yet, so you can keep your opinions to yourself about-zz who is going to make d'the decisions around here."

"So the covenant only counts when it suits your fancy? I am declaring it a medical necessity for you to get some rest, and your rest will be on that mattress. Do-zz you-zz understand-zz?"

"D'that wasn't kind."

"Neither were you! Now stop your sputtering and get into bed like you have been told to."

"No, I'm not going to. It ain't right."

"It's right if I say it is right! This is my decision, and your only choice. Do I tuck you in nice or do I have to get mean?"

"Anna…"

"I figured that threat would help you come to your senses. Honestly Bibb, for once can you do what I ask you to do before I have to start demanding it? You are the one that is hurt, not me. I have other reasons too, but the big reason is I want to deliver you alive to the surgeon."

"Surgeon?"

"Bibb, I'm no doctor, but your chest is a mess, your mouth is a mess, and your legs are a mess. Time may heal your top and your bottom, but something from your belly ain't pokin' out right. You need time to heal. Now get into bed."

"No, it ain't right. What don't you-zz understand about d'the word *No*?"

"I understand it well, Bibb. It's you that is slow to understand. Stop your whining and do what you're told to do."

"Anna, are we-zz having a fight?"

"No, Bibb, we-zzzzz are not. But you are, and all within your teeny-weeny heart. You are having a fight with your own pride, and you are losing. I am not having any problem at all. I am going to get my way, and you are going to learn to like it."

"Why are you-zz being so stubborn?" asked Bibb.

"Why are you-zz-zzz-zzzz being so stubborn?" asked Anna.

"I asked first."

"Asking first doesn't make you the Bed Boss."

The whole conversation stopped dead in its tracks when a knock was heard on the door. They both wondered if their neighbors had complained.

==0==

It was very late when the knock came on the door of Anna and Bibb's hotel room. Anna was scared, and quickly hid herself from view, whispering to Bibb that she was not presentable. Bibb took out his revolver and approached to the side of the door.

"Who's d'there?"

"Anna's mother."

"What do-zz you want?"

"Read and heed."

"Meet-zz me at the livery in five minutes."

==0==

Anna had already claimed her spot when Bibb returned to their rented hotel room. She didn't open her eyes, but she could tell that Bibb had extinguished the oil lamp when it became dark in the room. The squeaky groans of bed ropes underneath Bibb assured Anna that he went to where he was supposed to go.

Anna declared victory to herself as she snuggled up more warmly inside of what she delighted to call their cocoon on the floor. She loved the memories associated with it. She also decided it was going to the laundry in the morning. The other thing she loved was wearing her new clean clothes. Overall, she was as perfectly happy as a woman could be. Happy until…

"Anna, what-zz happened to your feet?" The question voiced in a soft tone just barely above a whisper came from just inches away. She discovered by this interruption of silence that Bibb chose to sleep backwards, with his head at the foot of the bed just above hers. Lying like that, if Bibb wanted to reach out and touch her face, he could.

"What about my feet?" Anna replied. She thought Bibb to be really acting strange.

"Do-zz d'they hurt?"

"Why would they hurt? Feet are feet, now go to sleep."

"Where did you get-zz d'those scars?"

"What are you doing looking at my feet? It is improper for a man to see a woman's naked foot."

"Do-zz d'they hurt?"

"No, Tommy, they do not hurt. They have been terribly scarred like that for many years. When I was young I accidently burned them walking through hot coals while camping with my family. You have no business looking at them." Anna was upset with herself because she had gotten careless in the warmth of the hotel room. Her new shoes had hurt her heels and she had unwittingly laid down to sleep bare-footed. Except for bathing, she had worn her moccasins since the time she received them from the Lakota widows. Until now, the condition of the bottoms of her feet had been hid from Bibb's eyes.

"I'm glad you have scars-zz. I'm more gladder d'they don't hurt. Your secret is safe with-zz me."

Anna was perplexed by his statement. He had insisted several times that the medicine man's predictions had no effect on his thinking. This comment hinted otherwise, and it may be all about prediction number three concerning him. She thought to herself that this maybe the moment he would finally confess the third prediction the medicine man had about her, if she asked nicely.

After at least five minutes had past, Anna could not keep quiet. Her curiosity had now gotten the better of her and she had to ask. "What secret is that, Bibb?"

"D'that you-zz aren't perfect. I won't-zz tell anyone."

Anna thought that the proverb finally came true: Curiosity finally did kill the cat. She should not have asked. On the bright side, Bibb did acknowledge his high opinion of her. He was very stingy with such revelations. There was no medicine man whispering this to him. He had asked about her feet because he thought they hurt, and that he cared. Her final conclusion before falling asleep was that men were not as complicated as women. Especially this man.

Thursday, October 20, 1887

First morning, second day, Miles City; Bibb moved his laundered bedroll to the preacher's couch for some peace and quiet (away from me). There will be no passenger train east until Saturday. Despite a protest, the sheriff convinced the stubborn Toivo twin to be on it. It irritates me that he would listen to sheriff and not to me in accepting the same suggestion. Stubborn and prideful — that man is the epitome of it. For what he has given to me, I can accept those flaws.

I enjoyed lunch with the same woman who met us upon our arrival in Miles City. She told me her story and I told her mine. Mrs. Westum said she now has a new husband but hinted she had a fear that his newness may not last. She and I had similar pains in our relationships, with the exception that her husband decided to live. We could be sisters in fate, but never friends. There is something… no, many things I do not like about her. I did like her shoes.

Bibb will never understand this, so there is no reason to tell him. Last night I secretly wanted one more dose of sleeping in the heart warming cocoon of my most cherished memories. Tommy is so delightfully blind. I love it. I love it! I love it!! Dear God, I so enjoyably overflow with such overwhelming delight in who I am and where I am. It almost feels wrong to be this happy inside. I was so hungry, and now my heart is full. I am alone in the room, but not alone in my heart. Who could have ever predicted this outcome of the covenant? Not me!

Kindness is not understood until it is tried — obey first and understand later. My daddy said that to me when I was little. My parents loved me so much, and they are no longer around for me to tell them how much I appreciate them now. I cried myself to sleep tonight.

==0==

ANNA THOUGHT SHE was dreaming. She was, sort of, until she realized that she really did feel something touching her feet. She opened her eyes slightly and saw Tommy sitting on the floor, dressed, and looking like he was ready to go somewhere. Dawn's light was just entering the room and Anna decided not to end the dream or give Tommy a reason to stop.

For the next half hour Tommy took turns rubbing down and massaging the bottoms of both of Anna's feet. He was strong and sometime his touch was a little too rough. Anna responded mildly, but nothing to give away the fact she wasn't sleeping. When the sunshine started to come into the room where Anna's eyes would have caught the rays, Bibb let her feet fall gently to the floor.

"Don't stop, Bibb. That really felt good."

"I got-zz to go, Anna. You sleep a bit longer. Hold your breath for a second."

Before she could ask why Bibb had picked up the cocoon, with the butterfly inside, and quickly placed it on the bed."

"Bibb…"

"Shhhh… go-zz to sleep, Anna. I will-zz be back in two hours." That little stunt winded Bibb and hurt his chest. It hurt, but he didn't want to say something that might start a conversation.

"Will you massage my back? It is sore too," asked Anna.

"No, I can't do d'that."

"Thank you for rubbing my feet." She hoped to hear "You-zz welcome" in response.

"D'they ain't your feet."

"Well then, whose are they?"

"God owns all scars. Your back and d'the rest of your body belong to you. I don't have d'the varmint's permission for none of d'that touchy stuff, and I ain't going to ask either."

"Bibb, will you anyway? I give you my permission."

"Nope. I got to go. You sleep in d'that bed where you should've been all night, if I had my way."

"Bibb, what's wrong with your ear? Come here and let me look at it."

"I got to go."

"Not like that. Come here. Come here now. I just want to look at it."

Bibb walked over and knelt down beside the bed where Anna could look at his ear. She fumbled with it for a few moments and then gave a little yank on it. "Bibb, I wanted to say more than just a simple thank you. I will sleep well while you are gone. Please be quiet when you return."

Once Bibb left Anna she immediately shed the cocoon and got under the covers of the bed. Once snuggled under, she put Bibb's bedroll back over the top of her. She nested the pillows so the light from the sun wouldn't shine in her eyes, and then started to purr as she started thinking her last thoughts before drifting off. She concluded it was one thing to be kind when asked, or in a conversation, but it is entirely a different thing to be kind when the other is sleeping or not even there. She couldn't wait to fall back asleep to enjoy another dose of delicious dreaming.

==0==

Bibb knocked and then stuck his head inside the door. "Good morning, Sheriff."

"So you're in a better mood this morning. What put a burr in your saddle yesterday? Come in, Bibb, and have some coffee."

Bibb looked around. He had expected to see the sheriff's wife there also, but instead there was a deputy in the far chair… with side arms… with a rifle. Bibb also noticed there was a man with his back to him lying on the cot in the jail as if he was asleep. The jail cell door was open. He also saw a hat hanging on the wall… a familiar hat… he had seen that hat somewhere before. "Sheriff, I had never seen Westum's wife before. Was d'that his wife?" asked Bibb.

"I never saw your wife before either. Was that your wife?"

"Please don't start such rumors! D'that woman…" Tommy started to sputter. "D'that woman… Sheriff, I ain't got-zz nothin' nice to say-zz, so-zz I won't-zz. Yes, we made a covenant to be kind to each other. We didn't kill each other on d'the way here, but you-zz have no idea how-zz much d'that promise taxed me… and taxed her."

"She signed in as Mrs. Toivo at the hotel. Would you care to explain?"

"You're going to say I'm lying, and you wouldn't-zz be d'the first or d'the last to d'think d'that. D'the Deadwood preacher told her she should borrow my name. D'that wasn't my idea. D'that woman… well… she certainly has a mind-zz of her own and… well d'that wouldn't be kind to say… Don't let her softness fool-zz you. She got a backbone of steel and a tongue as sharp as a porky quill. She could get even an earthworm upset."

"So you are trying to convince me that a preacher told her to go by Mrs. Toivo but she isn't your wife? Bibb, that's lame. Try again."

"I told you d'the truth. Anna Gorgon and I made a covenant before God. D'that's worser d'than marriage, and we-zz are bound until I do-zz my part and she does hers."

"Bibb, I know. I got your letter, and then some more information from folks in Deadwood. I got to ask, Bibb. What do you know about two of Westum's hands that were shot in the head?"

"I didn't know about it until-zz I got to Deadwood."

"Could Toak have done it?"

"I doubt it. I haven't talked to Toak since my first welcome into d'this town. I do know-zz he followed me to Deadwood from here. He may be in town now, or somewhere outside of it. If I was to guess, he would be camped by d'the river or on d'the rises overlooking Westum's ranch. He had several chances to kill me, but hasn't. D'that's encouraging, but Toak is d'the most patient man I know-zz. He has everything to live for, and he will kill-zz me first if he d'thinks I am out to kill him for d'the betrayal. But d'that wasn't your question. Do I d'think Toak killed d'the hands? No. He is good with a rifle, but not d'that good. He likes d'the ax."

"What does Toak have to live for and why would he risk bumping into you?"

"His wife's name is Redbird, and d'they have a baby and one more on d'the way. Redbird lives on my chicken farm with Humbird. Redbird was d'the one who named me Bibb."

"You're kidding me. Lakota don't settle down."

"Sheriff, I'm not d'the only man Toak has betrayed. Because of a like incident, Toak had his name taken away by his Indian nation. D'there's nothing out here for him. When Toak couldn't return to his tribe he hired himself out to Westum. You know d'the rest of d'that story. My relationship to Toak is rather complicated."

"And you didn't kill Westum's ranch hands?"

"I almost killed one last Monday. I didn't know it was one of Westum's men until I saw d'the brand on his horse. D'that was d'the horse I brought back. The man said his name was Tommy Carson. He will be walking back into town next week if he can't catch a ride. I'm not proud of d'this, but when I get hating I have a hard time controlling my temper. Mr. Carson shook hands with my friend Mr. Ax."

"So you didn't kill Carson then?"

"Mr. Carson is alive, but he won't be shooting anybody anytime soon. My Indian guides were upset with me for sparing his life. D'they wanted harsher justice on d'the man."

"So that was the burr in your side?"

"To tell you d'the truth, Sheriff, I would have been happier if I could have gone d'the rest of my life without seeing Mr. Westum again. My ribs are crying out for justice. Just d'the d'thought of d'that man hiring Toak on a lie, well, I best stop my opinions here."

"You have already got your revenge on him, Bibb. What more could you want?"

"What revenge? The man is still walking upright."

"Yes he is, but upright in a different way. You destroyed the man, Bibb. Can't you see that? The bully has had his rudder reset. He can never go back to what he was. Bibb, I understand why you could hate the man, but don't. Show the guy some mercy. He really has turned around his wagon, as well as this town. It was a genius move to put that widow on his trail."

"Is she doing what I asked her to do?"

"Ask her yourself. She has shown that man no quarter, and the poor Mrs. Westum has gained herself a new mother-in-law. Yes, she is happy with her husband now, but that widow has also had some stern words for her too. Bibb, I don't know how to say this any plainer: this town is witnessing a miracle in progress. Don't tamper with it. Lay low and take the Limited to Bismarck on Saturday."

"I was d'thinking of taking Anna with me to Bismarck in our buckboard."

"You're a fool if you do. If the outlaws don't get you, the weather will. We are only days from our first blizzard. Bibb, I will even sweeten the deal. I will make sure your horse and your woman make it to Bismarck without charge."

"How about you-zz sending her alone by train and I pocket my fare?"

"Bibb, let me tell you plain. There is nothing to negotiate. You're leaving my city by rail."

"In d'that case, Sheriff, I will d'think about it. Except for death, everything is renegotiable."

"There is nothing to think about, Tommy. You heard the sweet; now hear the bitter. Accept the offer or I will lock you up in jail until the train leaves, and then have you shackled in irons on the Limited for delivery to the Marshall in Bismarck. He wired me some wanted for murder arrest warrants with your name on them. I really don't want to arrest you Bibb. What is your decision?"

"Since you put it so delicately, Sheriff, I just might change my mind about taking d'the buckboard to Bismarck. At least you didn't d'threaten to shackle me to d'that Mrs. Gorgon. But d'that would be punishment for her, not me. I irritate her fierce. I don't even try to. It just happens."

"Bibb, you are not taking the buckboard. You are taking the Saturday train to Bismarck. The only decision for you to make is how you will go, first class or last class."

"Peaceful-like. What else do-zz you want from me, Sheriff?"

"Say it, Bibb. You will lay low and cause no ruckus in this town, yes? You will leave Westum and his men in peace? Bibb, this is the moment you say yes and then nod your head vertically."

Bibb stood up and gave his gun belt and ax to the Sheriff. "Will you keep these safe for me?"

"What are you planning to do until you leave?"

"I have just about had my fill of d'that Gorgon woman. I'm quite sure it's not entirely her fault either. She needs a little break from me and I need-zz a big one from her. We-zz had another heated discussion last night. I'm looking for some peace in my life, and I d'think I know where to find it. I can't deal with another day of scrambled egg feminine logic. D'that's plain painful. I'm ain't faulting her, Sheriff, it is just d'that I ain't used to it. Our quarters have been much too close for my liking."

"The same place you laid low last time?"

"Yes."

"If I need to talk to you will I be able to find you either there or at the hotel?"

"Or at d'the livery. If not at any of d'those places, I'll let somebody d'there know where I'm at."

"Peace?"

"Peace."

They shook hands and Bibb left to check on his animals. Once he was out of sight, the sheriff made his way down to the depot and reserved passage for Bibb, Anna, and their horses. He also went into the telegraph station and ordered a telegram to be sent to Major Ryder. It was rather short, only the same letter three times: WWW."

==0==

"Anna, I'm not interested, and yes, you look lovely."

"Why not, Tommy?" Anna got up and shut the hotel room door behind Bibb. She felt another leadership lecture bubbling up within her for her only pupil.

"Other d'than she would pull out a muff gun and shoot me without warning? You saw her eyes yesterday, especially after I gave d'the rider-less horse back! If she d'thinks her husband's life is in danger she would kill me dead without question, not to mention my prior d'threats against her. Anna, if you really have to do d'this, will you please go d'this alone? I have no interest in meeting d'the woman, and I promised d'the sheriff I wouldn't ruffle any feathers around here."

"So you talked to the sheriff this morning? I thought you said you spent time this morning in the livery with the horses."

"I should have told you. The sheriff talked me into taking d'the train back to Bismarck on Saturday. I also gave him my gun belt and ax for safe keeping."

"Bibb, if you want my trust you can't overlook details like that! If you're not going to lunch with me, then where are you going?"

"I plan to spend d'the day with Anna's family. I'm planning to stay d'there until Saturday morning. I will meet you here early d'then to help you finish packing."

"Unacceptable. Tomorrow night we shall dine together."

"You seem mighty sure about d'that, Anna. I don't-zz like it, but d'this ain't worth arguing over, and I have to eat anyway. Can I bring d'the preacher and his family? I'm quite sure d'they are curious about a woman who would risk riding alone with d'the likes of me across d'the plains."

"Acceptable, but afterwards your ear belongs to me."

"For how long?"

"Until I tell you I am done talking for the evening. I want to return to the spot we spent our first evening together here in Miles City. That was a lovely spot. I have some promises I expect you to agree with."

"I will certainly look forward to d'that, Mrs. Gorgon." His statement came across quite insincere. That was because it was quite insincere.

"Actually I think you will. Now go wait down in the lobby for me. When I come down, you can escort me to my lunch engagement with Mrs. Westum."

Bibb didn't have a good reason to say no other than he wanted to say no. He was about ready to leave when Anna told him to stay. Anna caught him rolling his eyes and she pounced on the prompt. "You can't go out looking like that! Put on the new pants and a shirt I bought you. They are over by the water pitcher."

"I was out-zz in public with d'these clothes d'this morning and not one person commented negatively about my duds. Anna, let us be reasonable here."

"I am reasonable, and the only part of us that isn't reasonable is you. Now change your clothes. Do you need my help?"

Bibb had enough churn in his belly to start their next fight, but had no grounds to counter her demands other than he just didn't want to. He decided it wouldn't hurt him to look nice for the preacher's family. Compared to what Anna had laying on the bed for herself his current ensemble was an embarrassment.

"I will need some help with d'the shirt, Anna."

Anna surprised him by walking from out from behind the blinder in a state of undress he had never seen before. It wasn't that she wasn't decent, but she was far from ready to leave the room. "Okay, Bibb, off with that stuff, and I'll get your new clothes ready to go."

In five minutes Bibb was down the stairs and waiting uncomfortably in the lobby. His head was spinning from what had just happened. What had brought on this familiarity that allowed for her to be comfortable like that in front of him? Was she just being a tease? Was this just another stunt she was using to control his behavior? Was it merely an expression of her lack of fear? Or was it done completely without thinking? Her tone of voice was no more elevated than if asking if the campfire needed another log. Tommy started to seriously wonder if she knew they were married.

Bibb ended up more confused and decided not to think about it anymore, but couldn't. Her behavior was really odd, but was it any stranger than what happened to them in the teepee? The only thing that was accomplished in the half hour while Bibb waited in the lobby was for him to become uncomfortably itchy due to his new shirt, and gaining a headache from trying to figure out Anna.

"That's what happens when men try to apply logic to the illogical," muttered Bibb to himself over a cup of coffee. Bibb loved structured thinking – all events lining up neatly into little boxes with ordered inputs and predictable outcomes. Anna? No. She loved to swirl all of those ingredients in a mixing bowl, bake it up, and come out with an answer that tasted good to her. Until then Bibb considered women intolerable and irrational, and best avoided. Now that he was experiencing one of those creatures up close, he promoted his "altared" fate to the rank of a humorless endless prank the varmint was putting on him. Bibb eventually concluded that God knew what He was doing, and made women like that on purpose – lest a man start thinking too highly of himself.

"D'that varmint was winning again. He always does," muttered Bibb as his coffee cup emptied. He couldn't get over how horses were so much more compatible than women. "Ladies really do think they are being logical when they aren't. I bet we men drive d'those female beasties nuts too. D'the varmint enjoys both, and hunts down both men and women alike," Bibb reasoned to himself.

Just as Bibb was finishing the condemnation of women as the bane of all mankind, the most graceful and well-dressed lady walked down the stairs and into the lobby. It was Bibb's Anna, and he couldn't take his eyes off of her. She was more than a beauty. She was stunning, and he was the one that was stunned.

Bibb stood up and immediately felt a sharp pain in his chest. At first the thought the hurt was from his jumbled ribs. Then Bibb had to second guess that conclusion when he heard a voice from within say, "Don't you dare call anything ugly that I have made for my own delight. Be kind." Bibb knew the varmint would have the last word. It does that, again and again and again.

As they walked out of the lobby together Bibb whispered to Anna, "I'm glad you asked me-zz to change my shirt."

His words tingled up and down her arms. To Anna that was a greater compliment than if he had remarked that she was beautiful. The man was a dear and didn't even know it. She had not stepped over the line. No, her attempt to persuade him in the simple task of changing his clothes worked. The man happily listened. The big things she wanted to change in him would come later.

==0==

"She ain't coming, Anna."

"A woman is never late. Bibb. Learn that and your life will go much easier for you, and quit being so antsy! Stop darting your eyes around the room and focus on something worth looking at. Bibb!" (She still didn't have his full attention), "Sit still and in the meantime let's enjoy this moment. This place is nice and the tea is good. Mrs. Westum will be here soon. Trust me." Anna's tone was very firm on this point.

"D'there is a difference between being late and not coming at all. And even if you insist you and all you other women aren't late, you are still late in everybody else's eyes. If you get to d'the depot and d'the train has already left, you ain't going, and there ain't no apologizing."

"I said nothing about conductors or trains. I was talking about you specifically. You need to learn that. Once you embrace that fact of life, Bibb, you can start enjoying us instead of living in a world of meaningless frustrations. Do you understand that? Bibb, quit looking down at the table and look at me!" She waited; he complied eventually. "So what if a person is late? It doesn't change the date of your funeral. I'm telling you this for your own good. I'm serious and you should thank me for sharing this wisdom with you. You should think of my words as a gift of kindness."

"Kindness? Anna, late is late. I don't care if you try to tell me different a hundred times."

"One hundred or two hundred times doesn't matter a wit to me. I don't have to learn that lesson, you do. It doesn't take any skin off my nose when you get angry about it. Learn it, live it, love it. It is your fate."

"D'that ain't my fate, Mrs. Gorgon. You might want to consider punctuality a high virtue."

"You're missing the point, Bibb. Women enjoy having people wait for them once in a while. It makes their entrances more dramatic."

"You can keep-zz your drama to yourself for your own amusement, Anna. When I want-zz drama I will go-zz to d'the opera. You need to learn to be-zz on time."

"Oh, Bibb, there is so much you need to learn. Beauty can never be rushed."

"At least I learned how-zz to read a clock and have respect for other people's-zz time!"

"You have no right to say such things about Mrs. Westum. She certainly must have a good reason for her delay. How far is it out to the Westum ranch?"

"Far enough to get all d'the skin scoured off the back of my-zz legs."

No matter what Anna said she sensed that they were not clicking in spirit. She tried a different level of communication with her man. "Do you hate her for that?"

"Anna, enjoy your tea. I'm going to do both you and Mrs. Westum a favor by-zz leaving before she gets here. And as for you, Mrs. Gorgon, if you want to be late go right ahead. You know my feelings about d'this. I also know-zz my feelings don't count for much with you."

His statement hurt deeply. "That's not kind, and that's not true. Bibb, take it back."

"Which of my statements were false?"

Anna answered in a huff. "Bibb, I promise that the first time you actually show me some real feelings they will count for something." Bibb's facial response revealed to Anna that she spoke before she thought. Her old Anna was so unkind. She felt ashamed, and for the first time she did not believe her own reflexive self-justification. She was speechless.

Bibb, exasperated, had been down this dark alley before and ended up bruised. To respond to any of her "real feelings" comments were often an overture for a fight. When Anna said something like that in public to him she knew he would back down. That was how she played the game and she always played to win. Bibb got up from the table and wished Mrs. Gorgon a good day and then added, "I may stop by d'the hotel tonight, but don't stay up for me. Mrs. Gorgon, d'the one d'thing I like about you is d'that I never leave your sight without something new to d'think about. And yes, Anna, I was unkind, and I apologize for it. Not just now, but last night too in d'the hotel room. I was wrong, and you-zz deserve better behavior out-zz of me."

Anna paused for an awkward moment. They were not on the trail anymore. She also took stock of her increased pickiness with the man. She so wanted that old reflex of hers to disappear forever. "And me towards you," responded Anna sincerely. "I will be better next time too. Bibb, you have been very good to me, and I have neglected to say so. I'm saying so right now."

"You mean d'that?"

"Stop by this evening sometime, Bibb, and yes, I meant that. Since you don't like drama, I shall say no more." He started to walk away when she interrupted his exit by kindly saying, "Schatz." It caught his attention, especially knowing it was a term of affection. "Before you go, please come back here for one quick moment."

Bibb complied, not sure what was on her mind. Upon his arrival, Anna reached out for his pinky and once secured gave it a little squeeze. Bibb replied, "Anna, you don't know how much I wanted d'that."

Anna replied, "Bibb, I am all in. I am your covenant woman. You are my covenant man. We will see this through. Together we will overcome my bickering and your shortcomings. Bibb… oh, never mind. Bibb, Peace?"

"Peace… and joy. Anna you really are a kindred spirit. Until later, stay safe…"

Next to them there was a man enjoying coffee all by himself. As Bibb walked out, Bibb took note of him as if his face was somewhat familiar. He wouldn't make eye contact with Bibb, in fact the man put on his hat forward on his head to conceal his eyes. Outside the restaurant Bibb realized who it could have been. Bibb was tempted to return inside to confront the man, but that would have caused a ruckus and more chastisement from Anna. No, the man was one of his drinking buddies from the sheriff's posse in Bismarck. Bibb was quite sure of it. The white ring of flesh, where is wedding ring should have been, gave him away.

Bibb decided to wait outside for a few minutes to see if the man followed him. No, the man stayed inside. What Bibb did not expect was five ladies, all dressed very finely, to walk past him to enter the restaurant. Mrs. Westum was in the middle of the gaggle. He was glad to go unnoticed. Bibb wanted none of that and quickly left, actually feeling sorry for his old drinking buddy.

Bibb knew the man's presence was not a coincidence. Either the major or the marshal had sent him, and now that poor guy would have to keep track of six simultaneous conversations he was sent to Miles City to overhear. Bibb thought if he had his guns he could shoot him now so the man could go on to glory without having to suffer verbal purgatory. At least the beverages in there were good.

==0==

Anna was quite reserved in response due to not knowing the other ladies that entered the restaurant with Mrs. Westum. Anna had hoped for a quieter and more intimate meeting where she could find out more about Bibb. That was not to be in this setting.

Before they got personal, Anna answered many questions about Deadwood, and particularly the social climate there. Anna was happy to tell her tales being careful to leave herself out of the stories. She returned the favor by asking the same about Miles

City. One lady started talking about schools, which bored Anna. Mrs. Westum noted that and pointed the conversation back to her host.

"Anna, why are you risking your reputation being caught in the same city with that Toivo boy?"

Anna took that question as a challenge. "That Toivo boy did a lot of growing up in this town, Mrs. Westum. He is ten times the man my husband was. Yes, my Mr. Gorgon was successful, but his means were bully tactics and cruelty. His personality led him to make the mistake of accusing that Toivo boy of a crime he didn't do. Does any of that sound familiar to you, Mrs. Westum?"

The normal chatter immediately ceased around the table. Every woman there knew about Mr. Westum's meeting with Bibb.

"Has the cat got your tongue, Mrs. Westum? You have nothing to say about that? I figure if that boy hadn't showed your husband some mercy you would be currently living as a trophy squaw with some band of Indians. Sure you don't have a comment?"

"Obviously my husband was wiser than yours, Mrs. Gorgon. Tell me, Mrs. Gorgon, aren't you that boy's trophy harlot right now? You just haven't yet been demoted into the second squaw phase of that scandal. You must still keep him happy, but I certainly can't see the attraction given all your catty baggage. Is the boy deaf?"

Anna thought of several very cruel retorts but changed her mind. "We digress from proper conversation, and that was my error, Mrs. Westum. I was unkind, and you deserved more respect. I did not leave Deadwood because of any physical attraction by me for him or him for me. I was run out of town by the local sheriff."

"For what cause?" asked one of the ladies.

"The attempted murder of my husband's killer. I was caught red-handed with the gun ready to shoot the man when I was tackled, wrestled to the floor, and then cuffed to the radiator. The sheriff didn't believe me when I said I was just being cautious. My choice became leaving town or trial. When I found out my late husband and Bibb were schoolmates, I asked the man to take me to Fort Rice. Everybody in town was both surprised and delighted that Bibb agreed, but only on his terms."

"What were his terms?"

"Entering into a covenant with him at the altar of God."

"Marriage?"

"No, worse. And showing my idiocy I fought it. I regret that I did not embrace his offer at first. Now I feel I have wasted most of my life up to this point. You think me a slave? No, but to the contrary. I have never been so free in my life. Mrs. Westum, I envy you. You still have your man, and I hear your husband has had a reversal of heart. Bibb is not marriage material and probably never will be. I have heard in my short stay here that your spouse is now and is getting better at being both a loving husband and a respected citizen. I hope that you experience in your marriage relationship the same hope, love, kindness, and peace I have gained over the last month. There could be no greater joy on this earth."

All the women were shocked by the turn in the conversation. "Are you serious, Mrs. Gorgon?"

"Serious enough to register at the hotel as Mrs. Toivo. None of this was free, Mrs. Westum. In my pride, I stood up to Bibb in every way, not taking one ounce of his snake oil, nor do I take any of it now. The man is an emotional invalid, but yet a dear saint. I have learned to prefer a dear saint over a manly man any day of the week."

"You're calling Bibb less than a man's man? And you lived?" said one of the other ladies.

"If you only knew; if you only knew. After God crushed him, God crushed me. I was humbled, not by Bibb, but by others. I am not the same woman that left Deadwood last month. I have the same body, but a different heart. You already witnessed I can be catty. For that I am truly sorry. That is not whom I am destined to become. An Indian medicine man said so."

"Anna, may I call you that? What happened?"

"Mrs. Westum, do you remember the dress I was wearing when Bibb and I arrived?"

"Yes, it was barely hanging on you."

"That dress was given to me as a gift from a Lakota matron."

"A gift?"

"And with it a double miracle. Mrs. Westum, afterwards why don't you and I take a ride in your carriage after our lunch? Please call me only curious, but I want to see where Bibb was beaten and tortured, and the road where he suffered so. Are any of the men who did that to Bibb still around?"

Mrs. Westum was staggered by her request. "Don't you know?"

"I was hoping to tell them they were forgiven. What they meant for evil, God used for good."

"Anna, they are all gone."

"When will they be coming back?"

"Nobody comes back from where they went. Anna, are you sure you want to go out there?"

"Yes, please."

"I agree, but only if you leave what you're packing here. We all know you purchased it yesterday. Mrs. Gorgon, considering the company you keep and by your own admission of a murderous predisposition, I am not willing to bring you armed and dangerous to visit the man who paid Toak the blood money to betray your man."

One of the other ladies quickly spoke up, desperately wanting to avoid another cat fight, "What happened with the Indian matron? And what miracle are you talking about?"

"Bibb would say I got bit by the varmint. Ladies, I already have said too much, and Mrs. Westum, I agree to your terms. Now please tell me every detail about this widow woman that follows your husband around. I heard about her from a man, but I want to hear about her through a woman's heart. Does she treat you harshly?"

==0==

Bibb stopped by the jail on his way to the preacher's home. He wasn't there, but the sheriff's wife was. Bibb asked if her husband had mentioned to her any of the rail arrangements. Since she was the one who actually purchased the trip, Bibb received more than a satisfactory answer.

Once Bibb had received and studied the tickets, the sheriff's wife interjected a question. "Where are you going now, Tommy?"

"I'm planning to go up to d'the preacher's home," said Bibb.

"You know that the preacher isn't home yet. If you don't mind me asking, what are you planning to do there?"

"Just a visit."

"Bibb, do you remember who took care of you after you were beaten?"

"D'the preacher's wife did, and also her daughter Anna."

"Before then, and who untied you from the whipping post and who helped put you in the wagon and who carted you to the cot over yonder? And what about the binding your wounds and helping relocate your dislocated shoulder? And what about buying the medicines to heal your legs? Is any of that coming back to your memory?"

"Yes, and what is d'this leading to?"

"Bibb, you owe me a favor and I'm calling it in."

"I owe you more d'than one. What's d'the first one?"

"Don't stay at the preacher's home tonight. My husband said you were thinking about it, but please don't. That man suffered extreme embarrassment and his credibility tarnished over what you did in Deadwood. He was all excited about your change of heart and said so from the pulpit. He was instantly made the laughing stock of this city when it was found out you hadn't been in Deadwood three hours before you killed again. We don't need any more rumors about you and your short lived conversions in this town. We especially don't need you staying the night on their couch with the preacher still out of town."

"But I have changed."

"Words are cheap, Bibb. And now you are renting a room with a woman that isn't your wife? Bibb, even the most gullible saint in this town would have to have some doubt. I am calling in that favor, Bibb. I know you want to, but don't. Nobody believes your words right now. But they will believe your actions if they are honorable after you leave town. My husband was already under pressure to arrest you for the murder of two of Westum's hands, and then you have the audacity of bringing in the horse of a third man. Bibb, do you see my husband's predicament?"

"It's not true, it's not fair, but it's done. I understand now, and I still owe you more favors. D'thank you for your advice. I was blind to it. One more question. Why did you take care of me?"

"That was my husband's decision. The 'Read and Heed' got to him."

"He saw d'that?"

"Bibb… wake up! He's a sheriff! Of course he saw that. That, and a threatening telegram directly from your Governor."

"What?"

"Never mind. I said more than I should. You go now."

==0==

Bibb was confounded by the new information he had received from the sheriff's wife. Those early hours in Miles City had been masked within his memory, most likely due to his physical distress. God must have blessed him with very poor recall when it came to his days of pain. He now had some additional questions for Major Ryder the next time they talked.

Bibb was determined not to arrive at the preacher's home with an empty hand. He found out that the preacher had been purchasing food and supplies on credit at the mercantile and asked the owner if he could apply payment to the account. Bibb asked the man what it would take to change the minus to a plus on the ledger, paid it, and then bought some beans and jerky to take with him."

"They will want to know who did this," replied the owner.

"I would rather you-zz didn't tell-zz d'them. Can't you call it an accounting error?"

"No I can't, but if pressed I will tell them somebody came by and did that for them. If they don't press, I won't stop the preacher's wife from assuming whatever she wants to. Your secret is safe with me. Oh Bibb, about that woman you are staying with…"

"The Widow Gorgon?"

"If you say so. Besides clothes for her and you, you need to know she also purchased a muff gun and ammunition. I already let the sheriff know. She is as scary as they come."

"I understand. I heard she was traveling with a no good lying murdering outlaw and she-zz probably wanted some personal protection from d'that reprobate."

"Tell me true. She isn't gunning for anybody in this town, is she?"

"D'the only person I know d'that she ever drew a gun on is talking to you. No, she only wants to be-zz able to protect herself if something d'threatening comes her way.

417

Tell d'the sheriff d'that her only aim is to get-zz home. She isn't going to let anything interrupt her goal of getting d'there."

The twenty minute walk up to the preacher's home seemed so strange. Along with Anna and her mother, the widow who was supervising Westum's personal revival was visiting at the preacher's home. They warmly accepted Bibb into their home, appreciated the food, and got back to business. While Anna was copying down the right hand page of the book, Bibb was busy copying the left hand side. When arms got tired, they switched places with the Anna's mother and the widow.

The time got away from them during their scribing party, and Bibb was reminded he needed to go when the yawns bloomed in his hosts. It was much too late to go back to the hotel room, nor did he really want another verbal challenge from that pistol packing woman registered under his name. If he was she, she would want the he to let the she sleep. He had learned over the last two weeks it was not necessary for him to even voice a word to get her upset, just being there did it to her.

Bibb borrowed the same blanket that he had when he laid healing up on the preacher's couch two months ago. Bibb said he would be back tomorrow to help, and reminded Anna's mother that the Toivos were planning to take them out to dinner the following evening. Bibb left for the livery.

==0==

Mrs. Westum obliged Anna's request to visit the ranch compound. Their ride out and back was much more soft-spoken, and Anna was very determined to keep her wits about her. Likewise, Mrs. Westum kept the conversation at an intimate level. She did not trust Anna one bit, but out of kindness and kindred life events she showed her guest passenger some deference. The tour of the compound was rather anti-climactic.

"Anna, did you see all you wanted to see?"

"Yes."

"And what did you see?"

"It looked like a barn for boys, decorated with all the rules of etiquette a bunkhouse full of ranch hands would happily enforce."

"Yes, and a similar disregard for personal hygiene too." They both laughed; a pleasant break in the pilgrimage.

Continuing on a theme previously discussed on their trip out to the ranch, Anna continued, "You know, and no offense is meant, but this place did not come across as special like I had pictured it would be. No, it was just like a hundred other bunkhouses. Functional, yes, dry and warm, but nothing special at all." Anna thought back to something said at lunch. "I bet there really wasn't anything special about Moses' mountain either… just another naked mountain popping out from the desert floor, or like what I just saw, another post holding up a roof outside a bunkhouse door. I guess what made it special was who went there and then what happened."

"Dearie, are you buying into the same stories the preacher might tell?"

"No, but I'm starting to believe Bibb believes them."

"What does he tell you?"

"Nothing much anymore. I told him I don't listen to liars, and that he was the king of them. That shut him up quick, and that suited me just fine. He probably doesn't do it on purpose, but all his stories seem to come across condemning in tone as if I was a defective human being. He never says anything like that directly but I know that is what he is thinking."

"Anna, that bump in the desert floor wasn't the only un-special pile of rocks described in the book Bibb carries with him in his saddle bag."

"What book is that?"

"You don't know? Tell me true. You really don't know about Bibb's book?"

"No, I don't, other than somebody came by late last night asking for a book. He had to go to the livery to fetch it. That was the first I ever knew he might have one. He never mentioned it nor did I accidently come upon something like that. That man doesn't answer questions well, and at the time we were having an animated discussion about his reluctance to accept my sage advice."

Their ride back from the ranch to Deadwood was filled with new revelations for Anna. Many of the coincidences Anna considered fictitious rumors were indeed fact. Mrs. Westum's unprompted revelations added logic that tied together many of the other tales. This new information also added to the credibility of little Heidi and her brothers. Mrs. Westum said that the inscription inside the book saved Bibb from death by lynching or a hanging for horse thieving. Anna had no choice but to conclude that her man had a lot of secrets, and an equal ability to keep his secrets secret. Maybe her low opinion of Bibb was because she only had discovered her man's sinister side. She felt that she had missed opportunities over the last month. Her disrespectful attitude had killed his desire to tell her even his most benign secrets. She did more to shut him up than her husband's bullet did.

==0==

Mrs. Westum delivered Anna to the hotel later that afternoon. Pleasantries were said but the unspoken desire on each of the women's mind was a sincere wish to never see each other again. There was nothing to be gained and a cart full of unacceptable risks if they did. Mrs. Gorgon feared Mrs. Westum to be very dangerous. Anna couldn't help but read between her host's comments that the Westum enterprise had suffered considerable degradation in their income and life style thanks to Bibb. She bemoaned the economics that forced her maid's termination and put a limit on her trips to the mercantile. Her husband was forced to return to work and suffer long hours of physical labor as his own ranch foreman. Mrs. Westum said they were happier, but Anna saw no evidence of it.

A woman was waiting at the hotel desk when Anna walked into the hotel. Anna had no idea who she was but by her attire and some uncharitable imagination Anna could guess what she was. The woman engaged Anna upon her entrance asking if her new boyfriend, waiting in the dining room, and she could buy Anna a drink. After accepting, Anna discovered from the woman that her boyfriend claimed he was a newspaper reporter.

"Sir, I'll accept your drink, but may not accept your questions. The last reporter I talked to came a hair's breadth away from being jailed for sharing a table with me. Are you ready to take that risk, and if so, what do you want of me?"

"Anna, I am aware of some of that, to include the fact that the reporter you referenced has been a burr in the Deadwood sheriff's sock for several years. It was just a matter of time for him to find himself in custody. Fortunately I enjoy a better working relationship with the law here. But that is enough about me. If you don't mind, make yourself comfortable. What are you drinking?"

"My traveling companion said that if it wasn't for my vanity I wouldn't give you pollywogs the backside of my shadow. My friend carries a somewhat nasty opinion of those in your line of work. I have to get along with the man, so if this conversation is to last beyond your next reply, tell me, what is in this conversation for me?"

"First is a drink. Second is your chance to tell your story your way, and third, how about a lunch date tomorrow at the lynching saloon. I hear you have a desire to eat a morsel there."

"Is that where she came from?"

"Call it what you will, but I wasn't going to be found talking to you unescorted. Is Bibb the jealous type?"

"And you call yourself a reporter?" replied Anna.

"I am not asking for new revelations, Anna. I want to confirm what I already heard second hand. The way I see it, Bibb would have to have a higher opinion of women in order to ever suffer a twinge of jealousy. The many stories I read, well, never mind. Then again, in a sick way, your escort has been quoted as saying he 'don't kill women no more because after they have been dead for three days they still keep talking.' If you ain't been dead over three days, I would like to ask you some questions." Before she responded he asked, "Tell me, Mrs. Gorgon, can you confirm that Bibb has a pretty low opinion of not just you but himself too? Was he shocked to find in you a woman who didn't bristle and flee at the thought of being romantically inclined towards him."

"Sir, with that insult I will drink the drink and be on my way."

"Are you admitting to being romantically involved with Bibb?"

"What is your given name? I want to make sure it is spelled correctly by the undertaker. Is that a threat? You bet it is. You won't live to see your next tomorrow if you print anything like that."

"I will take that as a simple no then. I already knew that." He displayed an unnatural smile that hinted of a touch of mischief. "Mrs. Gorgon, we can do this the easy way or the hard way. I want you to know the creativity I have in fabricating believable stories if you decide to keep your stories to yourself." The drinks were served as the man continued. "Tell me, Mrs. Gorgon your opinion. Would you confirm Bibb prefers Indian women because they are obedient and don't talk much?"

Anna shot back, "I will confirm that subject is closed as if the question was never asked." There was very little in Anna's body language to suggest a different conclusion, and he knew it.

The reporter's lady partner thought this was quite an interesting conversation. She was the same woman who had gotten to know Bibb better immediately before his meeting with Westum's lynching crew. She was savvy enough to know that her personal secret needed to remain a secret.

Anna, growing weary decided to redirect the questions back on him. "And what is in this for you?" ask Anna. "Are you prone to take facts and twist them to sell newspapers, or are you one of the rare breed that is interested in reporting the truth?"

"Your concern does not have to be an *or*, Mrs. Gorgon, and my experience is that the truth is often more twisted than fiction. My editor sells papers and Bibb is news. He is not just another outlaw. He is an enigma, and news about ghosts and government agents compel people to buy newspapers. You are part of that mystery."

"Bibb is no government agent, nor a ghost," Anna replied as if insulted.

"Nor are you? That is up for debate too. When was the last time you visited your grave? And for the record, were you surprised you lived see a dawn in Miles City? I was. You are an enigma too. But I misspoke. I was hasty in asking if you lived, rather witnessed, another dawn. Your rumored lack of a heart is well known, and the presence of a pulse within you remains unconfirmed."

"Your insults are easily explained by being born male. And to mimic your manly rudeness, that too is an unconfirmed rumor. I can see by your wedding finger that no woman would keep you around, and dare say from just ten minutes of knowing you it would be easy to start a rumor why. But if I start talking about your faults we would be here all day, and frankly you are boring me. I'll cut to the quick. Bibb is my escort back to the east and nothing else. Sounds as if you would rather print fiction rather than fact. What do you want me to serve up to you and your readers?"

"I'm in it for the money, honey. I sell papers. If what we report turns out not to be the truth, we print retractions. Better, if somebody lies to us, that is a whole new story and we sell more papers. This ain't hard. So what do you want, Anna? A story, no story, or let me make something up? I prefer you give me a story. That is so I don't have to deal with your enigma of the male variety. I have already had an unpleasant run in with him. He fired twice at me and missed both times on purpose. But that is me, and that is him. I want to ask about you. Since you asked a question about my name, let me return the favor. What is your given name? Is it the same name etched in stone over your tomb in the graveyard adjacent to the only church your body ever attended in Deadwood?"

Anna's stare was another whole story in itself too. She paused to think of her best response. Once she decided, she started her negotiations. "I will tell you one story. If you treat me fairly, you may take me to lunch tomorrow. If you don't, I will gladly attend your wake. I'm not threatening you, but merely agreeing with you that jealousy can be deadly. Bibb doesn't miss a third time. Do you understand me completely?"

"Yes I do, Anna. Tell me something that will sell a newspaper."

"Selling something or not is none of my concern, but I will answer your question. My given name was Hannah S. Higgins. I was born and raised on the East Coast and attended a boarding school at much more expense than my parents could afford. Upon graduation I escaped from my family's constant demands to make something of myself. That I did, but not in the way that my parents and family preferred I would. You see my family was a High-Church devoted bunch, and I was the one in the family that did not fit into that clan of goody-two-shoes."

"Then your name is really Hannah?"

"Not any more. I very much disliked that name. When I married the dashing Mr. Gorgon, along with changing my last name the Justice of the Peace banished forever any *H* from all my names. I suffered much teasing growing up being called the Horrible Hannah Higgins."

"But Hannah seems to be a sensible name, and your parents wouldn't have given it to you if they didn't think it fit."

"Fit? Are you kidding me? It was name of one of the most abused women in ancient history! I resented the name. That poor woman was under the heel of an abusive man, and when that man didn't get what he wanted from the woman he brought another woman into the home. Horrible Hannah of old had to feed the faces and wash the behinds of her husband's children which that opportunistic night-crawler bore to him – all while he and that other whippy woman went over to the next tent to make some more! And I was named after that? And don't be telling me that she was blessed with some prince or prophet later in life. Who cares? She was abused! The best her husband did for her was give her double portions to make her fat to appease his guilt. Her life was ruined by a man. If there is a consolation from the Good Book about my namesake is that she knew arrogance when she saw it, and she probably saw lots of it. At least she had the sense to give her child away rather than have it raised as a come lately surprise step-child in a household of competing women. How much worse can a man be to a woman? And my parents wanted me named after that? I guess it goes to show that you got to be careful what you name things. Yes, I had the Justice of the Peace rid me of that scar from the beginning and the end of my first name, and good riddance!"

"Mrs. Gorgon, I must say you were born with a colorful history that never dies." He meant that turn of phrase on purpose hoping to guide the conversation towards more ghoulish revelations.

The other lady interrupted. "Mrs. Gorgon, you might want to re-read that ancient story. There is a possibility you are seeing more in there that might be there. Just a suggestion, ma'am. I had parents I was upset with too, and it didn't bother them a wit. The only person it ate up with anger was me. I am sorry. I shouldn't have added my two bits. I'll be quiet now. You changed your name and you were happy with your decision to exercise that right. That settled it. I'm sorry I interrupted."

Anna, who had been tempted to throw a few verbal darts in her direction, was appeased by her postscript. She had offered the comment in humility and kindness and not as one in authority looking down to her. Anna turned her attention back to the reporter. "I was younger and more impulsive then. As for my present situation, well, a month ago nobody could have ever predicted what has happened to me since. We will just leave it there, kind sir. You now have enough to write your article. If Bibb does not object to my having lunch with you tomorrow you can plan on meeting me here at noon. Bring your humble lady friend to escort me to the saloon."

Anna had a light dinner alone after her two visitors left. Once finished, she decided to walk over to the gazebo swing prior to going up to her hotel room. She surprised herself with her own self-revelation. It had been years since she had changed her name, actually, buried it. It too had resurrected itself like a ghost, and not just today. The name Hannah made that miserable ditty all the worse. She refused to play it back in her mind while alone on the swing. What bothered her most was that her own life story was starting to line up with that of Hannah of old. Likewise, Anna had to deal with an abusive husband, the rent-by-the-hour painted honeys, two other serious women weaseling their way into her home seeking her husband's fortune and affections, as well as and her lack of children. Those facts she could accept because that man and those memories were all six feet below ground in a grave in Deadwood. The medicine man's prediction about her bearing a prince in her old age weighed heavily in her thoughts. Her only comfort was the cool breeze that made her hair dance as she sat there alone in the park. She knew the old medicine man would have no point of reference in the white man's ancient history to plagiarize such a cruel joke on a modern version of the Hannah saga, and then the audacity to say it as if it were a blessing. She could only concluded with certainty was that ditty that kept haunting her had to be the varmint's doing. Up to an hour ago there was not a person alive except herself that knew her given name. The good news about the recurring ditty is that she could resist it, tell it to go away, and it would. And no, her mind was not playing a cruel joke on her. She would never allow herself to be called Hannah again – never!

She decided this revelation given away to the reporter about her given name might waste a corner of the back end of some obscure newspaper, but who would care? At best, it would only add to the dunghill of stale outlaw trivia deposited in worthless newspapers. Would it affect her future? Not one wit. It may provide sermon material for some preacher that ran out of things to talk about. While on the range she remembered she had slipped up once about stating her original name, but had quickly changed the subject. If Bibb was to find out her given name it would be because he read it in the paper. She wasn't going to tell him again. She voiced within herself, "And so what if he found out? That man has no problem changing his name when it suits his fancy! He wouldn't dare throw this minor adjustment in my face. I would eat him up and spit him out if he did!" She thought how the word hypocrite wounded Bibb's spirit earlier, and planned to use it again if need be. She eventually did concede a difference, if all the tall tales were true. All Bibb's names were given to him – he had no part in the branding. Hers were taken at her choosing, and gained by inflicting her will.

==0==

The four words "LLL Hannah S. Higgins" was sent by telegraph to Major Ryder in Bismarck soon after the interview. By nightfall that same message was sent to a waiting investigator in the states' Department of State in Washington. She was an unknown and had been identified as a risk in the execution of emerging military strategies on the western frontier.

==0==

Later that afternoon the stock train left the yards with a package full of transcripts compiled by Bibb's old drinking buddy and faux newspaper reporter. It also contained confirmations of passenger ticket purchases on the Limited for Anna and Bibb, as well as the stock arrangements for the curious major to make. He was hopeful, if Bibb stayed away, that he would collect more information during a private lunch interview with the puzzling Hannah Anna.

The originator of the telegraph spent the evening reviewing the other interest items he had been sent to Miles City to discover. Besides two pages of general questions, the man had four other assigned key questions to have answered to complete his mission.

With luck FFF, YYY, AAA, and CCC would be on the wire (and he on the stock train heading east) by tomorrow night. He could not risk his life riding back to Bismarck on the Limited with Bibb and Anna that weekend.

==0==

Anna spent the evening in the hotel room writing memoirs of the most eventful month of her life. She was hoping Bibb would accept her invitation to visit, but doubted he would. Her revived mean streak that resided within her had done enough damage to relationships since arriving in Miles City. She was determined she would pack her nasty disposition away, and not just for the cruel things she had aimed at Bibb, but for everybody. The cat inside her needed to have more than its claws removed. The cat would have to suffer the same fate of the bunny inside her. It had to die.

The amount of new un-embellishments Anna learned about Bibb today was overwhelming. What else had he not told her? That man sure could drive her crazy. She wondered if she got him drunk he might spill his heart. She decided that was a stupid self-suggestion. He already proved he could control his tongue but not his anger. Considering her experience with him she believed he would be a quiet and mean drunk, and one that in a blink could be capable of mass mayhem. Liquoring him up was really a stupid idea, and in fact she decided to never tempt the man by drinking in front of him. He was unstable enough sober to risk having him drunk.

Anna's deeper frustration was knowing that Bibb chose the company of a different Anna in his life over hers. That bothered her, but she knew it should not. Anna loved competition, except when she was losing. Even if married, she didn't own the man. She didn't have the right to control him either. She had no right to say where he should go or what he should do when he got there. The only thing she agreed to was mutual kindness, and that proved much more difficult to her than first considered. Bibb was in uncharted territory. If she became as kind as she promised to be he could become terribly confused, and with that the risk of a reciprocating deeper commitment from the man. She, being honest with herself, didn't want a deeper commitment either, but she did want all the benefits of one. One thing for sure: this was not a game anymore. She had to be wise in applying her charms, a thought she considered before but not implemented.

Anna went to bed alone this night, and loved the privacy. As she looked up at the ceiling of her room she had to ask herself if she had fallen in love. That answer was certainly no, but she had a heartfelt concern for the man. Nor had she fallen *in hate* or *in I don't care* with the man. She knew what being in love was like and this was not it. She decided she too was in uncharted territory. She had been kissed by kindness.

Before she drifted to sleep two questions began growling inside her. "Hannah, are we lost?" Just as she was about to get angry with that question the other barked,

"Hannah, when are we going to get there?" She told the varmint to go away. She got the point. The prairies were now behind them. She was being called to become a kindhearted trail boss to take Tommy through a social wilderness he did not know. She may not like them, but the requests the varmint made of Tommy were always for good and never burdensome. She smiled, and whispered to herself, "Me too." She gladly accepted the call to willfully and wisely take her man to through his emotional and physical healing. She was called to be the means, and not the ends. The results were the varmint's concern, not hers.

Friday, October 21, 1887

Third Day, Miles City; I woke up alone and still tired. I miss Xue and her morning chatter. She had been a friend to me, but I was never a true friend to her. I originally thought it would be best for her to run the laundry, but she would still be alone. Maybe California is her better option. I wish, so wish she could see and know me now, and not as Deadwood Gulch's Gorgon the Gargoyle. My foreman told the truth. He was painfully right; and so was Xue. I know this now... I have had my feet scars touched twice... how shall I say... physically and spiritually. Xue had in-sight, Bibb has no-sight. When he doesn't think before he talks he is quite wise. Well, either him or that blasted varmint is to blame. Yes, I miss Xue. Not because of all she did for me, but what she was for me. How could I have missed that? I behaved badly in Deadwood and what I did cannot be undone. I shall never return to the Black Hills. The memories would be too pitiful and painful. My home is now in an unseen community over the eastern horizon.

I treated the preacher's family to the fanciest dinner that could be found in Miles City. I cannot fathom such craziness that entered that couple's mind to bring Bibb into their home while he was recovering from the lynching. That act was beyond unmerited charity. It was a reckless lapse in reasoning, or divine intervention only to be recognized in hindsight. Until I met her I was somewhat jealous of little Anna. She is so young and pimpled; a delightful school girl. I can now tolerate the healthy hooks she has put into my man. She asks way too many questions.

Our horses were loaded on the stock train, wagon sold, and feather retrieved. Bibb will stay the night at the preacher's home, unlike last night. He slept in the livery with his horse — not wanting to be alone with the Anna girl and her mother... or his Anna.

==0==

THE LIVERY OWNER knocked on the door of the sheriff's home just at dawn. His sleepy wife, armed with only a cup of coffee, invited him in. Shortly afterwards the sheriff emerged from the bedroom and greeted the man over a fresh plate of hot cinnamon and honey biscuits.

"Are you missing anybody? Everybody knows that Bibb didn't stay at the preacher's house last night."

"I didn't know that," responded the sheriff. "What else do you know?"

"I know he didn't stay at the hotel either. Are you sure you aren't missing any citizens of our town?"

"And...?"

"Sheriff, I found Bibb sleeping in my livery with his horse this morning. I was not fool enough to disturb him, but I thought you might want to know where he was. You might want to keep track of him a bit better."

"I disagree. Putting a leash on him would make him more dangerous."

"Nice try, Sheriff. I'm not buying any of that silly strategy. What did you think of that beauty he brought into town?" The ears of the sheriff's wife perked up as she waited for her man's answer.

"I grant you the premise she is a beauty, but she must also have a doozy of a personality. I find it telling that Bibb chose to sleep with his horse in a stable rather than spend the night in his own hotel room with her. A woman's beauty is but paint on an aging barn. Can you do me a favor?"

"What kind of favor?"

"I need to know what happened between those two last week. If you just happen to strike up a conversation with Bibb can you let me know what he says?"

"Why?"

"Because folks in this town want me to keep better track of the man. Help me out, will you? If so, you will be the first person I will buy a drink for once the Limited steams east with Bibb and that old barn on board."

Once the visitor left, the sheriff's wife casually asked her husband a question as she gathered up the dishes. "Old barn? Really? Why did you earlier agree with him that Bibb's partner was a beauty?"

"Because I needed a favor?" That response fell flat on the floor and died. He tried again. "Honey, it just might be true that her figure happens to be very easy on a younger man's eyes."

"But not your eyes, of course," she asked with the intent on getting a better answer. "At least she is out of that awful dress and has put on something respectable."

"What green dress? I didn't notice."

"Right." His wife gave him a look he recognized. She muttered under her voice that nobody but him said anything about the color green. Graciously, he was allowed another chance to answer.

"I can't help it. My passions are drawn to other things. Over the last ten years I find myself irresistibly drawn to cinnamon biscuit makers. Put a little flour on them and I'm compelled to surrender to their every wish. All others don't even catch my attention."

"Fibber, but you're forgiven." She took a little flour and patted it on her apron around her tummy. "Would you be interested in hearing my first wish?"

"I was talking about putting flour on the biscuits, not you, dear. What were you thinking?"

"Same thing you are, and don't you deny it. Be home for an early dinner. I got big plans to give you something special for dessert."

"Cinnamon biscuits? Yum!"

==0==

Bibb did not dare to return to the hotel too early. There was nothing there for him but trouble. Before he left the livery he changed the hay for his horses and swept out the main passageway in the barn. After that he spent time washing out their wagon. While he was cleaning it the owner of the livery stopped by and offered to buy the buckboard from him. It wasn't a good price, but it wasn't an insult either. It easily could have been a much lower offer since he knew Bibb was leaving the following day. It was a joy for Bibb to talk to a man who loved horses as much as he did.

Time at the livery was restful. Bibb was enjoying this short time in Miles City mostly because nobody was out to give him a hard time, and him likewise. There seemed to be a new rule in town: Don't cheat your neighbor. Bibb also noticed that nobody seem to give two figs about him – just another neighbor to be treated well like any other. Maybe he was wrong, but if so, he enjoyed being wrong.

As Bibb walked into the hotel, he committed to himself to be pleasant no matter what may be hidden behind door number three. His knock on the door was answered with a "Where have you been, Tommy?" from the other side. The door opened and Bibb was welcomed in with a smile.

"Did you sleep well, Tommy?"

"Yes, and I have some good news. D'the livery owner bought your buckboard. He will bring d'the money to d'the station in d'the morning. He gave a fair price considering d'the mud we dragged d'that d'thing d'through."

"I slept well too, Tommy."

"I'm glad you did and I'm ashamed I didn't ask. I tend to d'think about d'things before people. What did you do yesterday?"

"I wrote some thoughts down."

"What d'thoughts?"

"Bibb, it is too early to answer that question. Writing down a journal is one thing, and entirely another challenge to write down a perspective. Tommy, it's no secret to you how much those Indian women changed my outlook on things. I'm writing about them, and also those scouts."

"Well, if you leave-zz me out of it, you might have a good story to tell. All I said was one dumb d'thing after another. D'there is-zz no use in documenting d'the obvious."

"There was one or two days you were kind. I might mention those if I can just remember what you did, but for now I can't remember any specifics. Bibb, you have a chance to be kind to me now if you want."

"To do what, Anna?"

The Widow Gorgon told Bibb that she wanted to have dinner at the place where he had his famous table talk with Mr. Westum. Bibb refused saying that it was not a place where preachers would be welcome or comfortable, nor would the patrons enjoy having a varmint loose in the house. As a compromise Bibb agreed to wear the new pants she had purchased for him. He went and tried them on. They fit, but they itched terribly. He felt suckered into that agreement.

"Anna, tell me true. What is more important to you? Me wearing d'these new clothes or you going to d'the saloon?"

"That's a dumb question, Bibb. You wearing those pants, of course. I bought them for you. Besides that saloon is a dive. Mrs. Westum and I went by there yesterday."

"And what are you-zz planning to do today?"

"Well you already sold the buckboard, so I can scratch that item off the list. I also met a reporter in the lobby yesterday and he offered to take me to lunch today."

"You don't like reporters. Anna, you do remember d'that, yes? Obviously d'this reporter doesn't know about what you-zz did to his brethren in Deadwood. D'there is a fine line between fearless and foolish."

"Well, I might just tell him where the line is then."

"Be careful with d'them. D'their first obligation is to sell newspapers, and second to be allowed back to report-zz d'the next story. Once we leave, d'they don't have to worry about number two. Worse, if d'the truth interferes with d'their first priority, well, d'they will have something else to put in d'the obituary. D'they bury truth on-zz a regular basis."

"You're not jealous?"

"Of what?"

"A man taking me out to lunch?" inquired Anna.

"No, it-zz never crossed my mind. You-zz have a good time, and make him buy your meal."

"Bibb, I'm not happy with where you are spending your days and nights. Not happy at all."

Bibb now knew what generated the jealousy theme of her conversation and sensed trouble brewing inside that remark. It almost sounded like Anna wanted some assurance that he wasn't going to embarrass her somehow. "Anna, you may change your mind about d'that tonight. D'the preacher and his family are wonderful people. You will enjoy meeting Anna. I just want to warn you d'that she likes to ask questions. I didn't have to tell her how pretty you were. Her momma already did d'that better d'than I could. Is d'that your real concern?"

"You seem to have a hankering for women named Anna."

"Anna, d'there ain't no fish in d'the creek where-zz you're angling. I will be back here around four to wash up and walk you-zz down to d'the restaurant."

"Bibb, there must be something wrong with your ear. You're not hearing what I'm talking about. Come here and let me look at it."

"Anna, d'there ain't nothing wrong with my ear. D'there is nothing wrong with my-zz heart. D'there is nothing wrong with us. I am looking forward to dinner tonight and escorting my proven covenant keeper. All I ask-zz is d'that we not be late."

Anna smiled. "Okay Tommy. I will be ready before five."

"Anna, d'they're expecting us to be d'there a half hour before d'then."

"I know. I was curious if your ear was still mine and still working." She was happy. She got her man to say her favorite word: *us*. She also got him to put on the clothes she bought him. He knew why she wanted to look at his ear. The covenant was intact; their exchanged smiles confirmed it.

Bibb left the room and went down to the lobby wanting to take some time to think and write down some of his thoughts for little Anna's father. The warm cup of coffee did much to improve his disposition. While writing to the preacher, his own difficulties with his Anna kept interrupting his progress. He determined to finish the letter and once done ordered another cup of coffee.

Bibb smiled over what just happened upstairs. It was a predictable irritation that Anna would want another round of her favorite Dress-Me-Up-Dolly game with her newest favorite dolly. Bibb had learned that Anna could not or would not cease from her special form of verbal encouragements (not quite whining, but close) until he was wearing a new pair of itchy pants. His job was to give in, but not too quickly lest it encourage more of that same feminine behavior in the future. Bibb knew the itch would eventually go away as the pants were broke in, but for now they were quite a nuisance. What bothered him about her game was that she never compromised an inch; she delighted in getting him into accept everything she wanted as if she was giving away everything she wanted in trade. She never had the intention of going to that saloon with him; that was a combination of a serious bluff and a humorous bluster.

The time relaxing over coffee helped. Bibb reasoned that even if his Anna's ways were tainted with manipulation, her actions were based on heartfelt kindness. He decided to drop the manipulation offense (as if he had never done anything like that himself) and celebrate that he was now in a friendship that, without prompting, she saw his need and did something about it. Instead of complaining he should step out of his self-serving view of the world, open his eyes, learn to discover Anna's needs, and then maybe even do something to be useful, kind, or helpful for her.

This proved to be as difficult as it was unnatural for him. Obviously Anna's needs were not material. Her opinion about any need for a man in her life was well documented and often freely provided, and salted with many unneeded adjectives.

After a while, convinced that she needed neither money nor a man, Bibb thought back to the farewell party in Deadwood. Very few of the women there were sincere in their warm words to Anna, nor Anna to them. They knew each other, but they seemed to share a false friendliness. And then there was Xue and Anna's maid. No, there were no deep friendships there either. Then Bibb thought about Anna's endless story about combing the woman's hair in the medicine man's teepee. Bibb thought it very strange to hear that story over and over. No… he eventually thought. That was no accident; the varmint had his paw prints all over that.

Bibb discovered over the last of his coffee what Anna really needed. Anna needed a friendship that was deep enough to be unafraid to touch Anna heart and she touch back. Tommy already heard many times Anna's longing for a mother. Bibb now concluded that she also longed for a sister.

The waitress offered to refill his coffee cup, but Bibb waved her off. He decided that he would make it his task to find a friend for Anna. It was painfully obvious that he was totally unsuited for that task and gender repulsive. He had no men friends and even less female ones to qualify him to even begin the task. He pulled out a coin from his pocket, laid it on the table, and took a second to say a quick prayer. "God, please find for d'that woman a real friend."

Tommy's stroll up to the preacher's house was filled with many thoughts, and none of them comfortable. The varmint was getting ready to bite him over something. Bibb could just sense that critter crouching down with its teeth exposed ready to pounce and latch his jaws into him.

It was too quiet. By now the varmint normally would have bit him. Within his own heart Tommy started the conversation with the one he knew was watching his every step. These conversations really bothered Tommy because he could never tell if they were valid, sinister, or if he was just going nuts. Going nuts was a real possibility, except for the fact that these conversations were producing positive changes in his life.

"What did I do wrong now, God?"

"I heard your prayer, Terry."

Tommy was waiting for the shoe to fall. The bite was coming, but he wished he knew his offense. He eventually asked himself why the message in the mist called him Terry. Of course, Terry was the original name that his parents had named him. His twin Tommy was the compliant one that was friends with everyone in Fort Rice. Terry was the friendless renegade.

"Why did you call me Terry?" asked Tommy in prayer.

"For my glory, friend."

Tommy did not understand. What glory could God get by calling him Terry? Tommy was the one that could make friends. Terry was like Anna; both well skilled at using people, hurting people, and destroying relationships.

As he walked up the street Tommy remembered what the varmint had said once; it was going to stick closer than a brother. Then he remembered what Anna gave as her sign at the altar: she was going to "be this close." And now the latest words spoken to his heart called him friend. His twin Tommy won people's hearts by just breathing; it was something he was created to do. There was no glory in Tommy finding friends. But for Terry to find a friend… Yes, that was a God-sized project, and if He pulled that off, God would earn all the glory.

Tommy did not like the direction that this internal dialog was going. He tried to think about anything else, but it always returned back to his prayer. Bibb reminded God that his prayer was for Anna to find a friend. Bibb had agreed to be kind to that beastie, but to become her friend as implied in the mist was too much. Bibb told God he didn't sign up for that. He only signed up to be kind to the woman. "I really don't like her, God. She's just like me, and d'that stinks! Why don't you find somebody d'that can influence her for d'the better? Not me, God. No, not me. D'the woman drives me nuts. She needs a girlfriend, not another outlaw in her life! I don't like what you're hinting at. I don't like it at all. I can be kind to her… okay, I can do d'that. Being friendly to her is asking too much…" Bibb was reminded of the danger in praying. It changes the asker, not the object.

Before he knew it Bibb was already at the preacher's home and shamefully with nothing in his hands. Walking up to the door he realized that for the last twenty minutes he had been detached from his moorings and seriously arguing with himself. If God had said anything, it was less than ten words to him, and Bibb had added all the rest. Maybe Anna was right, he thought too much. The rational conclusion Tommy came up with was that he needed to think through the consequences of his prayers before he launched them up towards the God Almighty. He had a habit of both hearing and helping, and then lash the asker onto the sharp end of the spear attacking the problem.

==0==

Bibb and the preacher went off for a walk after lunch through his neighborhood on the southwest side of town. Bibb was quite anxious to talk about many things that bothered him. They happened upon the church and sat down on the front steps. Bibb handed him the note and asked him to read it and then give his opinion.

Preacher, there is a good chance I'm going nuts. I must ask you about some of my experiences. I figure you would know best about these things. I can't dare risk asking anybody else. The whole world already thinks I am unstable.

The problem is the varmint. It is like this critter that lives inside of me and it is always reminding me of what I am doing wrong. Not only that, but what I have done wrong in the past. It keeps sticking pins in me to turn past wrongs right, and to offer restitution to those I hurt. I would say it was some evil ghost bothering me, but no self-respecting demon would tell a reprobate like me to keep my promises, come clean, and be extra careful to give God and others all the credit for any good that happens.

This varmint doesn't talk like we do. It kind of drops hints around inside of my thinking that come and traps me when I get into some bad thoughts. It isn't even a whisper. It even sounds like your daughter, well not a girl like voice, but the same words and cadence as when she read to me from the book.

Worse than that, preacher, this varmint is getting bolder. It is getting more specific and it is telling me things almost too personal to mention. We need to talk about that. I ain't going to document those details in this letter. Sometimes I get so frustrated with the critter I tell it to go away. And it won't. It reminds me of what your Anna read, "I will never let you wander off nor forgets our promises." Or something like that.

One last thing. Lately it hasn't been a girly varmint talking to me. It is more like my dad. Preacher, my dad is long dead. I complained one night in what you might call a prayer. I wished that the varmint would let me have just one good night's sleep without reminding me I needed to be kind and treat people with respect and honor. I asked him to put the varmint in a cage. Then came this presence, I don't know, and he seemed to say that he wouldn't do what I asked. I don't know how to describe it. I asked him why, and he said that the varmint was going to be my good friend until the day I became exactly like the prince. I supposed, I didn't even really think fast enough - I just supposed it - and he whispered again that I was right even before I thunk it. It was that night I realized that this prince was the lamb you guys told me about. He told me his son knew how to listen good too, and that I should start a conversation with him once in a while.

Am I going nuts? How do I know if that is God talking to me, or just me talking to me, or if something sinister is trying to fool me? -Bibb

"You sure have a handful of questions there, Bibb. Where do you want me to start?"

"Does God talk-zz to people?"

"If He wants to. He can do anything He wants in any way He wants. He talks to me too, but not in the same way. He knows us from belly-button to backbone, and He also knows how to get our attention to where we will actually listen and obey. I am quite amused that you have gotten to know his Holy Spirit as a varmint. He talks to people in the way people will understand, and I suppose you know all about varmints. He speaks to my wife mostly by way of the book you let her copy. He speaks to my Anna in the breezes that blow past her brow during morning prayers on the porch. Everybody is different, and God is very creative in knowing how to best reach people. Not only is God very creative, He is also very consistent. There is one thing that God will not do."

"What's-zz d'that?"

The preacher didn't know exactly what Bibb had replied; he wasn't quite accustomed to the slurs and d'ats. "Bibb, one of the reasons I think it was God talking to you is because it was consistent with God's character. God will never violate His character.

God is good, and only good. None of his ways lead a man into sin or a violation of conscience. You can know for sure if it is sinister by a simple three question test."

"It bites me-zz once, it bites me-zz twice, and it bites me-zz again? D'that seems to be-zz pretty harsh. I'm sure glad-zz d'there aren't ten tests. D'that varmint will have me eaten alive. And why can't d'that varmint ever give me break and maybe say, 'Hey Bibb, you are doing great' or 'Do better next time'? No, d'that varmint demands perfection and when I accidently do something right it warns me not to take credit for it. That varmint is a bit of a snob if I dare say it. He wants all d'the credit for good d'that has been done or all d'the coincidences d'that saved our bacon from d'the frying pan. One d'thing is for sure, if I say something like 'D'that was lucky,' d'then I'm bit for sure. D'that varmint don't like d'that comment at all. D'that's worse d'than cuss'n'.''

"I'm trying not to laugh, Bibb," said the preacher. "But your experience with the varmint is so like God. Bibb, you need to understand that coincidences are events were Providence decides it is best to remain anonymous. But back to my point, you need to remember this first one test first. He is good, and in Him there is no evil. If anything is tainted with even a hint of evil, then it is not of God. His standard of behavior is perfection. God cannot tolerate sin."

"Do you mean like sleeping with a woman-zz d'that I ain't got any intention of marrying permanent like forever, not even to keep warm?"

"So Anna is not your wife? I heard a different story, Bibb, and I will want you to explain that later. The second rule is just as important. It is the 'Who gets the glory?' question. If anything you might think God is saying gives glory to yourself or another person, then it is not God. God is a jealous God, and is due all the glory. He does not share it with anybody. If somebody predicts something, and the predictor gets the credit for being wise, well I reckon that man is making it up, a good guesser, or as you said, something sinister."

"Did you know a medicine man did-zz d'that for us? He made-zz d'three predictions about each of us. I told Anna don't put no stock in-zz any of it. If it-zz comes true, I mean all of it true, d'then maybe-zz d'the medicine man relayed a whisper of God. Either way, we're not-zz to adjust our lives to any predictions. Predictions are predictions, not advice."

"Who told you that, Bibb?"

"Nobody. D'that just makes-zz sense. I didn't like his predictions about-zz me anyway. D'they were all bad. Not just a little bad, but-zz really bad. D'the quicker I forget-zz d'them, d'the better."

"God is the God of good sense. He also is the God of variety. He thinks of all sorts of ways to test us to see if what we say is what we mean. He will sacrifice anything or everything in our lives to build His character in us. His goal, like I read in your note, is to make us just like his Son."

"Is-zz d'that really true? Does He go out of his-zz way to zing me about my-zz boasts and promises? I hate-zz it! I will say something-zz like a promise or commitment, and it won't be-zz d'three winks later-zz d'that something will happen-zz d'that will make me either eat my words or keep-zz d'them. It is terrible! D'that varmint will not leave me-zz alone!"

"Bibb, you might gain some relief if you call Him by what He is. He might take offense being called a varmint. Then again, He might enjoy the bantering too. He made you feisty for a reason. Try calling him Holy, Counselor, or Comforter. You might get better results. The third test is not as dogmatic as the others. It is more of a disqualifier than a qualifier like the other two tests.

"I don't like none of-zz d'that bantering. Why can't-zz yes be yes, and no be no? D'that widow woman ties me-zz in such knots. She wants to talk about-zz d'three d'things all at once, and I get-zz so confused. But you said we would talk about-zz d'that later. Tell me true, what is-zz d'the d'third test, and-zz d'then tell me-zz if I am going-zz nuts."

"Are you a better man for listening to these promptings?"

"Yes, but-zz d'that might be by accident. D'that's still ain't saying nothing no how. It would be hard not-zz to be better d'than I was before."

"You sure have had a lot of accidents to all be accidents."

"I knows-zz. Her husband had an accident too. His death put-zz me in some deep-zz trouble. If I would have denied I killed him, d'then everybody would have d'thought me to be lying just because liars do d'that. I don't-zz want-zz to be known as a liar no more, so I said-zz nothing."

"That isn't what I heard, Bibb. We heard you killed him and brazenly put another notch in your hatchet. Yet it is mighty strange that the widow would marry her husband's murderer, and then one week later travel the length of the country with him. If you didn't kill him, who did?"

"It's a mystery. Preacher, what do you-zz d'think? Would God d'throw my ax to save my life and kill another man? D'that doesn't seem fair, and d'that is what-zz d'the sheriff would call-zz a weak alibi. Everybody else would call it a whopper. D'the best-zz d'thing I could do right d'then was to keep my-zz mouth shut. D'that wasn't hard to do given-zz d'the hole in my head. All I know is-zz d'that I woke up-zz d'three days later and-zz d'there was-zz d'this black veiled woman telling me-zz it was my responsibility to take-zz her home to Fort Rice."

"God takes no delight in the death of an unrepentant sinner. I would say no to the ax throw. Was your meeting three days later the first time you met the Widow Gorgon?"

"Yes, sir, sort of, and I am glad-zz you knew her name. You must already know some of d'the details and d'the problems I got. But d'that wid'r, I couldn't see her good – my one eye was bandaged and-zz d'the other full of tears. She was blackened from-zz toe to top. It was real spooky, like Death had come to take me away. I guess God had tied my tongue up pretty tight so I would listen for once. I remember-zz d'that night for another reason. D'that was-zz d'the first time-zz ever d'that varmint was almost nice to me. It told me it was my job to take-zz her home, and-zz d'that he would set a trail before me. He said-zz d'that d'the widow belonged to him, but she didn't know-zz it yet. It was just like-zz you said about-zz me when I slept on your couch. D'that was spooky."

"Bibb, how could you know for sure? Did God say something specifically or was there a sign."

"Preacher, d'there was so much peace about it-zz d'that-zz d'the decision was easy. D'there I was half dead, and d'that varmint kind of asked, kind of told me to obey him, and I actually felt-zz like I could. It was so strange. Maybe d'that varmint said 'Trial before me' instead of 'Trail before me.' D'that woman packs five hundred pounds of trouble into a hundred pounds of body. I'm glad she ain't fatter d'than she is. I take-zz d'that back, Preacher. She's a fine woman, as far as women go, and she ain't skinny skinny like a sick skinny. You have seen her. She is okay, I guess, for a woman."

"Bibb, you need to learn to keep those thoughts about women to yourself. She is a real beauty, and you don't have to deny it."

"D'that is hard for me, Preacher. If I start-zz d'thinking her pretty d'then other problems start. D'the Indian matron called her ugly."

"Bibb, I understand. Preachers very much understand that problem. It's better to agree with the matron than to burn inside with desires that cannot be rightly satisfied."

"Not just that, but we promised to be-zz kind to each other at a church altar in a public ceremony, and for-zz d'the most part she has kept-zz her promise."

"And what about you, Bibb?"

"I've been bad. I can't even sneeze and not-zz be bad (srpt). It is so hard-zz to be kind to her! It was easier (srpt) to be nice to her when-zz I hated her (srpt). Now-zz d'that we are almost friends (srpt), I'm more-zz worst-zz in-zz my d'thinkings-zz (srpt) and I-zz flip flopping-zz around like-zz a fish-zz out of water (srpt). She, oh (srpt), she-zz is so-zz much trouble-zz (srpt). I wish she-zz was ugly-zz and mean-zz (srpt). I can-zz deal with ugly and mean (srpt). She was ugly (srpt) and mean-zz when-zz we-zz left (srpt) Deadwood (srpt). She-zz was-zz easy to hate-zz d'then (srpt)."

That was an unintelligible earful. The man needed to slow down if he was to be understood, but nevertheless, the sentiment of his message was clearly received. "Bibb, you say she has changed?"

"She said she met d'the varmint."

"And…?"

"I don't know! I don't know-zz (srpt) nothing! But she has changed (srpt) and she ain't-zz so proud as she once was (srpt). Her-zz pride and vanity got-zz d'thumped bad right-zz (srpt) out of her. She's-zz actually nice now (srpt), and I don't-zz know (srpt) how to respond. She belongs to God, not-zz me. D'the varmint (srpt) said so. But-zz I still got-zz to do-zz d'the work (srpt) I promised I would do, and to do-zz d'that I got-zz to be-zz with her. It's just awful, Preacher (srpt). Here is-zz d'the real problem: How do I take-zz care of something-zz d'that belongs to God (srpt) without soiling it? It's like-zz holding a baby (srpt). I don't like-zz d'them either (srpt) because I-zz d'think I'm going to drop-zz it and break-zz it. D'that woman… D'that woman… never mind. I have said enough (srpt). Too much."

"Have you been intimate with her?"

"NO!" came an immediate denial as fast as his ax. "Her and d'that varmint would be in a race to see-zz who could kill-zz me first. Absolutely not! Uhohhh – what a-zz repulsive d'thought. D'that wasn't part-zz of our covenant. She ain't mine, and I don't want-zz no bunny business like-zz d'that to complicate-zz up my life. My best friend is-zz my horse, and I intend-zz to keep it-zz d'that way."

The preacher ears perked up when he heard Bibb say the word *covenant*. "Well then, Bibb, you will always have trouble then. Your best friend needs to be God's Son, the one who you know as Jesus. Another test to see if God is speaking is that the utterance, whisper, or still small voice – however God decides to communicate with you – will never deny that Jesus is Lord. Have you been true to your commitment to Him?"

"Preacher, I ain't no coward. Cowards run-zz home to-zz d'their mommas when life gets hard. D'that isn't in me. And yes, I have-zz been faithful to d'the best I know how."

"Your best? Is that all?"

That answer visibly irritated Bibb. "You talk just like-zz d'that big toothed varmint. It is never satisfied with just my best. His standard is set… It's-zz d'that Lamb. I will never make it, but-zz I will not-zz dishonor Him in my trying. It is-zz d'the least I can do. I'm not my own man; I am His man… well (srpt) what is left of me. And don't-zz you (srpt) tell Anna. D'that will ruin every d'thing."

"Which Anna?"

"My Anna. She don't like-zz none of-zz d'that God talk never."

"My Anna? I thought you said the widow belong to God."

"See! You got-zz me in knots too! God's gave-zz me d'that woman not-zz for me-zz to keep but to deliver to Fort Rice."

"Is that part of your covenant, Bibb? Tell me about it."

"Preacher, our covenant is-zz simple. Life for life. I deliver her and she delivers me-zz. I bring her from-zz her past to a new life, and she does-zz d'the same for me. Her need is relational, my need is physical. The second part was-zz d'that varmint's idea. We pledged before-zz God at his altar to be kind-zz to each other. What-zz a fool I was for not-zz counting-zz up d'that cost. D'the price is more d'than I can pay, and d'the difficult part of keeping my promise doesn't start until we reach Bismarck. On d'the prairie I am-zz d'the trail boss. She's fixin' to be d'the boss soon, too soon."

"Is there a third part?"

"We are bound-zz to our promises until dismissed by-zz d'the other at fulfillment, or die trying."

"How did this come about, Bibb? Covenants are not made by accident."

"I don't know. It was kind of like-zz a Jonathan and David idea, except I ain't-zz much of a man, and, oh, my, my, my, she certainly ain't one either. I just knew-zz d'that her idea of a contract wouldn't work. She is a terrible nitpicker, well-zz, until she was slapped... slapped twice."

"You slapped her?"

"Oh no... it was much worse-zz d'than-zz d'that. D'the 'Woman Who Must Be Obeyed' got her. D'that is also where she was forgiven. But-zz d'that is her story, not-zz mine. She knows humility now-zz."

"The 'She Who Must Be Obeyed'?" That is a strange title, and sounds fearsome.

Bibb replied, "D'that matron was rough, but d'those Indians have never heard about my Humbird." They both laughed, but discretely. Humbird might still be able to overhear them, even though hundreds of miles away.

"One last thing, Bibb," continued the preacher. "God is very creative in knowing how to best reach people. He can use lightning bolts from the sky if he wants to, but His favorite way is to use people. Sometimes he uses preachers, sometimes innocent teenagers, sometimes outlaws, and sometimes sheriffs. The same hot sun that melts candles also bakes bricks, and He knows which person is made of wax and who is made of clay. Bibb, you need to listen to this advice: You can bring death to some and to others you may bring life. You need to be open to the possibility that you may be used as God's means to show God's love to another person. If an outlaw can show mercy, the outlaw will never get the credit for that. God will. Westum proved that while you were gone. God specializes in small miracles. Some are no larger than the twinkle of an eye."

"Preacher, you never did answer-zz my question. Am I going nuts?"

"No more nuts than me, Bibb. Bibb, thank you. You answered more of my questions than you asked of me. That varmint of yours, well, that description is a new one on me. Keep those tests continually as part of your thinking. Don't worry about knowing any answers immediately. You keep true to the Prince. You will always have time later to discern if that critter keeps passing the tests. Keep looking beyond your own nose to see God's handiwork in your life. Keep keeping your promises, and God will lay out a trail in front of you."

"And trials."

"And trials too. Lots of trials and lots of trails. Bibb, I mean this with every fiber of my being. I am as proud of you as if you were my own boy. And I will pray for you just as if you were my own flesh. It takes no prophet to predict that the road ahead of you will be rough and stormy, but God has His hand all over you, son, like stink on skunk. You ain't pretty. You ain't refined. But Bibb, you are walking where God wants you to walk and doing what God wants you to do. There is no safer place to be."

"So you-zz d'think I should be kind to d'the varmint too?"

"And read the book too, Bibb. Read the book."

"So you are going to give it back? Preacher, d'this is when you say yes."

"Tomorrow, just before you leave. My wife and daughter would not forgive me if I gave it back now. They will be up all night copying more of it."

"So, until around half past four tonight? Your wife and Anna will be coming too, yes? Mrs. Gorgon is anxious to meet d'them."

==0==

"You know you can go up to the room, Mr. Toivo. You did pay for it."

"I know, but I'll wait. Can your maid deliver a message to Mrs. Toivo d'that I'm waiting in the lobby?"

"There is no need for that, Mr. Toivo. I see her coming down now." Tommy turned around and confirmed two things. First it was Anna, and second, based on the look on her face, she had heard him ask for the maid. Anna was actually amused.

"Tommy, let's go. For your sake, I want to get there early."

"Can we sit-zz down here a minute first?"

"Why?" Anna read his demeanor and sat down.

"Because (srpt), because I'm nervous."

"Bibb, sit down. You're looking awkward standing there. Tell me. Why are you nervous?"

"Because, well, just because."

"Why? And sit down, Bibb. I'm not going to tell you again. You're embarrassing me."

Bibb finally sat down next to her rather than across from her. "Anna, and you look very lovely, Anna. Anna, I'm glad I got to know you Anna when I did how I did Anna."

"Collect yourself, Tommy. Why are you so nervous?"

"Anna, it's because I-zz get nervous around women-zz, especially pretty ones. Anna, you-zz a lot-zz look-zz better tonight d'than you-zz looked in men's clothes." He was very frustrated. "Anna, let's-zz not talk-zz, Anna. Anna, please, let's go."

"You started this. And you are nervous because… ?"

440

"Because you're persistent. Because you're pretty, and because Anna's family not-zz will not, ohhhh, I hate-zz d'this when-zz I get-zz (srpt) like-zz d'this. D'they will not-zz squander (srpt) d'this opportunity to-zz ask you-zz some pointed questions (srpt)."

"About my morals? About our covenant? About our marriage? What about, Bibb?"

"Don't tease me about d'that, Anna, please. You know-zz you twist me-zz all about when you tease me-zz about long term stuff and us and, and touching my-zz hand and stuff and clothes and bedrolls and stuff-zz and stuff (srpt) like d'that. But Anna, you will get quizzed terrible about your destination, and I'm not talking about-zz Bismarck (srpt) or Fort Rice."

"That's what preachers do, Bibb. So what's your point?" She was enjoying this. She laughed inside at his frustration trying to spit out his words. The man was clearly in a dizzy tizzy.

Bibb saw her tiny smile and purposely took several deep breaths. He started again and much slower. "Okay, I just didn't want you-zz to d'think I was tricking you into something. I know-zz what d'they are like. Anna, I have another favor to ask." Bibb reached out his hand to hers. "D'this will be rough on me. Can we-zz agree on (srpt) something?"

"Are you asking me to pray with you? Bibb, are they planning to kill you, or you kill them?"

"Anna, can you just agree with me over something d'that is really bothering me?"

"Don't ask me to pray, Bibb."

"I'm asking you to agree with my prayer. If you don't like what I say, d'then let go of my hand."

"You're serious, aren't you?"

"Anna, please, for me?"

"Alright, but I'm not saying I will agree."

"Okay." Bibb took her hand. It was warm. His was clammy.

"Aren't you going to say something?"

"Yes, I will. Give me a chance. D'this ain't easy for me."

Anna waited as they sat next to each other. All of a sudden Bibb squeezed her hand tight surprising her. "God, make-zz me behave tonight and-zz my Anna beautiful. Amen." That burst of words was the quickest she had ever heard him speak, and with the last word he dropped her hand as quick as a snake strike.

"That's it, Bibb?"

"Yes, ma'am." Bibb was still talking fast. "I don't want to ask for too much, and I asked for a double helping for me and something easy for you. Let's go, Anna. I don't want to be late."

"Five minutes ago you said we had plenty of time. Bibb, you sure are a handful."

"D'the preacher was right. He said I would become just like d'the person I spend my time with. I d'think he was hinting about spending time with d'the Lamb."

"The Lamb?"

"Yep. Let's go, Anna. Please."

"I still want to go eat at the same place you and Mr. Westum had your famous discussion."

"We already decided d'that Anna. Let's go."

==0==

Anna and Bibb met the preacher, his wife and daughter at the door of the restaurant, all arriving at the same time. The preacher, being the gregarious one, introduced his wife and daughter.

The young Anna, with an unflinching stare as if a prelude to an act of worship, spoke to the older one, "Miss Anna, you're much, much, prettier than Tommy described."

Mrs. Gorgon was not expecting that reception and did what she could do to deflect the praise. She replied, "Tommy didn't call me an old potato sack again, did he? Bibb, you need to apologize! We will talk about this later. Let's go get our table."

"Anna," responded Tommy, "D'the Widow Gorgon is just being modest. She already knows she is prettier d'than a potato sack. She tells me so all d'the time."

Young Anna replied, "Miss Anna, Bibb doesn't lie any more. He told me you were both very attractive and good hearted, and I believed him. Obviously his first claim was an understatement, and I will forgive him. And as for his second claim he told me about your generosity with the Indian women. I hope I could be as generous as you someday. Miss Anna, was Bibb insincere or were you just being modest?"

"Anna, neither. I don't do modesty well. But for the record, both he and I were generous with our Lakota hosts. And secondly for the record, Bibb did not lie. Are you sure you're only sixteen?"

"Mrs. Toivo, may I call you that?" said the preacher, "I apologize for our young daughter. She is often too direct with her questions."

"Sir," replied Mrs. Toivo, "Bibb already warned me about that. He also warned me not to let her young age fool me. Anna, Bibb speaks highly of you, and now I see why. You may ask all the questions you like of me tonight. I may not answer them, but you certainly will not offend me by verbalizing your curiosities. Bibb, she is everything you said she was."

The dinner was delightful and the talk around the table even better. They even treated themselves to a dessert. It was quite possible that this was the first time young Anna ever tasted chocolate. Much of the talk was about Mrs. Toivo's childhood and then their recent journey from Deadwood. It was after the last spoon was put down that young Anna started her questions again.

"Mrs. Toivo, did Bibb tell you about his decision to accept the grand bargain?"

"No, I am not aware of any grand bargain, but I think I know what you're describing. I asked Tommy several times why his ways didn't match his reputation. Bibb is quite shy about it. Why don't you tell me about what he will not?"

Young Anna was clearly disappointed with that response. "Tommy, you didn't tell her? That was the most important moment of your life, and you said nothing?"

"Anna," Bibb responded softly to the young lady, "Mrs. Toivo has severe reservations about my-zz truthfulness. I wanted to wait-zz until she trusted my words. I do not fault her with her reluctance. I do not need to remind-zz you of my bad reputation as a liar. Why don't you tell her? She will believe you. You-zz have-zz my permission."

"Mrs. Toivo, do you think Tommy has changed?"

"Yes, and Tommy blames it on an old varmint and a new conscience. I never knew the old Tommy, but I am not a stranger to the trail of blood that follows him."

"Do you believe Tommy's change is genuine, or do you think he is faking it?"

"I think Mr. Toivo is a very frustrated man. His old ways seem to want to do one thing, and what he has confessed to me wants to do something else."

"What did he confess?"

"Anna," interrupted her mother, "Mr. Toivo can speak for himself on such matters."

"Anna," Bibb said to the young girl, "I trust Mrs. Toivo will give you-zz only truthful answers. She is a kind woman, and has my permission to speak her mind concerning me. She spoke d'the truth. I have-zz slipped up several times with not-zz being able to control my anger, but she was up to d'the challenge. I certainly have no regrets in-zz my decision to enter into a covenant with her. To my-zz shame, what I have received pales to what-zz I invested. Anna has been and continues to-zz be most faithful, and-zz her kindness is overwhelming."

"What did he confess, Anna?"

"He confessed he was a weak man, Anna, both mentally and physically."

"Specifically?"

"Anna, you are still a bit young for this conversation. I will tell you that Tommy was just as honorable with me as he was with you."

"And what did you confess to him?"

"You sure are a curious young lady. This is personal, but I will tell you anyway. It took me a long time, but I finally admitted my vanity to him. He had mentioned I was as vain as a peacock. He mentioned I was quite stubborn several times too, much to my irritation."

The preacher's wife started to laugh, immediately hushed by her husband's hand squeeze.

"What is so humorous, ma'am?" asked Mrs. Gorgon.

"I'm sorry. It just struck me as funny. Indirectly, I am absolutely convinced you are telling the truth. I know for a fact that the women Bibb cares the most about in his life end up with bird nicknames. Anna, it is quite the compliment. He would rather avoid most women completely."

"Did it feel good after you confessed?" asked the young Anna. Focused, she was annoyed by the conversational diversion.

"No, it did not Anna. Not at all. To the contrary, I was humiliated. But we were going to talk about Tommy, not me."

"Are you still vain?"

"Anna, Tommy… You remember him? He is sitting right here. Weren't you going to ask me about him?"

"How did Tommy respond to your confession?"

"Bibb was kind. In all the miles, Bibb has and still is retaining his promise to me."

"What promise was that?"

"We promised that he would do something big for me, and I would do something big for him, and no matter what happen we would always be kind to each other."

"Were you able to keep your promise to Tommy?"

"Not yet. I won't be able to do that until we return back east. And yes, I have tried to be kind."

"Were you able to be kind all the time?"

"Anna, I tried my best."

"Was your best good enough?" Mrs. Gorgon was getting more annoyed with her questions, but Bibb knew what was yet to come, and cringed.

"Anna, it was my best."

"Was your best good enough?"

"Anna, it really was my best."

"Was your best good enough?"

"Why do you keep asking that, Anna?" She didn't want to suffer the same question again.

"Because I want to know if you ever came to the conclusion you needed help keeping your promise to be kind. It is possible to be kind once in a while when it is convenient or kind if you can gain from it. But it is impossible to be kind all the time without asking God for his power and desire to be something you can't be on your own. Was your best good enough?"

"No, my best was not good enough, Anna. But Tommy was a good sport about it when I showed him my bad temper."

"Do you want to ask God for his help to make you kind all the time?"

"What are you suggesting?"

"I'm suggesting you accept the same grand bargain Tommy did. You saw the change providence has worked in him. You can have the same benefits!"

"If I get the same varmint that is tearing Bibb up, I say a hearty no thank you to that! You do not know how much that man has suffered from the varmint's bites."

"What are you scared of, Mrs. Toivo?"

"I just told you."

"No, you told me what Tommy was dealing with. What about you? Tommy told me that it was the only thing you lacked from becoming truly beautiful."

"Tommy told you what?" Bibb's nervous prayer in the hotel was now making more sense to her.

Bibb spoke up. "Anna, I d'think we have asked Mrs. Toivo enough questions. What did you-zz want to ask me?"

"I want to know what is taking you so long! Why haven't you told Anna yet about the source of your deepest joy? Tommy, I'm sorry to say this, but I am sorely disappointed in you."

"Anna," said Mrs. Toivo, "Bibb knows that if I'm going to be convinced of anything he tells me I have to be persuaded of his credibility first."

"Where hasn't he been truthful? Has he lied to you? And what are you waiting for? Are you waiting for Tommy to become perfect? And if you don't know if he is credible by now, what would it take? Lightning? Are you waiting for some voice to sneak up behind you when you are all alone and say 'Boo – I'm the Holy Ghost and I want you to be good and only good' from now on? Honestly ma'am, I do not understand your reluctance. Tommy's behavior has nothing to do with this. This is not a brain decision that is made by logical deductions, argument or persuasion. This is your heart decision, and decisions of the heart are more relational than rational."

"Young lady, have you ever thought of working as a saleswoman? You certainly are persistent."

"So why are you so reluctant?" replied the young Anna.

Anna was upset. "I will tell you why, young lady. It's because I'm not quite ready to do what Bibb did. I was told he traded control his life away in some mystical transaction where he no longer has the rights to his own decisions. I personally like being my own boss. Yes, Tommy seems happy, and changed his ways, but I'm not ready to give up my rights to an unknown unseen varmint."

Young Anna pleaded, "He can be known, and you only give up everything that is worthless, but in turn you gain everything that is precious. I still don't understand your reluctance. You're not giving up your mind. You're not giving up your talents. You're not giving up your riches. You will give up your vanity, and that is worthless anyway. I guess giving up vanity might be as hard as pride to give up. But Mrs. Toivo, it really is painless, and you get so much. Having a clean conscience is not as bad as Tommy says it is."

"I already have a clean conscience, thank you, little girl."

"Was your best good enough? You said 'No.' Did I hear you wrong? Did you lie to me?"

"Anna," Mrs. Toivo said trying to be kind, "This is my promise to you. Tommy and I will talk together about our conversation later tonight. We do not need to go into this any further."

"Will you write me a letter and let me know what you decided? I so want everything good that has happened to Tommy to happen to you too. Promise me that you will write me? I will be praying for you."

"You, and everybody else. I'm wondering why everybody has decided to pray for me lately."

The preacher's wife inserted herself. "Anna, I can answer that curiosity. It is because they are being prompted to. When God wants a precious daughter to accept His love, he encourages those who are able to show you His love to pray."

"Do they pray for me or at me? Sometimes I think some of your saints who deeply hate me secretly wish that God would strike me down with the pox."

Little Anna got up from her seat and walked over to where Mrs. Toivo was sitting. She stood by her as said, "Mrs. Toivo, I could never do that. I will pray that angels protect you until I get my letter from you." She bent over and kissed Mrs. Toivo on the ear and returned to her chair.

"I believe you, Anna. Bibb told me you had a pure heart." No response could have touched Anna's soul deeper than this kiss to her ear. Did Bibb tell her about his bite? No way, he never tells anything to anybody. There was no defense against the sincerity of this child's gentle caress. It was as unfair as it was unexpected. There was no condemnation from the girl. There was hope and encouragement. Anna knew in her spirit that she had just experienced a touch of the holy.

Bibb immediately saw that his Anna was getting misty eyed, and also why. He quickly took the opportunity to focus attention off of her on to himself. Bibb reminded the preacher of their big day tomorrow and they still had to finish packing. He thanked them for coming and that they both certainly enjoyed the evening. Anna never said another word after the girl's little kiss.

==0==

Walking back to the hotel Anna seemed to be without energy. Bibb responded by asking her if she would like to go to the swing at the gazebo. She nodded her head yes, and soon they were there.

Bibb enjoyed the quiet time swinging, but knew it wouldn't last. Anna eventually started a conversation. "Did you tell little Anna about me biting your ear?"

"Never, Anna."

"Did you say something about 'precious daughter' to her mother?"

"Never, Anna."

"Did you tell that Anna about 'good and only good'?"

"Anna told me d'that when I lay recovering on d'their couch after my beating. Her family says d'that phrase a lot. D'that is how d'they describe God, as if it is d'their name for him."

"Did you ever tell her to say 'Boo'?"

"Never, Anna. You are sounding like you d'think I conspired with d'them against you."

"Tell me then, is she normally as persistent as she was tonight?"

"Sometimes she's worse. You saw d'the genuine Anna. She really got angry with me – lots!"

"I thought those people weren't supposed to get angry."

"I gave d'them enough reasons. You know I'm good at d'that."

"Bibb, I will keep my promise to that girl, but not now or anytime soon. And I will write her. Don't push me. I know how much she means to you. I can't right now. Do you understand?"

"Better d'than you will ever know." In a whistle whisper to himself Bibb repeated that phrase back to himself. He had been there once, and it was not a pleasant place to be.

"Let's swing a while before we go back."

"Anna, you did remember d'they are expecting me to stay with d'them tonight?"

"I understand. Have I been that unkind to you?" asked Anna.

"Anna, I have no right to criticize you. You have been very, very kind to me. We-zz have had our moments, but Anna, your unkindness was never without my-zz first goading you."

"So you agree with that Anna, don't you?"

"What is to agree or disagree with? Anna, nothing has changed my-zz mind about you and our promises to each other. I am all in."

"You certainly disagreed with my insistence on me taking charge now that we are in Miles City."

"To tell you d'the truth, Anna, yes, I am scared about not being d'the trail boss anymore. I don't surrender my control easy. It's not just you, Anna. I wouldn't surrender even if General Grant demanded it."

"And?" snapped back Anna. "And where is the *and*?"

"Not-zz anymore. Not-zz anymore at all. I kept my promise and you kept yours. Our promises are d'the same but d'the details will now be different. We will be riding rails, not ruts. We will be seeing doctors instead-zz of medicine men. We will be in streets, not endless prairies. Not one promise I made will change out of my-zz deep and growing respect for you. I will not bring up any of what was said tonight until you-zz are ready to talk about it. I understand exactly what you-zz are going through. I have been d'there, and-zz it was terrible."

Anna said nothing. One glance confirmed to Bibb she had heard his recommitment to her. They sat on the swing together in silence for about a half hour. Bibb's many thoughts swirling inside him made him consider the place sacred in a strange way. They were set apart from the world. It was just them, nobody and nothing else. He dared not speak. That would somehow ruin the moment.

Bibb later became worried that he would arrive too late at the preacher's if they didn't return to the hotel to pack. He tapped Anna on the arm, interrupting her thoughts, and stated his concerns. "We still have a long way to Bismarck. Can we talk about all d'this and everything else later, Anna?"

"But I want to talk about it now," said Anna.

"Okay, but only if you-zz want to."

"Bibb, how did you put up with that for three weeks?"

"D'that wasn't my choice, Anna. God did it to me, and for me. He knew exactly what I needed."

"Her whining? How could you stand it?"

"I was close to death, Anna. What don't you understand about d'that?"

"So headstrong! That had to be extremely irritating."

"I needed somebody headstrong to change me into d'the man I'm becoming. D'that's no accident."

"And could never shut up when she has crossed the line! How did you stand it, Bibb?"

"Actually, Anna, after a while I saw d'that persistence was how God was showing his love to me. I couldn't do anything about it anyway. We were stuck together on purpose for our mutual benefit."

"What benefit?"

"God's presence in our lives, but we-zz got-zz to listen closely."

"There doesn't seem to be any deafness involved here."

"Denseness, not deafness."

"D'that is unkind. I thought you swore off being mean? Can you believe her boldness and not knowing her place? And where was the fear that should have come with being close to such a murderous outlaw?"

"Anna, d'that comes with confidence in knowing you're right. D'that's not a bad d'thing. I will confess it was rather irritating to be d'the object of d'the boldness. D'that got old quick."

"What did you do about it?"

"I listened."

"Well I am glad at least you learned that."

"I didn't say I understood. All I could do was listen. My head is swirling with everything..."

She cut off the last of his statement with her next one. "And talks too much too, never giving anybody a chance to say anything! So annoying! Controlling everything!"

"Sometimes d'things d'that are said are worth listening too. D'the words go down a lot easier when delivered by such an attractive face."

"Bibb, what is your problem? Why does everything go back to beauty with you?"

"Beauty is everything. I didn't know d'that before."

"Bibb, before what?"

"Before I lived with d'the woman we have been talking about. I didn't know d'that until she bit me."

"Did that girl bite you too? Bibb, were you intimate with her? Shame on you! Double shame on you! An under-aged preacher's kid! You are SCUM!"

"Who are we-zz talking about?" asked Bibb sheepishly.

"About that preacher's daughter! Bibb have you been listening or not?"

"Oh… oooh." Bibb knew he was in hot water.

"Who did you think I was talking about?"

"Your favorite subject?"

"BIBB!" She was so angry. She stood up and slapped Bibb hard across the face. It really hurt her hand; she slapped that hard. It really hurt Bibb too. Anna saw in addition to his reflexive reaction much involuntary tearing. Anna put her hands on her face in response to her own horror. "Oh no, what did I just do!?" She couldn't stand the sight in front of her. She turned and ran off the gazebo to stand and hide behind a weeping willow tree. She feared hearing the click of a revolver as she walked away from Bibb. No, she was the only person there with a gun. She was becoming sick.

Bibb did not know what to do, so he did nothing. He remained on the swing in silence. His thoughts were swirling again. The internal war between anger and kindness were at frontal assaults on each other's strengths. He justified lashing out since "justice was on his shoulder" but that would not appease the varmint on the other shoulder. So he decided to keep his tongue in cheek and wait for Anna to either leave the park or return to him. Besides, a cutting pain was burning his face, so sharp it reminded him of Westum's whips. Bibb wasn't in the mood to flinch. He decided to ride out the pain. Truth be known, he didn't trust himself at that moment and gripped the swing hard, to the point of whitened knuckles. Eventually the emotional pain overwhelmed the physical where he could lessen his grip.

Anna did return, composed, and stood before him. Her eyes were red. "Bibb, who were you thinking of, and did you really feel that way? Tell me true, and not what you think I want to hear."

"Anna, I will not tell you who, but I will tell you how I feel. You want feelings, well here it is: If you had some of d'that young Anna's faith, and d'that young Anna had some of your grace, I would be d'the richest man on earth. It is not fair to all d'the other men on d'this planet d'that I would have you two for friends. Now Anna, I made an honest mistake. I really, really d'thought you were talking about yourself, and what you-zz have been like (srpt) and what I've been like (srpt) for d'the last d'three weeks." Bibb was teary, and maybe not just from the slap. He continued in words more broken than usual, "What can I say? Is d'there anything I can say or do to comfort you, my Anna?"

"Forgive me for slapping you," Anna said softly and slowly. She wasn't her normal self.

"Done. What else?"

"Be my friend."

"Done. What else?"

"Walk me back to my room."

"Let's go. D'that will be my pleasure, Mrs. Toivo."

Bibb's quick prayer for peace and silence was answered.

==0==

It took all of three minutes for Bibb to put his stuff in the trunk, but all of Anna's shopping extended the activity for twenty minutes. Most of the time was deciding what to wear to the depot in the morning. After helping with this, and stacking that, Bibb decided that his part of the work had been satisfied. He took a chance and announced to Anna he would see her in the morning.

"Tommy, did it hurt?"

"It still hurts, but d'the stars have stopped d'their swirling around inside my noggin."

"You're exaggerating, Bibb."

Bibb had seen the swirling stars but only for the few seconds after the slap. He was not fool enough to claim any cowardly victimhood. "Yes, I am. Anna, d'that incident is-zz all forgotten."

"I haven't forgotten what you said! Recant! Did you really think I was talking about myself?"

"Anna, honestly, I really d'thought what had happened to me-zz was happening with you. I was going to be d'there with you in d'that terrifying first step of entering d'the grand bargain."

"You really thought I was that bad?"

"Anna, I cannot answer d'that question, nor want to. Anything I say will lead to another argument. D'this isn't about me. D'this is about you and you-zz talking to your own conscience. I have no place in d'that conversation. D'that is between you and your boudoir mirror when you-zz are all alone."

"Why did you say that Bibb?"

Anna's reply confused him. "Because d'this discussion really does belong between you and your mirror when you are all alone? I am not saying you-zz like mirrors. I am not saying d'that at all. I'm just saying it is a very personal assessment. Forget it, Anna. I was-zz just trying to say..."

"...To say that you understand?"

"Anna, I-zz don't know what I'm trying to say. I-zz am a simple man. I-zz hurt my dear friend tonight. I-zz hurt her bad enough d'that she lashed out at me. I-zz hate myself for d'that. I've-zz done it again, and I fear I have ruined another friendship. I-zz got to go, Anna. I-zz want you to know I failed tonight, but tomorrow is another day for me-zz to try my best-est at being kind once again. I-zz so want to see you-zz in d'the arms of your in-laws and you receive d'the joy d'that is stored up for you. I-zz hope nothing I have done will make you-zz want to quit our covenant. I-zz need you, Anna, and not-zz just for my healing."

"What was it like for you the night you gave in to the grand bargain? Tell me Bibb."

"You said I was-zz a liar and untrustworthy. When you d'think I'm better, let-zz me know."

"Tell me now."

"I was tore up d'then, and I am-zz tore up now. Maybe-zz later. I have-zz no tears left."

"It was that emotional for you, Bibb?"

"Anna-zz." Bibb fumbled around. "I-zz got to go. I-zz got-zz too many memories to sort."

"You go back to your safe place then. I will see you in the morning." She knew it wasn't the memories that made him want to flee. It was his fear of betrayal. His heart was exposed. She admitted to herself that her heart was exposed too. The moment was too dangerous for both.

When Tommy got to the door he stopped and looked at his covenant partner. She responded with a stare, but not the stare she had used to manipulate men in years past, but a glare ready to receive. Bibb could not reciprocate, but his eyes went to the floor.

"After d'the fight came peace. D'then came forgiveness. D'then came release. My life started over all clean. D'the hound left d'the fight bruised, bloodied, and with holes in his paws. D'that hound had won, but he won nothin' of value. All he got out of d'the deal was ugly me." Tommy fidgeted. "I said too much. You have my promise we will-zz talk about this later after I fix my lying and untrustworthy ways. I got-zz to go."

Bibb shut the door behind himself with all the care of dusting china. She went to the window and watched her man walk away into the night. Left alone in her room and while preparing herself for bed she rehearsed back all of his recent words. She also rehearsed back the ugly complaints she had voiced about the young Anna. She tried to comprehend how Tommy could have ever thought she was referring to herself and not that imp with all the questions! How could a man be so wrong?

Although tempted by habit, she stayed away from the mirror in her room. Sleep was not going to come easily tonight. Yes, Tommy was ugly, but clueless about his worth to her heart, or God's.

Saturday, October 22, 1887

Tommy and I headed east to Bismarck leaving late this morning on the Limited. Young Anna asked for (as predictable as dawn) but Bibb said "no" to giving her the Paymaster's Bible. It was a borrowed treasure, not a gift. Tommy showed no emotion at the farewell. If ever there would have been a time, that would have been it – but no, nothing came. "Us" is a duet, not a trio.

We repacked everything this morning after a very difficult night. The sheriff escorted me to the preacher's home early this morning after the incident. I am, and I greatly understate, irate because I felt my escort left me unprotected. He did not see it coming either. I will get over it. I lost nothing. Bibb lost a cherished treasure, and I can see in his eyes that he wants to get it back. Why? All he could mutter was some Indian words like Unktehi.

Men… and their blood sports. Where is his sense of propriety? Death follows Bibb everywhere. How does the man deal with his constant immersion in pain and trauma? When I lost my mother I cried for a year. Bibb either loses a pound of flesh or gains a notch.

In hindsight, nobody died. If Bibb would have stayed with me last night, one, two, or three of us would be dead. Yes, I will get over this violation. Young Anna's first installment on her promise to plead to heaven's gates for our protection proved ~~providential~~ beneficial.

I return to my innermost pain. Sadly, Bibb had no tear for young Anna this morning at the depot. I know why. He spent his last tears on me last night at the gazebo. I promise, double promise myself never again to pay that high price for another eye shower. There is no place in any relationship for that; I should have known that from Deadwood. What went around came around. I am thoroughly, thoroughly ashamed. I hate to agree with the preacher, but it was sin.

But today is a day of joy – I am free, free at last, and the man sitting next to me, dozing off as the jostling and clatter of the rails is rocking him to sleep, that man, my man, he loves me. He just doesn't know it yet. How do I know and he doesn't? He only knows himself by seeing where he has been. He is so lost and clueless living in the present; and I have no problem with that, in fact, I enjoy it; I so enjoy it. I know because I know. We are an "us" and I don't need the piece of paper in the bottom of the Toivo trunk to prove it. The real deal was sealed at the point of unconditional forgiveness. There were no loathsome negotiations. His answer? "Done."

I laugh… I hope he doesn't, but if my man ever asks for my hand in marriage I might surprise him by showing him a certain court document. He will be shocked to discover that his greatest benefactress in Deadwood was Mrs. Franklin. Mine too. If it wasn't so terribly cruel, I would want to delay the man's recovery. Our time spent together in our kindness covenant is pure joy.

==0==

453

THE REPACKING COULD always wait. Anna wanted to get more thoughts down on paper before packing away her quill at the bottom of the trunk. She was up past midnight writing down her thoughts. She spent much of her time trying to dissect the anatomy of the attraction Bibb had for that young Anna. Why would he give two winks about the teenager and not even a sneeze about her? Anna convinced herself she was not biased, but only personally curious, and definitely not jealous. What woman could be jealous of a mere girl? In the end, the Widow Gorgon agreed with her man about little Anna's overabundance of faith and lack of grace (that made her obnoxious) and her own lack of faith and abundance of vain social graces (which made her obnoxious). The remaining parts of his statements about her soul he said on the swing were nothing more than zings wrapped in kindness. His unmasked opinion of her was as revealing as it was hurtful. She stewed over the possibility that Bibb possessed several more low opinions of her that he wisely chose to swallow rather than say. She convinced herself that was a form of lying too. "What A Liar!!!!"

Anna had a lot of room in their trunk to store what she had purchased since arriving at Miles City. Her two new hats took up most of the real estate inside the container. She was also very fussy about how her new shoes were protected from scuffing. Her clothes were folded and refolded several times, and she took special care packing her prize dress and moccasins.

Although worthy of discarding, Anna could not bring herself to burn the clothes she and Bibb had shared coming across the plains. One looser fitting set of his clothes was worthy of sending to the laundry for resuscitation and resurrection. Anna paid extra for quick cleaning and was delighted to get them, along with his cleaned bedroll, back so soon. Bibb's flannel shirt and pants were warm and soft to the touch. They became her pajamas during her stay in Miles City. The pocket was also a convenient place to keep her muff gun. His other clothes were almost worthy of wrapping her shoes in. Once she was settled in the east, those pieces of tattered cloth would become forever a protected species residing in her rag drawer. Bibb may beg for them, but they would never be surrendered.

Once in bed, Anna swore there was a draft circulating in her room. She went to the window and checked outside. There was no breeze at all on this clear night. She relocked the window and returned to her bed. There was no air movement, but the sound, the faint noise similar to the sound of owls flying overhead whispered through the room. She got up and checked the window once again just to find the same results. She also put a towel under the door to stop a draft. Finally she lit a large candle and let it remain burning. The flame was perfectly happy to burn without a flicker, but the hushed sound remained. She was so alert that she got up and started to inspect her trunk again.

Eventually all was repacked to Anna's specifications, her flannel pajamas on, face washed (without the benefit of a mirror), and covers pulled back. She decided to keep the candle lit until the sea like sounds still tickling in her ears went away.

As she lay there she replayed all the conversations of the evening back into and through her heart. Twice she thought she should have slapped Bibb harder and just as many times she was so sorry she reacted that way. She should have never given young Anna permission to be so nosy. She was also angry with herself for not cutting off the questions earlier. Although there were some socially awkward moments, her desires were still accomplished. She had discovered much about the family Bibb had stayed with during his recovery from his beating.

She again got upset with Bibb. He also could have cut off Anna's questioning earlier! It turns out from his "Oh oooh" moment that he was actually siding with that girl! "Oh that man infuriates me! What does he want?" she muttered to herself as she begged for sleep to overcome her. She knew the answer but didn't want to say it. He had revealed it in his lightning prayer downstairs before they ate.

The longer she stared at the ceiling the more she knew the answers to her own questions. Bibb wanted to be rich. He said he would be rich if "That Anna" would gain some grace and if "His Anna" would gain some faith. She toyed with the idea of giving God an interview. If He passed her test, she would try Him out for a trial period of a week and then do an end of probation evaluation of His worthiness. She was serious, and her strategy and approach to God would be in the same way she hires a new clerk. If He turned out to be a profitable employee, she would renew His contract.

The candle started to flicker in the room and the ocean noises seemed to be in both ears now. Of all nights she wanted to sleep, why did this plague come upon her now? She got up out of bed and checked the window again with the same results. She was stopped dead in her tracks when the sea noises became audible to her:

> *Good and only good,*
> *You will belong to me,*
> *Kind and only kind,*
> *My Precious Anna Marie*

Anna immediately jumped back into bed and pulled the covers over her head, but to no avail. The chorus surrounding her repeated their rhyme! She yelled out at the top of her lungs from under the quilts, "Go away! Go away!"

Upon her command the words hushed, retreating back to that mystical sound of faint owl wings. She was both sleepless and angry. Frustrated, she got up and went back to her trunk and repacked her shoes. There was a difference this time, not with the trunk, but with the ditty. She was no longer a *Hannah* in the repeating rhyme. She questioned why and wondered if it was significant. Was it because she finally confessed (granted, the confession was just to a low-life reporter) that she was originally a *Hannah*? Bibb always lamented that the varmint heard everything, and maybe that critter granted the name she loved only after she admitted to the one she hated. The other thing that she noted was that she was no longer just a *precious* but now a *my precious* within the ditty. With everything that had happened to her, maybe being called a *my* by the varmint wasn't such a bad thing. Her thoughts went back to the party... Bibb asked for God's protection. "Well, if that critter wants to add a *my* in front of my name, that varmint can take ownership of my protection too! So be it!"

Once again satisfied with the packing, she went back to bed, and this time to fall asleep.

==0==

The blood curdling scream that came from Anna's room terrified all the guests at the main hotel in Miles City. The sleeping night clerk, startled, jumped up from where he was supposed to be awake on duty. He got up from his chair just in time to see an Indian with an ax run down the stairs through the lobby and out the door. Soon the halls were filled with curious eyes and Anna waving around her small gun in absolute terror.

The desk clerk told everybody to go back to sleep. It was four in the morning and there was nothing to see. To the contrary, there was plenty to see. What convinced people to retreat out of hall to behind their room doors wasn't the clerk's appeal, but Anna with a gun and in a state of rage. Until she calmed down they didn't want anything to do with that mad woman.

During her rant Anna had several unladylike words for the clerk. She was quite upset that the Indian had gotten past him and into her locked room without him noticing. Obviously the Indian had lifted the key from the front desk key box without him knowing.

The young embarrassed clerk had more than he could handle. He offered to report the incident to the sheriff in the morning. That appeasement was woefully inadequate for Anna's current mood.

That suggestion got him further in trouble. When the guests heard his offer to take her to the sheriff the other guests objected vocally. Their complaint was that they had paid for some semblance of protection and they were going to get it. He was not going to leave his post nor was he going to go back to sleep. The only thing the clerk was certain of was that he would soon be unemployed.

Ten minutes after the ruckus started, the morning biscuit lady happened to arrive at the hotel kitchen to start preparing breakfast for the guests. She was immediately pressed hard by the clerk to escort Anna to the sheriff's home. The press wasn't heeded immediately. She told both Anna and the clerk that as soon as the she had the oven fires going she would help out, but first things first.

The ten minutes Anna stayed within an eyelash of the cook's elbow did her a world of good. Her mind was on something else, even if it was how slow the cook seemed to be. That was cured by the cook enlisting her help to tend to the infant fires while she brought in more wood.

By half past the hour a much calmer Mrs. Toivo and the cook arrived at the home of the sheriff. They knocked on the door. Anna, impatient, did not get the results she wanted and found their bedroom window and knocked on the glass. A very tired sheriff came to the window, opened it, and asked Anna what her problem was. Errand completed, the biscuit maker went back to work.

"Open the door and I will let you know!" replied Anna loud enough to get the sheriff's wife's attention too. She had told her husband many times since Anna's arrival that she was not a woman to be trusted. She certainly didn't, and wouldn't stand for that woman talking to her husband alone.

"Please let her in, darling, and sit her down at our table." He continued, "Then you get back here and get dressed proper while I make the coffee. She wants something, and wants it badly. I so dislike rich women who entertain themselves by pushing their weight around."

The sheriff had no doubt in his mind what prompted his wife's directness. Her earlier words pointed directly at her husband about that Anna woman needed no additional embellishment or further explanation. The sheriff also remembered the attempted murder warrant that he could arrest her on if she got out of hand.

==0==

"Mrs. Gorgon, what gets you up so early this fine morning?" asked the sheriff as he returned the coffeepot to the stove. He spoke loud enough that his wife could hear everything said. "I hope you like your brew strong and black!" The sheriff's wife, unhappily getting dressed in the bedroom, uncharitably thought that the brew Anna was most familiar with was made in a caldron. Since she had nothing good to say, she continued to listen.

Anna got directly to her complaint. "Sir, I was awakened by an Indian in my room this morning. When I screamed, the lone Indian with an ax bolted out of my room, ran down the stairs, and escaped into the night. The night clerk can tell you the same thing."

"Are you injured, Mrs. Toivo?"

"Other than my damaged nerves, I am physically fine." Her words had the pain of violation voiced within them. She seemed emotionally unstable and very dangerous in this state of being. He looked to see where she was keeping her gun.

"Were you attacked physically?" asked the sheriff's wife as she entered the kitchen area to join Anna and her husband. There was no sleep in Anna's eyes. To the contrary, fire.

"No, he didn't dare. He saw I had my gun pointed at him."

"If he wasn't after you, what was he after?" asked the sheriff as he took over the questioning.

"He went through my trunk and threw all my packed belongings on the floor. He found what he wanted. It was something that belonged to Bibb."

"Do you know him?"

"I know of him. He said his name was Toak."

"Mrs. Gorgon, tell me slow. What happened?"

"I woke up when I heard noises in my room."

"How did the Indian get in? Was your room locked?"

"Absolutely! He must have taken the key from the sleeping desk clerk's key box!"

"And he went up the stairs, unlocked your door, came into your room, and started looking through your trunk? Anna, how could you see him?"

"With my own eyes when I woke up, Sheriff. I never blew out my candle last night."

"Did you confront him?"

"Yes, I told him to 'wash clothes' in his tongue. He was shocked."

"Wash clothes?"

"It's the only Lakota words I could remember at the moment, Sheriff, and it did get his attention. When he looked at me he saw that my gun was pointed directly at him."

"How did he respond?"

"He said in English that his ax was quicker than my gun, and told me to put it away. I did not. He said he came to make a deal with Bibb through me. He said 'Life for life. I no kill you if Bibb no kill Redbird.' Sheriff, Redbird is the name of Toak's wife."

"Why didn't you shoot him, Anna?"

"Because my aim stinks, Sheriff, and his ax is fast! If he would have made a move against me, I might have, but Bibb told me he wanted Toak to stay alive. Bibb told me that he needed Toak and Toak needed him."

"Obviously, since you are still alive, he did not make a move against you. What did he do?"

"I never took my gun away from pointing at him, and he never dropped his ax. He returned to going through my trunk until he found what he was looking for. Once he found it he had the strangest smile on his face."

"What did he find?" asked the sheriff.

"An eagle feather. I challenged him saying it was unwise to take a gift that the Lakota chief had given to Bibb. He responded with two statements. First was that he is only taking what was taken from him. Second he said the feather would be proof he offered Bibb life for life. Oh, he said a strange third thing. He said the feather was his name and his soul, and now he had it back."

"Why is he worried about Bibb killing his wife?"

"His wife and children, you mean. Toak said Bibb would be in Fort Rice one week before he could get there. He was very worried that Bibb would kill them."

"Why?"

"He didn't say, but I certainly can well assume that Mr. Westum had something to do with it."

"I don't think you are in any danger, Anna. Why don't you go back to the hotel and repack your stuff. You have a train to catch in the morning."

"THINK AGAIN, SHERIFF!" yelled Anna completely undone at the suggestion. "I am not going back to that room alone! That Indian still has a key and an ax and an attitude. Take me to the preacher's! No way am I going back to my hotel room alone!"

"I can take you to the preacher's, Anna," volunteered the sheriff's wife.

"No offense, ma'am, but I heard you're fast with the bandages but not so quick with an ax. I'm sorry, Sheriff, but you must take me to Tommy wherever he is. He said he was with the preacher but he could be on the moon for all I know. Sheriff, please take me there. Toak is somewhere out there right now, and most likely watching what is going on. That's all I ask. I will be a wreck anywhere else. Please take me there. Can we leave now?"

"We will both take you there, Anna." The sheriff's wife warmed her coffee again. "Anna, finish your drink while I get my public clothes on. Honey, come with me. I want some words with you."

The sheriff complied with his wife's strong suggestion. He wanted to talk to her too.

==0==

The preacher answered the door and invited the three of them in. The preacher's wife and daughter Anna were still awake, up all night with to task of copying the book. They woke Bibb who was right behind them on the couch.

Anna walked right in and stood next to her eye-rubbing outlaw. Anna thanked the sheriff and his wife for bringing her over. In short order, the sheriff and his wife started to gracefully excuse themselves explaining they needed to get over to the hotel.

As he left, the sheriff's wife mentioned to Bibb that Anna is quite herself now, but was not so an hour ago. She calmly explained that Anna had experienced the trauma of waking to an Indian with an ax in her hotel room.

"Bibb, it was Toak," said the sheriff. "Anna will explain the rest. By the way, Bibb, I'm taking this opportunity to return your guns and belt to you. Come get the rest of your stuff in the morning. Good night, or at least what's left of it."

The preacher's wife told Anna she could stay here with Bibb until breakfast was over. By the time she turned around and told her guests when she planned to eat, Anna had already sat on the couch, winked once or twice, and collapsed fast asleep.

"Bibb," said the preacher, "What are you doing still standing there? Go over and comfort that woman! Take her moccasins off of her feet and put a blanket around her. For being so fast you are so slow!"

"Preacher, can you wake us both up in time for breakfast? The only hope I have-zz of getting any more sleep today is right now. I'm so tired, and once she wakes she will be full of fire and vinegar. I should have seen d'this coming. D'this event complicates d'things a bit."

"Seven hours from now you will be on the train going east. I'll wake you both at dawn."

==0==

Anna and her father were both at the table working hard to finish their project while Anna's mother was in the kitchen preparing breakfast. The family had been working tirelessly since Bibb arrived in town to get as much of Bibb's book copied. Progress was good. They were almost done as they slugged through the last of the Minor Prophets.

"Dad, I had no idea how much noise people can make while they are sleeping. She is so pretty and so noisy at the same time. And Bibb, well, his snoring is to be expected."

"Anna dear, give them two hibernating bears a break. They are both lumped together in a new place, sleeping in an awkward contortion of almost sitting and almost laying down, and both wrapped up in a knot. People snore when they don't lay down to sleep normal."

"Dad, why are you letting them sleep together? They aren't married. Why don't the rules that you made for me apply the same to them while under your roof?"

"Anna, you would do well not to be so rigid in your rules. We make rules as a means to avoid breaking the principles. Yes, they are sleeping together, but they are not violating God's principles. My talk with Bibb convinced me that their covenant voiced to God has become more binding to them than any marriage vow voiced to any Justice of the Peace. And Anna, we really don't know if they are married or not, so don't be too hasty in your assumptions. Take a photograph of this in your mind's eye, Anna. You may never again see God's hand riding so hard on two people."

"Hard?" asked Anna.

"Hard and good. What God has joined together let no Indian break asunder."

"That isn't how that goes, Dad."

"That is how it goes this time, Anna. Don't be so unbending in your recitations that you can't see the reality of the Word's principles playing out in front of your own eyes. We're doing too much talking. Back to work, Anna."

"Dad, I love you."

"Anna, I love you too. You are one special woman. You are growing up to be more than what your momma and I could only dream of you being. Stop dawdling; get back to your copying."

==0==

Bibb and Anna stopped by the jail before going on to the hotel. They were both disheveled from the rough night, and their faces betrayed their mutual lack of sleep. Bibb asked Anna to carry his rifle and her muff gun while Bibb had his revolvers on his hips and an ax in his hand. Anna was so relieved Bibb was now at her side, and hip to hip is where she planned to keep him until they left Miles City together on the Limited.

When Bibb and Anna arrived back at the hotel the owner was waiting to greet them, and standing directly in front of his clerk. Bibb didn't mean it, but he looked like he intended to do some bodily damage to the man. The owner offered his sincerest apologies for the incident. He also mentioned that both the sheriff and his wife were there earlier and put their room back in order.

When Anna and Tommy returned to the room, still accompanied by the owner, they found the bed stripped of its sheets and Anna's clothes folded neatly on the bed. The trunk was turned right side up again and Anna's heirlooms and papers had been returned neatly to the bottom of the trunk. On top of the papers inside the trunk was Anna's envelope of cash she had withdrawn for the journey along with several bank drafts to get her reestablished upon arrival in Bismarck. It was obvious to all that Toak's motivation was not robbery. The owner excused himself gracefully.

As Bibb was placing her clothes back into the trunk (and Anna was advising him he wasn't doing it just right) a knock came to the door. Anna was immediately gun shy from the interruption and hid to the side of the room. Bibb inquired who was at the door. In response came an unknown woman's voice replying "Laundry Lady with a delivery."

Bibb opened the door and she handed him some sheets, blanket, his bedroll and a set of his flannel clothes. He thanked her, shut the door, and placed his stuff on the now vacated bed.

"Anna, were you-zz wearing d'those clothes you have-zz on as pajamas last night?"

"No." She avoided looking at the just delivered laundry as if it contained a secret.

"Did you-zz send d'this stuff out to be washed d'this morning?"

"No."

"Well, I reckon d'the same person who folded your clothes did d'that. I d'thought some of my stuff was-zz missing, but I wasn't quite yet ready to say Toak stole it."

"There is an explanation, Tommy. I broke my promise to you that I made the first time I put on your clothes."

"When Toak woke you up?" She nodded yes. "Well, d'that d'then explains d'these bedroll and sheets too. You were really scared, weren't you?"

"Terrified. Bibb, I'm so ashamed of myself. The sheets can always be washed, but what about me and all my broken promises? I really have been an enormous pain in your side, haven't I?"

Bibb didn't answer. While Anna watched with more than a passing curiosity, Bibb walked over, picked up his ax and placed it inside Anna's trunk along with his freshly laundered bedroll.

"Answer my question, Bibb." She repeated, "Please answer my question. I need your answer."

"I bet Adam smarted for weeks after God ripped a rib out-zz of his side to cook up something special for him. Little did he know d'that sting was only a down payment. But d'there is something poetic about-zz all d'this. I have a strange question for you-zz."

"What is it, Tommy?"

"Where is your muff gun right now, Anna?"

"In my purse behind you. Why?"

"Where-zz did d'that cold bowl of soup d'that is on your dresser come from?"

"I ordered it from the kitchen last night, Bibb. Why?"

"I d'thought it would be just like God to have Toak bring it up to you last night. Yours is-zz a better explanation d'than d'the one I was d'thinking of."

"What were you thinking, Bibb?" Anna was very curious. Her question seemed strange coming across her lips. Seldom in the last three weeks did that common question come out of her mouth without including a peppered accusation to put Bibb on the defensive. Not this time.

"Nothing. Just nothing. Let's finish up and get d'this trunk over to d'the depot. I want to go to d'the mercantile to buy-zz some hard tack and jerky for our train ride."

"Don't you dare, Bibb! I know what you're thinking! My days of HT, B & J are over. You need to eat better. We need to eat better, and the train has diner car. Forget that thought."

"What d'thought? About d'the soup?"

"What is your big concern about the soup, Bibb?"

"Nothing. Just nothing."

"Bibb, answer my question! Don't do this to me."

"Do what?"

"You tease me with a tidbit and then deny me. That is so cruel! No man has the right to do that to a woman."

"Shouldn't we agree d'that no person has d'the right to do d'that to another person, Anna? People have been known to get syphilis suffering d'that hurtful tactic from d'their best friend. Wouldn't you agree, Mrs. Gorgon? Is d'the soup cold? I'm d'thinking of having some."

"That soup was mine, not yours!"

"I'm glad to hear-zz d'that. It probably isn't as good as Bes's anyway."

Anna's mind chewed on several of Bibb's recent statements and it all started jelling together. She also now knew why he asked her where her gun was. "What are you trying to say, Bibb?"

"Nothing. Just nothing."

"You are trying to say something about what happened in Deadwood the night before we met for the first time, aren't you?"

"Anna, do you-zz remember d'the envelope I gave d'the sheriff when we arrived in town?"

"Yes. He looked at the contents and then put it away. So what?"

"D'the day after we arrived I visited d'the sheriff early in d'the morning. He asked me to surrender my weapons. When I pushed back on his request, he showed me d'the envelope. Inside d'the envelope I carried from-zz Deadwood was a warrant for my arrest from d'the magistrate in Deadwood. Along with d'that warrant was a directive d'that d'the Miles City Sheriff was authorized to have me arrested and jailed for your husband's murder. Included in d'the warrant was d'the actual complaint factually written out in legal speak. It explained d'the events and d'the charges outlining moment by-zz moment what-zz happened d'the night your husband died."

"What has any of that have to do with the cold soup? Why don't you answer the questions I ask instead of questions I didn't? You so infuriate me beyond my limits sometimes!"

"Anna, d'that wasn't d'the only warrant in d'the envelope."

"What else were you to be arrested for? You are nothing but an unrepentant reprobate outlaw! That is what you are! You were born for shame! And I think you live for shame too!"

"It was-zz an attempted murder warrant."

Anna was as angry as when she slapped him the night before, and Bibb carefully kept his distance. Anna continued by lashing out at him verbally.

"Who else did you try to kill, Bibb? Did you shoot a couple more people through the forehead? What was your weapon of choice this time? Rifle? Revolver? Whip? Ax? Bibb, sometimes I really do think you are an evil malicious child of the devil. What have you ever touched that wasn't soiled?"

"Actually, Anna…" Bibb took a breath as he was trying his best to control his temper. "Anna, d'the complaint said d'the attempted murder weapon was a muff gun, but originally it was d'thought to be a bowl of poisoned soup. Anna, it wasn't my name on d'that warrant. I couldn't believe it when I read d'the complaint. Tell me true. Did you really attempt to kill me in my sleep? D'the warrant said so, and with great detail to your motive, mindset, and methods. Your own Mr. Franklin helped write out d'the complaint. He's a man-zz I trust. Your best friend was d'the judge's wife, and he signed it. Anna, tell me true. Would you rather have me dead-zz or living? If so, d'that changes d'things. Although I need you for any hope of restoration of my person, you only need-zz to ask and I will-zz release you from your part of d'the covenant. Anna, I must know if you prefer me dead rather d'than whole. I want-zz to trust and believe you. Anna, d'this is new territory for me-zz. Never before have I ever willingly and wanted to surrender my safety, or very life, to somebody. My current desire is to trust you, and even more, my desire for you to trust me for your life. Life for life, Anna. I want to believe your words at d'the altar had erased your prior evil intentions. But-zz my faith is shaken and I want-zz to know your heart's desire. Anna, as God as witness to your reply, do you really want-zz me dead and rid of me? Better yet, tell God. You might lie to me."

"Bibb!" Anna cried out as she slumped onto the edge of the bed. She mumbled something into her pillow; Bibb hoped it had been said heavenward. After looking at Bibb, she buried her head in a pillow again and cried. "Oh God I'm guilty. I'm guilty of this and so much more," she prayed.

"Anna, if you're talking to God, don't-zz be looking at me or your-zz pillow. And-zz if you are, I'm-zz glad you are. I hold-zz no offense towards you. We-zz settled d'that last night at d'the swing." The crying increased. He realized immediately he had reinjured her soul by saying something when he should have remained silent. Then she all of a sudden she looked up.

Bibb was paralyzed by the look as she glared at him. He felt helpless in fear not to comfort and in a greater fear to hurt. Anna returned her face into her pillow and muttered more deliberate words. She did eventually stop talking, but she stayed motionless for a few moments while Bibb remained frozen. She turned to sit on the bed and motioned for Bibb to sit next to her. Once he complied, scared to death, she stared deep into his eyes demanding his full attention. "Bibb, everything I have accused you of, I have been worse. Tommy, tell me true, have you known this all week? Did you know about this before? Why didn't you say anything? How could you not say something?"

"Anna, it hurt me deeply when I read it. I could-zz never believe you wanted me-zz dead until I read d'the court's complaint. It very much complicates my feelings towards you."

"And you still love me, Tommy?"

"Anna, d'that's not a fair question. My promise to you was to be kind no matter what. I will keep d'that promise. No matter if you decided d'then or may decide again in d'the future to put a lead slug into me, I remain all in. Anna, I am committed to treat you kindly, now, or until d'the covenant is over, or until-zz you hug your momma, or Anna, most likely for d'the rest of my life. You are-zz d'that important to me. I have-zz to stop talking now. I don't want-zz to say something stupid."

"Bibb, how can I ever change from what I am? I want to start over. I so want to be a new person. What do I need to do to make things right? How do I make things right with you?"

"How about getting on-zz d'the train with me heading for Bismarck?"

"That won't fix the *me* in me though."

"Well, I know what will, but you won't like d'the taste of d'that soup. Anna, let me say d'this as kind as I can. I want-zz to be d'the richest man in d'the world."

"Hold me, Tommy." Bibb wasn't given a chance to reply before she wrapped her arms around the man. She began to weep, and cried until she had no tears left in her. Tommy didn't know what to do, but knew enough to keep his mouth shut. He held her until she broke the embrace.

==0==

The train was on time and so were the Toivos. Running all the way to the station, winded, and carrying a leather bound package for Bibb, young Anna arrived just as the conductor yelled out the final boarding call. On the platform the young Anna gave the outlaw the book along with a kiss on the cheek. Little Anna then turned to Mrs. Toivo and did the same. The last words that the Toivos heard as the train pulled out of the depot were "I'm praying for both of you! Write that letter!"

Once the train cleared the station with the Toivos on it, the sheriff walked over to the telegraph office with his wife. He instructed to operator to send another official telegram to the same place as before, but this time with the letters "GGG."

Walking back to jail, his wife asked him what that meant. He replied that it was code meaning Gone Gor Good. She replied, "You just made that up. Well, that is better than 'Gone for Bad.'"

"Let's go home. This day has already been too long, and it isn't even noon."

"What are you going to do with the list of things you wrote down that were in the Toivo's trunk? Were you just as surprised as me to see their signed JP document?" asked his wife.

"Honey, first things first, second things second. No, I've changed my mind. Let's stop in the diner for some lunch, and after that go home and catch a much needed nap."

"That's a good plan." She took her husband's hand and they walked into town together. She loved her husband's unashamed public displays of affection. Some might think it detracted from his manliness. She didn't care. As they passed the office she asked, "A penny for your thoughts, dear."

"Biscuits."

October, 1887, Final Entry

I have my life back! I have my life back abundantly! I have hope in tomorrow and I have joy in my today. I have gained my seventh fortune, and its value increases every day. Better yet, I am not alone. The sweetest word has been whispered in my ear, and shouted from the housetops. I was warned that hitching my wagon with the notorious would stain me forever. Well, paint me pink all over! I am so glad of our combined and inseparable reputations, and even happier that I will never have to tell anybody — the whole west knows. And what do they know, both red man and white? This Anna is no longer simply an "I" but part of an "us." It is done and cannot be undone. Does it count as a promise if a person wants to keep their pledge with all their heart and all their soul? I always thought promises were hard to keep because they always had to cost something. Not this one… this promise, my promise, our promise would be harder not to keep. And keep it I will! I will make him whole, and I will feel my mother's love.

And this "us" was no accident. How many people conspired to bring me this seventh fortune? Mr. and Mrs. Franklin, the doctor, Xue, the sheriff and his wife, Julia and her husband, the preacher and his wife, and those three notorious unfriendlies that signed the certificate? Lest I forget the matron, the chief, the widows and the scouts — shame for not mentioning them first. What of Bes, what of the Dowry girls? What of that reporter? No, too many involved to be a conspiracy, and for what gain? What reason would they have to give me everything and take nothing? What about that no good ugly outlaw? Yes, he had a motive but not an ounce of gumption to take advantage of my vulnerabilities. How can I not be kind to that man? He melted my heart so many times and he never knew it. That social invalid was more concerned about touching me right than touching me wrong. Conspiracy? Yes, now that I have had some time to think about it, there are paw prints all over this.

What I have learned this last month has been painful — the marks from the matron still mar the tops of my hands. I fear they will never go away, and maybe they shouldn't to keep me reminded of what I learned from the Lakota. And what did I learn? I learned that the poorest can be the richest, as my widow friends proved. I learned that little girls like Heidi can run in their sleep and force their mothers to hug them for all they are worth. I learned there is permanent joy in divesting and abandoning the desire to acquire. I have never been so dirty, and never been so clean. I have never been so cold and warmed at the same time. Modesty was my motto, and sorry, it still is — I will never wear Indian pajamas again. A full embrace can be heartfelt, but a pinky tug is priceless. A true friend intervenes when they see their sister headed for destruction, thank you Mrs. Franklin. From now on there may be more seen in a mirror than just a reflection, and certainly what goes around comes around. I learned not to abuse employees, forgive me Xue. I will never slap another. One last thought. The measure of a man may not be in what he can do, but what he chooses not to do. I should not compare, but I can't help it. A torn up Baby Bibb is worth more than ten silk-shirted Gorgons.

Lest one think all is roses, it is not. I fear for Bibb's life. He is like old ordinance found on the battlefields of so many southern states. Without warning he could explode physically or implode spiritually. He certainly believes in that varmint, and I am glad he does. I am not fool enough to forget I could have been slain on those plains given my unkind deeds and words. And given his temper and history, he is still capable of falling out of favor with man and God and go on a murderous rampage; and once off the straight and narrow, ten times worse than he was before.

The Lakota blessings... Oh my, what to do with them... Bibb promised me he would let me know the third blessing, but later, much later. It must be really bad, and I fear worse for Bibb more than me. I am at peace with them, but will not raise a finger to engineer their fulfillment. I will not plan to see them ever fulfilled, and in Bibb's case, not fulfilled at all. I dread the thought of losing that friend of friends. For me, sorry, the princess part is nice, but I cannot see myself as a mother now or ever. I am still on edge, and sometimes don't trust my own heart. Neither the chief or Bibb knew of the scars on my feet when the medicine man made his proclamation. Here the tears come again. The precious memory of Bibb rubbing my feet... If he only knew my deepest weakness.

Feather... The stolen feather. Bibb is hardly understandable, and when he mumbles it is unintelligible; and he mumbles about the feather a lot. He says it was no surprise when the scouts didn't see it... they put it there, and Bibb believes the scouts were instructed by the medicine man to tell the fifth Indian it was in the trunk. I asked him why and he said that Unktehi needed a thief at his side at Oglala, Wannagan, or Uncpapa. I asked him to explain and all I got out of that man was more mumbling about scissors, locks, blood, and convergences; all followed by denials that the medicine man's predictions should not be believed.

Mystery... Bibb can sure act strange sometimes, and yes, so does his covenant partner. All those Indian cultural undercurrents are part of our story, but what frustrates me is his keen understanding of them while totally misunderstanding me at every level. I admit some mystery is good. May I always remain a mystery, a delicious emotional, intellectual, and especially physical mystery to my Tommy. Tommy doesn't know me, but he enjoys me and I enjoy him. The covenant did not bind us; it freed us to become the fullest expressions of our best virtues. And there is that word again, us, a word that transcends time, circumstances, and trials... my most cherished word... a word that summarizes a new outlook on life within me. This time we have together is more precious especially because it is temporary. Bibb was loaned to me and I was loaned to him. Why? So we both could learn life lessons. We are being prepared to fulfill our life's longings; me for a mother; Tommy for a wife. Until then, my word is gold. I'm all in. I have never been so saturated in hope.

Precious... that word the preacher's wife threw at me. That persistent word is also key in the haunting tune that never leaves my subconscious mind. That word now tingles with a hope of a happy ending: My Precious Anna Marie. I am hardly precious now, but precious is something that I may become. Precious is much like humility; if you call yourself that, you aren't. May that word surprise me someday as a completely sincere and heartfelt compliment.

Varmint... I'm starting to believe Bibb ain't lying or making up all those stories about his fuzzy friend. I cooked my own goose when I first tried to get Bibb to tell me his secret. I would ask sincerely *about the varmint and he would look at me with the look I hated. He would ask me if I really wanted to know or if I wanted to mock him, and then I would mock him again. After a dozen verses of that song I was locked out. Yet Tommy accidently gave me hints every once in a while. When a subject would come up between us, it sometimes reminded him of a story the Anna girl had read to him, and he would get strangely talkative and retell the story to me. I don't know what demon pinched me, but just as he would be getting close to the point of the story I would get upset about something and mock that man again. I just kick myself for doing that. But those tales had tails, and the truth never stayed silent long. The principles would creep into that man's mind and blow back in the strangest ways, especially during his apologies. I'm not wrong about this. That varmint is fuzzy alright; fuzzy blonde hair, pimples, and a disposition that never lets Bibb get away with anything. It was her words in that varmint's mouth, the stories she read to him, and a book load of truths that got stuck in his gut. The varmint is real. I saw its twinkle in Bibb's eye that terrible morning when my most desperate prayer was answered. I call a lot of answered prayers coincidences in hindsight. Not that miracle. Bibb was right. The varmint doesn't fight fair; and seeing Bibb's fate, that varmint plays for keeps.*

Scars... Tommy told me that all scars belong to God. If that is true, then I have never seen a man with more marks of God's ownership on him than Bibb. Bibb said he had a close friend who, like me, had scars on both his hands and on his feet. I asked Bibb what happened to him. Tommy said he was murdered. I asked him who did it. Bibb said I knew the sorry person; a no good lying depraved example of human debris. I did not dare ask for a name.

Love... Bibb told me that love was a choice. My first wrong-headed thought when he offered to release me from the covenant was that he was acting like a coward. I had to rethink that. Bibb has many flaws but cowardice is not one of them. As much as he needs me he still offered me my freedom, and not a cowardly freedom from me as I first assumed. It takes great love to love the loveless, and a greater love to risk allowing those unlovely souls a free will. Well, I have made my choice too. I am all in. Will I give Tommy the same choice, a premature freedom from our covenant? Never, never, never, no never, and he will learn to like it. He said it himself: our fates are forever "altared." We are infamously bound, and not even death can change that.

The Altar... It is possible that the profane can become sacred. The moment was sacred with or without my cooperation. It wasn't me that made the place hallowed. It wasn't Bibb or the preacher either. It was the words that made it holy. Words like "kindness" and "I will." Words like "are you entering this covenant freely, without guile, and with a genuine concern for Anna Gorgon?" This old blind selfish girl was loved all the while she was still kicking that old cactus.

Friend... For the first time in my life I have a true friend, and he is the most unlikely of all persons in the world. Not of common upbringing or new found familiarity. It is not like I know him, or that he knows me. Our mutual mystery is not the substance of the bond... no... nor a familiarity... how can I describe it? The chains of this peculiar attachment, for me, are the most unlikely of all bonds in the world. It was, it is, and it will be the blind pledge of mutual kindness. One month ago I was dead, and now I am alive. I no longer feel hollow inside! I am overwhelmed in that joy. I am Anna, friend of Bibb, friend of the Lakota, and for the first time a friend to me. Alive! I am alive!

The hard part of our covenant lies ahead of us; Bibb will suffer much physically. And with me in charge of his healing, he will suffer emotionally too. He does not submit to others well, and especially to a woman. I will have to be wiser than my years, think like a matron, and love as a wife. I have no desire for the later. He has told me his goals, and once the covenant is complete I equally as much hope to fulfill my most secret of desires. He has told me many times that he longs for me to be delivered into the arms of my in-laws. Likewise, in my heart of hearts I want to deliver him chaste, unmarried, and fully trained to woo and wed his Humbird. That is what I promised God I would do for that man when he held me tight as we sat on the bed in our hotel room during our last hours in Miles City. May my own stubborn will, that so wants to dominate, not soil that promise with selfishness and short sighted desires. If Bibb can withhold the medicine man's third secret blessing from me, well then I can withhold this equally as mysterious heart throb from him. Here is my secret that I will keep from human ear and eye until Tommy's dying day, and my promise to the God of Anna's mother: I will gladly and fully commit to the grand bargain if providence allows me to see Bibb married to his Humbird. Okay. There it is: God-bait. Bibb said the Almighty likes specific prayers and now He has a big one posted on his debit ledger.

Go for it, Big Boy.

Historical Addendum

THIS BOOK WAS based on family narratives that have been passed down for generations. Anna (Hannah) Gorgon Ryder was my great-grandmother on my father's side. Historical documents supporting this narrative include all those mentioned in <u>The Hound of Tooty River</u>, plus Anna Gorgon's memoirs of these thirty days, Bibb's outer and inner letter to Major Ryder, and a quilt with some patches that legend says came from a much worn green dress. These items, which I saw earlier in my life, have all been lost or misplaced. I hope some relative will show up with them someday. Maybe this book will help in their discovery. Since the publication of my first book Hannah Ryder's Bible has been found.

There was also the family folklore. I am relating a story that is not my own, told to me when I was small enough to sit on my own grandfather's knee. It was well known about Anna's breakup with Mr. Gorgon over the syphilis problem. There was also her eventual marriage to Major Ryder, the tales of the balls and parties, and the widow Gorgon's long difficulty with Humbird. As for what I filled in when I had no source material I tried to stay true to the themes of the stories passed down. Is it embellished fabrications of myth? Most likely, but I hoped you enjoyed the legend as I remember it.

Most of the narrative of this book was sourced in Anna's journal with the exception of one story. Mr. Franklin had sent Anna one year after Xue left for California a curious essay found in the editorial section of the Deadwood paper. The title of the article was "Soaps, Scars, and Xue's." The piece was a very unflattering history of the Gorgons of Deadwood Gulch citing the trail of tears they cut through the city with their abusive business practices and mean-spiritedness, or as editorialized "The part of the wild west that the west wanted to forget." Anna was deemed the villain and Xue the saint. With the healing of time all that remained was the revelation of Anna's scars and servant Xue's giant risk taken on the eve of Anna's departure. That act of kindness will be forever remembered, and worthy to be remembered. Mr. Franklin added a handwritten postscript to the article that Awful Anna and Saint Xue were the sermon material in many pulpits for weeks after the publishing of the story in the paper.

In humility, when Anna was elderly, she told that story on herself to her family and relatives. Her point was to contrast where she had been to what she had become. She remembered the altar as the first time in her life that somebody invested their treasure in her soul without any expectation of return. No, not Bibb, but the preacher. She described his words as a seed planted between her toes that took a thousand miles to germinate. The other stories she told on herself, according to the recollection of my great aunts, were about the stones in the matron's hand, the stars dripping their twinkling beams of glowing radiance upon them as they camped, and the whiteness of the snow as she and Bibb crossed the cold plains. Besides vowing never to eat dried beans again, Anna often described as "cold in feet and warm in heart" her experience as she and her outlaw journeyed in that buckboard over those endless prairies surrounded by Indians. And the green dress... the gift from the chief through the matron's hand, her most precious of all her heirlooms.

Anna also told the story, to her shame, of the night she screamed and woke up the whole town of Miles City. Likewise, relatives told me that Anna could never tell the story without a tear how she regretted her fierce anger, even after fifty years had passed, the night while at the gazebo she slapped Bibb's injured face with all of her strength. She also recalled other turning points in her life, like fondly telling the story of Heidi the kick-sleeper. Anna never wanted children of her own until that night she spent with that precious child. It was the first time she had ever held a mere child, and found out there was nothing mere about any child.

==0==

The following is the best I can remember of the letter that Bibb sent to Major Ryder on Friday, October 21ˢᵗ, 1887. He wrote it because he was uncertain about what to do with the medicine man's predictions, other than it would be wrong to tell Anna. Yet he did not want to forget what was said. He trusted Major Ryder for the safe keeping of the record.

OUTSIDE LETTER:

Miles City, Montana Territory,
October 21ˢᵗ, 1887, I think.
Major Ryder, Bismarck Garrison, Dakota Territory

Sir, I am entrusting this letter and the enclosed sealed document to your care and safe keeping. This document may be of lasting significance or entirely folly. History will determine the veracity of the contents and to which of the previously mentioned categories these words belong.

Earlier this month Miss Anna Gorgon and I traveled from Deadwood to Miles City in route to Fort Rice. On Saturday, October the sixth, we happened upon a Lakota camp and were allowed to stay for two nights. On Monday the eighth we left camp with the blessing of the chief and words from their medicine man. Those words constitute what is in the sealed envelope. I ask you not to open that letter until I have passed away or at such a time I instruct you.

Now that your curiosity is stirred, because you are an inquisitive person, I will give you some information about it hopefully to satisfy. The medicine man made several predictions, three for me and three for Anna. They are general in nature, but specific enough that fulfillment would be recognized as certain in hindsight. They may or may not come true. Time will tell. I certainly am not going to plot my life around these predictions. The worst thing that could happen is that these predictions be taken to heart in such a way they become self-fulfilling prophecies. If they are truly from the source that the medicine man claimed then time will prove him right. If not, well, then the buffalo meat we ate the night before probably gave him both indigestion and a wild imagination. That is not for me to decide or waste another thought on.

Anna did not understand a word that the medicine man said. I did. I told her my three and the first two of hers. The third one about her was something I refused to share. The Widow Gorgon has ample evidence not to trust men, and I wasn't going to give her another stick to emotionally beat me with. (She is a spirited soul.) If she becomes aware of the third one, she might, dare say will (most certainly) consider it a fabrication on my part to trick her into intimacy. Trust me; I don't want any part of that. I have enough problems with a certain Anna of Fort Rice. Nor is the Widow Gorgon completely innocent and beyond engineering outcomes in her favor. She has a record of being drawn emotionally in by no good liars and scoundrels, and I don't want to encourage that weakness by making myself attractive or available. On this account, I believe I have succeeded. After all, her husband became the 24th notch on my ax.

I know you are driven by a need to know. Please resist that urge. Put this letter away somewhere safe and forget about it. There is nothing to gain by opening the letter now. I have not, nor intend to tell Anna of this correspondence.

As I continue in your service… Bibb.

==0==

INSIDE LETTER:

October 21st, 1887, Miles City, Montana Territory,
Major Ryder, Widow Gorgon, or their heirs, greetings,

On October eighth, 1887, the Widow Gorgon and I were guests of a chief of a Lakota band of Indians in extreme western Dakota Territory. Upon our departure the chief of the tribe plead a blessing upon both of us. In addition, the medicine man of that band pronounced six predictions, three for me and three for Anna Gorgon. The medicine man did not cite himself as the source of these predictions. I am not vouching for the validity of these predictions, nor the translation. Many of the words were said in high ceremonial language that I had to cipher by context.

Prediction One: Bibb would die without his name.
- *Bibb would die on the grassy plains*
- *Bibb would be taken to his final resting place on a horse he does not own*
- *He would be greeted by his father*

Prediction Two: Bibb would have "justice sitting on his shoulder" for the remainder of his life.

- *Wound for wound, blow for blow, blood for blood; all harm inflicted by Bibb on others would come upon his own body in like manner*
- *Injuries included all invisible hurts too*
- *Bibb would bring justice to the plains*

Prediction Three: Bibb would marry.

- *His wife would be badly scarred*
- *His wife would become beautiful in Bibb's eyes*

Prediction One: Anna would enjoy long life

- *A prince of warriors will give Anna a boy in her old age*
- *Anna will dine with governors and authorities, ambassadors and rulers*

Prediction Two: Anna would be transformed into something beautiful.

- *Beauty in women as defined by the Lakota*
- *She would become a wise wife*
- *Her hair would never be taken from her against her will*

Prediction Three: About the dress the matron gave her; (this one was very hard to translate)

- *A sign of renewal of lasting covenants; spirit-breathed sacred lashings (knots)*
- *That dress would appear when vows are made and vows are fulfilled*
- *The dress will have a role to play in fulfilling these predictions*
- *The dress will warm the son of the prince*

==0==

One additional historical footnote concerns Mr. and Mrs. Franklin. In response to an invitation from their unofficially adopted daughter Anna, they traveled to Bismarck the following summer. The reunion was a very emotional event for Mrs. Franklin as she confirmed first hand so many answers to her most private prayers. Anna wasn't her real daughter, but she was her real miracle.

Besides being a very gracious and perfect hostess, Anna took her guests along with Major Ryder to dine with Governor Church and his wife at their mansion. Yet the primary purpose of the lawyer's trip was for Anna to present written proof that Bibb did release her from the covenant. In return, Mr. Franklin remedied Tommy Toivo's legal problem of being married to two women at the same time. The annulment also resolved Anna's problem of being separated from her material fortune. Her seventh fortune, the one birthed within her soul on the plains, could never be lost. She had to admit to herself that treasure cost her nothing except an ounce of hair and a ton of attitude.

It was over a year later when Anna showed Bibb the annulment papers. She was stunned beyond words when Bibb told Anna his part of the story. She could not get over his matter of fact rendition of the events that happened the night she and Mrs. Franklin had hid at Xue's laundry, all told with the same gusto of reporting last month's market prices at the goat auction. Since leaving Deadwood she held the false assumptions that Mr. Franklin had forged Tommy's signature on their marriage certificate and that Bibb was unaware of their marriage. Yes, the varmint prevented a 25th notch.

Retelling the stories about great-grandmother Anna's stay in Bismarck before moving east would take another whole book to chronicle and best saved for another day.

CPSIA information can be obtained
at www.ICGtesting.com
Printed in the USA
LVOW12s0537090617
537522LV00001B/1/P